# *perfectly* IMPERFECT

BOOKS 4–6

NEVA ALTAJ

*Ruined Secrets*
Editing by Susan Stradiotto (www.susanstradiotto.com)
Proofreading #1 by Beyond The Proof (www.beyondtheproof.ca)
Proofreading #2 by Yvette Rebello (yreditor.com)

*Stolen Touches*
Editing by Susan Stradiotto (www.susanstradiotto.com)
Proofreading #1 by Beyond The Proof (www.beyondtheproof.ca)
Proofreading #2 by Yvette Rebello (yreditor.com)
Manuscript critique by Anka Lesko (www.amlediting.com)

*Fractured Souls*
Editing by Susan Stradiotto and Andie, Beyond The Proof
www.susanstradiotto.comv www.beyondtheproof.ca
Proofreading by Yvette Rebello, reditor.com
Manuscript critique by Anka Lesko, www.amlediting.com

Cover design by Deranged Doctor (www.derangeddoctordesign.com)
Interior Formatting by Champagne Book Design

PERFECTLY IMPERFECT
BOOK FOUR

# RUINED secrets

PERFECTLY IMPERFECT SERIES

Luca & Isabella

# AUTHOR'S NOTE

Dear reader, there are a few Italian words mentioned in the book, so h
the translations and clarifications:

*Tesoro*—treasure; endearment.

*Stella mia*—my star; endearment.

*Piccola*—little one, little girl; endearment.

# AUTHOR'S NOTE

Dear reader, there are a few Italian words mentioned in the book, so here are the translations and clarifications:

*Tesoro*—treasure; endearment.

*Stella mia*—my star; endearment.

*Piccola*—little one, little girl; endearment.

# Trigger Warning

Please be aware that this book contains content that some readers may find disturbing, such as gore, violence, and graphic descriptions of torture. There are also more steamy scenes than in the previous books in this series, and those include elements of mild BDSM, and the usage of toys.

# Prologue

Isabella

*Present*
*(Isabella 19 y.o.)*

THEY SHAVED HIS HAIR.

I don't know why that detail hits me so hard.

Reaching for my husband's hand, I entwine our fingers and drop my forehead onto the mattress. I don't know what I hate more—the hospital smell, the beep of the machine next to the bed tracking his heartbeat, or how still he is.

Minutes pass. Maybe hours, I'm not sure.

I almost miss it—the tiny twitch of his fingers in my own. My head snaps up, and I find two dark brown eyes watching me.

"Oh, Luca . . ." I choke out, then lean over him and place a light, quick kiss on his lips.

He doesn't say anything, just keeps looking at me, probably wondering how I dared to kiss him, but I don't care. I was so scared for him, and I needed the stolen kiss to assure myself that he's alive.

I let go of his hand, sit up straighter in the chair, and wait for him to start giving me an earful. When he speaks, his voice is rough and deep, even deeper than usual, and the words that leave his mouth make me go ice-cold.

"Who are you?"

I stare at him.

Luca cocks his head to the side, regarding me with his intense, calculating gaze. I'm very familiar with this expression, because I'm usually on the receiving end of it when he's not happy with something I've done. But there is one huge difference this time. It's his eyes. The same eyes that I've hoped for so long would look at me with love instead of indifference. They are gazing at me now without a sliver of recognition.

"I'm Isabella," I whisper. "Your . . . wife."

He blinks, then looks away at the window on the other side of the room and takes a deep breath.

"So, Isabella," he says and turns to me. "Care to tell me who I am?

# Part One

## "Before"

# CHAPTER

*Three Years Ago*
*(Isabella 16 y.o.)*

"ISA!" ANDREA YELLS MY NAME AS HER LOUD FOOTSTEPS POUND up the stairs.

I turn in my chair to see my younger sister running into my room. She's only two years younger than me, but sometimes behaves like she's starting elementary rather than high school. By the time she reaches me, she's out of breath.

"You can't run through the house yelling." I point a pencil at her. "You're fourteen, not four."

"He's here!" She grabs my hand and starts dragging me out of the room, a face-splitting smile lighting up her eyes.

"Who?"

"Luca Rossi."

My heartbeat quickens, just like it does every time his name comes up, and I scurry after my sister, ignoring my own words of warning. We run down the hallway and the big stone staircase. As expected, we get several disapproving looks from the maid and two of my grandfather's men along the way, but I can't make myself think about etiquette now. He's here!

We dash through the front double doors and circle the house until we reach the big azalea bush on the back side, just a few yards from the French window outside my grandfather's study. Like we've done so many times before, I crouch behind it and pull Andrea down beside me. It's an ideal hiding spot, with a clear view into Nonno Giuseppe's office.

"I should have changed," I mumble, looking down at my cut-off jeans shorts and plain T-shirt. "I can't let Luca see me like this."

Andrea sizes me up and raises an eyebrow. "What's wrong with your clothes?"

"I look like a schoolgirl," I say, quickly removing my hair tie and combing my fingers through my hair. Mom says wearing my hair down adds a few years to my appearance.

"Oh?" Andrea chuckles. "Newsflash, Isa—you are."

"Well, I don't have to dress the part." I pout and look up at the window, waiting. "If I'd known Luca was coming over, I would've put on that beige dress."

The door to the study opens and Luca Rossi, one of my grandfather's capos, enters the room. I grab Andrea's hand and squeeze. I've been obsessing over him since I was six years old, when he jumped into the pool and saved my life after that idiot Enzo threw me in it. I don't remember ever being as scared as when my head dipped below the water, and my socked, fancy dress pulled me down. I wasn't a good swimmer, and I fruitlessly kicked my legs, trying to get to the surface. When I was sure I would die, two large hands suddenly grabbed me and pulled me up.

Never will I forget those smiling eyes as Luca carried me toward my hysterical mother. His expensive suit was dripping wet, and the strands of his long dark hair were plastered to his face. That evening, I told my mother that when I grew up, I would marry Luca Rossi. Maybe I fell in love with him that day.

"He's even hotter than last time I saw him." I sigh.

Luca has always been beautiful, and girls and women have often fallen over their own feet when he entered a room. It must have been his serious, slightly indifferent stance where other people were concerned, women included, that made him so interesting. He would walk into the room, do what he came for, and leave. No meaningless conversations. No lingering for gossip. If he had to stay longer for some event, because it was expected, he would either sit with my grandfather talking business, or lurk in one of the corners, observing the crowd. I loved watching him then, his huge body leaning on the wall, his dark eyes skimming over the room, observing everyone. Every sharp line of his perfect face has been carved into my brain. Over the years, however, his features have changed. His face matured, the lines becoming harsher and partially hidden with a short beard. His dark eyes have changed as well, getting a somehow harder, more sinister look in them. The only thing that has remained the same is his long, dark hair gathered in a bun on the top of his head. In our circle, it takes a certain kind of character for a man to wear his hair long and not be judged. But Luca Rossi has always been something else. Something *more* than other men.

"You're nuts." Andrea elbows me into my side, "He's double your age."

"I don't care."

"And he is married, Isa."

Pain pierces my heart at the mention of Simona, Luca's wife. Four years ago, I spent a week in bed, crying my eyes out, when I heard he was getting married. Although only twelve at the time, all I wanted was to be his wife one day. Like most girls, I dreamed about my wedding and in each of those childhood fantasies, it was always Luca standing next to me as my groom. People said Simona got pregnant on purpose to manipulate him into marriage, but it didn't make it hurt any less. I felt betrayed. He was mine!

I grab the branch in front of me and squeeze. "I hate that woman."

"I heard Aunt Agata telling Mama that she saw them fighting again," Andrea whispers, "in a restaurant full of people."

"About what?" I ask, without taking my eyes off Luca's handsome face.

"It sounded like they fought because Simona forgot to pick up Rosa from preschool." Andrea mumbles.

"How can a mother forget her child?" I stare disbelievingly at her. Even though Simona is a bitch, I didn't think she'd be capable of doing that.

"She was probably at one of her Botox appointments." My sister laughs.

I shake my head and turn back to watch Luca. He's sitting in a chair on the other side of my grandfather's desk, with his profile to us. Based on the grim expression on both of their faces, something serious is going on. I know my grandfather very well. When Giuseppe Agostini, the don of Chicago's Cosa Nostra Family, has that face on, it means nothing good is cooking. A scowl on Luca's face isn't new, though, but this time, it causes a lump to form in my throat. I haven't seen him smile in years, and he's been around the house a lot since becoming a capo.

"I'm going back." I brush away a stray tear and turn to leave.

Every time I see him, it gets harder. It's as if a weight settles over my chest. I know he'll never be with me. And still, I can't make myself stay away. Andrea calls me crazy for obsessing over someone so much older. Maybe I am. But I can't help it. It started as hero-worshipping when he saved my life.

In the last couple of years, however, that child adoration has transformed into something else entirely.

"Don't be sad, Isa." Andrea wraps her arm around my waist. "There are other men who'd worship the ground you walk on. You are the granddaughter to the don of the Cosa Nostra. When the time comes for you to marry, there will be a line of suitors waiting here for you. Someone will come by, sweep you off your feet, and you'll forget all about Luca Rossi. It's just a teenage crush."

"Yeah." I nod and put a fake smile on my face, the one I've been practicing with Mom. "You're right. Let's go back."

*One year ago*
*(Isabella 18 y.o.)*

The crowd is scattered around the garden, drinking and laughing. My grandfather must have invited everyone in the Chicago area with Italian blood to my birthday party.

"That waiter is super cute." Catalina, my best friend, nudges me with her elbow. "I think I'm going to grab another piece of cake and check him out a bit better. You want to tag along?"

"Nope, I'm good," I say.

"But, look at him! He's got dimples when he laughs."

I glance over at the man standing next to the food table, conversing with one of the guests. He's in his early twenties, with short blond hair and a really nice smile.

"You go." I nod toward the cutie who's captured her interest. "I'll wait for you here."

Catalina giggles, winks at me, and rushes to the tables laden with food. She approaches the cute waiter and starts to flirt, and for a moment, I wish I were able to do the same. Too bad I only have eyes for one man.

I look toward the opposite side of the garden where Luca is sitting with my grandfather and Lorenzo Barbini, my nonno's underboss. They seem to be discussing business, not really paying too much attention to the festive atmosphere around them. Luca hasn't even glanced my way since he got here, which is nothing new.

It wasn't always like this. When I was little, I'd run across the lawn the moment I saw him arrive. He would catch and spin me around when I jumped into his arms, making me squeal in delight. But he stopped doing that the summer I turned thirteen.

I remember that day as if it happened yesterday. The moment I saw him exiting his car, I dashed outside and ran across the driveway to him. He didn't open his arms to catch me that day. Instead, he just brushed his hand down my hair and went inside the house. That's all I got during his next few visits—a light brush of my hair. I guess he decided I was too old for spinning around, or maybe that it wasn't proper. Then, even those light stokes of my hair stopped. In the last few years, I was left with simply watching him from a distance.

Like now.

"Isabella!"

I throw a look over my shoulder to find Enzo, Catalina's idiot cousin, barreling in my direction.

"Shit," I murmur and turn around, intending to head inside the house. Before I can make my escape, he comes around and steps into my path.

"So beautiful." He wraps his hand around my wrist and bends his head to rest on mine, inhaling as he does so. "And smelling like flowers."

"Leave me alone, Enzo." I try to wriggle free, but his grip is strong, and he pulls me tighter.

"Oh, come on, Isa! Why are you always acting like an iceberg?"

"Enzo! You're drunk!" I look around, searching for Andrea or anyone else who could get me away from him. There are dozens of guests milling across the garden, but no one is close enough to come to my aid. I could yell, but I don't want to make a scene because there are too many important people here tonight.

"Of course, I am." He laughs. "It's your eighteenth birthday. It's only natural to drink to that, yeah? Come on, let me give you a birthday kiss."

"Get away from me." I sneer and try to wiggle away again.

"But it's just one kiss. Come on, Isa, don't be such a—"

He stops midsentence, his eyes focusing on something behind me, then he tilts his head up until his gaze stops well above my own. The color in his face starts rapidly draining. A hand adorned with a thin, white gold wedding band reaches from behind me and wraps around Enzo's wrist in a vice-like grip. Enzo lets go of me, but the newcomer's long, strong fingers squeeze the idiot's wrist tighter until he whimpers. I don't pay attention to Enzo. My heartbeat picks up as I stare at the two bracelets encircling the other person's wrist. One is a wide silver cuff and the other a black leather band. I bought both with my pocket money five years ago and gave them to him. I didn't know he actually wore them.

I take a deep breath, trying to keep my racing heart from exploding as I move my eyes from the bracelets back to the wedding band on his finger. Something dies in me again, just like the first time I saw the ring on his hand.

"Touch her again," Luca's smooth, whiskey-like voice says above me, "and you die."

Enzo nods maniacally and whimpers again. "Yes, Mr. Rossi."

"Get lost," Luca barks and releases Enzo's hand.

I stare at Enzo's back as he runs toward the gate. I don't dare face my savior. If I do, I might fall apart. Until this morning, I still believed there might be a small chance I would get to be with Luca someday. That sliver of hope evaporated the moment my father informed me that he agreed to give my hand in marriage to Angelo Scardoni, the youngest of my grandfather's capos, when I turn twenty-one. I always knew I would end up in an arranged marriage because it was the only option for the Cosa Nostra don's granddaughter, but I still hoped.

"Everything okay, tesoro?"

"Yes." I nod, keeping my eyes fixed on the gate. "Thank you, Luca."

"If he pesters you again, let me know."

"I will."

"Okay." There's a slight touch at the back of my head as if he lightly brushed my hair. "Happy birthday, Isabella."

I wait until I no longer feel Luca behind me, then turn around slowly and watch him as he walks away, leaving me to stand with an overload of emotions brewing within, with nowhere to go. Something squeezes in my chest. I wonder how it would feel to have him walking toward me for once. Maybe start a meaningless conversation, even if it's only in passing. This is the most we've spoken to each other in the past two years. I've often feared he's forgotten I exist.

I hear my name being called and turn to see Catalina waving at me to come over. Throwing one last look at Luca's retreating form over my shoulder, I head toward the tables with food, running my fingers along my hair where his hand brushed it.

# Chapter

Luca

*Three months ago*
*(Luca 35 y.o.)*

I lean my elbows on the steering wheel and watch the video playing on my phone.

A pair of black pants and a red dress, obviously discarded in a hurry, are lying on the floor in the middle of the room. A man in a white shirt is sitting at the edge of the bed, while a blonde-haired woman is kneeling between his legs, sucking his dick. The room they are in is . . . my bedroom. And the woman who's currently choking on her bodyguard's dick is my dear wife.

I put the phone in my jacket, take my gun from the glove compartment, and leave the car.

It's half past one in the morning, and there's no one in the hall. My footsteps echo off the dark marble floor and up the wide stairwell. When I reach the third floor, I turn right and walk down the hallway to my daughter's room to make sure she's not home. Rosa is having a sleepover at her friend's, as she usually does when I have to leave home for a couple of days for work. She and her mother never got along well.

I open the door to Rosa's room and peek inside. Empty. I close the door, then continue to the other end of the hallway, toward my bedroom.

Simona is still on her knees in front of the bodyguard when I enter. The lamp in the corner is giving off more than enough light for me to clearly see the man's flushed face above Simona's bobbing head. I lift my gun, aiming at the center of his forehead, and pull the trigger. The loud bang makes the nightstand rattle, and blood sprays all over the white, satin sheets. Simona screams, then jumps up and away from the body now sprawled across the bed. Her face and hair also bear red splotches, and there are some on her breasts and neck. Seems like some of her lover's brain matter ended up in her hair as well. She is still wailing when I walk casually over to her and grab her upper arm.

"Let me go!" she yells as I drag her out of the room and down the hallway. "You killed him, you monster!"

Simona keeps shrieking all the way down the two flights of stairs, trying to squirm out of my grasp. I ignore her protests and head toward the wide-open front door. Two of my security guards run inside, but stop at the entrance, their eyes bulging out upon seeing us. A maid comes out around the corner from the hall where staff have their rooms and freezes midstep. She's clutching her knitted cardigan around herself with her gaze locked on Simona's naked and blood-splattered body. I pass the guards and drag my screaming wife outside, and down the four stone steps to the driveway.

"You'll receive the divorce papers in the morning," I spit out and release her arm.

"What? Luca, please! It was a mistake." She reaches over as if to take my hand.

"Don't you dare fucking touch me! Get the fuck out of my house."

"You can't do this!" she wails. "Luca!"

I turn and go back inside. For some reason, I'm not even angry. The only thing I feel is disgust. With her, but also with myself for not ending things with the bitch sooner.

"Send a maid to bring her something to put on, and call a taxi," I tell Marco, who is standing by the door. "She's not to come inside the house."

"Of course, Mr. Rossi." He nods quickly.

"There is a body in my bedroom. Have someone take care of that, too," I say as I move toward the stairwell. I'm halfway to the second floor when my brother's voice reaches me.

"Luca? What's going on?"

Damian is standing on the landing to the second floor, wearing only his boxer briefs. Behind him is a dark-haired girl wrapped in a blanket, peeking over his shoulder.

"Simona and I decided to split," I say as I'm climbing the stairwell. "She's leaving."

"Naked?"

"Yes." I stop in front of him and cast a glance at the girl cowering behind his back. "Good evening, Arianna."

"Hi, Luca." She smiles nervously.

"Does your father know where you're spending the night?"

"Nope," she mumbles.

I shake my head and look back at my brother. "Franco is going to kill you."

"Arianna is twenty-one. I think she can make her own decisions, Luca." He smirks.

"She's also engaged," I say and keep heading up the stairs. "I'm going to crash. I have a meeting at eight tomorrow."

"Luca?" he calls after me. "Was that a gunshot we heard earlier?"

"Yes."

"Care to elaborate?"

"Nope. Go back to bed, Damian."

When I reach the third floor, I drop by my bedroom to collect the phone charger and a change of clothes for tomorrow, then head into Rosa's room to sleep.

# CHAPTER

*Two months ago*
*(Isabella 19 y.o.)*

I SIT AT THE EDGE OF THE BED AND TAKE MY GRANDFATHER'S FRAIL hand in mine. I'm trying to be careful not to nudge the attached IV, supplying fluids to keep him hydrated. I gently rearrange the tube and move the pole so I don't accidentally bump it with my knees. The nightstand on the left is covered with all sorts of medicine bottles. At least ten of them. The air in the room feels stale, permeated with the smell of pharmaceuticals that seems to cling to everything.

"Nonno," I whisper. His cheeks are sunken, and there are big black circles around his eyes. He looks really bad. "How are you feeling?"

"Like I've been hit by a train."

"You had a heart attack. It's to be expected. You'll get better in a few days."

He smiles sadly. "We both know that's not true." I start to say something, but he squeezes my hand and continues, "We need to talk. It's important."

"It can wait until you're feeling better."

"No, it can't wait." He shakes his head. "When I'm gone, there will be chaos. You know that."

"You are not dying anytime soon. The Family needs you." I press my lips together tightly. "I need you."

Giuseppe Agostini has been leading the Chicago branch of the Cosa Nostra Family for twenty years, but he's also been the rock of our own family.

While he had his own wing, we all lived in the same house. I can't imagine not having him here.

"It's the circle of life. The old are meant to go, and the young stay."

"You're sixty-nine. That's not old."

"I know, stella mia. But, it is what it is." He sighs and squeezes my hand. "You know how things work in our world. If a don dies without a successor defined, there will be an internal war within the Family. I called the capos to come the day after tomorrow, so I can name my replacement."

I don't understand why he's telling me this. He's not dying. It was just a minor heart attack. People live for years after that happens.

"The man I plan to name will need the connection to our family to ensure no one will confront him and make matters worse," he continues, "Do you understand what I'm saying, Isabella?"

"No, I don't think so."

"We need to tie our families together. By marriage."

Things finally start to make sense and chills run down my spine. "You want me to marry? Right away?"

"Yes. Will you do that, Isi?"

Tears start to gather in the corners of my eyes. He's the only one who ever calls me that.

"Did you talk with Angelo already?" I ask.

I have nothing against Angelo. He's a nice guy, and we've been on a few dates, but I never felt anything for him, not even a spark. And I hoped I'd get a few more years of freedom.

"Yes." He nods. "I told him that the engagement is off."

"Off?" I blink. "I don't understand."

"Angelo is a good kid, but he's too young to be a don, Isi. The rest of the Family would never stand by him."

I draw my brows together, confused. "Who am I marrying then?"

"The only man who can take over all the shit I'm going to throw at him and not crumble under the weight of it."

My breathing becomes shallow, and my heart starts thumping so hard I'm afraid it's going to burst out of my chest.

"You're marrying Luca Rossi," my grandfather says the words I've been longing to hear for more than a decade, and I can only stare at him.

"But . . . he's already married," I say, dumbfounded.

"He and Simona are divorcing. It should be done in a matter of days. I know you're only nineteen, and he is so much older than you . . ."

I shake my head and bend down to wrap my arms around his frail form. "I will gladly marry Luca, Nonno."

Luca

I knock on the door of Don Agostini's study.

"Come in," a faint voice calls from the inside.

The Family has known for quite some time that Giuseppe hasn't been well. I've been meeting with him at least once a week to update him on the real estate business, so I've witnessed the deterioration firsthand. Still, the sight that greets me makes me falter. He looks as if he's aged twenty years since the last time I saw him.

"Luca." He nods toward the chair on the other side of the desk. "Please sit."

"How are you feeling, Boss?" I ask as I take a seat.

"Awful, as you can see." He smiles. "I'll be short because Lorenzo and the other capos are coming in less than an hour."

I've been wondering what he wants to talk about since I got his call yesterday. At first, I assumed it would be business, as usual. But if that's the case, it could be discussed after the meeting with the capos.

"I had a heart attack two days ago," he says. "It was a minor thing, but as the doctor so nicely put it to me, I need to start getting my things in order. Fast."

"All right. How can I help?"

"By taking over."

"Okay." I nod.

Giuseppe has been giving me more responsibilities over the last two years. He's also transferred the real estate dealings to me completely, saying he couldn't handle everything. I guess he plans to delegate another part of the business. "What do you need me to take over?"

"The Chicago Family of Cosa Nostra, Luca."

I stare at him. Saying that he caught me by surprise would be an understatement. Everyone expected the next don to be Lorenzo Barbini.

"What about Lorenzo?" I ask.

"Lorenzo is a good underboss. He's been organizing and overseeing the operations well so far," Giuseppe says. "However, he's not capable of making decisions that have the Family's best interests in mind instead of his own. I always planned for it to be you."

"Well, some warning in advance would have been appreciated."

"Consider yourself warned."

"Is that why you called all the capos today?" I ask.

"Yes, one of the reasons."

"And the others?"

"Just one more. I'm moving up the timeline on an important matter." He pauses, eyes locked onto mine. Despite his frail appearance, his gaze remains steady and scrutinizing. What is he hoping to find? "Isabella's upcoming marriage," he continues after bit.

"To Angelo Scardoni?"

A smile pulls across his face. "To you."

I close my eyes, then open them widely. They said it was his heart, not his brain, that was going bad. "Isabella is nineteen," I say. "I'm not marrying a child."

"She's not a child. Her mother married at eighteen. I don't see a problem."

"Well, I do. I could be her father, technically."

"You're not even thirty."

"I'm thirty-five." And he knows that very well, but he just waves his hand through the air like it's nothing of importance.

"Isabella is a good girl, maybe a little stubborn sometimes, but she's extremely clever and very well versed in social interaction and Family affairs. Not to mention exceptionally beautiful."

That she is. I've seen her quite often, and I can't deny the obvious. With her long chestnut hair falling down her back in soft curls, a pert nose, and huge dark eyes that are almost too big for her face, she is stunning. She isn't very tall, but she has an amazing little body, a ridiculously tiny waist, and the most perfect ass I've ever seen. And the fact that I've noticed a nineteen-year-old's ass at all is all kinds of fucked up. I've also known Isabella since she was a kid, and the idea of marrying her sounds completely insane.

It seems that Giuseppe doesn't catch my reluctance because he continues speaking. "She'll be a good wife to you. And if you let her, a good partner."

"Partner in what?"

"In life, Luca. When you're in a position of power, a wife you can lean on and trust is indispensable. For men like us, it's rare to find a partner with whom you can share the good, as well as the bad. And there will be a shitload of bad, trust me."

I shake my head. Who would have thought the don would be romantic. "The only person one can truly trust is themselves, Boss. And, sometimes, his closest blood kin. I've learned that lesson well."

"Not all women are like Simona." He reaches with his hand to take a glass of water from the desk, and I can't help but notice the way his fingers are shaking. "What happened between you two? I know you never got along well, but a divorce?"

I recline back in the chair and cross my arms in front of me. "I caught her giving her bodyguard a blow job. In our bed. I suspected it for quite some time, so I set up a camera in the room."

"Christ. Is he alive?"

"Nope. And she barely escaped the same fate."

"I wondered why she went along with the divorce so easily. How's Rosa dealing with the situation?" he asks after a pause.

"Simona was never interested in her. Rosa was only a means to an end. A tool to make me marry her."

"I'm sorry. I hope Isabella will get along well with your daughter."

"So you're serious about the marriage thing?"

With his head bowed slightly, the don looks at me over the rims of his glasses. He opens a drawer, takes out a stack of papers, and throws them onto the desk in front of me. A marriage agreement. I can't believe I just managed to get rid of one wife, and he's saddling me with a child bride before my divorce is even finalized.

"What am I going to do with a nineteen-year-old, Boss?"

"Whatever you do, you will do it with respect. Isabella might be young, but she's still my granddaughter, and a person who will help secure your place as the new don. Keep that in mind."

I stare at the stack of papers in front of me. Clenching my teeth together, I give him my resigned nod.

# CHAPTER

# *four*

IS IT POSSIBLE FOR THE SAME DAY TO BE THE HAPPIEST AND THE SADDEST of my life?

I tilt my head and regard my reflection in the mirror while standing on a small stool as two seamstresses kneel on the floor, adjusting the length of my wedding gown. There wasn't enough time to order a custom dress, so my mother took me to the most prestigious wedding salon in the city and picked the most expensive dress available. It had to be adjusted to fit my rather impressive behind.

Andrea and I were similarly built when we were younger, but when puberty hit, my sister kept her slender figure and I didn't. It's as if my body is made of two halves that don't really fit together. I love my narrow waist and flat stomach. My breasts are average but firm. Having a petite upper body allows me to purchase the smallest size T-shirts and tops. The bottom half of me, however, is a different story all together. My ass and hips are at least two sizes too big for my torso. Diets never helped much because they only caused my breasts and my already thin arms to get smaller before my ass would get the memo.

Andrea is always telling me I'm crazy and she'd kill for a butt like mine, but I don't see it. Although I've never struggled with any self-esteem problems, I wouldn't say no to a smaller booty and slimmer thighs. I sigh as I look at my reflection again.

"What do you want to be done with your hair, Miss Isabella?" the hairstylist asks.

"Leave it loose," my mother suggests from the chair in the corner of the room. She's been overseeing the preparations since five this morning.

"Loose is okay." I shrug.

Luca didn't come to see me. Not on the day my grandfather announced that we'll be getting married, and not any time during the following weeks. I guess he considered it not necessary since we already knew each other.

I assess my reflection again, noting the long, white, lacy dress and expensive tiara on top of my head. My dream is finally coming true. But, I never thought it would be such a bitter experience. Based on what I overheard the morning I eavesdropped outside of my grandfather's study, I should have expected it.

"*What am I going to do with a nineteen-year-old,*" Luca said. As if I was a stray dog someone brought in off the street. One he couldn't throw out, but he didn't want there either.

I'm glad I only overheard the tail end of the conversation. God knows what else he said before that.

There is a knock on the door and my father's head peeks inside. "You're beautiful, Isa." He smiles and turns to my mother. "Emma, we need to hurry or we're going to be late."

"We'll be down in a minute," she says, moving somewhere behind me.

The staff leave the room first, my mother following, then Andrea and I exit last.

"Smile, Isa! You're finally marrying Luca," she whispers. "It still feels surreal."

"Yeah."

"Oh, come on. It's your wedding day for God's sake. I expected you to be ecstatic. People will expect you to be happy."

"I'm just nervous," I lie. I haven't told her about what I heard Luca say in Grandfather's study. "Here, better?" I ask and offer one of my favorite fake smiles.

"Perfect. I love that one, I've never really managed to pull off the right mix of happiness with a tiny bit of shyness. You were always Mom's best student." She laughs.

Yes, it's all about appearances in our world.

## Luca

My divorce is official as of yesterday afternoon. And now, not even twenty-four hours later, I'm standing in front of an altar, waiting for my new bride. Unbelievable.

The church's tall door opens, and Isabella, on her father's arm, steps inside. I take the opportunity to study my future wife as she approaches. Maybe it's the light, but her face looks different from the last time I saw her for more than a fleeting second. She's still breathtaking. Still the same long hair, huge eyes, and sharp cheekbones. I can't pinpoint exactly what it is, but there's something amiss. She gives the impression that she's happy. A small smile is on her lips, and her head is held high—a picture-perfect image of a radiant bride. I move my gaze back to her eyes, and that's when I see it. Her face might be showing happiness and joy, but the emotion doesn't reach her eyes. Instead, they seem . . . empty.

She takes the final step to stand beside me, her gaze focused solely on the priest. Of course she doesn't want this either. What nineteen-year-old would want to be tied to a man almost twice her age? She must be scared about what's happening. I should have gone to speak with her beforehand, met her properly prior to the wedding. It's not as if I'm planning on us having a marriage that fits the true sense of the word, but still.

As the priest starts speaking, I reach out to take her hand in mine, and hear her sharp intake of breath. Isabella looks down at our joined hands, then lifts her gaze to stare right at me. Her eyes are not vacant anymore, and as she watches me, I can almost see the fire burning in their dark depths. I like that much better than the dead look.

After the priest finishes and we exchange rings, I lean down and place a quick kiss on her cheek. When I straighten and look at her, I find her watching me with that empty stare again.

I lift my glass and sip the seltzer without taking my eyes off the corner of the room where my young wife is standing with her sister and mother.

The moment we arrived at the country club, where the wedding lunch is being held, Isabella left my side and went to the opposite end of the room.

She hasn't looked in my direction once. I should be relieved. Instead, I've been watching her for more than an hour, noticing every man who gives her a passing glance. It pisses me off. Not only the looks other men are giving her, but also the fact that it's bothering me.

"What an unexpected turn of events," Lorenzo Barbini says as he steps up next to me.

"Oh?" I take another sip of my drink. "Do you mean the wedding or the fact that Giuseppe named me his successor?"

"Both, to be honest. I thought the plan was to have Angelo Scardoni marry his granddaughter."

"Plans change," I say.

Lorenzo has been Giuseppe's underboss for almost fifteen years, which is longer than I've been a capo. It's understandable that he was surprised by the don's decision. Everyone was, including me. Usually, when a don dies or decides to step down, it's his son or son-in-law who takes over the leadership. If that's not the case, then the reigns are passed to the underboss. My new grandfather-in-law chose to forge a new path.

"Are you sure you can handle everything your new position will entail?" he asks.

I've never aspired to lead the Family. Making arms deals, managing transactions so everything runs smoothly, and bringing in money was my main focus. Presently, the operations I oversee account for more than fifty percent of our earnings.

"Do you think you'd make a better don?" I ask.

"Let's be real here, Luca. You're a businessman and you do a great job. But you rarely attend Family events, and I'm pretty sure you have no idea how to handle internal affairs."

He's right. I don't give a damn about their dinners, or who banged whose wife. Assuming the head position of the Chicago Cosa Nostra means resolving a bunch of private matters, meddling in debt issues between high-level members, and arranging marriages within the Family. Other people's personal drama is not something I enjoy. But how little I care about the social aspect of the job doesn't mean I'll allow anyone to question my abilities.

"Yes, I assume you'd be better versed in handling that part, considering that sitting at parties is all you've been doing recently. Tell me, Lorenzo, would you run the Family the same way you're running our casinos? Because from what I know, you've been dealing with significant losses for months." I smile, enjoying the shock that spreads over his face. "Losses, might I add, that were covered with the profits I brought in from the gun deals. Maybe you should focus on taking care of your own shit before you aspire to take on more responsibilities?"

"He who flies high, falls deep," Lorenzo mumbles into his glass.

I smile and grab the knot of his tie, pulling him up slightly. "I didn't hear you well." I bend, getting into his face, "Can you please repeat that?"

Lorenzo's nostrils flare as the redness starts spreading over his face. He stares at me with bulging eyes for a few moments, then grits his teeth.

"I said, your information is wrong," he sneers, "There is nothing wrong with the casino business."

"Oh. My bad, then." I release his tie and nod toward the corner of the room. "Seems like your wife is looking for you."

Lorenzo gives me one angry stare, then marches away, and I turn my eyes back to my young wife. Franco Conti, the capo in charge of laundering money, is speaking with Emma, Isabella's mother. I haven't collaborated with Franco much, since he only handles money that comes from our casinos. Damian is in charge of laundering what my operations make, and I plan on keeping it that way. Standing next to Franco is Dario D'Angelo, the oldest son of Capo Santino D'Angelo, talking with Isabella. She smiles at something he says, then turns toward her sister, and I notice the way Dario's gaze passes down her body while she's not looking. Grinding my teeth, I pivot around and head to the bar. Who she talks to shouldn't concern me. I'm halfway to my destination when I hear female laughter ring out behind me, so I peer over my shoulder. Isabella and her sister are giggling at something Dario has just said.

It shouldn't bother me that another man can make her laugh. But it does. It's like a damn itch in my side. I ignore the urge to walk over and shoo Santino's son away from Isabella. Instead, I join Orlando Lombardi, another capo who handles the Family's gambling business, at the bar.

"Did you hear about last week's shitstorm in New York?" he asks when I take a seat next to him.

"I'm not into gossip." I motion for the barman to bring me another seltzer. "Too much shit to deal with here."

"Ajello annihilated two Camorra clans in one night. Forty-seven people. Looks like they tried sticking their fingers in his business." Orlando leans close to me. "One of my nieces is married to a guy who works as a foot soldier for Ajello. She heard Ajello was shot during the skirmish."

I take a sip of my drink. What the don of New York does doesn't concern me in the least, I have no business with him. But I can't say I'm not a bit curious. That man has always been a mystery. "Is he dead?"

"No. But that's all I know," Orlando says. "His ranks are too tightly stitched, and his men are loyal to a point of madness. My niece only overheard the conversation when her husband talked over the phone with someone."

I'm trying my best to keep my eyes focused on my drink, but can't fight the compulsion to take another look at Isabella. When I do, I find her watching me. The moment our gazes connect, however, she turns back to Dario.

"You know, I sometimes think that man doesn't exist," Orlando continues. "How come no one has ever met him?"

"Giuseppe did," I say and glance at my wife again. She's still talking with the idiot. "Last year."

"No! Why did he never mention it?"

"Because Giuseppe doesn't need to share what he does with anyone."

"He told you," he says with an envious glint in his eyes. "What was the meeting about?"

"One of our soldiers went to New York to visit a girlfriend who was there for work. And he didn't ask permission to enter Ajello's territory. Giuseppe met with Ajello to resolve the issue."

"And did they? Resolve the issue?"

"Yes." I nod but keep one eye on Isabella.

"Ajello released the guy?"

"In a way," I say. "He sent back his head via FedEx."

"Jesus fuck."

Santino's kid is still standing with Isabella. I lower my glass to the bar and stand up. "I'm off."

"Leaving in the middle of your own wedding reception?"

"I have a meeting with Sergei Belov this afternoon."

He widens his eyes at me. "I didn't know you were doing business with the Bratva."

"Well, we already established that you don't know that many things, Orlando."

I leave Orlando staring daggers at my back and head to collect my wife.

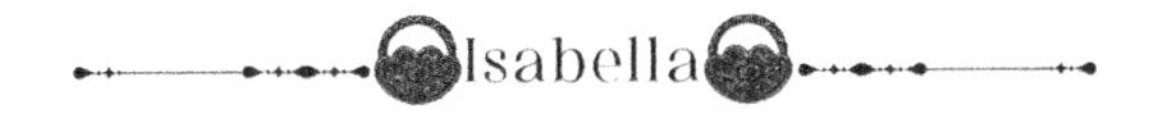

## Isabella

I stare out the window of the limousine, watching the buildings as we pass them by, and try to smother the need to turn and face Luca. He made sure he sat as far away from me as possible, on the other side of the back seat. We've been driving for almost an hour, and he hasn't said a word to me. Instead, he's been engrossed by typing something on his phone.

My thoughts fly back to the church and our wedding this morning. I was so damn excited when the priest said "You may kiss the bride". It's not that I expected Luca to devour me in front of all those people, but I did want a real kiss. And what did I get? A light peck on the cheek. Next, he might as well have taken out candy from his pocket and given it to me. It hurts, the way he's acting.

I sigh and continue looking outside, wondering what the hell I should do now. Just say *who cares* and see where this situation leads us? Live with a husband who remains a stranger because we ignore each other? Nope, I won't allow it. My self-pity party ends here. I finally married a man whom I've secretly loved for years, and I'll be damned if I let him sweep me under the carpet. Luca may not care about me now, but I will make him fall in love with me, or I'll die trying.

He has a problem with our age difference. I clearly heard him say that. Well, I can't do anything about how old I am, so it's one of the obstacles I'll need to overcome. I guess I'll have to give him a wake-up call. I may be young, but I know what I want. Him. Loving me. And I'm ready to fight for it.

The limo stops in front of a big white mansion, and Luca exits and comes around to open my door. Gathering my skirt, I take his extended hand, and get out to regard my new home. It's smaller than my grandfather's house, where I grew up, but still huge.

"Take Mrs. Rossi's suitcase upstairs," he says to the driver and motions for me to follow him inside. "I suppose you'll want to change and rest, so I'll take you to your room. Damian will show you around the house before dinner."

"Your brother?" I ask as we enter the big foyer.

"Yes. I have work to do."

"Oh?" I might be in love with him, but it doesn't mean I'll allow him to treat me like a doormat. "I don't remember marrying your brother, Luca."

He stops in his tracks and turns to me. "What does that mean?"

"It means that you will be the one to show me the house and introduce me to your staff," I say in a cold voice and enjoy the way his eyes widen in disbelief. Didn't expect me to have a backbone, did he? Well, surprise. "Where's your daughter?"

"Rosa is at her friend's house. She'll be home for dinner."

"Good. Please take me to my room now."

Luca cocks his head to the side, eyeing me with interest, then heads to the big stairway as I lag a few paces behind. I always admired the way he walks. His stride is slow, like a wolf on the prowl. Letting my eyes travel up his body, I check out his long legs and broad shoulders, and stop at the top of his head where his hair is gathered in a bun.

So many times, I've daydreamed about taking out that hair tie and threading my fingers through those black strands. I wonder how long his hair is now. The only time I saw it loose was after he jumped into the pool to save me all those years ago. His bun must have come undone in the process, spilling his mane free. It was shoulder-length back then.

I remember everything about him. Observing Luca in secret was all I ever could do, so I made sure to catch every single detail and store it in my mental vault, labeled with his name. The way his body changed over the years, becoming brawny, harder. Since I turned sixteen, I imagined that huge body wrapped around mine, holding me tight. Loving me.

I was seventeen the first time I pleasured myself, and I did it by imagining it was his hand between my legs instead of mine. From that day on, I've been doing it every single night before going to sleep. Sometimes even during the day. Whenever I've felt lonely or sad, I would lock myself in my room, get under the blanket, and imagine Luca lying next to me while I orgasmed. If people knew, they may think I'm silly for being in love with a man without actually knowing him that well. I don't care.

When we reach the third floor, Luca nods toward the door on the left and opens it. "My room," he says.

I take a glance, noticing an enormous bed under the window. Most of the furniture is made of dark wood that works well with the pale beige walls and curtains in the same shade.

"This room is not used," he says, opening the next door. The room seems the same size as his, but the furniture here is mostly white, with curtains and a rug in a soft peach color. There's a connecting door on the left wall that probably leads to his bedroom. He quickly shuts the door and ushers me down the corridor until we reach the last two rooms.

"Rosa's room." He nods to the one on the left with a big "Do Not Disturb" sticker on it, then turns to the door on the right and opens it. "This is you."

It's a nice space. Big, with several tall windows and light wood furniture. My suitcase stands in the middle of the carpet next to a big fluffy sofa.

"I'll come by at six to take you downstairs to have dinner," he says and leaves.

I look around one more time. So, he placed me as far from him as possible on this floor. It won't do. I walk to my suitcase and grab the handle. Rolling it in front of me so my dress doesn't catch within the wheels, I leave the room and head toward the other end of the corridor. Luca is just entering his room when he hears me coming. He takes a step back and watches me approach.

"Something wrong with your room?" he asks.

I stop in front of the room adjacent to his and tilt my chin up. His hooded eyes are peering at me, glaring with expression that I can't quite read.

"Not at all," I say, roll my suitcase inside and close the door behind me.

I look at the door that connects my bedroom to the room Isabella has claimed and listen to the sounds coming from the other side. There is no way she's staying that close to me. I'll let it be for now, but first thing in the morning, she's going back to the room across from Rosa's. I hear her move around, and then the water turns on in her ensuite bathroom. My teenage wife is taking a shower just a few yards from me, and suddenly, my mind conjures up images of her perfect little body under the spray.

I shake my head. What the fuck is wrong with me? I'm imagining having sex with a teenager. And one that's probably never slept with a man before. Jesus. I march out of the room and slam the door shut behind me as if it'll help erase the images of Isabella naked and wet. Or the temptation to pin her body between mine and the tiles of the shower wall while holding her wrists above her head.

It's quarter to six when I get back from the meeting with Sergei Belov. One of my weapons suppliers got a hold of several crates of military-issued crossbows, but no one knew how they worked. Belov was the only person who came to mind that might know how to handle that shit. Based on his grinning face when I showed him the sample, he had plenty of experience with them. Somehow, I wasn't surprised. But he did stun me when he asked if I could get him a tank. Then, he shrugged and said, "Asking for a friend." They must have more than one lunatic in the Bratva.

I climb the stairs to the third floor and knock on the door of Isabella's temporary room. She opens and looks me over, focusing on my jeans and black shirt. I notice a glint of astonishment in her eyes.

"No dressing up for dinner here?" she asks as we head toward the stairway.

"I hate suits."

Isabella's eyebrows lift in surprise. Wordlessly, she descends the stairs in front of me, giving me an unobstructed view of her behind. A pink sleeveless top that ties around her neck is molded to her torso and narrow waist, and it only emphasizes her perky round ass, clad in tight black trousers. It takes tremendous willpower to move my eyes away from it.

When we get to the ground floor, she stops in front of the staff lined up on the right side of the foyer.

"This is Isabella. My wife," I say and introduce them one by one, starting with the housekeeper, then the maids, two drivers, the gardener, and finally the kitchen staff.

With that done, I turn to the other side where my security people stand and introduce them, as well. I don't expect her to remember any of their names because there are more than thirty people that work here.

"This is the second shift," I tell her. "I'll introduce you to the first shift when they arrive in the morning."

"Thank you." She nods and follows me to the dining room that spans a quarter of the ground floor on the east side.

I remember the first time I brought Simona here after we were married at the city hall. She was overwhelmed with the number of security guards and the size of the house itself, and she jumped and squealed when anyone carrying a firearm passed by her. Isabella, on the contrary, takes all of this in without batting an eye. I guess it's nothing new to her. She was raised in a house twice the size of mine and with significantly more armed guards.

Damian is already in the dining room, sitting at the table to the left of the head seat. He sees us come in and stands up, extending his hand.

"Finally." He laughs. "I started wondering if Luca decided to hide you in your room forever."

"Isabella, this is my brother," I say and watch closely for her reaction.

My brother is twelve years younger than me and, as women like to call him, "drop-dead gorgeous." People usually focus on his blue eyes, styled hair, and impeccable clothing, while underestimating him in the process, thinking him as a playboy. He does his best to uphold that impression with his behavior. Not many people know what a genius is hiding under that expensive haircut. Damian has a knack when it comes to numbers and the real estate market. Because of that, he handles the finances of my business dealings. He also launders millions of dollars on a monthly basis.

"Just Isa, please," my wife says.

"I have to say, I couldn't think of a name that would fit you better, Isa." He smiles at her. "Bella."

I shake my head. He's already turned on the charm.

"No flirting, Damian. Where's Rosa?"

"She said she'll eat in her room."

I turn to the maid waiting close by. "Get my daughter down here. Right now."

As we sit at the table waiting for Rosa, I lean back in my chair and observe as Isabella and Damian discuss how she likes the house. They clearly hit it off right from the start, which I expected since they're close in age. I wonder if she'll try seducing him like Simona did.

"You weren't at the wedding," Isabella says.

Damian smiles. "Yeah, I try to avoid Family gatherings."

"What he means is he doesn't want to run into his exes," I throw in. "Especially since half of them were already married when he slept with them."

"Makes sense." Isabella smirks at my brother. "Are you still sleeping with Franco's daughter?"

Damian swirls his wine and stares at her. "How do you know about that?"

Isabella just smiles and reaches for the carafe with juice.

"I'm not sitting at the same table with that woman!" My daughter's high voice reaches me.

I turn around in my chair and fix Rosa with my stare, making sure she sees in my eyes what I think about her yelling. "Come here."

"No. I told you . . ."

"Right this second, piccola."

She stomps her foot on the floor, juts her chin, and marches over to the table, taking a seat on the other side of Damian.

"Now, apologize to Isabella," I say.

"No."

Jesus. Doesn't puberty hit around twelve or so? Rosa is only seven, but I'm starting to believe she's going into it prematurely. When I told her that Simona and I were divorcing, her comment was "Good riddance." The two of them never had any kind of relationship, and Rosa spent more time with our cook than with her own mother. I talked with Rosa last week and explained the situation with Isabella, and she seemed reasonable, but I guess we'll have to discuss it some more. No matter how or why Isabella ended up here, I will not allow anyone to disrespect her, my daughter included. And I certainly won't allow yelling in my house.

"Are you sure?" I ask.

"Yes."

"Okay. You can go back to your room."

"What?" She bulges her eyes at me. "And dinner?"

"No apology, no dinner."

"Dad!"

"You are free to go." I nod toward the door, and motion with my hand to the maid to serve the food.

"Fine," Rosa snaps, jumps up from the chair, and marches away.

I follow Rosa with my eyes as she leaves and notice Isabella watching me, her mouth pressed into a thin line. I wait to see if she'll comment, but she doesn't say anything, just turns away and focuses on her plate. She probably thinks I'll let my daughter go to sleep without dinner, and I don't plan on reassuring her.

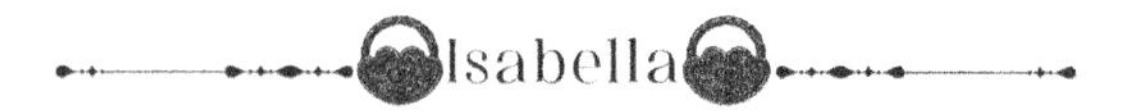


I thought finding the kitchen would pose a problem, but when I get down to the ground floor, one of the maids I met when I arrived is dusting the lamp in the corner.

"Anna, can you show me where the kitchen is?" I ask as I approach her.

She blinks at me with a slightly confused expression on her face, then nods quickly. "Of course, Mrs. Rossi. This way."

I follow Anna down the corridor on the right until we reach the rear of the house, where she stops in front of a white door. "It's here."

"Thank you," I say and step inside.

The kitchen is spacious. Counters and an island on the left. On the right, there is a long wooden table that can seat at least ten people. That's probably where the staff eat. I head over to the cabinets, where a willowy woman in her fifties is polishing glasses by the sink.

"Can I help you, Mrs. Rossi?"

"Would you mind making me a sandwich? I'd do it myself, but I have no idea where you store the ingredients."

"Right away." She nods and rushes around, taking out a plate and bread, then asks, "Do you want something specific?"

"It's for Rosa. Just make them how she usually likes them. Thank you."

The maid busies herself preparing the food, but I notice her throwing looks my way every couple of seconds. When she's done, she brings over a plate with two sandwiches and a napkin, offering these to me.

"Ham. With extra cheese."

"Thank you, Grace. Good night."

Her eyes widen at hearing me say her name, but she quickly composes herself. "Good night, Mrs. Rossi."

I carry the sandwiches to the third floor, walk down the hallway, and knock on Rosa's door.

"I'm not here!" comes from the other side.

I roll my eyes. It's like I'm listening to my sister. Andrea gets extremely cranky when something is not going her way. I grab the knob with my free hand and open the door. Rosa is lying on her stomach across the bed, fully engrossed in whatever's happening on the phone set in front of her.

When she sees me standing in the doorway, she springs up, staring at me. "What are you doing in my room? Get out or . . ." Her eyes land on the plate in my hands. "No mayo?"

"No mayo." I approach the bed, place the plate next to her, and turn to leave.

"How did you meet my dad?"

I stop. "He jumped into the pool and saved my life."

"You're lying."

"Nope," I call over my shoulder. "Ask him yourself if you want."

"He really saved your life?"

I smile inwardly and turn around. "Want to hear about it?"

"Yes!" she exclaims, her eyes wide. "Tell me."

I plop down on the small sofa in the corner of the room and lean back. "I was a little bit younger than you. It was my sixth birthday party. All of us kids were running around the garden playing. One of my shoelaces was untied, and when I kneeled to tie it right next to the pool, my friend's cousin ran by me and pushed me into it."

"You fell into a pool?"

"Yup."

"And Dad saved you?"

"Jumped right in, clothes and all. The pool wasn't deep, but I was little and could have drowned."

"Wow," she says, then tilts her head, regarding me. "Is that why you married him? Because he saved your life?"

I laugh. "No. I married him because my grandfather and your father agreed that it would be for the best. It's how things sometimes work."

"So, you don't love him?"

Do I? To truly love someone, I would need to love the person the way they wholly are, the best and the worst about them. I've been in love with the idea of Luca since I can remember, and I've been obsessing over him for the last few years like a crazy woman. Is that love? Or just a crush? I've never felt anything similar for another man, that's for sure.

"I like him." I nod.

"I heard Tiyana's sister say my dad is hot. What does that mean?"

I blink, slightly confused about how to explain. Rosa is only seven, even if her attitude screams preteen at times. "It means he looks nice."

"Oh. Okay." She takes a bite of her sandwich, her gaze never leaving me. As she chews, she narrows her eyes as if she's judging me. "Will you yell at me?"

"No. Why would I do that?"

"Simona always yells at me." She shrugs. "When Dad's not around that is. He doesn't allow yelling."

She calls her mother by her first name? I'm still trying to process that fact and the implications it carries when the door opens. Luca steps inside, carrying a tray with a sandwich on a plate and a glass of milk. He halts in the doorway, zeroing in on the sandwich in Rosa's hand.

"Isabella beat you to it," Rosa says between bites and points her finger at me.

"Okay, I'll be going now." I stand up and head toward the door. "Good night, Rosa."

Luca doesn't move from the doorway where he's glaring at me like a hawk. I look up and meet his gaze, and our eyes lock in silence for several long heartbeats until he finally steps aside. Making sure my movements are deliberately slow, I tread down the hallway until I reach my room. Something, call it intuition, tells me he's still watching me as I slip inside my room without looking back.

The moment the door closes behind me I exhale and lean my back against it. I thought it would be easy to pretend I'm indifferent, but I have a feeling that a single kind act on my part will result in him pulling away even more. I can't risk it. Not yet.

Being so close to Luca after all these years and knowing he doesn't want anything to do with me . . . hurts. In a way, it was easier when I knew I didn't have a chance. I never expected anything. And now, when I finally have him so close, it feels like he's even farther away than he was before.

I close my eyes and remember the day of my eighteenth birthday when he called me tesoro. Apparently, the word didn't really carry the affection I imagined. It was just a word said in passing. Yet, I thought about that moment and his light touch on my hair for days after it happened.

Well, I'm not giving up. He better prepare for war, because that's what I'm going to serve him. I will fight him and his indifference, every step of the way.

"You better be ready, Luca Rossi," I whisper to the empty room, "because all's fair in love and war."

# CHAPTER

## *five*

Luca

I THROW MY JACKET ONTO ONE OF THE RECLINERS IN MY ROOM AND SIT down on the edge of the bed, listening to Donato's mumbling coming from the phone. There have been some problems with one of the properties we bought and I spent last night and the whole of today in my office downtown, trying to get that shit sorted out. I really don't need another fuckup today.

"Oh, for the love of God, Donato. Can't you deal with at least some of the shit by yourself?" I say into the phone, squeezing the bridge of my nose. "How many crates?"

"The truck just came in. We opened the first few, but it's likely several more are the same, Luca."

"Fuck." I close my eyes in frustration. What the hell am I going to do with a whole fucking shipment of the wrong caliber ammunition?

A low, moaning sound reaches me from the direction of Isabella's room and I look up, staring at the door connecting our rooms. I haven't seen her after yesterday evening when I found her in Rosa's room. She brought my daughter dinner. I'm not sure what to think about that. Or about the fact that I've been thinking about her the whole day. Fuck. I need to tell Viola to move her things back to the room across from Rosa's.

"What should I tell the Romanians?" Donato asks, pulling me away from thinking about my young wife.

"Call Bogdan. Tell him I'm expecting him at the warehouse at eight tomorrow morning."

"What if he says he can't come?"

"Then, I will come to him and personally put each and every fucking bullet up his ass. Tell him that." I throw the phone onto the bed. Damn Romanians.

I cross my bedroom, heading toward the bathroom, but stop in front of the connecting door to the room where Isabella is sleeping. There it is again, another quiet moan like the one I thought I heard a few moments ago. I inch closer to the door, wondering if something's wrong, but there's only silence from the other side. The door handle feels cool when I grasp it and open the door as quietly as possible, taking a peek inside.

At first, I think Isabella must be unwell, because the only thing I can see through the darkness is her body on the bed, twisted slightly to the side. I open the door a bit more and some of the light from my room spills inside, allowing me to see her more clearly. The moment I do, my hand tightens on the handle.

Isabella lifts her head off the pillow and looks directly at me while her hand keeps moving inside her silky pajama pants, right between her legs. I watch, mesmerized, as she lifts her ass up and a moan escapes her lips. My breaths quicken and I feel myself getting hard as she opens her legs wider and slides her other hand under the waistband. I should turn around and shut the door in my wake, but I can't make myself leave. I'm glued to the sight of my teenage wife as she pleasures herself, her eyes fixed on me the whole time. She lifts her pelvis again and starts panting, her lips partially open. I grip the doorjamb with my other hand when she arches her body and throws back her head as tremors shake her frame. It lasts a few seconds before she sags down onto the bed. She exhales slowly, removes her hands from inside of her pants, and flashes her eyes at me one more time as she slides under the blanket.

I stare at her for some time, then turn around and bang the door closed.

"Good morning," I smile at Rosa and Damian as I sit down at the dining table where coffee has already been served.

"You seem to be cheerful today. Any particular reason?" Damian asks and reaches for his coffee.

Of course I am, and there's a very specific reason. Every time I think about the shocked look on my husband's face when he opened the door and saw me playing with my pussy, a smile pulls at my lips. Yes, he went back to his room and banged the door after him, but based on the way he gripped the doorway while he watched, we're off to a good start.

"No reason." I nod toward the empty chair on my left. "Where's Luca?"

"There were some problems he had to deal with, so he left early. He was in a really strange mood, though," Damian says, looking at me over the rim of his cup.

"Oh? How so?"

"Cranky. Snapping at the staff. He rarely does that. I wonder what could have riled him up."

"He's in a stressful line of work." I shrug, a picture of innocence.

"Yeah, it must be that," he says casually, but I see the way he's looking at me with a tiny smile on his lips.

"I'll need a driver," I say. "My grandfather's not feeling well. I want to drop by and check on him."

"Sure. But we'll have to wait for Luca to come back to see who he'll assign as your security detail."

"I won't need a bodyguard today. I'll be going straight to the don's house and back, I don't plan on stopping anywhere else or leaving the car along the way."

"Luca won't like it if you leave the grounds without one, Isabella."

"Dad always has to have the last word, Isa," Rosa throws in, laughing.

Good to know.

A maid brings in a huge basket of freshly baked pastries and places it in the middle of the table. Rosa jumps up, grabbing two croissants, but before placing them on her plate throws a sideways look at me.

"Is something wrong, Rosa?" I ask and reach to take some pastries for myself.

"I'm really hungry," she mumbles.

"Then you should eat those before they get cold." I nod at the croissants she's still holding.

"Both?"

"You said you're hungry."

"But I'll get fat."

My head snaps up. "Oh, sweetie, you won't get fat. Where did you get that idea from?"

Rosa bends her head and shrugs. "Simona told me I need to watch how much I eat because of my meta . . . hm, metalism."

Jesus Christ. Something is seriously wrong with that woman. I place my palms on the table and lean toward Rosa. Damian keeps observing the situation without commenting, as if he's waiting to see what I'll do.

"You mean metabolism, sweetie. You're a child. Kids need to eat a good breakfast because they're still growing." I reach out and, taking the croissants from her hands, lower them onto her plate. "You don't have to worry about your metabolism for at least a decade. Okay?"

A small smile pulls at Rosa's lips, and the next second she digs into her breakfast. When I lean back in my chair, I notice Luca's brother watching me and I raise an eyebrow at him. Damian smirks and gets back to his coffee.

## Luca

I walk inside the warehouse where my men are unloading the rest of the crates that came last night. Donato is following a few paces behind me. Bogdan and two more of his guys are standing next to the truck, arguing.

"What happened with my shipment?" I nod toward the crates left on the truck.

"Gavril swapped the model numbers on some containers," Bogdan says and turns to face the tall guy on his right. "I told you to check everything twice!"

"How many crates?" I ask.

"Twelve. I'll have the correct ammunition in two weeks. Three, in the worst-case scenario."

I look back at Donato. "When did we promise to deliver those?"

"On Monday."

I turn back to Bogdan. "I need the correct ammo on Sunday."

"I can't get anything within the next ten days, Luca. All my trucks are already loaded and have routes planned out. How about the weekend after next?"

How unfortunate. I walk to the open crates lined along the truck, take out a Beretta, then reach for a magazine in the adjacent container. "I have a feeling you are not taking our arrangement seriously, Bogdan." I load the magazine inside the gun. "Let's change the narrative."

"Oh, come on. You know how it is. Mistakes happen."

"Indeed." I cock the gun. "The thing is, Bogdan, I've been in an extremely bad mood recently. I didn't need this today."

I lift the gun and shoot the asshole who apparently caused this clusterfuck, hitting his forehead dead-center.

"What the fuck!" Bogdan yells, staring at the dead guy now at his feet.

"You see, I've just mistaken Gavril for you. Mistakes happen," I say and shoot Bogdan's other guy. His body drops next to the first one. "Should I continue? It's only you left. I'm pretty sure I won't make a mistake a third time."

Bogdan's eyes bulge, his mouth opening and closing like a fish out of water.

"I want my ammunition here on Sunday. Can you do that for me?"

He nods.

"Good. I'm glad we've found a language that makes it easier for you to understand." I throw the gun back in the crate. "Ask around and see if you can get me a tank."

My arms supplier just stares at me.

"Can you?" I ask again.

"A tank . . . as in . . . an actual tank?"

"Do you sell imaginary ones as well?" I shake my head. "Belov sounded interested when we met. Says he's asking for a friend."

"They're all insane, those Russians," he mumbles.

"Let me know what you find out."

My phone rings as I'm getting behind the wheel, showing Isabella's name. She probably asked Damian for my number, since I never offered it to her. But I certainly made sure I have hers. It's a shitty move, I know, but I've already been thinking about my wife way more than I should. I don't need her calling me, especially now when all I can think about are the sounds she was making last evening.

I let the phone ring and throw it onto the passenger's seat. Maybe if I avoid her, I might be able to forget how edible she looked last night. The moment I come home I'm ordering her to move out of that damn room.

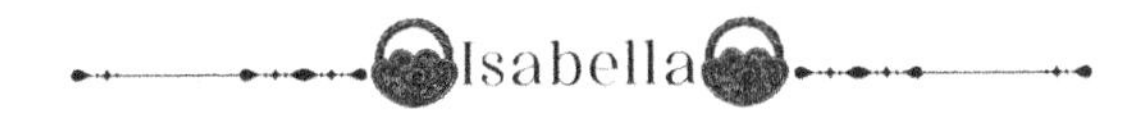


It's already five in the afternoon, and Luca still hasn't returned. I tried calling him several times, but each call went unanswered. Finally, I decide I'm done waiting for him, so I head down to the ground floor and approach the security guy standing at the front door.

"Can you please get me a car and a driver?"

"Of course, Mrs. Rossi. Did Mr. Rossi approve it?"

"I don't need my husband to approve anything for me. Please get me a car."

He fidgets, visibly unsure of what to do, and it looks like I'll have to help him decide.

"Are you disobeying my direct request, Emilio?"

"No, of course not, Mrs. Rossi. I'll get you a car immediately." He quickly takes out his phone.

I don't like pulling rank with the staff, but sometimes it's necessary. Being a woman in mafia circles is not easy. I watched my mother be ignored too many times when she tried to join the "men's conversations" at Family dinners. Even though she has a degree in economics, no one except my grandfather has ever asked for her opinion. The mafia world is ruled by men, and women are often perceived as less important and weak. It is imperative I make my position clear from the beginning if I want to be treated as equal. I've never had a problem with authority in my grandfather's house. Here, on the other hand, even though I'm a capo's wife, they still see a nineteen-year-old girl, and that's not something either Luca or I can afford. He might not have wanted me, but he got me, and I will not end up as a burden or a trophy wife.

I resigned myself to becoming a capo's wife a long time ago. I've been groomed for it since I was ten. While other girls my age were having playdates and obsessing over their latest celebrity crushes, I was learning how to feign interest even when a conversation bored me to death. I learned how to smile and what to say to make people open up and spill information they wouldn't normally share. As well as how to make myself seem a little stupid, if the situation required it. There were key lessons on how to pretend to be having a great time even when the only thing I wanted was to go to my room and be alone. But the most important training I ever received was to never show weakness. Never cry when someone can see, and never show if their words hurt you. In a tank full of sharks, I can't allow myself to bleed, or they would eat me alive.

While my friends stalked cute boys on Facebook and Instagram, I spent hours sitting with my mother at social events, listening to her and learning as she explained who was who in our world and about their roles in the Family. But most of all, I discovered everyone's dirty laundry, and there were lots of it. I smile inwardly at the recollection. How I would love to see the faces of all those men who believed my mother to be just another pretty, harmless face. They had no idea how dangerous she was.

I haven't officially met more than half of the people in the Family, but thanks to my mother, I knew who had affairs with whom, who enjoyed gambling a bit too much, and whose tongue would loosen when they had a few shots. Those may sound like trivial things, but in Cosa Nostra, information means power. And power is the main currency of all the games in the mafia world.

A silver sedan with tinted windows pulls up to the front of the stone steps. The driver gets out, opens the back door and nods at me. "Mrs. Rossi."

"Thank you, Emilio." I smile at the security guard and descend the stairs, heading toward the car. "To the don's house, Renato."

The driver looks at me with surprise, but he tucks his chin and closes the door after me. I quite enjoy the shock on people's faces when I address them by their name. The first lesson my mother taught me was to remember every name of every person I ever meet.

Luca

I knock at the door of Isabella's room, not getting an answer.

She called me several more times today. However, I was still too pissed with myself about last night, so I kept ignoring her. As if not talking to her would somehow erase the image of her arching her back as she masturbated in front of me, or the fact that I had to take a long, cold shower immediately after leaving her room.

I knock again. Nothing.

"Isabella?" I open the door and find her room empty.

I already checked the living room and the library on the ground floor, but she wasn't there. Maybe she's with Rosa. I walk down the hallway and open Rosa's door. My daughter is sprawled on the bed on her back, watching some crap on her phone again.

"Dad?" She looks up at me. "Can I pierce my eyebrow?"

"What? No, you cannot pierce your anything. Are you watching that TikTik again?" I'm going to uninstall that shit from her phone. It's a bad influence.

"It's TikTok, Dad." She giggles. "What about tattoos?"

"You're seven. Forget about tattoos or piercings for the next fifteen years, Rosa."

"When did you get your tats?"

Twenty years ago. But there's no way I'm telling her that. "When I was thirty. You can get yours when you're thirty, as well."

"No!"

I raise my eyebrows at her, "Yes. Have you seen Isabella?"

"She was downstairs for lunch. But I haven't seen her after that." She shrugs and looks back at her phone.

Perfect. Where is that woman? I head down to the second floor where Damian has his rooms. His bedroom is empty, so I go to his office next.

"Where's Isabella?" I ask from the doorway.

"I have no idea," Damian mumbles without taking his eyes off the laptop screen. "The real estate prices went up again. We should sell some of the properties we don't use."

"She's not in her room or anywhere else in the house."

"Then she's probably still at the don's house. I'm selling those apartments we have downtown. They only eat away at the money since you won't allow me to rent them out, and if we—"

"What!"

He looks up at me. "You don't want to sell them?"

"What the fuck is she doing at the don's? Who went with her?" Surely, she wouldn't be so reckless as to leave without a security detail.

"I don't know. I gave her your number and assumed you assigned a bodyguard?"

I close my eyes and curse. She went there without any protection and it's my fault. "I didn't take her calls."

Damian's eyebrows lift. "Why?"

"I've been avoiding her. Who took her to the Agostini mansion?"

"You don't avoid people. Did something happen?"

"Will you answer my fucking question?"

He leans back in his chair and folds his hands behind his head, smiling. "Why are you so concerned all of a sudden? You never cared when Simona went somewhere without informing you."

Because I didn't give a fuck if something happened to Simona. However, the idea of Isabella leaving the house without a bodyguard ignites a surge of panic in my chest.

I take a step inside and pin him with my stare. "Damian."

"Jesus fuck. It was Renato's shift."

I grind my teeth. "Find out who let her leave the grounds without a bodyguard and let them know that if that happens again, there will be consequences. Then, call Renato, and if they're still at the don's, tell him to stay put until I get there."

"Why not send one of the security guys?"

"Do it," I snap and leave the room, hearing Damian laugh the moment I shut the door behind me.

It takes me thirty minutes to get to the Agostini mansion, more than enough time to analyze my erratic behavior and come up with zero conclusions. The chances that something could happen to Isabella between the don's house and mine are almost non-existent, and still, I keep hitting the gas like a maniac. I could've sent Marco to drive over and bring her back. I planned on assigning him as Isabella's bodyguard anyway, but I had this strange compulsion to make sure she was all right.

And the idea of her spending time alone with another man doesn't sit well with me. Maybe I'm feeling overprotective since she's so young. Yeah, that must be it. There's no other explanation.

The guards at the gate let me pass without stopping. When I reach the house, I park next to a silver sedan. I recognize it instantly as one of mine. And that's before I spot the dipshit leaning on the hood.

"Head back home," I bark at Renato the moment I'm out of my car. "And if you ever take my wife off the grounds without a security detail again, you're dead."

"Yes, Mr. Rossi." He straightens, nods, and rushes to get inside the vehicle.

I walk around the mansion to the garden on the far side where I've always seen Isabella while visiting the don and head toward the gazebo. Isabella is sitting in a white iron chair with her back turned to me, and her sister sits opposite her. Andrea sees me first and says something to Isabella, probably warning her about my presence. I expect my young wife to tense or turn around in surprise. Maybe even be a little scared since she knows very well that she shouldn't have left without a bodyguard. Instead, when she turns her head, she looks completely unperturbed.

I grab the arm of the chair and turn it around with Isabella in it, ignoring the screeching sounds the chair legs make against the stone.

"Luca." She blinks at me innocently. "I wasn't expecting you here. Do you want something to drink?"

I grab the other chair arm and bend until we're face to face, staring at her enormous eyes. "Why did you leave the house without letting me know?"

"Oh? Am I obliged to share my daily schedule with you?"

My grip on the chair tightens. Yes, I want her to share her daily schedule with me. I want to know what she does and where she goes. And that's absolutely idiotic.

"No," I make myself say. "But you can't leave the house without a bodyguard."

"Well, if you returned any of my calls, I would have discussed it with you." She shrugs. "But if it distresses you, I won't do it again."

"Good."

"Does that mean you'll answer when I call from now on?"

Oh, she really likes to push my buttons. It's pissing me off. And it also turns me the hell on. I wonder if she would be just as feisty lying under me, with my cock buried inside her. Just thinking about it makes me instantly hard.

"Maybe," I bite out.

Isabella tilts her head up slightly, and there's a barely noticeable curve to her lips. "Works for me."

"Are you done with your visit?"

"Yup," she says, and the corners of her lips curve a little bit more. "Are we taking the chair with us?"

I let go of the chair and move aside. Isabella gives me a smirk as she walks over to give her sister, who gawked at us in silence through this whole ordeal, a goodbye kiss on a cheek.

"See you on Saturday," Andrea says and cuts a quick glance in my direction.

I follow two steps behind Isabella as she heads across the lawn toward the driveway, trying my best to keep my eyes off her ass. She's wearing white jeans today, paired with a silky navy-blue shirt and high-heeled sandals in the same color. As I leer at my wife, the heel of her left shoe catches on something in the grass, and she stumbles slightly. Instantaneously, I spring forward and grab her around the waist, steadying her. Isabella's body tenses under my hand, but it lasts only for a second or so.

"Thank you," she says, regains her balance and keeps walking, as my hand falls away from her.

I look down at the uneven ground and then at her heels, which are at least four inches high. She'll break her leg in those things. I take two quick steps and wrap one arm around her middle. Placing the other behind her knees, I lift her up. There's a barely audible gasp of surprise, but other than that, she doesn't say a word as her arm settles around my neck. I avoid eye contact and keep my teeth clenched as I carry her, heading to the front of the house.

"Where's Renato?" she asks after I put her down next to my car.

I open the passenger door. "I sent him back."

Isabella arches an eyebrow, then gets inside the vehicle and looks straight ahead through the windshield.

As I reverse, I ask, "What's on Saturday?"

"Our friend is having a birthday party."

"You're going?"

"Yes. Is that a problem?"

"No," I say and squeeze the steering wheel. "You will take two bodyguards."

"Of course."

We drive for some time in silence, but I keep thinking about that party. It will probably be at her friend's house. They'll eat junk food and watch movies. And gossip.

"Where is it?" I ask.

"Where is what?"

"The party. At your friend's house?"

Isabella looks at me and laughs. "We're not twelve. The girls and I are going to a club."

My knuckles turn white from my death grip on the wheel. "Which one?"

"Ural."

"That's the Bratva's club."

"Correct." She smirks.

"You're not going."

"Of course, I am. My grandfather signed the treaty with them, so we're friends with the Russians now. It's perfectly safe," she says. "Milene Scardoni is coming too, and since she's bringing her sister, there's no reason for concern. No one will dare approach us while Bianca's husband is there. You can come as well if you want."

"I'm not going to a teenage birthday party."

"Well, I can't say that I expected you to. You wouldn't fit in anyway."

"How so?"

"You're too old, Luca."

I grind my teeth and focus on the road in front of me, pressing the gas pedal to the floor.

I open the top drawer of the dresser and regard my collection of sexy underwear and lacy nightgowns.

Most of them I purchased the same day Nonno told me I was going to marry Luca. I was so damn excited that I dragged Andrea to the mall to shop for all the lingerie I could find. As I tried on set after set, I imagined Luca tearing each one off my body. When we returned home, I had two huge bags filled to the brim with silk and lace.

Lifting one of the white babydoll nighties, I consider it but change my mind and put it back into the drawer. White won't do. Too innocent. Let's go with the black today. I put on a short black nightgown and matching panties, turn off the lamp and climb into bed. It's showtime.

Just like the previous night, not even a minute after I start, the door connecting my room to Luca's opens, revealing his large form framed in the soft light behind him. He stands at the threshold, his hands gripping the doorframe on either side of him. I can't see his face, only the illuminated shape of his body, but I know he's looking at me.

I let my hand travel even lower and slide one finger inside my pussy, panting. Luca leans forward slightly, but then grips the doorframe even harder as if he's at war with himself about whether to come inside. Is he hard? I widen my legs a bit more and tease my clit with my other hand, imagining his cock inside me instead of my finger. The breath leaving my mouth hitches as my movements become faster, and soon, tremors start rocking my body.

I bite my lower lip and, without taking my eyes off Luca, slide another finger inside. A gasp leaves me as I orgasm, riding the wave for almost a full minute. When I come down from the high, I slowly slide my hand out from my panties, and bring it to my mouth, licking the tips of my fingers. A strange growling sound comes from the direction of the door. I tilt my head to the side, watching Luca's looming figure in the doorway, and spread my legs even more in a silent invitation. He doesn't move from his spot, just stands there stone-still, clutching the frame. Watching me. There's a muffled Italian curse, and then he turns away and goes back inside his room, slamming the door shut after him.

# Chapter

## *six*

I hear Isabella's door to the hallway open and barely restrain myself from rushing out to intercept her. I should have prohibited her from going to that club, locked her in her room, and thrown away the key. There's no reason for me to give a fuck where she goes. She'll have Marco and Nicolas with her, so she will be perfectly safe from harm. And I made sure they know to deter any man who may dare approach her. Still, I keep staring at the laptop without actually seeing the numbers on the screen. I'm too focused on the sound of high heels clicking on the hardwood as Isabella walks by my door.

Five minutes pass. The rumble of a car as it leaves the driveway reaches me through the window. I keep staring at the screen. Seven days. That's how long it has been since she became my wife and she's been fucking with my brain since. It started the first night I caught her pleasuring herself. Until that moment, I had myself convinced she was still a child and that thinking about her in any other way would be sick. Well, I haven't been able to think of her as an adolescent after that, even though I've tried, because she keeps playing with her pussy every single night. And like the sick fuck I am, I come to watch every time.

I avoid her at all costs during the day, occupying myself with work, but I can't stay away at night. The moment I hear her first moan, I'm drawn to that damn door. And then, I open it and stand on the threshold like some psycho, watching Isabella arching her body with her hand between her legs. The first few nights she wore pajamas, but then she switched to short silky nightgowns, her lacy panties the only thing obstructing my view. They were pink last night, and I barely managed to keep myself from rushing to that bed, tearing the lacy fabric from her body, and using *my* hand on her pussy. Or even better, my mouth.

Two more minutes elapse. I close the laptop. She's seen me watching. And not only that, but she also doesn't stop when she notices me lurking in the doorway. She captures my gaze and holds it like I'm her prisoner, not averting her eyes for even a second until that last moment when the tremors take over her body before she comes. She knows I'm watching every time, and that fact gets me even harder. I've had to find my own release after—in the shower, gripping my cock and imagining I'm inside her until I explode all over my hand. A thirty-five-year-old man pumping his cock in a shower while fantasizing about a nineteen-year-old girl. Jesus fuck.

Just because Isabella acts like someone much older doesn't make it better. Neither does her pretending the next morning that nothing happened. She comes downstairs for breakfast, all regal and composed—impeccable manners and calm face—as if everything is perfectly in order.

Another minute trickles by. There's no way I'm going to that party after her. To a club full of other men. Younger men. I close my eyes and take a deep breath. Fuck.

Jumping up from my desk, I grab my holster and the jacket from the chair, curse again, and leave the room.

There are at least a hundred other women in the club, most of them wearing tight short dresses. And who has the tightest and the shortest one? My wife. And as if that wasn't bad enough, it's white, making her glow like a fucking lighthouse under the neon lights.

I grab a glass of seltzer from the bar, squeezing it in my hand. I don't drink alcohol, but as I watch Isabella from my spot in the dark corner, I'm seriously tempted to start. She's standing at a tall round table, her sister on her right, and Milene Scardoni and two girls I don't recognize on the left. Nicolas and Marco are a few paces behind her, watching the crowd. I notice Bianca Scardoni perched at the end of the bar, clutching her Russian husband around his neck and smiling as he whispers something in her ear. Mikhail Orlov at a nightclub. I shake my head. Now I've seen everything.

There's a group of guys at the table next to Isabella's. I noticed them the moment I came in. One of them in particular. He's in his early twenties, blond, and wearing a tight black T-shirt. He's leaning his elbows on the table in a way that showcases his meager-looking biceps. My grip on the glass in my hand tightens. Milene and the other two girls are looking in his direction and giggling, but he's focused on my wife, or more specifically, her cleavage. Isabella doesn't look at him. She seems to be interested in Bianca Scardoni and her husband. As I watch, the blond kid calls the waiter, says something in his ear, and motions with his hand toward Isabella. The waiter nods and leaves. Did that little shit dare send my wife a drink?

The glass in my hand shatters.

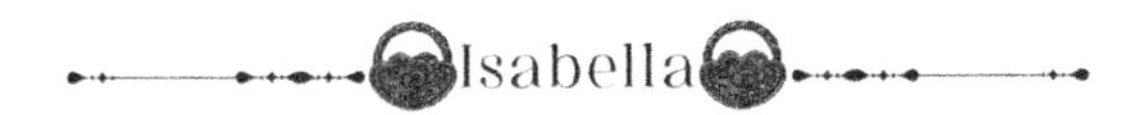


I can't take my eyes off Milene's sister and her husband. They've been at the bar since we arrived, and despite the crowd, they seem oblivious to anything happening around them. I don't ever remember seeing a man look at a woman the way Bianca's husband looks at her. It's as if she is the single most important being in the whole universe. I want that. I would kill to have Luca look at me that way, to be his sun and sky and everything in between.

I was at their wedding. Everybody was. It's not often that the Bratva and Cosa Nostra decide to ally themselves in such a way. I still remember the collective gasp when it became clear who Bianca Scardoni was marrying. Everyone assumed it was going to be the blond, cocky guy—Kostya. But, when the huge, dark-haired man with a badly scarred face and an eye patch stepped up in front of the wedding officiant, I was in shock, along with everyone else. Bianca doesn't seem to give a damn about her husband's ruined face or that he's missing an eye, because she's gazing at him like he's the most beautiful man on earth.

A waiter approaches, obstructing my view of the couple, and places a bottle of white wine on the table in front of me.

"Miss," he says, "the gentleman from that table has sent this for you."

I don't get the chance to reject it because a hand reaches over from behind me, grips the bottle, and thrusts it back into the confused waiter's chest.

"*Mrs.* Rossi is not interested," Luca's deep voice barks above my head.

I take a deep breath. He came. I feel this silly need to squeak with happiness, but I bottle it up and school my features, glancing at him over my shoulder. "You were in the neighborhood?"

"Yes," he says, his eyes focused on the table next to ours.

Yeah, right. I sigh and take a sip of my orange juice.

I've been drunk just once in my life, from barely two glasses of wine on the night of my eighteenth birthday. After the guests left, I stole a bottle from the kitchen and dragged Andrea to my room so she could keep me company at my personal pity party. I was lucky there was no one except her to witness it, because from what Andrea told me in the morning, I giggled like a crazy person at first, talked about Luca for two hours, then cried and vomited in the toilet for the rest of the night. The only two things I remember were singing "Total Eclipse of the Heart" by Bonnie Tyler, and Andrea holding my hair while I puked my guts out. I haven't touched alcohol since. Not because I have something against it, but because I don't want to risk blurting out anything Luca-related with someone else around.

As I sip my juice and watch the crowd, I wonder if he's going to do anything, maybe start a conversation or touch me. He doesn't. Instead, he stands right behind me, unmoving and silent, looming like a gargoyle. The guy from the nearby group throws a look in my direction, and the next instant, Luca's arms materialize on either side of me, his hands griping the edge of the table. I close my eyes for a second, trying to calm my inner turmoil. Surrounded by his body on nearly all sides, inhaling his cologne, and not daring to touch him is making me crazy. What would he do if I turned, placed my hands around his neck, and pulled his head down for a kiss? Dear God, I've been imagining how it would feel to be kissed by Luca for so long, but it's too soon. He needs time to get over his issues with our age differences. I won't risk him pulling away even more. I give myself a couple of seconds more to relax, then open my eyes.

"What happened to your hand?" I ask, looking at a piece of cloth that seems to be a kitchen towel, wrapped around his left palm.

"I cut myself on broken glass," comes the answer from above my head.

Where did he find broken glass, for God's sake? "It's still bleeding. You should head home and get that cut cleaned."

"I'm fine."

He's fine. I roll my eyes.

I turn toward Andrea, who's pretending to be interested in something in front of her, but I know she's listening. "I'm going home. Do you want to stay?"

"Yeah, I'll head back with Milene."

"Marco and Nicolas will stay with your sister," Luca says.

"They can go home. Gino is with her." I nod toward my sister's bodyguard who's leaning on the wall further back, then give Andrea a kiss. "I'll call you tomorrow."

After saying goodbye to the other girls, I turn and leave, with Luca following right behind me—my silent, towering shadow. We're almost at the exit when the guy who was ogling me earlier and three of his friends cut us off. He says something in Russian and smiles, nodding in my direction. The next moment, all of his buddies lunge at Luca.

I stare, petrified, as one of them swings his fist at Luca's head. Luca ducks and grabs the guy's shoulders, then smashes his knee into the man's stomach. One of the remaining two guys grabs Luca from behind, and the other one punches his fist into Luca's side. A hand wraps around my upper arm, pulling me backward into the gathering crowd.

I scream and try to escape, not taking my eyes off Luca, who's managed to get free and is in the process of making mush out of his attacker's face. The person holding me tugs at my arm again, and I turn to see the guy who sent me the drink. I knee the bastard's balls with all my might. He cries out and doubles over, clutching his crotch.

When I look back to where Luca was earlier, the fight seems to be over. One of the assailants is lying on his side, unconscious. Luca has the other guy pressed face first to the floor, holding the man's arm bent behind his back. I don't see the last asshole immediately because the huge frame of Bianca's husband is obstructing my view. Mikhail has his hand wrapped around the guy's throat, keeping him pressed to the wall. The man's feet dangle a foot off the ground. Luca rises and pushes his guy toward the security staff who drag him toward the exit.

I run toward Luca as he turns to look for me. When I approach, his arm shoots out, grabbing me around my waist and pulling me to his body. He takes my chin with his free hand and tilts my head up.

"Did he hurt you?" he asks in a low voice.

"No," I choke out.

Luca nods and exhales, his nostrils flaring. "You're not wearing that dress ever again."

"Okay." I blink at him. Is he going to kiss me? Our faces are so close, and based on the way he's staring at me, it seems like he might. I stop breathing and wait.

"Let's get your sister and friends," he says and releases my chin. "I don't want to see any of you in a Russian club again."

Looks like I'm not getting that kiss after all. As we walk back toward the table to get Andrea and the girls, I barely manage to bottle up the need to scream in frustration.

Luca doesn't say anything during the thirty-minute drive home, and I pretend I'm engrossed in watching the street through my window. When we arrive at the house, he opens my door for me and follows me inside and then up the two flights of stairs until we reach our bedrooms. Looks like we're back to cold shoulders and silent treatment.

"I'm going to shower and then I'm coming to check your hand." I say casually and go inside my room.

If the situation was different, I would have taken care of his cut before doing anything else, but I need time to decompress from the emotional overload before I can continue acting indifferent. Why is he making this so hard, damn it?

After I'm done with the shower, I dress in one of the short silky nightgowns that reveals my cleavage, and head through the door connecting our rooms. I have no intention of making this easy for him.

I don't see Luca anywhere in his bedroom, but the door to the bathroom is open so I turn that way and stop at the threshold. He's standing at the sink in nothing except loose black sweatpants, and for a moment, I find it hard to draw my next breath. I've never seen Luca shirtless, and I can't take my eyes off the perfection that is his body.

He is more muscled than I could have guessed. Those dress shirts hide way too much. Other than his build, they also hid the ink. There's a black geometric pattern forming a sleeve around his right arm, while on his left shoulder and bicep, there's another black and gray design. The front of his torso is free of ink, but I can see there's something that looks like a huge bird in flight on his upper back. However, what catches my attention the most is his hair. It's wet and hangs loose, reaching his shoulder blades. The only time

I've seen his hair unbound was thirteen years ago, and seeing it like this now hits me right in the chest. The moment feels somehow intimate.

He's holding his hand over the sink under the spray of water. I gasp as I see his condition. "Oh God."

There's a deep gash in the middle of his palm, and the blood is still oozing out of it. I can't determine exactly how much because it's quickly being washed away.

Luca looks up at me, his eyes stopping at my nightgown's deep V-neck for a few seconds, then he quickly shifts his gaze and turns off the water.

"It looks worse than it is," he says without giving me another glance.

"That will need stitches."

"Damian will patch me up when he comes home."

He takes a towel, wraps it around his palm, then reaches for the first aid kit next to the sink. Stepping inside the bathroom, I stand beside him, take the first aid kit from his hand, and start taking out compresses and bandages. Choosing the largest pack of dressings, I tear the packaging and fold the gauze several times.

"Remove the towel," I say, willing my stomach to stop churning. It's an understatement to say I'm not very good with blood.

Luca does as I say, and I quickly press the folded gauze to the gash. Keeping it in place with my left hand, I roll the self-sticking bandage around his palm.

"Tighter."

I nod, back up the roll, and pull a little more on the bandage, trying to control my erratic breathing. He's so close that if I lean forward just a little my forehead would be pressed against his chest.

"Tighter, Isabella," Luca says next to my ear.

My fingers start shaking slightly, and I'm sure he notices it but he doesn't say anything. When I'm done, I secure the bandage, take a deep breath, and lift my eyes to find him watching me. His face is set in hard lines, his jaw tight. *Do something, damn it! At least fucking touch me,* I want to yell at him. Instead, I just stare as he turns away and leaves the bathroom.

I want to scream. I have to fight with all my will not to run after him and hit him on his chest as hard as I can. Maybe then he would perceive even the slightest amount of the pain that tears me from the inside out every time he turns his back to me. I want to jump into his arms, bury my hands in his hair, and kiss him frantically. Everywhere. But I do neither of those things, only return to my room.

Will he be waiting for me to start my evening show so he can come to watch again? It's okay to observe, but not to touch? Do I have the fucking plague? Well, fuck him. He can wait all night long.

I leave my room, descend the two flights of stairs, and turn left into the kitchen. It's almost one in the morning and there's no one around, so I start opening the cupboards one by one until I find a stash of wine. I take the first bottle I see, pick up the bottle opener and a glass on my way out, and climb the stairs back up to my room.

I fill the wineglass almost to the brim and leave the bottle on the nightstand. On the bed, I sit with my back against the headboard, glass in one hand, and grab my phone from beside the wine bottle. I have a playlist of rock ballads I listen to when I'm feeling down, so I put it on. Drinking alone and humming along to Bon Jovi. Pathetic. Well, nothing new there.

I'm on my third glass when the door between our rooms opens. Looking up from my phone, I find Luca standing in the doorway, staring daggers at me.

"No show tonight," I say, and close my eyes.

For a few seconds, there's only silence, and then I hear the muffled sound of bare feet padding across the floor in my direction.

"You are too young to drink alcohol, Isabella."

I can't help but laugh. What a hypocrite. I open my eyes. He's standing by my bed, his arms crossed over his chest and lips pressed into a thin line. His hair is tied up again. What a shame.

"So, you're saying I should throw this away?" I raise my eyebrows and nod toward the glass in my hand.

"Yes."

"All right." I shrug. Smile. And then splash the contents of the glass into his face. "Any other requests, husband?"

Luca closes his eyes for a second, but when he opens them, the look he gives me is so full of rage that it would have probably made me pee myself if I wasn't drunk. There's also a vein in the side of his neck, one I've always found incredibly sexy, which is currently pulsing. Oh, he is really mad. Suddenly, his hand juts to grab me behind my neck, and he leans forward so our noses are almost touching. The way he's grinding his teeth makes me fear he'll shatter them if he doesn't stop soon.

"You should have told me that this is what it would take to make you touch me." I tilt my chin up. "If I knew, I would have done this the first night."

He removes his hand from my neck immediately. "You are a teenager," he barks. "I don't plan on touching you in any way."

"If that's the case, I'll have to seek out someone else. Someone who *will* fulfill my needs."

"Try," he whispers. "You won't like what will happen." The way his eyes flare makes me tense, but I don't pull away.

"I might be a nineteen-year-old, Luca, but I know what I want and what I need. I want more than my own hand making me come at night." I lean into his face. "If you're not interested, I'll find someone who is. And you don't have the right to deny me that since you obviously won't do anything about my problem."

Luca stares at me with bulging eyes, his breathing becoming quicker and his nostrils flaring, then he turns his head to the side. There's a loud bang as he hits the headboard with his fist.

"Fine," he says between clenched teeth and turns toward the door to his room. "Have fun."

He walks toward the door, and I try to keep my tears at bay, at least until he leaves the room. I can't believe he would rather let me fuck someone else. When he reaches the door, he stops, gripping the doorway with both hands. He bends his head and stays in that position for quite some time.

A mumbled curse. Another *BAM* echoes through the room as he hits the frame with his palm. A few more curses, and then he turns around and marches back to me.

He reaches the bed in two long strides and, for a long moment, just stands there at the footboard, staring down at me. I suck in a breath and hold it, waiting. It feels like my heart has stopped beating. Suddenly, he leans forward and wraps his hands around my ankles. With a sudden jerk, he pulls me toward himself. The glass I've been holding slips from my hand and falls onto the thick carpet next to the bed.

There's a tick in Luca's jaw and his brow furrows as he bends and grabs the hem of my nightgown in his fists. His forearms ripple with the flex of corded muscles as he tears my nightie in one swift tug. He's angry. It's obvious in his every move and by the way he's clenching his jaw muscles. I don't care. I've been waiting for this so long, and I'm going to take it any way I can get it and love every moment of it.

My breath hitches when he kneels on the floor and places my legs over his shoulders. He buries his face between my legs, and inhales. I bite my lower lip, feeling my wetness soak through the lacy panties, the only barrier between my pussy and his mouth. But he doesn't remove them. Instead, he presses his lips onto the lace, just over my core, and exhales. I grab onto the bedcover and arch my back, almost coming just from feeling his warm breath. The rough skin of his palms brushes my thighs as he slides his hands up to my waist and slips his fingers into the waistline of my panties. His forearms flex again, and there's another tearing sound. He removes the scrap of fabric that were once my panties and a moment later I feel his tongue.

The first lick is slow. Teasing. I squeeze the bedcover harder as tremors pass through my body. He licks me again, then thrusts his tongue inside my opening for a moment before he starts sucking on my clit. I'm already panting, but as he adds his finger, I feel the pressure building more and more. A second finger enters me, and I close my eyes, whimpering. I rip out his hair tie and thread my hands in his hair. The feel of it between my fingers is more than I ever could have imagined. It's still wet, either from his shower or the wine I threw at him. His tongue circles my clit, then he sucks at it, and at the same time, he does something with his finger inside me. I let out a loud moan as my whole body starts shaking. I feel weightless, like I'm floating on air. When he places his thumb on my clit next to his tongue and applies a little pressure, I explode.

My legs are still quivering when he lowers them off his shoulders, and I have no energy left to move any part of my body. Luca rises, sliding his arms under my back and knees, and shifts me to the center of the bed.

He covers me with a blanket and bends down to whisper in my ear, "If I see any other man touch you, he will die. It will be a very unpleasant death." He adjusts the blanket around my shoulders. "And you won't be satisfying your own pussy anymore. When you need your problem, as you called it, taken care of, you come to me. You got that, tesoro?"

"Yes," I rasp.

He nods and heads back into his room, leaving me sated, and absolutely shocked.

# CHAPTER

Isabella

If I expected Luca's cold treatment to cease after what happened last night, I would be gravely mistaken. When I make it downstairs for breakfast, he's already there with Rosa and Damian. Rosa throws the last few pieces of food in her mouth and rushes off to her room to pack her things for the day she's spending with her mother. Luca gets up shortly after her, saying he has work to do, and vanishes, leaving Damian and me at the table.

"What's going on between you two?" Damian asks the moment Luca is out of view.

"Nothing." I take a sip of my juice. "Why do you ask?"

He leans back in his chair, crossing his arms, and smiles. One thing I've noticed about Damian is that nothing escapes his attention. He might come across as nonchalant, always smiling and joking around, but his eyes betray him. There is pure intellect and calculation hidden there. He's playing his role of a carefree younger brother quite well. If I wasn't so skilled at pretending myself, I might have missed it.

"You're in love with my brother," he says.

Yes, he's definitely more observant than I thought.

"So what?" I ask and continue eating. There's no point in denying it.

Damian laughs and shakes his head. "Since when?"

"Years." I shrug. "What gave me away?"

"The way you look at him when you think no one is watching. Does he know?"

"Nope. And you won't tell him."

"I wasn't meaning to. Your relationship is not my problem. But why not tell him?"

I debate if I should explain or not. He already knows I'm in love with Luca. Maybe he'll have some insight regarding his brother's idiotic behavior.

"Because he treats me like I have the plague," I say. "He can't get over our age difference. He sees me as a child."

Damian starts stirring his coffee with a spoon even though I saw him doing so not a minute earlier.

"Yes, I see how that could be an issue for him," he finally says and looks up at me. "Luca and I are half brothers. His mother killed herself when Luca was a baby."

I blink. I didn't know that, and I was certain that Damian and Luca had the same parents. How come I've never heard about this? "Okay. How does that reflect on my situation?"

"Luca's mother was eighteen when she married our father. It was an arranged marriage." Damian says. "Father was forty."

I close my eyes. Shit.

"From what I know, Luca's mother wasn't mentally stable," he continues. "Couldn't deal with the obligations that came with the position of being a capo's wife, or being married to someone so much older than her. Our father was a hard man. She was young and sheltered. Eventually, she crumbled under the pressure."

"So, what did your brother expect when he agreed to marry me? That we'd be living like roommates until he deems me old enough to upgrade my status to a wife and have sex with me?"

Damian cringes. "Probably."

"Oh, he's in for a surprise, then."

"Don't push him too much. You've already managed to mess with his head quite well. Luca is hell to deal with when he's agitated."

"I don't think I messed up anything. He still doesn't give a fuck about me."

Damian takes a slow sip of his coffee but doesn't remove his eyes from mine. "Do you know what my brother did when he found Simona in bed with her bodyguard?"

I gulp my juice. "She cheated on him?" Who in their right mind would cheat on Luca?

"Luca shot the bodyguard in the head, and threw Simona out, naked, in the middle of the night. When the maid told me what was happening, I came out of my room to see if he was okay." He shakes his head. "Luca told the staff to clean up, greeted the girl I had over, then climbed up to the third floor, and went to bed. The next morning, he said he hadn't slept that well in ages."

"So?"

"So, imagine my surprise when I saw him storming out of the house last night, furious. I asked what was going on, and he said, and I quote, 'She went to a fucking club,' then got into his car and was gone in seconds." Damian bursts out laughing and gets up from the table. "I never thought I'd live to see a day when my brother chased after a woman."

I follow Damian with my eyes, wondering if he could be right. Luca jealous? Because of me?

"I'm not buying anything before trying out the product, Bogdan," I say into the phone and flip through the papers on my desk. I've spent the whole morning in my downtown office, going over the cash flow of our real estate business.

"It has a twenty-inch barrel and a rifle-length gas system. A candy, believe me," he says.

"How much?"

"They're a steal at seven hundred dollars apiece," he says, "but I'll take six fifty for each if you get more than five hundred."

"I'll take four hundred for six hundred dollars per piece."

"No way, Luca. I'm selling last year's model for that price."

"All right. I'll check with Dushku, then. Maybe he can work with that price."

"You're not going to the Albanians!" he barks. "We agreed on exclusivity two years ago."

"We also agreed that you will be delivering the goods I ordered," I say.

"It was a one-time fuckup, and you were very clear in showing your displeasure."

"I'm glad to hear that." I turn the page and skim the numbers on the next one. "I'll take four hundred pieces at six hundred dollars a pop. Or I go to Dushku."

you, Luca," he says, then mumbles something in Romanian. "Okay. ng else?"

sample for me to try out first. If I like it, we are a go. Send me ten more crates of grenades, as well. And Bogdan, if I receive the wrong goods again, you're done. Are we clear on that?"

There's more mumbling in Romanian and then, "Very. I'll call you next week to confirm the shipment details." Bogdan bites out and cuts the call.

There's a knock on my office door, and Donato comes inside. "Luca. What's going on?"

"We have a problem, Donato. Have a seat." I nod toward the chair on the other side of the desk and put the stack of papers in front of him. "This is the cash flow statement from the real estate business."

He takes the printout and starts looking over the numbers. "This seems fine."

"On its own it's good, but not when it can't keep up with the revenues from gun sales." I take the sheet of paper with the expected profits I calculated from the weapons deals and place it over the one he's looking at. "We need the real estate figures to double so Damian can launder all the money. Sit down with Adam and find me some properties that require significant investments. Damian says he can clear at least five million a month through renovations expenses."

"Okay." He nods then looks at me sideways.

"What is it?"

He fidgets in his chair like he usually does when he's delivering bad news. Even though both of us hold the same spot in the hierarchy, no one really considers him a serious player. The only reason he's still holding the capo's role is because he and the don are childhood friends. Donato is too old and too passive to do any actual work, so I'm doing most of it and he's just overseeing execution.

"Barbini reached out to me yesterday," he says.

"And what did Lorenzo want?"

"He was asking about your plans for when you take over."

That didn't take him long. I expected Lorenzo to make a move, but I assumed he would wait until Giuseppe stepped down. "Plans for what exactly?" I ask.

"Family business."

"I'll let the Family know when the time comes. For now, we operate as the don wants."

"Oh. Okay. I'll tell him that." He nods and hurries out of the office.

I pick up my phone and start scrolling through the missed calls from this morning, stopping when I reach Isabella's name. She's called me twice, the first time around ten and again two hours ago. I let it ring through both times. Leaning back in the chair, I tilt my head and stare at the ceiling, wondering what I'm going to do with her.

I have no idea what came over me last night, but no way am I doing it again. And I am not having sex with her until she is twenty-one. It may sound ridiculous, but I can't stomach the idea of fucking a nineteen-year-old. She might not look like one in the dark while sprawled out on the bed, with her hand between her legs. But then I see her in the morning light, looking even younger with her eyes still puffy from a lack of sleep, and I feel like a piece of shit. This madness stops now. What she does in her room, is her business. Whatever insanity that possessed me to tell her to come to me when she needs her "problem" handled is gone now. I'm not opening that door between our rooms again. If she wants to fuck, she'll have to wait, or find someone else. I don't give a damn.

The phone on my desk rings.

"Yes?"

"Mr. Rossi," my secretary says from the other side. "Your wife is here."

What the fuck is she doing here? "Send her in," I say through gritted teeth and march to the door. A brief glance outside and I find all my employees have stopped what they were doing to gawk at Isabella. They probably heard Magda announce her.

"Back to work!" I snap at them as I watch Isabella approach, her heels clicking on the marble floor. She's wearing a white sleeveless dress that hugs her chest and flares down from the waist, reaching her knees. Her hair is tied at the top of her head in a long straight ponytail, and oversized sunglasses hide her eyes.

She stops in front of me, removes the shades, and tilts her head up. "Good afternoon, husband."

"Get inside." I step aside, letting her pass, and shut the door. "Where's your bodyguard?"

"You haven't assigned me one yet. I tried calling you, but you didn't return my calls." She sits down on the sofa in the corner of my office and tilts her chin up. "We had a deal. You take my calls. I take your bodyguard."

"Did Renato drive you here?" He is a dead man.

"No. He said he can't take me anywhere without a bodyguard."

"So how the fuck did you get here?"

"Taxi."

"Are you out of your mind?"

She leans back and smiles. "I'm here because of our agreement."

"What agreement?"

"The one from last night," she says, and I stare as she lifts her ass, pulls the skirt of her dress up and removes a beige thong. "I have a problem. And I need you to solve it."

She launches the thong across the room where it falls on my desk.

"I've changed my mind." I round my desk and sit down. Grabbing the lacy undergarment, I sling it back at her. "You're allowed to use your hand. Go home. One of the security guys will drop you off."

She blinks at me, takes the thong, and places it into her purse. "Well, after last night, I decided that my own hand won't do."

I watch as she walks to the door, scrolling through her phone along the way, then puts the phone to her ear. "See you at dinner," she calls over her shoulder.

"Who are you calling?"

"A problem solver," she says and opens the door. "Hey, Angelo. Do you have plans for this afternoon? Perfect, let's meet—" The door closes, shutting out the rest of her conversation.

I glare at the door and start counting to ten to calm myself. One. Let her go. Two. Not your problem. Three. I spring out of my chair, nearly ripping the door off its hinges as I rush out and straight across the open floor space beyond, ignoring the employees who, once again, have ceased whatever they're doing. When I reach Isabella, I wrap my arms around her middle and lift her up. Turning around, I carry her back toward my office. With her back plastered to my chest and her feet dangling several inches above the ground, her ass is pressed right to my cock, which is getting harder by the second.

"Angelo, looks like something came up, I won't make it today." She's still talking on the phone like nothing strange at all is happening. "Yes, I'll call. Promise."

She most certainly won't be calling him ever again. I'll make sure of that.

As I enter the office, I shut the door with my foot and let her slide down my body until her heels reach the floor. She starts turning to face me, but I tighten my arms around her, drawing her body to mine.

"Throw away the phone," I whisper in her ear and slide my palms down and over her hips.

I hear her sharp inhale of breath before she lets the phone fall out of her hand.

"The bag and the glasses," I say as I continue moving my hands lower.

Her bag hits the floor, and the sunglasses follow. When my hands reach the hem of her dress, I start moving them back up, pulling the material along her thighs. "Let's see if my hand can do a better job than yours, hmm?"

"I doubt it," she utters and moans as my finger enters her.

I place my right hand at her clit and start massaging in slow, round circles. Meanwhile, I move my left hand towards her center and insert one finger into her wet pussy. The way her gorgeous ass is pressing against me, I'm ready to blow my load. I barely manage to stifle a groan as I fight to regain control.

Shifting my left hand even lower, I remove my finger and hear her hiss in frustration. I push it back inside, then carefully add another. Jesus, she's tight. Slowly, I curl my fingers and quicken my movements on her clit. Isabella starts to pant and drops her hands, placing them over mine to increase the pressure. I feel her walls spasm around me, so I massage her clit faster, enjoying her mewls as she comes all over my hand a few seconds later.

I bend my head until my lips almost touch her bare shoulder and inhale her scent. She smells like vanilla.

"Can you walk, tesoro?" I whisper.

"Yes."

"Okay. Let's go to the bathroom." I start to pull my finger out, but she keeps her hand over mine, not letting me withdraw.

"Not yet," she says in a raspy voice, pressing harder on my hand, and it almost makes me snap and fuck her on the spot.

"All right."

I wrap my free arm around her middle and lifting her up, carry her toward the bathroom on the left, keeping my finger buried inside her. Her breathing is shallow and hitches a little with every step. We reach the bathroom and come to a stop in front of a small sink. I lift my head, our gazes meeting in the mirror, and I can't decide what I like more—the flustered expression on her face, her huge eyes burning with fire as she regards me, or the sight of my hand over her pussy as my body looms over her.

I reach for the towel and, putting it between her legs, slowly pull out my finger, watching her as she inhales and closes her eyes. After I clean her up, I throw the towel into the sink and grip the edge of the counter on either side of her, lowering my head until my chin rests on her shoulder.

"So, did I resolve your problem?" I ask, holding my eyes fixed on hers in the mirror.

"Yes. Thank you."

"Good. If I catch you calling the little Scardoni boy again, I'm going to break his legs. And his hands. Is that clear?"

The corner of her lips lift upward, but she doesn't reply. Oh, she really likes to defy me.

I move my hand between her legs again and press lightly on her still-sensitive pussy, making her gasp. "Is that clear, Isabella?"

"Yes." She exhales.

"Perfect." I remove my hand and straighten up. "I'll call security. Two of the guys will drive you back home."

I leave the bathroom, sit at my desk, and grab the phone to call security. Isabella walks out two minutes later, her dress straightened and hair no longer in disarray. She bends over to collect her things from the floor, giving me a view of her naked ass, then puts her sunglasses on and heads to the door.

"I like the feel of your hands and mouth on me," she says over her shoulder. "But you know that's not enough. Don't you, Luca?"

She doesn't wait for my reply, just leaves me to stare at the door she vanished through and to wonder how a nineteen-year-old girl managed to so royally fuck up my head.

The ringing of my phone wakes me up. I open my eyes and stare at the ceiling, trying to ignore the ache in my fully erect cock—the result of the dream that haunts me every night. Me, weighing Isabella down with my body, my cock buried inside of her. I thought she'd skip the evening show after what happened in the office this afternoon. She didn't. I tried restraining myself when I heard soft moans coming from her room. And failed miserably. Barely two minutes after the first moan, I stormed inside Isabella's bedroom and feasted on her sweet pussy until she came all over my face.

The ringing stops, then starts again. I grab the phone to see Donato's name on the screen. The numbers in the corner show it's three in the morning.

"What happened?" I ask the moment I take the call.

"I'm at the warehouse. We caught one of the security guards stealing ammunition."

"So?"

"What do you want me to do with him?"

I squeeze my temples between my thumb and middle finger and shake my head. "Kill him, Donato."

"Kill? Are you certain?"

Jesus. How the fuck he ended up being a capo, I'll never understand. I start to tell him to have one of the guys kill the thief then change my mind.

"I'll be there in an hour," I say and cut the call.

I need something to shake loose the frustration.

In the shower, as the water pours down on me, I grip my aching cock and imagine pounding into Isabella from behind, with her ass right there in front of me. It doesn't take any time at all to find my release. Despite jerking off, I'm still wound up as I dress and head outside.

When I reach the warehouse where we store the guns, I head right toward the man sitting in the far corner. Donato is standing next to him, along with another of my guards, both holding guns pointed at him. I'm amazed by the fact that Donato knows how to hold the gun at all.

"Is that the thief?" I ask.

"Yes." Donato nods. "Gianni caught him while—"

I don't wait for him to finish, just draw my gun from the holster, point it at the thief's chest, and fire four times. Donato gasps and stumbles backward, staring at the blood soaking the front of the man's shirt. I turn around and head back to my car, still pissed and sexually frustrated as fuck. Damn that woman. Damn her to hell.

# CHAPTER

I reach for the water carafe in the middle of the table, watching Luca from the corner of my eye. He's been in a sour mood for the last few days, but it hit its peak this morning. He hasn't said a word since he came down for breakfast.

We've been at this status quo for almost three weeks now. We have breakfast with Damian and Rosa, and then he goes to work. Every day at two, I go to his office, where he wrecks me bit by bit with his fingers in the best possible way, and in the evening, he enters my room and devours me with his masterful tongue. He sates me so well the only thing I'm able to do after is fall into a deep sleep.

However, nothing else has changed. He still mostly ignores my presence during the day. He hasn't touched me in any way unless he is "solving my problems," and my patience is slowly running out.

"Is your downtown office just a front or a real business?" I ask as I fill my glass with water.

"It's real," he says without lifting his head, focused intently on the plate of food in front of him. "Real estate business is the best way to launder big amounts of money," he adds after another bite.

"And who's in charge of that?"

"Oh, that would be me," Damian chimes in with a mischievous smile.

I raise my eyebrows. He's barely twenty-three, and we're talking about laundering millions. Luca must have great deal of confidence in his brother's abilities.

"Are you involved in the arms dealing as well, or do you just handle the financial part?" I ask.

Luca's head snaps up. "How do you know about our arms dealing business?"

"Please." I snort. "Where do you think I've lived my whole life? Under a rock?"

"You're the don's granddaughter. You should have spent your days browsing magazines, shopping, and going to spas."

"I'm sorry to disappoint. Spas were never my thing." I shrug. "And because I am the don's granddaughter, I've been groomed for my role since I was ten."

"And what role would that be?"

"The wife of a capo," I say and take a croissant from the basket.

"Who should do nothing but go shopping and to spas and browse magazines."

"Well, I didn't expect to be married off to a chauvinistic grump, but it is what it is."

Across the table from me, Damian chokes on his coffee when he bursts out laughing. "Sorry I just . . ." He snickers. "Chauvinistic grump." He laughs again.

I turn my head and find Luca watching me through narrowed eyes. "I want you to stay in your room this afternoon," he says.

"Why?"

"Simona is coming to take Rosa, and I have a meeting I need to attend. I don't want you two confronting one another, especially when I'm not here."

I reach for the milk and fill the glass for Rosa. When I went to see her earlier, she said she's not feeling well and decided to stay in her room. "You're afraid I'll bite your ex or something?"

"I'm not concerned about what *you* may do, Isabella."

Oh. He's concerned about what his big, bad ex will do to his delicate young wife. How sweet of him. I wish I were drunk again so I could allow myself to throw something else in his face.

"I'll take Rosa her breakfast, then make sure I'm locked away safe in my room when your ex-wife comes." I grab the plate I've prepared for Rosa, turn on my heel, and march toward the stairway.

Damian's laughter rings out behind me.

"Do you want me to get you tea or something?" I ask Rosa.

"No," she mumbles into her pillow.

"Maybe we should call a doctor." I put my palm on her forehead, but it doesn't feel like she has a fever. "Did you eat something strange yesterday?"

"No."

"Diarrhea? Do you feel like vomiting?"

"No, just my stomach hurts. I'm okay."

I sit on the edge of her bed and lightly squeeze her shoulder. "So, this has nothing to do with the fact your mom is coming?"

"She wants me to call her Simona," she says. "And I don't want to go with her. She always takes me to a mall. It's boring."

"Well, can you ask her to take you to the park? Or to see some movie? How about that?"

"She hates parks because I get dirty. And she says she doesn't like movies because her eyes hurt. I want to stay here."

"You'll be bored here, too."

"I won't. I can call Clara. She said she'll bring Tomas next time she comes."

"Who's Tomas?"

"Her cat. He has a little leash so we can walk him around the garden. And Grace will make us sandwiches."

"Did you tell your dad that you don't want to go with Simona?"

"No. He wouldn't understand."

"Of course, he would. Want me to call him to come upstairs?"

"Yeah."

I nod, grab my phone, and call Luca.

"What?" he barks.

A picture of politeness. "Please come upstairs. Rosa wants to talk to you."

"I'm just getting into my car."

"Well *un*-get and come talk with your daughter. It's important."

I cut the call and rub Rosa's back. "He's coming. If you don't feel like doing something, you should always tell your dad. Okay?"

"Okay."

"I'll be in my room. Come get me if you need me. If you want, we can watch something downstairs later. Or we can call your friend. Deal?"

"Okay."

I squeeze her shoulder again and leave her room.

## Luca

"She's your mother, piccola." I brush the back of my palm down Rosa's cheek. "You should spend some time with her."

"I don't want to," she bites out, staring me down. She's trying very hard to keep her tears at bay, but I see how her nose scrunches a little, and a stray tear slides down her cheek. "Please don't make me go with her."

"I will never make you do anything you don't want to, Rosa," I say and gather her in my arms. Rosa sniffs, then wraps her arms around my neck, burying her face in the crook of it. She's always loved doing that, even when she was a baby.

"Promise?" she whispers.

I take her chin between my thumb and fingers and tilt her head up to look into her eyes. "I promise."

"Simona told me she would write to some kind of service that will take me away and make me live with her. I don't want to live with her, Dad."

I squeeze my hand into a fist. "She told you that, huh?"

"Yes."

"That's not true, Rosa. No one can take you away from me. She's just trying to manipulate you."

"Why does she want me to go anywhere with her? She doesn't love me. Why can't she just . . . go away?"

Sometimes I wish I could just kill Simona and be done with it, but I can't do that to Rosa. Simona is still her mother. I press my daughter's face to my chest and wrap my arm around her back. "She loves you in her own way, Rosa. She just doesn't know how to show it."

I'm not sure Simona is capable of loving anyone except herself. Sometimes I wonder if I should have just taken Rosa without marrying my ex, but I didn't want my child to grow up without a mother like I did. I thought Simona would change, so I stayed with her for Rosa's sake. She didn't.

"Can I call Clara to come over?" Rosa asks into my chest. "We can ask Grace to make us tuna sandwiches. And those ginger cookies with cinnamon."

"Only if you leave some for me. You and Clara ate everything the last time."

"Uncle Damian ate them! We told him to leave you some, but he said his sugar level was low and he needed them more than you."

I laugh. Why am I not surprised?

"Isa said she'd watch a movie with me," Rosa adds and leans back to look at my eyes. "I really like Isa, Dad."

"You do?" I brush my thumb over her cheek, removing her tears.

"Yeah. I was working on some math problems we needed to finish during vacation yesterday and asked her to help me. She worked with me the whole morning. Isa is super smart."

"Yes, she is." I nod.

It's the truth. My young wife is one exceptionally intelligent woman. I can't help but admire the way she plays me, day after day, without backing down or faltering her stance. And with every passing day, it's becoming harder to continue resisting. Sometimes, I find myself watching her, debating whether I should just say, "to hell with it," grab her and crush my mouth to hers. I don't remember a time I've been so crazy about a woman before. It's like she's slipped under my skin and made her home there, and it's getting exponentially worse with every day that passes. Every stubborn look, every clever remark, every defiant tilt of her chin—it all contributes to her working her way even deeper into me.

I quickly shake my head and place a kiss at Rosa's head. "I have to go to work but call me if you need me, and I'll come right back. Okay, piccola?"

"Yeah." she nods.

When I leave Rosa's room, I find Isabella downstairs talking with one of the maids. She spots me coming, and her eyes instantly flick away before I can pin her with my gaze. As if my presence makes no difference to her one way or another, she continues her conversation without missing a beat.

"I'll call Simona to reschedule her visit," I say in passing.

"How nice. Does that mean it's safe for me to roam the house this afternoon?"

I decide to ignore her snarky remark and head toward the front door. I'm not sure if Isabella would be able to stand up to Simona, especially if my ex is in one of her moods, and I won't risk them meeting unless I'm there. Simona is a bitch and just the idea of her saying something that might hurt Isabella makes the rage boil in my stomach.

I close the book on world economy, one of the courses on my curriculum next semester, and put it into the desk drawer. Since I have nothing to do around here, I've decided to use the time to go over the main subjects and get myself prepared for when classes resume. I doubt my husband knows I'm attending college as an online student, and since he's never actually asked what I do during the day, I've never offered the information.

My phone rings as I'm heading to the bathroom to shower and change before going over to Luca's office. The display shows the number from the gate guard. Strange. I don't remember inviting anyone over.

"Mrs. Rossi," he says when I take the call. "I have Ms. Albano here. She's insisting on being let inside."

What the hell is Luca's ex doing here? He said they'd rescheduled her visit.

"Did you call Luca?" I ask.

"Twice. He's not answering."

Typical. "Let her in, Tony," I say, leave my room, and head downstairs.

As I pass the big mirror at the landing on the second floor, I glance at my reflection and groan. If I'd known Simona would be coming, I'd have put on something else, maybe jeans and a white blouse. And heels. As it is, I'll be meeting my husband's first wife in pastel blue sweatpants and a matching T-shirt, with Hello Kitty face plastered all over my chest. Barefoot. How nice.

I'm halfway to the front door when I hear high-pitched yelling on the other side. The front door opens, and a tall blonde woman rushes inside, her heels clicking on the floor. Our security guard runs in after her.

"I told her to wait outside, Mrs. Rossi," he says. "She wouldn't listen."

"It's all right, Emilio." I nod and return my gaze to Simona Albano, *formerly* Rossi.

I have seen her numerous times at different social gatherings. It was impossible to miss her. Each time, I felt this piercing pain in the middle of my stomach. I envied her so much. The last time I saw her was six months ago, and since then, her lips have doubled in size, her boobs are bigger, and she's lost at least ten pounds. She looks like a clothes hanger for her expensive, beige-with-black-polka-dots dress.

Standing with her hand on her hip, she looks me up and down, pausing for a few seconds on the Hello Kitty image on my chest, and bursts out laughing.

"Dear God, I knew you were young, but I had no idea they made Luca marry a child." She gives me a condescending smile.

"What do you want, Simona?"

"It's Ms. Albano to you."

"You came into my house uninvited," I say. "I'm going to call you whatever the fuck I want."

Simona blinks, looking a bit dumbfounded. She tries to sneer at me in the process, but all she ends up doing is cracking her Botox-infused lips. "I came to pick up Rosa."

"Rosa doesn't want to go. Luca told me he called you and rescheduled it."

"I changed my mind. Where's my daughter? I'm taking her shopping."

"Did you clear it with Luca?"

"I don't have to clear anything with him," she snaps.

"Of course, you do. You signed all parental rights over to him. Rosa is not leaving unless her father says so."

Anger flashes in Simona's eyes. She takes two steps forward until she's standing right in front of me, and her lips stretch into a sneer that transforms her face from beautiful into something grotesque. "Get me my daughter! Right now!"

"Have a nice day, Simona." I turn to Emilio, who's standing in the doorway. "Please walk her to her car and make sure she leaves the grounds. And make it clear to Tony that she is not allowed through the gate again unless Luca has cleared it."

I turn to leave when I feel a hand grabbing my upper arm. "How dare you throw me out? This was my house!"

"*Was.* Past tense." I look down at her hand, then back into her eyes. "Get your hand off me."

"Who do you think you are, you little bitch?" she snaps and starts shaking me.

I'm not a violent person. I believe in resolving problems with discussion, but I won't allow anyone to manhandle me. Especially my husband's ex-wife. I look down, focus my gaze on her toes peeking out from her strappy sandals, then smash my right heel onto them with all my might. Simona screams and lets go of my arm. I use the opportunity to grab a handful of her hair, pulling her head back. She screams again and tries scratching my face, but I move to stand behind her and pull her hair down even further, making her arch her back.

"Don't you dare touch me again!" I bark and drag her toward the door where Emilio is standing, his mouth gaping. "Get her out." I let go of Simona's hair, turn on my heel, and head to the kitchen. I need some sugar because I'm coming down from an adrenaline high and my legs are starting to shake. As I pass the stairway, I hear chuckling and lift my head. Damian is standing next to the banister with his phone in front of him.

"Don't even think about posting that anywhere. I mean it, Damian."

"It's for my private collection of catfight videos." He grins and disappears down the hallway.

## Luca

My phone rings with Damian's name flashing on the screen. I let it ring where it's lying on my desk and continue reading the real estate listing I was checking out. He was right. Selling those apartments was a good call. If we had waited, we'd have lost 10 percent. He's probably calling to say "I told you so." I'm not in the mood. It's almost half past two, and Isabella still hasn't come. What if she decided to call the Scardoni pup after all? The ringing stops, only to start again a few seconds later.

I curse and grab the phone. "I'm busy, Damian."

"Simona was here."

"What? When?"

"She just left."

"We agreed to postpone her visit until next week." I hit the table with my palm. "And she knows she shouldn't come into my house unless I'm there."

"Yeah, well, you know Simona."

"What happened? Did she take Rosa?"

"Nope. Isabella didn't let her. She told Simona she can't take Rosa anywhere without your permission."

"Jesus fuck. They met?"

"Yeah. It wasn't pretty."

I stand up from the chair, gripping the phone. "What did Simona do to her?"

"Calm down. Everything's okay."

"Don't tell me to calm down." I take my wallet and car keys from the table and rush out of the office. "I'm on my way."

"Isa is fine. She's watching *Say Yes to the Dress* with Rosa."

"Don't lie to me, Damian. Simona knew I wasn't there, and she came with a purpose. I know my ex all too well."

"I recorded the whole ordeal. I'm sending you a video."

"You recorded it? Why the fuck didn't you throw out that bitch instead?"

"It seemed Isa didn't need my help." He laughs. "She threw her out herself."

"What?" I hit the button on my remote as I approach my car. The doors click just as I'm reaching for the handle.

"Just watch, Luca." Damian cuts the call.

I get into my car and play the video Damian sent. When I come to the part where Simona grabs Isabella's arm, I grip the steering wheel, then reach down and start the car, only to turn it off two seconds later. I watch with growing amazement as my tiny wife grabs my ex, who's more than a head taller, and pulls Simona toward the front door by her hair. The video ends with her casually walking across the hall.

I play the video again, and then one more time. Smiling, I lean back in the seat and shake my head. Little hellion. I step out of the car, intending to call Simona to let her know what I think of her visit, when my phone rings again. The display shows Francesco's name. I don't get calls from Isabella's father often.

"Francesco? What's going on?"

"The don has just been admitted to the hospital," he says. "Another heart attack."

"Fuck. Is it bad?"

"Yes. Can you get Isa there? I haven't told her yet. I was afraid she'd come by herself."

"Sure."

Once he gives me the address, I jump behind the wheel and floor it.

I find Isabella just as Damian said—watching TV with Rosa in the library. Her left arm is lying on the back of the sofa, and as I approach, I notice a red bruise above her elbow. I'm going to kill Simona if she dares come within a five-yard radius of my wife ever again. Without thinking, I reach out and brush her skin with the back of my hand. Isabella's head snaps up, surprise in her eyes, and I quickly remove my hand.

"Go get your purse," I say and drop a kiss on the top of Rosa's head. "I'll wait for you in the car. We have to go."

"Where?"

"To the hospital. Your grandfather's had another heart attack."

She stares at me for a second, then jumps up from the sofa and leaves the library at a run. I expect her to change or put on some makeup, but she rushes back down the stairs with her purse and shoes on before I reach the front door.

"How is he?" Isabella asks as we get in the car.

"I don't know. Your father just gave me the address and hung up. We'll ask when we get there."

She nods and leans back in the seat, clutching her purse in her lap.

It takes us thirty minutes to reach the hospital and five more to find a parking spot. As soon as I park the car, Isabella gets out and rushes toward the entrance. I run after her, and when I reach her, I take her hand in mine. "Stay close to me."

Isabella looks down at our joined hands, nods, and lets me lead her inside. As we enter the lobby, I scan the people in the waiting room. When I don't notice anything suspicious, I guide us to the information desk and ask for directions.

The closer we get to the hospital unit the nurse indicated, the stronger Isabella's grip on my hand gets. We round the corner and spot two men in front of the door at the end of the hallway and Isabella's father sitting on a chair across from them. Immediately, Isabella lets go of my hand and runs to him.

She embraces her father while he speaks in her ear, probably updating her on her grandfather's condition, and I expect her to break down and start crying at any moment. Instead, she nods, sits down in the chair next to Francesco, and stares at the door in front of her. It amazes me how collected she seems on the outside, because I know she's freaking out on the inside. She couldn't hide the fear in her eyes while we were driving to the hospital. My place is there, sitting next to her and holding her hand, but it doesn't feel right. I'm sure she wouldn't welcome it. Not after the cold shoulder I've been giving her. I've truly been acting like a piece of shit.

Isabella seems to act with more maturity than Simona, who's ten years older. When Damian told me the two of them met today, I assumed I'd find Isabella crying in her room when I came home. I never would have imagined that she'd stand her ground. Damian's video proved me wrong and showed that she managed quite well. My young wife has turned out to be quite a surprise, and I'm finding it hard to continue keeping her at arm's length.

The fact is, I'm attracted to her, and I don't mean just physically. I like the way she stands up to me each and every time—never pulling away and meeting me on the middle ground instead. The way, day after day, she keeps playing the game of indifference that I started, makes me even crazier for her. Maybe I should just let go of my self-restraint and start fucking her senseless. It's not like she doesn't have the experience. That's obvious from the way she's acting. And that realization makes me furious. Why do I care if she's had sex before? And what the hell am I going to do with this idiotic urge to find every man who's touched her and strangle them? Maybe it's her unpredictable behavior that's messing with my brain. She riles me up to the point of my dick exploding one moment, and the next, she's an ice queen, ready to brush me aside for the next schmuck who'll fix her "little problem".

The door to the don's room opens, and Isabella's mother and sister walk out. They exchange a few words, then Isabella heads inside, but not before throwing a quick look in my direction.

*Dear God, he looks so old.*

It's the first thing that flashes through my mind as I enter the room and see my grandfather's fragile form on the bed. I can't reconcile this image of him with how I remember him from my childhood—a burly, tall man, with a deep voice and commanding presence. He always seemed so strong, until his heart started failing him.

"Isi, come here, stella mia," he says.

I sit in the chair next to the bed and take his hand in mine. It feels so light and breakable. I want to say something, but I can't seem to find the words.

"Have I ever told you how much you remind me of your grandmother?" He smiles weakly. "The same big eyes. The same unbreakable spirit that seems so grand for such a tiny person."

He sounds like he is saying goodbye, and I find it hard to rein in the tears. So, I let them fall.

"Don't cry, Isi. I had a good life, and it's time to move on. You have to be strong now, stella mia, because when I'm gone, all hell will break loose. Luca will need you. Especially with the mess Bruno Scardoni has created."

I shake my head and sigh. "I don't think Luca needs anyone, Nonno. He manages quite well on his own."

"Men can be stubborn sometimes. And your husband is the most stubborn one I've ever come across." He raises his hand and brushes my cheek. "I have a confession to make, Isi. I hope you won't get mad that I didn't tell you sooner."

"I can never get mad at you, Nonno. You know that."

He regards me with his dark, slightly misty eyes, then smiles. "I knew, Isi," he says. "I knew for years."

"Knew what?"

"That you were in love with Luca. Still are, from what I can see."

I open my mouth to say something, but he places his finger over my lips. "I paid that bodyguard. The one Luca caught in bed with Simona. It's not like she wasn't cheating on him before, but she was careful not to be caught."

"Nonno!"

"Luca is a good man. And I wanted him for you." He smiles. "So, I made sure you got him, stella mia."

I burst out crying.

"Barbini is going to confront him, Isi. Lorenzo didn't say anything in front of me, but I saw it in his face. Tell Luca to be careful."

"I will," I say through the tears. "But you will be okay, Nonno. Dad said they're taking you to surgery and the doctors will fix your heart. You're not going anywhere, yet."

"I love you, stella mia."

The door behind me opens and two nurses come in. I squeeze my grandfather's hand and kiss his cheek.

"I love you, too," I say and brush away my tears. "We'll be waiting outside when you come out of surgery. Okay?"

"Okay."

I leave the room and sit next to Andrea, who's whimpering on my mother's shoulder. My father is standing a few paces from us, quietly talking with the doctor. As I turn my head to the right, I see Luca standing at the far end of the long hallway, leaning on the wall with his shoulder. I should go and talk to him, but I don't think I can manage that distance on my shaking legs. Taking the phone from my bag, I press his number and watch as he takes the call.

"The surgery will last several hours. You don't have to stay," I say. "I know you have work to do."

"I'm staying, Isabella."

He puts away the phone and holds his position, looking back at me. Sighing, I lean my head against the wall and close my eyes.

I hear hurried steps from the direction of the elevator and lift my head to see Lorenzo and Orlando Lombardi approaching. They couldn't have waited until the don was out of the hospital? Bastards. I push away from the wall and head in their direction.

"What do you want?" I stop before them, barring their way.

"We came to see the don," Lorenzo says.

"Giuseppe is in surgery. When we have news, I'll call you."

"Who the fuck do you think you are?" Lorenzo barks into my face. "You can't forbid us from seeing him." He steps forward as if I'll let him pass.

I wrap my hand around his upper arm, stopping him, and get in his face.

"This is a personal matter, Lorenzo. I won't let you or anyone else intrude on Giuseppe's family in this moment. Leave."

"Channeling a don already, Luca?" he spits out. "You couldn't wait to jump into the role, could you? Let go of me!"

"Jesus, Lorenzo." I shake my head and turn to Orlando. "Get him out of the hospital or I will. And I really don't want to make a scene."

"Luca?" Isabella's voice reaches me from behind. "What's going on?"

"Out. Both of you," I say through gritted teeth and release Lorenzo's arm. "Right fucking now."

I watch until Lorenzo and Orlando disappear into the elevator, then turn to Isabella, who's standing a few paces behind me, her arms wrapped tightly around her waist.

"I heard yelling. Is something wrong?" she asks.

"No. They just dropped by to see how Giuseppe is doing. Don't worry."

She nods but doesn't move. She looks so small and so young. I close the distance between us and wrap my arms around her, pressing her to my body.

"He's going to be okay, tesoro," I say into her hair.

"I'm scared," she whispers into my chest.

"I know."

"Mom is freaking out. I better go back," she says but doesn't let me go.

I squeeze her a little tighter. "I'll stay here to make sure no one comes to disturb you. Okay?"

Isabella nods and pulls back, looking up at me. Her eyes are red, but there are no tears. I don't know how someone so young can have such self-control. I'm certain she's keeping her tears at bay with sheer will.

"Thank you," she whispers and walks back to her family.

The doctor comes out at around eleven in the evening, and Isabella's family gathers around him. Based on the looks on their faces, the chances are not good, but the don is still alive. They return to their chairs, and sometime later, Andrea and Isabella's parents stand up and start walking down the hallway toward me.

"How is he?" I ask Francesco.

"In the ICU. It doesn't look good. If he lives through the next twenty-four hours, there's a chance he'll pull through." He puts his arm around his wife's back. "We're going to grab something to eat. Can you stay with Isa?"

"Sure. Bring something for her, as well."

"She said she can't eat."

"Just bring it. I'll make sure she eats it."

When they leave, I walk down the hallway to where Isabella is sitting and crouch in front of her. For a second, I think she must have fallen asleep in the chair, but then she opens her eyes and looks at me.

"How are you holding up?" I ask.

She doesn't answer, just shrugs and closes her eyes again. I can't bear seeing her like this. Beat. Lethargic. With an empty look in her eyes. Reaching out, I cup her cheek with my palm, and her eyes snap open. There it is. That spark I was looking for. I caress her skin with my thumb, noticing how perfectly soft it is. Slowly, she lifts her hand and, after a few seconds of hesitation, cups my cheek just as I have with her. She sighs and leans forward, pressing her forehead to mine.

"What am I going to do with you, Luca?" she whispers.

The sound of approaching steps reaches me from somewhere off to the side, and I assume it's her parents and Andrea returning, but when I rise, I find the doctor from earlier standing a few feet away.

"Mrs. Rossi," The doctor says, an expression of regret all over his face.

"No." Isabella stands up next to me.

"His heart wasn't in a stable condition," the doctor continues. "It stopped while he was waking up from the anesthesia. We couldn't bring him back."

"No." Isabella grabs my hand and squeezes. "Please, no."

"I'm so sorry, Mrs. Rossi. Your grandfather has passed away."

Isabella stumbles. I catch her around the waist and turn her toward me, burying my hand in her hair and pressing her face to my chest. Her parents and sister round the corner and rush toward us. The doctor meets them halfway and gives them the news. Isabella's mother presses her hand to her mouth, and bursts out crying. I look down at Isabella, who is clutching my shirt in her small hands, her silent tears hitting me right in the chest like a sledgehammer. There's nothing I can do to take away her pain, so I just hold her even tighter.

# CHAPTER

## *nine*

THE RAIN STARTS AS WE'RE LEAVING THE CEMETERY. MORE THAN two hundred people attended the funeral, and as the drizzle transforms into a downpour, they run toward their cars for cover. Isabella doesn't change her tempo, and instead stays walking by my side, her head bent. I take off my suit jacket and place it over her shoulders. Her steps falter for a moment and she stops, looking up at me. I can't see her eyes because she's wearing a pair of oversized sunglasses, but I'm pretty sure her cheeks are not wet as a result of the rain. Looks like she's finally allowed herself to cry, but only when there's no one else around.

I open the car door and watch as Isabella gets into the back seat in silence. When she's inside, she moves to the other end and leans her head against the window. She hasn't said a word since this morning. I get inside the car, lean over and wrap my arm around her waist, then pull her onto my lap. A surprised yelp leaves her lips, but she doesn't protest, just places her cheek onto my chest and snuggles into my body. Her ponytail has loosened, so I remove her hair tie and bury my fingers into her soft hair, massaging her scalp.

When the car stops in front of the house I get out, holding Isabella in my arms as I carry her inside and up the stairs to her room. I put her down next to the bed, expecting her to change, but she just removes my jacket and her sunglasses and slides under the covers. I hate this feeling of helplessness, the inability to make the situation easier for her even just a little bit. So, I do the only thing I can—I carefully remove her heels, arrange the covers around her shoulders and then climb up into the bed behind her. Wrapping my arm around her bundled form, I pull her into my body and stay that way until I hear her breathing even out and she finally falls asleep.

As I stare out the window and look at the setting sun, a realization forms inside my head. Am I falling in love with my wife?

*She's nineteen*! My brain yells.

I quickly unwrap my arm from Isabella's waist, get up and leave the room, urging myself to forget about that ridiculous idea.

I don't remember much of the past two days. What I do remember is Luca carrying me to the car as we left the hospital and me trying without any success to make him put me down. That first night he slept on the sofa which is under the window in my room. The day of the funeral is a complete blur in my mind. I remember the rain and some random moments like Luca holding me inside the car and getting inside the bed fully clothed, but not much else. I'm pretty sure he slept on the sofa last night as well but it looks like he left while I was still asleep.

The sound of a lawn mower invades my thoughts through the open window, and it feels like its rumbling is drilling into my brain. I should get up and close the window but I can't make myself move. Instead, I stay lying on my bed, staring up at the ceiling. My nonno is gone. I can't grasp that fact. This morning when I woke up, I reached for my phone, wanting to call and ask how he's feeling. Like I've done every morning. Only this time my hand stilled halfway to the phone when I remembered.

There's no one around, so I let myself break down and spend the following hour crying my eyes out.

Nonno would be so mad if he saw me now with my puffy face and red eyes. He always insisted on facing whatever life throws at you with your head held high and steel in the spine. I look up at the big clock on the wall. It's seven p.m., and I haven't yet told Luca about my grandfather's warning regarding Lorenzo.

I get out of bed and head into the bathroom to splash some water on my face. Hopefully, it will make me feel a little better. Five minutes later, I leave my room and go to the second floor, hoping to catch Damian in his office.

"Isa?" Damian looks up from his laptop. "Are you okay?"

"I'm fine, thank you. When's Luca coming back? I need to speak with him."

"No idea. He has a meeting with the capos on Friday, so he's trying to tie up loose ends."

"They're swearing fealties to him in four days? That's fast."

"Lorenzo was starting to make trouble," he says. "We had to hurry."

"That's what I wanted to talk with Luca about. Grandfather told me to warn him. Who else?"

"What do you mean?"

I walk up to Damian's desk and take a seat across from him. "Who else is against having Luca as a don? And who's undecided?"

Damian watches me with interest, takes a pen from the table and starts rolling it between his fingers. "Don't take this the wrong way, but why do you ask?"

I smile. "Humor me."

"Orlando Lombardi is against. He sided with Lorenzo and insisted on the Family dropping the arms and gambling deals, and transferring all the efforts into drugs. Luca said no."

"The Bratva has most of the drug business," I say. "It wouldn't be wise butting in, especially after Bruno Scardoni almost killed Bianca's husband." Damian's eyes widen in surprise. Yeah, he wouldn't be the first to underestimate me. "You need to call Orlando Lombardi. Tell him it would be extremely unfortunate if Lorenzo found out what he's been doing every second Saturday morning."

"And what would that be?"

"Banging Lorenzo's wife while she is, supposedly, at her regular manicure appointment," I say. "Who else?"

Damian crosses his arms over his chest and leans back, smiling. "Santino D'Angelo is undecided."

"Well, Santino is not fucking anyone except his maid, and his wife knows about it. Shame," I say. "But his oldest son, Dario, is neck deep in debt. With the Albanians."

"Gambling?"

"Yes. The last bit of information I have is that it's close to three hundred grand, but that was last month. It's probably more now. Dario has a huge influence on his father."

"If we buy out his debt, perhaps he'll be able to steer Santino in the right direction?"

"Most probably." I nod. "Any other problems?"

"None for now." He leans forward, resting his elbows on his desk. "Where did you get this information?"

"Definitely not in spas or from fashion magazines." I smirk. "Don's position is not only about doing the job well. It requires closely watching those who want to stab you in the back, and involves a good deal of blackmailing in order to steer people in the desired direction. My grandfather had Orlando Lombardi's driver on his payroll, as well as two of the maids working for Santino D'Angelo. He had at least one person in each capo's household, and paid them triple their salary to update him on anything that might be useful."

Damian's body stiffens at my words. "He had someone here, as well?"

"Your previous gardener."

"Domenico? The ancient guy who spent half of his time trying to get under Grace's skirt?"

"Well, I don't know whose skirt he was trying to get under while he was here, but he was providing some rather nice intel. He's working for Franco Conti now."

"I'll be damned." He shakes his head. "Giuseppe had his own little nest of spies."

"Yes. My mother and I have been handling them for the last two years since my grandfather got sick. We can continue doing so, but Luca will have to take over the funding."

"I'll talk with him."

"He also needs to call all the big shots in the Family over, after he officially takes over the don position. A month or two from now would work fine."

"My brother is not a fan of parties."

"He'll have to throw one anyway. It's expected."

"You can give Luca a shitload of weapons of any kind, and he'll find a buyer in under an hour. But he has no idea how to organize a party."

"Good thing he has me, then." I smile and rise to leave. "I'll need fifty grand."

"Fifty grand for a party?"

"It may end up being closer to seventy-five, but let's start with fifty for now."

## Luca

I fire another round into the target across the field, testing the weight as well as the accuracy of the scope, then put the rifle down on the makeshift table in front of me.

"It'll do," I say and turn to Bogdan. "We're taking four hundred as previously agreed."

"You can wire the deposit to the usual account."

"No deposit for the next three shipments."

"What? I don't take orders without a 20 percent down payment."

"You do now." I take out my phone and start walking toward my car. "Until I'm convinced there won't be any mix-ups of the containers in the future. That's how *I* work."

"Then you can forget about the fucking guns," he yells after me. "I'm not loading anything without seeing my money."

"It was a pleasure doing business with you, Bogdan," I say as I get into my car and dial Damian. "How's Isabella?"

"Better. I had an extremely interesting conversation with her earlier today."

"About?" I turn on the ignition, ignoring Bogdan who's banging on my window.

"It looks like your little wife may prove to be one useful asset."

"In what way?"

"She took it upon herself to organize your big party. It's going to be quite an event since she plans on spending seventy-five grand on it."

"I'm not hosting a party, Damian."

"Isa says you will." He laughs. "And she also made me spend three hundred and twenty grand."

"Are you fucking insane? On what? Wait a second." I roll down the window Bogdan has been banging on for over a minute and fix him with my stare. "Yes?"

"Only the next three shipments, Luca." He points his finger at me. "After that, we're going back to a 20 percent up-front payment."

"All right. Don't forget my grenades." I roll up the window, put Damian on speakerphone and reverse the car. "What did you do with the money, Damian?"

"Paid off Dario D'Angelo's gambling debt to the Albanians."

I had no idea Santino's son's gambling problems were so serious. Why the hell would we be paying off . . .? Oh. I'll be damned. "Does this mean we'll have Santino's support?"

"Yup. And Lombardi won't be a problem anymore, either."

"You bought his debt, too?"

"No. I called Orlando to let him know that we expect his 'yes', or else he may want to change a certain 'manicure appointment' in the future."

"Orlando doesn't get manicures. His hands look like they belong to a butcher."

"No. But Lorenzo's wife does. According to Isa, every second Saturday. Orlando has been fucking Lorenzo's wife under his nose for who knows how long." He laughs. "Your wife and her mother are running a damn spy network within the Family. They have someone in every capo's household. Domenico was in ours."

"That old scumbag who kept hanging around the kitchen all day?"

"Yup. Your woman is dangerous, Luca."

Indeed. And in more ways than I thought.

The moment I get home, I run up the stairs and go straight to Isabella's room, intending to give her a lecture. When I enter, however, she's not there. I turn around, about to head out in search of her in Rosa's room, when I hear the shower turn on.

"Isabella." I bang on the bathroom door. "We need to talk."

"I'm taking a shower. It can wait."

"You can shower later." I bang on the door again. "I talked with Damian. You're dropping your spy hobby starting now."

"You're welcome, Luca," she shouts over the sound of running water. "I was happy to help."

"This is not a fucking game! If anyone even suspects what you and your mother are doing, it won't end well!"

"You said you don't allow yelling in this house."

"New rules." I beat my open palm against the door. "Open the door, or I'm breaking it."

The water shuts off, and a few seconds later, the lock turns. I cross my arms over my chest, waiting for the door to open before I continue. When it does, all I can do is stare.

"I'm listening," I say and lean my shoulder onto the doorframe, enjoying the way Luca's eyes are eating me up as they travel down my naked body.

"Cover yourself up." A muscle in his jaw ticks as he bites out his words.

"I was in the middle of a shower, and I plan on continuing after you're done with your tirade."

"Tirade?" He takes a step forward and looks down at me. "It's not a tirade, Isabella. It's an order. One that you better follow."

He's trying really hard to focus on my face, but his eyes keep wandering downward every couple of seconds.

"Or else?" I ask.

He places his palms on the doorframe on either side of me and bends his head to whisper in my ear. "Do not provoke me, Isa."

Isa? Oh, he must be really angry if he let that slip. I tilt my head up so my lips are nearly brushing his earlobe. "But I enjoy doing so," I whisper back, then lick the shell of his ear with the tip of my tongue. "Very much."

He takes a deep breath. There is a strange cracking sound to the left of me, but I don't move, enjoying the feel of having him so close. The need to lean into him, to press my cheek to his, and bury my fingers in his hair is eating me alive, but I fight it. I need him to come to me of his own accord—because he wants to and not because I pushed him over the edge into mad lust. I'm already toeing the line as it is.

Standing before him naked was a gamble. I half expected him to succumb, but he's still resisting. Stubborn, stubborn man. *What do I have to do to make you see me, Luca? Not the girl they made you marry, but the woman who's been in love with you for so, so long.* I don't have any more ammunition left. If he doesn't want me after all the things I've done to seduce him, is there a point in continuing to try?

His head tilts slightly to the side and I feel the tip of his nose touch the side of my neck. My body goes still while my heart starts thundering in my chest as I listen to his breathing. Having his body looming over mine, and not daring to touch him, makes me want to scream in frustration. *Do something, damn you!*

"Go back to your shower, Isabella," he says, then disappears through the door into his room without saying another word.

I stare at the door joining our rooms, closed now, and wonder how it's possible to hate a fixture with such passion. Oh, how much I loathe that door and everything it represents. Sighing, I lean my back onto the doorjamb and only then do I notice it. The trim on the other side is askew, its upper part separated from the wall. I move closer to inspect the damage and trace the surface of the board where his hand had been with my fingertips, then head back to my shower, a wide smile plastered on my face.

# Chapter Ten

Luca

I grab the counter in front of me and look up at my reflection in the mirror above the sink. There's something wrong with me. It's the only explanation.

Tonight, after leaving Isabella naked in her room, I got into my car and drove downtown while my dick was on the verge of exploding because of how hard it was. I planned to call an escort and just be done with it. I drove around for two hours, only to get back home and find release courtesy of my own hand in the shower. Again. Thinking about the nineteen-year-old in the next room.

Damian says I'm acting irrationally, but he doesn't understand my fear. I'm not a tender man, and my tastes where sex is concerned are not something a nineteen old girl would be okay with. If I let myself go, Isabella will probably get scared.

I always had to hold back with Simona. One time when I slipped, she avoided me for two weeks. When we passed each other around the house, she would stare at me with the look of a terrified gazelle and bolt.

I don't think I could stomach seeing the same fear in Isabella's eyes.

There's something that attracts me to this girl like a magnet, but I can't pinpoint what. It's not only her body, which is every man's wet dream—small with her tiny waist and the most gorgeous fucking ass I've ever laid my eyes on. Nor is it just her pixie face—all sharp lines and huge eyes. I can't grasp it. I have no idea what it is, but for some reason, I can't stop thinking about her. I keep trying to convince myself that this madness will pass, but it's only getting worse.

Then, there's my sick jealousy. I assigned Marco as her bodyguard for two reasons. First, because he's the most reliable I have and won't hesitate to get in front of a bullet for her. And second, because he's fifty-two. Still, every day I find it harder and harder to let her go anywhere with him alone. A few days ago, when I was heading out to meet with Donato, I saw Isabella and Marco leave. I had to make myself get into my damn car and drive off immediately or I would have called Donato and canceled just so I could take her to see Andrea myself.

I have no idea what's going on with me. When the fuck did I start losing my shit?

After washing my face, I get into bed, but sleep eludes me. I find myself staring into the darkness, wondering what I'm going to do with the little spymaster in the other room.

It's well into the night when I hear the faint sound of a door opening. Keeping my body still and pretending I'm asleep, I crack my eyes open just a little. Isabella is standing at the threshold of our connecting rooms, a blanket wrapped around her from neck to toes. She stays there for a few moments, then tiptoes toward my bed. Carefully, she climbs up and slowly lies down, curling on the empty side with her back to me.

I wonder if Luca will be mad when he wakes up and finds me in his bed. He probably will, but I don't give a damn at the moment. I kept tossing and turning for hours, trying to fall asleep, but my eyes kept wandering to the sofa where Luca slept the last few nights. He didn't say anything when he came in that first time, just tossed a pillow on the end of the sofa and laid down. He didn't even undress. The sofa was way too small for him, and it couldn't have been comfortable, but he stayed the whole night. In the morning, when I woke up, he was gone. I could do the same, just sleep here a little bit and go back to my room before he notices me.

The mattress dips behind me and my eyes snap open, but I don't dare to move. If he thinks I've fallen asleep, maybe he won't throw me out. An arm wraps around my waist and pulls me back until I'm pressed against Luca's hard chest. He throws one leg over mine and tightens his hold, spooning me with his huge body. I can barely breathe, too shocked by his unexpected act. The blanket is the only thing separating our bodies, but I can still feel his warmth seeping into me, as well as his hard cock pressing into my backside.

He doesn't say anything, just lies still behind me. Slowly, I reach over and take his hand, moving it off my hip to inside the folds of the blanket until it rests between my legs. His fingers brush my core through the lacy material of my panties, and I suck in a breath.

"Not tonight, tesoro," he whispers next to my ear. "My self-control is barely hanging by a thread."

He starts to pull his hand away, but I hold onto it and press it harder to my pussy, tightening my legs and caging it in place. "You want to know what I think of your self-control, Luca?"

"Isa . . ."

"It can go to hell." I grind my ass right over his hard cock, and hear him growl.

"You are"—his hand tugs on my panties, sliding them down—"playing with fire, tesoro."

Luca presses his cock to my behind as his finger enters me. I gasp, arching back against him.

He leans into me and removes his finger. "Last chance, Isa."

"I will enjoy burning with you, Luca," I rasp, kicking my panties from around my ankles.

He throws his blanket off. It lands somewhere across the room as he tugs on the one I have wrapped around me, and it follows suit. His lips press onto my shoulder, then skim the side of my neck. I start turning toward him, but his arms come around me, hands sliding lower, between my legs.

"How many men, Isa?" he utters, teasing my clit with his thumb.

"What?"

"How many have you slept with before now?"

His finger enters me again, and I ride it as my nails dig into his forearm. "Does it matter?"

"No." A bite on my shoulder, then a lick. "But I still want you to tell me." Another bite. "Names, as well."

"I'm not telling you."

"The names, Isa."

The pressure he's putting on my clit makes me whimper, and then he curls a finger inside of me. I pant as tremors rack my body, my thighs trembling.

"I'm going to strangle them all," he says and moves his mouth to my neck, biting at the sensitive skin there.

I come with a loud moan, but he keeps massaging my pussy. My body continues to shake like I have a fever. Luca adds a second finger into me, and I gasp. He continues to press firmly onto my core and pump his fingers in and out. When I think I can't take much more, he pinches my clit, and I come again. I'm still trembling as he removes his boxer briefs and then places a kiss on my shoulder. He turns me onto my back, covers my body with his, and positions his cock at my entrance. For a second I go completely still. I can't help it. Then I force my body to relax as a combination of anticipation and fear consumes me.

Luca's head lowers, his lips landing on mine. Dear God, I've dreamed about kissing him for so long, imagining how it would feel. So much that it became an obsession. For some reason, in my mind, it always ended up as a slow, tender kiss, where he would tilt my head slightly and carefully taste my lips. Almost a chaste kiss, similar to those I had with a couple of boys I went out with. I was so wrong because there's nothing chaste about this kiss. It's hard and raw, like the man himself. Luca's kiss is him staking his claim. Threading my hands in his hair which is falling on either side of my face, I brush my fingers through the silky strands and let him possess me with his lips.

One of Luca's hands moves between my legs, spreading them wider, and the tip of his cock slowly enters me. I suck in a breath and close my eyes, my body rigid. *Relax,* I say to myself. It doesn't work. Luca stops, starts massaging my clit, then tries again. This time, *his* body goes rigid.

"Isabella?" he says into my mouth. "Is there something you need to tell me?"

I bite my lip and shake my head. "No."

"Look at me."

I do, and find him regarding me with his jaw set in a hard line. "Have you had sex before?"

I've been dreading this moment. It was a struggle to get this far because of his obsession with the difference in our ages, so I was afraid he would never succumb if he knew I was a virgin. I hoped he wouldn't notice.

"No," I utter and fist my hands in his hair to keep him from pulling away. "Please, don't stop."

He watches me, then shakes his head. Closing his eyes, he presses his forehead to mine. "Jesus, tesoro."

"Please, Luca," I whisper. "Please, don't stop."

"I could've hurt you, Isa. Do you have any idea how it would make me feel? Did you even think about that?"

I wrap my legs around his waist, opening myself even more for him, and slide my hands down his back. "Do it." I dig my nails into his skin. "Or I'll find someone else to do it for you."

Luca's nostrils flare as he stares into my eyes. I inhale to prepare for the pain, I expect him to thrust himself into me to the hilt. Instead, his hand slides between our bodies and he starts to circle my clit with his finger while his cock remains at my entrance.

The pressure begins to build inside of me, my breathing coming faster as his finger continues to tease me. Soon, I'm so crazy with the need to feel him inside me that I forget my anxiety and fear. His cock slides into me—impossibly slow—and there's a slight pinch of pain, but it lasts only a few seconds. Then, I'm engulfed by the sensation of his rhythm as he rocks into me, stretches me, fills me. It's slightly uncomfortable at first, but it quickly transforms into pleasure that consumes my whole being.

It's not just having him inside me, making me tremble. It's his body pressed against mine and his hands caressing my cheeks. It's Luca's eyes, piercing and dangerous, holding my gaze the whole time, and the tips of his hair tickling my shoulders and face. The way he grits his teeth because he's holding back for fear of hurting me. I never expected that from him. Even though he's mad for not telling him it's my first time, he's still trying not to hurt me. And that fact makes my heart swell with happiness.

With his breath fanning my face, Luca keeps rocking his body. In. Out. In again. My walls are stretching, taking more of him inside with every thrust. His hand moves up my body, grabs the back of my neck and squeezes.

"Is this what you wanted, Isabella?" he asks, then bites my shoulder.

"Yes," I choke out, "But now I want more."

Luca slides his cock out, then slams into me, hard, and I gasp as spasms begin in my core. A strange satisfaction overcomes me, and the next moment, my brain explodes into beautiful nothingness just as he comes inside me.

I'm bathing in the feeling of having Luca's body lying over mine when he pulls out and gets up. He disappears into the bathroom on the other side of the room for a moment, returning with a towel in his hand. Taking a seat on the edge of the bed, he cleans me up. Once he's done, he leans his elbows on his knees, and remains nearly motionless, gaze focused on the towel smeared with my blood. After a while, and without saying a word, he grabs the blanket off the floor and covers my naked body. His touch is gentle, but I can feel him pulling away as he starts putting on his sweats and T-shirt.

"Don't you dare try manipulating me again, Isabella," he says in cold voice. Not giving me another glance, he walks to the door and leaves the room.

For a few moments, I just stare at that damn door—yet another barrier he slammed in his wake—then bury my face in the pillow and cry.

# Chapter

Luca

"So, we all agree with the decision that Luca Rossi is going to take over the Family?" Francesco asks.

Under Giuseppe's rule, Isabella's father was a consigliere to the don. I plan on keeping him as my adviser.

The men sitting around the table turn toward me. Donato nods first. Franco Conti follows, then Angelo Scardoni. Orlando Lombardi and Santino D'Angelo are next. It appears Isabella was right. Francesco turns to Lorenzo Barbini. Lorenzo looks up at me, seeming outwardly relaxed, but I notice the way he's clenching his jaw. Prior to Giuseppe's death, I was reporting to him and to the don. From this point forward, he will be my subordinate. It doesn't happen often that a capo takes over the Family. By appointing me as his successor, Giuseppe basically declared that he didn't find his underboss fit for the role. It must be a hard pill to swallow, but with five other capos in agreement, Lorenzo has no other choice. He nods.

Francesco comes to stand before me, and bends to place a kiss on the back of my hand. As a consigliere, he is the first one to swear his loyalty.

"Don." He nods and returns to his seat.

As an underboss, Lorenzo is next. He approaches with his spine rigid and his face set in hard lines, but he bends and kisses my hand. The capos follow one by one. When everyone is once again seated, I lean back in my chair and regard them.

"I heard there were some discussions regarding branching out into the drug business," I say and fix my gaze on Lorenzo. "It won't be happening.

We're keeping the same setup we had under Giuseppe. Donato and I will keep handling the gun deals and laundering the money through real estate. Lorenzo, Orlando and Santino are staying in the gambling business, with Franco laundering their income. Everyone will be reporting to Lorenzo, no changes there, either."

I turn toward the young Scardoni. He's barely twenty-five and only recently became a capo following the death of his father. "Angelo, you will work with Franco and set up more businesses we can use to launder the money. We're running close to the limit with what Franco and Damian can process."

He nods.

"If I ever hear that you've set foot in Mexico again," I continue, "or that you've met with Mendoza's men, you're dead."

"Yes, Boss."

I turn my gaze to the other men around the table. "I don't want any more problems with the Russians. Next week, I'm meeting Roman Petrov to assure him we will keep the truce the Bratva agreed to with Giuseppe. Petrov let the fuckup that Bruno created slide because he knew Scardoni's deal was outside the official channels. But he won't do it again." I look at Francesco. "How much money did we lose during the three-month war with the Russians earlier this year?"

"If we include the infrastructure damaged or lost, a little over seven million," he says.

I curse. "No more quarrels with the Russians. Unless you want to see one of your daughters or sisters married off to the Bratva."

After everybody nods, I rise from the table. "That's all."

I open the notes app on my phone and look up at Damian. "Do you want me to hire private security for the banquet, or will you have your own men in place?"

"We'll have our men at the gate and inside the house. Hire ten people to patrol the grounds, just in case."

I make a note in my planner. "I'm meeting the catering people today to pick the cake and decide on the menu. Do you have wine preferences?"

"Nope. Take whatever they think will work best with the menu," he says and looks up from his laptop. "Luca upgraded your security detail. You'll have two bodyguards from now on. Marco and Sandro."

"It would've been nice if he informed me about that himself," I mumble.

Three days. He's been avoiding me for three days, ever since I sneaked into his room. I barely see him. If I do, it's usually only during breakfast. He goes out and returns well after midnight. There must be a lot to handle since he took over as Don, in addition to his own business, but still. I considered resuming with my daily visits to his office, but have decided to wait a few more days.

"He's busy," Damian says.

"Of course, he is."

"And extremely agitated. Care to share what the hell is going on with you and Luca?"

"Why do you think it has anything to do with me?"

"Please. I know my brother better than he knows himself. You're the only person who ever riles him up so much." He starts chewing on the end of his pen. "I wonder how you do it. Luca doesn't lose his shit that easily."

"I told him if he doesn't want to sleep with me, I'd find someone who will." I shrug.

"Interesting. So, you two had sex, I take it?"

"Yes. Now he's avoiding me."

"I told you not to push him."

I put the organizer on my lap and cross my arms. "I'm done being treated like a flower arrangement in this marriage, Damian."

"You don't seem like a delicate flower to me, Isa."

"Because I'm not. And it's time your brother realizes that." I press my lips together and look back at my notes. "What about the music?"

"Anything but jazz. Luca hates it."

"How unfortunate." I smile.

"You're mean." Damian laughs. "Remind me never to get on your bad side."

"I don't usually have a bad side, Damian. Apparently, it only surfaces when your brother's around."

"You know, sometimes I don't get you two and all this drama. Why can't you act like mature people and have a normal relationship instead of circling around one another in this cat and mouse game? There's more than enough shit to deal with without it."

"I couldn't agree more. Hopefully, Luca will get the memo." I stand up. "I'm off. If you change your mind about the wine, call me."

I leave Damian's office and head downstairs to look for Marco just as Luca comes through the front door. He looks me up and down as I pass the foyer, his eyes focusing on my behind. I barely managed to squeeze into these white skinny jeans. With the way my butt is straining the material, they might not be appropriate for a business meeting. I don't give a fuck. I've been feeling like crap for days and wanted to doll up. They're my favorite pair, and they go amazingly well with my beige top and nude heels. After everything that's happened with Luca, I needed a moral boost.

"Where are you going?" he asks.

"I have a meeting with the catering company," I say and head toward the kitchen. "Have you seen Marco and Sandro?"

Silence stretches for a few heartbeats before he barks out, "I'm taking you."

I stop and turn around. "I thought you were busy."

"You thought wrong. Go upstairs and change."

"Why?"

"You won't be wearing those in front of people." He saunters over until he is standing right in front of me and nods at my skinny jeans.

"Can you be more specific? People as in strangers or . . ."

"Anyone but me. Is that specific enough for you?"

I raise my eyebrows. "They're jeans."

"Extremely tight jeans. Go find an oversized shirt and put it on. Or change the pants. Whatever."

"Why?"

"I don't want men ogling your ass."

"Well, my ass is rather huge, it's hard to miss." I laugh.

"Your ass is a fucking piece of art." He bends his head until his eyes are level with mine. "And it's only mine to look at, Isabella."

I blink at him. A piece of art? And only his to look at? "Are you jealous?"

His lips press into a tight line as he regards me while that vein of his keeps pulsing on his neck. "No."

"Perfect. Then it shouldn't bother you what I'm wearing and who ogles my ass," I say and turn toward the front door, intending to head to the car. Luca's hand shoots out and grabs me around my waist, pulling me to him.

"Go. Change," he whispers into my ear.

My breath catches and I close my eyes, trying to compose myself. He's finally started showing some reaction to me, which means we're getting somewhere, but he still hasn't touched me intimately since the night I gave him my virginity. The stubborn mule is still fighting it.

"If you want me out of these jeans, Luca," I say and lean back into him, feeling his hard cock at the small of my back, "you'll have to remove them yourself."

Luca's breath fans the skin on my neck as he tightens his hold around my middle. "What did I tell you about trying to manipulate me, Isa?"

Grinding my teeth, I turn and look up at him, this stubborn man who just won't let me through his shield no matter how often I hit and slash at it. I wonder if it'll always be like this between us. When will I finally be able to stop hiding the feelings I have for him? I've suppressed them for so long, they want to burst out of my chest. I reach up and hook my finger into his hair tie, pulling and releasing his hair so that it spills down and around his face. He doesn't say anything, just regards me as I tilt my head up until the tip of my nose touches his.

"You're so damn stubborn," I whisper, "but I will keep banging at this fucking wall you set between us, Luca, until it crumbles into dust."

His fingers get a hold of my chin, tilting it slightly until my lips are almost touching his. "You may not like what you'll find lurking behind that wall, tesoro," he says, his breath teasing my lips.

"Oh? But what if I do?"

The phone in Luca's pocket rings. He doesn't stop looking into my eyes as he takes it out and puts it to his ear. "What?"

I don't hear the reply from the other side, but it must be something serious because Luca suddenly straightens, his hand falling away from my face.

"I'll be there in an hour," he says and cuts the call. "I have to go. Reschedule the meeting with the catering company for tomorrow. I'll be taking you."

"All right." I nod as butterflies flutter in my chest.

He watches me for a few moments, and I hold my breath, my eyes focused on his lips. Instead of kissing me as I'd hoped, he turns and walks out the front door, leaving me to stand in the middle of the foyer, clutching his hair tie in my hand.

## Luca

*I am done,* I say to myself as I'm driving down the highway. Fucking *done* with pushing Isabella away, trying to stifle this mad need to grab her every time I see her, to envelop her in my arms and never let her leave my side. As soon as I get back home, I'm throwing her over my shoulder and fucking her senseless the moment we get inside the bedroom. *Our bedroom.* Starting tonight she'll be sleeping in my bed. *Our bed.* I'm calling my mission of waiting for her to turn twenty-one a failure. I can't keep her at arms length anymore. And I fucking don't want to. We're turning a new leaf, everything else be damned. Tonight, when I get home, everything will change.

I'm exiting off the highway onto a narrow road and driving uphill when I notice two black SUVs in my rearview mirror, taking the same turn. The route leading to the warehouse where we keep heavy weaponry is usually deserted. There's nothing around for miles except a few abandoned factories, so seeing two cars following me immediately raises a red flag. My hand slips inside my jacket, freeing my gun from the holster. I put it on the dashboard so it's within reach and maintain my speed. There's an intersection in about a mile, and I decide to wait and see if they'll turn off or stay on this road. I pass the crossroads. The SUVs stay on my rear and start speeding up, closing in on me. The road continues uphill, with a rockface on my left and a ravine on my right. The only option I have is to keep driving forward. There are no other intersections for miles.

That call was a scam. A setup. There was no explosion like the guard said. Looks like someone wants me dead. I floor the car.

I manage to keep my distance for a couple of miles, but the SUVs start gaining on me after that. A shot rings out. Then several more. I throw a look in the rearview mirror and spot the passenger of the nearest vehicle leaning out of the window, aiming his gun at my tires. Another shot echoes. Trying to shoot back is not an option, there are too many bends in the road. The best course of action I have is trying to lose them. A couple of more miles, then the road will start going downhill and get wider. I'll have more options for maneuvering there. Another shot. The car swerves under me. Fuck. They've hit one of my tires.

I fight to maintain control of the car and manage to straighten it, but then one of the pursuing vehicles rams me from behind, making my car lurch forward and lose traction, throwing the vehicle into a sideways skid. With a flat tire, there's no way I can escape them, so I hit the brakes, managing to stop just before I reach another curve in the road, and grab my gun. I have my hand on the door handle, intending to get out and start shooting when the other SUV rams into the side of my car. The last thing that I see before my car tumbles down the ravine is the glaring face of a man I haven't seen in years.

"I'm not sure we can risk having the banquet outside in September. I'll order some tents to be placed on the lawn," I say as I motion for Damian to pass me the salad bowl.

"Tents?" Rosa squeaks. "So, it will be a camping party?"

"No." I laugh. "These are just white party tents. They're not for camping. They'll just provide cover in case of rain or shade from the sun."

"Oh. Can I go anyway?"

I look at Damian, but he just shrugs. "You have to ask your dad," I say. "If he's okay with it, then you can come. But you'll still be able to see everything from your window, even if you have to stay inside."

"Can I invite Clara? We can watch it together?"

"I don't see why not. There'll be a huge cake." I wink.

"Did Luca say where he was going?" Damian pipes up. "I've tried calling him, but he's not answering."

"No. Someone called earlier, and he said he had to go. I don't know who it was, but it sounded urgent. Maybe he's in a meeting and turned off his phone?"

"Luca never does that."

"Will there be a band?" Rosa asks. "Or a DJ?"

"I've hired a jazz band."

"Oh no, that's boring. And Dad hates jazz."

"I know." I laugh at the same time as Damian's phone rings.

He looks at the screen and takes the call. A moment later he abruptly gets up from his chair. For a few seconds, he just listens to the person on the other end, his face going ghostly white, then nods.

"We're coming right away," he says and disconnects the call. "Rosa, go to your room."

"But I haven't—"

"Now!" he shouts.

Rosa jumps up off her chair and dashes upstairs as I stare at Damian. I've never heard him raise his voice.

"We have to go." He takes my hand and starts pulling me with him across the entry hall toward the front door.

"Damian? What happened?"

"There's been a crash. Luca's car went off the road and into a ravine," he says, and I stumble as my heart stops beating.

"Is he . . . alive?"

"Barely."

There's a piercing pain in my chest as if someone has thrust a knife into me. As soon as we get into Damian's car, he hits the gas. I'm finding it hard to breathe, so it takes me a few tries to form the words. "How bad?"

"Head trauma and second-degree burns."

"Burns?"

"His car caught fire. I don't know anything else."

I watch the road in front of us, trying to control the urge to scream.

The smell of antiseptic and medical supplies infiltrates my nostrils. People quietly talk around us. Someone is crying in one of the rooms. The sound of my heels clicking on the tiled floor echoes as we run down the corridor. Every single thing I see and feel gets tangled up in a mess of sensations. All I can make out for sure is Damian's hand squeezing mine as he drags me behind him, his long legs covering the distance much faster than my own. A man in a white coat comes around the corner and heads toward us.

"How is he?" Damian chokes out when we reach him.

"Mr. Rossi suffered significant trauma to his head. We managed to get the swelling under control, but we won't know if there will be any lasting damage until he regains consciousness."

I grab Damian's forearm and ask the doctor, "When do you expect him to wake up?"

"It's hard to say until he's out of recovery. He might end up perfectly well, or there may be serious long-term effects."

Damian is sitting on a chair next to me, talking with someone over the phone, but all I can do is stare at the wall in front of me. We've been here for twelve hours now. Luca came out of surgery an hour ago, but he's still in the recovery room.

"They finished processing Luca's car," Damian says. "The car was totaled, but there's some evidence that the scratches and dents on the side and rear may have happened before he crashed."

I stare at him. The preliminary report said Luca lost control of the car and slid off the road into the ravine, rolling twice. It was pure luck that a fire truck was passing by and noticed his wreck and the fire. "What does that mean?"

"It means someone pushed him off the road. Based on the tire marks, probably two vehicles. Looks like someone may have rear-ended him, while another vehicle hit his side."

My heart skips a beat. Someone tried to kill my husband.

# Part Two

**“After”**

# Chapter Twelve

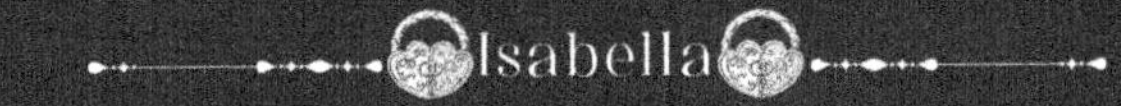

Isabella

*Present*

I SLOWLY APPROACH THE HOSPITAL BED WHERE MY HUSBAND IS LYING, numerous wires hooked up to his body and connected to a machine on the right. My hand grips the bed rail to prevent my legs giving out from under me, and I nearly collapse into the nearby chair. Most of his head is tightly wrapped in bandages, they must have shaved his hair. I press my hand to my mouth to keep the sobs from escaping.

I don't know why that detail hits me so hard. I managed to keep it together while he was in surgery and during the hours he spent in the recovery room. I've put on a stoic mask and pretended I wasn't falling apart while his life was hanging in the balance. Somehow, I managed to get through it without spilling a tear.

I reach for his hand and entwine our fingers, and dropping my forehead onto the mattress, I cry. Minutes pass. Maybe hours, I'm not sure. Different scenarios roll around my mind, each worse than the one before, and I weep harder until my whole body is shaking.

I almost miss the tiny twitch of fingers in my own. My head snaps up, and I find two dark brown eyes watching me.

"Oh, Luca . . ." I choke out, then lean over him and place a light, quick kiss on his lips.

He doesn't say anything, just keeps looking at me. When he finally speaks, the words that leave his mouth make me go ice-cold.

"Who are you?"

I stare at him.

Luca cocks his head to the side, regarding me with his intense, calculating gaze.

"I'm Isabella," I whisper. "Your . . . wife."

He blinks, then looks away at the window on the other side of the room and takes a deep breath.

"So, Isabella," he says and turns to me. "Care to tell me who I am?

I take a slow deep breath, trying to suppress the panic rising in the pit of my stomach. It's hard to know how long he was unconscious in the car, and then there were hours of surgery. It's perfectly normal for him to be slightly confused.

I place my hand over his, noticing the way my fingers shake. "I'll go find the doctor. He said to call him the moment you wake up. Okay?"

After he nods, I turn around and walk to the door, trying my best to appear calm. In reality, I'm choking down the urge to run in search of the doctor, yelling for him to come right away. When I find Dr. Jacobs, he rushes to Luca's room, asking me to stay outside. I sit in the chair and wait. And wait. I'm not sure how long the doctor has been inside when Damian comes and joins me.

When the doctor finally exits the room, we both jump from our chairs and stare at him.

"Physically, Mr. Rossi is good," Dr. Jacobs says. "Taking into account the seriousness of his condition when he arrived, I would say he's doing exceptionally well. I did a basic exam, and all his motor functions seem to be working quite well. We'll do a more thorough examination, of course, and another CT scan to make sure the swelling continues to recede, but other than some bruises and burns, he seems fine. Except for his memory loss."

I stiffen next to Damian. "Is that . . . permanent?"

"I don't know. He could wake up tomorrow and be his old self. Or it may happen in six months. Or his memory could come back in pieces."

"Does he remember anything?" Damian asks.

"He knows where he is, as well as which month and year it is. He can list the main cities, solve math problems, and he can read and write. When I asked him about some landmarks here in Chicago or elsewhere, he described how to reach them in great detail. But he doesn't remember anything personal. He doesn't know his name or recall any family members. He can't tell me the names of any childhood friends, and he doesn't know where he lives or what he does for a living."

Dear God.

"We have good psychologists here." Dr. Jacobs continues, "Once we get him out of the ICU, they can help him deal with this problem, and also give you guidelines on how to support him."

"So it might help him remember?" I ask.

"No. It will help him manage the situation. Only time will tell if he'll recover his memories."

"Okay," I say, then turn to Damian and grab his forearm. "Take the doctor to the side," I say in Italian. "Explain to him that under no circumstances is he to share the information about Luca's memory with anyone. He needs to leave it out of the reports. You'll need to threaten him. Make sure he understands that if he shares this info with anyone, he won't live long enough to regret it."

"And if he declines?" Damian asks, in Italian, as well.

"If he declines, he'll need to be dealt with right away."

Damian stares at me like he's seeing me for the first time. "I've never killed anyone, Isa. I deal with the finances. Luca is in charge of . . . the rest."

I take a step forward and look him right in the eyes. "Do you have any idea what will happen if this comes out? If anyone suspects that Luca is unfit for his . . . position, he's as good as dead. No one, other than you and me, can know."

Damian just gapes at me. He knows very well how things work in Cosa Nostra. If the don is not capable of doing his duty, he needs to step down. If he doesn't, someone will kill him in a matter of days.

"We have to tell Rosa," he says.

I take a deep breath, hating myself for making this decision, then shake my head. "No. She may slip in front of her friends. This is too big. We can't risk it."

"How the fuck do you plan on keeping this hidden, Isa? Luca doesn't remember who he is. How will he lead the Family? There are business meetings. He has Lorenzo coming to report to him every week. There are—"

"We'll figure it out," I say and squeeze his forearm. "Luca's memory will come back in a couple of days. Go talk to the doctor."

Damian leads the doctor to the side, speaking to him in hushed tones. The doctor watches him with a grim face. I hope to God Damian can convince him to keep his mouth shut. The alternative, the good doctor will have to die. I'll do whatever it takes to protect my husband, which means if Damian can't kill him, I'll have to. The thought of killing another human being has never crossed my mind, and I get lightheaded just from the sight of blood. But if saving Luca's life means I need to take another's, I'll do it.

## Luca

I regard the woman sitting on the edge of my hospital bed, holding a tablet in her lap. The screen shows a photo from some event I don't remember. She turns it toward me, pointing at the people, telling me their names, roles, and sometimes even the names of their pets.

Isabella. My amazingly beautiful and very cunning young wife, who's been spending hours stuffing information in my head to make sure no one realizes that I don't remember shit.

Every morning she comes to see me, trying to fill the blank spaces in my brain with pieces of my life. My brother, Damian, always arrives around noon and takes over, vomiting business information at me, describing how I act in certain situations, and explaining who does what in both our legitimate and Cosa Nostra dealings. He leaves around three, probably to take care of tasks I should be doing, and Isabella resumes teaching me what I should already know.

She's all business when it comes to my reeducation. At first, I thought she was doing this for her own benefit because maybe she's afraid of losing her status as the don's wife if anyone finds out and decides to remove me from the position. But when I get one of the small details right, she smiles in a way that makes her eyes twinkle, and I'm not so sure anymore.

"Okay, let's go through the house staff again," she says and tries to hide a yawn.

I reach up to remove a strand of hair that's fallen over her face, hooking it behind her ear, and she goes still. Slowly, she raises her head and looks at me, surprise in her eyes. One thing I've noticed, and it has been baffling me from the beginning, is the fact that during the whole six days she's spent here, she hasn't once tried to touch me. Is it because we don't have that kind of relationship? She told me that ours was an arranged marriage. Or is it something else? Whatever the reason, I don't like it.

"That's enough for today," I say. "Go home and rest."

"You're being released in the morning. We need to go over the staff one more time."

"Security, first shift. Marco, Sandro, Gio, Antonio, Emilio, Luigi, Renato. Sergio and Tony at the gate. House staff: Grace and Anna in the kitchen. Maids: Martha, Viola . . ." I keep listing the names until I cover both shifts, all thirty-two people. "We're good, Isabella."

She stands, wearing a smile that doesn't quite reach her eyes. "Okay. I'll get going, then."

As she turns to leave, I wrap my hand around her wrist and wait for her to face me. "Is everything okay?"

She looks down at my hand holding her forearm, then up until our gazes meet, and nods. Her eyes flick to the side of my head. The doctor removed my bandages this morning, revealing a long, partially healed incision that starts behind my ear and curls down toward my neck. Isabella notices me watching her and quickly looks away.

"Is it that awful?" I ask. It didn't look that bad to me when I inspected it in the mirror after the doctor had left. Only six stiches.

"What?"

"The scar?"

"No, it's just . . ." She lifts her eyes to mine, reaches up with her hand, and lightly brushes her fingers over the hair tied at the top of my head. "I was worried they had shaved it all off," she says in a strangled voice.

"Just the bottom part." They got rid of everything below the crown, leaving the rest.

"I like it. Very stylish." She plays with one of the strands that has escaped the bun.

I was rather surprised when I realized I had long hair. I didn't expect that for some reason and considered cutting it. But after seeing that it makes her happy, I decide I'm keeping it.

Isabella leans forward to look at the back of my head, and a faint vanilla fragrance envelops me. I turn my head, burying my nose in the crook of her neck, and inhale. She tenses but doesn't move away, just steadies herself a little more and sighs.

"Did your family make you marry me, Isabella?" I ask and cup her cheek with my hand. "You're way too young."

"No."

"Then why did you marry me?"

She doesn't reply right away, just nuzzles my neck with her nose for a few moments. "Because I'm in love with you, Luca," she whispers, then goes rigid, like she didn't mean to say those words.

"And me? Am I in love with you?"

Isabella steps away and smiles. "Of course you are," she says and brushes my cheek with the back of her hand. "I have to go. Don't forget to call Rosa."

"I won't," I say.

I've been calling Rosa twice a day, in the morning and in the evening. She'd usually be the one who talked while I mostly listened. About her friend Clara who has a cat. About the construction workers who came to fix the façade and one of them ending up in the rose bush. About movies she watched. It has been the hardest thing so far—talking with my child without having any recollection of her. Almost as hard as shaking my head when Isabella showed me a photo of a dark-haired girl with shoulder-length hair, asking me if I recognized her.

I don't remember my daughter.

"Damian and I will be here first thing in the morning," Isabella says and leaves the room without looking back.

# Chapter Thirteen

Isabella

I stand next to Damian in the hospital hallway, staring at the door as we wait for Luca to come out of his room.

Dear God, what the hell possessed me yesterday to tell him he was in love with me? I spent the whole night awake, trying to think of a way to correct that fuckup. What kind of person am I, lying to a man who's lost his memory about something so important? I didn't mean to say it. It just kind of burst out of me. I was so fucking scared this whole week, worrying that Luca's condition may change for the worse, or that someone from the Family may make an appearance and find out about his memory loss, that I wasn't thinking straight and just blurted out that nonsense. So, now what? Should I come clean right away? Or wait until we get home?

The door opens, pulling me from my internal turmoil, and Luca comes out, dressed in a dark gray shirt and black pants. I think he's lost a couple of pounds during his stay, but it's barely noticeable. He still looks the same—larger than life. After a few words with Dr. Jacobs, Luca nods at Damian, and then his eyes land on me. I offer him a small smile and turn toward the exit when I feel his arm around my waist.

"Is something wrong?" he asks.

"No. I'm just nervous."

"Don't be." He bends and whispers in my ear, "You've taught me well."

He kisses me on the top of my head, and I close my eyes, swallowing the tears that threaten to spill. This lie will probably make me burn in hell, and Luca will most certainly hate me when he finally remembers everything. But walking down the hallway with his arm around my back feels so right, and the heart in my chest literally makes a leap. That kiss. The way he watches me with affection instead of reluctance. His warmth next to my side. I've wanted this for so so long. I don't want to go back to the cold treatment. Not now, when I almost lost him. As we leave the hospital and walk toward the car, I make my decision.

I'm not telling him the truth.

As we pull up to the house, and Damian parks the car, I nod toward the man standing at the front door. "Emilio." I tell Luca. "The one at the gate was Tony."

"Emilio. Tony." He repeats.

"Rosa's waiting for us inside."

Luca grinds his teeth and nods. "How . . . how do I call her? Do I have a pet name for her?"

Something squeezes in my chest upon hearing his question. "You call her 'piccola,'" I choke out and take his hand in mine.

"And you?"

I blink in confusion. "Me?"

"Yes," he says and passes his free hand through my hair. "Do I have a pet name for you as well?"

I bite my lip, and stare into his eyes, then whisper. "You sometimes called me 'tesoro.'"

Luca nods and leans forward. "Thank you, tesoro."

"You're welcome." I choke out, barely able to keep my emotions at bay.

When we enter the house, I face Luca and force a smile. "Welcome home." I place my palm on his chest, raise onto my tiptoes, and place a quick kiss on his chin. "Viola by the stairs. Martha on the left," I whisper. "Ask Viola how her son, Fabio, is doing."

We move toward the stairs, the maids watching us approach. They dip their heads slightly, a welcome home to Luca.

"Mr. Rossi, it's good to have you back."

"Thank you, Viola. How's Fabio?" he asks.

"Better, Mr. Rossi. His leg is healing fine. Thank you for asking."

Luca nods and places one hand on the stair railing when the sound of running feet reaches us.

"Dad! Daddy!" Rosa shouts, running toward us across the foyer.

Luca turns just in time to catch her as she throws herself into his arms, and I watch Luca's face, holding my breath. My hope that seeing Rosa would trigger something in his brain and help him remember quickly fades when Luca turns to me with a haunted look in his eyes. I hold utterly still, carefully schooling my features. He still doesn't remember his daughter.

"They wouldn't let me visit you in the hospital!" Rosa weeps, clinging to his neck. "I was so scared."

"Hospitals are not places for kids, piccola," Luca whispers, gently holding the back of her head with his bandaged hand.

"Did they really open your head? Uncle Damian said they did and had to patch it back together with iron nails because your head was too thick for them to sew it."

"Well, you know your uncle is an idiot. Don't listen to him."

"I knew it." She laughs. "Can I see?"

Luca turns his head to show her, and Rosa makes a disgusted face. "Yuck, Dad. That's nasty. And what's with the hipster haircut? You're too old for that. Isa, did you see this?"

"Yup," I say and notice Luca watching me. "I love it."

"I have to go. Clara will be here in fifteen, and Grace is making us a cake." Rosa kisses Luca's cheek. "Love you, Dad."

"I love you too, Rosa."

She dashes off to the kitchen. Luca stares after her with a somewhat shuttered look in his eye, and my heart squeezes. How do you deal with the fact you don't have any recollection of your own kid?

I open the door between our rooms and peek inside. "Luca?"

For a second, panic rises in my stomach. What if something's happened? The doctor said they did a thorough evaluation, and with the exception of his memory loss, every other test came back with positive results. Still, I'm constantly on edge. The sound of running water in the bathroom reaches me, and I exhale in relief.

"Luca?" I cross the room to the en suite. "Is everything . . .? What the fuck are you doing?"

His head is under the tap and he's reaching for the shampoo bottle on the counter. "Washing my hair," he states the obvious.

I grab the shampoo. "Are you out of your fucking mind? You have second-degree burns on your arm. Dr. Jacobs said you can't let the bandages get wet."

"You curse quite a lot when you're mad."

I curse again, squeeze a bit of shampoo onto my hand and start lathering his hair, making sure I don't let the water reach the back of his head. Rinsing takes quite some time because he has a lot of hair, even with a fair bit of it shaved off.

"Don't move." I open the cupboard to grab a clean towel, then proceed with drying his hair. Luca doesn't say anything through the whole ordeal, just regards me with a strange look in his eyes. When I'm done, I comb through his hair and turn around to look for a hair tie, but there isn't one in sight. I take off mine and gather Luca's hair, securing it at the top of his head. "All done."

He straightens, caging me with his arms against the counter, and slowly bends until we're at the same eye level.

"Do you sleep here? In this room?" he asks, and I tense.

"Yes."

Luca smirks and cocks his head to one side. "Then tell me, Isabella, why aren't any of your clothes in the closet?"

Shit. I should have thought of that. The way he watches me, with his eyes staring right into mine like he can uncover all my secrets with one look, is highly unnerving. "Because I have a lot of stuff." I blurt out "I'm using the wardrobe in the room next door."

"Hmm." He lifts his hand and places it under my chin. "Tomorrow morning, I'm having Martha and Viola move your clothes in here."

What? Why? "Sure. Anything else?"

"Yes." He tilts my head up a bit more. "I prefer your hair like that."

"Down?" I ask and he nods. "Thank you. Consider your preference noted."

He narrows his eyes at my comment. Did I miss some meaning there? I'm not sure how to act around this new Luca because he's not behaving like he used to.

"I'm going to take a shower," he says. "Are you coming?"

My breath catches. God help me, but I like this new version of him so much better. "Yes."

## Luca

My wife is hiding something. What it is, exactly, is a mystery, but it has something to do with our relationship. I went through every part of the bedroom and each piece of furniture when I came in here, and I didn't find a single thing of hers.

Isabella removes her dress, then her bra and panties, and my breathing stills. She's an amazingly beautiful little thing. I let my gaze travel down her firm little breasts and narrow ribcage, then from her tiny waist to her generous hips and shapely legs. She has the body of a fucking goddess. "Turn around," I rasp and barely manage to keep my hands to myself when she does. Even though I don't remember shit, I'm sure my eyes have never landed on a more perfect ass.

"Now you." She turns to face me and starts unbuttoning my shirt. When she's done, I remove the shirt and throw it next to her dress on the floor. The rest of my clothes follow soon after.

"You lost some weight," she says, placing her hand on my chest.

"How much?"

"A few pounds." Her palm slides down my stomach and then moves to my hip. "Five, maybe six."

I checked the chart at the hospital. I lost six pounds since being admitted. She knows my body well, and still, something feels off. Based on how comfortable she is with being naked around me, I'm fairly certain we've had sex before, so it can't be that. *What are you hiding from me, Isabella?*

Her touch leaves me as she gets into the stall. For a few moments, she fumbles with the shower head, adjusting its position, then turns on the water and looks up. "Keep your arm out of the spray."

I join her inside. Isabella watches me, but keeps her eyes focused on my face instead of my hard cock, pretending she doesn't notice it. We both know where this is leading. It's been inevitable from the moment she started removing her clothes, but we keep dancing around it. She lathers her hands with soap and presses her palms to my chest, massaging, and it takes tremendous self-control to keep myself from reaching out and grabbing her. Somehow, I manage and close my eyes instead, enjoying the sweet torture as her hands travel across my chest and then down, but when I feel her fingers brushing my cock . . . well, my patience hits its limit.

"Enough." I turn off the water, reach out and press my palm to her pussy. Slowly, I slide a finger inside. Isabella gasps but doesn't pull away, her huge eyes glued to mine. Smiling, I slightly curl my finger inside her.

"Hands on my wrist, Isabella," I say, "and don't you dare let my finger slip out."

I wait until her hands wrap around my wrist. With my palm cupping her pussy and finger still buried inside of her, I take a step back, pulling her with me. It takes us a couple of minutes to leave the bathroom and reach the bed, step-by-*tiny*-step, and by the time we do, Isabella is panting, but she doesn't let go of my hand.

I move to stand behind her, press my chest to her back and bend my head to whisper in her ear.

"On the bed," I say and slide another finger inside her. "Slowly."

Isabella lets go of my wrist and starts crawling toward the middle of the bed. I follow, hunched over her, keeping my fingers buried in her.

"Stop." I wrap my left arm around her waist, ignoring the pain the strain inflicts on my burned skin. "I'm going to remove my fingers now," I say next to her ear.

"Please, don't." She presses her legs together and moans.

"Don't worry." I place a kiss on her shoulder. "I'll be only a second, and then I'll make it better."

"Promise?"

"I promise." I kiss her neck next. "Front? Or from behind?"

"Front."

Isabella whimpers when I slowly slide out my fingers, then turns onto her back and hooks her legs around my hips. I just watch her for a few moments. Her hair is tangled, her mouth slightly open, and her chest rises as she pants.

"Please, Luca."

I want to take her in one hard thrust, but I felt how tight she is. So, instead, I place the tip of my cock at her entrance and slide in just a bit.

Isabella growls in displeasure and digs her nails into my back, pulling me closer. My little wife—always so composed and calm—just growled at me.

Our eyes lock, and I crush my mouth to her lips, thrusting all the way inside. She gasps but doesn't close her eyes, watching me.

"You like the feel of my cock filling you up, don't you, Isabella?"

"Yes." She breathes out, then squeezes her legs around me.

I slide out, then drive into her again, hard. "How much?"

Isabella doesn't reply, just moves her hands up my back and pulls the hair tie from the knot at the top of my head. My hair falls, framing my face, and she threads her fingers through it as her body arches up. I pull my cock out, press my fingers over her pussy, and start teasing her clit. Her hands in my hair grip the strands, pulling, and it takes a lot of control not to bury myself inside her again.

"I asked how much, Isabella?"

"So, so much." She gulps air with a hiss. "I wish it could stay inside me all the time."

An answering growl rumbles from my throat as I slide back inside her. When I bury myself to the hilt, a sigh of relief leaves her lips. My God, I can definitely get behind the idea of having my cock buried in this woman. Permanently. The bed squeaks under us as I pound into her, soaking up her every grunt and sigh.

The need to take her from behind is growing too strong to ignore. "Turn around," I say and slide out.

Isabella turns and rises onto all fours, perching her ass. Holy Mother of God, I almost come from just seeing that perfection. I grab her around the waist and bite her right butt cheek. Then I slap that sweet ass twice in quick succession. A yelp escapes her, then another one when I bury my teeth in her other ass cheek. Moving my hands around her hips to her front, I find her clit and tease it as I thrust my cock inside. I feel her walls gripping my length. Moaning, she lowers her head to the pillow, raising her ass even higher, and I lose it completely. I begin to thrust faster into her sweet pussy, then smack her ass cheek again and watch as my handprint appears, marking her. Gripping her hips, I continue my punishing pace. A muffled scream leaves her when I slam into her and her inner walls grip my cock, the sensation causing my orgasm to hit me before I'm ready to be done with her. Still, I can't help but relish the feel of my seed pouring inside, branding her.

Isabella's body is still shaking when I pull out and lie down next to her. With my hand around her waist, I bring her against me, pressing her back to my chest, then slide my hand across her front until I cup her pussy with my palm.

"Don't even think about moving." I whisper into her ear and keep my hand covering her pussy. "I want my cum in you the whole night."

Slowly, I slide one finger inside and Isabella sucks in a breath.

"I don't know how we've slept before," I say, "but this is how we'll sleep from now on. Is that clear?"

She nods and glides her palm down my forearm and lower until she covers my hand and presses it, pushing my finger deeper.

"If your hand is anywhere else when I wake up," she says, "I'll be very displeased, Luca."

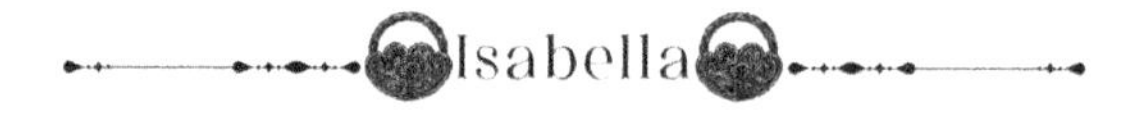


When I open my eyes next morning, Luca is sitting at the edge of the bed, unwrapping the bandage from his left arm.

"The doctor said you should go to the hospital to have your bandages changed," I say.

"No time. I'm going to the office with Damian. We need to be there in an hour."

"You were discharged less than twenty-four hours ago. Maybe you should take a few days off."

"I don't remember shit, Isabella. I need to get up to speed on my own life. There's no time to waste."

"You say that as if you don't believe your memory will return."

"Dr. Jacobs said it might happen in months. Or years. Or never. I don't plan on sitting at home and hoping for a miracle that may never happen," he says.

"That's a very . . . pragmatic way of looking at the things."

He tilts his head and looks at me sideways. "Do I have a choice?"

"No. I don't think you do." I crawl over the bed until I'm sitting behind his back and place my chin on his shoulder. "Is it bad?" I nod at his arm.

"Not so much," he says and looks at me from the corner of his eye. "Don't faint."

"I never faint," I say as he unwraps the last of the bandage and removes the dressing.

"Dear God, Luca." I suck in a breath and quickly bury my face in his neck. The skin on his arm, from just below the shoulder all the way to his wrist is mottled red, and looks like it was scrubbed raw. "Do you need help?" I mumble into his neck.

"No, I'll manage."

He starts putting some kind of balm over the burns on his arm, but his movements seem too sharp, and he's rubbing the sensitive skin way too much.

I slide to the edge of the bed next to him and take the jar. "Let me do it."

I'm not good with blood or wounds of any kind, but the rough way he's going about it will only make it worse. Taking a deep breath, I scoop a good amount of the balm with my fingers and carefully start applying it to his wounds, first focusing on the less damaged parts. Then, I move up his arm, leaving the worst of the burns to be treated last. Not a very wise decision. When I come to his bicep, my hand is shaking so much that I have to pull away for a moment to calm myself. I don't want to risk hurting him more. Luca's hand wraps around mine, and he moves it back to his wounded skin.

"You're doing great," he says.

I nod and resume applying the balm, trying my best to be as gentle as possible. When I'm done, I place a thin piece of sterile gauze over his damaged skin and bandage his arm. Only then do I let myself sag.

"I'm sorry," I say and close my eyes. "I don't deal well with this kind of stuff."

His hand cups my face and a kiss lands on my lips. "I think you deal quite well with anything that gets thrown at you, Isabella," he says against my mouth. "Unexpectedly well, I might add."

"Not really." I kiss him back. "I'm just good at pretending."

"Are you pretending now?"

"No."

"Good. I don't want you pretending with me." His lips move across my cheek, toward my ear. "But I know you're hiding something from me, Isabella," he whispers.

My eyes snap open. "I'm not hiding anything."

"Yes, you are." He bites my ear slightly and stands up. As he walks toward the wardrobe I enjoy the view of his powerful body moving with grace. Watching Luca move around has always been one of my favorite things, but I usually had to do it in secret. Being able to do so freely feels strange. I still can't believe he's finally mine. Well, at least until he remembers he doesn't like me. Then, he'll probably hate me for lying to him. But I don't care. It will be worth it.

# Chapter fourteen

## Isabella

I place my fist to my forehead, switching my gaze between Luca and Damian every few seconds. We're fucked.

"I don't have the slightest idea, Luca." Damian raises his hands in the air and sighs.

"How the fuck am I going to discuss the next shipment with the Romanians if I don't know the terms we agreed to?" Luca asks.

"Well, you'll have to improvise."

"Do you even know what we ordered?"

"Not a clue. I just launder the money you throw my way. You're in charge of everything else. I don't know the quantities, the rates, or the payment terms."

"What about Donato?" I throw in. "He should know most of that stuff. You just need to find a way to wring the info out of him without actually asking."

"I'll take him with me,"—Luca nods—"say I'm planning on passing the reins over to him since I'm busy with the Family shit, and that I want to see how he'll manage."

"That could work. What about trying the goods?" Damian asks. "Do you remember how to assemble and shoot your toys? Because Donato only knows how to handle his own gun. Barely."

"Yes."

"Good. That leaves us Orlando Lombardi as the last pressing issue for now. Everything else can be dealt with without a face-to-face meeting. At least for now."

"What about him?"

"He's throwing a party for his son, Massimo. He just turned eighteen, and the party is on Wednesday. You two are invited." Damian points his fingers to me and then Luca. "And everyone will be there."

"You're not going?" Luca asks.

I place a hand on Luca's arm. "He's persona non grata in the Lombardi household. At most of the Family households, actually. He wasn't at our wedding for the same reason." I smile and look at Damian. "He was sleeping with Constansa, Orlando's youngest daughter, while in a relationship with the older one, Amalia."

"You were fifteen when that happened!" Damian widens his eyes at me. "How do you even know about that?"

"When Orlando caught him in Constansa's room, he had to escape through the window," I add. "Everyone talked about his naked ass running across the garden while Orlando chased him with a shotgun."

"I had my boxer briefs on, for God's sake." Damian rolls his eyes.

"Any other love affairs I should know about?" Luca asks.

"We should go over the real estate business one more time." Damian answers, pointedly ignoring Luca's question.

"Damian."

"All right, damnit, I'll make you a list." Damian waves his hand dismissively and opens his laptop. "Let's go through the real estate we sold this month and what we'd like to consider purchasing."

I lean back on the sofa and watch Luca as he listens to Damian dumping heaps of information on him—details on money laundering schemes, commission rates, numbers, rental terms, explanations of agreements they have with the biggest clients he may end up meeting. They already covered people at the office while Luca was in the hospital, but Damian goes over their names and roles one more time. Luca doesn't speak much, only asks a question here and there, and keeps listening, absorbing. I don't know how I would deal with this if it were me in a similar situation. I'd probably lose it after two days. But not Luca.

The other day, Damian found a video from a reception held last year for the real estate businesses. Luca spent the whole morning watching a two-minute segment where the camera caught him, studying the way he moved and talked. He's extraordinary. It's been ten days since he came back from the hospital, and he hasn't slipped once.

When Luca told me Lorenzo was coming by to update him last Friday,

I was scared shitless. Trying to fool the second most important man in the Family is not the same as deceiving the household staff. Damian and I did our best to fill him in on everything they could potentially discuss, but our knowledge was limited. Still, Luca pulled it off, somehow.

We have three days until Massimo's birthday party, not nearly enough time to go over everyone we might meet there. I'll have to start combing social media and downloading images of people I haven't shown him so far.

"If you two don't need me, I'm going to find Rosa," I say and rise off the sofa. "She wanted to buy new curtains for her room, and I promised I would take her."

I head toward the door, but as I'm passing Luca, he stands up, grabs me around my midriff, and pulls me against him.

"I'm coming with you," he says and slides his hand to my butt.

"We have work to do, Luca," Damian barks from his spot behind the desk.

"It can wait."

I look up to find Luca watching me. Based on the glint in his eyes, he's interested in something other than picking out curtains. Smirking, I slide my hand under his shirt and brush the tip of my finger across his lower back. We had sex twice this morning—in the bed first, then in the shower—but it was rather quick since Luca was in a hurry. I can't wait for tonight when we won't be rushed. My absolute favorite part is when he spoons me after we're both spent and sated, and slides his finger into me. It felt a little strange the first night, having his finger in my pussy while I slept, but I got used to it pretty quickly. Now, I don't think I could fall asleep any other way now.

Before the crash, he barely touched me, especially when someone else was around. He only relented when I pushed him into pleasuring me. And he only kissed me once—when we slept together that first time. His behavior has taken a one-eighty after the crash. Sometimes, I find it hard to connect this Luca with the one from before.

## Luca

"Didn't we come for curtains?" I turn to Rosa, who's browsing the bed throws.

"I'm too old for a pink room. I want to change everything," she says and picks a faux fur cover in a shade of gray. "I love this! Can we get it?"

"If we have to." The thing looks like a yak hide.

"Yes! I'll see if they have cushions to go with it."

"We should buy one for our room," Isabella adds.

I look down at her, placing my hand under her chin, and tilt her head up. Big brown eyes meet mine and she laughs. Jesus, she is so beautiful.

"No dead animals. Real or fake," I say.

"You're no fun."

"Oh?" I squish her to me, pressing her into my body. "We'll see about that tonight."

"Well, I see you're up and about," A high-pitched voice exclaims behind me. "I thought you were half dead."

Keeping my hand around Isabella's waist I turn around to look over at the blonde woman standing a few paces away. I remember her from the photos Isabella showed me. "I'm sorry to disappoint, Simona."

She narrows her eyes at me and then looks down at my arm around Isabella. Damian only briefly filled me in on my first marriage because we were more concerned about business-related details.

"I'll come to pick up Rosa on Thursday," she says, and Isabella lightly squeezes my waist once, then one more time.

"No," I say.

"No?" Simona sneers. "You can't keep me from seeing my child."

"You get Rosa on the weekends," Isabella says.

"I don't remember asking you anything."

"Enough!" I snap. "You will not talk to my wife in that tone. Are we clear?"

"What? She was—"

"Are we fucking clear, Simona?"

She scrunches her nose at me and tilts her chin, but shuts up.

"Rosa will be ready at ten on Saturday," I say and look down at Isabella. "Let's go find Rosa and check out those glasses you said you liked."

I walk toward the other end of the shop until I'm sure we're well out of Simona's earshot, then glance at Isabella. "You need to fill me in on my relationship with Simona. Damian only told me I have full custody, and that she takes Rosa a couple of times a month. Why did we divorce?"

"She was supposed to be in Europe till the end of the month, so we thought it wasn't the most pressing matter," she says and cocks her head. "Damian will have to be the one to fill you in on Simona and her issues. He knows much more, and anyway, I'm not a fan of your ex, so I'd prefer not to discuss her."

"Why not?"

Isabella arches her eyebrows. "Isn't that obvious? She had you first, and I hate her for that."

I take a step forward and place my hand at the back of Isabella's neck. "What about your exes?"

"What about them?"

"Who had you first, Isa?" I take another step forward, then one more, making her walk backward until her back hits a wall. Her eyes regard me without blinking, and the corners of her lips curve up.

"I already told you that, Luca," she says and smirks. "Before."

"You know I don't remember." I slide my hand into her hair and tug. "Tell me."

A knowing smile spreads over Isabella's face as if my frustration amuses her. I grit my teeth and bend until my face is right in front of hers. "Speak," I bite out.

She raises her hand and grips my chin, still wearing that smug smile. "You," she whispers and presses her lips to mine. "It has always been only you for me, Luca."

"Good." I bite her lower lip and slide my palm down her back to the waistband of her skirt. It's one of those with an elastic waist. How convenient. "Can you see Rosa?"

Isabella's breath hitches when I slide my hand under the waistband of her skirt and squeeze her butt cheek. "She's . . . at the cash register," she chokes out, looking behind my back to the opposite side of the store. "Waiting in line."

"How many people are ahead of her?"

"Five."

"Perfect." Beneath her skirt, I move my hand to her stomach and dip it lower, between her legs, pressing over her pussy.

"Luca," Isabella whispers. "There are people here."

"I know." I place my free hand on the wall next to her head, move her panties to the side and position my finger at her entrance. She's already wet. "Take a slow, deep breath."

She blinks at me, then inhales, and my finger enters her at the same moment.

"Good?" I ask.

Those big brown eyes watch me with intensity, then grow wider when I push in even deeper.

"I asked you something, Isabella." I bend my head to bite at her earlobe lightly.

"Yes," comes her barely audible answer.

I slowly remove my finger, then slide it back inside. An adorable little moan leaves her lips. Her breathing quickens as I fuck her with my finger. Based on how my hand is completely drenched with her juices, she's close.

"And now, how many people before Rosa?" I ask as I curl my finger.

Isabella takes a deep breath then tilts her head to take a quick glance behind me. "She's next."

"What a shame. Looks like we'll have to finish at home."

Isabella's hand grips my wrist. "Don't you dare," she says through her teeth.

"You want to come here?" I whisper next to her ear. "With all these people around?"

"Yes," comes her breathy answer.

I smile and thrust my finger inside her, pressing onto her clit with the heel of my palm. Isabella moans and comes all over my hand.

# Chapter

Isabella

The bedroom door opens, and Luca comes in, carrying a thick folder with a bunch of papers inside.

"You stayed late today," I say.

"Yeah. And I have homework as well." He drops the folder and his jacket on the recliner next to the bed and bends down to me. Holding my chin between his fingers, he places a quick kiss on my lips. "What are you reading?"

"Economics."

He raises his eyebrows. "I'm going to take a quick shower and come join you. We can read our shit on economics together."

When he disappears into the bathroom, I try to get back to my reading, but my mind keeps wandering back to that quick kiss. So casual. Natural. He called me his wife that morning at the furniture store. In front of Simona. I think it was the first time he's ever called me that. And it felt so good.

Will everything change when his memories return? Will he go back to his old, detached self? I've never thought about myself as a selfish person, but in this moment, I realize I am. Selfish, greedy, and mean. Because somewhere deep inside me, there's a poisonous seed of hope that he'll never get his memory back. And I am utterly disgusted by that realization.

Ten minutes later, Luca comes out of the bathroom, his hair is loose and he's wearing gray sweatpants, and a white T-shirt. Laid-back looks good on him. Well, everything looks good on Luca. The burns on his arm seem to be healing well. The skin is still red, but looks much better than it did when the bandages were removed.

Luca sits down next to me, leans back onto the headboard, and wraps his arm around me. "Come here."

He pulls me to him until I am sitting between his legs, with my back pressed to his chest. Then, he leans over and picks up the folder he left on the recliner and places it on the bed next to him. I open it and skim over a bunch of numbers on the first page. "Cash flows?"

"Yup," he says as he reaches for his jacket. He takes a pair of glasses from the pocket and puts them on.

I stare at him.

"What?" he asks and grabs the first piece of paper.

"You wear glasses?"

"For reading, apparently. I found them in a drawer at the office today, and the numbers started making much more sense when I could see them clearly." He tilts his head and narrows his eyes at me "You didn't know your husband needs glasses?"

"My husband never told me," I say, then lift my hand and thread my fingers through his hair. He looks hot in glasses. "I guess the cat is out of the bag now."

"Hmm. You and your husband had a really strange relationship, Isabella." He leans in and kisses me.

*Oh, Luca, you haven't the slightest idea of how much.* I brush the back of my hand over the side of his face, then take my book and lean back onto his chest. Not five seconds later, his right hand slips under my silk nightgown and into my panties. He places his finger at my entrance and slowly slides it in. I gasp and look over my shoulder to find him focused on the cash flow printout in his left hand, seemingly immersed in the numbers.

"Luca?"

"Yes?" he mumbles, not looking up.

"I can't concentrate with your finger inside me," I state what should be obvious.

"Well, too bad. Because it's staying there, Isabella."

"You expect me to be able to read like this?"

He finally looks up from his report, his face the embodiment of seriousness. "You'll get used to it. I enjoy having my fingers inside you, so every time you sit next to me, that's where they'll be. Do you have a problem with that?"

I blink at him. "No."

"Perfect." He nods and turns back to his papers.

"What if there's someone else around?" I ask.

"In that case, I may reconsider."

He may reconsider?

With the book on World economy in my hands, I try to ignore his warm palm over my pussy and his finger inside me. It doesn't work. I know how skilled his hands are, and it's driving me mad. Trying to keep the rest of my body still, I slowly squeeze my legs together. Luca's still engrossed in the report as I start rotating my hips just a little, enjoying the feel of my walls brushing his finger.

"Isabella."

I don't stop but turn my head and find him regarding me over the rim of his glasses.

"What?" I arch an eyebrow.

"Behave."

"And what if I don't wish to behave?"

Luca tsks, lets his papers fall to the floor, then takes the book from my hands and launches it across the room. "Take your clothes off."

"You first," I say. "But keep the glasses."

A deep rumble leaves his lips. When he grabs the hem of his T-shirt to remove it, I can't help but sigh at the sight of his biceps bulging in the process. I get a hold of his sweatpants, but a second later end up on my back, with Luca holding the hem of my nightgown.

"Not the silk one!" I shout, but it's too late. He's already tearing the material. That's the fourth one this week. "Damn it, Luca!"

While he's removing his pants and boxer briefs, I take off my panties so they don't meet the same fate as the nightgown. When I look up, I find Luca regarding me with hooded eyes.

"You're so fucking sexy," he whispers, grabs me around the waist and pulls me to him. "I want you to ride me, but don't you dare come until I say you can."

Wetness pools between my legs.

"Why?" I straddle him and press my palms on his chest, positioning myself above his fully erect cock.

His hands grab at my butt cheeks, squeezing. "Because I said so."

I bite at my lower lip and lower myself, taking his thick length inside of me inch by inch. "And what if I can't control myself?"

Luca tilts his head up and snags my chin, his eyes staring daggers at me. "You will."

I smirk. There's something unbelievably sexy about him ordering me around, especially when he wears those glasses. "If you say so, Mr. Rossi."

The moment the words are out of my mouth, I feel his cock twitch. I lower myself until I'm fully seated in and rock my hips, already close to coming. Luca lifts his hand to my lips and pushes his thumb into my mouth. I suck on it in the same rhythm as I move my body while the pressure in my core builds.

I glide my palms up his hard chest and rock my hips, enjoying the way my walls stretch to accommodate his size. As I reach his hair, I sink my hands into his dark strands, making sure I don't accidentally touch the wound on the back of his head. They removed his stitches last week, but I'm sure it still must be sensitive.

"Why are you so fixated on my hair?" he asks as he trails his hands down my back, the rough skin of his palms causing goose bumps with his every touch.

"I'm not," I breathe out, then lean down to nip at his chin.

"You keep taking the elastic out every time you have the chance, Isabella." His hands travel down to my ass. He lifts me and slams me back down onto his cock. "Why?"

"I like seeing your hair down, that's all," I say.

The truth is, it makes me feel special. Luca never wears his hair loose in public. Before his accident, I only saw him with his hair unbound a handful of times, and it always felt as if I got a glimpse of something forbidden. I'm so crazy in love with him that I get excited by something as inconsequential as the fact that he now almost always removes his hair tie when we're alone.

I straighten and grind against him, enjoying the sight of him under me.

"Don't you dare come." Luca says through gritted teeth and squeezes my ass.

I smirk.

Suddenly, Luca grabs me around my waist and lifts me up until he's holding me just an inch above his cock. I wrap my hands around his thick forearms and bury my nails in his skin, glaring at him. The devil just smiles.

"Frustrated looks good on you, Mrs. Rossi," he says and lowers me a bit until the tip of his cock enters me. I try moving down so I can take all of him back inside me but fail. Leaning forward, I fix him with my gaze and move my right hand to his hard length. Then, I squeeze it. A deep rumble leaves Luca's mouth and the next moment I find myself lying on my back, with his big body looming over mine. He gathers my wrists into his right hand and moves my arms above my head, keeping them locked there.

"Now, you can come," he says and slams into me with such force that I scream and come instantly. He keeps pounding as I ride my orgasm until his seed spills inside me.

# Chapter sixteen

Luca

"Camilla, Orlando's wife," Isabella whispers as we walk across the room at Massimo Lombardi's eighteenth birthday celebration.

"She's the one who's addicted to sleeping pills?"

"Nope. That's Lorenzo's wife, Ludovica," she says, then continues with the rest of Orlando's family. "Next to Camilla are his daughters Constansa, the taller one, and Amalia. Don't mention Damian in front of them."

From the way Isabella is holding herself—pressed to my side, her arm tightly wrapped around mine, whispering in my ear with a smile on her face—people will probably presume we're having a very private conversation. Her feet must be killing her in the heels she's wearing. She purchased them yesterday, specifically for this occasion. The damn things are more than five inches tall, but she said it was necessary because of our height difference. Even with the added inches, I still need to bend my head to hear what she murmurs.

After a short talk with Orlando, we take drinks from a passing waiter and move toward the corner of the room. Several people approach us along the way, and thanks to the hours I've spent with Isabella going over photos and videos, I recognize most of them. For a few, I have trouble connecting the faces to names, so I discreetly squeeze Isabella's waist and she jumps into the conversation, giving me hints. It's astounding how she manages to make it look so natural. Unforced.

Lorenzo stands on the other side of the room with a red-haired woman and a few men I don't recognize. They weren't in the pictures Isabella showed me. The woman seems familiar, but it takes me a few moments to recall her. Lorenzo's wife. She's changed her hair. She was blonde in the photos. Lorenzo looks up and our gazes connect. I'll have to speak with him later, or it may come across as suspicious. Lorenzo has been the biggest challenge so far since neither Isabella nor Damian could fill me in on all dealings I've had with him.

A man in his late fifties starts heading our way from across the room, a woman in her early thirties on his arm.

"Franco Conti. Second wife, Ava," Isabella says into her glass.

One of the capos who's in charge of laundering the money from gambling, I recall.

"Damian said you haven't met his wife yet. She wasn't at our wedding," Isabella adds before they reach us.

"Franco." I nod. "I see you finally decided to let us meet your wife."

After the introductions, Isabella starts chatting with Ava while Franco stands beside me, watching the crowd.

"I'm concerned about Angelo," he says. "I'm not sure he's fit for the role you gave him."

"Why?"

"Numbers are not his forte."

I look around at the grounds, pretending that I'm thinking about what he said while I'm trying to filter through the plethora of information in my brain. Who the fuck is Angelo? I squeeze Isabella's waist lightly.

"Angelo Scardoni is here?" she exclaims next to me. "I wanted to ask him about Bianca and how she's doing with being married into the Bratva."

Oh, yes. The youngest capo whose sister married the Bratva's enforcer a few months back. I forgot his name.

"He will have to learn," I say, having no idea what role I assigned him. It probably has something to do with the money laundering.

"Did you talk with Lorenzo?" Franco asks.

"About?"

"He was extremely . . . unhappy when you vetoed his drug business idea."

From what Damian told me, we have never dealt in drugs. Damian mentioned that Angelo Scardoni's father tried something behind the old don's back, and it didn't end well. I can't recall all the details. "Lorenzo's happiness is not my concern," I say.

"Are you sure that's wise?"

I turn to him, making certain my face shows what I think of his impromptu question.

"I apologize, Boss." Franco quickly looks down.

"If you overhear Lorenzo mentioning his idea again, to anyone, you will let me know."

"Of course." He nods and takes his wife's arm. "I'm glad to see that you're well. The Family was worried."

"They have no reason to be."

When Franco and his wife leave, I look down at Isabella and find her holding her phone, texting someone. I step behind her, wrap both of my arms around her waist, and rest my chin on her shoulder. "Who are you texting?"

She looks at me sideways, her eyebrows raised. "Why?"

"Is it a male someone?"

"Yes."

"You won't text any men unless they are related to you by blood." I lightly squeeze my arms around her and growl into her ear. "Or I'll kill them, Isabella."

"Jealous?" Her lips curl in a barely visible smile.

"You have no idea how much."

"I'm texting Damian. There are some people here we didn't expect, and I need him to let me know if there's any important information you should know."

"My little scheme master." I drop a kiss on her exposed skin.

Isabella goes still. "You shouldn't do that, Luca."

"Kiss you?" I let my mouth travel upward to her neck and kiss her again. "Why?"

"You're not exactly known for displaying affection around other people. Especially not at the Family gatherings."

"Too bad. I enjoy showing everyone you're mine."

"Everybody already knows that, Luca. Most of them were at our wedding."

"They might know,"—I turn her so she's facing me—"but I want them to see as well."

Holding her around the middle, I lift her off the ground and press my mouth to hers, as a surprised little yelp leaves her lips. She doesn't kiss me back right away. I've probably shocked her. The thing is, I find myself rather surprised by my act as well. I never intended to make a scene, which is exactly what I'm doing based on the dumbfounded looks on the faces around us, but I couldn't resist this unexplainable urge to claim her in front of everyone.

Maybe because I saw other men watching her, their eyes skimming every part of her that's on display in that skin-tight burgundy dress.

I bite her lower lip lightly, and Isabella finally starts kissing me back, slowly at first, but then, her hands wrap around my shoulders and the nape of my neck, and her kiss becomes greedy. That's much better. I feel something wet on my face and open my eyes to find Isabella's eyes still closed but tears rolling down her cheeks.

I gently lower her back down and take her chin between my finger and thumb. "Tesoro? What's wrong?"

She presses her lips together tightly and shakes her head, her eyes still closed. More tears fall from them.

"Too much pressure. Stress," she says. "Don't mind me."

She sounds sincere. I don't believe a word. "I'm taking you home."

"Yeah. Let's go through the garden." She opens her eyes but avoids looking at me. Instead, she nods toward the balcony door. "I don't want anyone witnessing my breakdown."

"Okay," I say and take her hand in mine, leading her outside.

Something's wrong. I might have lost my memories, but I haven't lost my mind. She will tell me what the fuck I did to make her cry in front of fifty people. Because, even though I can't say I've known her long, one thing I'm completely sure about is the fact Isabella would never let the members of the Family see her cry.

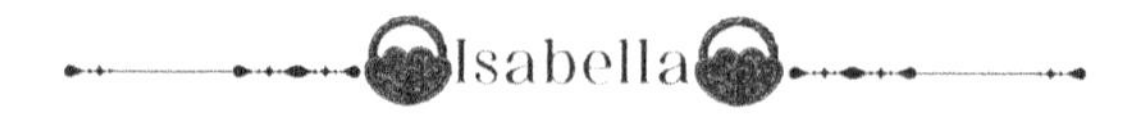


I sag into the passenger seat and exhale. Shit. Luca walks around the front, sits behind the wheel, and starts the car.

"Feeling better?"

"Yeah." I nod, open my clutch and retrieve a small mirror and tissues to clean the mascara marks from under my eyes. Waterproof, my ass.

"Care to tell me what just happened there, Isabella?"

"I already told you. Stress overload." I keep wiping my cheek with the tissue but the black stains just won't come off, damn it. "Just forget it."

The road ahead of us is free of other vehicles, but Luca slows down and then turns into a gas station parking lot. In the rearview mirror, I notice the car with our security detail make the same turn, and park a few spots away.

"Why did you stop?" I ask.

Luca doesn't say anything, just leaves the car and heads toward the building. One of the security guys exits the other car, but Luca motions with his hand for him to get back inside. A couple of minutes later, he returns and drops a package of wet wipes onto my lap.

I look at the package, then up at my husband, who sits with his elbows on the wheel, staring through the windshield. Slowly, I take a wipe and proceed with cleaning my face. "Are we waiting for someone?"

"Yes. For you to start talking, Isabella."

"Jesus Christ." I throw the used wipe into my purse and close the small bag. Why won't he just leave it alone?

As far as I'm concerned, we can stay here all night because there's no way I'm telling him I was so fucking affected and happy to have him kiss me in front of everyone. Like I matter. Like I have dreamed of him doing for so long. Like . . . he's in love with me. Just to realize that he probably did that only because he believes we're a couple happily in love. Before, he didn't even find it fitting to kiss me on our wedding day.

"I have nothing else to say. Can we please go home?"

"All right." He starts the car.

The thirty-minute drive passes in complete silence. When we arrive, Luca parks in the driveway, and comes around to open my door. He still doesn't say anything. Maybe it's better this way. Tonight has been exhausting, and I'm not in the mood to fight with him. And on top of it, my feet have been killing me for hours. So, prior to getting out of the car, I take off my heels and hold them in my hand as I head toward the house. I take maybe three steps before Luca scoops me into his arms and carries me toward the front door.

He doesn't put me down when we get inside, as I expected, but proceeds to climb the two flights of stairs. Inside our bedroom, he lowers me onto the bed, then turns around and disappears into the bathroom. A few seconds later I hear the shower turn on.

Instead of waiting for him to finish, I hurry into my old room and take a quick shower there. When I leave the bathroom, I look at my old bed, then at the door between the rooms. I don't want to sleep alone, but maybe it would be better to avoid more questions, so I shut the adjoining door. Turning down the covers, I get into my old bed and snuggle under the blanket.

I've just closed my eyes when a loud bang makes me spring up. I search for the source, and my eyes land on Luca standing in the doorway between the rooms. He's completely naked, his hair is loose, and by the look on his face, he's angry as hell. The door next to him is hanging askew by only one of its hinges.

"It wasn't locked, damn it!" I snap.

He stalks over to the bed, grabs me just under my ribcage, and hauls me up. Then, he throws me over his shoulder.

"Really mature," I mumble as he carries me to our bedroom. When we reach the bed, he deposits me onto it, then lies down over my body, holding himself on his elbows. Caging me in.

"You sleep in this bed," he says through gritted teeth. "Nowhere else. Is that clear?"

"Even when we have a fight?"

"Even when we have a fight, Isabella."

"Okay," I say, brushing my fingers through his hair. It's ridiculous how soft it is, I could spend the whole night just passing my hand through it.

"What did I do to make you cry?" he asks and bends his head. "It was the kiss, wasn't it?"

"Luca . . ."

"Did you feel uncomfortable because people saw us kissing?"

I gape at him. "Why would I?"

"Because I'm so much older than you, and you find it awkward to kiss me in public. Why didn't you tell me?"

"What?!" I stare at him with wide eyes, wondering how the hell he came to that conclusion. "Of course, not!"

"Don't lie to me, Isabella. I want the truth."

He wants the truth? Fine. I take his face into my hands and look directly into his eyes.

"I've been in love with you for years. Years, Luca," I say. "I lived for those short moments when you'd come for a meeting with my grandfather. I basically stalked you around the house, hiding behind furniture or bushes in the garden, just so I'd get to look at you."

I squeeze his face, then continue.

"Before we got married, every night for two years, I fell asleep only after pleasuring myself and imagining you were next to me. I've never been with any other man except you because, even when you were off limits, I didn't want to sleep with anyone else," I say and kiss him. "I've loved you for as long as I can remember, Luca. And being kissed by you in front of the whole Family was my dream come true. I cried because I was happy."

"So you don't think I'm too old for you?" he asks, staring down at me.

"Luca, baby, I don't give a damn how old you are. I've never wanted any other man in my whole life."

Luca's hand cups my jaw and he watches me through narrowed eyes for a few moments. Then, he slides his hand down and under my nightgown to cup my pussy. "No one's had this except me?"

"I already told you, you were my first." I tilt my head and kiss him again. "In fact, you're the only man who has ever touched it."

His body goes still above mine, and for a few seconds, it looks like he isn't even breathing as his eyes bore into mine. And then he snaps. Grabbing the hem of my nightgown, he pulls at the silky fabric until a tearing sound follows. My panties meet the same fate soon after. If this continues, I'll need to shop for new underwear every week. Or stop buying it all together.

He presses his right hand to my pussy and teases my clit while his left hand travels down my body, trailing from my neck, across my chest and stomach, until it's between my legs, too. His eyes never leave mine while he slides his finger inside me, still massaging my clit with his other hand.

"Only mine," he whispers and adds another finger, making me gasp.

A self-satisfied smirk pulls at his lips. He slides down and buries his face between my legs, replacing the finger on my clit with his tongue. My breathing hitches as the pressure in my core keeps building, but just as I'm on the brink, he removes his hand. I whimper at the loss of his fingers, then moan when he sucks on my clit and almost come undone. As I'm about to go over the edge, his mouth vanishes, too. I stare frustratedly at him as he looms over me, his eyes narrowed.

"If I find you in that other bed ever again, you won't like the consequences," he says. "Do you understand, tesoro?"

I tilt my chin up and smirk. "And what will you do?"

Luca leans forward, the corners of his lips curling upward in a wicked smile. He slides his finger inside me again, painfully slow. I grab at his hand, pulling on it with all my might, trying to get his finger to move faster without effect. He just smiles wider, then pulls his hand away.

"Luca!" I get a hold of his wrist and pull his hand back between my legs.

"Yes?" He presses the tips of his fingers to my pussy, pinches my clit, then removes his hand again. I feel like I'm going to break from frustration.

"Please," I whimper.

"If you ever dare to sneak out of my bed again," he says and bites my earlobe, "I'm going to torture you for hours. Understood?"

"Yes."

"Good girl," Luca whispers into my ear, then buries himself to the hilt inside me.

My breath hitches and I pant as he rocks his hips, filling me up more with each thrust. I grab at his upper arms, squeezing, enjoying the sensation of his muscles flexing under my palms. The pressure at my core builds and when he slams into me with a roar, I shatter.

I'm still shaking when Luca slides his cock out and grabs me around the waist, turning me around.

"Have I ever told you how obsessed I am with your ass?" He squeezes my butt cheeks and scrapes his teeth across the skin, then bites.

"Maybe once or twice," I breathe out, then moan when he licks the spot where his teeth had been.

"Every time you enter a room and my eyes fall on your sweet ass, I have the urge to tear your clothes off you and do this," he says and his cock enters me again.

Grabbing onto the sheet, I widen my legs a little more, then gasp when he starts pounding into me. His hand slides down my side and across my lower belly. He rocks his hips while his finger finds and teases my clit. I can't get enough air in my lungs as he continues to hammer me from behind. My walls start spasming around his length while my arms and legs shake uncontrollably. When he buries himself fully, his seed filling me, I moan and come again.

"You're shaking like a leaf," Luca says as he lies down next to me and pulls me to his body. "Are you cold, tesoro?"

"I don't know," I mumble and nuzzle my face into his chest. My whole body is trembling, but I think it's the aftereffects of having two of the most amazing orgasms, one right after another.

"Here." He covers us with a blanket. "Better?"

I tilt my head up and nip his chin lightly. "Yes. But you forgot something."

"Oh? Did I?" He slides his hand down until he reaches my pussy and brushes the tip of his fingers over my folds. "What might that be?"

I bite his chin again, then turn around so that my back is pressed to his chest. "Don't keep me waiting," I say.

His palm cups my pussy, and I take a deep breath in anticipation. Nothing happens.

"Luca!"

"Yes?" I feel his breath at my nape. "Do you need something, tesoro?"

"You know I do."

"Tell me."

Oh, how he enjoys torturing me. I place my hand over his between my legs and press on it. "I can't fall asleep without your finger inside me, okay?"

It's slightly embarrassing to confess, but it's the truth. Last night he was going over some Family matters with Damian, and they stayed in his office until well after midnight. I spent the whole day with the catering company and was dog-tired, but when I went to bed, I couldn't sleep. I tossed and turned until Luca joined me somewhere around two a.m., and only when his finger slid inside of me did I manage to fall asleep.

"I know," he whispers into my hair and pushes his finger into me. I suck in a breath. My pussy is still sensitive, but when his finger is seated fully in, the feeling of comfort washes over me. I sigh, close my eyes, and fall asleep.

# Chapter *seventeen*

Isabella

There's a squeak of the closet door, followed by some rustling. I open my eyes just a crack, squinting at the sunlight coming through the window. Luca is standing by the bed, putting on his pants.

"What time is it?" I ask.

"Half past seven. I'm taking Rosa to buy some things for school. I don't want to wait until later. It will be madness the closer it gets to the end of summer. After that I'm driving her to Clara's. They'll be camping in the backyard."

"Have her take a jacket. It may rain today." I turn over so I'm on my stomach, fold the pillow, and prop my chin on it so I can still watch Luca. "I'm seeing my sister later. Are you coming back for lunch?"

"Probably not. I have a meeting with Franco Conti at noon, and after that, another sit down with the real estate agent."

"I'll have lunch with Andrea, then."

"You'll wear the blue dress today. The one that ties around the neck," he says and pins me with his gaze. There's a challenge in his dark eyes.

I tilt my head to the side, watching him. What an odd way to say it. Not "Will you wear the blue dress for me?" or something similar, and he knows I've noticed.

"Okay," I say and watch as his eyes flare. "Can I wear the nude heels with it?"

A look of satisfaction crosses his face, but it lasts just for a second before he hides it. Interesting.

"Yes." He nods and starts buttoning his shirt.

I regard him, and a realization slowly forms in my head. My, oh my . . . if I'm right, and I'm pretty certain I am, my husband has been hiding some rather interesting things about his preferences. I decide to test my theory.

"I'd like to put my hair in a bun today," I say, choosing my words very carefully, and regard him closely for his reaction. "Will you allow it?"

His fingers on the button still. Slowly, he turns toward me, and our eyes lock.

"No. You will leave it down," he says, his eyes daring me.

"Okay. Will you allow it tomorrow? Please?"

"I'll think about it." He takes his jacket off the chair, grabs his keys and wallet, and heads toward the door, but then he stops at the threshold. I see his hand form a fist like he's warring with himself about something, then turns to face me. For a few seconds, he just watches me, the knuckles on his fisted hand going white. "Starting today," he says, "I will be approving all your outfits. When I'm not here and you need to go somewhere, if you plan to change, you'll call me to approve it first," he says at last and keeps his gaze on mine, waiting for my reaction.

"Of course, Luca." I nod.

He unfolds his fist, a tiny, satisfied smile forming on his face. I wouldn't have noticed it if he wasn't facing me, but his pants tightened across his crotch upon hearing my answer. This is turning him on. As soon as he leaves, I grin and roll onto my back. I knew Luca was holding back with me, but up until this moment, I didn't grasp how much. But I do now, and I'm ready to play.

"I hear you and Luca made quite an impression at Lombardi's," Andrea says over the rim of her cup.

"How would you know when you weren't there?"

"Milene called and gave me a full report. With all the sizzling details."

"It was just a kiss." I shrug. "Nothing particularly saucy about it."

"Luca Rossi caught kissing in public? The man no one has ever seen so much as touch his previous wife? I'm amazed it wasn't covered in the morning news."

"People tend to exaggerate things," I say. "Why weren't you there? You said you were coming with Mom and Dad."

"I was grounded." She scrunches her nose. "Dad caught me sneaking out the night before."

"What?" I slam my cup down. "Alone?"

"I wouldn't have been alone. I was going out with Catalina."

"Where?"

"To a club."

"Please tell me you were going to take Gino."

"Of course not. God, I hate that guy. He acts like he's my father. And Dad lets him! Why couldn't I keep Leandro as my bodyguard?"

"Because he's too old to run after you when you slip," I snap. "You're too reckless. Sneaking out in the middle of the night. Running away from bodyguards. You need someone to rein you in, and I'm glad Gino is managing."

"He's prohibited me from going to Perla's birthday party next week!" she barks. "How can he prohibit me from anything? He is a fucking bodyguard! When I told Dad, he said he agrees with everything Gino decides."

"Where's the party?"

"At Baykal."

"You were planning on going to one of Bratva's clubs? After what happened at Ural the last time? Are you out of your mind?"

"That mess was your fault." She grins.

"You can't go to the Bratva's club! For God's sake, Andrea!"

"Kostya would have been there." She shrugs. "Catalina has been seeing him. Kind of."

"Dear God! Does her father know she's going out with one of the Bratva's men?"

"No. And you won't tell him! It's nothing serious, they're just . . . talking."

"From what I've heard, half of the city's female population have been through Kostya Balakirev's bed. He's not the type of man to just talk with a woman."

"That's not true."

"He slept with Amalia Lombardi last month. And their cook. I'm not absolutely sure, but I think he slept with Amalia's mother, as well. He's worse than Damian."

"It scares me sometimes, you know? How much shit you remember about people."

"You can never anticipate when knowing someone's dirty laundry may come in handy." I look down at my phone. "I have to call Luca. I'm going shopping with Milene this afternoon and have to change. He wants to approve what I'm wearing."

"He what?" Andrea widens her eyes at me.

"I've been unearthing some very interesting things about my husband recently." I smile. "One of them is that choosing what I wear really turns him on."

"He's controlling you?"

"No. I'm letting him control me. And enjoying every second of it."

"Isa, that's . . . kinky."

"Yeah, I guess it is." I grin and call Luca.

He answers on the first ring. "Where are you?"

"Having coffee with Andrea at my parents' house."

"Did you take bodyguards?"

"Marco and Sandro are waiting for me in the car. Don't worry."

A few moments of silence, and then, "Are you wearing the blue dress as I instructed?"

"Yes," I say. "I'm going home to change. I have some errands to do. I'll send you a picture of what I put on before I leave."

"Good. Call me the moment you get home."

"I will."

Luca

The man across the desk keeps talking, showing me and Damian images of houses and condos on his tablet, and listing the benefits and downsides of each. With a load of money from arms deals waiting to be laundered, we need to increase the number and size of the properties that pass through our company. Fast.

"We need bigger properties, Adam. And more." I throw the paper with the prices onto the desk.

My phone rings, showing Lorenzo's name. I look up at Adam and nod my head toward the door. "Leave. I'll call you later."

When the door closes after him, I take the call and put it on speakerphone so Damian can hear as well. "Lorenzo."

"One of Octavio's bookkeepers has been taking money on the side," he says. "That needs to be taken care of, Boss."

"All right."

"Do you want me to handle that?" asks Lorenzo.

I look at Damian who shakes his head, then I reply, "No. I'll take care of it."

"We're keeping him in the back room in Octavio's casino."

"I'll be there in forty minutes." I cut the call and look up at Damian. "How do we take care of thieves?"

"Kill them," he says. "You can assign someone else to pull the trigger, but Giuseppe handled thieves personally. It was a statement."

I lean back in the chair and think it over. Even though I don't remember killing anyone, the idea of taking someone's life doesn't seem to trouble me. "I'll do it. Do you want to come?"

Damian cringes. "I'd rather not. But I'll draw you a floor plan. You'll have to go inside Magna through the back entrance since they have metal detectors at the front door."

"I know."

His head snaps up. "You remembered something?"

"No. I don't have any recollection of going there or meeting people, but I do know how the inside looks."

"That's bizarre," he says and starts chewing on the pen he's holding. "What are we going to do if your memory doesn't come back?"

"We'll just keep going as we've been doing so far. I don't think anyone suspects anything."

"You don't find that possibility disconcerting?"

"It frustrates me, yes, and I hate that I don't remember my daughter or my wife. But the doctor said I can't do anything about it. And I can't waste my energy dwelling on things I can't change." I stand up and head toward the door. "Instruct Adam to search for more real estate. I'm going home after I dispose of that bookkeeper."

Getting to Magna doesn't pose a problem. I spent two days driving across Chicago with Damian, who pointed out all our businesses, as well as other locations where I may need to go at some point. I remembered everything about the city but couldn't connect the names of the casinos with any particular location until I saw it.

My phone pings as I'm parking the car in the back alley. It's a selfie from

Isabella, showing her standing in front of the big mirror in our bedroom. She's wearing a flowing brown dress with white flowers, and there is a mischievous smile on her face. Smirking, I type a quick reply. *Approved, tesoro.*

I send the message, put my gun in the holster under my jacket, and leave the car. Emilio parks his car behind mine, but I raise my hand, signaling him to wait for me here, and head to the metal door on the right. A man in a dark suit is standing by the entrance with his hands clasped behind his back.

"Boss." He nods and opens the door for me.

I walk down the long corridor and turn left, heading into the back room. It's strange how everything around me seems familiar but I have no recollection of ever being here. It was the same with my house the first day I came home from the hospital. I remembered the layout but not who had which room. It was as if someone had erased random parts of my memory and left only crumbs for me to follow.

Two men are flanking the double doors at the end of the corridor. They open it when I approach, letting me inside a medium-sized room which smells of stale booze and sweat. Lorenzo is sitting behind the desk at the far corner, but he quickly stands up when I enter. A man I don't recognize is leaning on the furthest wall, probably one of the Family's foot soldiers. I'll have to tell Isabella and Damian to dig up some photos of the soldiers for me. Until now, I haven't had time to go over the lower-ranking men in the Family hierarchy.

In the center of the room, a man in his late fifties is sitting on a wooden chair. His shirt is wrinkled and there are specs of blood on it. Based on the bruises on his face and his swollen lip, he's been roughed up a bit while waiting for me. The thief, I presume. The moment he sees me, he starts fidgeting in his chair as much as the ties around his hands and legs allow.

"Boss." The man I don't recognize nods, moves away from the wall, and stands next to the bookkeeper.

"What proof do you have that he's guilty?" I ask, turning to Lorenzo.

"We found double books on his desk. According to them, he stole close to twenty grand last month."

"You're sure they weren't planted?"

"They were in his handwriting," Lorenzo says and crosses his arms. A small smile forms on his lips. "If you want, I can take care of the thief, Boss."

Yeah, I'm sure he'd love that. I don't need Isabella and Damian to tell me that Lorenzo isn't happy with me becoming the head of the Family. I can see that quite well myself. He thinks he's hiding it well, but I've been paying close attention to everyone around me, looking for subtle tells or double meanings. A man in my position can't afford to miss anything because only one slip will be enough to initiate my downfall.

"Yes," I say and take two steps until I'm standing behind the tied-up man. "You do that."

The smile on Lorenzo's face widens as he reaches inside his jacket for his gun. He likes the idea of me being reluctant to kill a man and letting him do the job instead. Especially in front of a foot soldier. I turn, wrap my right arm around the bookkeeper's chin and place my left hand at the back of his head. One strong twist. The man's neck snaps.

I unwrap my arms from the bookkeeper's neck, then turn to face Lorenzo, who's staring at me, obviously surprised. It would have been easier to just shoot the guy, but Damian said this was supposed to be a statement.

"Make sure the body won't be found," I say and leave the room, feeling two sets of eyes boring into my back.

When I get inside my car, I dial Isabella, turn on the speakerphone, and start the engine.

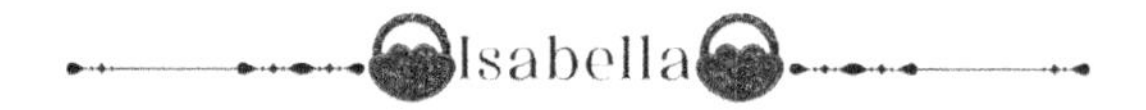


I've just finished removing my makeup when my phone rings. Luca's name flashes across the screen, and I hit the button to accept the call, putting it on loudspeaker.

"Where are you?" comes a clipped question from the other side.

"You're in a nice mood," I say as I toss the soiled wipes into the garbage. "Did something happen?"

"Seems like Lorenzo is playing games."

"It was expected. What did he do?"

"I don't want to talk about my underboss now. Where are you?"

"In our bedroom."

"Take off your clothes."

I put the cosmetics and face oil down on the dresser, remove my dress, then my underwear. "Done."

"The bed. Lie down on your back."

I smile, walk to the bed with the phone in my hand and lie down as instructed. "Okay. Now what?"

"Put your hand between your legs. You're going to stay that way and tease yourself until I arrive."

"And when will that be?"

"In twenty minutes. And Isabella . . ."

"Yes?"

"Don't you dare come before I get there."

What? "I'm not sure I can manage that, Luca."

"Well, if I find out you came earlier than I allowed, we will start again, and this time, it will be an hour instead. Do you understand?"

"Yes."

"Good. Turn on the speakerphone and leave the phone next to you."

"It's on. You'll be listening?"

"Of course. You can start."

I let my hands slide down my body to my pussy and start teasing my clit in slow circles.

"Do you know how many times I pleasured myself imagining it was you next to me?" I ask.

"Tell me." Comes a gruff answer.

I press onto my clit, then add another finger. "Are you sure?"

"Isabella."

Oh, I love when he says my name with that commanding tone. It's a request, as well as an order at the same time. Luca gives off much more emotion with his tone than with actual words.

"The first time I did it, I was seventeen." I moan and keep teasing my pussy. "I've done it every single night and sometimes during the day. So, I would say at least a thousand times."

"And what was I doing to you in those fantasies of yours?"

"You would come into my room." I smile and slide one finger inside me, enjoying the tingling and building tension at my core. "You would wear a suit. That all-black combination that makes you look both edible and dangerous at the same time. You would approach me slowly, tear off my dress, and throw me onto the bed." I place my other hand on my clit, massaging it as I push my finger even deeper, imagining it's his cock. "Then, you would bury your face between my legs and eat me out until I screamed."

"Without taking off my suit?" he asks.

"Yes." I bite my lip and pull out my finger, afraid I'll come.

"And what would I do, then?" There's a strain in his voice. I can hear it loud and clear.

"Are you hard, Luca?" I ask and press my palm over my pussy, hoping it will help subdue the need to thrust my finger back inside myself.

"Answer me, Isabella!" he barks. "What would I do next?"

"You'd place your body over me, your weight pressing me into the mattress. Then, you'd kiss me, and I would taste myself on your lips."

"Would I still be clothed?"

"Yes. I'd remove your jacket and shirt first. Your breathing would quicken as I dig my nails into your shoulders and kiss you in the center of your chest. Then, I'd help you remove your pants."

I can't take it anymore, so I slide two fingers inside myself and gasp.

"What did you just do?" he asks.

"Nothing." I breathe out and slide my fingers even deeper, moaning.

"Did you come, Isabella?" he snaps.

"Not yet," I whisper. "Are you close by?"

"I'm passing through the gate," he says. "What happens next?"

I smile and keep playing with my pussy, enjoying the sounds of his labored breathing coming from the other end of the line.

"You'd gather my wrists in your hand and pull my arms above my head. Just like you usually do." I moan as the pressure between my legs builds. "And you would bury yourself inside me in one thrust. Hard. To the hilt."

The door on the other side of the room bangs open. Without removing my hand from my pussy, I lift my head from the pillow and look between my bent legs at the threshold. Luca is standing in the doorway, gripping the frame on either side of him, his jaw set in hard lines as he stares at me.

I take my lower lip between my teeth and start circling my clit with my free hand. My fingers are still inside me, so I slide them out and move them to my mouth, licking each one of them slowly.

"Tell me, Luca,"—I smile—"how hard does this make you?"

A deep growl comes from him. He takes a step inside, kicking the door closed behind him, and walks slowly toward the bed, removing his clothes along the way. The jacket. Then, his charcoal shirt. The pants. He's looking at me the whole time. When he reaches the bed, he is completely naked, his cock fully erect. I wet my lips and widen my legs a bit more.

"You're the sexiest fucking thing that has ever walked this earth." His voice is a low, primal rumble as he grabs behind my knees and pulls me toward him. Wrapping his arm around me, he turns me around so I'm on all fours on the bed. In the next instant, I feel him entering me from behind.

"So wet." He brushes his palm down my back. "Did you orgasm before I got here, Isabella?"

"No." I gasp as he buries himself all the way.

"Good. You're not allowed to come unless I'm here with you." He slides out, then slams back inside again.

"Am I allowed to play at least?"

"Only when I say so." Another slam, his cock filling me completely. The pressure that has been building in my core intensifies. "You do not touch your pussy unless I give you permission. Do you understand?"

I press my lips together and lower my head, my breathing coming hard through my nose.

"Do. You. Understand?" He keeps pounding into me, punctuating each word with a hard thrust making me gasp for air.

"Yes!" I scream.

Luca's rapid pounding thrusting doesn't stop. He looks at me and commands, "Come."

I scream again as the orgasm suddenly hits me. Luca groans and explodes into me.

# Chapter eighteen

Luca

My phone on the nightstand buzzes. I put my glasses on and take a look at the message from Donato, saying the gun delivery has been fucked up again. I'll need to ask Damian if he knows what happened the first time, but that can wait until I get to the office. A piercing pain jolts through my skull between my temples, and I suck in a breath. It's gone just as quickly. Maybe I should go see Dr. Jacobs for a checkup. This isn't the first time it's happened.

Isabella wriggles in my arms, then places her palm over my hand between her legs and presses on it. She certainly has become addicted to having my finger in her pussy. Yesterday we took Rosa and some of her friends to a movie. The kids sat in the first row, but Isabella and I stayed in the back. Once we were alone, she took my hand, slid it under her skirt, and whispered that her pussy needed it. The small sigh of relief that left her lips as I thrust my finger inside her made me so hard I barely managed to stop myself from dragging her off like a caveman. She fucking whimpered when I had to remove my finger at the end of the movie.

I brush the palm of my free hand down Isabella's back, squeeze her ass lightly, then run my fingers over the skin on her side. "I can count your ribs, Isabella. Have you lost weight?"

"I'm trying to slim my butt a bit. I'm on a diet," she mumbles.

"What?" I put a knuckle under her chin and raise her head to make her look at me. "Did you ask for permission to starve yourself?"

"No." She blinks at me, looking slightly confused. "I thought men liked skinny women."

"You thought wrong."

"My butt is huge, Luca. I want to be a size down before the party."

Squeezing her chin, I lean forward until I'm in her face. I don't want her ass to get smaller. I want it larger. "How much weight have you lost?"

"Ten pounds."

"You have two weeks to put that weight back on, Isabella," I say, scowling at her.

"It will all go to my ass. It will get even bigger."

An image of Isabella, with her beautiful behind a size or two larger, fills my mind and my cock swells. "Good."

"Fine." She rolls her eyes. "I guess those new pants I bought yesterday will go to waste. I barely managed to get into them as it is."

"Fuck the pants." I move my hand to her backside and squeeze her ass cheek again. Her butt does seem smaller. "I want this as it was."

"Is that an order?" She smirks.

"Yes."

The smile on her face widens. "I like when you order me around."

I curl my finger to expand the pressure against her walls and press my thumb to her clit, loving the way she squeezes her thighs together to hold my hand in place.

"It turns me on so fucking much when you wear these glasses, Luca."

I growl and keeping her flush to my body, I turn us over on the bed until she is lying under me, and lean closer to whisper in her ear. "And what else turns you on, tesoro?"

"The frustration I feel for those few seconds when your finger slides out of me during the night, just before your cock replaces it." She breathes out and mewls when I do just that, but I keep my fingers on her clit, teasing her.

"This is tyranny," she says, sliding her hands through my hair.

"I know." I bend my head to bite her neck, pinching her clit at the same time.

"Damn it, Luca!" She fists my hair.

It amuses me to no end that she gets frustrated when I don't bury my cock inside her right away. I position myself at her entrance and start sliding my cock into her greedy little pussy. God, the sounds she makes. Sometimes I think I could come simply from hearing her moans.

"Is it better now?" I retreat, then push into her.

"Yes . . . Yes . . . Yes . . ." She pants to the rhythm of my pounding into her while her body shakes under me, climbing the high. I pinch her clit again, then massage it. She squeals a little when I pinch her clit again and squeezes her legs around me.

"I love the sounds you make, tesoro." I bury myself within her with a groan. "So damn much."

She whimpers and grabs my shoulders as she comes. I thrust inside her again and explode, marveling at the feel of my cum filling her up. The best feeling ever.

"Come here." I wrap my arm around her waist and press her back to my chest. She's still trembling when I cover her pussy with my palm and slide my finger back inside her.

"I wish I could have your finger, or your cock, inside me all day," Isabella sighs.

"You don't like the feel of your pussy being empty?"

"Nope." She cocks her head and looks at me. "You've made an addict out of me."

"Perfect."

"I might need to start stopping by your office during the day. To get my fix."

"I like that plan." I smile, then nuzzle her neck. "And I'll arrange something else for you in the meantime."

"What do you have in mind?"

"You'll have to wait and see, tesoro."

"Can I dye my hair red?" Rosa asks from the opposite side of the dining table.

"No." Both me and Damian reply in unison.

Rosa leans back in her chair and crosses her arms over her chest, her chin tucked in.

"When you grow up, you can dye your hair, sweetie," I say, "You're too young for that now."

"But I want to," she mumbles.

"Why? Have some of your friends dyed their hair?"

"Nope. I still want to do it."

I sigh and shake my head. It's exactly as if I'm listening to my sister. "How about a new haircut? I can take you next week. We could do our nails too."

Rosa's gaze snaps to me, her eyes wide. "Really?"

"Sure." I nod. "I'll call my stylist and tell her to book another spot. Do you have a specific hairstyle in mind?"

Rosa fidgets in her chair, then shrugs. "I want it short," she says, then looks up at me. "Do you think Dad would let me?"

"If you explain that you'd really like to have it short, of course he would."

There's a sound of footsteps approaching, and Luca rounds the corner, coming into the dining room.

"Dad!" Rosa jumps in her chair, "Can I cut my hair short? Isa said she'll take me with her. Can I? Please?"

Luca stops behind Rosa and places a kiss at the top of her head. "Sure, piccola. Now, go to the kitchen and help Viola with food. I need to speak with Isabella and Damian."

"I want to hear, too!"

"It's business stuff, Rosa. Go. Please."

Rosa scrunches her nose, gets up from her chair, and leaves reluctantly.

As soon as she's gone, Luca turns to Damian. "Salvatore Ajello requested a meeting," he says. "Who the fuck is Salvatore Ajello?"

I stare at Luca while panic starts gathering in the bottom of my stomach. "When's the meeting?"

"Tomorrow," he says. "Who is he?"

"The don of the New York Family," Damian says. "Do you have anything on him, Isa?"

"A ton of gossip. Nothing useful. And I don't know anyone who does." I don't think many people even know what the don of the New York crime family even looks like. If you need to contact the New York Cosa Nostra, you call Arturo DeVille, the underboss. Never the don. I turn my eyes back to Luca. "Did he call you personally?"

"Yes. He just said he wants to discuss business, no other details."

"I know they mostly deal with drugs. I heard my grandfather mention it once, but that's it. My father might know more." I look at Damian. "Did Luca meet with Ajello before?"

"Not as far as I know. And he would have mentioned something like that."

"Then it's safe to ask Francesco," Luca says. "I'll call him to let him know we're coming over for a coffee." He bends and bites my ear lightly, then whispers,

"Go, change. That pink dress I like. I'm taking you with me, and we can go somewhere for lunch on our way back."

I stand up from the table and head toward the door, but then stop and look at Luca over my shoulder. "I think I'm going to wear the navy one."

"Isabella."

I smile inwardly at his tone. It riles him up no end when I decline to follow his orders. "Yes?"

"The pink dress."

"If you insist." I smile and resume walking.

I'm halfway to the dining room door when I hear Damian whisper, "You need to loosen up your reins, Luca, or she'll flip out."

I smile. If only Damian knew how much his brother's commands turn me on . . .

When I get inside the car with Luca twenty minutes later, wearing the pink dress, of course, he's unusually quiet, seemingly focused on his thoughts. I let it slide, but when he doesn't say a word until almost halfway to the Agostini mansion, I decide he's brooded enough.

"What is it?" I ask.

"Nothing."

"Luca," I sigh, "just spill it."

He grinds his teeth and squeezes the steering wheel. "Am I too extreme? Do you need me to 'loosen the reins,' as Damian put it?"

"Is this about the clothes thing?"

"Everything," he says and looks at me. "Do you need me to loosen the reins, Isabella?"

"No. But maybe you could reciprocate in some way." I smirk and lean to whisper in his ear. "I've been thinking, if you get to keep your finger in my pussy while I sleep, I get to do this while you drive."

Smiling, I reach my left hand over and place it on his crotch, putting a little pressure in just the right spot. The car swivels slightly while his cock hardens under my palm. Luca turns his head to look at me and his nostrils flare. I press a little harder and he inhales sharply.

"From now on," he says, "when you're driving with me, that's where your hand will be. The whole time. Am I clear Isabella?"

"Of course, Luca."

He looks at me sideways and I see a corner of his lips curve slightly. "When we get back home, I'm going to fuck you so hard, you won't be able to walk."

"I'm looking forward to it." I squeeze his cock.

Luca

"Salvatore Ajello?" Francesco's hand stills halfway to the coffee cup, his eyes wide. "Crime families rarely go into business ventures together. Too much possibility for a conflict of interest. And I've never heard of the New York Family reaching out to someone for collaboration. From what I've heard, he rarely leaves New York. And members of other families are strongly"—he clears his throat—"discouraged from visiting his region unless specifically invited."

"What if someone ventures there without invitation?" Isabella throws in.

During the drive, we agreed she'll ask the questions, so as not to raise any suspicions in the event I slip up and mention Ajello in front of Francesco at some point.

"He ends up being sent back home. In a body bag. Sometimes in more than one bag," Francesco says, then turns to me. "Be careful, Luca. That man is not to be taken lightly."

"Have you met him?" Isabella asks.

"No. But your grandfather did. He didn't like him. He said, and I quote, 'There are ruthless people, and then there is Salvatore Ajello.' He didn't elaborate other than mentioning that he'd never met a man who seemed so dead inside."

"Sounds promising." I smile. "How old is he?"

"I have no idea. He was a capo until he took over the Family two years ago, so I assume he's in his forties or fifties. There are no photos of him that I know of. I've never heard of him visiting any public event. The way he took over the don's position created quite an uproar. He stormed into the Family meeting and killed the old don and the other six capos."

"A maniac." I snort. Perfect.

Francesco leans over the table. "If you do agree to collaborate on something with him, it could potentially make us millions. Nobody can confirm it, but rumor has it he owns half of New York."

"We'll see." I shrug and take a sip of my coffee.

# Chapter nineteen

Luca walks through the front door as I am descending the stairs and the moment his eyes land on me, his eyebrows furrow. He passes his gaze down my white shirt and tight beige miniskirt, then moves his eyes back to lock them with mine. I smirk and lean my hip on the banister, enjoying the look of displeasure that passes his face. Without breaking eye contact, he slowly climbs the stairs and stops on the step below me.

"I thought I picked the navy dress for you today, Isabella," he says and wraps his arm around my waist, pulling me into his body. "Did I not?"

"You did." I tilt my head up and smile, "But I wanted to see what would happen if I didn't do what you said. Maybe I was looking forward to being . . . punished for my misbehavior."

The corner of Luca's lips curves up and his hand moves lower to squeeze my butt cheek.

"To the bedroom," he whispers next to my ear, then squeezes my butt cheek again. "Run."

I squeal and dash up the stairs. When I'm in the middle of the second staircase I look down and see Luca climbing them in a relaxed manner.

"It seems like you're too old to chase after me." I smile.

Luca's eyes flare. The next moment he's running up the stairs, taking two at a time. I laugh and sprint the last few steps to the landing, then turn left. I've just reached the bedroom when I feel two strong arms wrap around my waist from behind.

"I guess I'm not that old," Luca says next to my ear.

The sound of a door banging closed behind us reaches me as Luca grabs the waistband of my skirt.

"No!" I yelp, but he already has my skirt torn along the stitches at the side. Jesus!

"Now," he whispers and places a kiss at the side of my neck, "About that dress . . ."

His hand grabs my right ass cheek, and then he slaps it. The burning sensation spreads over my skin and I bite at my lower lip, as wetness pools between my legs.

"What about the dress?" I choke out, then suck in a breath as his left hand slides down my stomach and inside my panties.

"When I tell you to wear something,"—he places his finger at my core and slides it inside—"you obey, Isabella."

"And if I don't?"

"If you don't, a punishment is in order." Two more slaps. Then a kiss, on my jaw this time. "But, based on how drenched your pussy is, it seems you quite enjoy my educational methods."

"I think I do." I smile, then moan when he adds another finger.

A deep rumbling comes from behind me, followed by the sound of my panties being torn. I hear him fumbling with his belt, and then his fingers leave my pussy. Suddenly, Luca turns me around and grabs me under my thighs, lifting me up. I wrap my arms around his neck, then suck in a breath as my back gets plastered against the door.

"I can't express how much I enjoy having my cock buried in your pretty pussy, Isabella," he says and thrusts his rock-hard length inside me.

"The feeling is mutual." I moan then bury my hands in his hair, squeezing as he pounds into me.

I walk to the closet and glance at Luca over my shoulder. "So, about this dinner. Is it some special occasion?"

"Do I need a special occasion to take you to dinner?"

"I guess not. How about the white dress? The one with the gray belt?"

"You're wearing jeans tonight," Luca says.

"Oh?" That's strange. He always picks dresses.

"The tight black ones. And that silk pink blouse. No heels."

"No heels?" I turn to face him. "What kind of dinner it is with jeans and no heels?"

"It's better if you don't wear heels the first time." There's a smug smile on his lips.

"First time for what?" I take the pants out of the closet and pull them on, before reaching for the pink blouse.

"You'll see."

I shake my head, wondering what he has in mind now. I'm just tying the blouse when I feel Luca come to stand behind me. He places his hands on my waist and starts unbuttoning my pants.

"I thought we were going to dinner."

"We are." His hand slides into my panties, his fingers stroking my clit for a few seconds before one of them slips inside of me. "You know, I've found a solution to your problem."

"Which problem?" I breathe out, then shudder when he presses on my clit with his thumb.

"Your need to have either my cock or my finger inside of you. I can't be here all the time, so I've found an alternative to make sure your pussy doesn't feel alone."

"What . . . alternative?"

He takes a black leather box from the top shelf and puts it in my hands. "Open it."

I lift the lid and look at the object resting on a velvet cushion inside. It's an elongated C-shape, with one end thicker and the other smaller, made of silicone. "What's this?"

"It's a pussy plug." He takes the object from the box. "Pull your panties and jeans down."

I place the box on a shelf and slowly follow his instructions. I'm a little skeptical because sex toys are not something I've ever been attracted to. His thumb brushes my clit a few more times, getting me wet.

"Perfect," Luca whispers in my ear, then pulls his finger out.

I moan at the loss.

"Miss my finger?"

"Yes."

"It'll get better in a second, tesoro."

He places the pussy plug between my legs, the narrower side at the front, and the thicker side right at my entrance. He teases my opening with the tip of the bulkier end, then slides it inside me. I gasp and grab the shelf to steady myself. The object isn't as large as his cock, but it's much larger than his finger. I take deep breaths as Luca continues until the whole thing is inside me and the narrow tip is pressed to my clit. It's an odd feeling having a foreign object lodged in me this way, but not uncomfortable.

"Pull your pants up," he says. "We'll be late for dinner."

"Do you want me to remove it? Or will you do it?"

"The toy stays, tesoro."

"What? Inside?" I look at him over my shoulder in shock, but he just smiles.

When we're both dressed and ready to go, he saunters over and presses his palm over my pussy. "Looks like a perfect fit. No one will even notice it since it was specifically designed to be wearable."

The situation still has me reeling when he adds, "Let's go."

I take a first, tentative step. The silicone is soft, and the pussy plug doesn't impede my progress, but my walls do brush the sides of it with every shift. It's almost like having Luca's finger in me. The narrow end nested between my folds is touching my clit, rubbing it discreetly with each movement. Another step, then one more. The odd feeling dissipates as I walk, and by the time we reach the stairway, the strangeness is gone completely, replaced with an unexpected sense of . . . comfort.

"So?" Luca asks next to my ear. "Do you like it?"

"Yes."

"I knew you would."

Walking down the two sets of stairs makes me feel it even more, enough that I have to suppress the need to sigh. When we reach the car and I carefully sit down, the sensation changes again. The thick end pushes a little deeper inside me, and the other side presses onto my clit. I expected there to be at least some irritation with me sitting down, but the shape of it seems to work perfectly with my body.

"How long?" I ask when Luca gets behind the wheel.

"What, tesoro?"

"How long do I get to . . . wear it."

He smiles. "Addicted already? I knew you would be. You're too used to having my finger inside you." He slides his palm between my legs and applies light pressure on the new toy, making me moan. "You wear it whenever I'm not in a position to keep my finger or my cock in you, Isabella. Is that clear?"

"Yes."

"I'll wake you up in the morning before I leave for work and help you place it. And I'm the only one allowed to remove it. You can do it yourself only when you need to go to the bathroom."

"Okay." I lean toward him to whisper in his ear, "You are one kinky man, Luca."

"So I am. Does it bother you?"

"Not even a little." I kiss him and slide my hand down his chest until it rests on his crotch. "I like your wickedness."

"Isabella, behave."

I smile. "Are there bigger sizes available?"

"Yes. Why?"

"This one feels like having your fingers inside of me," I say and lick his earlobe. "I'd like to have one that would make me feel like I have your cock there."

When I feel him harden under my palm, a grin spreads across my face. The fact that I can make him hard just by saying such things to him turns me on so much.

"It would feel amazing having you remove it just to replace it with your cock." I add, "I would probably come in the process."

He sucks in a breath and grabs the back of my neck. "If you continue, there won't be dinner tonight, Isabella."

"Will you?" I squeeze his cock lightly. "Get me a bigger one?"

"Yes. But you only get to wear it when I say so."

# Chapter

Luca

I take a sip of my coffee, pretending to be engrossed in something on my phone while I watch my surroundings. I agreed to meet with Ajello at seven p.m., but when I proposed a restaurant downtown, he rejected the idea, picking a small family-run café in the suburbs. Strange choice, but I accepted. What's even more interesting is he insisted on taking a table outdoors. If he arrives with a convoy of bodyguards, it's bound to attract the attention of anyone passing by. Whatever. I only brought Marco, but he's waiting in the car.

Out of the corner of my eye, I spot a man crossing the street. I'm not sure what possesses me to keep my gaze focused on him because there's nothing that stands out. He appears to be in his late twenties or early thirties, has dark hair, and is wearing a black suit without a jacket. Tall. Athletic. Women would probably find him handsome, but then again, nothing overly special. The only out-of-the-ordinary thing about him is a black leather glove on his left hand. As he enters the coffee shop's patio, heading in my direction, I notice that he has a slight limp in his gait. It's very subtle, and I wouldn't have spotted it if I wasn't so focused on him. He approaches the table, takes the chair across from me, and sits down.

"Mr. Rossi." He leans back in his chair. "I'm glad to be meeting you in person, at last."

"Mr. Ajello, I presume?" I ask and look around the café trying to spot his security detail.

"I don't use bodyguards, Mr. Rossi." His lips curve upward, and there is something extremely disturbing in his smile. It's not that it seems fake. I've grown accustomed to fake smiles. That's how our society works, apparently. People smile sweetly one moment, then stab you in the back the next. This, however, seems as if he knows what a smile should look like and mimics it instead. But there's nothing behind his smile. No emotion. No scheme. It's trained. Like a dancer must learn steps to the music, this man has learned to smile for a conversation, when needed. Only the movement is that of muscles matching the beat of an imagined song. Choreographed.

"So, let's get to the point of this meeting," I say.

The waitress comes to take our order. Ajello doesn't even look at her, just waves his gloved hand, keeping his gaze on mine.

"A straightforward man. I respect that." He nods. "I've been widening my construction operations lately, a very comfortable way for laundering drug money, and I have a business proposition for you, Mr. Rossi."

"I'm listening."

"You buy and sell real estate to launder your money. It must be tiring, searching for available properties to purchase all the time. Wouldn't it be easier to have a constant supply of top-notch locations?"

"It would." I nod "Are you offering to supply?"

"Yes."

"What amount of net worth are we talking about?"

"Twenty million. Monthly."

I think about his offer. "Why me? Why not someone else?"

"You're the head of your Family. A don. You know how things work in our world, but you're also a businessman. Bogdan doesn't like you, which is a compliment in my book. He also says you drive a hard bargain."

So, he also has dealings with the Romanians. Good to know.

"I'm interested." I nod.

"Perfect. I'll send you the details." As he stands up, he places his hands on the tabletop, and I notice that the last two fingers on his gloved hand are in a slightly unnatural position, as if he can't fully extend them. "I hope we'll have a fruitful collaboration, Mr. Rossi."

I regard him as he leaves, wondering why he murdered all the other capos. If his only aim was to take over the New York Family, killing the previous don would have been enough.

Leaving money for the coffee on the table, I rise but immediately grab the side of the chair as pain slashes through my temples. It lasts for a second or two, and then it's gone. The fucking headaches are getting worse. I'll go in for that checkup as soon as I'm done with the damn banquet.

Now, I can't wait to get home, and back to my wife. I wonder if I was always this crazy about her, or if it's something that's built up after we were married and before the crash. It seems unhealthy, how I can't stop thinking about her even for a moment. Even when I'm working, Isabella is constantly on my mind. Her eyes. Her hair. The way she likes to snuggle into me every night. But most of all, it's her strong-minded personality. Her courage. She keeps amazing me every single day, this slip of a girl, who keeps playing this game, fooling the whole Family. She knew what was at stake from the beginning. I didn't. It was only a few days ago that Damian explained it to me. If anyone finds out that Isabella has been covering for me, hiding my condition, the Family will proclaim her a traitor—someone who's been acting against the Family's interests. A punishment for such an act is usually death.

If I'd known this sooner, I never would have allowed her to get tangled up in this shit. There's no coming back now. I'm not afraid of dying. But if the truth does come out at some point, and if anyone even so much as thinks about hurting Isabella, they better come at us with all they have. Because I am going to annihilate any man who tries harming a hair on my wife's head.

# Chapter Twenty-one

Luca

"LORENZO INSISTS ON SEEING ME TOMORROW," I SAY AS I'M unbuttoning my shirt. "I don't know why he insists. We can talk business at the banquet on Saturday."

"He wants to make himself feel important. Low self-esteem complex," Isabella says from the bed. "Especially now, with you as the head of the Family."

"Do you want to come? He's booked us a table at Mirage."

"Of course, he has," she snorts. Getting off the bed, she stands behind me and wraps her arms around my waist. "He knows you'll be paying the bill. Is it okay if I come? It's a business meeting after all."

"I don't give a fuck that it is." I take the box I picked up this morning from the specialty shop I've started visiting frequently and place it on a dresser. "I've bought you something."

"What?" She peeks around me, and I see her eyes widen upon seeing the leather box. "Is it . . . ?"

"Yes." I take her arm and pull her around to stand in front of me. "Want to try it on?"

"Is it much bigger?" she asks and reaches for the box, but I catch her hand in mine.

"It's bigger. Close your eyes."

She shuts her eyes immediately, and I smile. Who would've expected someone as young as her to be so eager and responsive to all my unconventional ways. Moving my palms down her generous hips, I slide her panties down and wrap my fingers around the object lodged in her pussy. Two days ago, I decided to punish her for not putting on the dress I requested and removed her pussy plug. She whimpered and begged me to put it back, pressing her small hands over her pussy the whole time. I buried my cock inside of her instead. My little addict. Isabella can't bear the thought of not having my cock or something else that reminds her of me inside her. Her reactions make me so hard that it feels like I'm going to explode.

As expected, she starts complaining the moment I take out the toy, so I temporarily push my finger inside her. "Keep your eyes closed," I say and open the box.

I take the new pussy plug from the box. I've already washed it and put a good amount of lubricant over the thick end because it's significantly larger than the one she's accustomed to.

"Spread your legs slightly. Yes, just like that." I place the tip of the new pussy plug at her entrance, pull out my finger and start sliding the sleek black toy inside her pussy.

"Everything okay?" I ask when her breathing hitches. "If it's too much, I'll stop."

"Don't stop." She breathes out and squeezes my wrist. "I want it all in. Now, Luca."

I slide it fully inside, then adjust the thinner tip so it presses on her clit. "Good?"

"What if it slides out?" she asks.

"It won't, tesoro." I press my palm over her pussy. "Let's try walking, hmm?"

She steps forward and I follow without taking my hand off her. "See? It won't slide out. You just need to get accustomed to a bigger size. Let's try a few more steps."

When she starts walking toward the bed, I let go of her pussy. "How does it feel?"

She turns to face me and lowers herself to the bed. Her movements are slow, her eyes closed as if she's savoring the feeling. When she's seated and moans, I can barely restrain myself from grabbing and fucking her senseless.

"How does it feel?" she repeats my question, biting her lower lip, and opens her eyes. "It feels like I have your cock inside of me, Luca."

"You need to be really wet to use this one, Isabella. If you're not, use lubricant. If you hurt yourself, I'll throw it away. You hear me?"

"Yes."

I take her chin, tilt her head up, and trace her bottom lip with my thumb. "Now, let's remove it."

"No."

"Yes, Isabella. When I'm around, you get my cock," I say and start unbuttoning my pants. "On the bed, please."

I lower myself over her and reach to pull out the pussy plug. With the toy gone, I slide my cock inside her heat. Isabella pants and moans as I bury myself in her.

Instead of pounding into her hard, I slowly slide out, then in again, watching her face the whole time, enjoying the sounds of pleasure that leave her lips. My young little wife whom I've corrupted with my wicked ways. I don't know what I felt for her before, but I know what I feel now, hearing her moan my name. I thrust into her again, and she starts shaking under me, but I keep sliding in and out, letting her ride the orgasm, and only allow myself to come after she's done. When her body goes limp beneath me, I bend my head to whisper next to her ear, "I am so fucking in love with you, Isabella." Then, I crash my lips to hers.

I watch him as he sleeps, his thick eyebrows, mouth that does the most sinful things, hair falling freely over his face. *My Luca*. I lean into him, tucking my face into his neck and inhaling his scent.

He told me he loves me last night. I never dared to hope those words would fall from his lips. It was always an impossible dream. And now that I've finally heard the words I've been so desperate for, instead of being overjoyed, I'm scared shitless. What if his memory comes back? I don't think I could take it if Luca goes back to being his old self. It would be even worse than before the accident if he knows I tricked him into believing the farce I've created.

An arm wraps around my midsection, and suddenly I'm facing the wall with my back pressed to Luca's chest.

"What did I tell you? How do you sleep?" he asks, his words whispered in my ear.

"With your finger in me," I say as his finger circles my clit and then slips inside, making me gasp.

"If I ever again catch you lying next to me in any other way, there will be consequences, Isabella."

"What kind of consequences?"

"I'm going to keep you in bed"—his finger slides out then in again—"the whole fucking day,"—he pinches my clit—"torturing you like this, without letting you come."

His finger vanishes from my core, and I cry out, grabbing his hand and pressing it over my pussy. "Please, Luca."

"Please, what? What do you need?"

"Your cock. Inside me." I squeeze my legs together, trying to relieve myself of at least some of the yearning in my core.

He turns me, his big hands holding on to my waist, and positions me above his cock, its tip teasing my entrance. I try sinking onto it, but he keeps me clutched in his grip, denying me the gratification.

"Do we have an understanding, Isabella? About the sleeping arrangement?"

"Yes." I nod, gripping his forearms. "Please. I can't take it anymore."

"Is this better?" he asks as he lowers me onto his cock.

I breathe deeply, marveling at the feel of him filling me up so completely. I start rotating my hips, trying to take even more of him inside. Luca's hand comes to rest where our bodies are joined, and he massages my clit as he pumps into me from below. I'm already close when his hands come under my ass, and he lifts me only to slam me down onto his cock again. A scream escapes me as I feel the orgasm nearing. I close my eyes. He raises my body again, and I arch my back when his length invades my pussy in the next moment. Up. Down. Up. Down. The pressure in my core skyrockets, and I come with another scream.

When I slump onto his chest, his cock still feels hard, and his breathing is labored. I tilt my head up and raise my eyebrows at him. "Why didn't you finish?"

"I like the feel of my cock inside you too much," he says through gritted teeth.

"Luca . . ." I reach out and place my hand on his cheek, trying not to laugh. "You'll give yourself a heart attack from the strain, baby."

"No!" he barks. "And don't you dare move. I'm holding on by a thread."

"And how long do you plan on us staying like this?"

"For as long as I can control myself. Don't fucking move, Isabella."

He's crazy. I won't let him do this to himself.

"I need to tell you something," I say.

"What?"

"When I went to the hairdressers yesterday, I removed the pussy plug."

His eyes widen and his hands squeeze my ass cheeks. "You did what?" he growls. "For how long?"

"Two hours."

His breathing quickens, and he stares at me, his nostrils flaring. "You left the house with nothing to remind you how my cock feels?"

"Yes."

I didn't, actually. I planned to. I wanted to see if I could manage without it for so long, but I only got to the car before the need became too much, and I rushed back to the bedroom. If someone told me previously that I'd be using sex toys, especially in such an extreme way, I would've thought they were nuts.

The vein on his neck starts pulsing. Wrapping his arm around my middle, he rolls us until I'm on my back, then gathers my wrists with his hand pinning them above my head.

"You,"—he slams into me—"will never,"—another thrust—"fucking ever . . ."

I moan as my pussy starts spasming around his cock again. It should have been too soon, but seeing Luca losing it like this, turns me on beyond measure.

". . . leave the house without it." Another thrust. "Do you understand, Isabella?"

"Yes, Luca."

He groans as his orgasm hits when the words leave my lips, and I shatter.

# Chapter Twenty-Two

## Luca

"Turn right here," Isabella says when we reach the intersection. "It's there, just next to the big flower shop."

I follow her directions and park in front of the building with a glass façade. Even from the outside, it's visible that the restaurant is high-end kind of place. Each car parked in the lot is priced at more than a hundred grand. I can't see the inside because the glass is mirrored, but I know it has black wood finishings and tall ceilings with fancy iron chandeliers. In the center, there's a huge round space with an open ceiling where the best tables are set. I know all that without having any recollection of ever visiting the place. I've been here. Before.

It's taken me some time to accept the concept of *before*. The first few days after the crash, I was sure my memory would come back. Every time I woke up, I expected the recollections to hit me, certain that my loss was temporary. When Isabella and Damian started filling me in on the details of my life, I assumed that some of it would trigger my brain and start an avalanche of memories. It didn't. Neither did coming home. Facing my daughter was my last chance for something to spark my memories. There was no spark, however. No trigger of any kind. I saw the girl with long black hair running into my arms, and I felt not even an inkling of recognition. The moment I held Rosa in my embrace, I decided I would accept the situation as it was. I stopped dwelling on the possibility of my memory and old life returning someday. In a way, I decided to cut my losses and focus on the now. The *before* became only a time marker.

"Have I brought you here at some point?" I ask as I help Isabella out of the car. She's wearing a navy silk dress that's adorned with lace and flows over her upper body and flares out from the waist. I've chosen it for her. I keep picking dresses that have flowy skirts because the idea of another man ogling her ass makes me go ballistic. Her pretty behind is only mine to look at.

"Nope." She shrugs. "I came here once with Angelo."

"Angelo Scardoni?"

"Yes. We were kind of engaged."

I grab her hand and turn her to face me. "What?"

"It was just an agreement that my father set up when I was eighteen. Nothing came out of it, as you already know," she says and smiles. "But I have to say, you are sexy when you're jealous."

"So why did he take you to dinner?"

"Because I wanted to go out with someone, hoping it would cure me of my crush on you, Luca." She raises her free hand and takes my chin between her fingers. "A hint for you. It didn't. Nothing and no one managed to make me even slightly interested in anyone other than you."

"He's ten years younger than me," I say through my teeth.

"But he isn't you. I've always wanted you." She squeezes my chin. "You. No one else."

I stare at her, then grab her around the waist and bring her flush with my chest. Then, I slam my mouth to hers.

I know we're fucked the moment we step inside the restaurant and my eyes find the table at the center where Lorenzo is sitting. He's not alone. Sitting next to him is a man in his midthirties, with sandy blond hair and glasses. He stands up when he sees us approaching, a wide smile on his face. Davide Barbini. Lorenzo's nephew. And one of Luca's friends from school.

My heart explodes into an insane tempo while my brain works in overdrive as I try, and fail, to come up with a way to get us out of this shitstorm. Damian and I never briefed Luca on his childhood friends because none of them had anything to do with Cosa Nostra. None, except Davide Barbini, who moved to Italy two years ago and should have stayed there, damn it!

There's no time to warn Luca because we've nearly reached their table. They'd notice if I tried to say something to him. And we can't just turn around and leave. Fuck! Think!

A fifteen-step distance divides us from our demise, and I have nothing. There's no way Luca can pull off a whole meal without slipping. Ten steps. There will be high school jokes and mentions of other friends from that time. We're doomed.

Six steps. The sound of high-pitched laughter reaches me from our right. My head snaps to the side, my eyes finding a blonde woman sitting at the table in the corner, laughing at something one of her friends said. Simona. I never would have thought that seeing Luca's ex would make me so happy. I could kiss that bitch right now. Two steps. Lorenzo rises from his chair. It's now or never.

I pull my hand out of Luca's, turn toward him abruptly, and start yelling into his face. "How could you!"

I stare at Isabella, stunned. What the fuck?

"You did it on purpose, didn't you?" she continues. "Asking me to accompany you, when you knew she would be here!"

Everyone at the restaurant, including Lorenzo and the blond man with him, have gone deadly quiet. I have no idea who the guy is.

"Isabella, calm down," I say, reaching for her hand. I don't know what's riled her up so much to make a scene with at least sixty people watching.

"Calm down?" she shouts, pointing with her finger to her left. "I know you've been cheating on me with your ex, but to insist we come to the same restaurant where you knew she'd be?"

"What?" I look to the table she's pointing at and see Simona sitting there, looking as shocked as everyone else.

"I let the incident with the maid go," Isabella keeps shouting, waving her hands through the air. "But this . . . this is too much! I'm not staying here a second more."

An incident with a maid? What the fuck is she talking about? We both know it's utter nonsense. Something's going on here. From what I know about

Isabella—and I think I know her very well by now—she'd never make a fool of herself in front of an audience. Not without a reason.

"Isabella," I say and try to place my arm around her, but she moves away a step.

"Fuck you, Luca," she sneers at me and storms toward the exit.

I watch her leave, then turn toward Lorenzo and the blond guy. They too are staring at the door Isabella just went through.

"Looks like you have a problem, Luca." The blond guy laughs and looks directly at me just as a jolt of pain pierces my brain. I don't worry about the fact that he knows who I am. Instead, I turn my back to them and head for the exit.

"We'll talk tomorrow, Lorenzo," I call over my shoulder and leave the restaurant, stalking after my exhibitionist wife.

I find Isabella standing next to our car, leaning on the door with her eyes closed. Another pang hits me as I walk toward her. When I reach her, I place my hands on either side of her, caging her in against the car.

"You made a fool out of yourself there, tesoro." I bend until our faces are at the same level.

"I know," she says, keeping her eyes closed. "And with Simona there to witness it, I'm sure the whole Cosa Nostra will know what happened within an hour."

"It was because of that guy who was with Lorenzo, wasn't it?"

"Davide Barbini." She nods. "You two went to school together. If we'd have stayed, it would've been a disaster. We needed an out."

"So, you made a fool of yourself because of me?" I lift my hand and place it at the back of her neck.

Isabella's eyes open and she looks at me, holding my gaze. "There are not many things that I wouldn't do for you, Luca. You should know that already."

I watch her for a few moments, etching her defiant eyes and stubborn chin on my very being it seems, then I crash my mouth against her lips in a soul-shuttering kiss.

# Chapter Twenty-Three

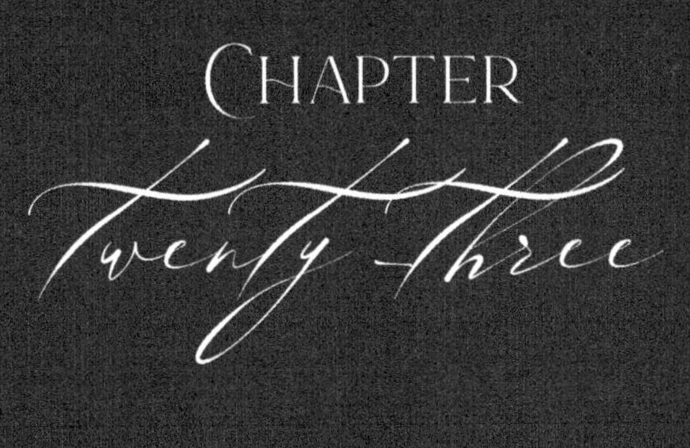

## Luca

It happens suddenly as I'm buttoning my shirt the morning of the banquet.

Isabella's in the bathroom, taking a shower. I woke her up early by sliding my cock into her while she was still asleep. With all the people arriving to make preparations for tonight, she'll be busy the whole day, and there won't be any time for us until late into the night. There's no way I could let her go the entire day without having my cock inside her.

It starts with another sharp pang, but this time the pain doesn't dissipate right away. Instead, it keeps slashing across my temples in waves so strong I have to sit down on the bed. I squeeze my eyes closed, waiting for it to pass, but the pain keeps building until I feel like my head is going to explode. Then, as suddenly as it started, the pain is gone. I should feel relief, but I can't move from my spot on the bed while I'm trying to sort out the chaos raging in my brain.

When I allowed myself to consider the possibility of regaining my memory, I always assumed it will be a gradual process—remembering one person at a time, or certain events, randomly. I never expected it to hit me like a sledgehammer, but that's how it feels. One moment all I know is the last two months of my life, and the next, the past thirty-five years materialize out of nowhere.

The bathroom door opens, and Isabella rushes out, clutching her phone to her ear while she's adjusting her dress. "Let them in, I'll be right down," she says into the phone, then looks at me. "The decoration company is early, I have to go."

"All right." I nod, staring at her.

"Are you going to the office?"

"Yes."

"Don't be late for your own party." She points the phone in my direction. "If I finish up early, I might drop by your office around noon."

I get up and walk across the room. When I'm standing before her, I take her face in my palms and just stare at her.

"Luca? Is something wrong?"

"No," I say, not breaking our locked gazes. "Why?"

"You have a very strange look in your eyes."

The phone in her hand rings again. Isabella sighs, then tilts her head up to press her lips to mine. "I really have to go," she says into my mouth.

I follow her with my eyes as she hurries out of the room—my extraordinarily brilliant wife, whom I so wrongly accused of being too young to deal with me and my line of work. Two months. For two fucking months she guided me about while I didn't have a damn clue who all the people around me were. She managed to trick the whole damn Family into believing there was nothing wrong with her husband. Or, it seems, everyone except one person.

I grab my jacket off the chair, take the car keys and my wallet, and head for the door. Tonight's banquet is bound to be much more interesting than I imagined because, along with my life, I also remember the face of the man who tried to kill me, and he'll probably be here.

Yes, it will be a very exciting evening.

There's a knock at the office door, and Isabella's head peeks inside. "Am I interrupting?"

"I'll call you later, Franco," I say into the phone and motion for her to come in.

She walks to my desk, removes her sunglasses, and places them and her purse on the wooden surface. I study her, focusing on how her gray dress dips into her cleavage, leaving nothing to the imagination.

"I don't remember approving that outfit for today."

"Because you haven't." She stands before me, bends, and starts unbuttoning my pants. "So, I came to make amends."

My cock instantly gets hard. "All right. I'll allow it this time. But you won't do it again. Is that clear?"

"Yes, Luca."

My cock swells even more. It's unbelievable how much it turns me on when she's obedient because I know there isn't a single submissive bone in her body. Isabella is not a woman who'd ever let a man control her in any way, yet, she's compliant with my orders. What's even a greater turn-on is knowing that she likes it.

"You may proceed." I lean back in my chair.

Isabella kneels between my legs, takes out my cock and brings her lips to the tip. She licks it, then takes it into her mouth and starts sucking. I grip the sides of the chair, trying to restrain myself from coming into her mouth right away.

"Are you wearing your pussy plug, Isabella?"

She gives my cock one slow lick, then looks up and smiles. "No."

"Why?"

"I came here intending to get something better inside of me." She slides her hand down my length and squeezes it lightly. "I left my panties at home, as well."

I growl, then bend to grab around her waist and hoist her onto my lap, right over my rock-hard dick. She moans as I slide into her, wriggling her hips and taking all of me.

I paw her ass, lift and slowly slide her back down as she moans and grabs my shoulders. The feel of Isabella on my lap, with my cock lodged inside her, is priceless. Unfortunately, the position doesn't allow much space for maneuvering. I swipe my right hand over my desk, pushing the folders and other stuff off the top.

"Luca!" Isabella yelps, looking down at the papers littering the floor.

Holding under her thighs, I get up off the chair and deposit her sweet ass on my desk. The laptop is lying open right behind her back. She may hurt herself if she leans back, so I grab the thing and send it to the floor, as well.

"Are you out of your fucking mind?" She stares at me.

"On the contrary, tesoro." I cup her butt cheeks in my palms and pull her toward the edge of the desk. "Lock your legs behind me and hold on."

The moment she obeys, I thrust myself back inside of her. It feels so fucking good when her walls clutch at my cock while she watches me with those magnificent eyes. I'm not sure what I love more—Isabella's breathtakingly sinful body, her unrelenting and steely spirit, or her brilliant mind. I'm crazy about everything where my young wife is concerned.

A mewl leaves her lips when I start pounding into her, and I soak up every single sound as I demolish her. When I feel her walls trembling around my cock, I stop holding myself back and let go, filling her up with my cum.

My desk phone rings. It somehow escaped the same fate that befell the laptop and the folders. I maintain my hold on Isabella as I sit back down on the chair, then reach for the phone.

"Donato, I'm busy," I answer the phone.

Isabella starts to move, trying to stand up, but I squeeze my arm around her to keep her flush to my body. I like the feel of my cock inside of her.

"There's a problem with the newest arms delivery," Donato says. "We're two crates of grenades short."

There's a lick at the side of my neck. Then, on my jaw, a bite.

"Deduct the amount equal to the cost of six crates, and wire Bogdan the money."

Hands in my hair. A kiss at the corner of my mouth.

"Six?" Donato gulps. "What if he raises an issue?"

I turn my head and our gazes meet. She smiles mischievously and presses her lips to mine.

"Just remind him of the last discussion he and I had," I say into Isabella's lips, throw the phone on my desk, and wrap my hand around her throat.

"What are you wearing tonight?" I ask, sliding my hand up to cup her jaw.

"No restrictions?" She arches her eyebrows.

"No restrictions." I press my lips to hers. "But only for tonight."

She smiles, wraps her arms around my neck, and removes my hair tie. "You were right, you know? I *am* obsessed with your hair," she says and tunnels her fingers through the strands. "My first memory of you is like this. It was wet then, though."

"I know, Isa."

Isabella's fingers go still. Fuck. I never meant that to slip out. I planned on telling her tonight that I remember everything.

"Damian told me I saved you, pulled you out of the pool when you were six," I add.

"You did." She smiles. "I should head back. There are still some last-minute checks to be made, and I have to change."

"Make sure it's not something too revealing, or I may change my mind."

Her lips widen more. "What if it is?"

I tilt her head sideways to whisper in her ear, "There will be consequences, Isabella. You know that."

"Yes."

"Good." I lean forward and press the intercom button on my desk phone. "Magda, bring me today's listings."

"Right away, Mr. Rossi."

Isabella shifts, intending to get off my lap, but I tighten my arm around her, keeping her in place.

"Luca? Your secretary will be here any second."

"I know." I kiss her shoulder, grab her butt cheeks and reposition her on my, once again, hard cock. "And you're staying right where you are. Is that clear, Isabella?"

She's silent for a few moments, then turns her head so her lips are just near my ear. "Yes, Mr. Rossi," she whispers, and my cock hardens even more.

"Do you have any idea"—she starts moving her pelvis forward, then back, slowly—"how much it turns me on"—a slight rotation of her hips—"when you order me around?"

I grit my teeth, trying to stay composed, but a growl still manages to leave my lips. "Tell me."

"It makes me so wet that I'm seriously considering wearing two pairs of panties if you continue." She bites my earlobe. "You know what makes me even wetter?"

Jesus. Don't say it.

"When I obey, Luca."

I explode inside of her the instant my name leaves her lips. "Fuck."

There's a knock at the door, and Magda enters holding a stack of papers in her hand but then stops midstep. Her gaze passes over the overturned laptop on the floor, the papers scattered about, and finally stops on Isabella sitting on my lap. The desk provides some cover, but she can't have missed Isabella's dress pulled up to just below her breasts.

"I-i-is it a bad time?" she stutters.

Isabella straightens on my lap and throws a look over her shoulder. "Not at all, Magda. Please leave the papers on the sofa."

My secretary rushes to drop off the papers, then hightails it out of the office in record time, closing the door with a bang.

"I need two minutes," I say through my teeth. I can't believe I came without waiting for her. Like I'm some teenager.

"No time. I have to go back home."

I squeeze her ass. "You're not leaving this office with a lower orgasm score than me."

Holding her under her ass, I stand up and carry her to the bathroom, where I clean us up, then carry her back. I set her onto the desk, sit down in my chair, and place my hands behind her knees. "Lie down."

"What if someone comes in?"

"They'll turn around and leave." I fix her with my gaze. "Down. Spread your legs."

"If you say so, Mr. Rossi." She smiles and lowers her back onto the desk.

I fasten the last button at the back of my neck and look at myself in the mirror. The beige material of the dress hugs my body from the high neckline to slightly below the knees, emphasizing my curves. I turn and look at myself from the side, and then from the back, focusing on my hips. The shapewear that I put on under the dress works wonders. My butt seems at least two sizes smaller. Maybe even three.

When I first got dressed for tonight, I regretted the fact I let Luca convince me to gain back the weight I'd previously lost. I kind of got carried away and instead of putting on only those ten pounds, I packed on fifteen more. It wasn't that hard, I just stopped counting calories as rigorously as I usually do. I wish I didn't. The most hilarious thing is that I'm still wearing the same size shirts. All that extra weight, and my breasts became only slightly fuller. Everything else ended up in the bottom part of my body—some on my thighs, but mostly my hips and ass. Just like I feared it would.

I wasn't insecure about my body until the moment I saw myself in the mirror, wearing this dress. My eyes zeroed in on my behind, making me think of a patient whose butt implant surgery had gone terribly wrong. I almost took off the dress, initially, thinking I'd put on something less tight. But then I remembered the crazy body-shaping underwear I bought on a whim. It's really tight and rather uncomfortable, but I don't care. Maybe I should start wearing it every day, at least until I manage to lose a few inches around my hips.

It's genetics. My mother has a similar pear-shaped build—narrow upper body and significant behind. Grandma was the same. But I seemed to have ended up with the most well-endowed . . . back end. Thank God Luca usually wants me to wear dresses. That allows me to hide the size my butt has reached. I doubt he's noticed it when we're intimate. Men don't usually notice that kind of thing during sex.

The image of Simona comes to my mind. She's much taller than me, but I don't think that, even at fifteen, I would have been able to get into her current size pants. Luca keeps saying he likes my body, and I don't think he's lying, but still . . . He must have been attracted to his ex-wife if he chose to be with her. If he was attracted to her body, how can he like mine, which is the total opposite?

Enough. Now is not the time for insecurities when there are close to fifty people arriving shortly and expecting everything to be perfect. Maybe I should check the guest list one more time, just to make sure I didn't miss anyone I should brief Luca on. I comb my hand through my hair, which I've left down, check my reflection in the mirror one last time to make sure the lines of the shapewear are not visible, and leave the bathroom.

Luca is sitting in the recliner at the opposite side of the room, typing on his phone. When I enter, he lifts his head, checking me out.

"You're the most beautiful thing I've ever set my eyes on," he says with a satisfied smile on his lips, then moves his gaze lower, but he stops midway. "Turn around."

I raise my eyebrows but make a slow turn. As my eyes return to him, he isn't smiling anymore.

"Are you on a diet again, Isabella?"

"No. Why?"

"Your ass is smaller."

So, he's noticed. "I'm wearing shapewear underneath the dress," I say. "Do you like it?"

"Shapewear?" He scowls. "What the fuck is that?"

"It's worn underneath clothes to make the body look slimmer." I pass my palms down my legs one more time, checking for the visible seams. "It's damn tight but it works great."

Luca's nostrils flare and his eyes narrow. "Remove that crap."

"What?"

"Now, Isabella."

I grit my teeth, pull the dress up to my waist and take off the slimming shorts I had on underneath. Throwing them away, I straighten my dress again.

"There. Satisfied?" I snap. He doesn't say anything, just watches me. Maybe he doesn't like the idea of shapewear. "I only planned on wearing it until I got back to my old weight, okay?"

Luca still doesn't say a word. The stretchy material of the dress clings to my body, showing every extra pound I've gained. I wait for him to tell me to put the shaping shorts on again when he suddenly stands up from the recliner and, leaving the phone, stalks toward me. Is he mad at me? He can't be mad because I've gained weight, can he? The expression on his face is really strange. I take a step back, then a few more until I end up in the bathroom again, with Luca following me inside. He bends his head, his breath brushing my cheek as his hands come to his belt, and he starts unclasping it. I watch with wide eyes as he unbuttons his pants and releases his cock that's already fully erect.

"Turn around," he says.

I turn my back to him, slightly confused, and feel his hands land on my ass.

"Jesus." He sucks in a breath. "I could come just from looking at you."

"You . . . like it?"

"Oh, tesoro." He grabs my hips and presses me against his body. "Why did you put that slimming crap on?"

"I . . . my ass is enormous, and this dress is really tight. It shows everything. I thought you wouldn't find it attractive."

"Hmm. Want me to demonstrate to you what I think about your body?" He bends his head to whisper into my ear, "Just to make sure there are no misunderstandings?"

"Okay?"

"Take a step forward so I can see you better." He moves his hands from my butt cheeks to my hips. "Perk your ass slightly."

When I do as he says, he takes a deep breath. "Fucking perfection."

His hands leave my hips, and I hear a groan behind me. I look up into the mirror and lock eyes with him. His right arm is moving furiously and I realize that he's jerking himself off to the sight of my ass. He screws his face up, as if he's in pain, but then a pure euphoric look comes over him as he comes. I turn around to find Luca holding his cock in his hand, cum all over his fingers. He reaches for one of the towels, cleans himself, and buttons up his pants.

"Does me coming just from looking at your ass clear things for you, tesoro?"

I nod, slightly shocked.

"Good. Are you wearing your pussy plug?" he slides his hand under my dress and presses his palm onto my panties, cupping my pussy.

"You know I am."

"Perfect. Then let's go downstairs."

## Luca

ISABELLA TAKES A GLASS FROM THE WAITER AND LEANS TOWARD ME.

"Emiliano Caruso," she mumbles. "Damian said you two worked together on some project in January, but he doesn't have any details. Emiliano has been trying to climb the hierarchy ladder for years. He wants Donato's spot, but my grandfather wouldn't let him have it. He was the main suspect in a case involving illegal dog fights a few years back, and Nonno didn't want anyone who'd ever been on the police radar."

I nod, brush my hand down Isabella's back and place a kiss on the top of her head. We've been mingling for almost two hours. She's been giving me details on every guest as they've arrived, and I've let her, even though it's not necessary anymore. I'm not quite sure why I didn't tell her this morning that my memory has come back. Maybe because I wanted to see her in action tonight. It's amazing how much information she keeps in her brain. Over the past two days, she's filled me in on every member of the Family expected to attend the banquet, their roles, family members, and dirty laundry. People would be shocked if they were aware how many details of their lives were stored in Isabella's pretty head.

"Why did you send Rosa to her friend's house for tonight?" Isabella asks. "She was so excited about the party, especially the cake."

"I didn't want her here in case something bad happens," I say.

"It's a party, Luca. We have a ton of security. Nothing bad is going to happen."

I look down at her and brush my thumb along the line of her chin while my lips curve into a smile. "We'll see."

Isabella's eyes widen. "What are you not telling me?"

Several excited shouts come from the other side of the room, and we both look toward the commotion near the door.

"Shit!" Isabella grabs my hand and squeezes it. "What the fuck is Davide Barbini doing here? He wasn't on the guest list, and I strictly forbade the guys at the door to admit anyone who's not on it."

"It looks like Lorenzo brought him in," I say and watch my underboss standing next to his nephew while the people gather around to chat with the newcomer.

"I still don't understand what the hell Davide is doing in Chicago," she whispers.

"Yes, quite interesting, don't you think?" I smile and take her hand in mine. "Let's go say hi."

"What!" she whisper-yells. "Damian was only able to share some general info on him. What if he mentions something that happened when the two of you went to school?"

"I'll improvise."

"You'll improvise?" she snaps. "Are you crazy?"

I stop, turn her toward me and lift her chin with my finger. "Trust me, tesoro," I say and place a kiss on her lips.

The group with Lorenzo and Davide has moved to the center of the room, where more than a dozen round tables have been set. As we walk in their direction, I cast a glance at the corner where Marco is standing, and when our gazes connect, I give him a discreet nod. He tilts his head, speaking into his headpiece, and in my peripheral vision, Emilio locks the front door and blocks it with his body.

By the time we reach the center of the room, two of my security guys are positioned at each exit point. Just as I instructed. It might be overkill since this is a no-weapons-allowed event, but I don't want to risk it.

"Davide," I say and clasp him on the back. "I'm so sorry we didn't get the opportunity to catch up the other day. Let's eat and you can tell us about your life in Italy."

He opens his mouth to say something, but I push onto his shoulder until he sits down on the chair.

"You can join us, Lorenzo." I turn toward my underboss. "If I remember well, you said you have something important to discuss."

Lorenzo smiles and takes a seat next to Davide. The quick calculated look the two of them exchange doesn't escape my notice. Isabella doesn't say a word, just keeps squeezing my hand and doesn't release it even when we walk around the table and take our seats opposite them.

"I hear you had an accident two months back," Davide says. "I hope it wasn't anything serious."

"Not at all. A mild concussion. Some burns and scratches."

"You were always thick-headed, Luca." He smirks. "Remember that time when we stole your father's car and headed to Luigi's? When we crashed not even a mile after we left the grounds?"

Isabella's hand squeezes mine under the table and I can feel her fingers are trembling. I recline in my chair and cock my head, regarding Davide, then turn my gaze to Lorenzo. He's looking at me with an evil glint in his eyes and a barely visible self-satisfied smile on his lips. Yes, it looks like I was right in my assumptions.

"You don't remember?" Davide continues, but I keep watching Lorenzo, whose smile is getting wider by the second.

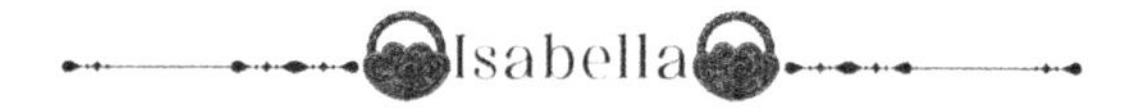

We are so fucked.

I keep my eyes glued to the table in front of me, trying to think of a way to get us out of this fuckup. Why doesn't he just say he remembers and be done with it? I can then try changing the direction of the conversation afterward.

"I can't say I remember that, Davide," Luca says next to me, and my head snaps up.

Why did he confess that? I turn my gaze on Lorenzo and find him smiling. He doesn't look surprised by Luca's answer. In fact, he seems . . . excited. The realization sets in, and I squeeze Luca's hand with all my might. How the fuck did Lorenzo find out about Luca's memory loss?

"How can you not remember?" Davide presses.

"Because it never happened, Davide," Luca says in a cold voice.

My body goes rigid. How would he know that? Did Damian tell him about that event?

"That's the story Philip told us while we were playing cards at his place." Luca continues. "It was the summer after freshman year, as I recall. Good old days."

I feel this strange falling sensation, and I'm spiraling as panic settles inside me. Oh my God, he remembers.

I don't dare look at Luca, I can't bear to see the loathing on his face. He probably hates me now. It's over. Squeezing my lips together, I rein in the tears that threaten to fall and try pulling my hand out of Luca's grasp. The grip he has around my fingers only gets stronger. Taking a deep breath, I somehow gather the courage to look up at him, but instead of a look of anger which I expected to find, I see a smug smile pulling at his lips. His hand lifts to my face, and he brushes away a stray tear with his thumb. My eyes widen as he leans forward to place a quick kiss on my lips, then turns to Davide.

"I wonder, Davide," he says, "what were you promised in exchange for running me off that road?"

With his face turned ghostly white, Davide stares at Luca. A chair screeches, and in the next moment, Davide launches toward the nearest door. Marco catches him halfway there.

The room has gone silent.

"Boss." Marco turns to Luca. "Where should we put him?"

"Kitchen will do," Luca says. "We have a tiled floor there, it's easier to wash away the blood."

Marco nods and starts dragging Davide toward the door on the opposite side of the room. Most of the guests were in the middle of their meals, but now, everyone has stopped eating, and dozens of eyes are staring at Davide, who thrashes and yells as he tries to free himself. Marco backhands him, then keeps hauling him in the direction of the kitchen.

The door on the left suddenly flies opens and three men walk in, followed by Emilio and Tony. I don't recognize the first two, but the one that follows is one of Lorenzo's bodyguards. Their hands are tied behind their backs, and they have bruises all over their faces. Emilio nudges one of them with his gun, and the guy stumbles. I shift my gaze to Lorenzo, who's sitting rigidly in his chair, staring at the tied men.

"To the kitchen, as well. I'll take care of them later." Luca crosses his arms over his chest and turns to Lorenzo. "I wonder, what did you promise Davide? A capo's position when you take over the Family after I'm out of the picture? Was that the plan?"

"I have no idea what you're talking about," Lorenzo mumbles.

"No?" Luca smiles and leans into Lorenzo's face. "There was one thing that kept bugging me. Why haven't you tried again? And then it came to me. You knew I didn't remember anything. Tell me, what gave me away?"

Lorenzo watches him for a couple of seconds, then grits his teeth. "I found the doctor who treated you when you were admitted to the hospital."

"But you needed to be sure, didn't you? Before you revealed it to the Family. So, you brought Davide with you to the lunch yesterday to see how I'd react. And when that failed, you brought him here. I'm so sorry for ruining your plan."

"You took my place!" Lorenzo sneers. "It was mine! I spent decades licking Giuseppe's ass, and then you barged in, married this cunt, and fucked up everything!"

Someone gasps at a table nearby, but other than that, the room remains eerily silent.

Luca leaps from the chair, grabs Lorenzo's hair and smashes his face on the tabletop. The plates and silverware clatter from the force of the blow. Lorenzo flails, reaches for Luca's hand and tries to wriggle free, but Luca just slams his face into the table again. And again. The tableware clinks and rattles each time. Two of the plates and several glasses end up falling to the floor, the shattering of china and crystal adding to the symphony of brutality.

The gasps and murmurs among the guests continue while my husband does his best to beat the living shit out of Barbini. Eventually, Luca pulls Lorenzo up, still holding him by the hair. "Apologize to my wife."

I lean back in my chair, staring at the bloody mess of Lorenzo's face. He looks up, then spits in my general direction, bloodied spittle soiling the white tablecloth.

The eyes of the people in the room dart between Luca and Lorenzo, waiting for what will happen next.

"You know, I'm okay with you trying to kill me," Luca says, and he looks down at the table. "That's business. You tried. Failed. I shoot you in the head, and we all go back to our merry lives." He reaches for a corkscrew on the table, then steps closer to Lorenzo.

"But no one disrespects my wife, Lorenzo," Luca barks, then looks up at Marco and Emilio who are standing behind the underboss. "Hold him down."

Luca's men grip Lorenzo, keeping him in the chair. As I watch, my husband plunges the corkscrew into the side of Lorenzo's neck, just under the ear. Lorenzo screams and tries to get up off the chair, but Marco and Emilio push him back down and keep a hold of him as Luca rips the corkscrew out. Blood sprays from the wound, soaking the front of Luca's shirt, as well as Marco's hands. Several of the guests shriek.

"Did I hear an apology?" Luca bends his head as if to hear what Lorenzo is saying, but the only sounds that leave Barbini's mouth are choking noises. "Nope, I don't think it was an apology," he says and thrusts the corkscrew into Lorenzo's neck again, from the front this time.

I shut my eyes, not able to watch the bloodbath anymore. But I can't shut out the whimpering. The choking sounds. I swallow bile.

A minute or so later, the choking sounds cease, and I will myself to open my eyes. Luca is standing in front of Lorenzo, corkscrew in hand. His right arm is covered in blood. His front, too. I move my gaze to Lorenzo, or really his body, and gasp. There's a long red line around his neck, blood pouring from at least a dozen puncture wounds and flowing down his torso. Bile gathers in my throat from seeing all the blood. Grinding my teeth together, I take a deep breath and force myself to remain still. I am not fainting with the whole Family watching.

Luca turns around, pins me with his gaze and throws the bloody corkscrew on the table. I follow him with my eyes as he covers the distance between us in a few long steps and stands before me while everyone stares at him.

"I'm sorry for ruining your party, tesoro."

I blink at him. Should I say something?

"Let's go upstairs." He takes my hand with his blood-free one and leads me toward the foyer and then up the two flights of stairs.

When we reach the bedroom, Luca heads straight to shower. I walk toward the bed, sit down at the edge and wait, my eyes glued to the bathroom door. I've just witnessed a man being slaughtered in front of me, but instead of processing that, I'm freaking out because Luca, obviously, remembers everything.

What happens now? Will he throw me out? Divorce me? I don't think I can live in the same house with him if he goes back to his old self, but just the thought of not being close to him makes me want to scream. The sound of the water stops, and I hold my breath.

The bathroom door opens and Luca steps out, naked. His hair is wet and falling on either side of his face, just like in my first memory of him. I stand up and watch him approach, waiting. When he's right in front of me, he lifts his hand and takes my chin, tilting my head up.

"I'm sorry for lying to you," I whisper.

He bends his head until our noses are barely an inch apart. "About what?"

"About you being in love with me," I choke out.

The corners of Luca's lips curve up. "But you weren't lying, Isabella." His hand leaves my chin to travel down along my neck and chest, then around my waist to the small of my back. "You see, I was already crazy about you, way before the crash."

My breath catches. I open my mouth to say something, but nothing comes out.

"I'm so sorry for being a moron, Isa. For pushing you away, even after I fell in love with you" The arm around my midsection tightens, pressing me against his body. "I was afraid that you were too young."

"You were wrong," I say, while happy tears gather at the corners of my eyes. I never dared to hope that I'd hear those words leave his lips.

"I know." He presses his lips to mine. "Will you let me show you how sorry I am?"

"Maybe."

Luca's eyes flare. "Maybe?"

I raise my arms to brush my fingers into his wet strands and look straight into his eyes. "You're going to fuck me. First with your mouth. Then your hand. And finally, with your cock."

"All right."

"But, Luca . . ." I squeeze his hair. "You're not allowed to come until you have me absolutely sated."

A wicked smile spreads across his lips, and the next moment, I find myself thrown onto the bed.

"I don't think I've ever told you,"—he says as he crawls up over my body—"how utterly in love I am with your cunning mind."

"Just my mind?" I ask, then gasp when a tearing sound fills the room. "For God's sake, Luca. Stop destroying my clothes."

"I will destroy anything that comes between me and your body." A kiss lands at the side of my neck, then his mouth moves lower, across my collarbone and chest, to my breasts. I reach behind my back and quickly unclasp the bra so it won't also end up destroyed.

Luca's huge hands cup my breasts, squeezing lightly. "I love your pretty boobs." He bites at my left one, then the right. "As well as the rest of your body." He trails kisses down my stomach. "And your greedy little pussy."

He takes the waistband of my panties, and an instant later, a bundle of torn beige lace lands on the floor. I grip at his hair, panting, as he slowly removes the pussy plug. A moan leaves my lips when he buries his face between my legs and sucks on my clit.

"I've changed my mind, I need your cock, now," I whimper. The need to have it inside me is making me insane. Luca grabs my legs and throws them over his shoulders.

"Not yet." His tongue slides between my folds, and I shudder.

Luca laps at my pussy, switching between licking and sucking as if it's an ice cream, and the pressure between my legs builds until I feel like I'm going to melt from the inside. I arch my back, pulling at the long dark strands between my fingers, pushing his head down even more. My body is already shaking when he starts slowly sliding his finger inside. I come before it's even halfway in.

"You even taste like fucking vanilla, Isa," Luca says as he licks away all my wetness, then lowers my legs and hovers over me. His finger is still inside my pussy, pumping in and out, milking me even more.

"So, you're not mad that I lied?" I whisper against his lips.

"You weren't lying. I already told you,"—he adds another finger, thrusting deeper—"I fell for you way before I lost my memories, tesoro. For your stubborn personality. For the way you stood your ground and fought me every time I acted like an idiot."

"Yes, you did that quite often." I grab his thick arm and ride his fingers.

"I'm sorry." There's a bite on my chin, and another one at the side of my neck. "From now on, I promise I'll treat you like I should have from the start."

"And how would that be?"

His fingers still for a moment, but then he thrusts them inside so hard I gasp. "Like a fucking queen, Isabella."

His words. His fingers. Him. It's too much.

I come again, tears in my eyes and a wide smile on my lips.

Luca's arm encircles me, and he flips me around until I'm on my stomach. "And now, I'm going to royally fuck you. With your magnificent noble ass on display the whole time." He grips my hips, lifts my pelvis, and buries himself inside of me.

I grab at the headboard and hold on with all my might as Luca rocks into me from behind, trying to match my breathing to his tempo. Him, inside—I take a deep breath. Exhale when he slides out. I don't think I'm getting enough air because I'm feeling lightheaded. It could be due to the lack of oxygen or maybe because I'm going to come for the third time in under ten minutes, and my body has trouble processing that. Luca's hand moves between my legs, and his fingers find my clit. He slams into me again, pressing onto my bud at the same time, and white stars burst behind my eyelids. I scream as I come, the sounds mixing with his groans as he explodes into me.

A kiss at the base of my neck, then another one. "Are you asleep?"

I open my eyes and throw a look over my shoulder. "Yes. And I'm half dead, so you can forget about it."

It's been an hour since he destroyed me in the best possible way, and I still can't make myself move.

"Are you sure?" He pushes his finger even deeper inside of me.

"Yes, I'm—"

*BANG!*

I go stone-still. "Was that a gunshot?"

"Sounds like it." Luca moves his lips to my shoulder.

"Are you not going check what's going on?"

"We have over forty security men on the premises at the moment. Let them earn their paychecks."

Another gunshot rings out somewhere in the garden, and then the sound of male yelling reaches us through the window.

"You piece of shit! I'm going to fucking kill you!"

I look at Luca. "That sounded like Franco."

"Jesus fuck." He shakes his head, reaches for his phone, and calls someone. "Marco, is my brother still alive?"

"He was two minutes ago when he ran out of the house in only his pants. Unbuttoned," Marco's voice comes across the line. "Mr. Conti found him with Miss Arianna in the library."

"Perfect. Should I come down?"

"I think it would be a good idea, Boss."

Luca ends the call and looks down at me. "I'm going downstairs to deal with Franco and shoo the rest of the guests out of our home. I'd hoped they leave after the bloodshed."

"Are you kidding? It'll be the main source of gossip for the next six months."

He slides his hand to my ass and squeezes my butt cheek. "I'll be back in twenty. Then we'll continue."

"Of course, Luca." I smirk.

His eyes flare and he bends his head until his lips touch mine. "I love you, my beautiful, cunning Isa."

# Epilogue

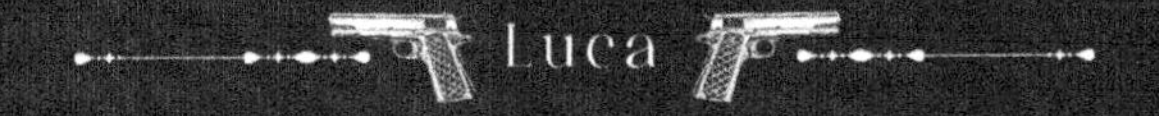


*Four years later*

My phone on the nightstand rings. I put down the folder I've been holding and pick up the phone with my left hand since my right one is cupping Isabella's pussy, my finger buried inside. And unless there's a fire or something similar, I don't plan on removing it. I look at the screen showing the caller's name and furrow my eyebrows.

"Who is it?" Isabella mumbles sleepily.

"Salvatore Ajello," I say and take the call. "Yes?"

"Mr. Rossi. We may have a problem."

"Something regarding the last construction project?"

"No. This is a personal matter," he says. "There's something of yours here. Something that shouldn't have been in my city, Mr. Rossi."

Jesus fuck. If someone from our Family was crazy enough to enter the New York region without permission, he's dead, and there's nothing I can do about it.

"Who is it?" I ask.

There are a few moments of silence before he finally answers.

"Milene Scardoni."

PERFECTLY IMPERFECT
BOOK FIVE

# STOLEN

PERFECTLY IMPERFECT SERIES

# *touches*

*Salvatore & Milene*

# AUTHOR'S NOTE

Dear reader, there are a few Italian words mentioned in the book, so here are the translations and clarifications:

*Cara*—dear; endearment.

*Vita mia*—"my life"; endearment.

# Trigger Warning

Please be aware that this book contains content that some readers may find disturbing, such as: gore, abuse, and graphic descriptions of violence and torture.

# Prologue

## Salvatore

*Seven years ago*

A hammer comes down onto my hand, its metal head burying into flesh that's already a swollen mess, and a fine spray of blood splatters across the table.

I wait until the worst of the pain recedes, then lift my chin and glare at the man looming above me.

"No." I bite out.

Marcello, one of the capos, watches me for a couple of seconds before he throws a glance over his shoulder at the don who is leaning against the wall to the right. It's dim in the room, no buzz or glare from the fluorescent tubes on the ceiling. The only illumination seeps from an old lamp on the corner of the table, but when the don lights his cigar, his face glows red from the flame as he nods.

Marcello turns back to me and tightens his hold around my wrist. "I think you should reconsider," he sneers and brings the hammer down heavily onto my fingers once more.

Searing pain shoots up along the length of my arm, zinging through my shoulder and sending a lightning strike straight to the back of my head. The sensation takes hold in my brain, making a home for itself inside my skull. I clench my teeth in an effort to block it out.

"Fuck you, Marcello," I rasp.

He laughs and shakes his head. "You really are something."

Marcello sets the hammer down on the table and takes a gun from his holster. I assume he'll simply shoot me in the head, but instead, he points the weapon at my leg. "I think I've fucked up your hand enough. You probably can't feel it anymore. How about this?"

Two gunshots ring out, and I roar in agony as bullets tear through flesh and bone. Black spots blur my vision.

"Last chance, Salvatore," he barks.

I take a deep breath, ignore the worthless bastard, and make direct eye contact with the don, who is still standing at the same spot in the dark corner. It's too dark for me to see his eyes clearly, but with the lamp so close to my face, I'm sure he can see mine. My unharmed hand is tied to the arm of the chair, but I rotate my wrist enough to raise my middle finger at him, the rope chafing my skin.

"He won't cave, Marcello," the don says and turns to leave. "Just kill him and be done with it."

Marcello waits until the door closes, then circles around the chair I'm tied to and leans down to whisper into my ear. "I've always hated your guts. I don't know what the don was thinking when he let you take your father's place two years ago. Making a twenty-four-year-old a capo, as though we're running a fucking kindergarten or something."

"I understand how that must unnerve you, Marcello." I take a deep breath while the dark patches continue to cloud my vision. "Especially since I've made more money for the Family in my two years as a capo than you have after twenty in the same position."

"I should leave you here to bleed out." He spits on the floor and sends another bullet into my foot.

"That wouldn't," I choke out, "be wise."

"Why not?"

"Because if I don't die . . . you will."

He laughs. "Yes, we shouldn't risk it."

Three rapid gunshots echo through the room, and I gasp as a sharp, burning pain explodes in my back. I manage one forced breath before everything fades to black.

# one

## Salvatore

*Present*

"MOVE, YOU IDIOT!"

My head snaps up as I step to the side, avoiding an elbow to my kidney, and stare at the woman in scrubs who rushes past me. She's running toward a car that screeches to a halt a few feet in front of me in the middle of the hospital parking lot.

A teenage boy, not more than fifteen, jumps out of the driver's side. It's clear he's not been to a hospital before, given he's driven to the parking lot and not the emergency entrance. He opens the door at the same time the nurse reaches the vehicle. For a few seconds, they both stare into the back seat.

"Is that . . . the head?" the boy stutters. "Why is . . .? Mom, you said we had time."

A woman's moans fill the air as the boy, horrified and as white as a sheet of paper, keeps his eyes on the back seat.

"Kid! Hey!" The nurse grabs the boy's forearm and shakes him, but he's not responding. "Kid. Focus!" She slaps him lightly on his face. "Get inside the hospital. Find a doctor and drag them out here."

"Aren't . . . aren't you a doctor?"

"I'm just a nurse. The information stated your mom was having contractions, not that she was in full-blown labor. Go. Now!" she snaps, turns toward the car and kneels down on the concrete, placing her hands on the seat in front of her. "It's okay, Mama. Breathe for me. It's okay. When the pain comes, I need you to push, all right? What's your name?"

The woman in the car whimpers and says something I don't catch, probably answering the nurse's question, then cries out again.

"I'm Milene," the nurse says. "You're doing great, Jenny. Yes, breathe. One more time, the head is already out. Just one more push, but make it count."

The nurse looks over her shoulder at the hospital entrance, then off to the side until her gaze lands on me. "You! Suit guy!" she yells. "Come here!"

I cock my head and take in the sight of her. The first thing I notice are her eyes, but not the color. I'm too far away to see that detail. There is a mixture of panic and determination in them that captures my gaze. In any other situation, I would have ignored a similar request and walked away. Other people's lives don't interest me in the least. But I find myself unable to move my gaze from the girl. It takes quite a lot of determination to keep a level head in a situation like this. Slowly, I approach the car, my eyes not leaving the nurse who is, once again, focused on the woman in the car and doling out instructions. The nurse's hair is a very light shade of blonde, and it's gathered into a ponytail, which hangs in disarray.

"Give me your jacket," she says without looking in my direction, as the woman in the car lets out a deep groan. "That's it, Jenny. That's it. I have her."

Her voice is trembling only slightly, but it's impossible to miss the panicked look on her face. It amazes me, how she keeps it together. And, after everything I've seen and done in my lifetime, not many things amaze me anymore.

Suddenly, a baby's cry pierces the space around us.

They say a child's first cry should melt even the coldest of hearts, but it does nothing for me. Not that I expected it would. I've just witnessed a new life entering the world, but it elicited exactly the same emotional response as the changing of a traffic light.

None.

I take off my jacket, intending to lay it over the car door and leave, but my gaze falls on the nurse's face and my breath catches in my throat. She's looking at the baby in her arms, smiling with such awe and joy it makes her face glow. It's so unguarded and so sincere I can't force my eyes away from her lips. I felt nothing at the supposed miracle of life, but a strange sensation suddenly tightens my chest while looking at her, and with it, a foreign feeling of . . . wanting. I squeeze the jacket in my hand, trying to decipher the meaning of this unbidden urge to grab the girl's face and turn her to me so I might claim her smile for myself. I don't have a good name for what's overtaken me. Perhaps . . . yearning?

From the corner of my eye, I catch sight of two women in white coats exiting the hospital and running in our direction. Behind them, a male nurse is pushing a gurney.

"You did great, Jenny. I'll put her on your chest. Open your shirt," the nurse says, then turns to me, her hand extended. I give her my Armani jacket and watch as she leans inside the car to cover the baby.

"Jesus, Milene." One of the doctors who'd just arrived gasps. "We'll take it from here, honey. You did great."

The blonde nurse—Milene—nods and rises up from the asphalt. Her joyful expression is replaced by confusion, as though she's only now registering what's taken place. I have an urge to grab the person responsible for extinguishing her smile and punish them for it, but there is no one to blame. It's the situation itself. Still, the need to kill someone doesn't leave me.

The young nurse heads toward the hospital entrance but stops after a few steps and leans against a parked car. With her head bent, she stares at her trembling hands which are smeared with blood, then frantically starts brushing them on the front of her scrubs. She's very young. Early twenties. Maybe twenty-two or twenty-three, at most. It was probably her first delivery, but she held herself together well and I can't help but admire her for it. When her hands are somewhat clean, she pushes off the car and resumes her trek, but stumbles. Taking a step to the side, she leans against the next car and closes her eyes.

I should leave. Just turn around, go to my car, and drive home. But I can't. It's like my whole being is focused on the blonde nurse. She seems so lost and vulnerable. So instead of doing the reasonable thing, I cover the distance between us and stand right in front of her. Suddenly, a crazy compulsion to reach out and touch her face overwhelms me but I stifle that ridiculous urge and just observe her instead. Her eyes open, and she looks up at me. Dark green.

"The jacket guy," she says and closes her eyes again. "You can leave your name and address at the information desk. I'll make sure they send your jacket back."

Her voice sounds steady, but her hands are still shaking, as is the rest of her body. Post-adrenaline crash. I throw a look over my shoulder. There are only thirty yards between us and the hospital entrance, but I doubt she can manage the small distance in this state. Her legs are trembling so badly I expect them to fold under her at any second. She could trip on her way back to the building and hurt herself. I'm not sure why that possibility bothers me.

I bend and scoop her small frame into my arms. A yelp of surprise escapes the girl's lips, but she doesn't immediately complain. She simply wraps her arms around my neck and stares back at me with wide eyes. We're halfway to the entrance when she starts to wriggle, almost knocking me off balance.

"Put me down." More wriggling, "I can walk, damn it."

I continue to march forward with her in my arms as she keeps hitting my chest with her tiny fists, trying to slip from my grip. Although she can't weigh more than a hundred pounds, her fidgeting does make the task bothersome. If she doesn't stop, we could both end up facedown on the pavement.

I turn my head, and our noses accidentally touch. She has freckles, I notice.

"Stop," I say, and the wriggling ceases.

She opens her mouth, as if she's about to argue with me, but I squeeze my arms around her in warning. No one is allowed to disobey my orders. The girl closes her mouth and scrunches her nose at me but says nothing. Wise. I turn my head back toward the entrance and walk on.

"Was he hot?" Andrea, my best friend, asks.

I lodge the phone between my shoulder and cheek and take out some leftovers from the fridge to have for dinner.

"I guess," I say and pile the food onto my plate. I haven't eaten anything since breakfast.

"What kind of answer is that? Was he or not?"

"He was. Tall. Expensive suit. Dark hair, a little salt-and-pepper in places. He smelled nice." Very, very nice. I can still smell his cologne on my T-shirt.

"Gray hairs? How old was that guy?"

"Midthirties. Probably going prematurely gray." I place the plate in the microwave, setting the timer to one minute. Not nearly enough time for the food to warm up sufficiently, but it'll have to do. I'm too hungry to wait any longer than that.

"And he didn't say anything? His name?"

"Nope. Just carried me inside the hospital lobby, set me down, then turned around and left."

"Well, I can't say that I'm surprised. You've always attracted weirdos." Andrea laughs. "Is that anesthesiologist, Randy, still stalking you?"

"Yup." I sit at the small table in the corner with my plate and dig in. "He sent me flowers again yesterday. Carnations this time. I mean, what the fuck? They're for funerals."

"Was there another creepy note?"

"Yeah. Something about my skin shining like moonlight. I threw up a little in my mouth." My cat jumps onto the table, sticks his nose in my cup and laps my water. I tap him with a kitchen rag on the head. "Down, damn you!"

"Do you think that Randy guy is dangerous?" Andrea asks. "He's been stalking you for months."

"I don't think so. He'll find someone else to pester soon, hopefully. What's going on in Chicago?" I load another heaped forkful of food into my mouth.

"I saw your brother the other day. He still thinks you're in Illinois."

"Good. Please make sure you don't slip up in front of him. Angelo will flip if he finds out I'm in New York."

"You should come back to Chicago, Milene. It's not safe. What if someone from the New York Family finds out you're there?" She switches to whispering. "Ajello doesn't allow members of other Cosa Nostra Families on his territory without approval. You know that very well."

"I doubt the notorious Don Ajello would tire himself out over poor little me," I mumble between bites, "and anyway, I have to finish my residency. I'll be coming back as soon as I'm done." The cat jumps up onto the table again, steals a piece of meat off my plate, and dashes toward the bathroom. "One of these days, I'm going to strangle this cat."

"You've been saying that for weeks." Andrea laughs.

"He came home with a fucking chicken wing yesterday. And a piece of fish two days before. The neighbors will think I've trained him to steal food for me." I yawn. "I'll call you tomorrow. I can't keep my eyes open."

"All right. If you run into that sexy stranger again, be sure to get his number."

"Yeah, sure."

I cut the call and drag myself to the bed on the other side of my apartment. The whole thing is smaller than my bedroom back home, but it's paid for with my own money, and I wouldn't change it for the world. I haven't told Andrea or anyone else yet, but I don't plan on going back to Chicago. Ever.

I'm done with all the Cosa Nostra crap.

A sharp rap sounds on my office door. I look up from the laptop to see my head of security enter and nod toward the chair on the other side of the desk.

"Did you find the girl?" I ask.

"Yes. And you won't believe this." Nino sits down and crosses his arms in front of his chest. "She's Milene Scardoni. The youngest sister of one of Chicago's capos, Angelo Scardoni."

I lean back in my chair. What an unusual turn of events. "You're sure?"

"Yes. She's the only Milene who works at St. Mary's. I checked her social media as well." He takes out his phone, scrolls through it for a couple of seconds, then slides it across the desk toward me. "Not many photos there, but I found two where she's with her sister. The one who married into the Bratva. They look very much alike. And I found several photos with Rossi's sister-in-law, Andrea. It's her, Boss."

I pick up the phone from the desk and look down at the screen. The photo is a couple of years old. Her hair is shorter. She's standing with another girl of about the same age. Milene is smiling, and her palm is fully extended in front of her mouth, sending a kiss toward the camera. With full lips and a tiny nose, she is beautiful. But, it's not her flawless features that attract my attention. It's her eyes. Big, luminous green orbs that seem as though they are looking right at me, twinkling with joy and mischief. I move my thumb over the screen until I reach her lips and trace their contours.

"The sister of a Chicago capo. In my territory." I put the phone back on the desk, but I can't stop staring at the image. It seems so genuine, her smile. How would it feel to have someone smile at me like that?

"Do you want me to send someone to drag her in here?" Nino asks. "Or will you call Rossi so he can handle the problem himself?"

I force my eyes away from the screen, unnerved by the fact a random woman who I've just met has managed to invoke such an unhealthy interest. I stand up and walk toward the large window overlooking the city. Calling

Luca Rossi, the Chicago don, would be the best course of action. He'll send someone to collect her and take her back to Chicago.

"No," I say, staring at the street below. The rain had begun an hour earlier. It started as drizzle but grew into a full-blown downpour. I wonder how much darker her hair is when it's wet. "Put someone on her. Do you know where she lives?"

"I checked. Some dump in the suburbs."

"Alone?"

"She has a cat."

"I want cameras planted in her place," I say. "Kitchen, living room, bedrooms, but not in the bathroom."

Nino says nothing, so I turn to find him regarding me with a slightly shocked expression on his face. We've known each other for two decades, so it's no wonder my request stuns him. I'm baffled by it too.

"I had a look inside from the fire escape," he says quickly. "It's a two hundred-square-foot studio. Just one room."

What the hell is a capo's sister doing, working her ass off as a nurse, living in a studio in the suburbs?

"Put two cameras to cover the whole space," I say. "I want it done in the next twenty-four hours, and set the recordings to stream directly to my laptop. No one else is to have access."

"Consider it done." Nino gets up to leave but looks at me over his shoulder. "If I may ask, where did you unearth her?"

"In front of St. Mary's. I was going home after a semiannual checkup." I turn back to the window. "She called me an idiot, almost knocked me over, and then delivered a baby in the middle of a parking lot. She also confiscated my jacket in the course of this escapade."

Nino bursts out laughing behind me. "Well, I see why you found her interesting."

Yes. I find Milene Scardoni very interesting.

# Chapter Two

Salvatore

I LIE BACK IN MY BED, POWER UP THE LAPTOP, AND CLICK THROUGH TO the surveillance feed from the Scardoni girl's apartment, as I have done every evening for the past week. The first evening I did it, I told myself it's just a benign interest, convinced it was just some passing fixation. I would have a quick look, turn off the feed and go to sleep. I ended up watching the whole recording. And I've done the same every damn evening since. The need to see her is too strong to ignore.

Backtracking the recording to this morning, when she would have returned from her night shift, I hit enter and play the video.

The place is a goddamned shoebox, and two cameras are enough to cover every inch. I watch Milene as she comes in, almost stumbles over the sleeping cat in the middle of the entranceway, and disappears into the bathroom. Ten minutes later, she comes out, wearing an oversized T-shirt, drags herself to bed, and slides beneath the blanket. She pulls the corner close in a comforting embrace. Not a minute later, her idiot cat jumps onto the bed. It's a muddy gray, skinny, and part of its tail seems to be missing. Did she pick it out of a dumpster? The cat prowls toward the foot of the bed, then taps and scratches Milene's feet, which are poking out from under the covers.

There is no audio, so when Milene springs up off the bed, I can only see her lips move. From the expression on her face, she's yelling. The cat dashes under the bed. Milene lies back down, but the instant she pulls the blanket up again, the cat returns. It stalks toward Milene's head, extends its front paw and bats her nose. She doesn't react, even though the cat touches her a few more times. The damn thing is persistent. Milene reaches out her hand to grab the cat around its middle, hugging it close to her side and buries her face into the pillow.

I zoom in on the video and watch her sleeping form, illuminated by the midday sunlight streaming in through the window. The cat turned around at some point and has its head pressed against Milene's neck.

Why the hell is she living in that dump? I had Nino check her accounts. Her brother is depositing a huge sum of money every month, but she doesn't withdraw anything. She only uses her second account, the one where she receives her meager monthly paycheck. I wonder if Scardoni knows she's in New York. Probably not. I should have called Rossi the moment I found out who she was. Instead, I kept spying on her, night after night, and it became an urge. It's ridiculous. But I can't stop.

Trying to ignore the phantom pain in my left foot, I skip the recording ahead to around seven in the evening when Milene startles and sits up in her bed. She stares at the front door for a second, wraps the blanket around herself as she gets out of bed, and heads in the direction of the entrance. She's halfway there when that stupid cat dashes toward her, grabs the corner of the blanket that's dragging along the floor, and darts between her legs. Milene stumbles. The cat jumps onto the dresser and pushes a decorative basket onto the floor, along with a stack of papers and other items. Milene regards the mess at her feet, shakes her head, and proceeds toward the door.

A delivery guy holding a huge bouquet of red roses in his arms comes into view. They exchange a few words, then he leaves with the flowers, and Milene heads into the kitchen with some kind of note in her hand. She stops next to the trash can, reads it, and frowns. Rolling her eyes, she throws the note in the garbage.

I take my phone from the nightstand, send a message to Nino instructing him to find out who sent the damn flowers, and resume watching.

I follow Milene as she scrambles some eggs on the stove, drumming my fingers onto the laptop the whole time. Did she send the flowers away because she didn't like roses? The thought of some other man sending her flowers burns in the pit of my stomach. Maybe it was the color. I grab my phone again and call my secretary. When she takes the call, I let her know what I need. There are a few moments of utter silence before she quickly mumbles she'll have the florist call me right away. My phone rings five minutes later.

"Mr. Ajello. It's Diana from the flower boutique. Please let me know what you need, and I'll arrange everything for you," she chirps.

“I need flowers to be sent tomorrow morning.”

“Of course. Would you like something specific? We have amazing red roses from the Netherlands and—”

“I’ll take everything you have, except red roses.”

“Oh? All of our roses except the red ones? Absolutely. Where—”

“I said everything, Diana,” I say. “Write down the address. I need them delivered at six in the morning.”

When I finish the call with the florist, I place the phone on the keyboard in front of me and stare at it. I’ve never bought flowers for anyone. So where the fuck has this insane need to do so now come from?

“Shit,” I mumble, fumbling with the deadbolt lock.

I forgot to turn on my alarm and almost slept in. The knob turns finally, and I open my front door, intending to dash down the hallway but stop at the threshold. There won’t be any running down the corridor, that’s for sure. I’ll be lucky if I manage to reach the stairway because it looks like some delivery company fucked up. Big time.

Both sides of the entire length of the hallway passage—which is around eighty feet long—are filled with huge bowls and vases, all overflowing with flowers. Each arrangement consists of a different type of flower—white roses, yellow roses, peach roses, daisies, lilies, tulips, and a bunch of others I don’t recognize. Every bouquet has a big satin bow tied around the vase in a color that matches the flowers.

“Jesus,” I mumble, staring at the sea of flowers, wondering how I’m going to reach the stairway without knocking any of them over.

“Milene!” a raspy female voice yells.

I turn my head and find my landlady standing at the top of the stairwell with her hands on her hips.

“I need you to get these out of the hallway. People need to go to work,” she continues.

“They’re not mine,” I say, looking over the explosion of colors.

“The note says they are.”

My head snaps back to the right. “The note?”

She lifts a hand holding a pink envelope. "The delivery guys said to give this to you."

"It must be a mistake."

"It has your name on it."

I step into the corridor, trying my best not to knock anything over, and head toward her. I have to walk in a zigzag pattern around what must be at least a hundred vases.

"Let me see," I say and lean over a large arrangement of white roses to grab the envelope. She's right. It has my name on it. I glance over my shoulder, gaping at all the flowers, then slide the note from the envelope.

*Pick what you like.*

*Give away those you don't.*

I blink. Read it again. Turn it over. There is no signature. Who the fuck buys thousands of dollars' worth of flowers and tells the recipient to give away what they don't like? Was it Randy? I don't think so. Besides, the note doesn't have a cheesy one-liner, and he always writes one. I look down the hallway again and do a quick calculation. Each of those vases must have cost a hundred bucks. Probably more. So, the total would be . . .. My head snaps back to the landlady, my eyes wide. Holy. Fuck.

"I need those out of the hallway," she grumbles and turns to leave. "You have thirty minutes."

What the hell am I going to do with all this? And who's the maniac who bought what looks like an entire flower shop? This is a special level of crazy.

I take my phone out and call Pippa, my friend from work.

"Can you get me the phone number from one of the guys working in the hospital laundry service?" I ask.

"Laundry service?"

"Yup. I need a favor. And a truck," I say, looking at the flowers. "A big one."

# Chapter Three

Salvatore

I close my laptop and regard the man kneeling in the opposite corner of my office. Nino is holding him by the hair, yelling into his face.

"I asked, who do you work for, Octavio?" he shouts and punches the man in the face. "You ratted on us? To the DEA?"

"It wasn't me, Nino. I swear it wasn't me!"

"Who else is working with you, selling info?" Another blow. Two teeth fly across the office in a mess of spittle and blood, leaving red stains on the wall.

"I want a name, Octavio!" Nino keeps yelling.

I take the phone from my desk and open the surveillance app, bringing up the feed from Milene's apartment. During the past week, I periodically began checking the live video stream over the course of the day. I still watched the entire day's recording in the evenings, but that had ceased to provide me with a strong enough fix. I've developed an inexplicable need to know where she is and what she's doing.

The screen lights up with the view of Milene's place. She kept the white roses and daisies, and they're on her kitchen table. I expected to find Milene watching TV or reading, which is what she usually does in the evenings when she's not at work. Instead, I see her rushing around the room, wearing only a matching set of black lace lingerie. With my elbows on the desk, I lean forward and squeeze the phone in my hand.

Milene removes a silver dress from a hanger in the small closet and a pair of black high heels from the bottom. She puts the dress on first. It's short, tight, and glitters like an old-style disco ball. I grip the phone in my hand even harder. The T-shirts she wears in bed hang lower than that dress. It barely covers her ass. Milene slips on the heels and shoos away the ragged feline sleeping on her coat. Picking up the jacket, she leaves the apartment.

"Nino, who's on the Scardoni girl?" I ask.

Nino looks up, his attention shifting away from his methodical task of breaking Octavio's fingers. "It should be Pietro's turn."

I find Pietro's number and call him. "Where is she?"

"Getting into a cab," he says.

"Follow. Let me know where she goes." I cut the call, take out my gun, and walk over to Octavio, who's still kneeling but is only half-conscious.

"The name of the other snitch, Octavio," I demand.

"I don't know, Boss. I swear . . ."

I raise the gun, shoot him once at point blank range in the head, and turn to Nino. "Call maintenance. I need my office cleaned by morning. I have a meeting at eight. Did he have a family?"

"A wife."

"Send someone with money. A hundred grand should do it. Make sure she knows what will happen if she doesn't keep her mouth shut."

"Okay. Anything else?"

"Have someone paint over that." I nod toward the wall behind Octavio's body. "His brains are all over it."

"Are you going out?"

"Yes."

"Should I send backup?"

"No," I say and pin him with my gaze. "Don't you send anyone to follow me. I've already told you to lose that habit of yours."

"I'm your chief of security. How do you expect me to do my job if you don't let me?"

"Up to now, I've been pretending not to notice the guys you put on my tail. Not tonight, Nino."

"Okay, Boss."

As I'm heading toward the garage, Pietro calls and gives me the address of a bar downtown. When I get in my car, I check the location on my phone. Almost an hour away. Fuck. I hit the steering wheel with my palm and rev the engine.

I lean back against the bar and lift my glass to take a sip of my drink when I notice a man in navy pants and white shirt entering. Shit.

"For God's sake, Pip." I groan. "Did you seriously invite Randy on our girls' night out?"

"Of course not." Pippa follows my gaze. "I might have mentioned it at some point. We were on the night shift together on Wednesday, but I definitely didn't ask him to come along."

"Fucking great." I take a big gulp of my drink and watch Randy approach, a broad grin plastered on his dull-as-dishwater face.

"Girls! What can I get you?"

"We're good, thanks," I mumble.

I've told Randy so many times that I don't want to go out with him, but he won't leave me alone. If this goes on much longer, I don't know what I'm going to do. I can't tell him off for asking me out and sending me flowers. That would be rude. Also, he's a doctor who's been working at St. Mary's for five years, and I'm just a nurse completing the residency program. If it comes down to a public confrontation, everybody will take his side. Anaesthesiologists are hard to find.

"Would you like to go see a movie next week?" he asks.

"Randy, please. I've already told you that I'm not going out with you."

"I have to pee," Pippa jumps off her chair.

"Now?" I glare at her. I don't want to be alone with Randy.

"I really need to go. I'll be back in five."

The moment Pippa's gone, Randy places his hand over mine. "Come on, Milene. Just one date."

"No." I pull my hand away "Can you please leave?"

"Why are you being so difficult? It's—"

Randy stops midsentence and looks over my shoulder. At the same time, an arm wraps around my waist.

"Sorry I'm late," a deep baritone resonates next to my ear.

My body stiffens. I recognize that voice. He only spoke one word in the parking lot, but it's hard to forget a voice like his. I turn my head and look up. The jacket guy. I blink at him, slightly stunned. It was early evening when we met before, and I wasn't exactly in the best mental state, so I'd failed to fully take in his appearance. This time, my attention is more focused, and I'm seeing him clearly. Black suit, with a black shirt underneath. Both surely expensive. His face is all sharp lines and edges, as if carved in hard granite. He has an aristocratic air about him. The jacket guy is seriously hot.

"Milene?" Randy asks. "Who's your friend?"

I smile at Randy. "This is Kurt. My boyfriend."

"Boyfriend?" Randy asks while still staring at the jacket guy behind me. "Pippa said you broke up with him."

"We had a fight, and I was angry, but we're back together now." I grin.

The arm around my waist tightens, and I find myself plastered against the muscular chest at my back.

"And we're getting married in December," the jacket guy says as he looks down at me. "Aren't we, Goldie?"

Kurt and Goldie? I press my lips together, trying not to laugh. "Yup. December first." How can he keep a straight face? "So you really need to stop asking me out, Randy. Kurt doesn't like that one bit."

Randy looks at the jacket guy, mumbles a sort of goodbye, and reluctantly heads toward the exit. The arm around my middle vanishes and I feel a pang of disappointment.

"Thanks for the save," I say, reaching for my glass on the bar. "So, it's a small world after all."

The jacket guy regards me for a second, then moves even closer, leaning against the bar next to my stool. He has more gray than I thought, mostly at his temples, but also some up top. It's unusual, but somehow the effect complements his face and those light brown eyes.

"Why Kurt?"

"I rewatched *Tango and Cash* yesterday. It was the first name that came to mind." I shrug. "What's your real name?"

"Kurt works for me just fine, Goldie."

"Oh, a man of mystery?" I bring the glass to my lips, but it's him I'm drinking in with my eyes. I don't remember ever meeting a man with such a powerful presence before. He commands attention just by being in the room, and his looks seem to have little to do with it. "So, what do you do in life, Kurt?"

"You could say that I'm in management." He tilts his head, and a strange look lights his eyes, as if he's trying to figure me out. "And you? Delivered any more babies recently?"

"God, no. I'm still trying to process the first one." I take a sip of my drink. "I was scared to death."

"Yes, I could tell."

"You could? Shit. I thought I'd hidden it quite well."

The bartender leans in between us, asking if we need anything. I nod toward my glass for a refill while Kurt waves him off with his left hand, showing a black leather glove. Is he one of those germ-obsessed paranoids? His right hand is resting on the bar. No glove. Strange.

"Did you always want to be a nurse?" he asks.

"Yup. Since I was in third grade."

"Why?"

"That's a good question." I nod. "I don't know why. It's something I always wanted. How about you?"

"I'm carrying on the family business. It's what was expected."

"Yeah, I know what you mean." I drain my glass.

It was expected of me, as well. In my case, though, it meant being wedded to a husband chosen by the don. Well, not happening. My sister was lucky. Bianca ended up married to a man she adores, but there is no way I'm going back home to risk becoming a bargaining chip in the Cosa Nostra deals.

"Is that guy your ex, or something?" my mystery stranger asks, and I shudder.

"Randy? Christ, no." I make a disgusted face. "Just a creep from work I can't shake off. He's been sending me flowers and pathetic notes for months."

"What kind of notes?"

"The last one said my hair reminds him of *sunrays*." I snort.

His gloved hand enters my field of vision, and my breath catches as he takes a lock of my hair, wrapping it around his finger. It's a rather intimate act, touching someone's hair, and it should bother me. It doesn't. Not even a little.

"Not a romantic soul, are you, Goldie?"

"No, not really, Kurt." I say, trying to keep my voice steady while my heart races.

He's so close I can smell his cologne. It's the same scent as when we met in front of the hospital, very discrete and slightly spicy, and I can't help but lean forward just a little. His facial expression remains completely neutral as he asks, "And you also don't like flowers?"

"I have nothing against flowers. I just don't feel comfortable getting them from creeps," I mumble into my glass. "And it looks like I've somehow obtained a second one."

"A second creep?" he asks, still playing with my hair.

"Yup. Earlier this week, someone decided to buy out the whole flower shop and left more than a hundred bouquets in front of my door."

"It wasn't Randy?"

"I'm pretty sure it wasn't him. There was no cheesy line and no signature on the note. Randy always makes sure he signs his cards," I say looking into his eyes. "My friend, Pippa, says I always attract strange guys."

His head bends slightly. "You think she's right?"

"Maybe." I hold my breath, wondering if he's going to kiss me. The friend in question picks just that moment to come back from the restroom and sit on the chair on my other side. Pippa always has the best timing.

"I guess it's time for me to leave," the jacket guy says and moves away from the bar.

I don't want him to leave, but instead of protesting, I simply nod. "See you around."

He cocks his head to the side, keeping me a prisoner to his gaze, and brushes the back of his gloved hand down my cheek.

"Maybe." He lets go of my hair and turns away.

I watch as he walks away, his tall frame navigating through the crowd, which seems to part naturally, letting him through. He has a slight limp, I realize. It's very subtle. A mere variance in his footsteps that might not catch another's eye. I didn't notice it before.

I wonder whether he'll turn around, but he leaves without looking back.

"Whoa." Pippa sighs next to me. "Who was that?"

"I have no idea," I whisper.

I step inside the sparsely lit living room and look around me. The house is a disaster—clothes strewn across the living room floor and empty takeout boxes piled on the counter. The stale atmosphere clings to my airways, thick and vaguely noxious. It's as though no one has bothered to open a window in months. The place is disgusting. I walk over to the dining room table and pull out a chair. Turning it to face the front door, I sit down to wait.

Twenty minutes later, the front door opens, and Randy Philips, Milene's creep, walks inside. He doesn't notice me right away because I've turned the lights off. However, when he flicks the switch and sees me sitting in his dining room, he stops dead in his tracks.

"Hello Randy," I say.

His eyes widen, and he takes a step back. "What are you doing here? How did you get in? I'm calling the police."

"I wouldn't recommend that." I lean back in the chair. "I came to chat. That's all."

"What do you want?" He sizes me up, then moves closer.

"I want you to forget about Milene," I say. "You don't talk to her. You don't even look at her. When she comes into a room, you turn around and leave."

"What if I decline?" He takes another step in my direction.

Randy's a big guy, a little shorter than me, but with at least fifty additional pounds. His bulk, however, comes mainly from the extra weight he's packing around his middle. He looks smug, like he's sure he can take me on. Drawing conclusions that aren't well-founded can get you killed. Most people fail to take that into account.

I see the precise moment he decides to lunge at me. Before he has a chance to do so, I get up, grab the chair, and smash it against his head. Randy crumbles and falls to his knees, palms pressed heavily against the floor. As he restores his balance and presence of mind, I reach into my jacket, take out my gun, and begin screwing the silencer onto the barrel. It won't extinguish the sound of the gunshots completely, but it'll definitely quieten them. I don't want any of the neighbors interrupting our discussion.

"I really hoped it wouldn't come to this, Randy, but you're leaving me no choice."

He looks up, and when he sees the gun, crawls backward on all fours. I aim to his left and pull the trigger, sending a bullet into the wooden flooring an inch from his hand.

"Stop," I say, and he freezes. "The only reason you're still breathing, Randy, is because I heard you're a doctor, and I have a lot of respect for medical professionals. So, I'm giving you one last chance to comply."

He nods quickly and whimpers, his eyes wide and filled with panic.

"Good. Tomorrow morning, you'll resign from your position at St. Mary's.

If I ever hear that anyone catches sight of you within ten miles of the building, or Milene, your life is over. Do you understand?"

"I understand."

"Perfect." I aim at his leg and shoot him in the thigh.

He screams and falls to his side, pressing his hands onto the bleeding wound. His knuckles turn white from the strain.

"Just a small reminder that I'm serious. You can call 911 when I'm gone, tell them you ran into a burglar." I unscrew the silencer and conceal my gun, then head toward the front door. "Ten-mile radius, Randy."

As soon as I'm in the car, I take out my phone and open the surveillance app. Milene is sitting on her sofa, eating chips and focused on a sitcom on the TV. The cat is sitting on her lap, trying to pull one of Milene's snacks from the bowl with its paw. With her busy daily schedule, the girl needs better nutrition. Since I've been watching her, she's only cooked for herself a handful of times, and only when she has a day off. Based on what I've seen, she's awful at it. Other than those few instances, she's been eating fast food. Sometimes, when she has longer shifts, she crashes when she gets home without eating a thing. If that goes on, she'll get sick.

I send a message to Ada, my housekeeper, with instructions on what I need her to do, and place the phone in its holder next to the steering wheel, so I can watch and drive at the same time.

# Chapter

"Jesus fuck!" I yelp and jump over the cat who's sleeping unaware, sprawled lengthways along the floor right in front of the entryway. I almost squished him underfoot. Again.

Shaking my head, I go to the kitchen area, my mind on leftovers from the day before, and then sleep. The night shifts are killing me. I open the fridge, reaching my hand up to the top shelf, and blink twice. I close the fridge and turn around to make sure I'm in the right apartment.

My kitchen.

My cat.

The two-day-old pile of dirty dishes, also mine. No, I didn't walk into the wrong apartment. I open the fridge again, gawk at its contents, and take out the phone from my back pocket to call Pippa.

"Did you drop by my place while I was at work?" I ask.

"Nope."

"Are you sure?"

"Of course I'm sure. Why?"

"I think someone broke in last night."

"What?! Did you report it? What did they take?"

"Ahem. They didn't take anything." I bend to inspect the contents of the shelves, blinking several times to be certain I'm not imagining things. "They've . . . stocked my fridge."

"I'm not following."

"Someone broke in, filled my fridge with vegetables, a ton of meat, milk, eggs, and"—I reach for the plastic container on the middle shelf and lift the lid—"home-cooked soup."

I'm greeted with silence on the other end of the line, then the sound of giggling. "Yeah, must be little home elves. You're funny."

"I'm serious. I haven't seen a fridge this full since I left home."

"You probably stocked it yesterday and forgot. Fridges don't miraculously fill themselves."

"I'm sleep-deprived, not demented, for God's sake. I'd remember going to a store and spending half my monthly paycheck on food." I reach out to take a block of cheese from the middle shelf and turn it to get a better view. It's one of those fancy, moldy varieties. "There's even a huge package of Gorgonzola there. Posh burglars."

"You're serious?"

"Of course I'm serious." I throw the cheese back on the shelf and slam the fridge closed. "I'm calling the police."

"To tell them what?"

Shit. She has a point, they'd only laugh. "Do you think it was David?"

"Your ex? I thought he left for India with his yoga group when you two broke up. Man, that guy was super strange, and obsessed with food. I can totally imagine him sneaking into your place."

"Jesus. I was certain I got the extra keys back." I sigh and squeeze my nape. "I'm going to crash, but I'm messaging David when I wake up, and I'm changing the locks first thing tomorrow."

I cut the call and head to bed. A stray thought passes through my mind as I'm falling asleep—wasn't David a vegan?

Tilting my head to the side, I watch Milene as she gets ready for work. She brushes her hair in front of the mirror, then gathers it near the crown of her head in a high ponytail. I prefer when she wears it down. I turn my phone face down and focus on the two capos across from my desk, Cosimo and Rocco, who are arguing about hiring yet another construction company.

"Atticus works on government projects, as well," Cosimo snaps. "They have strict internal and external audits. What if someone decides to check out all the companies they work for and combs through our documents?"

"All our contracts are solid. They won't find anything suspicious." Rocco shrugs.

"Oh? And if they dig deeper?" I ask. "Checking up on our investors, for example? Did you think of that, Rocco?"

"Shit," he mumbles.

"Exactly. We're not doing any business with Atticus." I nod toward the door of my office. "We're done for today."

When they leave, I return my attention to my phone, and switch on the second camera feed. Milene is filling her lunch box with some meat she obviously grilled herself because half of it appears to be charred. I'll need to tell Ada to get more groceries and send Alessandro to fill her fridge again next week. She changed the locks, but locked doors have never posed a problem for Alessandro. The moment she leaves her place, I power off my laptop and head to the garage.

I drive forty minutes to reach the hospital where Milene works. Parking close to the entrance, I lean back in my seat and wait. Sometime later, she comes around the corner, and I follow her with my eyes until she disappears through the wide sliding doors. I turn on the ignition, reverse, and leave the parking lot.

This obsession I have with the girl hasn't waned like I expected it to. In fact, it's only intensified. At some point in the last couple of days, I've switched from checking the camera feed a few times per day to leaving it on constantly, except for when I'm in meetings. Even then, if the conversation goes on for more than three hours, I'll pull it up and have a quick glance. It's barely enough to alleviate the anxiety that builds whenever I'm unaware of her location for an extended period. Milene Scardoni, for whatever reason, has become a drug coursing through my veins. The more I get, the more I want. I need to see her again, in person. It won't be today, but soon.

I stop at a red light a few blocks from home and check the rearview mirror. A familiar black car has been following me for the past fifteen minutes, staying in the same lane and a few vehicles back. Looks like the wife of the Boston don has sent another one of her pets to follow me. She needs to have her men trained better, because disposing of her incompetent spies is becoming bothersome. After the traffic light switches to green, I turn right and drive for half an hour until I reach a half-constructed office building. I make another right and head into the underground garage, which should have been finished last week. Based on the boxes, painting supplies, and rolls of electric cables strewn along the walls, the completion is way behind schedule.

After parking next to the service door leading to the stairwell, I take my gun from below the seat, and leave the car. I pass a concrete pillar on my way to the stairs and enter the building, leaving the door ajar.

Less than thirty seconds later, a man in black jeans and a black T-shirt sneaks inside the garage. He keeps his back to the wall and creeps toward the service door with a gun in hand. As he reaches the threshold and presses the palm of his free hand to the doorjamb, I step out of the shadows and put a bullet in his temple. The blood sprays across the freshly painted wall, and the man's body drops to the ground. I lower my gun and, taking out my phone, approach the body.

"Yes?" a female voice answers.

"Nera. I found something of yours."

"Oh. How unfortunate." There is a short silence on the other end before she continues, "Well, I guess we're even. Should we put a stop to this situation for now? I'm having some issues here in Boston. I need to focus on that for the moment and can't exactly spend the time and effort on hunting the spies you're sending."

"Yes. That would be wise. Please pass my best wishes for a quick recovery to Don Leone."

"I will," she says, and the line goes dead.

I step over the dead body at my feet and call Nino.

"I have another of Nera Leone's spies. Send someone to dispose of the body. It's in the garage under the Brooklyn office building."

"Right away. Should we expect more?"

"No. Nera and I came to an agreement to pause spying on each other for the time being."

"Will we be sending a message again?" he asks.

"Yes. The head is enough this time. But wrap it in a fancy red paper. It's her favorite color."

"That woman always gave me the creeps."

"You know the views Cosa Nostra has on women being in a position of power. She needs to be ruthless to put up with all of that."

"You think she'll uphold her promise."

"Yes. Nera is a snake, but she won't go back on her word. Too bad she'll be dead soon."

"You think someone will kill her?"

"As soon as her husband dies. She'll keep the reins until then, but the moment the don dies, she's done." I put the phone away and return to my car.

# Chapter five

Milene

"I can't wait to get home." I sigh and close my locker. "I've switched shifts with Harper for tomorrow. I'll be pulling a double."

"Why?" Pippa asks.

"She said her mother's sick and needs a visit. I couldn't very well say no."

"You're too soft sometimes. Harper never agrees to switch with anyone." She shakes her head. "Did you run into that sexy stranger again? The one from three weeks ago?"

"Nope." I wave to the girl at the reception desk as we pass.

"I can't believe he didn't ask for your number."

"Maybe he wasn't interested." I shrug. "He saw Randy pestering me, decided to help, and that was all."

"I'm still shocked Randy quit. It was so sudden."

"I heard he mentioned a family emergency and left town," I say as we pass through the exit doors. "Thank God."

Suddenly, Pippa's no longer walking in step with me. I stop and turn to find her staring at something, her eyes wide.

"Pip? Are you coming?"

"Um . . . about your mystery guy."

"What about him?"

"Looks like he might be interested after all." She smirks and nods toward the parking lot.

I follow her gaze, and the corners of my mouth twitch in an involuntary smile. Fifteen yards from us, the jacket guy is leaning against the hood of a big silver car, his arms crossed in front of him.

"Holy fuck. Is that a Bentley?" Pippa whispers in my ear as she nudges me with her shoulder. "Go over now. Make him marry you. You'll never have to work again." She giggles.

I snort. What she's suggesting is the exact thing I've been trying my damnedest to avoid. "See you tomorrow."

The jacket guy watches me as I walk toward him, and I find myself wishing I was wearing something a little more flattering than hospital scrubs. The midday light brings out the gray in his hair, and once again, I'm amazed at how attractive he is. Today, he's wearing a simple gray shirt with nothing over it. His stance emphasizes his wide shoulders and bulging biceps. He's built like a professional swimmer—toned muscle, with a narrow waist and broad chest. I reach his direct orbit and smile.

"Well, hello again, stranger. If you are still a stranger," I say. "Just passing by?"

"Kind of." He straightens and puts his hands in his pockets. "I was wondering if you'd like to have lunch with me."

"I don't usually go to lunch with men whose names I don't know, Kurt."

I expect him to smile at that, but instead he just returns my gaze. "Coffee?"

I wonder why he doesn't want to share his name. I mean, he could have given me a fake name from the start. It's not like I'd ask for his ID to confirm. Maybe he thinks I'll find him more alluring this way? If that's the case, he's not entirely wrong.

"Coffee might be doable." I shrug and motion toward the small place nearby where most of the hospital staff, including me, are at least semi-regular visitors. "There's a café across the street."

He nods and follows me in silence as we cross the road. We pick one of the tables on the patio, covered with a garish red and white gingham tablecloth. The jacket guy pulls a chair out for me and takes a seat at my side.

"So, are you stalking me, Kurt?"

"No," he says. "I had some business in the neighborhood and saw you leaving the hospital as I was getting into my car."

"What a coincidence."

The daughter of the café owner comes to take our orders. A cappuccino for me and a double espresso, no sugar, for him. I've always wondered how people can drink coffee without sugar.

"How's life treating you, Goldie?"

There is something unusual in the way he watches me, waiting for an answer. As if he genuinely wants to know and isn't just asking for the sake of making conversation. It may sound stupid since I've only truly exchanged a handful of words with him, but I have the impression he rarely gives his undivided attention to anyone.

"Pretty much the same," I say. "People getting stabbed. Overdoses. A bunch of broken bones. One poisoning."

"Poisoning?"

"Jealous wife. The husband was cheating." I grin. "She wasn't happy at all."

"Did he live?"

"Yup. We pumped his stomach when he came in."

"What did she use?"

"Some cocktail of kitchen chemicals." I raise an eyebrow. "You?"

"No poisonings here. Just meetings and a ton of emails."

I squint my eyes at him. Even though he looks like a businessman, with his expensive clothes and a watch that likely costs more than a year's worth of my rent, he doesn't strike me as the kind of guy who'd be dealing with paperwork. He holds himself in a certain way, even now when he's seemingly relaxed, and it makes me certain he's not an ordinary manager.

"You didn't just happen to be in the neighborhood, did you, Kurt?" I pick up the coffee the waitress has placed in front of me and take a sip.

"No." He leans forward, reaches over and removes the pin that's holding my hair in a bun at the nape of my neck, causing it to cascade down my back. "You have really unusual hair, Goldie."

There is nothing unusual about my hair. Except for the fact that my sister and I share its light shade, but no one else in our family does. Blonde hair is not common in the Italian community. Bianca and I are the only ones who take after our Norwegian grandmother.

He takes a few strands between his gloved fingers, lightly brushing the locks.

*Tell him to stop! He's crossing boundaries. You can't let a random stranger do that.*

I ignore the voice of reason completely and look at the strand of hair he's holding, noticing he's only using the first three digits, while the other two remain slightly rigid and bent. I wonder what happened with his hand.

"So, you were waiting for me," I say. "Why?"

"Is there anything wrong with my wanting to take a beautiful woman out to lunch?"

"That usually comes after the necessary introductions, Kurt." I smirk.

"Do you have something to hide? Is there a reason why you don't want to tell me your name?"

"What could I possibly have to hide?" His gloved fingers release my hair and brush against the skin along my upper arm in the process, sending an excited shudder throughout my body.

"I don't know. Are you an ex-con? A politician with a wife and three kids at home?"

"I don't have so much as a speeding ticket to my name. No wife or kids, either."

"Why not?" I raise an eyebrow. "How old are you?"

"Thirty-four. Having a wife and kids was never something I planned."

"And do you have a set plan for everything?"

"For most things, yes." He looks into my eyes. "Would you like to apply for the wife position?"

I burst out laughing. It's not the question itself, but the way it's delivered in a completely serious tone. "Sorry, Kurt. I'm not exactly on the market. You'll have to search for a likely candidate elsewhere."

"Do you have something against marriage? Are you afraid of commitment?"

"Nope." I shake my head in bewilderment over discussing marriage with a man I've just met. "I have a well-founded fear of ending up tied to a man I don't love. Too many bad examples in my family, I guess. At one time, my sister Bianca and I had an agreement that we'd never get married. We planned on being cat ladies, living in houses that smelled like pee." I reach for my cappuccino. "That was until she upended her half of the bargain and married a scary Russian guy. I changed my perspective on marriage for real after that."

"How so?"

"Strangely, I saw how good it could be. Those two are . . . like damn soulmates or something. I've never seen two people so fucking in love. They could be on a Hallmark card." I take a sip of my coffee. "I can't explain it. You'd have to see it to understand."

"You plan on marrying a scary Russian guy, as well?" he asks.

"Of course not." I laugh. "I don't like scary guys. What I'm saying is that I won't settle for anything less."

"And you said you weren't romantic . . ." His finger lands on my bare forearm and traces a line down to the blue veins at my wrist. I swear my heart truly skips a beat.

"Maybe I am, a little." I shrug, aware of his finger moving upward again and trying to suppress the need to simply close my eyes and enjoy his touch.

"Has that guy been bothering you again?" he asks. "The one from the bar?"

"Randy? Nope. I heard he suddenly left the city, hasn't even called. Thank God."

"Good." He nods and moves his finger to the back of my hand. "Is anything else new?"

"Other than a bunch of bizarre stuff happening? No."

"What bizarre stuff?"

"Well, I could start with me going on a date with a man whose name I don't know." I grin.

"So, this is a date?"

"You tell me."

"Maybe it is." He takes my hand, turns it palm upward, and resumes tracing patterns on my skin. "I don't go on many dates, so I'm not exactly sure how to classify this."

I arch an eyebrow. "You don't go on dates?"

"No. In fact, I don't think I've ever been on a date. Maybe in high school."

I double over, laughing. "You're shitting me, right?"

He's lying. Has to be. When a man looks like he does, there must be a ton of women lining up to throw themselves into his arms. He looks down at my hand, which slipped away from his while I was giggling, and wraps his fingers around my wrist. Pulling it closer, he continues to trace the lines with his fingertip. Love line, life line, I'm never sure which is which.

"What other bizarre stuff?" he asks.

I blink and shake my head. His touch is very light, but it still raises goose bumps on my skin. Not just my arms, either. And I certainly don't plan on removing my hand.

"Well, there's the flower incident. I still have no idea who sent them."

"Yes, I remember you mentioning it. What did you do with all the flowers?"

"Asked the hospital laundry department guys to help me take them over to St. Mary's. We brought the flowers to the rooms of long-term patients," I say. "I kept some. I shouldn't have since I don't know who sent them, but they were too pretty."

His finger moves up along my forearm. "What else?"

"My ex broke into my place last week and stocked my fridge." I look up at him. "He says he didn't do it, but I don't believe him."

David isn't exactly a relationship type of guy. I find it super strange he'd try to get back together with an act like that, but I can't think of anyone else who could have done it.

"Your ex?" he asks. "Were you together long?"

"With all the off-and-on periods included . . ." I think about it. "Maybe a year."

The finger on my forearm stills for a moment.

"A year," he says, then continues with his pattern. "That's a long time. Does he live nearby?"

"Yeah, but he's in India right now. A yoga retreat or something like that. He probably sent someone to handle the fridge thing for him. Why do you ask?"

"I hear India's nice. He should consider staying there. It would be good for his health."

I squint my eyes at him. "Why? Because of the tropical climate?"

His fingers move back down to my palm. "Because of the air."

God, I love this man's voice. My eyes land on his watch and, reluctantly, I pull my hand away from his. "I have to go. I have an appointment with the vet for my cat."

"I'll drop you off." He takes out his wallet and leaves fifty dollars, which is way too much money, then stands up. "What's wrong with the cat?"

"He's been puking since last night. I think he ate one of my hair ties again."

As we're crossing the street, a bunch of teenage boys rush toward us from the other side, shouting and fooling around as they often do. The jacket guy's hand lands on my hip, drawing me closer to his side, and he holds me tightly as the kids fly by in a flurry of waved arms and banter. Damn, I'm a sucker for guys with a protective steak.

"Is that normal?" he asks. "I heard dogs might eat anything, but not cats."

"I don't think so. He has issues," I say as we walk toward his car. "But at least he's stopped stealing food from the lady next door."

"Why keep the cat if he's got issues?"

"He kind of moved in without asking. I couldn't throw him out."

We reach his car, and I turn around, suddenly wondering how wise it is to get into a car with someone I barely know. As the thought hits me, he raises his hand and takes my chin between his fingers, tilting my face upward.

A finger lightly brushes the skin on my cheek, and I find myself leaning into his touch. His head bends until his mouth is next to my ear, his lips making slight but electric contact.

"You are one extremely unusual creature, Goldie," he whispers into my ear. His voice is rough and hypnotizing, sending a shiver down my spine. "And I like unusual things very much."

His other arm wraps around my waist, and in an instant, I find myself sitting on the hood of his car, my legs astride his body.

"There's nothing unusual about me," I say, watching his amber eyes. He has a small scar on his forehead above his eyebrow, and I reach out to touch it. Our faces are so close that his breath brushes against my lips. If I were to lean forward a little, my lips would touch his. I move my finger from his eyebrow down the side of his face and then bury it in his hair at the back of his neck. At the same time, his finger slides upward from my chin to my bottom lip.

"I beg to differ, Goldie." His finger vanishes from my mouth, replaced by firm lips.

The kiss is slow. Controlled. Just like him. I tighten my hand at his neck and marvel at how his lips savor mine. It's as though he's discovered a new and exotic land. I've always thought that hard and forceful kisses were the most intense. I couldn't have been more wrong because the way he's exploring my mouth is downright sinful. Would he make love the same way? For some reason, I don't believe he would. His other hand reaches down to the small of my back and under my top, sliding upward along the ridges of my spine, igniting the firework flashes with each and every gentle touch.

"Come to my place," I whisper into his mouth, not quite believing my boldness. I don't invite strangers home, and I've only slept with men I've been dating, but here I am, inviting a nameless man into my bed to do whatever he wants with me. It's reckless. Crazy. Why don't I care?

He angles his head, watching me intensely. His hand is still holding my chin, his finger caressing my lower lip. "Are you sure?"

I open my mouth to say yes when a whizzing sound pierces the air as the windshield behind me shatters. I scream. The arm around my waist tightens, the hood disappears from beneath me, and I find myself pressed fully against the side of the car, my face flat against a rock-hard chest. Another shot echoes through the air. The bullet sends shards of asphalt up like sparks just to the left of us. A car screeches to a halt somewhere nearby and is closely followed by a second one. The chest vanishes, and suddenly, I'm being bundled into the back seat of a vehicle.

The jacket guy is speaking to the driver in a disturbingly even voice. "Take the girl home. Make sure you're not followed."

"Boss," the driver nods toward my protector's upper arm. "You're bleeding."

My eyes snap to his side, and I see the dark crimson stain spreading across his sleeve.

He ignores it completely and turns to someone who's now standing behind him, out of my field of vision. "Find that fucking sniper."

He throws one rapid glance at me and brings his palm down on the roof of the car. In a split second, the vehicle lunges forward, and I'm pressed to the back of the seat, feeling for the first time what it must be like to blast into space.

# Chapter *six*

Salvatore

"You got reckless, Boss," Nino says. "Standing there for two hours, waiting for the girl where anyone could see you. And in the middle of the day. It was only to be expected."

"Did you find the shooter?" I ask.

"It took us most of the night, but yes. Just a gun for hire." He looks at the bulge of the bandage beneath my sleeve. "And not a very good one."

"Did he say who hired him?"

"Stefano worked him over pretty good, but he kept saying he doesn't know who hired him. Could it have been Nera Leone?"

"It's not her," I say. The wife of the Boston don is a great schemer, but she keeps her promises. "Where are you holding the shooter?"

"In the old safe house."

"I'll come over later. What about the girl?"

"She went to work this morning, as usual. We have two men on her constantly, but so far nothing suspicious has occurred. I don't think anyone other than the hitman saw her with you. She should be safe." He looks at me pointedly. "If you keep your distance."

He's right. But the problem is, I don't want to keep my distance.

It takes me two hours to go over the updates on the shipments of drugs with Arturo, my underboss. I leave the operational part of the narcotics business to him, so if everything works as it should, he only needs to bring me up to speed once a week. I spend the next hour with Cosimo, Rocco, and Giancarlo—the capos in charge of our construction division. They report to me daily. Dusk has already fallen when I head over to the safe house.

An hour later, I turn my car onto a dirt road that's hidden from prying eyes by a thicket of trees and follow the track downhill. Soon, I reach a rusty gate and flash my lights four times. A man in black tactical clothing emerges from behind a tree, unlocks the gate, and drags it open.

"Is Stefano still here?" I ask when he approaches the driver-side window.

"Yes, Boss." He nods. "How's the arm?"

"Just a graze," I say and proceed along the trail, past the overgrown bushes that sweep the side of the car. A rickety house comes into view, and I park on the gravel out front.

When I enter the safe house, I find Stefano sitting in a recliner, dressed only in his black suit pants. His chest is bare and glistens with sweat and blood, most of which appears to have dried to a dark, crusty brown. Across from him, tied to a wooden chair, sits a man in his late forties. He's still alive, but Stefano has taken him right to the edge, it seems.

"Got a little carried away, Stefano?" I ask.

"Boss." He jumps off the recliner and comes to stand next to our unfortunate guest. "Sorry. I heard he shot you, so I might have been a little rougher than normal."

Sometimes, my men are like an old maids' church choir. They love to gossip among themselves. I don't give a fuck, as long as they keep the information within the right circles. They know better than to let any news—personal or business—spread if they don't want to end up like Octavio.

I walk toward Stefano's vacated recliner, sit down, and regard the shooter. He's conscious, but unresponsive. It happens when you overdo a beating, eventually numbness and dissociation set in, and you're left with a lump of throbbing, inert flesh. Stefano should have switched tactics hours ago if he wanted results. But he's young. He'll learn.

When I took over the New York Family, I changed the way things work. I delegated most of the operational stuff—things that don't require my personal involvement—to Arturo and the capos. That left me only with high-level decision-making in terms of general business oversight. I kept a close hold on the Family stuff, however, including the handling of thieves, snitches, and outside threats.

"Cut off his hand," I say to Stefano.

The man starts talking the moment the saw bites at the skin of his wrist two minutes later.

"The Irish!" he screams. "It was the Irish."

"Who, specifically?" I ask.

"Patrick Fitzgerald."

I lean back in the chair and regard the prisoner. It's nothing new, someone's always trying to kill me, but the Irish are becoming a serious problem. When they attacked the Bratva in Chicago four years ago, their attempt ended with half their own men dead, the leader included. It looks like they've set their sights on my city now. They'll have to be dealt with, and fast.

"Did you tell the Irish I was meeting a woman?" I ask.

The shooter stares at me, then shakes his head quickly. I give Stefano a nod. He takes a knife and thrusts it into the man's side, hopefully avoiding any vital organs. The prisoner screams.

"I . . . I might have mentioned her," he says between whimpers.

"Did you give them her description?"

"Yes."

I close my eyes. If the Irish think there is something between us, they might come for Milene. "What else?"

"I told them she works at the hospital."

I open my eyes and stare at the peeling wallpaper behind him. It's not the fact that he's passed the information along that stuns me, but the anxiety that builds in my gut. When I think about how easily this man's bullet could have caught Milene, it turns into full-blown rage. This bastard missed her, but the next one might not. For a few minutes I stare at the wall, making sure my features don't betray anything of my internal turmoil.

Unfamiliar emotions wash over me. I feel like a sailor caught out on the stormy sea. I let the feelings overtake me, taking them all in. The urge to destroy rises inside me like the tide. It's anger. Fury. An unrelenting maelstrom.

I get up, walk toward the prisoner, and take the knife from Stefano's hand. With the blade at the sniper's neck, I swipe hard, slicing his throat from ear to ear.

After I leave the safe house, I get inside my car and taking out my phone, pull up the surveillance feed from Milene's place. The cat is hanging from a half-shredded curtain, evidently chasing some bug. Milene is not there. Anxiety immediately builds deep in my chest.

I call Aldo. "Where is she?"

"Still at work. I'm parked in front of the hospital, I'll let you know the moment she heads home."

"Don't let her out of your sight." I cut the call and stare into the distance. I'm not sure for how long. Eventually, I pick up the phone again and call Luca Rossi, the don of the Chicago Family.

"Mr. Rossi. We may have a problem."

"Something regarding the last construction project?" he asks.

"No. This is a personal matter," I say and lean back in my seat. "There is something of yours here. Something that shouldn't have been in my city, Mr. Rossi . . ."

"Say that again." Pippa lowers her purse and stares at me.

"Someone shot at us." I grab a bottle of water from my locker and take a sip.

"In the middle of the day? Did you call the police? And why are you so . . . unperturbed?"

It's not my first rodeo, but Pippa doesn't have to know that. "My mysterious stranger threw me into his friend's car and sent me away. I can't say what happened afterward. The driver dropped me off and hightailed it."

"Was it a random shooting?"

"I don't know. It's possible they were aiming at the jacket guy."

"Why would someone shoot at him? You said he's just a businessman."

Yeah, I've wondered about that, too. "I'm not even sure whether they were shooting at us or if it was a stray bullet. Everything happened so fast. One moment we were kissing, and the next, the windshield behind me shattered, and then I ended up in the back of another car."

"What?" She widens her eyes at me. "You kissed him? Was it good?"

"Technically speaking, he kissed me." I grin in spite of myself. "And yup, it was good."

"Are you going to see him again?"

"I don't know. We didn't exactly have time to exchange numbers." I close the locker and lean back against it. "There is something about him. I can't put my finger on what it is exactly, but I'm attracted to him like a bee to honey. And believe me, there is nothing sweet about that guy."

"He certainly is hot."

"It's not just that. He's . . . weird, in some strangely attractive way. He was completely serious the entire time, as if we were in a business meeting, discussing stock fluctuations. But the way he looked at me . . ." I sigh. "Have you ever gone out on a date and talked nonsense to break the ice? There, outside the coffee shop, I rambled on about work while his eyes studied mine. And, Pippa, he listened to me. Not because he was being polite, but as though he really wanted to know." I close my eyes and shake my head. "I like him. Like, really like him. But I don't like being shot at. And I would have really appreciated it if he'd shared his name this time."

I slide the key into the new lock, but the front door opens without me having to turn it. Did I forget to lock up this morning? I step into my apartment and freeze like a waxwork model. My brother is sitting at the kitchen table, his arms crossed, staring at me.

"What the fuck were you thinking, Milene?" he asks through his teeth.

I cross the small space and drop heavily down on the sofa. "How did you find me?"

"How? That's a funny story, really. Last night, Rossi called me, furious. He wanted to know what the hell my sister was doing in New York. I said it must be a mistake since my sister was in Illinois."

Shit. How did our don find out I'm in New York? I squeeze my eyes shut for a second, then look up at Angelo. "I knew you wouldn't let me come to New York, but St Mary's is the best hospital. I was lucky to get the chance to work there and didn't want to miss it. I'm sorry."

"You're sorry?" he snarls. "You're fucking *sorry*?"

"I have three more months of my residency left, and then I'll leave, I promise. Don Ajello won't ever find out."

Angelo regards me with his jaw pressed tight, the veins in his neck pulsing rapidly, and shakes his head. "How do you think I got your address, Milene?"

An icy chill passes down my spine as dread spreads a numb sort of panic throughout my body.

"Ajello sent your address to Rossi, Milene. Along with a copy of your residency details, showing you've been here nine fucking months!" He yells so loudly that my poor cat jumps from the sofa and dashes into the bathroom.

All I can do is stare at my brother, incapable of speech.

"Do you realize you've almost started a goddamned war?"

"But . . . I'm just working at a hospital. It's not like I'm selling drugs on Ajello's turf or anything. Why does it matter?"

"He's the fucking Don of the New York Family, and you went against his specific decree. It sends the message that you don't recognize him as an authority figure in his own region. And by extension, neither does the Chicago Family." He slumps his shoulders and squeezes the bridge of his nose between two fingers. "You being a capo's sister only makes the situation a hundred times worse."

"I . . . I never saw it that way, Angelo." I bury my hands in my hair. "Jesus."

He sighs and looks up at the ceiling. "Do you remember Enzo, Milene?"

"Catalina's idiot cousin who died in an accident last year? What does Enzo have to do with anything?"

"He didn't die in an accident. Ajello found out he came to New York for a weekend "mancation"—strip clubs, drinking, having a good time. Nothing to do with the Family business. Enzo's body was delivered to Rossi the following day. It came in several bags, Milene."

"Bags?" I gape at him.

"Yes. There were three. The note said it was easier for FedEx to handle smaller packages. It worked out to be cheaper."

I wrap my arms around myself. "Is he going to kill me, too?"

"He has every right to, and no one would be able to do anything about it." He looks at me. "But he's demanded another compensation. Rossi agreed."

"What kind of compensation?"

"A marriage."

My head snaps up. "No," I whisper.

"I'm sorry. You've brought this on yourself."

"I am not getting married!" I yell while trying very hard to keep the tears at bay, but they come anyway, blurring my vision.

"There's nothing I can do, sis." Angelo gets up from the chair and walks toward me, crouching at my feet. "If it were just you, I could have arranged to get you out of the country or something. But it's the whole Family on the line here."

My brother's right, there isn't anything he could do. Saying no would mean war. People would die because of me and my stupidity. I knew the risk of coming to Ajello's territory and decided to come anyway.

"I fucked up big time, didn't I?" I sniff.

"Yes, you did. I'm sorry."

"So, who am I arranged to marry?"

He grabs my hand and just watches me for a few seconds, then sighs in. "Don Ajello, Milene."

Panic explodes inside my chest. "What? I'm not marrying a man who chops people up and mails their body parts."

"If you don't, Ajello may attack. And, even though the Bratva will likely side with us because of Bianca, it will still be a fucking bloodbath."

I close my eyes and take a deep breath. Our sister's husband is the Bratva's enforcer. If the Russians are dragged into this, he'll be sent to the front line. I can't do that to Bianca.

"When?" I choke out.

"He'll be here with the marriage officiant at noon."

My tears flow so fast they fall like rain onto the wooden floor, each one splashing against the last.

Exactly at noon, a sharp knock sounds at the door, but I remain seated and motionless on the sofa, still wearing my work scrubs. Angelo answers it.

My brother tried to convince me to change into something more appropriate, but I told him to fuck off and die. In the three hours I've spent on the sofa, I've gone through shock and disbelief, then denial and self-pity. Now? Now, I'm royally pissed off.

Angelo opens the door, and a huge bald man in his fifties marches confidently into my apartment. I can't suppress a shudder. It could be worse. It could be much worse. My inner monologue is still repeating the thought when the bald guy moves to the side, revealing another figure. I spring to my feet in an instant. It's the jacket guy.

My enigmatic stranger walks in as though he's lived here all his life, and I can't decide whether to laugh or cry. The son of a bitch knew who I was the entire time. He was probably the one who informed Ajello. Bastard.

"Milene," my brother says and nods toward the mysterious asshole. "This is Don Salvatore Ajello."

My jaw drops. What the fuck?

"Nice to meet you at last, Miss Scardoni," he says in his even tone.

I stare. Blink. Then stare some more, paying no attention to what is going on around me.

"For such a tiny woman, you've created quite an uproar," he adds, his words snapping me out of my stupor.

I press my lips together. The nerve he has, pretending we don't know each other when he's well aware that he had his tongue thoroughly inspecting my mouth not forty-eight hours earlier. I guess he's waiting for my reply. Well, he's not getting it.

"Milene!" Angelo nudges me with his elbow. "She's just nervous."

I let my lips widen in a sarcastic smile. Salvatore Ajello ignores my brother's comment and regards me. Even though I keep on smiling, I communicate all the loathing I feel through my eyes. And there is loads of it.

My gaze is focused on the road, which comes in and out of view through the windshield as wipers periodically clear the glass of the steady rain.

Milene hasn't said a word since I walked into her place, other than to answer "Yes" to the officiant's question. I expected her to be surprised, but I didn't expect this. Being ignored is a new experience for me, and the fact she's the one doing it makes me want to hit something. Instead, I grip the steering wheel harder. It doesn't help. I take a deep breath, trying to quell the raging fire within. Pissed. No, that's not the exact term. Livid. I am fucking livid, even though it's not a reasonable reaction.

A mewling sound reaches my ears from the back seat. The damn cat had completely slipped my mind until Milene left her building, holding a carrier with the dumb animal inside.

I park the car in my spot in the underground garage below my building and get out, intending to open the door for Milene, but she's already out and opening the back door to take out the cat. Walking around the car, I open the trunk and take out her bag as she moves to stand to my right. She grabs the handle with her free hand, wrapping her fingers around it right next to mine, and pulls, trying with all her might to take the bag from me. I keep hold until she releases the handle and huffs. As we walk toward the elevator, Milene makes sure she stays two steps behind me, and doesn't say a word.

When we reach my penthouse, I lead her across the living room and down the hallway to my bedroom and open the door. Milene stops at the threshold and casts a quick glance around the room.

"Not happening," she says and takes a step back into the hallway.

"What, exactly?"

"Me sleeping in your room."

I meet her gaze. "How do you know this is my bedroom?"

"Please." She snorts. "Massive dark wood furniture? A bed the size of a football field? It screams 'self-centered, selfish bastard.'"

"Is that how you see me?"

"Yes. Am I wrong?"

No, she isn't wrong. "And where would you like to sleep?"

"Back at my place."

"You know that's not an option."

She lifts the cat carrier and wraps her arms around it, creating a barrier between us.

Maybe I should give her some space. For now. "All right."

I exit my bedroom and head down the hallway toward the second bedroom, leaving her to follow.

"Lunch will be in the dining room at two," I say when I step inside, turning to find her watching me through narrowed eyes. "Is something wrong?"

She lowers the cat carrier to the floor, then crosses her arms and juts her chin out. "You mean, other than you making a mess of my life, Salvatore?"

A feeling of immense satisfaction passes through me upon hearing her say my name. I take two steps forward until I am standing right in front of her. "Would you prefer I killed you?"

"Well, I can't say it makes much of a difference."

"You're exaggerating."

"Oh? My life might have seemed small and meaningless to you, but it was *my* life." She chokes on the words. "Why didn't you just tell me to leave New York? You knew who I was from the start."

"I planned on doing that. It would have made things much easier." I reach out and take a strand of her hair between my fingers. "However, the situation has changed."

"Why? In what way?"

Because I've decided I won't let her go anywhere. "It's nothing you should concern yourself about now," I say.

"Yes, let's not overwhelm my limited brain with stuff only men can understand." She moves her gaze to the strand of hair I'm still holding and grabs at my hand, trying to pry my fingers open. "Let go of my hair."

"You always knew you'd end up married to someone in the Family, Milene. So, what's the problem?"

"Well, therein lies the rub—I didn't," she mumbles as she keeps pulling at my fingers. "I left Chicago because I hoped I'd somehow avoid that destiny."

I let go of her hair and take her chin, tilting her head up. Her green eyes bore into mine as her breathing picks up slightly. "You can't run from Cosa Nostra, Milene." I say and move my hand.

"No. I guess I can't," she whispers and takes a step back, escaping my hold. Grabbing the carrier again, she walks past me toward the bed and puts the cat down next to it. "I'm going to take a shower."

I follow her with my eyes until she disappears into the bathroom, wondering if I've made the right decision. Maybe the Irish wouldn't have come for Milene, and by marrying her, I've only made her a more lucrative target. But I wasn't satisfied with watching her from afar anymore.

I want Milene Scardoni like I've never wanted anything else before.

I let the cat out of his carrier, then flop down on the bed and stare at the ceiling. Calling this a disaster would be an understatement. What am I going to do? Live the rest of my life here, with him? I don't know who he is. He doesn't know me. Who the fuck still thinks arranged marriages are a good idea? It's like we've forgotten five hundred years of history and returned to the Middle Ages, for fuck's sake. Yes, I messed up. He didn't have to marry me to prove his point. He could have let me go back to Chicago, and everything would have been a bed of roses. Why the fuck did he want to marry me?

Was it some kind of a whim? We didn't even exchange rings. Maybe he just wanted to teach me a lesson? No, he has more important things to do than that. Sex? Nope, it wasn't that either because I was ready to have sex with him anyway without this shitstorm. Well, it's not going to happen now, that's for sure. Maybe he's bored, and he'll let me go when he's had enough of me.

I roll over on the bed to bury my face in the pillow and groan. He didn't do this out of boredom, and I very much doubt he'll let me go. This shit is for real.

Me. Married.

To the fucking Don of New York.

# Chapter seven

Salvatore

THERE HAVE BEEN SOME ISSUES WITH ONE OF THE CONSTRUCTION projects, so when I return to the penthouse, it's already nine in the evening. I thought I'd be agitated by not knowing what Milene was doing during the day, but having her in my home made it easier. As I pass by the kitchen, I nod to Ada, who's taking dishes out of the dishwasher, and head into my bedroom to have a shower.

When I exit my bedroom half an hour later, Ada's putting on her coat, readying to leave.

"Where is she?" I ask.

"In her room. She hasn't come out since you left, Mr. Ajello."

"Did you take her lunch?"

"Yes, but when I went in again to bring her the litter tray for the cat that she had asked for, the plate was sitting on her nightstand, untouched," Ada says. "I took her dinner at seven, but she didn't touch that, either."

"Has she eaten anything since this morning?"

"No. I offered to make something else, but she said she wasn't going to eat anything made under your roof. I've put the food in the fridge."

Grinding my teeth, I nod. "You can go, Ada."

I wait for Ada to leave and then head to Milene's room, furious as hell and with no experience as to how to deal with it. I never get mad. Annoyed, yes. Irritated, sometimes. But where that woman is concerned, every emotion jumps straight into overload. I open the door and see her sitting cross-legged on the bed, typing something on her phone.

"This childish behavior ends now!" I roar, and her head snaps up, her eyes suddenly wide. "Ada left the food in the fridge. If you don't eat something, I'm going to fucking force-feed you!"

Milene blinks, still gaping at me, and it dawns on me. Shit. I'd been so damn angry about her not eating that I completely forgot. Milene's gaze travels down my arms and the hands holding my crutches. Then, it moves lower until her eyes reach my left leg . . . where the pant leg of my sweats is tied in a knot just below the knee. It completely slipped my mind that I've never told her about my leg. As her eyes lift to meet mine, I steel myself for what I'll see there because if I find even an ounce of pity, I'm going to smash the room.

She gets up off the bed and comes over to stand before me, her chin tilted up at a slight angle. "I'd love to see you try, Salvatore." She raises her eyebrows and slams the door closed.

I stand there, staring at the door that almost hit me in the face, and feel the corner of my lips twitch slightly upward.

I walk back to the bed and sit down on the edge, trying to collect myself. It never crossed my mind that part of his leg might have been amputated.

Salvatore Ajello is always trending where gossip is concerned. Even though only a few members of our Family have met him, people love to talk. Probably because there is never enough info about him. He doesn't visit public events, and there are no pictures of him anywhere. His underboss, Arturo, acts as the "face" of the New York crime family. When anyone needs to contact the New York Cosa Nostra, they call Arturo. Never the don.

If there was a recent accident resulting in such serious injury, someone would have heard about it. The rumor mill would have run rampant for months. So, it must have happened before he became the head of the New York Family.

"Jesus," I mumble and bury my hands in my hair.

Losing a limb must be hell to deal with. I've met a few amputees during my studies and residency, and most of them had trouble adjusting to their new realities. Salvatore doesn't seem to have a problem with that. What kind of nurse am I not to have suspected? I noticed his limp and that it had become a little more pronounced when we arrived at the penthouse, but I didn't make the connection. He probably controls the way he walks when there are other people around. I assumed it had to be an old injury or something congenital. That is if I even thought that much about it.

He's a really peculiar guy, my new husband. The way he acted so calm and unshaken that day when someone shot at us in the parking lot was truly frightening. I have a feeling not many things would shake him to his core. Except, apparently, me not wanting to eat.

I grip my phone at my side. I should call Bianca and tell her what's happened. She'll freak out. Distressing a woman who's six months pregnant isn't wise, but I'll have to tell her. Tomorrow. I'll call her tomorrow because I'm still processing this shit myself. As I scroll through my contacts list, wondering if I should call Andrea, another name comes across the screen, and I stop. Nonna Giulia. My late father's aunt is always up-to-date with the latest gossip. Being a hundred and one years old, she knows everyone in Cosa Nostra. I press the call button.

"Milene, tesoro!" she chirps on the other side.

"Hey, Nonna. How are you?"

"Sunbathing in Cancun. You cannot believe the male hotties they have here."

I snort. Nonna's a little whacky. "Listen, I wanted to ask you something. Have you ever met Salvatore Ajello? The don of the New York Family?"

"I know who Ajello is, tesoro. I'm still what you would call compos mentis." She snickers. "Why do you ask?"

I sigh and give her a summary of the latest events in my life. When I'm done, there is a long pause on the other end of the line before she finally answers.

"Holy fuck, Milene," she whispers.

I've never heard Nonna curse before. "So? Do you know him?"

"I knew his father. He was a capo. Salvatore took his place when his father was murdered. It was nine or ten years ago," she says. "Something happened in New York a few years later, and the whole establishment ended up dead. The don, the underboss, five capos. Salvatore took over. I think that was six years ago."

"You've never met him?"

"Once, but it was decades ago. There was a wedding and his father brought him along. Salvatore was eight, I think."

I try to imagine Salvatore as a child but can't make the leap. "How was he?" I ask.

"Strange," Nonna says. "There was an accident toward the end of that day. One of the light fixtures broke free from the ceiling and fell onto a table, trapping a man beneath it. Women screamed. Blood was everywhere. People rushed around, trying to help the poor soul, but he was already dead. It was awful."

"Dear God."

"Salvatore was sitting at a table nearby, eating cake and observing the events, absolutely unaffected by what had happened. It was as if there wasn't a man with a metal rod sticking out of his chest sitting not even fifteen feet away from him. At first, I thought the kid must have been in shock, but he stood up and casually walked toward the buffet table to take another piece of cake. He passed the bloody scene as though it didn't bother him in the least," she says. "There is something *wrong* with him, Milene. Please, be careful."

When I end the call, I spend some time mulling over what Nonna said. I've already noticed Salvatore is a bit odd, so she hasn't told me anything new. What interests me more is the fact that he became a don at what? Twenty-eight? That's unheard of.

The cat jumps down off the bed and rubs his flank against my legs. He's probably hungry. I forgot to tell Ada to order cat food. For now, something from the fridge will have to do, and I'll buy some cat food tomorrow. It would be a good idea for me to eat something, too, but my stomach has shrunk, and the idea of food seems unappealing. However, I'm pretty certain Salvatore wasn't bluffing when he said he would force me to eat. Bastard.

I take the cat in my arms and head toward the door. "Let's go and find something to eat, Kurt."

The first word that comes to mind as I walk through the penthouse, is "enormous." The space must be at least four thousand square feet, maybe more. Considering its location, this place must be worth millions. How loaded is Salvatore, I wonder. My family has money, and I became accustomed to owning expensive things quite early in life, but this is a whole new level of rich. I'm not much of an art expert, but the paintings lining the walls must have cost a fortune. Hopefully, the furniture isn't as expensive since my cat loves to sharpen his nails on the upholstery without a care in the world.

The penthouse is divided into two sections. The first one, where my room is located, seems to be a private area with two bedrooms on each side of the wide hallway. Large white double doors separate it from the common area, where the kitchen, living and dining rooms are located. Everything is immaculately kept, and the open floor plan emphasizes the vastness of the space.

I find Salvatore sitting at the breakfast bar which divides the kitchen from the living area but ignore him pointedly. Opening the door of the state-of-the-art refrigerator, I rummage through its contents, searching for something my cat might eat. I find a plastic container of meat on the middle shelf, so I open it, take a piece and touch my tongue against it, to check whether it's too spicy or too salty. It's not, so I put the cat down and grab a bowl from the stand on the counter. I place a few pieces of meat inside, removing the bone with my fingers and walk toward the corner of the kitchen to place the bowl on the floor. Instead of going to the dish, the cat jumps up on the counter and leaps onto the top of the fridge. His nose twitches once, twice, and then he sprawls on top of it.

"Damn it, Kurt!" I snap.

The cat stares haughtily at me from his spot atop the appliance.

"Kurt?" Salvatore's deep voice echoes behind me.

"Yup. I've decided it's time to name my cat since I'm keeping him."

I turn and head into the open concept dining room to get a chair, avoiding Salvatore, not wanting to know whether he's watching me or not. I'm so mad at him.

"And it has to be 'Kurt'?"

"Yes." I chose that name so I can always be reminded of what a liar my husband is.

I carry the chair into the kitchen and climb on it, intending to get Kurt down. However, the second I reach for him, he leaps across onto the counter, runs the length of it, and jumps on top of the bar in front of Salvatore. They engage in some kind of a standoff, the cat observing him with interest while he scowls at him. I open my mouth to warn Salvatore to watch his plate, but Kurt's already snagged a huge piece of food and dashed away.

"Was that . . . fish?" I ask.

"Yes. Why?"

I groan. "That upsets his stomach."

As I watch Kurt chew the piece of fish in the corner of the kitchen and think of what will await me in the litter box tomorrow, I decide I'm done for today. I take the container with the rest of the meat from the fridge and head back to my room.

Milene leaves the kitchen and walks across the living room, carrying the leftovers from lunch, obviously planning to eat them in her room. I decide that won't do. "No eating in the bedrooms."

She stops in her tracks, turns slowly and graces me with one firm, agitated look. "Ada brought me lunch and dinner there."

"But you didn't eat it, did you?" I point to the bar stool next to mine. "You eat here."

"I'm most certainly not eating at the same table as you."

I grab the back of the chair and turn it so it's facing her. "Here," I bark. Milene lifts her chin, and yet she does as I ask.

"You have control issues." She sits next to me and starts eating directly out of the container.

It amazes me how unexpectedly normal she is. If I didn't know it already, I never would have guessed that she was a Mafia princess, accustomed to luxury. She seems so ordinary, living in that dump of an apartment, working as a nurse, and keeping that idiotic cat. Why not spend the money her brother was sending her? She keeps her nails short and unpainted, and her hair is gathered at the top of her head with a simple rubber band. I've seen it hang loose, and it's a simple cut, nothing fancy. Then, there is her face. Zero makeup. No false eyelashes. I have never come across a woman within our circle who hasn't had her hair perfectly styled, had makeup flawless and was wearing an outfit that came off the runway. Still, the woman sitting next to me in a loose T-shirt and jeans is more beautiful than any of the others. Milene Scardoni is a rare specimen.

"I need to do some shopping tomorrow," she says between bites.

"You'll take bodyguards."

"Bodyguards?" She looks up at me. "As in plural?"

"Yes."

"I'm going to a fucking supermarket. One will be enough."

"You will take the bodyguards I assign to you, or you can order online. Your choice."

"Perfect." She turns back to her food. "I'm going to buy tampons and cat food with two gorillas trailing after me."

"Four gorillas," I say.

Her head snaps up. "Four? Are you serious?"

"Don't argue with me, Milene. It won't get you anywhere. It's going to be my way, or it's not happening."

"You"—she points her fork in my face—"need professional help."

"Alessandro will be waiting for you in front of the door at nine. You'll be escorted by him. The rest of the team will follow in a second car."

"Two cars. Fucking great." She shakes her head and resumes eating.

It looks like I'm being ignored again since she keeps shoveling food into her mouth, clearly trying everything she can to avoid making eye contact with me.

"You haven't asked what happened to my leg," I say and see her fork still halfway to its destination.

"What happened to your leg?" she asks just before taking a bite of meat.

"Gunshot wound. Transtibial amputation."

She lifts her head and looks at the bandage visible beneath the cuff of my T-shirt sleeve. "Seems like people enjoy shooting you."

"It happens."

"How many times so far?"

"That I've been shot at?" I reach for my glass of water. "I stopped counting. But if you mean how many times I've been hit—eight. Actually, nine, if you count this last one, but that one was just a graze."

Milene's eyes bulge. "Holy shit. Are you trying to break a Guinness World Record or something?"

I ignore her retort. "When you married me, you became a target, too," I say. "Do you now understand the need for four bodyguards?"

"Wonderful." She sighs and looks at my left hand lying on the bar surface. "Gunshot wound, as well?"

So, she's noticed that I removed the glove, as I usually do before going to bed. I follow her gaze to my hand, regarding the numerous scars covering my slightly deformed fingers.

"Hammer," I say. "The nerves in the last two fingers are damaged beyond repair. I can't feel those. The rest are mostly okay, but I have trouble with fine motor skills."

"Why do you wear a glove?"

"I don't like being reminded of my weak spots," I say. "My left hand is the dominant one."

"What about your leg? Is that a weak spot, as well?"

"No. I have a top-of-the-line prosthesis and have adapted well. A textbook case. And it has been over seven years. Most of the time, I forget it's there." I reach out to take a lock of hair that's fallen across her eyes, and tuck it behind her ear. "Does it bother you? That I'm missing part of my leg?"

"Nope." She smiles. "But you being a lying bastard, does."

I lean forward and take in the contours of her face. This smile doesn't compare to the way she laughed at the coffee shop two days ago. The coffee-shop smile, I liked. I don't like this one. It seems . . . angry.

Reaching for my crutches, I stand up and lean to whisper into her ear. "But I've never lied to you, Milene, have I?"

"Withholding the truth is the same as lying."

"Not in my world, cara." I place a light kiss on the exposed part of her shoulder where the T-shirt she's wearing has slipped and head toward my bedroom.

"I have a night shift tomorrow," she shouts after me. "I need to be at work at nine."

"You won't be working at the hospital anymore, Milene."

"What! You can't forbid me from working."

"I just did."

The sound of a chair scraping across the floor is followed by rapid tramping of bare feet. Just seconds later, she comes around me and stands there, blocking my path.

"Please, don't do this," she says through gritted teeth.

"I'm sorry, cara, but I won't risk your safety."

Milene's nostrils flare, and she takes a step closer to stand right in front of me, our bodies almost touching. She tilts her chin and looks straight into my eyes.

"You've ruined my life," she whispers.

I bend my head until our noses touch, just like the day we met in the parking lot. "I know."

She doesn't say anything. Eyes locked, we stare at each other for a long time, the tips of our noses the only point of contact between our two bodies. After what seems like an eternity, Milene turns abruptly on her heel and disappears into the guest bedroom.

# Chapter eight

Milene

I'M BROWSING THE SOAP AISLE WHEN THE PHONE IN MY POCKET vibrates, indicating an incoming message.

**09:23 Bianca:** Angelo just told me. What the hell were you thinking, going to New York? I can't believe you lied to me! Are you okay?

I sigh and hit the microphone icon to record a voice message. Bianca and I usually text each other since she can't speak, but it would take me half an hour to type everything I want to say.

"I'm sorry for lying to you, twinkle toes. I'm okay, I guess. Still trying to come to terms with the fact that everything I've worked for is all just . . . gone. Did you know I delivered a baby in a parking lot earlier this month? It was scary, Bianca, but at the same time it was the best feeling ever. Salvatore said I can't work anymore. That controlling son of a bitch . . . Just a second." I turn to face the mountain of a man who's standing a few paces behind me. I thought Salvatore was strange, but this guy beats him by a mile. He didn't utter a single word on the way here.

"Alessandro, right? Do you mind?" I motion with my hand for him to move away. "I'm trying to have a private call here."

My bodyguard takes one step back and crosses his arms, regarding me with a piercing black gaze. I roll my eyes and continue.

"About Salvatore. I'm so mad at him!" I whisper-yell into the phone. "We'd already met. Salvatore and me. Three times. He never told me who he was, and I thought he was just a guy, you know? I only realized who he was when he came to my place to sign the marriage papers yesterday. I liked him, Bianca. I really liked him. We went on a date, kind of, and then he ended up being the fucking don of the New York Family."

I take a chocolate-scented body wash from the shelf and sniff it.

"I'm not sure what I think of him. I hate him for making me marry him and ruining everything I had planned. If I could turn back time, I would never have come here. But part of me still kind of likes him, and that's making everything so much more frustrating."

I put the chocolate wash back—too sweet-smelling—and pick up one with a coconut scent.

"Looks like someone's trying to kill him, so I'm saddled with four bodyguards. Four! I'm in a fucking supermarket with four guys in dark suits trailing behind me. Jesus. Talk about taking someone's life and turning it one-eighty in twenty-four hours. How's Mikhail? Lena? How are you? Does your back hurt? I miss you, honey. I'm sorry for lying to you, but trust me, I'm paying for it with interest."

I send the message and head to the cash register, with Alessandro trailing after me and another bodyguard following a few yards behind. The third is standing in a corner, observing the space. The fourth guy stayed out front by the entrance. What an overkill. What if I decide to go jogging? Would all four of them come along, snapping at my heels?

This morning, I caught Salvatore as he was leaving and told him I had to go to the hospital to hand in my resignation. He said it was already handled. Handled! As though it were a subscription to a fucking online magazine and not my life's dream! What am I going to do now? Maybe, I could find some small private hospital to finish my residency and work there. It wouldn't be as much of a high security risk as working in a big hospital like St. Mary's. Yes, that would work perfectly.

"No," Salvatore says and returns to his meal.

"What? Why?"

"They wouldn't allow bodyguards to accompany you in a hospital. Any hospital."

"They can stay outside."

"Not good enough."

I put my fork down and take a deep breath. "What do you expect me to do all day long?"

"You can do whatever you want."

"I want to work."

"Anything except for that."

I have this maddening urge to wrap my hands around his neck and squeeze. "I'll go nuts with nothing to do. I can't live like that."

"I'll give you some funds. Start a charity or something."

"A charity?" I gape at him. "I sew wounds and insert catheters. I have no idea how charities work or how I'd even set one up."

"Google it."

Google it. Great. "Why did you insist on marrying me?"

"I've already told you. I have my reasons."

"Will you share those reasons with me?"

He looks up at me, those piercing amber eyes sending laser beams directly into mine. I want to look away, but I can't.

"No," he says and goes back to his dinner once again. "We're going to an auction next week. There is a painting I'm planning to buy. Do you have a dress?"

"I'm not going anywhere with you, Salvatore."

"Yes, you are."

"I said no."

"It doesn't matter what you say, Milene. I want you to come with me, so you're doing so voluntarily, or I'll be dragging you. It's your choice."

I grip the fork in my hand and lean forward until my face is right in front of his. "Fuck. You." I sneer.

He watches me for a moment, then his hand shoots out and grabs my chin before I can move a muscle. "I will, cara."

I lean away, escaping his tender hold. "Keep dreaming. You're not coming anywhere near my pussy."

I might be wrong, but it seems like the corner of his lips curl upward a little bit. "If you don't have a suitable dress, Alessandro will take you to buy one. I don't want you going in that short disco-ball creation you wore at the bar. You need something that will cover your ass this time."

"Oh? So you ogled my ass?"

"Of course I did," he says, picks up his plate and carries it over to the dishwasher.

I watch as he walks away toward the private part of the penthouse, enjoying the view of his backside in charcoal dress pants, despite my better instincts. That ass is sexy as fuck, and it goes perfectly with his narrow waist and wide shoulders. I don't remember ever meeting a man who wears suits the way Salvatore does, as if he were born in one. He's seriously hot and . . . Stop, damn it! As handsome as he is, it doesn't change the fact that he's an asshole. I'd better remember that.

# CHAPTER

## Salvatore

I'VE JUST FINISHED BREWING MY COFFEE WHEN MILENE COMES OUT of the hallway and trudges across the living room toward the kitchen. Her hair is a mess, her feet are bare, and she's carrying that defective animal under her arm like it's a purse. In the kitchen, she mumbles something as she passes by me, bound for the fridge. She opens the door and takes out a carton of milk, then crosses to the counter. The cat is still under her right arm and currently giving me the evil eye.

After the lunch yesterday, she disappeared into her room and didn't come out. Obviously, she's trying her best to avoid me. I take the tangled strand which has fallen over her face and move it away, making sure the back of my fingers brush the skin of her cheek. Milene throws me a sideways look, which I assume is meant to be angry, but the overall impression is somewhat ruined with her yawn.

"What happened to you?" I ask.

"I binge-watched the last season of *Stranger Things* last night. Finished at four and couldn't sleep."

She looks over to the coffee machine in front of her, then switches her gaze to the coffee I've prepared for myself and leans forward to inhale the scent. She tentatively reaches out to wrap her hand around the cup and slowly pulls it along the counter. Once she has the coffee in front of her, she looks at me from the corner of her eye, probably awaiting my reaction. Without breaking eye contact, she reaches for the milk and pours a bit into the coffee. My coffee. Which I drink black. Finishing up with the milk, she stretches toward a container of sugar, but it's out of her reach. Our gazes remain locked.

counter until it's in front of her. It's a screw-top, so she'll need to put the cat down.

Instead of doing so, she thrusts the scrawny animal into my arms and proceeds to open the jar. The cat looks even worse up close. Part of its left ear is missing, and it seems like one of its eyes is looking in the wrong direction.

"This is the ugliest cat I've ever laid my eyes on," I say.

Milene's head snaps up, her eyes widening. "That was mean."

She reaches for the cat. The damn thing picks that exact moment to wake up from its lethargic state and leaps onto the counter, scratching my wrist with its hind paw.

"It's not Kurt's fault. You scared him," Milene says, takes the cup with *my* coffee and turns to leave. She takes two steps toward the living room but suddenly stops, turns on her heel, and marches back. She places the coffee on the counter, takes my right hand, and turns it to inspect the inside of my wrist.

"Do you think I'll live?" I ask, observing the three-inch long scratch.

Milene glides the tip of her finger over my skin along the scratch and looks up at me. "Yes, unfortunately."

I grab her around the waist with my free hand and crash her body to mine. She yelps, then presses her palms against my chest as if to push me away. Only she doesn't. A small shudder passes through her body when I slide my palm under her T-shirt and continue up along her spine.

"Whose is this?" I ask and bend my head to bury my nose in her hair.

"What?" she breathes out.

"This is a man's T-shirt." It's one of the oversized shirts I've noticed she likes to sleep in.

"I'm not sure. Probably David's."

My hand stills in the middle of her back. She's wearing another man's T-shirt. "What about the others? Are those his, too?"

"Some. Why?"

I grab the material of her shirt and pull the damn thing over her head.

"Hey!" She covers her naked breasts with her arms and stares at me. "What the fuck is wrong with you? Give that back."

She won't be wearing another man's things ever again. I walk toward the other side of the kitchen to throw the T-shirt into the trashcan, then head toward her bedroom.

"You can't throw away my stuff," I yell after Salvatore.

He ignores me and keeps walking until he reaches the door of my room, then marches inside.

"Hey!" I dash after him. "You have no business there! Salvatore!"

I find him standing in front of my closet, looking over its contents. He grabs the stack of folded T-shirts I use to sleep in from the middle shelf, crosses the room, and walks out.

"Are you crazy? Give me my clothes back. Right away!"

I'm still standing in the middle of my room with my arms pressed over my boobs when he comes back two minutes later, carrying another pile of T-shirts under his arm. Without any explanation whatsoever, he returns to the closet and lays the shirts on the shelf where mine had been.

"What is this?" I snap. "Another of your power games? You can't go around throwing away other people's belongings! Salvatore, are you even listening to me?"

"No." He closes the closet doors and approaches me, holding one of the shirts he brought in his hands.

I'm just about to lay into him again when he holds up the T-shirt and pulls it down over my head.

"Arms," he says, holding the shirt.

"You need help," I say through clenched teeth.

Salvatore bends until our faces are at the same level. It's ridiculous, how pretty those amber eyes of his are. Or how absolutely excited it makes me every time he pins with his piercing gaze.

"Arms, Milene."

I press my lips together, unwrap my arms from my chest and slide them into the sleeves he's holding out for me.

"Satisfied?" I snap.

He looks me over. The hem of his T-shirt almost reaches my knees.

"Very," he says and casually walks out of the room.

"Control freak!" I shout after him.

When I'm sure he's gone, I grab a handful of the white cotton and press it to my nose. It smells like him. There is no way I'm going to wear this maniac's clothes. I close my eyes and inhale again. What the hell am

I doing? I quickly take off the T-shirt, throw it onto the floor and head into the bathroom to take a shower. I'm getting rid of every single one of those.

When I leave the bathroom twenty minutes later, however, I grab Salvatore's T-shirt off the floor and tuck it under my pillow.

# Chapter Ten

Milene

I grab the remote, turn on the TV, and flop myself down onto the big couch in the middle of the living room to channel surf. Nothing catches my eye, so I leave it on the Food Network, where some guy is making homemade pasta. I grab a throw pillow to place under my head and stretch out.

Four days. I've been holed up in the penthouse for four fucking days with absolutely nothing to do, and it's really getting to me. The only people I see are Ada and Salvatore. Ada doesn't talk much. She pays me lip service occasionally to ask whether I need anything, then goes straight back to work. I hate cooking, but I was so desperate for something to do earlier I asked if she'd like any help with lunch. Ada looked at me as though I'd offered to gut the neighbor's dog. I guess she caught the sight of me frying eggs this morning when I almost set the kitchen on fire. It was an accident! I left the pan on the stove and went to chase Kurt, who was scratching his claws on the carpet in the living room.

And then, there's him. My dearest husband. The bane of my existence. All those mysterious looks he gives me. Casual touches I pretend I don't like, but secretly enjoy. The excitement that overwhelms me every time he walks through the front door in the evening. It's making me insane. I don't want to feel those things for someone who's basically smashed my life to smithereens.

Yawning, I turn down the TV volume and close my eyes. Last night I dreamed about him kissing me, then woke up abruptly and couldn't make myself go back to sleep because I kept thinking about him. It seems like my fate is to spend my life sleep-deprived. Before, it was because of work. Now, it's because of him.

"Damn you, Salvatore Ajello," I mumble into the pillow.

I've just dozed off, when I feel a light touch along my jaw, moving up the side of my face and tracing my cheek toward the lower lip. I reach out to shoo away the cat, which enjoys toying with me while I sleep, but instead of the soft fur, my fingers wrap around a strong male hand. My eyes snap open.

"Feisty, even while sleeping," Salvatore's deep baritone voice booms as he looks down at my hand still holding his. I let go immediately and jump off the couch, intending to hightail it out of the room. The moment I turn away, Salvatore's arm reaches out to grab my waist, pulling me back against his hard chest.

"Let me go," I mumble.

The arm around my middle tightens even more. His breath is warm on the side of my neck as he bends his head to whisper into my ear. "No."

I close my eyes and inhale deeply, trying to ignore the butterflies fluttering in the pit of my stomach. It appears my whole body is suddenly charged with electricity, simply from being near him. As I open my mouth to tell him to go to hell, his lips kiss the side of my neck, and I barely manage to stifle a sigh.

"You didn't join me for breakfast this morning," he says into my ear. "Are you avoiding me, Milene?"

"No," I lie. Of course I'm avoiding him. Being attracted to a man you hate is torturous.

"Oh, but I think you are." His grip around my waist intensifies, while his other hand moves to wrap around my neck. "Tell me, cara, does my presence affect you?"

"Yes," I say while clenching my teeth. My skin itches all over as if a low current is steadily overwhelming my nervous system. My body is a live wire, but my head is spinning in confusion as I try hard to block out the image of him naked. "Every time I see you, I have an urge to launch a blunt object at your head."

"So violent . . . I thought Mafia princesses were sweet-tempered by default. Demure . . ."

Salvatore's lips continue to graze my skin, and I find it really hard to keep my composure while his soft touch tingles the fine hairs on my neck.

"Sorry to disappoint. You got the short end of the stick. Maybe you should send me back to the shop since you're not satisfied with what's under the hood."

Suddenly, he turns me around so I'm facing him and gripping my chin, tilts my head up.

"You're not going anywhere, Milene." His lips gently brush against mine as he speaks, and I fist my hands to stop the powerful urge to pull his mouth forcefully onto mine. "Night, cara."

He releases my chin, turns away and leaves without turning back.

# Chapter eleven

## Salvatore

I LEAN MY SHOULDER ON THE BOOKSHELF AND REGARD MILENE. I'VE been doing so quite a lot in the last week. She is sprawled on the couch, watching another cooking show. My gaze travels along her body and stops at her legs which are dangling over the armrest. A pair of extremely ugly sandals with multicolored sequins adorn her ridiculously small feet. The cat is stretched out next to Milene, with its head turned toward the TV. Something is seriously wrong with that animal.

Before I moved Milene in here, I would go to the office early in the morning and usually return to the penthouse late in the evening. But now, I keep finding some idiotic reasons to leave the office and drop by my place at least twice a day, just to get a glimpse of her. Milene tries her best to ignore my presence when she sees me watching her, so I started coming upstairs for lunch every day.

"You can't cook," I say. "Why do you watch cooking shows?"

This morning when I came to breakfast, Ada approached me and asked if I would consider installing extra fire extinguishers in the kitchen. When I asked why, she said my wife offered to help her make pasta sauce yesterday and managed to start a fire in the pan because she left it to heat for too long.

"Well, I watch *Animal Planet*, too, and you don't see me chasing rabbits around or laying eggs in the sand, do you?" Milene says without taking her eyes off the screen. "Are you going to dictate what I watch now?"

"Maybe." I don't give a fuck what she watches, but I quite enjoy rattling her cage.

Milene cocks her head to the side and arches an eyebrow at me. "Is that some compulsion? Ordering people around just because and expecting them to dance to your tune?"

"It's how things work around here, Milene."

"So, you say jump and people ask how high?"

"Pretty much."

She scrunches her nose. "Your life must be a really boring endeavor."

Yes. I never realized just how much until she barged in and made a mess of my entire existence.

"Grab your purse," I say.

"I don't need a purse for lounging on the couch."

"We're going to have a look at one of the lots I bought."

"Not interested. But thanks for the invite." She throws a placating smile at me and shifts her attention back to the TV.

I straighten and walk toward the couch. Milene pretends she doesn't notice me when I stop in front of her. I bend, grab her around the waist, and lift her onto my shoulder.

"What the fuck!" she yelps. "Put me down!"

Ignoring her protests, I head toward the front door. I want to spend time with her, and she has no say in it.

"You controlling, rude, overbearing asshat . . ." She rattles on with her insults, while she pounds on my back with her fists. It's . . . quite amusing.

I carry her toward the elevator and get in.

". . . absolutely no care whatsoever about other people's wants . . ."

I hit the button for the garage.

". . . find a therapist who'll help you with your issues . . ."

The elevator dings when we reach the underground level. I step out and pivot toward my car as another vehicle parks next to mine, and Nino gets out.

Milene continues to babble, ". . . a fucking Neanderthal with zero . . ."

I pass my head of security—who stares at us with his mouth agape—open the passenger door, and deposit my wife onto the seat.

"Put on your seat belt, Milene."

She tilts her face up and presses her lips together, then gives me the middle finger. I close her door and walk around the hood to get into the driver's seat. Milene is sitting with her arms crossed, staring through the windshield at the concrete wall.

"Milene," I say.

She snorts.

Reaching over, I grab her chin and turn her head. We stare at each other for almost a minute. The defiance in her eyes turns me on so fucking much. I don't want to break her spirit because I enjoy the ways in which she tries to defy me. But she needs to understand there is a leader in every pack. And in this particular menagerie, that would be me.

"Seat belt," I whisper.

Milene exhales through her nose, reaches for the seat belt, and tries three times before she finds the buckle. She is still looking at me, her eyes boring into mine. I move my thumb to lightly brush the line of her lower lip, then lean away and start the car.

I turn around, looking over the green expanse as far as my gaze can reach. The vast field is surrounded by trees on three sides. It's beautiful.

"I thought you said you bought a lot," I say, "not half of the state."

"I bought several. I still haven't decided what I want to build on this one, so I'm acquiring all the available land. Just in case." He takes my hand and leads me back to the car. "Are you hungry?"

I expected the lot he mentioned to be somewhere in the city, but we drove two hours to reach it.

"I'm starving," I mumble, looking down at our intertwined fingers. I should pull my hand away. But I don't.

"There's a restaurant twenty minutes from here," he says as he opens the passenger door for me. "I eat there when I come this way."

"Some posh place, I presume?" I ask when he starts the car.

"Yes. Why do you ask?"

I gape at him. "I'm in fucking jean shorts, Salvatore. Even if they let us in, everyone will stare."

He gives me one of those pinning looks of his, then reaches for his phone and calls someone.

"Jonathan," he says into the phone, "I'm coming for a lunch with my wife in fifteen minutes. We don't want to be disturbed."

He doesn't wait for the person on the other end to reply, just ends the call and throws the phone onto the dash. Rude much? And what will this Jonathan guy do, anyway? I assume he's the manager.

I shake my head and train my eyes on the road in front of us. "You have a very strange way of handling phone calls."

"How so?"

"What happened with 'Hello, how's your day?' or 'How are you?' You know, common courtesy."

During the two-hour drive over here, his phone rang at least seven times. With each one, he said exactly two words: "yes" when he took the call, and then either "yes" or "no" after listening to the person on the other end of the line. He'd cut the call right afterward.

"I don't care how they are or how their day is going, Milene."

I turn my head and stare at him. I kind of assumed that was the case, but I didn't expect him to be so blunt and admit it. "You are one exceptionally rude person."

"What I am, is *un*interested."

"Uninterested." I nod. He's absolutely nuts. "About the people who work for you, or people in general?"

"In general. With one exception," he says and levels me with that unnerving gaze of his. "You."

I blink in confusion and quickly avert my eyes. Should I be flattered or terrified?

Probably both.

"Whoa." I stop in my tracks as we pass through the restaurant's rear French doors.

The place is situated near the edge of a forest. It's a big one-story colonial style mansion. What leaves me speechless, however, is a huge garden in the center, placed under an enormous iron dome covered with vines and greenery. The tables and chairs are all done in white wood, with flowerpots scattered around to create a jungle-like aesthetic. It's magnificent. And completely empty of people, excluding the manager who greeted us at the doors.

Based on the size of the parking lot and the number of tables, the place can accommodate more than a hundred people. It's lunch time. How come there is not even one table occupied?

Salvatore's hand lands on the small of my back as he ushers me toward a table on the side of the garden area, set next to a lemon tree planted in a red terracotta pot. He pulls out the chair for me and takes a seat opposite.

"Is something wrong with their business?" I ask in a quiet voice.

"No. Why?"

"Well, I'm under the impression you need guests to run a restaurant business."

"They have more customers than they can handle," Salvatore says and takes the menus the waiter brought. "What do you want to drink?"

"Lemonade."

"A lemonade and a mineral water," he tells the waiter. "And tell Jonathan we'll take a few dishes the chef already has prepared."

The waiter nods and vanishes.

"Mineral water?" I raise an eyebrow.

"I don't drink when I drive." He leans over the table and reaches for my hand.

A pleasant shiver passes through me when he traces the lines on my skin in the same way as he did when we went for our "date." And like before, I don't remove my hand, even though I want to.

"So, if this place is usually packed, where is everyone?" I ask looking around.

"They left."

"Left? Where to? Why would they . . .?" I snap my head back and gawk at him. "You shooed away a whole restaurant full of people?"

"You said you wouldn't be comfortable with them staring at you." He pulls my hand closer . "Now they won't."

My heartbeat skyrockets. That's the most fucking romantic thing a man has ever done for me.

"So, a hundred or more people had to leave in the middle of their meal because of my shorts?"

"No. They had to leave because no one gets to make you feel uncomfortable."

I lean onto my elbows, coming up to his face with only a few inches separating us. "I didn't feel particularly comfortable with my head dangling upside down while you so graciously carried me to the car as if I was a sack of potatoes. In fact, it was a rather uncomfortable experience, Salvatore."

"Then let me rephrase my declaration. No one, except me."

Ugh. I roll my eyes and sit back down in my chair.

"Tell me, do you really chop people up for fun?" I ask.

It's been bugging me from the start. When Angelo told me that Salvatore sent Enzo's body back in three bags, I assumed he was some super aggressive, violent guy who did that kind of stuff in a mad rage. That's the absolute opposite of the extremely composed man who's currently watching me from the other side of the table. I have the impression that he wouldn't bat an eyelid if a fucking UFO landed in the middle of the restaurant.

"No," Salvatore says and reaches for his water.

"I knew it." I smirk. Of course he doesn't. I've always been good in judging person's character.

"I do it because nothing sends a stronger message than a severed head delivered to your doorstep, Milene."

My jaw drops. I've been married off to a complete lunatic.

Salvatore cocks his head to the side and pins me with his gaze. "Are you scared of me now, cara?"

I take him in, his big body casually leaning back into the chair, those amber eyes boring into mine. After hearing that declaration, I should jump up from my chair and run away screaming. Only, I don't. Something must be wrong with me, because for some unexplainable reason, I am not scared of him.

Two waiters approach the table, carrying huge oval platters in each hand, saving me from giving Salvatore my answer. As they place them on the table, I notice both are trying really hard not to meet Salvatore's gaze. I guess that's understandable. People tend to avoid eye contact with someone they think is crazy. But what puzzles me is that neither the waiters nor the manager who greeted us when we arrived ever glanced at me. Why would they avoid looking at me? I'm a nice person.

I shake my head, take a sip of my lemonade, and cough. How many lemons did they put in, a whole pound?

"Excuse me?" I call to the nearby waiter.

He stills while arranging the plates on the table, then turns his head to Salvatore. Why would he do that?

Salvatore gives him a nod.

The waiter straightens and finally gives me his attention. "Yes, Mrs. Ajello?"

"Can I have some sugar, please?" I ask and lean my elbows on the table again, glaring at my husband who's been watching me the whole time. I wait for the waiters to leave, then raise my eyebrows. "What was that?"

"What exactly?"

"That nod. Because it looked like you were giving the waiter permission to address me."

"And what's wrong with that?"

"Are you for real?"

"He's not from the Family, Milene. Therefore, he is not permitted to look at my wife unless I allow him to."

I have no comeback to that, so I just stare at him.

"What would you like to eat?" He nods toward the plates and the ton of food lining the table in front of me.

"I'm not picky." I shrug and place something that looks like rice and green leaves on my plate, together with a huge piece of fish.

"Don't you want to know what it is first? What if you don't like it?"

"Someone took time to make these . . . whatever you call them. They cooked them and brought them over. I didn't have to make any of this." I stuff a spoonful of food into my mouth. "So, what's not to like?"

"You really hate cooking."

"Yup." There is something that looks like fried onion rings on one of the plates. I reach out and take a piece, then yelp. They're scorching hot.

"Let me see." Salvatore seizes my hand and turns my palm up.

I try pulling out of his grip, but he holds my hand tightly. My heartbeat picks up, and butterflies flutter in my stomach again as he lifts my hand to his lips and places a kiss on the tips of my fingers. The moment his grip loosens, I quickly retrieve my hand and pretend I'm engrossed in my meal. Why does he keep doing that? Shouldn't the seduction come before the marriage? He's already forced me into marrying him, so I don't see the point.

He can keep trying. I'm not sleeping with him. I would rather die than sleep with him. I take another bite and chew slowly while my inner devil mocks me.

*Liar, liar, pants on fire. You've been imagining how it would be. Wondering if he would also be controlling in bed. You've been ogling him in secret like he's a candy for days, and . . .*

I put my fork next to the plate and grit my teeth. *Stop*! I yell at my internal self. That bitch has the worst taste in men. *Just . . . fucking stop.*

"Are you all right, Milene?"

My head snaps up. "Yup," I murmur and keep shoveling the food in my mouth. "Why?"

"You had a very interesting facial expression for a moment. It seemed like . . . frustration."

"Well, I'm forced to be with you, Salvatore. Wouldn't you be frustrated if someone forced you to spend time with yourself?"

He leans over the table and takes my chin, making me look at him. "Is it really that awful? Spending time with me?"

No. And that's exactly why I'm so frustrated. "Yes," I say.

His thumb traces a line along my chin and up to my lower lip. If I saw his picture somewhere, I would have said he's ridiculously handsome and that's it. But the image wouldn't be able to convey the potency of his presence in person. I quickly pull away from his touch and focus back on my meal, eating some more of the delicious food. Trying my best not to let my eyes wander to him. It doesn't really help because even though I'm not looking at him, I can still sense his gaze on me.

Why did he insist on marrying me? I'm pretty sure I'm not his type. I mean, he's like a walking commercial for Armani or Prada, or a similar high-end designer, in his impeccably tailored gray suit and black shirt. And that slicked back dark hair, with snow-white strands splattered here and there, which tempts me to thread my fingers through it and count the grays. I don't know why I'm so attracted to him. I like blond guys. Chris Hemsworth. Brad Pitt. The angelic-looking type. I steal a quick glance at Salvatore and snort. He could give Satan a fucking run for his money. He's just missing the damn horns and a pitchfork.

Suddenly, his gloved hand enters my field of vision and takes a strand of my hair that's fallen out of my ponytail and is hanging next to my plate. He holds it between his fingers for a few seconds, then moves it behind my shoulder.

"You find something amusing, Milene?"

I put my fork down and lift my head. Salvatore is leaning over the table, his face barely inches from mine, and his unnerving eyes are staring right into my own. My breath catches. I force myself to hold his gaze while keeping my expression blank. It's not easy.

It's both horrifying and exciting how someone is able to ensnare a person with only a look like Salvatore does. I'm afraid that if he tried to pull me into the depths of hell while looking at me like this, I would willingly follow. Not good. Not good at all.

"I don't find anything amusing in this situation, Salvatore." I sigh. "Listen, I understand. I really do. I fucked up, and you wanted to punish me for it. Nobody messes with the big bad New York Don—point taken. But let's be honest, here. This,"—I point my finger to him, then to me—"this is not going to work. It's better we part ways. You send me back to Chicago, saying I suck in bed, or whatever, and annul the marriage. I get out of your hair and go on with my life. And you can continue beheading people, sending their bodies around via FedEx, or whatever, without me to mess with your schedule. What do you say?"

Salvatore places his left hand at the edge of the table and tilts his head, regarding me in silence. Is he considering my proposition? Oh God, please make him say yes.

The table between us suddenly flies to the side, knocking me backward in my chair. Dishes and cutlery crash onto the cobbled ground. Pieces of food and broken glass scatter everywhere within a five-foot radius. I stare at my husband with wide eyes as he gets up and takes two casual steps until he's standing right in front of me.

Leaning back in my chair, I tilt my head up. "That would mean no, I assume?"

"That would mean no, Milene," he says in that cold tone, grabs me around my waist and lifts me up over his shoulder.

"Salvatore!" I yell with my head once again dangling behind his back as he carries me. "Put me down! Right now!"

He takes a couple of more steps, then stops. Thank you, Jesus, there is some sense in him after all.

"The food was excellent, Jonathan. Tell the chef we enjoyed our meal and put the damages on my account."

"Of course, Mr. Ajello," answers a strangled voice, and Salvatore resumes his trek through the restaurant. The fucking son of a bitch keeps walking!

"I have your shoulder lodged in my stomach," I snap. "I'm going to puke all over your fancy suit if you don't put me down, Salvatore."

A ping sounds as the car door unlocks. Salvatore settles me onto the passenger seat, walks around the car, and gets behind the wheel as if everything is perfectly in order.

"If you have a mental health diagnosis, now is the time to mention it," I say, staring at his perfect profile.

He turns his head and I find myself a prisoner of his intense gaze again. His hand shoots up and grabs my chin. I suck in a breath and stare at him as he leans close to my face.

"It doesn't really matter, cara. Because you're stuck with me," he says through his teeth, then crushes his mouth to mine.

It's so angry. His kiss. My response—even angrier. I grab his neck, intending to squeeze it, but instead my hands slide upward, fingers tangling in his hair. There is not enough air in my lungs as I try to keep up, taking everything he's giving. God, his mouth . . . so hard, but somehow soft at the same time. Teeth biting at my lower lip. His fingers, still holding my chin. It's madness. I can't think. I don't want to think. When he kissed me in that parking lot it was like a sea breeze, but this is a tempest. I find myself wrapping my arms around his neck, trying to get closer to the stormy sea that is Salvatore Ajello. His other hand cups my cheek, then moves to my nape, squeezing. The lips on mine go still.

"It looks like we're not incompatible, Milene," he says into my mouth, then abruptly releases me and starts the car.

I fix my gaze onto the road in front of us, wondering what the hell just happened.

# Chapter Twelve

Salvatore

THE HUGE LOT WHERE I'M PLANNING ON BUILDING A NEW WAREHOUSE is in the industrial district. It's far enough away from the city to provide privacy, but at the same time, close enough to the main roads not to be problematic when it comes to our distribution needs.

"I want the main warehouse in the center. Put eight or so more around it and fill them with random goods to act as a front," I say.

"Food?" Arturo asks.

"No. Something with a longer shelf life. Car parts. Tools. Furniture. Use your imagination. If someone comes poking their nose in, I don't want anything to raise their suspicions. For example, tons of rotten food."

"All right." He nods. "How much should we transfer when the warehouse is fully prepped?"

"Forty percent, max."

"Why not all?" Rocco throws in.

I turn around and look at my capo. Rocco is good with managing the operational part of our construction projects, but he's not very bright where general business is concerned. I allowed him to take over as capo two years ago when his father stepped down, but I'm not sure if it was the best decision.

"Never put all your eggs in one basket, Rocco," I say and check my watch. I need to head back, or I'll be late for the auction.

"Nino told me you assigned Alessandro as your wife's bodyguard," he says as he follows me toward our cars. "Was it because he's not attracted to women?"

I stop in my tracks and pivot so suddenly he nearly runs into me. "I don't give a fuck about who he's attracted to, Rocco. I assigned him because he'll make a damn good bodyguard."

He backs up ever so slightly. "Yes, but . . ."

"Are you questioning my decision?"

His face goes ghostly pale. "No, Boss. Of course not."

"You sure?"

"Yes." He takes another step back. "I'm sorry, Boss."

"Good." I get inside my car and peel out of the lot with the accompaniment of screeching tires and the scent of burning rubber, heading out to the highway leading back to the city.

During the drive, I give Ada a quick call to ask what Milene's doing, and she confirms my wife is in the penthouse chasing the cat. The anxiety in the pit of my stomach lessens, slightly. Still, I press harder on the gas.

Rocco's words cross my mind as I'm waiting for the streetlight to change. He's always been very homophobic and considers any man who doesn't indulge in every willing pussy to be gay. I wonder if he's right about Alessandro. I can't remember ever seeing him with a woman, or even talking about one. In fact, for the five years he's been working for me, I don't think I've heard Alessandro Zanetti talk more than a handful of times.

When he first became part of the Family, I was suspicious. He'd obviously received military training, and I even considered the possibility that he might be an undercover cop, so Nino did a thorough check of his background. It seemed solid. A couple of years of military service, then an honorary discharge due to injury. I don't remember the nature of the injury which Nino mentioned, but it certainly hasn't impacted Alessandro's abilities. From what I've seen, the man is in perfect physical condition. Over the years, I've tested him several times by assigning him to carry out terminations, just to gauge his reaction in case he was, in fact, a plant. The way he disposed of his targets using surgical precision and not a second's hesitation, confirmed what I already suspected. Before he joined Cosa Nostra, Alessandro was a professional hitman. So, I made sure his skills wouldn't go to waste.

When Milene walks through the double doors and enters the living room, I let my eyes wander over her white stiletto heels and the white dress that hugs her curves and emphasizes her figure. Her hair is loose, the soft curls falling to the middle of her back. She's put on makeup and looks devastatingly beautiful.

"Will this event go on all night? If that's the case, I'll need to swap these shoes for another pair with smaller heels," she states as she approaches, fumbling through her purse. "I've gotten too used to wearing sneakers."

"No."

"Thank God." She stops in front of me, lifting her eyes to mine. "Are you all right?"

"Why?"

"You have a slightly bewildered look on your face. It doesn't quite work with your controlling personality, Tore, sunshine." She smirks.

"Tore?"

"Your name's too long. It takes an age to pronounce, and by the time it's out, I've often forgotten what I wanted to say. Or do you prefer I keep on calling you Kurt? It may confuse the cat, though."

Very funny. "Tore will do," I say. "Give me your hand."

"You've already taken my life. I'm not giving you anything else."

"The hand, Milene. Left one."

She lifts her hand. I take two thick gold bands from my pocket and slide the smaller one down onto her ring finger.

Milene raises her eyebrows. "I thought we were skipping the ring part."

"We're not skipping anything, cara. The rings were late."

And I made sure the jeweler knew how I felt about that. Nino said the man will be staying in hospital for at least two weeks.

Still holding Milene's hand, I revel in the sight of the ring that marks her as mine on her delicate finger. I lift the second band so it's in front of her face.

Milene cocks her head. "You didn't strike me as the jewelry type."

I'm not. I never planned on getting married, and the idea of wearing a wedding band had never crossed my mind. Until now.

She takes the ring. "Left hand or right?"

"Right." I want it visible at all times, not hidden under the glove. It wouldn't fit over my deformed knuckle anyway.

Milene takes my right hand in hers and slides the ring onto my finger. When she's about to let go, I wrap my fingers around her hand. She looks at me sideways but doesn't pull away when I lead her to the door.

As we walk into the gallery, all eyes turn toward us and follow our steps as we cross the foyer to the main room where the auction will be held. The crowd is made up of the same people who typically frequent these auctions, and this is the first time I've ever brought a woman with me. I've also never brought bodyguards. However, since Milene is with me tonight, Stefano and two other men stick to our tail.

It does not escape my notice how most of the men react to my wife. They try their best to hide it, but I see them checking her out when they think I'm not looking, so I let go of her hand and wrap my arm around her waist instead. Milene looks up at me and pushes away a lock of hair that's fallen over her face. My eyes catch the glint of gold on her finger. The wedding band I've chosen seems absurdly large on her delicate hand. Something subtle might have been a better choice, but I like it the way it is.

"Is this wise?" she asks.

"What, exactly?"

"Being out in public when there are people trying to kill you?"

"Someone's always trying to kill me, Milene. I don't intend to hide in a hole because of that. What kind of message would it send?"

She shakes her head and sighs. "Men."

I lead her to the row of seats at the rear, which is ordinarily reserved for me alone, and over to the last two seats on the side furthest from the door. Stefano stands behind Milene as instructed, and the other two bodyguards take their places on the left- and right-hand side of the entrance.

Milene is sitting next to me with her spine ramrod straight and her hands clasped in her lap, seemingly uninterested. But her eyes are moving left and right, regarding various people entering the hall in silence and taking their seats. She focuses her gaze on a group of men who have just entered, mumbling something in a low voice. I tilt my head to the side to hear better.

". . . what's with the funeral atmosphere?" she murmurs, "Are they mourning the heaps of money they are going to spend on trinkets?"

I lean back and extend my arm along the back of Milene's seat. It amuses me to no end how grumpy she can be sometimes.

The big screen on the opposite wall lights up and I observe my wife as the auction proceeds. As paintings are sold, with the quality and expense of each piece steadily increasing, her eyes grow wider. She flinches when the assistants bring out a large textured canvas in shades of black, gray, and red.

"That's disturbing," she whispers.

I shift my gaze to the painting, which shows a beheaded stag standing on top of something that looks like a pile of kitchen pots. The price tag reads twenty thousand dollars.

"Will anyone actually buy that thing?" Milene asks.

"Wait and see."

No one bids. Not unexpected. They know they have no chance of getting it. The man who's taking phone offers at his desk in the corner lifts his hand.

"We have one hundred thousand," he exclaims.

"What?" Milene says. "Who would give a hundred grand to have that in their home."

"The Chicago Bratva's pakhan," I say. "His wife painted it. She has one piece on offer at each auction, and he's been buying all of them, no matter the price. Everyone else stopped bidding on her paintings some time ago."

"People are so strange sometimes." Milene shakes her head.

The painting I've chosen comes up next, a still-life piece from a lesser-known English painter from the nineteenth century. When I place my bid, Milene slowly raises one eyebrow, but refrains from commenting. Once the paintings are done, the auction proceeds, as always, with the jewelry. I usually leave at this point, but today I've decided to stay and take in Milene's reaction to the pieces on offer.

I've just about concluded that she's entirely indifferent to precious metals and gemstones when an antique gold bracelet is brought out. In terms of design, it's nothing special. There are no gemstones or diamonds of any kind in it, just a solid gold circlet with discrete floral elements engraved on its surface. The only thing special about it is that it's from the twelfth century. Milene's eyes widen, and she leans forward, peering at the close-up displayed on the giant screen above the podium. She completely ignored all the diamonds, rubies, and pearls we've seen so far, but now she's gaping at the most ordinary looking piece without blinking. The note under the image shows a starting price of $650,000. Making sure Milene can't see what I'm doing I raise my hand. My movement is barely perceptible, but the auctioneer's senses are finely tuned.

"Damn," she mumbles, still looking at the bracelet. "These people are insane."

Someone from the first row raises the bid to $660,000. I tip my finger again, $670,000. The man from the first row follows. I could keep going, but I'd rather head home sooner than later. I raise my hand again and mouth the amount.

"We have one million," the auctioneer declares. "Any further bids?"

"Jesus fucking Christ," Milene says, staring at the auctioneer. "I'd really like to meet the lunatic who'd pay a million dollars for a bracelet."

The auctioneer closes the bidding, and I message my banker. He's always on standby and knows to wire the money immediately and without question, regardless of the amount.

"Come on." I stand up and take Milene's hand, leading her toward the desk at the front.

"One million. Does that happen often? I mean, who does that? Art, I understand. There are people who like having that kind of stuff on their walls—your kind of crazy, you know—but come on."

She continues her bemused babbling in a quiet voice as I approach the desk to sign the papers and to confirm the painting is to be sent to my usual address. When the clerk accepts the documentation, I point to the rectangular velvet box. Once he brings it over, I take out the bracelet.

"And what if someone steals it?" Milene continues. "Is that kind of stuff insured? One million. It's absolutely outrageous, if you ask me."

I turn and find Milene looking back at the auction room, staring at the big screen where the image of the bracelet is still being displayed.

"Where would someone wear something like that? What if . . ." She rattles on, standing in front of me with her hands on her hips.

I put the bracelet around her right wrist and fasten the clasp. It's one of those simple hook clasps. I don't think I'd be able to manage anything daintier. When I look at Milene again, she's staring at her arm, open-mouthed.

"So, that's what it takes to get you to stop talking," I say. "I'll keep it in mind."

"I can't take this," Milene says the moment we're inside the penthouse.

I knew it was coming. She hadn't uttered a single word on the drive home or looked at me even once. Her attention was focused through the passenger-side window on the neon lights as we passed them by.

"It's beautiful, but I really can't. Maybe if it was worth three zeros less."

"You're keeping it." I say and head into the hallway leading to my bedroom.

"I . . . what would I do with this? It should be in a damn museum or something."

"Do whatever you want with it."

"Tore!"

Behind me, heels *clink* against the floor tiles, then Milene curses. I glance over my shoulder and catch her taking off her shoes. Given the cut of her dress and the way she's bending forward, I'm gifted with a fine view of her breasts. I tilt my head for a better angle and imagine my wife lying naked in my bed, her milky skin contrasting with the dark sheets and her pale hair tangled around her head.

"Please, be reasonable." She sighs and straightens up. "Please."

"I never do anything without a reason, Milene. You should know that by now," I say and close my bedroom door behind me.

Milene

I regard the bracelet on the nightstand with caution, as if it were about to attack me. I've been staring at that thing since the moment I got into the bed, wondering what I should do with it. Where do you keep something that's worth a million dollars? Under the mattress? Should I try to lift one of the floorboards and stash it beneath? Why the hell did Salvatore buy it? Does he expect me to wear it around the house? He's crazy.

There must be some kind of safe in the penthouse. I take the bracelet, leave my bedroom, and walk down the hallway to knock on Salvatore's door. Nothing. I try one more time. Nothing again. Turning on my heel, I head toward the living room.

I find Salvatore sprawled on the sofa in front of the TV, watching a game and holding a bottle of beer. Just an ordinary guy in sweatpants and a T-shirt, watching football. What a misleading picture.

"Do you have a safe?"

"Yes," he says without taking his eyes off the screen.

"Can I put the bracelet there?"

"No."

"No?" I march around the sofa, careful not to knock over his crutches. He removes his prosthesis in the evenings. Standing right in front of him, I cross my arms. "Why not?"

"Because I bought it for you to wear it. Not to have it be stuck in a safe." He points the bottle toward the TV behind me. "I'm watching that."

"Why would you buy me something like this?"

"I've already told you."

"Yes, yes, you have your reasons. What are those reasons? Are you feeling bad for making me quit my job?"

"Not particularly." He takes a sip of his beer and looks at me. "That was for your safety."

His hair is wet and slicked back, but a few strands have fallen across his forehead, and I have a crazy urge to reach out and move them away.

"Are you trying to lure me in, then?"

Salvatore sets the bottle down on the floor and folds his arm behind his head, watching me. His white T-shirt is stretched tightly across his chest and wide shoulders. He looks like an ad for men's cologne.

"To lure you in?" he asks. "Why?"

"To be with you?"

"I don't have to lure you in, Milene. We're already married. Or did that slip your mind?"

"You know what I mean."

"No, I don't think I do."

"Fine. Whatever." I shake my head. As I turn to leave, his arm shoots out and grabs me around the waist. He pulls me down on top of him, my face directly above his.

"Do you really believe"—he raises his left hand and brushes the back of his fingers across my cheek—"that I need to buy you jewelry to lure you in?"

I take a deep breath, trying to calm my traitorous body that's been twitching and trembling with excitement since the moment we touched. There is no way I'm answering his question, but I'm afraid he already knows the truth.

"Do you, Milene?" he tilts his head and places a light kiss on my chin.

"No." I close my eyes.

Another kiss. A little to the right this time. "Then why did I buy it?"

I squeeze the bracelet in my hand and press it to his chest. "I have no idea."

Salvatore's hand covers mine, and he pries my fingers from around the gold circlet. I let go of the bracelet and open my eyes to see him toss the million-dollar antique behind the sofa as if it were an empty soda can.

I gasp. "Are you crazy?"

"Why"—he buries his fingers in my hair, pulling my head lower until my mouth almost touches his lips—"did I buy the bracelet, Milene?"

"Because I liked it?" I whisper against his lips.

"Because you liked it," he says as he presses his mouth to mine.

There is nothing delicate or light in his kiss. It's hungry. Hard. Perhaps it's even a little hostile. His hand moves down my back and under my shirt to squeeze one of my butt cheeks. I can feel his hard cock pressing upon my core. It's so enticing that a small moan escapes my lips as wetness pools between my legs. He bites my lower lip, hard, then squeezes my ass again. I rock my hips, brushing my mound over his rock-hard length. An image of him inside of me flashes through my mind, and my panties become instantly drenched, begging to be removed.

Something falls to the floor with a thud, followed by a loud meow. I open my eyes to see Salvatore watching me. It feels so damn good, being pressed against his hard body, his arm pinning me to him. And I hate myself for enjoying it.

"I'd better go and get the cat before he breaks something," I say, waiting to see if he'll call me out on taking this opportunity to flee.

"All right." He unwraps his arms from my body, and I immediately want to weep at the loss. "Don't forget the bracelet."

I nod and straighten to a sitting position. While quickly scrambling off his gorgeous body, I feel my ass brush his cock one more time.

I pick up the bracelet from the floor and dash to the kitchen to collect Kurt, undecided whether I should kiss him or strangle him for interrupting.

# Chapter Thirteen

## Salvatore

I take a sip of coffee while waiting for Nino and Arturo to take their seats across from my desk. "Bogdan called earlier this morning."

"I don't think we need more ammunition at the moment," Nino says. "The last shipment came in two weeks ago."

"It wasn't about the orders. He wanted to let me know that he'd heard Fitzgerald had ordered a shitload of weapons from Dushku."

"The Bratva won't like that," Arturo says. "Not after what happened four years ago between them and the Irish. If Petrov hears Dushku is selling to the Irish on the side, he won't be happy."

I lean back in my chair, debating whether to give Petrov a call. "The more important thing right now is what the Irish may be planning to do with all those weapons. Bogdan figures they aren't for resale."

"You think they're prepping to attack us?" Arturo asks. "They don't have enough men to inflict any serious damage."

"Well, I don't want any kind of damage at all, Arturo," I say and turn to Nino. "Double the security on all locations. I want two additional soldiers with each transport. Tell the men to expect trouble. Any suspicious activity needs to be reported immediately. And put a tail on Fitzgerald. On his second-in-command, Deegan, as well."

"All right." He nods.

"Where are we on locating the second snitch?"

"He's lying low. There haven't been any leaks since we dealt with Octavio."

My phone vibrates on the desk with an incoming message from Ada. I instructed her to report to me every two hours on what Milene is doing.

The message says my wife is currently in the bathroom, trying to give the cat a bath because the idiotic thing spent the night sleeping in the flowerpot.

"How many people knew where that takeover was happening when the DEA showed up?" I ask as I lower the phone back onto the desk.

"Around twenty," Nino says.

"And how many of them have been with us for less than two years?"

He thinks about it for a moment. "Nine. Why?"

"They weren't around when we made an example of the last person who blabbed about our business. If they had been, going to the authorities wouldn't even have crossed their minds," I say. "Split those nine into two groups and send them somewhere. Make it known that someone from Cosa Nostra will be meeting with Mendoza in person, but provide a different location for each group. Then, we wait to see where the cops show up."

"What will we do when we catch the snitch?"

"We'll have a little demonstration," I say.

I planned to have lunch with Rocco and the construction site's manager, but that's been canceled at the last moment, so I leave my tenth-floor office and take the elevator up to the penthouse. I told Ada to prepare lunch for just Milene today, but she usually makes far more food than necessary, and I'm already agitated about the fact I haven't seen her since yesterday evening. When I get to the dining area, I find the table set for one, but instead of eating there, Milene is sitting at the breakfast bar with her phone leaning against a water bottle, watching a video.

"Is there something wrong with the table?" I ask.

"Nope." She shakes her head and stuffs a bite of lasagna into her mouth without raising her eyes off the phone.

"So why are you eating lunch here?"

"We were always forced to eat lunch at the dining table back home, even when we were eating alone. I have trauma."

I take a plate out of the cupboard, head over to the dining room table and grab some food from the serving tray, then sit down on the barstool opposite Milene. She looks up at me but quickly switches her attention back to the phone. Apparently, we'll be ignoring what happened on the couch from last night.

"I found a how-to video on setting up a charity." She points her fork toward the phone. "It seems like too much bureaucracy for my taste. Isn't there anything else I could do?"

"You don't have to do anything."

She lowers her fork and shoots me an exasperated look. "I told you, I can't sit here all day."

"If it'll make you feel better, I can call some of my men, so you can insert IV needles and such."

"Ha ha." She rolls her eyes. "I'm serious."

"So am I."

Milene blinks at me, then shakes her head and mumbles something. I'm not a hundred percent sure, but I think she just called me batshit crazy.

"How fast can you type?" I ask.

"On the phone?"

"Laptop."

"I don't know. I've never actually timed it, but I'd say average speed. Why?"

"It'll do." I reach for the bottle of water.

She takes her phone from its resting place. "What for?"

"If you're done with lunch, go and change into something more appropriate for business." I nod at her yellow T-shirt, the name of some band emblazoned across the front. "You're coming to the office with me."

"What am I going to do in your office? Water the plants?"

"You have twenty minutes, or I'm leaving without you."

I put on a classy, navy dress I haven't worn in at least two years and look at my reflection in the mirror.

Salvatore didn't mention the couch fiasco. Good. As far as I'm concerned, it never happened. He caught me by surprise. What the fuck is wrong with me, grinding my pussy like an animal in heat against the cock of the man who destroyed my life? Who does that?

If he needs recreational sex, he can find it elsewhere because he won't be getting any from me. That . . . episode was a one-off. I have to live here, but that's all we'll do—cohabitate. I'm sure he has a long list of women, all lined up and waiting to be summoned and fucked. He can do as he wants. It doesn't bother me at all. Not even a little. It will probably be some tall, sophisticated type. They can discuss art and other aristocratic shit I have no clue about. Maybe he'll take her to his auctions. Buy her million-dollar trinkets.

I grind my teeth and fasten the wide white belt that goes with the dress. I don't care. He can fuck whomever he wants. I pull the belt so tight I almost bruise my hips.

"'You have twenty minutes, or I'm leaving without you,'" I mumble, imitating Salvatore's abrupt tone when he issued the order to me earlier. What a control freak. If I wasn't dying of boredom, I would have told him exactly what I thought about his offer. But I've been going out of my mind in this ridiculous penthouse, and I'll do anything to escape, if only for a few hours.

The dress is a little loose around the hips, but it'll do. I quickly collect my hair in a low bun, put on my white heels, and grab my purse before rushing out of the room. It can't have been twenty minutes, but when I reach the living room, Salvatore's already leaving.

"Wait, God damn it!"

He turns and watches me approach, checking me out from head to toe.

"Does your business highness approve?" I motion with my hand down the length of my outfit.

"I approve," he says and exits through the front door, leaving me to follow.

I'd assumed he had an office somewhere downtown, but when we get inside the elevator, he presses the button for two floors down. The doors open to reveal a wide entry hall decorated in white marble and dark wood. Immediately in front of us and close to the wall, a desk is positioned with a computer and several stacks of folders sitting on it. A woman sitting behind it jumps to her feet once she sees us exit the elevator.

"Mr. Ajello." She nods and remains standing, staring at me with wide eyes. She's pretty, in her late twenties, and impeccably dressed in a coral pantsuit and white shirt, which is so perfectly pressed you could cut your finger on its lapel.

To the left, there is a long hallway with several doors on each side, but Salvatore heads in the opposite direction toward the large ornate wooden door, nodding to the woman at the reception desk as he passes. He holds the door open for me, and I enter the office dominated by a massive wooden desk next to impressive floor-to-ceiling windows. The right wall is composed entirely of bookshelves, while on the other is a plush leather sofa and two matching armchairs. A painting of a sunset hangs on the wall above the sofa.

Salvatore walks around the desk to power up the laptop, then sits down on his office chair and motions for me to come over. I approach the desk, intending to take one of the two guest chairs set up before it, but he shakes his head.

"Come here."

Raising my eyebrows, I walk around the desk. As I move to stand next to him, he grabs me around the waist and pulls me down to sit on his right thigh. I yelp and look at him in surprise, but he just rolls the chair closer to the desk while still holding me with his arm and slides the laptop in front of me.

"Open the email app," he says.

I reach for the mouse and lean forward to search through dozens of icons scattered around the screen for the one that will open his email. The desktop is a mess and completely at odds with Salvatore's personality. He lifts his right hand off my waist and covers mine, moving the mouse toward the upper left corner of the screen.

He clicks on the envelope icon to bring up the inbox window. "Let's start with emails that arrived today."

I find it rather hard to feign indifference while sitting on his lap with his arm again wrapped around my middle, but somehow, I manage to keep my cool and open the first unread email from the list.

"That's the paperwork for another lot I'm planning to buy," he says next to my ear. "Forward it to my lawyer. Greg Atkinson. Tell him to make sure he checks whether everything's clean. I don't want a repeat of the situation from February."

"What happened in February?" I ask as I type.

"The previous owner's illegitimate son surfaced, claiming ownership."

I finish the email, send it, and open the next one.

"I assume you don't have an uncle in South Africa who needs money for brain surgery."

The arm around my waist tightens. "No," he says, his lips lightly brushing my earlobe.

I need him to stop touching me. It's making me crazy.

*So why don't you tell him to stop, then? I'll tell you why. Because you're a hypocrite, Milene. You like it, just admit it.*

I'm not admitting it, not even to myself. *Shut up!* I tell my inner voice, mark the email as spam, and move on to the next.

"That one's from my banker," Salvatore says. "Forward it to Greg, as well. Tell him to make sure he reads the new contract and checks whether they've offered better conversion rates, as we requested. If they haven't, he can let them know we'll be closing all our accounts by the end of the month."

As I type, I cast a quick glance at his gloved left hand resting next to the laptop. He probably can't type with it, or if he can, it likely takes ages. How did he end up in a situation where someone smashed his fingers to smithereens with a hammer? Jesus, it must have hurt like a bitch.

I open the next email and skim over the list of renovation supplies and the prices listed next to each item. "You plan on redecorating?"

He doesn't strike me as a DIY guy, but why else would he need tiles, paints, and the other things listed there.

"Not exactly." He angles his head to the side and his nose ends up pressing against my neck. "Tell them we'll take the same amount as last month, except for the white metro tiles. I need triple the quantity of those, and I want a better price. Include Arturo on the CC."

I stop typing midsentence and turn to him, my eyes wide. "You're ordering drugs via email? Are you insane?"

With his finger under my chin, Salvatore gently tilts my head. My heartbeat quickens as his eyes focus on my lips.

"Maybe," he says, then lowers his hand and focuses back on the laptop again. "Let's proceed."

We spend almost four hours going through his emails before he moves my hands from the keyboard and closes the laptop. "That's enough for today."

I get up and pick up my purse off the desk, trying to ignore the sense of loss at the break in contact.

"Well, I'll head back upstairs," I say.

"Okay." He leans back in his chair. "I have to make a few calls, then I'll be up as well."

"Yup. See you later." I leave the office in haste, as though getting away from him might help suppress the crazy urge to leap back onto his lap and press my lips to his. I can't sacrifice my integrity at the altar of this maddening attraction. I want to hate him, damn it, not imagine him screwing me senseless every single night.

Fucking hell.

After a long bubble bath, I spend an hour sorting through my clothes, setting the appropriate business attire to one side. If Salvatore decides that I should continue helping out with his emails, I'll need to go shopping because my pile of business-suitable clothes consist of two dresses, four blouses, and one pair of black pants. I haven't really had the opportunity to wear suits or skirts in the past couple of years, and most of my wardrobe is jeans, shorts, and casual tops. There are a few dresses I bought on a whim and wore maybe once when I went out, but those aren't suitable, either.

I put the clothes back into the closet, shoo Kurt off my pillow, where he's been sleeping for the past hour, and head into the kitchen to grab something to eat. Hopefully, Salvatore has already eaten, and I won't run into him. Yes, I'm chickening out, but it's easier to avoid him than to resist the insane attraction I feel whenever he's close. The thing that frustrates me most is he knows exactly how his proximity affects me. He's been playing with me for days, all those "I-want-to-fuck-you" looks and stolen touches, followed by feigned indifference. And I'm not sure of the rules of this game.

Thankfully, the kitchen is empty, so I inspect the contents of the fridge. There are leftovers from lunch, but I decide to have a lighter meal and reach for the box of strawberries on the top shelf. I've almost finished washing them when I sense Salvatore behind me. I don't even have to turn to know it's him. And it has nothing to do with the fact there are only two of us in the penthouse. I have a tingling sensation at the back of my neck every time he's near. My body's strong reaction to him is unnerving.

"Those look sweet," Salvatore's velvety voice echoes next to my ear. "Can I have one?"

I take a deep breath and turn around slowly. My eyes land on the sculpted form of his bare chest, mere inches from my face, since he's wearing only sweatpants. I lift my head and catch him watching me. He must have had a shower because the scent of woodsy body wash clings to him. His hair is wet and in a state of complete disarray, as though he's passed his fingers through it a couple of times and considered it combed. I find it hard to believe, but he's even more sexy like this than when he's all polished and dressed in a suit. I clear my throat and lift the bowl of washed strawberries between us.

Salvatore cocks his head, then pins me with his gaze and slowly blinks. My heart rate quickens, and I barely stifle a sigh. It's ridiculous, how such a small act can make me weak in the knees. He looks down at the bowl in my hands, takes a step forward and cages me against the counter with his arms. I press my lips together, take a strawberry from the bowl and lift it to his mouth. His eyes never leave mine as he wraps his lips around the berry, sucking the tips of my fingers into his mouth in the process.

"What's your agenda, Tore?" I ask.

"My agenda?"

"I'm not going to sleep with you, so you can stop with this seduction thing you have going on. Playing with me, walking around shirtless. It won't work."

"This is my home, I can do whatever I please." He leans forward and bends his head. "And if it won't work, does it matter whether I'm shirtless or not?"

His eyes remind me of a hawk's, sharp and focused, with prey in their sights and preparing for the kill. He's doing this on purpose.

"It doesn't." I shrug. "I'm absolutely indifferent where you're concerned."

One corner of his lip curls upward a little. I wouldn't have even recognized it if I wasn't so accustomed to seeing him with a face that's constantly grim.

"I can't wait to have you in my bed, Milene," he whispers, and a shudder passes through my body.

"That will never happen. I don't even like you." I turn my back to him, place the bowl of strawberries on the counter, and pop one into my mouth, pretending to be focused on the cityscape visible through the window.

Salvatore's body leans onto mine, and his hand comes to my waist. Hard lips press to the side of my neck, then teeth, biting lightly at the sensitive skin.

"Are you sure you're indifferent toward me, cara?" he whispers and bites at my neck again.

I grab the edge of the counter and close my eyes. His mouth is now on my nape, kissing and nibbling. I need to fucking move away from him, but I can't make myself do it.

"I'm sure," I choke out and will my eyes to open.

"Let's test that conviction of yours. Shall we?"

He moves his hand down my belly and inside my shorts. I take a deep breath and concentrate on the path his palm is taking. It feels so good I almost crumble.

His hand travels lower to between my legs and applies pressure onto my pussy. I suck in a breath, then exhale slowly as his fingers keep stroking me over the drenched fabric of my panties. Jesus. I close my eyes again, wondering where my composure has gone.

"Liar," he whispers into my ear as he gently takes my earlobe between his front teeth. "Good night, Milene."

Gently, he withdraws his hand from my shorts, and a few seconds later, I hear him leave the kitchen. Only once I am sure he's gone do I open my eyes and bolt toward my own bedroom.

# Chapter fourteen

Salvatore

I LEAN MY SHOULDER ON THE SUPPORT COLUMN THAT MARKS THE kitchen area and cross my arms over my chest, watching Milene as she stirs whatever she is cooking on the stove. Why does she keep trying when she burns everything or sets something on fire whenever she attempts cook?

"If I remember correctly, you are forbidden to approach the stove," I say.

She sends me an exasperated look over her shoulder, then goes back to her stirring. "Kurt has diarrhea. The article I read said to feed him boiled chicken."

"Why didn't you ask Ada to prepare it?"

"I'm capable of boiling two pieces of meat by myself."

"Is there a medical issue your cat doesn't have?"

"He's had a hard life, Tore. Stress can lead to many medical issues. It's obvious he was bullied."

"Bullied?"

"Of course. Didn't you see his tail?"

"Yes." And its eye. And ear. And it's also missing some hair on the back. That cat looks like it survived a nuclear catastrophe.

Milene reaches for a plate and fishes out two pieces of meat—enough to feed at least five cats—from the pot and cuts them into small cubes. When she's done, she blows on the meat for almost a minute, then places the plate on the floor in the corner. Meanwhile, the pot is still on the stove with the burner on. Shaking my head, I walk over and turn it off.

"Why are you not at work?" she asks casually as she washes her hands.

Too casually. It looks like we'll be ignoring what happened in the kitchen last night as well. I find her insistence that there is no attraction between us rather amusing. Like she thinks it'll disappear if we pretend it's not there.

"I needed something from here," I say.

It's not a lie because I do need something—my regular fix of her presence. I couldn't wait two more hours for her to come downstairs to work on my emails. I had to see her.

Now.

"And how is your black empire holding these days?"

"Better than ever," I say. "Why?"

She shrugs, then jumps up to sit on the counter. "I was just wondering. Why do you keep dealing in drugs? You have an enormous real estate business. Why take the risk?"

After throwing a look at the stove to make sure Milene hasn't left anything else on the burner, I stride across the kitchen until I am standing right in front of her. Placing my hands on either side of her, I cage her against the counter. The sunrays coming through the window fall directly on her face, making her freckles even more noticeable. "Are you worried about me, Milene?"

"You get shot often," she says. "Maybe branching out would be wise. Minimize the exposure and all that."

I raise my hand to place it under her chin and tilt her head up. "You haven't answered my question."

"No."

"No?" I lean forward until our faces are barely an inch apart.

Her lips widen in a smug smile.

Oh, how she likes to test me. I slide my hand down and wrap my fingers around her slender neck, the black of my leather glove creating such a contrast with her milky skin and pale hair.

"Tell me, Milene." I whisper into her ear. "Aren't you worried I might decide to drop this . . . seduction thing, as you called it, and take what I want?"

Her breathing quickens. I wish I didn't have the glove on, so I could feel her pulse under my skin. Would it be only slightly faster than normal? Or would it be erratic?

"No. I'm not afraid of that," she says, her lips brushing my earlobe.

"Like every predator out there, you revel in the thrill of the hunt. But know one thing, Salvatore. This prey will not fall into your claws willingly. Ever."

I close my eyes and inhale her scent. "You shouldn't have said that, cara." I tilt my head to the side and press my lips on the soft skin of her neck. "You really . . . really shouldn't have."

"Why?" she breathes out.

"Because that declaration, Milene . . . is every predator's wet dream," I whisper into her ear, then let go of her neck and turn to leave. "I'm expecting you at the office in two hours."

# Chapter Fifteen

Salvatore

Tormenting Milene has been as satisfying as it is frustrating. While I enjoy toying with her and wondering when she'll finally succumb, the entire endeavor has turned on me because I can't get her out of my head. I don't let anything stand in the way of business, but recently, I've been thinking more about Milene than about investments and the problems which should concern me.

It's been a week since I first asked her to go with me to the office, and she's been coming every afternoon since. She's insisted on taking one of the chairs to sit on while replying to emails. I said no. She tried to argue, but when that didn't succeed, she relented and now she automatically sits on my lap once she's walked through the door. Like now.

I watch as she approaches, a perfectly neutral expression on her face. She lowers her perky ass onto my thigh and pulls the laptop closer.

"Another contract," she says. "Any comments on this, or should I forward it to Greg?"

"Just forward it."

Milene nods, sends the email and opens the next one. "A local school is asking for a donation. What should I say?"

"Just ignore it."

She turns her head and eyes me over her shoulder. "You're loaded."

"So?"

"So, you can afford a small donation."

"I can. But I don't see why I should start giving money away." I let my gaze fall from her eyes down to her chest. She's wearing a white silk blouse.

The first two buttons are undone, and from beneath its sheen, the ghost of a pale pink bra is taunting me.

"Because you want to be a better person?"

"I don't need to be a better person, Milene. I'm quite satisfied with what I am."

"And what is that?"

I lift my eyes off her cleavage and focus on her face. Her hair is down today. I move away the blond strands to reveal the delicate skin of her neck.

"Plain bad." I tighten my hold around her waist, enjoying the way she tenses. To unnerve her even further, I plant a light kiss at the back of her neck, brushing my lips across her soft skin. I meant what I said in the kitchen that day. She doesn't know it yet, but she will end up in my bed very soon. "Tell them they'll receive laptops for the high-achieving students but that I'll be sending someone to make sure the tech actually ends up in those students' hands. If I find out that even a single item is being used someplace else, they won't see another cent from me ever again."

She nods and starts typing, but her fingers tremble slightly as she does so. I kiss her neck again, a little higher this time—under her ear, and enjoy the way she shudders.

"You're distracting me, Salvatore."

"You need to work on your concentration," I say and move my right hand down her thigh until I reach the hem of her skirt. "Let's practice."

Milene opens her mouth to say something, but as my palm slides between her legs and presses against her core, she gasps instead. I brush the tips of my fingers over the lacy material, then apply slight pressure once again.

"What are you doing?" she whispers.

"Helping you."

"With what?"

"Working on your concentration." I push her panties to the side, feel her wetness, and gently rub her clit in a circular motion, increasing the pressure at just the right moments.

Milene doesn't move for a while. She simply sits stone-still on my lap, then takes a deep breath and places her hands over the keyboard once again. I watch as she takes another breath, hits enter, and resumes her quiet clickety-clack against the keys.

She's pretty quick. Much faster than I'd expected. For the first time I can remember, I'm up-to-date with my correspondence. I can type, but with one hand, it's mere pecking, and it takes far too much time. I usually focus on only the most pressing matters and handle the rest via phone. I once tried typing with both my left and right hand, but the results were a mess. It took longer to fix the mistakes than it does to just use one hand to type.

"What do you want me to do with those documents Greg sent?" Milene's tone is even when she asks, but I detect a slight tremble in her voice. She's trying very hard to feign indifference and pretend my exploring fingers aren't affecting her in the least.

I bury my nose in her hair and inhale. "Leave it. I'll check them tomorrow," I say flicking my thumb over her clit.

A low whimper leaves Milene's lips. "Please, stop."

"Why?" I brush the tip of my finger along the wet lips of her pussy. "You don't like it?"

She turns around in my lap and bites her lower lip. "I don't."

"All right." I start pulling my hand away but her legs clench, trapping my hand in place. The mix of anger and confusion on her face is priceless. I wonder if she's aware her ire is misdirected. It's not me she's mad at. She's furious with herself because she's enjoying this. Her eyes move lower and come to rest on my lips.

The moment her hold of my hand loosens, I slide my hand inside her panties and tease her again. A gasp leaves her lips when I slide a finger into her. She widens her legs, her breathing quickening. Warm breath fans my face as I slide my finger in and out. A tiny mewl leaves her mouth, and my cock swells upon hearing it.

"I'm so looking forward to fucking you senseless, cara," I say, looking into her eyes.

"Dream on," she chokes out, then whimpers when I add another finger.

"I already do. I imagine myself slamming into you, wrecking your sweet pussy every fucking night." I thrust my fingers all the way in, enjoying her erratic panting. "But I only end up frustrated because you are so damn stubborn."

"I don't like you!" she says through her teeth.

"No? Well, it looks like your pussy likes my hand quite a lot. But maybe I'm wrong." I pull my fingers out and lift my hand off her pussy.

Milene stares at me with her teeth clenched together and her eyes wide. She looks like she's going to combust.

Someone knocks on the door. Milene quickly turns her head away and looks back at the laptop screen.

“Enter,” I say and remove my hand from under her skirt.

Nino walks in but falters when he sees Milene sitting on my lap. I motion for him to come, and he takes a chair on the opposite side of the desk.

“We have a new development regarding the snitch,” he says. “Leaking the info worked.”

“Do you know who it is?”

“No. But he was in the group of five men.”

“Their phones are clean?” I ask.

“Yup. No way to discover who it was unless someone confesses.”

“Take all five to the old safe house and lock them in a room under video surveillance. All together. No guards inside. No food, no water.” I lean back in my chair, pulling Milene with me. “But before you do that, take the one who’s least likely to be the snitch and tell him what’s happening. Let it be known that if no one confesses by morning, all five will be dead in a ditch.”

Milene’s body tenses. Maybe I shouldn’t discuss such things in front of her. “We’ll continue tomorrow, Milene.”

She looks at Nino, then back at me before getting up and leaving the office and I can’t help but notice how pale her face is. When she closes the door behind her, I turn back to Nino.

“At least one of them must have seen the rat using the wrong phone or acting strangely, but they’ll need the incentive to remember. Put two of your men to monitor the feed. Let’s see whether they start accusing each other. The culprit might float to the surface.”

“And if he doesn’t?”

“As I said, kill all five of them. There will be no rats on this ship.”

“Consider it done.”

“Tell me about Fitzgerald. Anything new on that?”

Nino’s giving me updates on Fitzgerald’s whereabouts when the phone on my desk rings loudly. I glance at the caller ID and see that it’s the security desk downstairs. For a moment I consider ignoring it, but then decide to take the call after all.

“Mr. Ajello, I wanted to inform you that your wife has just left the building.”

“What?” I spring up from the chair. “Alone?”

“Yes. I . . . should I have stopped her?”

I squeeze the receiver in my hand. “Is she still downstairs?”

“No, she successfully hailed a cab and left.”

"If you're still there when I get down," I sneer, "I will fucking shoot you in the head, Steven."

I grab my phone and car keys off the desk, and head toward the door.

"Boss?" Nino calls, hurrying behind me. "What happened?"

"My wife happened," I snap, get into the elevator with Nino on my heels, and call Milene.

"Yes?"

"Where the fuck did you go without a security detail?" I yell.

"You said you had work to do. I'm heading to Pippa's for coffee. I'll be home in two hours."

"Tell the driver to turn around and get back to your bodyguards. Now, Milene!"

"I'm not taking four bodyguards to my friend's tiny place. The taxi will drop me in front of Pippa's building, and I'll come straight back afterward."

I hit the button for the garage. "Tell the driver to make that fucking U-turn!"

"Don't yell at me, Salvatore. I'm not going anywhere risky, and I'll be back soon. If you feel that next time I should take security, we can discuss it later and find some sort of compromise."

Oh, I'll give her a compromise. "The address?"

"Why?"

"I'm coming to get you. Do not leave the taxi until I'm there."

"Stop overreacting. We'll talk when I return." She cuts the call. I dial her number again, but the call goes directly to her voice mail.

She hung up on me. No one fucking hangs up on me. I close my eyes, take a deep breath, and head toward my car.

"Boss?" Nino speaks up behind me.

"Find me the address of Pippa something!" I get inside the vehicle, leaving the door open as I continue my conversation. "She works at St. Mary's as a nurse."

"I'll have it in five minutes," he says and stares at me. "Boss, are you all right?"

I put the key into the ignition. "Why wouldn't I be?"

"You were yelling the whole way here. You never yell." He nods toward my hands on the wheel. "And your hands are shaking."

Of course, my hands are shaking, I'm so full of rage it feels like I'm going to explode, and I have no idea how to process that shit.

"Find me that address. Now!" I slam the door closed, start the car and hit the gas.

I ignore the red light as I exit the garage, pressing down harder on the accelerator. The way I am acting is completely unreasonable, but I don't give a fuck. I can't stand the idea of not knowing where she is. It's gnawing at me from the inside out, like a rat in a cage. I grip the steering wheel with all my might and take a deep breath, trying to calm down. It's not working. Where the fuck is she?!

Milene

"What the hell happened?" Pippa jumps at me with questions before I'm even inside her apartment. "Why did you resign? Where have you been for the past few weeks? I came to your place twice. I thought you'd been kidnapped."

"Sorry, I just didn't want to talk about it over the phone. It's a long story." I flop down on the sofa and, leaning back into the soft cushions, close my eyes. I've missed this. The ordinary world. A normal life. I spent fifteen minutes in front of the building, taking deep breaths so I could calm down enough to come upstairs.

When I left Salvatore's office, it seemed as though the walls were suddenly closing in on me, and I couldn't draw a breath. I couldn't make myself go up to the penthouse. I had to get out and go somewhere, anywhere but there, so I called Pippa. I guess spending four years trying to avoid everything about Cosa Nostra has made me soft. I've forgotten how a lot of problems are handled. Killing five men, four of whom are innocent, is normal in our world.

"Talk!" Pippa says and sits down on the sofa next to me.

"Remember the mysterious guy?"

"Yes."

"Well, we like each other," I say, aware how utterly stupid the rest of the explanation will sound. "And I decided to follow your advice."

"What? You married the guy?" She stares at me. "But you've known him for, like, a month!"

"We *really* like each other." I shrug.

"Whoa, Milene. That's . . . it's crazy."

Yeah. She doesn't know the half of it.

"So, you've been with him this whole time? Who is he? Is that why you resigned? I . . . wow. I still can't believe this. You never seemed like an impulsive person."

"I realized my life had become too boring, and I should . . . you know, spice it up a bit."

Pippa laughs and shakes her head. "Oh, you definitely spiced it up, babe. Did you at least get his name before you married the guy?"

"Yes. It's Salvatore."

"Italian? Nice. I can't wait to tell the girls at work."

A loud bang echoes against the front door, and it flies open to reveal Salvatore standing on the threshold. His lips are pressed into a pale thin line, and the darkness in his eyes shows he's mad as hell. It's as though tiny daggers are shooting out of his pupils, all directed at me. How on earth did he find me so fast?

"Milene," he says with forced calmness.

I see it on his face, though. He's ready to drag me back, by the hair if necessary. I let out a sigh. I shouldn't have left without security, but I was freaking out. Now we're here, and he's going to make a scene.

"I have to go, honey," I tell Pippa and rise off the sofa. "I just wanted to drop by and say hi, but I'll call you, and we'll go for coffee one afternoon. Deal?"

She looks at Salvatore, who casts a long shadow on the floor of Pippa's apartment, and back at me. "Is everything okay? You can stay here if you want."

"Everything is fine." I lean in to kiss her on the cheek. "I'll call you next week."

I walk toward the door and lift my chin to meet my husband's stare. He's still waiting to pounce like a lion with its prey in sight, but I'm not backing down. "Later," I say in a low voice.

He doesn't say anything, just takes my hand and leads me toward the elevator.

When we get inside the car, he leans his forearms on the wheel and stares off into the distance. With both of us looking straight ahead, we sit in menacing silence for at least five minutes before he finally breaks it.

"You will never do that again," he says and hits the steering wheel with his palm. "Never, Milene."

I lean back in the seat and close my eyes. "I freaked out, Tore. I had to get out of that building."

Strong fingers wrap around the back of my neck, and I open my eyes to find Salvatore's face a couple of inches from mine.

"Why?" he asks through his teeth and slightly tightens his hold on my neck.

"Hearing someone state they're willing to execute five people as though they're speaking of tossing out overripe fruit, well, that may worry a person. I suppose you can understand that a little."

"You know very well how things work in the Family, Milene."

"Yes. Which is why I left. Or tried to, at least."

He curses, then presses his mouth against mine in a hard and angry kiss. I gasp, both shocked and confused.

"Never. Again," he says against my lips and again squeezes the back of my neck. "Understood?"

"Okay." I nod.

He watches me through narrowed eyes, and I wonder if he's going to kiss me again. But he just nods, then releases my neck and starts the engine.

# Chapter sixteen

Milene

"Milene!"

I spring up in the bed and blink away the sleep. Salvatore is standing in the doorway of my room, hair in disarray and shirt unbuttoned. It's pitch dark outside.

"Dress," he says, starting to button his shirt. "We need you on the eleventh floor."

"What's there?" I ask as I rush to turn on a lamp, then move to the closet to take out a pair of leggings and a T-shirt and pull them on.

"The infirmary. The Irish attacked my men while they were loading the drugs. They'll be here in ten minutes."

"You have an infirmary here? How many floors do you own?" I rush to the bathroom to brush my teeth.

"I own the building," his answer reaches me.

When I return, Salvatore is still fumbling with the buttons. In the four minutes I've spent in the bathroom, he's only managed to fasten the top two. I watch as he tries to do up the third, but it keeps slipping from between the fingers of his left hand, so he curses.

I walk over and shoo his hands out of the way. He stands still as a statue while I work my way down the row until the buttons are all done.

"There. All set," I say and look up.

His eyes are fixed on mine for several long seconds. Then, he abruptly says, "Let's go."

When we exit the elevator on the floor below, I follow Salvatore through the door into a large room which has floor-to-ceiling white tiles. My jaw drops as I take in the sight. To the left, there are three gurneys with high-end medical equipment beside each. Toward the back, the space is separated by a glass wall with an operating table visible inside. The wall on the right is lined with large white shelves that are stocked with medical supplies.

I expected a small room with perhaps a cart holding bandages and similar first aid items, maybe an IV stand, not a miniature hospital. As I turn toward Salvatore, baffled by everything I'm seeing, the doors to a huge service elevator located on the opposite side of the room—different to the one Salvatore and I used—open, and a group of people, more than half of them covered in blood, file out.

"Where the fuck is Ilaria?" Salvatore barks at Nino, who is half dragging Alessandro as he exits the elevator. The big guy is holding his hand against his bleeding belly. A gunshot wound?

"I'm here," A female voice announces from somewhere. I turn to see an elegant, tall woman in her late fifties coming out of the main elevator. Her perfectly coiffured hair is sandy-blonde. She's wearing dark blue dress pants with a silky blouse and a white cashmere coat overtop. When she reaches us, she peruses me and sighs.

"I guess this is the wife. We'll do the introductions later," the woman says, taking off her coat. She heads to the sink to scrub her hands, then takes a plastic doctor's gown from one of the drawers, snaps on a pair of gloves, and moves swiftly toward the group of wounded men.

"Who's that?" I look at Salvatore and head to the sink to scrub my own hands.

"My mother," he answers.

I stare at his back, stunned for a moment, as he walks away to join the group huddled around Alessandro. All I can do is blink rapidly as I shake my head a bit to recover from that little bombshell.

His mother?

I finish getting prepped and run toward the chaos at the other end of the room, where Salvatore's mother is already instructing Nino to take Alessandro into the small operating room.

"Hold this." Milene grabs my hand, pulling my palm over the bundled gauze compressed onto the wound in Carmelo's shoulder. "Damn it, Tore. You need to press harder."

Carmelo looks at her, then at me, his eyes wide. I ignore his gawking and watch as Milene moves to Filippo and pulls up his shirt to inspect the laceration across the side of his body.

"Superficial. Do you want me to sew you up, or do you want Ilaria to do it?" she asks.

Filippo looks at me, and I shake my head. I won't have my wife touching any other man unless it's absolutely necessary.

"Doc can do it, Mrs. Ajello," Filippo says quickly.

"Okay, I'll go see if they need me in the OR."

She stops to check the IV next to Alessandro's bed, goes to change her gloves and the sterile coat, then heads into the small room where Ilaria is trying to dig out the bullet from Pasquale's thigh. They fumble with his wound for twenty more minutes. Milene bandages his leg while Ilaria throws her gloves in the trash, dons a new pair, and opens the sliding door.

"Next!" Ilaria yells, then looks at Carmelo. "Long time no see, Carmelo. What do you have for me today, hmm?"

It takes two more hours for Ilaria and Milene to take care of the wounded, and by the time everyone's been treated, it's already eight in the morning. Due to his stomach wound, Alessandro will have to stay in the infirmary for a few days. Carmelo's and Pasquale's injuries are less serious, so they will be released tomorrow. The other four men were sent home as soon as they'd been treated. Seven wounded in total. I can't wait to get my hands on Fitzgerald.

The service elevator opens, and Nino walks out, followed by two of the nurses I have on the payroll for just these types of situations. They'll keep watch over Alessandro, Carmelo, and Pasquale until tomorrow afternoon, when another pair will take over.

"Let's go upstairs. I've told Ada to prepare us something to eat." I pass Ilaria her coat. "You can sleep in one of the guest rooms, or I can have someone drop you off."

"No need. Cosimo will pick me up at nine. I want to check on Alessandro one more time before I go."

"Does he need to be moved to a hospital?" I ask.

"No. He was lucky. The bullet didn't damage any organs. I'll drop by to check on him twice a day till Monday. He should be good to leave by then."

I nod. "I'll get Milene and we'll go up."

Ilaria looks at me as though she wants to say something but leaves without uttering a word. I turn around in search of my wife and find her changing

Pasquale's IV, chatting away as he looks at her like she's an angel. It takes all of five seconds for me to reach her, scoop her into my arms, and carry her toward the elevator, signaling to one of the other nurses to take over.

"Tore? What are you doing?"

"I'm taking you home."

"I was in the middle of a conversation."

"I could see that," I say and use my elbow to press the button for the twelfth floor. "You won't be talking to my men unless necessary. Or any men, for that matter."

"What?"

"You heard me."

"Don't be ridiculous."

The elevator chimes as we reach the top floor, and the doors slide open. I set Milene down, but instead of letting her exit, I press the stop button and take a step toward her, caging her within the cab by pressing my palms against the walls on either side of her head. "No talking to my men, Milene."

"Jesus, what's gotten into you all of a sudden?" She tries to slip free, but I grab her around her waist and pull her body to mine.

"Do. Not. Test me," I whisper, placing my hand at the back of her head and pulling her face toward mine. "Because if I see anyone else looking at you the way Pasquale just did, I'll end them."

"For God's sake, Salvatore. That's absolutely . . ."

Pressing my mouth against hers, I swallow her words, and slide my left hand under her T-shirt. Milene gasps and stiffens for a second, but then her hands move around my neck, drawing me in.

My lips brush against hers before I pull back a hair's breadth to look her in the eyes. "I will end him, Milene. Whoever it may be," I say and slide my hands down the sides of her body to her thighs. I grip and lift her up, pressing her against the back wall. "Got it?"

Milene nods and wraps her legs around my waist, then moans when my hard cock presses against her sex. I don't remember ever wanting a woman so madly that she occupies my every waking thought.

"Why is there a cat in your living room currently sharpening its claws on the Persian rug?" my mother says from somewhere behind me.

"We're busy, Ilaria," I say and keep attacking Milene's lips.

"So I can see."

Milene wriggles in my arms, so I let her down reluctantly and my eyes follow her as she exits the elevator and dashes across the hallway, past Ilaria, and into the penthouse. Damn that cat.

"You let her bring a cat here?" Ilaria asks.

I walk by her and head right toward the living area. "It's not a cat. It's the devil's spawn. And, wasn't Cosimo supposed to be meeting you?"

"He's on his way," Illaria replies.

Ada set the dining table for breakfast, so I pick a chair that gives me an unobstructed view of the living room. Milene stands in front of the bookshelf with her hands on her hips, trying to coax Kurt down from the top of it. It has something that looks like a piece of sausage in its mouth.

"How old is she?" Ilaria asks and takes a seat next to me.

"Twenty-two."

"Young. She did good down there. Is she a medical student?"

The cat leaps off the shelf and scurries under the sofa. Milene twists, crouching to look under the furniture.

"A nurse." I reach for my coffee and take a sip.

"Why did you marry her, Salvatore? Cosimo said it was because of some agreement with the Chicago Family, but we both know no one can *make* you do anything."

"I'm not exactly sure, Ilaria." I tilt my head, leering at Milene's firm ass as she continues to peer beneath the sofa. "She's completely screwed up my brain. I've started acting irrationally."

"How so?"

"She went to see a friend a few days ago. Alone. I flipped. Yelled at Nino all the way from the office to the parking lot."

"That doesn't sound like you."

"I know."

Milene finally catches a hold of the cat and carries it into the kitchen.

"You eat there!" She points at the bowl in the corner.

The cat looks at her, jumps onto the counter, and then on top of the refrigerator, where it resumes chewing on the sausage. Milene throws her hands up into the air, leaves the cat sitting on the fridge, and comes over to take a seat next to me.

"So, you never told me your mom is a surgeon." She takes a piece of pastry from the platter in the middle of the table. "That was amazing to watch, Mrs. Ajello. Are you the one who's always patching up Tore's men?"

My mother's eyebrows shoot up on hearing the nickname.

"Salvatore has a general medical practitioner for everyday stuff. They only call me when there are serious wounds," she says and casts a sideways glance in my direction. "I don't mind, so long as the bullets I'm digging out are not from inside my son."

"Yeah, I hear that happens quite often." Milene stuffs the rest of her pastry into her mouth and gets up from the table. "I'm gonna crash. Do you need me in the office this afternoon?"

"No. I have a meeting with Arturo in an hour that'll take most of the day," I say.

"What about sleep? We've been up since two."

"Are you inviting me to join you, cara?"

Her eyes widen before she scrunches her nose at me. "You know the answer to that question." She turns to Ilaria. "It was nice meeting you, Mrs. Ajello. I hope the next time we see each other will be under less dramatic circumstances."

The moment Milene is out of sight, my mother crosses her arms and fixes me with her gaze. "Cara?"

"Yes. Why?"

"I've never heard you use an endearment for anyone."

"There is a first time for everything."

Ilaria's eyes narrow. "And the two of you are not sleeping together?"

"I don't see how that is any of your concern."

"So, you aren't."

"No. Not yet."

"You don't do relationships, Salvatore. I very much doubt you know how to behave in one. As far as I know, you've only used women to fuck, so what's so different about this girl? You two are already married. Why play roommates?"

"I've already taken away all of her choices in life," I say. "When we do, eventually, sleep together, it'll be because she's decided to take that step."

"What I saw happening in that elevator is not first base action." She shakes her head. "The air around the two of you is practically buzzing with sexual energy. I have half a mind to lock you two in a room and leave."

"She's still mad at me."

"For marrying her?"

"I don't think the marriage itself bothers her that much. It's everything else that goes with it." I pour myself another coffee. "I made her resign from the hospital where she worked."

"She didn't want to leave the job?"

"No. Perhaps if the situation were different, we could have worked something out, but with the Irish on a killing spree, I can't risk it."

"So, you would have let her work if the Irish were out of the picture?"

"Maybe. If she'd agreed to transfer to gynecology or pediatrics. Somewhere with no adult male patients."

"Are you telling me you're jealous?"

"I'm not jealous." I take a sip of coffee. "I just have an uncontrollable urge to kill any man who even looks at my wife."

My mother watches me for a few seconds, then places her hands on the table and leans forward. "I truly hope this is a passing infatuation," she says. "God help her, if you're truly fixated."

"That sounds ominous."

"Because it is. You've always had issues connecting with people, ever since you were a child. She's too young to handle someone like you."

"Ilaria, please, you make it sound like I'm a psychopath."

My mother sighs and shifts her gaze to something behind me. Her eyes remain glued to that spot for a couple of minutes, and she appears to be deep in thought.

"You're my child, Salvatore. I love you the way you are," she says, then looks directly into my eyes. "But we both know you're not what most people consider normal. If I'm right, and if you do feel something for this girl, you'll make her life very difficult. You know you become unreasonable when you fixate on something. You'll need to either control yourself or explain certain things to her. Otherwise, she will eventually run."

"What is it you think I'll do?"

The phone in her coat pings.

"I wish I knew. Your brain is wired differently, son. Remember that." She takes out the phone and looks at the screen. "Cosimo's here. I'll check on Alessandro, then I'll be gone."

"It's interesting that you claim to hate Cosa Nostra, yet you're in a relationship with one of my capos."

"Of course I hate it. You almost died because of this fucking Family," she barks, her mask of civility slipping a little. "I still don't know how you survived.

You have no idea what waiting in that hospital hall did to me, praying for the surgeon to come out and tell me you'd live."

"I lived, Ilaria. And that was seven years ago."

"You did, barely, and not without consequences," she snaps, looking down at my left leg, but quickly averting her eyes.

Losing part of my leg affected Ilaria more than me. She still hasn't quite come to terms with it. I always make sure to wear my prosthesis when she's around because the last few times she saw me without it, she left with tears forming in the corners of her eyes. She was fighting them back, but I saw all the same.

Ilaria takes her coat, giving my shoulder a squeeze. "Call me if you need to talk. I'll drop by this evening to see how Alessandro is doing."

# Chapter seventeen

Milene

I WAKE UP WITH A TINGLING SENSATION AT THE BASE OF MY SKULL, AND I'm instantly aware that someone is watching me. I don't even need to open my eyes to know it's Salvatore.

"What time is it?" I mumble.

"Three in the afternoon."

Dear God, his voice has an even more devastating impact on my half-asleep brain. Deep and sexy, it makes me want to bury myself beneath the blanket and simply take in the sound of his baritone. Not the words, but the timbre. I wonder whether his tone drops even lower when he's having sex. No, I'm not going down that rabbit hole.

I blink several times before fully opening my eyes and find Salvatore leaning his shoulder against the doorframe, the sleeves of his black shirt rolled up to the elbows, and his top two buttons undone.

"Did you check on the guys?"

"Yes. They're good." He looks at Kurt, who's curled up on the pillow above my head. "Do you know your cat sleeps with its tail over your face?"

"He's been doing that from the start. I tried to make him sleep at the foot of the bed, but it hasn't worked.

"You should try again."

"Why?"

"Because when you move into my room, I don't want the cat on my bed."

"I don't plan on moving into your room."

"But I do, Milene."

He leaves, and I press my thighs together, despising myself for wanting to spend every night in his bed.

I remember the episode in the elevator and how good it felt to be crushed against his body, his cock pressed to my pussy. Just thinking about the moan I had to stifle turns me inside out. I do my best to ignore the urge to run after him and leap into his arms. Instead, I make my way to the bathroom to wash my hair.

Lifting the handheld showerhead, I bring it down until the jet of water pulsates against my pussy, and slide a finger of my free hand inside my aching core. I let waves of pleasure overcome me, shivering with delight while imagining Salvatore before me, his finger within me instead of my own. I come with a moan.

While eating a late lunch, I shoot a message to Bianca, asking what's new with her. I also try calling Andrea, but she doesn't answer. Salvatore is nowhere to be seen. He's probably either sleeping or in his office, plotting revenge on the Irish. Finished with my food, I head to the infirmary to check on the wounded men.

Nodding to the duty nurse organizing the medicine locker, I walk over to Alessandro, who is resting in bed at the furthest part of the room. He's scrolling on his phone, but when I approach, he lowers the device.

The way his eyes bore into mine is extremely unsettling. It's as if he is analyzing my every action and reaction. The look in his eyes indicates he's ready for anything and I've noticed that he does this with everyone. The way he observes people with such intense focus is unnerving.

I once met another man, a war veteran who returned from his fifth tour of duty in Afghanistan, with almost the same look in his eyes. He acted as if he was still in enemy territory, ready to fight insurgents hiding around every corner.

"How are you feeling?" I ask, checking his IV. He doesn't respond, but simply watches as I replace the saline bag and scribble a note on the chart at the foot of the bed.

"Fine," he finally says.

"Oh." I frown theatrically. "He talks."

Alessandro gifts me with another one of his dark glares, then takes his phone and continues swiping. I roll my eyes and head toward the next bed.

I'm in the middle of changing the dressing on Pasquale's thigh when the phone in my back pocket vibrates. It's probably Andrea, so I let it ring and continue bandaging the wound. As soon as the ringing stops, however, it starts again. I secure the bandage and pull out the phone. Salvatore's name lights up the screen.

"Where. Are. You?" he bites out the moment I take the call, his voice deathly quiet.

"On the eleventh floor. Why?"

He hangs up. Has something happened? I collect the medical supplies and carry them to the other side of the room. As I'm returning the unused bandages to the cupboard, the door to my right opens with a bang, and Salvatore comes inside. I've never seen him leave the penthouse in anything other than an immaculate suit or without his prosthesis, but now, he's wearing only his sweatpants and leaning on his crutches. Based on the surprised expression on Pasquale's face, this is not a normal occurrence. The moment Salvatore's eyes find me, he heads in my direction. He doesn't stop, even when he's almost in front of me, and find myself backing up until I hit the wall.

"Salvatore?" I look up into his face.

His eyes are narrowed, his breathing quick, and his nostrils flare.

"I was looking for you, and you weren't there," he says through his teeth. "You do not leave the penthouse without informing me first."

"But I'm on the floor below you."

"That doesn't matter."

"Am I a prisoner here?"

"Nope." In his eyes, there's a controlled kind of crazy. "I need to know where you are at all times."

It's silly. He's expecting me to let him know whenever I want to leave the apartment? For a moment, I think he's messing with me, but then I see his expression. He's deadly serious.

"Why?" I ask.

"I just do. Are you done here?"

"I want to check on Carmelo, as well."

"Ilaria will be here later. She'll make sure he's okay. Let's go."

I shake my head and follow him to the elevator. When we reach the penthouse, he doesn't say anything. There is no explanation for his strange behavior. I walk behind him as he heads into his bedroom and pause in the doorway.

Salvatore sits down on the bed and unties the knot on the left pant leg of his sweats. He pulls up the material and reaches for the prosthesis that's leaning against the wall. It takes him a long time to put it on. Much longer than it should. Rolling on the liner sleeve is quite a feat with only one fully functioning hand because the fabric keeps slipping from his fingers. I wondered why he didn't wear the prosthesis in the evening after he's taken a shower. It's probably too much trouble to do it up twice a day.

"Is something going on?" I ask.

"What do you mean?"

"You insisting I let you know every time I leave the penthouse. Are you expecting that the Irish may try getting inside this building?"

"This has nothing to do with the Irish." He curses when the liner slips from his fingers again. "And no one can get inside this building."

"Then why? Do you think I'll run away or something?"

He doesn't reply but continues fumbling with the prosthesis. When he puts it on he stands up and approaches me, lifting his hand to the back of my neck.

"You can try running," he says and tilts my head up, "but I will catch you every time, Milene."

He's still shirtless and being so close to him is messing with my already confused mind. The guy has a fucking eight pack. How can I keep up the pretense of being indifferent when my eyes want to wander to his stomach and count each ab again to make sure? I thought that shit was a myth.

"Can you please put on a shirt?"

"No." He takes another step forward, making me step back. The hand that's clutching the back of my neck slides down until it stops at the small of my back. The tiny hairs on my skin rise as goose bumps cover the length of my body.

"Tore?"

"Yes?" Another step, followed by one more, until I end up with my back against the hallway wall.

"What is it with you always cornering me?" I ask, trying to distract myself from thoughts of placing my palms flat against his chest. "Does it turn you on or something?"

"Maybe. Why don't you check?" He takes my hand and presses it against his crotch, and I suck in air. He's hard as a rock.

"Stop with this sexual intimidation, Salvatore," I choke out.

"I don't see you trying to get away." He bends his head, watching me, then brushes his finger down my cheek. "Or letting go of my cock, for that matter."

I gasp and quickly remove my hand.

"Tell me, Milene, if I were to put my hand down your panties right now,"—he glides his right hand along my hip toward the front, trailing his finger in a line from my navel to the waistband of my shorts—"how wet would I find you?"

I should tell him I'm dry, or turn and leave. Or ask him to stop. Instead, I bite my bottom lip and hold his gaze without blinking.

Slowly, I undo the first button of my denim cutoffs. Salvatore dips his head and presses his lips to mine, but it lasts for only a second.

"The next one, cara," he says against my lips, and I undo one more button. This time, he takes my bottom lip between his teeth and sucks it gently, driving me mad with desire.

"Next."

I undo the last two buttons and take a deep breath, waiting to see what he'll do. His finger trails lower, beneath the frill at the top of my panties, and presses against the wetness there.

"Soaked. You should have told me it was this bad, Milene." He rubs his fingers fast over my clit, and my breathing quickens. "Why are you so damn stubborn?"

"I'm not stubborn," I whisper. "I'm mad at you."

"You can continue being mad at me. I don't mind." He braces his left hand next to my head. "Turn around and place your palms against the wall."

*No! Remove his hand and walk away,* my brain cries. Unfortunately, my mind's ability to wield control over my body has been severed, because I find myself doing exactly as he commands. The moment I turn, he presses his body against mine, his hand slides inside my panties again, and I barely manage to keep the moan from escaping. Or maybe not, as a tiny whimper does escape through my barely parted lips.

"I quite enjoy this little game we've been playing." His finger pushes, and presses, and circles, causing my already wet entrance to become even more soaked.

When he applies a little extra pressure, I grind my teeth, giving in even as I try to hold on to the last of my resistance before it ebbs away. Did I scream a little? Maybe, but the out of body experience I'm having due to his deftly skilled fingers is making it hard for me to think. Slowly circling my clit this time, applying pressure in all the right places, I'm like a puppet on his string. My breathing quickens, my heart races in my chest.

"But as with every such game, there can only be one winner in the end." He presses onto my clit just a little harder, his movements faster, and beneath his controlled and methodical touch, the last of my resistance is quickly seeping out.

"You think you're going to win?" I bite my lip again and press my forehead to the wall. More. I need more, but I'd rather die than confess it to him. A demon. Yes, he's a demon, sent to torment and play me like an instrument with his infernal fingers. With every press of his fingers, I lose another piece of my mind.

"Well, that's the thing, Milene," he whispers into my ear and slowly moves his finger to my entrance. "I've already won. All that's left is for you to accept it."

"You haven't won anything, Salvatore."

"Are you sure about that, cara?" he asks and slides two fingers inside me.

I suck in a breath and moan as my eyes roll up in my head. He pushes his fingers even deeper while his other hand moves to rub my clit rapidly. His fingers curl to massage my inner wall, finding my G-spot. This time a very loud moan fills the air as pleasure overwhelms my system.

As Salvatore pinches my clit a little harder and rubs faster with both hands, I reach an orgasm like I've never experienced before. Wave after wave of spasms rack my body, drowning out all rational thoughts. It feels as if my mind fully disintegrates in that moment.

His lips brush the side of my neck. Light kisses pepper the column of my throat all the way up to my earlobe. Softly, he whispers, "That was with my fingers, Milene. Tonight, when you're trying to sleep, imagine how it would feel to have my cock inside you instead."

He slides his fingers out gently, his hand vanishes, and between breaths, he's gone as well, leaving me panting in the middle of the hallway, with my forehead and hands pressed against the wall.

"Damn him," I mumble and take the phone from my nightstand, checking the time. Four a.m. Groaning, I put the phone back and bury my face in the pillow, trying to cast the memory of being pressed against the wall out of my head. No amount of mental gymnastics is successful.

I get out of bed and go to the kitchen. Maybe I should get wasted and pass out on the sofa. It wouldn't take much since I don't often drink. Three glasses of wine would do the trick.

I take out an open bottle of white wine from the fridge and walk to the cupboard next to the sink to get a glass. As I'm reaching for it, I hear Salvatore coming inside the kitchen and my hand stills on its journey toward my holy grail. A few moments later I feel a light touch against my back.

"Can't sleep?" comes the whispered words behind my ear, followed by a light kiss that makes the fine hairs on the back of my neck stand to attention in a flash.

"No."

"Me neither." Another light kiss against my neck. "Grab two glasses. And bring the wine."

"Bring it where?" I utter.

"Into my bedroom," he says and moves his lips to my shoulder, biting slightly. "I'll behave."

"Oh? Like you're behaving now?"

"So stubborn." He kisses the skin on the side of my neck. "We can talk. If that's what you want."

"Yes." I grip the stems of two glasses between my fingers and lift the chilled bottle from its resting place. When I turn, I find him looking at me, a curious glint in his eyes. "Just talk, Tore."

"Just talk, Milene."

I nod and move past him into the hallway, which has taken on a new aspect since earlier events. I'm aware of his eyes on me as he follows a few steps behind. The door to his bedroom is closed, so I lean down to press the handle with my elbow and feel my T-shirt rise. I turn to find Salvatore standing right behind me, holding his finger under the hem of my shirt, ogling my ass.

"Tore! We had a deal."

"But I haven't laid a finger on you, Milene," he says without lifting his eyes from my backside. "Red looks good on you, cara. I especially like the frills."

"I'm glad you approve of my choice in underwear. Now stop it."

I open the door and move inside his bedroom, knowing full well I haven't come here to talk. At some point during the night, between tossing and turning while I was trying to sleep, I finally admitted to myself—I can't resist anymore. My integrity be damned. I can't keep going on like this because, if I do, I'm going to lose my mind.

I pass Milene, who's setting the glasses down on the dresser next to the door, sit on the edge of the bed, and lean my crutches against the wall before sprawling out on the satin sheets. Milene pours the wine, then sways her hips as she moves toward the nightstand next to me and sets down my glass. Walking around the room, she sips the Sauvignon Blanc while checking out the space. I hope she likes it, because she'll be spending every night here with me from now on.

"You really like art," she comments, standing in front of a wide landscape painting on the wall facing the bed.

"Yes."

"An expensive hobby." She takes a sip of her wine and continues perusing the rest of the paintings.

I wonder how long she'll keep on pretending we're just going to chat. We both know how this will end. My wife, I've come to realize, has an almost pathological need to stand behind her decisions, even when she knows they're wrong. From the info Nino uncovered, Milene's father was a tyrant who went to great lengths in forcing his will upon his children. She's probably compelled to do anything, even fight against herself, to maintain a semblance of control over her life. She wants me, but she's afraid it would mean she's somehow failed. I've been patient with her, letting her dance around this situation for quite some time, but it ends tonight.

"Come here, Milene."

She turns around, takes another sip and raises an eyebrow. "To your bed?"

"Yes. Come here or I'm going to chase you across this penthouse until you do."

"I'm pretty sure I can outrun you." She smirks.

"Teasing a handicapped person, cara? That doesn't suit a medical professional." I cross my arms behind my head, noticing the way her eyes rivet on my biceps.

"The only way you're handicapped is that you can't understand the meaning of the word *No*, Salvatore."

I focus on the curve of her lips for a few moments, then ask, "How about we play a little game?"

"I'm not interested in your games."

"Afraid you'll lose, cara?"

Her eyes snap to mine as she covers her mouth with the glass. "I'm not afraid of you, or your games," she says. "What did you have in mind?"

No, she doesn't seem to be afraid of me. "I'll tell you something about yourself. If I'm right, you remove a piece of clothing."

Milene laughs and a warm feeling spreads through my chest upon hearing it.

"And if you're wrong?" she asks.

"I remove one of mine."

"You don't know me. You'll end up naked in under five minutes."

"Then you have nothing to worry about."

She leans her back on the wall and takes another sip of her wine, smiling. "All right."

The gray T-shirt she has on is one of mine. I wondered if she would wear my shirts after I threw away the shit that belonged to her ex. I barely restrained myself from setting the whole closet on fire that day. The mere idea of Milene wearing something that belonged to another man nearly sends me on a murdering rampage. The sight of her in *my* clothes, however, pleases me immensely.

I move my gaze up her body until it reaches her mouth. She's still smiling.

"You lied when you told me you don't know why you wanted to become a nurse," I say and watch for her reaction.

Milene's body goes rigid, her hand holding the glass stills halfway to her mouth. "You're wrong."

"Am I?" I cock my head to the side. "Why not a doctor? A neurosurgeon? Cardiologist?"

"I don't know." She shrugs and looks down at her glass.

"Lying will get you disqualified from the game, cara," I say. "What did you see that made you want to be a nurse?"

Milene closes her eyes and leans her head against the wall. "My sister, Bianca, was in a car accident when she was eleven. She almost died because the paramedic who came to help had no idea what he was doing." She shakes her head. "Some idiot recorded the whole thing on a phone and posted it online. I was at a friend's house when it happened. Her brother showed me the video. I watched the guy as he tried and failed to intubate my sister while she lay in the middle of the sidewalk. Only when the other paramedics arrived did they manage to bring her back." She takes a deep breath and opens her eyes but keeps staring at the ceiling. "My father was driving the car when they crashed. He was drunk."

Yes, Bruno Scardoni was an epic son of a bitch.

"So, what do you want me to take off?" Milene asks and lowers her eyes to meet mine.

"Your choice."

She bends and reaches under the T-shirt and slowly removes her panties. When she straightens, I nod toward the piece of red lace she's holding and extend my hand. "Those are mine now."

Milene curves an eyebrow as she launches her panties right into my face. "You got lucky with that one. Next."

The red lace falls onto my chest, so I deliberately lift it to my nose and inhale, enjoying the sight of surprise on Milene's face. "You are allergic to fish," I say and then add, "and to peanuts."

Her lips widen in a smug smile. "That's two misses, Tore. I eat half a jar of peanut butter a week, and we had fish at that restaurant where you made all the other guests leave. I expected you to be more attentive for someone who—" She stops in the middle of the sentence, and surprise flashes in her eyes as she comes to a realization.

"Yes, I guess I should be more attentive," I say and remove my sweats for the fish. For the peanut butter, I take off my shirt. She only has the T-shirt left, and I'm in my boxer briefs. "Looks like we're even at the moment."

Milene's eyes travel down my chest and stomach and stop at my crotch, or more specifically, the bulge there. "Playing games with me turns you on?"

"It's not the games, Milene," I say. "Just you."

Her gaze snaps back to my face, those green eyes glaring into mine, lips pressed tightly together.

"Tell me, Milene, why were you so scared of getting into a relationship with someone from Cosa Nostra?"

She blinks and quickly shifts her focus to the painting above the bed. "I have no idea what you're talking about."

"You are a very bad liar, cara. Lie again, and you remove your T-shirt as a punishment." I reach for my wine on the nightstand. "I noticed a very interesting thing when I went over the info Nino collected for me. This last guy you were with, David . . . he was a yoga instructor."

"So?"

"Before him, it was some pastry chef. Before that one, a florist. Even when you were in high school, you always picked the most . . . tame partners. You never even went out on a date with anyone from our circles."

"You had your chief of security dig out my high school crushes?" She gapes at me.

"Yes."

Milene leaves her empty glass on the dresser behind her and grabs the board at the foot of the bed. "You had no right!" she snaps.

"Were you afraid everyone in Cosa Nostra is like your father? Terrorizing people because of his own inferiority complex?" I continue, "Or was it because you didn't feel safe?"

"And I'm safe with you?" The corners of her lips curve upward. It's concerning, how much that little smirk turns me on. I watch her as she climbs onto the bed, then crawls over my body to straddle my waist until her face is only inches from mine. "You think you're better than the other men in Cosa Nostra, so I have nothing to fear? Is that it?"

"You *are* safe with me, Milene." I take a sip of my wine and leave the glass on the nightstand. "But not because I'm better than the rest. Just the opposite, in fact."

"Oh?"

I grab her chin and fix her with my stare. "You're safe with me because I'm the worst it can get, cara. And no one will dare touch what is mine."

"You missed again." She hooks her fingers in the hem of my boxer briefs. "I was never afraid that I might get hurt if I ended up with someone from the Family."

"What else?" I ask and regard her as she moves down my body, pulling my boxer briefs along my legs. She doesn't flinch when she reaches the stump midway of my calf, just continues sliding them down my right leg and then throws the underwear over her shoulder.

"I was terrified by the possibility I might fall in love with someone from Cosa Nostra," she says and crawls up my body, avoiding my now fully erect cock until she's sitting on my stomach with her bare and completely drenched pussy pressing onto my skin.

My cock is so fucking hard it feels like it's going to explode. "And why would that pose a problem?" I ask and lift my hand to trace the line of her lips with my finger.

"Because I don't think I'll survive watching a man I love die, Tore," she whispers, looking down into my eyes.

"Well, it's a good thing you hate me, cara. So, I guess you're safe from the heartache."

"Of course I hate you," Milene says through her teeth.

I behold her sitting there on me, her blonde hair falling down her face and over her breasts. My beautiful, stubborn liar. She takes a deep breath and closes her eyes, and when she exhales, it sounds like a sigh of defeat. A second later, those mischievous green eyes open. Keeping a hold of my gaze, she grabs the hem of her T-shirt and pulls it off.

"Looks like it's game over for both of us, cara," I say and move my hand to the back of her neck, pulling her down.

"Fuck you, Salvatore," she whispers and crashes her mouth to mine.

I roll her onto her back, my body looming over hers, and drink in the sight of her. Finally, my little hellcat has succumbed. I rarely feel satisfaction, or any kind of excitement, but this, having my wife under me, can't compare with any other sensation I've ever experienced. Milene wraps her legs around my torso, pressing her warm and waiting sex against my cock. I thought I might take this slow, savor the moment, and torment her a little by making her wait. I intended to drag it out for an hour or more before purposefully sliding my cock into her heat until it fills her completely. A rather odd plan because I've never wanted to take it slow with a woman before. For me, sex has always been a means of release. But not with her. Everything is different with my Milene.

I move my hand down her front and press my fingers onto her pussy. She's so wet, silently begging me to fuck her into the stratosphere.

My cock is already close to bursting, veins pulsing. As Milene buries her nails into my back, I lose my composure entirely. I want her to moan, scream, and pant. I want to hear her yell my name . . . I want everything, and I want it now! I remove my hand and bury my cock inside her in one thrust. Perfect. Milene gasps and squeezes her legs around me. I slide in to the hilt, marveling at the sensation of my cock filling her.

Bending my head, I move my hand to grip her nape. "Look at me."

Milene's eyes open and she stares at me, her deep and heavy breaths fanning my face.

"Who owns you, Milene?"

She presses her lips together and squints her eyes a little. I withdraw my cock till it's almost completely out of her trembling pussy. Milene's legs tighten around me, trying but failing to keep me deep inside.

"I said . . ." I tangle my hands into the hair at the back of her head. "Who owns you?"

She pants, wrapping her hands around my neck and pulling me toward her, but she doesn't utter a word. The urge to push myself all the way back in is infuriating, but I don't move an inch, enjoying the way she's begging with her eyes and her body.

I squeeze the blonde strands a little harder. "Who, Milene?"

"You!" she cries out.

"Me." I slam inside her. "Don't you ever forget that."

Her hands travel up my neck, tugging at the back of my head, and she tilts her chin to stare up into my eyes. "I'm still mad at you, Salvatore."

I slide out and slam back in, then lean to whisper into her ear, "I don't believe you."

Her hold on me tightens. Moving my hand between our bodies, I find her clit and tease it. Milene's breathing quickens. I pull out my cock slightly, then thrust all the way in, massaging her both inside and out.

"Faster," she breathes.

I place my lips at the curve of her shoulder, kissing the soft skin. "Are you still mad at me?"

"Yes."

I slide my cock out completely, replacing it with a single finger. She wraps her hands around my upper arms and buries her nails into the skin.

"What is it, cara?" I ask and add another finger. "Is something bothering you?"

Oh, the look she gives me. Frustration in its purest form. Still, she doesn't reply. Stubborn. So, fucking stubborn. I curl my finger inside of her and press onto her clit with my thumb.

Milene moans, and the hold she has around my arm tightens. "I want your cock," she says finally.

I remove my fingers from inside of her pussy and bend to gently bite that lower lip she likes to chew. "Are you still mad at me?"

"No, damn you!" she cries out, and I slam my cock inside her once again, all the way up to my balls.

I push into her, slowly at first, my eyes locked onto her face. Then faster, until the bed creaks beneath us, and the headboard bangs against the wall as our bodies rock together.

Milene screams and presses her palms to the board above her head as she widens her legs, panting. My hand moves up her body to wrap around her throat, and I thrust into her even deeper and harder than before. Mine. I slide out only to slam back inside. Only mine. I stare at her—into her half-closed eyes, at her mouth that's red from her biting her lips. The mouth that fascinates me so much.

"Smile at me," I bark as I rock into her.

Her eyes find mine and lock on, but her lips remain puckered. I lightly squeeze my fingers around her neck and bend my head until we're face-to-face.

"Smile. At. Me." I pound into her—once, twice, three times. It's like air to me, her smile. I need to see it. If I don't, I'm going to lose my mind. "Smile, you stubborn woman."

Milene squints her eyes at me, and then she smiles. It's like the first ray of light after a thousand hours of a long night, piercing the darkness inside my chest and filling me with warmth. I kiss that stubborn mouth and enjoy the feel of my cock as it stretches her inner walls until her pussy spasms around my length.

She screams as I push my dick even deeper into her, and it drives me more insane. I slide out and thrust back inside, feeling her body shake. I bite her chin and graze my teeth down the side of her neck.

"I want you to smile at me every day," I say next to her ear and slam into her again. "Every." Slam. "Fucking." Slam. "Day."

"Why?" she breathes out, then moans as she comes.

Because I need it. Because every time she does, something happens inside my chest. Because it breathes air into my lungs and makes my heart race.

"Because I'm ordering you to," I bark, staring her down.

She watches me for a few seconds, then squeezes her legs around me and bursts out laughing.

I take a deep breath and thrust into her one final time, unable to keep my orgasm at bay as I pump weeks of my frustration into her. Not for one second do I take my eyes off her smiling mouth.

"Are you okay, cara?" Salvatore reaches out and traces the back of his hand along the line of my jaw.

Nope, I am not okay. My legs are still trembling slightly, my pussy is sore, and my whole body aches all over. The best feeling ever. "I hope I'll be able to walk tomorrow," I say and lift my head off Salvatore's chest to find him watching me.

I place the tip of my finger at the corner of his mouth and push upward slightly. I don't think I've ever seen Salvatore smile, so I don't understand why he seems to be fixated on me doing so. He almost "sextroyed" me for it earlier.

Salvatore bites the tip of my finger, then kisses it. "I will carry you around with me if necessary."

"Piggyback?"

"If you insist."

I imagine how his men will react and laugh. "You are such a contradiction, Tore."

"Does that pose a problem?"

"No. I kind of like your strange ways." Moving my hand upward, I thread my fingers through his hair. "When did you start to go gray?"

"A few years ago. It runs in the family."

"Your father's side?"

"No. I got it from Ilaria." He tilts his head to the side, giving me greater access to his neck. "I still remember the day she discovered the first gray hair on her head. I found her crying in the bathroom. I was sure someone had died. She was twenty-nine, I think."

I raise my eyebrows. "From what I've seen, she comes across as a very composed person."

"It's a front," he says. "She's very well versed in pretending, since she's been doing it for years. My father and her were a bad match. I'm glad she has Cosimo now. He makes her happy, which means I can't kill him if he fucks up."

He says this as though he's reading the weather report aloud. Facts. Conclusions. Zero emotions. For a second, I think he's joking, but he looks down at me, and I see in his eyes he's deadly serious.

"What happened to your father?" I ask.

"He was killed during a Family disagreement."

I sigh and lower my head back to his chest. "My father was killed, too. Four years ago."

"I know. It was the fuckup with the Bratva."

"Yeah. He almost killed Bianca's husband." I shudder. "I hate Cosa Nostra."

"You and Ilaria can set up a club." His hand settles on my arm and he traces random patterns on my skin. "But if there was ever anyone who had his life fucked up by the Cosa Nostra, it's Arturo."

"The underboss?"

"Yes. His parents, along with four other people, were killed in a police raid at one of the casinos. The previous don was heavily invested in the illegal gambling business." His hand moves down to my ass, then back up. "Arturo ended up raising his sisters. He was twenty."

"Jesus. How old were they?"

"Five years old, twins."

"Whoa." I blink. "Did he have help with that, or . . . anything?"

"An aunt who came occasionally, but that was all."

We remain silent for a long time, me staring at the wall, and Salvatore still tracing lines across my back.

"I wish I'd been born into another family," I whisper. "A normal one."

"I'm glad you weren't." He squeezes my ass and looks at me with his calculating eyes. "Because our paths wouldn't have ever crossed."

I place my palm on his chest and glide it up to wrap my hand around his neck. "That's extremely selfish."

"I know. But it's the truth." His other hand comes to take my chin and tilts my head. "Would you prefer I lied to you?"

"No, I wouldn't." I throw my leg over his middle and climb to lay atop of him, feeling his cock swell rapidly against my stomach. "Seriously?"

"You denied me for weeks." His hand comes into my hair. "I plan on collecting everything you owe me, Milene."

"And you think you'll manage to get everything tonight?" I straighten up, straddling his waist.

"You're working off the interest at this point, cara."

"Oh? And how much do I owe you in total?" I raise an eyebrow and slide down his length. My pussy is sensitive, but I don't really care because having his hard cock filling me, straining the parts of my body which are already tender, is worth it. It's only a sliver from being painful, which makes it even better.

"I could have killed you when I found you in my city." His left hand comes to my waist, and he slides it up over my stomach and breasts to once again wrap it around my throat. "I didn't, so I'd say you owe me everything."

A shiver runs through my body on hearing his words, and I lean forward slightly, my throat pressing onto his palm. There is something disturbingly sensual in having his hand wrapped around my neck, knowing he can feel every draw and release of my breath, and, if he wished to, he could cut off my supply of air altogether.

It should scare me. I don't deal well with giving a man, any man, a semblance of control over me, ever. Still, for some reason, this doesn't bother me. Maybe it's because his touch is feather-light, his fingers barely pressing on my skin, as though he doesn't truly want to scare me, and as if this is a game. Yes, such a contradiction—my husband. Ordering four innocent men to be executed, then offering to carry me around the apartment because I'm sore.

I press my palms on Salvatore's chest and slowly rotate my hips. It's my turn to tease, so I lift myself slightly and slide back down again, hard, watching him as intently as he watched me. I change my pace and shift forward so I can take even more of him inside, and he arches his hips to rock into me from below. I moan as my nails dig into his chest and ride him faster, a mixture of satisfaction and excitement washing over me. Salvatore Ajello, the most feared man in all of Cosa Nostra, is coming undone beneath me.

His arms wrap around my back, pulling me down to him. He rolls us until he's on top again, pounding into me, neck muscles straining with the effort. He is so beautiful—in the way the exotic, dangerous animals are. The closer I get, the more likely I'll be eaten alive.

Salvatore's hand slides between our bodies and finds my trembling pussy. I'm already close, so when he pinches my clit and thrusts inside—hard, I scream as tremors rack my body.

"I love when you scream, cara," he says and suddenly pulls out.

I stare at him. He did not just do that!

"You don't have to worry about the hitmen, Salvatore," I snarl, winding my legs around his waist and grabbing at his throat with my hand. "Because I'm going to be the one to end your life if you don't get your cock back inside me."

Salvatore dips his head until our noses touch. "That sinister streak of yours is sexy as fuck," he says and slams back into me so hard, I unintentionally squeeze his neck. His eyes flare, and a growl leaves his lips. I tighten my hold on his throat a little more, smiling. Hawkish eyes watch me from above as he pulls out, only to thrust back in even harder, making me moan.

I release his neck and let my hands travel over his shoulders, wrapping my fingers around his bulging biceps. Salvatore slams into me again. I dig my nails into the skin of his arms. Another growl, and hard lips press down onto mine. I smile into Salvatore's mouth and grip tighter, digging deeper into his flesh with my nails. Drawing my next breath, I bite his lower lip.

He completely flips. His palm slides between my breasts and around my neck, then he threads his fingers into my hair and pulls. I gasp for air while a waterfall of pleasure washes over me as he continues his powerful thrusts, making the headboard bang against the wall once more. Stars explode behind my eyelids, and I come at the same time as him.

As the waves of bliss pass through me, we're kissing again—our breaths heavy and the surrounding air filled with the scent of our lovemaking.

I open my eyes and find Salvatore looking down at me. His fingers are still tangled in my hair. I raise my hand and move one of the black strands that has fallen over his forehead.

"That was a lot of pent-up aggression, Salvatore," I say and brush the back of my palm down his cheek. "Where am I with my debt now?"

"Right where you were two hours ago."

"That doesn't sound quite fair."

He lowers his head, leaning toward my face. "I don't give a fuck."

I sigh, then pull his head down until our lips touch. "So, I still owe you everything?"

"Everything, Milene," he whispers without lifting his mouth off mine.

# Chapter eighteen

Salvatore

I ground to a halt at the threshold as I'm leaving the bathroom, staring at my bed. Empty. Milene was still sleeping when I went to take a shower, so she's probably gone to her own room to do the same. She should be here. I grind my teeth and head toward the closet.

I have a meeting with Arturo and Nino in fifteen minutes, and one thing I truly hate is being late. Once I put on my prosthesis and get dressed, I quickly head down the hallway, only to stop in front of Milene's door. The sound of a hairdryer can be heard from the other side. With a shake of my head, I continue toward the elevator but pause after a few feet. Squeezing my hands into fists, I take another step and stop again. Fuck! I turn around and head back toward Milene's room.

"Hey." She turns off the hairdryer when she sees me enter. "Do you need something?"

Yes. Her in my room. In my bed. The fact she's not there inflicts a feeling of restlessness in the back of my head which I can't shake off.

"No," I say. "I have a meeting, so I'll skip breakfast today."

"Okay." She leaves the hairdryer on the dresser and comes over. "Is something bothering you?"

"No. Why?"

"You seem . . . angry." She places her hand on my forearm and brushes it lightly.

"I don't get angry, Milene."

She arches her eyebrows. "You could have fooled me."

I grab her around the waist and pull her to me. She smiles. It's one of the smiles I like—the one where her eyes seem as though they're twinkling.

People rarely smile at me, and I don't really want them to. I just need them to do what they're told.

Squeezing my arm more tightly around her, I smash my lips against hers, stealing that smile. It's mine. She's mine. Along with everything else she has to give. Every smile, every kiss, every moan. They're all mine.

"I can't . . . breathe," Milene mumbles against my lips.

I ease my hold slightly.

Her eyes dim a little, and she looks puzzled. Concerned, even. She brushes the back of her hand down my cheek. "Are you sure you're okay?"

"Of course I am."

Milene nods, kisses the side of my chin, then steps into her walk-in closet.

"I need to take Kurt to a vet. He's been scratching his hind leg like a maniac for three days."

"If that thing brought fleas into my home, I'm going to strangle it."

"He doesn't have fleas," she throws back over her shoulder. "It looks like some kind of allergy. There's a veterinarian's office two blocks from here. I found them online. I'll call to see if they have some availability today."

"Call Nino when you know the time. He'll have the bodyguards waiting for you downstairs."

"Four?"

"Yes."

"Jesus." She sighs and shakes her head.

"Call me before you leave, and when you get back."

"Yes, *Mom*."

I grit my teeth. She doesn't understand. I don't fucking understand it, either. I only know I need her to call me. "I'll be in the office."

"I'll come by as soon as I'm done with Kurt," she says.

Arturo and Nino will be arriving in a few minutes, but instead of heading to my office, I move to stand behind Milene. She's still rummaging through her closet and grumbling something about a yellow T-shirt. I bend my head to bury my nose in her freshly washed and dried hair.

"Chocolate?" I ask.

She looks over her shoulder and smirks. "Nope. Coconut."

"Hmm." I wrap my arm around her waist and pull her to me. "Are you sore?"

"A little." She gasps when I slide my hand inside her panties. "You kind of demolished my pussy last night."

I circle her clit with the tip of my finger, teasing it with fast strokes until

I feel her getting wet. Her breathing quickens, and I slowly move my finger lower and slide it inside. Milene grabs the shelf in front of her and opens her legs wider, letting out a sweet moan.

"Does this hurt?" I ask and slide my finger a little deeper.

"No," she breathes out and grabs my wrist. "More."

"Will you call me as we agreed?"

"Yes!"

"Good girl." I slide my finger out, circle her clit a few more times, then push two fingers inside her in one thrust. Milene gasps and shudders as she comes.

"You see how nice it is when we agree on things?" I kiss her neck and remove my fingers from her pussy. When I leave the room, she's still clutching the shelf while taking rapid, shallow breaths.

"So, do we know who the snitch is?" I ask Nino, who's sitting on a chair next to Arturo.

"It's Tomaso," he says. "The guys cornered him, and he broke after two hours."

"Send someone to question him. I want to know who his contacts are, how they got in touch with him, and what he told them. You have"—I check my watch—"nine hours."

"Okay." Nino nods. "Then what?"

I look at Arturo. "I want all capos and team leaders in the old safe house at ten this evening."

"All right. What should I tell them? What's the occasion?"

"A demonstration of sorts."

"No specifics?"

"No, we'll leave it at that," I say. "Where are we on Fitzgerald?"

"He hasn't been leaving his lair." Nino shakes his head. "I have two men outside his house at all times, but so far, no activity."

I lean back in my chair, weighing our options. "I want you to nab one of Fitzgerald's men and bring him to me. Someone close to him. Unharmed. Make sure no one notices when you grab him, I want to keep this encounter on a need-to-know basis."

"Where should we bring him?"

"Into the safe house downtown. Do we have any other pressing matters?"

"Do you plan on going to the City Museum opening next week?" Nino asks. "If you do, I'll have to organize the security detail."

"No."

"What about Rocco's wedding? Everyone will expect to see you there."

I'm not really in the mood for mingling with the Family, but gossip surrounding my marriage has already picked up, so I guess taking Milene to meet them is in order. "We'll go."

"How many bodyguards?"

If it were just me, I wouldn't be taking any, especially to a Family wedding. "Stefano and Aldo."

"Okay. Anything else?"

"No. That's all."

When Nino and Arturo leave, I pick up the phone to call Milene. She messaged me two hours earlier after getting back from the veterinarian. Barely an hour later, I found myself feeling on edge. It's idiotic. I know she's two floors up—in the penthouse—because I called Ada to make sure she was there, and yet, I still have a powerful compulsion to check on her again.

"I was meaning to call you," she says the moment the line connects. "Why is Ada moving all of my things to your room?"

"Because I told her to."

"And it didn't occur to you that maybe you should talk to me first?"

No. "I want you to move into my room, Milene."

"You're seriously lacking in social skills. You know that, right?"

"Yes."

She sighs. "Kurt is coming, too, just so you're aware."

"I'm not going to sleep in the same bed with a cat. Especially one with fleas."

"He doesn't have fleas. The veterinarian says he's depressed."

A depressed cat. "Should we sign it up for a group therapy?" I ask.

"Ha ha."

"What do you do with a depressed cat?"

"He suggested taking in another one, so they could play."

"No."

"He's suffering, Tore!"

"I said no, Milene." Another cat and I will be the one who's suffering.

"There's a rescue close by. We can go have a look after lunch."

"No. More. Cats."

"You *are* a bad person."

"Yes."

"Please? Just one. You can choose."

"We're not taking in another cat, Milene," I say and cut the call.

"Oh, look at the ginger one!" I grab Salvatore's hand and pull him toward the last cage in the line. "He looks like a mini Garfield."

"That one is a little problematic," the lady who runs the rescue says, observing Salvatore with concern. My husband isn't the typical clientele—stoically standing there in his charcoal Armani suit, wearing a scowl on his face while regarding the cat in question. I guess she's right. He certainly doesn't give the impression of someone who likes cats.

"Problematic?" I ask. "In what way?"

"No more mentally defective animals, Milene," Salvatore grumbles. "One is enough."

"Well, he's a little grouchy," the lady says. "Not very good with people."

"Sounds exactly like you, Tore." I place a hand on his arm. "Can we take him?"

"No."

"But look at him! Isn't he cute?"

"No."

"Tore!"

He looks at the cat, then moves his gaze to glare at me. "You said we'd come here to look."

I cock an eyebrow and smile. "I lied."

Salvatore watches me, his eyes glued to my lips. He does that a lot. He always studies my mouth when I smile.

"Just take the damn thing, and let's go home," he grumbles.

"Tore!" I yell from the guest bathroom. "He won't come out from the shower stall."

I nudge the food bowl toward the cat and coo at him, but he keeps sitting stubbornly in the corner.

Kurt came to see the new resident as soon as we arrived, hissed at him, and went back to my old bedroom. Saying things are not going as I expected would be putting it mildly. I sigh, leave the cat in the bathroom, and head toward the dining room where Salvatore is already eating.

"We need to name him," I say as I sit on the chair next to him. "How about Riggs? Like Mel Gibson's character in *Lethal Weapon*.

"I don't particularly care for the way you name your animals."

"I'm glad you like it." I scoop a spoonful of mashed potatoes from a bowl on the table and drop them onto my plate.

"What's with you and the obsession with eighties movies?"

"They made the best films back then. Want to rewatch *Escape from LA* with me?"

"I don't watch movies, Milene."

I lower my fork and stare at him. "You don't watch movies? What do you do in your free time?"

"Go to a gym on the third floor. Watch a game from time to time. Sleep."

"And . . . that's it?"

"Yes."

"It's no wonder you're surly all the time."

His hand shoots out and grabs at my chin, tilting my head to the side until our gazes meet. "I'm surly?"

"Extremely."

"And watching action movies from the eighties will fix that?"

"Maybe?" I smile. "Want to try?"

His gloomy gaze moves to my lips. "We can watch a movie this weekend," he says and lets go of my chin to return to his meal.

"Are we going to do emails after lunch?" I ask.

"Yes."

"Okay. I'll go to check on Alessandro first."

"I'll come with you."

"You don't need to," I say with my mouth full. "It'll only take a minute, and I'll go to the office straight after."

"I said I'll come."

I lower my cutlery and sigh. "Do you think I'm going to flirt with Alessandro or something?"

"No. I don't like the idea of you alone with another man."

"Don't you think you're overreacting?"

"Probably. I still don't want you alone with him."

I sigh. "I find it really hard to understand you sometimes, Salvatore."

"I know." He picks up his glass of water and leans back in his chair, fixing me with his gaze. "I have some business to attend to tonight and won't be home before two a.m. I need you to call me to tell me everything is okay."

"All right. I'll call you before I go to sleep."

He nods, but I notice his jaw is set in a hard line as though he's unhappy with my answer.

"Is there something wrong?"

"No," he says, clutching the glass in his hand as though he's trying to break it.

"Tore?"

He sets the glass on the table, turns toward me, and squeezes the bridge of his nose. I don't know what's going on, but he seems unusually agitated all of a sudden. I can't figure out why.

"I'm leaving around eight." He looks me in the eye. "You will call me every hour while I'm not here."

"What for?"

"To check in," he deadpans. "So, I know everything is okay."

I gape at him. "You want me to check in every hour? While I'm kicking back in the living room, watching a cooking show?"

"Yes."

"Are you expecting someone to storm the building? Did they announce an imminent earthquake?" I ask.

"No."

"Then why?"

"Because I told you to."

"Would a text message suffice instead?"

"No. I need to hear your voice."

Okay. We need to talk about this. I stand up and place my palms on his cheeks, looking into his eyes. "Can you explain? Please?"

His piercing light brown gaze bores into me. "I'm not sure you'll understand, Milene."

"Try me."

Salvatore's hand comes to the waistband of my jeans. He hooks his finger on a belt loop and pulls me down to sit on his thigh. I raise an eyebrow in question, waiting for him to explain, but he just watches me for a few seconds, lips pressed tightly together.

"I have . . . a problem," he bites out the words. I already figured Salvatore didn't tolerate weakness, and it seems very hard for him to be confessing one now.

"Do you think I'm cheating on you when you're not around?"

"No. It doesn't have anything to do with that." He places the tip of his finger onto my forearm, stroking my skin lightly. "When I was in the office today, even knowing you were here, I felt compelled to call and confirm. I can't control it, Milene. I've tried."

"Is it like some kind of anxiety?"

"Yes, but ten times worse."

"Do you have this . . . compulsion with anyone else? Your employees?"

"Just you."

I blink at him in confusion. "Why? And why so suddenly? Have I done anything to trigger this?"

"It's not sudden, Milene. I've barely managed to control it for these past weeks." He reaches out with his other hand and strokes my cheek. "You will call me every hour. Please."

"Will it go away?" I ask. "This compulsion."

"I don't think so." His face is grim, and I see he doesn't enjoy asking this of me. He's right, I don't understand.

Salvatore gives the impression of a highly composed individual, but the more I think about it, the more I realize that many of his reactions have not been exactly normal. Like in the parking lot when someone shot at us. No one should be that calm and controlled under fire, but then freak out when I go to the floor below without informing him beforehand. I've also never seen him smile. He's a little odd—I knew that from the start—but this doesn't seem like a silly quirk. I think he actually has a problem, and I'm not sure he's telling me everything.

"Well, I hope it won't get worse, because I'm not letting you into the bathroom when I have to pee." I lean forward and touch my nose to his. "How often do you need me to call you?"

He closes his eyes and brushes his nose against mine. It's such an unexpected and tender gesture, so completely at odds with his character, that it elicits a tenderness in my heart, like a warm hug comforting me from within.

"When I'm in the office, every two hours," he says and looks at me. "But when I'm not in the building, every hour, on the hour."

"And what do you want me to tell you when I call?"

"Whatever. Doesn't matter."

"Okay." I nod and stroke his hair. "What will we do when I have to go somewhere?"

"I'll be accompanying you from now on."

"You can't always go with me, Salvatore. What if I need to visit the hairdresser? Or get a manicure? I have girlfriends. I like going for coffee with them from time to time."

His body goes rigid. "How often?"

"Beauty salon stuff, once a month. Girl time, twice a month."

"All right. I'll deal with that somehow." He squeezes his hands around my waist. "But tonight . . . every hour, Milene."

"I'll call," I whisper. "Where are you going tonight?"

"To one of our safe houses. I have a situation to resolve."

"Do I want to know the specifics?"

"You don't." He places a quick kiss on my lips. "Let's go work on those emails."

The sound of the doorbell reaches me as I'm trying to coax Kurt out of the kitchen cupboard. He's been hiding out in a large, stainless-steel pot for twenty minutes, and every time I've tried to get him out, he's only hissed and bared his fangs. I also have two long claw marks on my forearm from when I tried to take him out.

"Ada, can you get that?" I yell over my shoulder, then turn back to the devil's eyes before me. I will not admit defeat before this cat! Grabbing the lid from the shelf below, I put it over the pot and, with the cat still inside, take the vessel by its handles. I'll carry Kurt to the bedroom and deposit him on the bed to avoid further injury.

Pot in hands, I turn around and come face-to-face with Salvatore's mother.

"Ilaria." I gulp, then smile. "How nice to see you. Would you like some coffee?"

"Sure," she says and takes off her coat.

"Perfect, I'll just . . . take this away." I nod down at the pot in my hands.

Kurt picks that exact moment to let out a pained meow. I groan, lower the pot to the floor and carefully remove the lid. Kurt leaps out of the pot, hisses at me again for good measure, and dashes toward the hallway. When I stand up, I find Ilaria staring at me with wide eyes. I guess she's not accustomed to seeing people carrying cats around in stockpots.

"Desperate measures," I murmur, setting the pot down in the sink and head toward the coffee machine. "Milk? Sugar?"

"Both." She takes a seat at the breakfast bar.

"Salvatore's not here," I mention over my shoulder. "He had some business to attend to."

"I know. I came to check on Alessandro, but I wanted to talk to you first."

"Oh?" I carry the coffee over and take a seat opposite her. "About anything in particular?"

"How's this thing between you two going?"

"By 'thing,' you mean the marriage?"

"Yes. Being forced to marry someone you don't know is not every woman's dream," she says and looks down at her cup. "Believe me, I have experience."

"You didn't know Salvatore's father until you married him?"

"No. So, you see, I can relate to you and your situation."

"Hmm." I take a sip of my coffee. "Salvatore and I knew each other before he decided to trap me in this marriage."

Ilaria's hand holding her cup of coffee stops midway to her mouth. "What?"

"Oh, he didn't tell you?"

"No," she whispers.

"We met a handful of times. I'm pretty sure he was stalking me. We even went on a date. A kind of date, anyway."

She stares at me. "Salvatore doesn't do dates."

"He told me." I snort. "Also, I'm not a hundred percent certain, but I think he broke into my place and filled my refrigerator with food."

The realization came only a couple of days ago when I stumbled on Ada preparing soup. I asked why we needed soup when no one was sick, and she said it was because Salvatore had told her I liked it the last time. The only soup I've eaten in the past two years was the one I found in my miraculously stocked fridge. I still don't know what to think about that revelation. It's cute in a very bizarre way.

Ilaria keeps on staring at me for a few moments, then slowly lowers her cup. "Has he been acting . . . strangely?"

"Well, your son is a very unusual person, Ilaria, and I don't know him well enough to gauge what behavior is 'normal-strange' or 'strange-strange.'" I shrug. "He wants me to call him and check in every two hours. Would that be considered 'strange-strange?'"

"Yes. Did he say why?"

"Because of some compulsion to know where I am at all times. Do you think it's some kind of OCD? Like when you need to touch your wallet every few minutes to make sure it's there, you know?"

Ilaria closes her eyes and takes a deep breath. "It's not OCD," she says and looks at me with a grave expression on her face. "I think he . . . likes you."

I burst out laughing. "He did force me to marry him, so yes, I assume he likes me."

"Salvatore doesn't like people, Milene. He respects them, or not. But he doesn't *like* them."

I furrow my brows in confusion. "That's crazy. He likes his men. I saw how concerned he was when the Irish attacked, and some of them got hurt."

"Salvatore's men are extremely loyal to him. He respects their loyalty. Maybe even cares about them in his own way." She leans forward and takes my hand. "But he doesn't feel anything for anyone."

"Of course he does." I blink at her. "He's not a fucking statue. Yes, he sometimes has weird reactions, but . . . he loves you. You're his mom."

"Salvatore cares about me, yes." Her eyes crease in a sad smile. "Will you call him, as he asked?"

"He hasn't actually asked. It was more like a demand." I smirk. "But he said please, so yes."

"He said please . . .," she mutters, then squeezes my hand. "I'm going to check on Alessandro."

As she takes her coat and purse, I wonder if this might be the weirdest interaction I've ever experienced.

# Chapter Nineteen

Salvatore

There are four guards in front of the safe house tonight, which is expected, considering how many people are coming.

"Boss." They nod in unison as I pass them, the one closest to me opening the door.

Nino's waiting by the window in the first room, nursing a drink, while Aldo and Stefano are sitting at the table in the corner but quickly rise as soon as they see me.

"Did Tomaso talk?" I ask.

"He gave us everything within the hour." Aldo motions with his hand toward the door on the right. "Do you want to talk to him, Boss?"

"No. How badly did you rough him up?"

"Three fingers missing. Some beating. He was relatively easy to break."

I nod and scan my surroundings. "Get me one chair in the middle of the room. Do you have pliers and heavy-duty scissors?"

Aldo looks at me with confusion in his eyes, but then collects himself. "Would gardening shears do?"

"Yes."

The phone in my pocket vibrates. As I take it out, some of the anxiety that's been building begins to ebb.

"Milene."

"Riggs vomited all over the carpet."

"What?"

"How the hell should I know, Salvatore? It looks like hair and half-digested cat food."

"I was expressing my irritation. Not asking for the cat vomit analysis."

"You need to work on expressing meaning through your voice. Your intonation sucks. I have to go and clean this up." She cuts the call. Apparently, she took the fact I told her it didn't matter what she talked about literally.

I put the phone back in my pocket and find Aldo and Stefano gaping at me. "We adopted a cat. It's defective," I say and turn toward the door just as Cosimo and Arturo come in. "Get that chair and bring Tomaso. Tie him nice and tight."

It takes fifteen minutes for everyone to arrive. Nino instructs them to stand along the wall opposite the chair where Tomaso is sitting, tied and gagged. After Arturo nods, signaling that all twelve people we've been waiting for are present, I walk over to Tomaso and turn toward the group of capos and team leaders for our ranks of soldiers.

"Tomaso here thought it was a good idea to cozy up to the authorities and leak information regarding our drug shipments," I say, looking at the men who are standing around in utter silence.

I take off my jacket, put it over the back of the chair behind me, and roll up my shirtsleeves. "Nino, remove the gag and open his mouth. And keep it open."

Tomaso whimpers and shakes his head left and right, trying but failing to avoid Nino's hands. Once Nino succeeds in opening the guy's mouth, I take the pliers and the shears off the table and stand in front of the snitch.

"People tend to forget things, so I figured it might be a good time to remind everyone what we do with snitches," I say.

It takes me a few tries to catch Tomaso's tongue with the pliers. When I have it in my grip, I pull it out and cut it free from his treacherous mouth with the gardening shears. Blood sprays all over the front of my white shirt as Tomaso screams. I turn around to face the group—every man staring at the screaming Tomaso—and throw the pliers, along with the still-attached pink lump of flesh, onto the floor in front of them.

"I don't tolerate traitors," I say. Walking around the chair until I'm standing behind Tomaso, I place my right hand below his chin and my left one on top of his head. "Remember that."

With those words, I force Tomaso's mouth closed and keep it that way.

He flails, choking on his own blood, and I wait until his body goes still before letting go of him.

I grab a rag off the table to wipe my hands. The blood comes easily off my right hand, but the glove on my left is completely saturated. I take it off and drop it on the ground, right into the puddle of more blood pooling beneath the dead man.

"You're dismissed," I say and reach for my jacket.

Milene is already asleep when I get home. I lean my shoulder on the doorjamb and just watch her for what seems like hours. Would she look at me differently, if she saw me doing all those obnoxious things so I can keep this organization standing? Would she let me touch her with hands that were soaked in blood barely two hours earlier? I know she's aware of how things are handled in Cosa Nostra, but I don't think I can risk having her witness it. It should concern me, the fact that her opinion matters this much. I don't give a fuck that people are calling me a monster behind my back; it goes with the job description. But not her. I grip the doorway with all my strength, ignoring the pain that shoots from my left hand all the way to my head. Never her.

I feel a light touch on my chin, followed by a finger tracing the line of my jaw. Firm lips soon find my own. I smile sleepily and turn my head toward the heat I feel at my side. Opening my eyes, I discover Salvatore looking at me as he lounges in bed.

"You talk in your sleep," he says.

"I know." I reach out to stroke his hair. "I hope I didn't spill any secrets."

"You don't get to keep any secrets from me, Milene." His finger moves down my neck, lower and lower. "I've already told you that you owe me everything." His palm slides between my legs. "And that includes any secrets you might have."

I smile, then gasp as his finger enters me. "You can't demand that."

"Yes, I can." Another finger slides inside. "I own you. Your body. Your mind." His thumb presses onto my clit and he teases me with his masterful fingers. "Your smile. And your secrets."

"You don't get to own a person." I grab at his shoulders and ride his hand. The things he can do with his fingers defy all logic and reason.

"I don't?" He thrusts his fingers so deep that I choke on my breath and whimper when he curls them inside me. He hits the sensitive spot on my upper wall, and I come in an instant—violently.

I'm still panting, trying to catch my breath, when he covers me with his body, pressing me into the bed.

"You weigh a ton, Salvatore," I choke out, then gasp when his fingers are replaced by his steel-hard cock.

"Who . . ."—he slides the tip inside, but so very slowly I want to groan in frustration—"owns you, cara?"

I meet his hawkish gaze, smile, and move my hand to his neck. When I tighten my hold, Salvatore lets out a growl and thrusts his cock all the way to the hilt filling me so completely that consciousness leaves my body. It feels as if I'm flying.

"You," I whisper and slide my palms down his back all the way to his hard ass. "And do I own you, Tore?"

He doesn't reply immediately, just keeps pounding into me until my walls clench around his cock, and I come again from his punishing pace. Dipping his head lower, he places a kiss on my shoulder and whispers in my ear.

"I'm afraid you do, Milene." He slams his lips to mine and thrusts into me at the same time, filling me with his hot cum.

I sit up in bed and watch Salvatore as he walks toward the closet on the other side of the room, takes out a shirt, and puts it on. He has four gunshot scars on his back. One is near his shoulder, two on the left side, and another a few inches to the right of his spine. With his leg and the graze to his right bicep, the total amounts to six.

"Where are the others?" I ask.

"What?"

"Gunshot wounds."

He turns and fumbles with the buttons on his shirt. "Right thigh and left leg."

"Holy fuck, Salvatore. When did you get all these gunshot wounds?" I get up from the bed and take over the buttoning of his shirt.

"The one on my shoulder is from a few years back. The thigh shot was last year." He says this like he's reciting a grocery list. "My left leg, and the three on the back were inflicted on me during the same incident. Seven years ago."

My fingers go still on the middle button. Three bullets in the back do not come from an ordinary gunfight. That was an execution. "Who did it?"

"The old don gave the order," he says. "But it was one of the capos who carried it out."

"Why?"

"The previous establishment became greedy. They decided to keep the lion's share of the money for themselves."

That's insane. I couldn't have understood correctly. "They were stealing from the Family?"

Cosa Nostra Families have a very strict way of operating, and it's based on trust above all else. The don and capos are in charge of organizing business, but they are only entitled to part of the profits. The rest of the money is distributed to all other members, all the way down to the foot soldiers. The shares depend on the person's position in the organization, but the don and the capos never take more than 40 percent of the total income. I don't know how many people there are in the New York Family, but back in Chicago, there were at least a hundred.

"Yes," he says. "And I found out."

"So, they decided to kill you?"

"In the end, yes." He bends his head and brushes his cheek against mine. "They tried to bring me into their little scheme first. I was a capo then, and I'd already started to build up my own construction business. It was bringing in a lot of money."

"What happened?"

"I said no. They tried giving me an incentive to change my mind." He reaches with his hand and traces a line along my jaw with his finger. "They were very enthusiastic in their efforts."

"Your hand?" I ask and place my palm over the one that's caressing my chin.

"And my leg."

"Jesus, Tore." I blink to keep the tears at bay. "How does anyone survive something like that?"

"Nino found me in the warehouse where I was invited for a 'meeting.' He has a habit of following me, even when I've told him not to. When I was released from the hospital, Arturo helped me lie low until I was well enough to discuss the matter with the don and the capos again."

"What did you say to them?"

"Nothing in particular. I only demonstrated where they'd gone wrong." He presses his lips to my fingers. "When you really intend to kill someone, you aim for the head."

"You killed the don?"

"And all six capos."

A shudder passes down my spine. The fact that I like a man who represents everything I wanted to run away from is hard to accept. "Tore?"

"Yes?"

"How many people have you killed?" I whisper. "Personally."

His finger moves under my chin and raises my head. Our eyes lock. "Do you really want me to answer that question, cara?"

I stare at those amber depths and feeling like the largest hypocrite on earth, I slowly shake my head. No, I don't want to know. But not because I'm afraid it'll make me like him less. It's because I'm afraid I'll like him the same, whatever the answer is.

"THIS IS HILARIOUS," PIPPA SAYS, LOOKING BACK OVER HER shoulder at Stefano and Vincenzo, who are trailing a few paces behind us. Two more bodyguards are following a little further back.

"Yeah, tell me about it," I sigh and turn to enter the next boutique.

"I feel like there should be a camera crew following us, as well." She giggles. "Why would anyone need four bodyguards? You said your husband was a businessman, not the president."

"He is a bit extreme." I approach the dress rack and fish the phone out of my purse to call Salvatore.

"Milene."

"About the dress for Rocco's wedding. How about gray?" I ask, looking at a long and flowing gown. "Or should I go with something more colorful?"

"You can wear whatever you want, as long as it covers your ass."

"Well, thank you, sugar pie, that was really helpful." I snort and cut the line.

"You're really into him," Pippa comments, looking past me at the dress. "What was that, the third time you've called him since we started shopping?"

Actually, it was the fourth. I called him while she was in a restroom, as well.

It's been two weeks since Salvatore asked me to call him whenever we're not together. In the beginning, I wasn't exactly punctual. He never commented on it or reprimanded me for being late with my "check-ins." I think he was feeling bad for asking me to do it in the first place, but, every time I was late calling, I noticed a slight strain in his voice, as if he was on edge. After that, I decided to be more diligent with my communications.

"Yup." I nod. "I really am."

It's the truth. Weird or not, I enjoy spending time with Salvatore. I don't even mind his quirks. If there wasn't his continued insistence that I do not work, I wouldn't harbor any lingering resentment to the marriage, arranged or not.

"Shit," I say as I'm taking the dress to the cash register. I think I'm falling for my husband.

After a quick coffee at the mall, we drop Pippa off at her place and head home. The car enters the garage, and while I'm taking my phone out to call Salvatore and tell him I'm back, the elevator doors open, and he steps out. As I'm reaching across the back seat to collect the shopping bags that are piled next to me, the door opens, and Salvatore slides in beside me.

"Out!" he barks at the driver and Stefano in the front seat.

As soon as they exit the car, he grabs me around the waist, pulls me onto his lap, and puts his nose in my hair. I try to turn my head, but he just tightens his grip around my middle, pressing me to his body.

"Four hours, Milene," he whispers into my ear.

"I called you every hour."

"I know." He presses his face to my neck and inhales. "Do you think I'm crazy?"

"A little?" I snort, wrapping my arms around his neck and pressing my lips to his.

"Is that a problem?"

"Not really." I shrug and kiss him. It should concern me. The thing is—I don't mind Salvatore's OCD behavior or his need to know where I am. I don't mind calling him, either, even more than every hour if that's what it takes to quell his anxiety. In fact, I kind of . . . like it. "You know, something came to my mind when Pippa and I passed a flower shop earlier."

"What?" he asks as he nips at the side of my jaw.

"You were the second creep. The one who sent me a ton of flowers."

"Yes."

I lean away and pin him with my gaze. "A hundred vases?"

"Ninety-six. That's all they had."

"One would have been more than enough."

Salvatore watches me for a moment, then bends forward and touches his nose to mine. "It's all or nothing with me, Milene. You should have figured that out by now."

Yeah. I guess it is.

I comb my fingers through Salvatore's hair, watching him from my spot astride his waist as he reaches to pick up his bottle of beer from the floor. It still surprises me, seeing him so relaxed.

We've been lounging on the sofa in the living room for almost an hour—him watching the game and me sprawled across his chest, texting Bianca. She stopped replying to my messages about ten minutes ago, meaning Mikhail probably came home. God knows, those two can't keep their hands off each other.

"I can't believe you like beer," I say.

"Why?"

"I don't know. You always seemed more like the fine-wine type to me." I trace the line of his jaw with the back of one finger. "It's the suits."

"I have nothing against wine. But it goes better with cheese than it does with football." He tilts his head and kisses my finger. "What did your sister say? Any news from home?"

"The same. I'm still waiting for her to reply to the last text."

Salvatore lifts his hand and traces his thumb over my bottom lip. "Ask her to pass on a message to Petrov for me."

"To the Russian pakhan?"

"Yes. He should know that the Albanians have started to do business with the Irish."

I type a quick text and send it to Bianca. "Anything else?"

"Nope." He takes the phone from my hand, places it on the coffee table, and removes the throw pillows from the sofa, throwing them on the floor.

"Did the poor pillows do something to offend you?"

"Yes." He throws the last one over the back. "They take up too much space."

"Maybe we should shop for a larger couch." I bend my head and plant a kiss on the side of his jaw.

"Couldn't agree more."

His arm comes around my waist, and he pulls me down so I'm lying on my side, pressed between his body and the back of the sofa. I reach for the waistband of my leggings and take them off, before removing Salvatore's sweatpants and boxer briefs. I do the same with my panties, tossing them next to Salvatore's clothes on the floor.

He takes my hand, lifts my fingers to his lips, gently kisses each one in turn, then proceeds to move his lips across my wrist and along my arm, sending tremors throughout my body. He does all of this very slowly, holding his lips over the spot for a few seconds before moving on, as though every kiss is meant as a statement. It's captivating, the way he caresses my skin, because Salvatore has never seemed like a patient lover. The attraction between us has always been an explosive force, both hard and intense.

"You have no idea what you do to me, Milene," he whispers when he reaches my shoulder, and I tremble. "No fucking idea."

His lips meet mine, and I wrap my arms around his neck, squeezing him to me with all my strength. I don't think he realizes how much he's messed up my own mind. It's scary. I don't even know what I feel anymore. Am I in love with him? With this controlling, grouchy, closed-off man? Someone I haven't even seen smile once in all the time I've known him? I'm afraid I am.

My hands travel down his neck and over his shoulders to rest on his chiseled chest, and, without breaking the kiss, I throw my leg over his waist and move so I'm seated on top of him.

"I want to make love to you," I say into his lips and feel him go still under me. "Will you let me?"

When I open my eyes, his steady gaze is fixated on me. "Yes."

I smile and brush my fingers over his lips. Ilaria was right. He doesn't deal well with feelings. It's as though he's unable to grasp the meanings of the various emotions and has trouble processing them. I move down his body until his cock is pressing against the wetness of my sex. Inch by inch, I take him inside me, reveling in the way he gradually fills me up. It's large, his cock. Having all of him inside me feels as though my walls are going to burst. I love that.

When he's fully in, I bend to place my lips at the center of his chest and move up to trail kisses along his neck until I reach his strong jaw. I'm rotating my hips methodically and continuously, but as delicately and as slowly as I can, just to keep him on the edge. When my mouth reaches his, I lift my hips up until only the tip of his cock remains inside. Salvatore regards me, his eyes glued to mine and his hands gripping my hips, but he doesn't move. I smile, then slam down onto his cock and simultaneously bite his lip. He inhales sharply and places his left palm lightly against my cheek while his other hand wanders to where our bodies are joined.

"I've been wondering, cara," he says and presses his thumb to my clit, making me moan.

"What?" I lean back and continue rotating my hips.

His fingers pinch my clit lightly, and I shudder but resist the need to move faster. Instead, I maintain the slow tempo, enjoying the way his hazy, lust-soaked eyes fixate on mine.

Salvatore's hands move to my ass, and he squeezes, making me whimper. In the next heartbeat, he slams into me from below so hard I gasp.

"You've never been scared of me," he says. "Why?"

I smile, as he continues to rock into me, his tempo building.

"Answer me, Milene."

"I was too mad at you to be scared!"

"That"—he thrusts his cock into me again with such force I explode in an instant like fireworks and thunder—"is the most idiotic answer I've ever heard."

# Chapter Twenty-one

## Salvatore

Arturo has been providing updates about our business dealings in narcotics for the past hour, but my mind has been wandering. Milene went to get a manicure with her friend and called less than an hour ago from the salon, yet I got restless a mere twenty minutes later. Even though she has four bodyguards there to protect her I still find it hard to concentrate.

My phone pings with an incoming message. It's from a jeweler I placed a special request with two days ago, letting me know my order is ready to be picked up.

I somehow manage to sit through the entire meeting, then tell Arturo he's free to go. The moment he's out, I leave the office and go to my vehicle.

The store is nearby, so it takes me less than half an hour to get there and collect my purchase. When I get back into my car, I put the red velvet box on the dash in front of me. Just looking at it lessens my anxiety. I'm not sure how Milene will react when I tell her what it is. I might be pushing her too far already. It still amazes me that she's willing to deal with my shit. But still . . . that little box on the dashboard might be too much.

My eyes scan the clock on the dash. Two minutes after six. She should have called already. Anxiety rears its ugly head once again.

I squeeze the steering wheel, close my eyes, and take a deep breath. Another. And one more. If anything's happened, Stefano would have informed me. She probably lost track of time. My phone rings. I open my eyes and grab the phone.

"Tore?"

"Yes?"

"You know that crystal vase in the hallway?" Milene says in a small voice. "How much was that thing worth?"

A couple of thousand. "Not much. Why?"

She sighs. "Thank God. When I came home, Kurt was chasing Riggs, and they kind of . . . broke it. I had to clean up the broken pieces, and some of them were very small, so please make sure you don't go barefoot there. I'm not sure if I caught every last shard. Where are you? Should I wait for you to eat dinner?"

"I had some errands to run, but I'll be there soon."

"Okay, I'll—Get down, you bastard!" The sound of something crashing travels down the line. "No, not the curtains! I have to go."

I put the phone down next to the velvet box and start the car.

Walking into the penthouse, I stop at the threshold to take in the chaos in the living room. Several unraveled rolls of toilet paper are strewn across the floor, with small bits littering the furniture. It looks like a tornado hit it. A large pot, which was home to a ficus, rests on its side in the corner of the room with soil scattered around its base. One end of the curtain pole hangs halfway to the floor, the satin drapes falling off it. There are also claw marks visible along its length.

A clang comes from somewhere in the kitchen, and I turn in time to see Kurt jumping from the counter onto the breakfast bar and then to the dining room table. Milene appears a moment later, giving chase.

"Come here, damn you!" she yells and tries to grab the cat, but it jumps down and dashes toward the hallway.

Milene's shoulders droop, and she looks up at me. "I'll clean everything, I promise! I have no idea what's gotten into Kurt. He's gone insane. Running around like a banshee for almost an hour." She comes toward me, shaking her head. "I'm trying to catch him. Maybe he'll calm down if I put him in the bedroom for a bit."

As she stops in front of me, I take a good look at my wife. Her white T-shirt is torn at the side. Her ponytail hangs askew, with several locks of hair dangling loose. She has claw marks on her right hand, and there are stains of an unknown origin across her front. She really looks like something the cat dragged in.

"Tore?"

I raise my hand and take her chin between my fingers, staring into her eyes. "You're so beautiful."

She blinks at me, looking slightly confused. "Um . . . thank you?"

The sofa is thirty feet away, but the dining table is closer. It'll do. I grab her around the waist and lift her up, carrying her toward it.

"What are you doing?" she asks next to my ear, sounding genuinely puzzled.

When I reach the table, I set her on her feet. Grasping the tablecloth, I pull it off, making the dishes and cutlery clatter and smash noisily against the floor.

"Jeans," I say, looking down at her.

Milene raises her eyebrows, unbuttons her jeans, and slides them off. The moment she removes her panties, I take her around the waist and sit her down on the table.

"Down." I press my palm against her chest until she's lying on the surface, her legs dangling over the edge. With my free hand, I pull up a chair, sit down, and lift her legs over my shoulders. "Close your eyes," I say before grabbing her ass and tugging her toward me so I can lick her perfect pussy.

Milene moans. I lick her again slowly, kiss gently, and suck on her clit until she starts to pant. She widens her legs, so I slide a finger inside as I continue to tease her with my tongue. She's soaked. Arching her back, she lets out a scream of pleasure. Without removing my finger, I lick her sweet spot, pressing a little harder with my tongue. Her body shivers, and I again suck her clit into my mouth.

I've never gone down on a woman before and never had the desire to do so, but with Milene, I want everything. I revel in the way her body reacts to each stroke and movement. I tease her pussy with my tongue for a few more minutes, and when I'm sure she's close, I press my mouth to her clit again and suck hard, curling my finger inside of her at the same time. She comes with another rising scream, and her legs shake violently around my shoulders. I place one more kiss against the lips of her pussy and watch how her body recovers. Milene is lying back, eyes closed, her chest rising and falling in rapid tempo as though she's trying to draw in enough air.

"Milene?" I ask and brush my palm down her naked thigh. "Are you alive, cara mia?"

"No," she whispers, slowly rising into the sitting position and staring at me. "Move back."

I slide the chair back and watch as she gets down off the table, kneels between my legs, and starts unbuttoning my pants.

"You don't have to reciprocate, Milene." I brush the back of my hand down her cheek.

She takes out my cock, which has been painfully hard since the moment I placed my mouth on her pussy, and looks up at me. "Try stopping me." She smirks. "And see what will happen."

With those words, she wraps her lips around the head of my cock, gripping the shaft with her slender fingers. She starts off slow, licking the sensitive underside, sucking the tip, then swallowing more of me with her hot mouth. Her pace becomes gradually faster, and I grab the back of her hair as she bobs more furiously, watching her lips as she takes me in. I try to hold back but find that I can't. Just the sight of Milene on her knees between my legs with my cock in her mouth is more than enough to make me come, so when she squeezes me and hollows out her cheeks, I explode in her mouth.

Keeping hold of her bunched hair, I lift her head up until our eyes meet.

"Swallow," I order.

She smirks and follows the order. The sexiest fucking thing I've ever witnessed.

I trace a line down Salvatore's chest, circle my finger over his rock-hard stomach, then tilt my head to place a kiss on his shoulder. His arm tightens around my middle, pressing me closer to his body.

"Bianca texted me today." I move my finger upward over his chest again. "Petrov sends his thanks for the intel on the Albanians."

"I wouldn't want to be in Dushku's shoes right now." He reaches with his left hand to move the hair that's fallen over my face behind my ear, then places his hand on his stomach.

"Does it still hurt?" I ask and move my finger to his hand, tracing a line over one of the prominent scars there.

"Sometimes."

"How many breaks?"

"They couldn't determine." He turns his hand and entwines his fingers with mine. "I managed to train myself to shoot with my right. Now I'm even better than I was with my left. My handwriting sucks, though." He looks down at me. "As does my typing, which you've probably noticed."

"And the leg? A gunshot wound to the calf rarely requires amputation."

"I was shot once in the ankle and twice in the calf, from short range," he says. "There wasn't any chance of saving it."

I close my eyes and bury my face in the crook of his neck. "Promise me something."

"What?"

"Please don't get shot again."

"It's not like I'm running around with a target drawn over my back, Milene." A kiss lands at the top of my head.

"Yes, you are," I mumble into his neck. "I asked Nino why there's no security detail on you. He said you don't allow it."

"If someone is persistent enough in trying to kill me, they'll do it. Security detail or not."

My head snaps up. "So, what, you'll do as you've been doing so far and wait for it to happen?"

"No. I'll try my best to kill them first."

"Then, try harder damn it!"

Hi tilts his head, regarding me with interest. "Would it bother you if I got killed?"

"Jesus fuck, Salvatore!" I snap. "Would it bother me? Are you for real?"

"Yes. I want to know."

"You want to know." I blink, not believing what I'm hearing. "He wants to know if it would bother me if he got killed."

"It's a simple question, cara."

He needs to have his head checked. "Yeah, it would bother me." I shake my head in frustration. "Would it bother you if I got killed?"

Salvatore's body goes still. "Do not. Ever. Ask that. Again."

"You started this with the idiotic questions." I take his face between my hands. "No more gunshot wounds. Promise me."

"I'll try."

I sigh and close my eyes. He'll try. Perfect.

"Does that mean you'll start taking security detail?"

"No."

Of course not.

"Then deal with the Irish," I say through my clenched teeth and press my lips to his. "I want them dead."

"I'm already working on that." He takes a strand of my hair and wraps it around his finger. "Why are you so bloodthirsty all of a sudden?"

I stare at him, amazed by his cluelessness. He does have a problem with realizing and processing certain things if he can't see that I'm in love with him.

"Must be PMS." I sigh, hoping he'll accept my answer and not question me any more, and place my head on his chest.

Salvatore's hand lands at my nape and slides downward, lightly brushing my skin with the tips of his fingers. I close my eyes and enjoy the sensation. I'm half-asleep when his hand halts at my neck.

"I bought you something," he says in a serious tone. "But if you don't like it, I'll take it back."

"You suck at giving presents," I mumble into his chest.

"I know." He buries his fingers in my hair. "Do you want to see it?"

"Did it cost a million dollars? A hint for you—if the answer is yes, you can take it back now."

"No."

"Okay."

"It's in my jacket. I'll be right back."

I watch as he reaches for the crutches, rises, and heads toward the door. I use the opportunity to ogle his tight ass, clad in black boxers. Very nice indeed. Salvatore sleeps in just his underwear, something I wholeheartedly approve of. He returns a few minutes later, throws the jacket on the bed, and sits down. Taking out a red velvet box, he places it beside me on the pillow. I sit up and open the box to find a simple gold bracelet. It's thick, yet somehow still delicate.

"It's beautiful, but you don't have to buy me jewelry. You know I rarely wear it. I haven't even had the opportunity to wear that ridiculously exuberant bracelet you bought," I say.

He stiffens beside me. "I need you to wear this one," he says. "At all times."

"Okay." I shrug and open the clasp to put it on.

"It has a GPS chip inside," he adds, and my head snaps up.

Milene remains silent at first, and then her gaze moves between me and the bracelet in her hand. "Why?"

"The calls are not enough anymore. I almost flipped out today while you were with Pippa. Barely managed to sit through a meeting because I was wondering where you were. I need to know where you are, Milene. At all times."

"You knew where I was. I called every hour," she says. "There were four bodyguards with me. You could have called them to check."

I called Stefano twice. It didn't really help. I became anxious less than fifteen minutes later. "Alright. I'll find a way to deal with my issues some other way."

I've shocked her. It's apparent from the way she flips her gaze between me and the bracelet.

"Can you explain those . . . issues more clearly? Please."

I take her hand in mine and trace a circular pattern on the middle of her palm. "It starts as a slight unease—nothing special, a little discomfort, but it quickly transforms into a restlessness that's hard to control," I say. "Then, I become distracted. Edgy. I can't concentrate. My brain constructs different scenarios, each worse than the last, and it's all I can think about. I can't block it out."

"What scenarios, Tore?" Her eyes search mine.

Not taking my eyes off hers, I press my lips together. "You," I say through gritted teeth. "Hurt. Or kidnapped."

"You understand your fear is unfounded, don't you? Especially when we're in the same building."

"It doesn't matter." I reach out and take her chin. "I need to see you, to be sure you're really okay. If that's not a possibility, I need to know where you are. Every fucking second."

I don't mention that I also have this crazy urge to touch her all the time. I can't stand being in the same room with her without placing my hand on hers or wrapping my arm around her waist. If she's sitting nearby, it has to be on my lap. I can't process the idea of her being near and not having her skin against mine. It's like dangling a bottle of water in front of a man dying of thirst. A physiological need I have to fulfill, or else I'll go insane. I've been resisting that compulsion so far, and only succumb when I'm close to losing my mind. For now, that is.

Milene regards the bracelet, then meets my gaze. "So, my wearing this would help?"

"Yes."

She sighs and offers it to me, extending her left hand. "Okay."

I take the bracelet and fix it around her wrist. The moment it's fastened, the feeling of restlessness building inside me dissipates almost completely. "You're going to wear this at all times, even when you're in the shower or asleep. And you'll continue calling me, as we agreed."

"I will."

I nod and, wrapping my arms around her middle, pull her toward me. "Good."

# Chapter Twenty Two

Milene

"The bride doesn't look excited," I comment, looking at the dark-haired woman in her early twenties sitting next to Rocco. Instead of looking happy, she's sitting with her head lowered and eyes focused on her hands which are folded on her lap. "Arranged marriage?"

"Kind of," Salvatore says next to me. "Her brother has a gambling problem. He spent everything they had and then borrowed money from Rocco. He spent that, too."

I inhale sharply. "Rocco took her as a loan repayment?"

Salvatore nods once. "Yes."

The groom sits next to his bride, talking to a man on the other side of the table and laughing as if the marriage will be the best experience of both their lives. His arm is resting on the back of his wife's chair. There is no missing the way she is leaning forward as if she's trying to move away from him as much as possible.

"That's sick," I say.

Rocco's handsome, so why force a woman who obviously doesn't want to be anywhere near him into marriage? There must be a reason why she looks so . . . scared.

I move my eyes away from the newlyweds and scan the room. Yup, people are still staring at me. From the moment we arrived, I felt like some exotic animal in a zoo—people looking at us constantly. I expected some stares since it's the first time I was meeting members of the New York Family, but I didn't anticipate seeing fear in their eyes. Most of them have kept well away from where Salvatore and I are standing, but they haven't stopped gawking at us. Or, more specifically, at Salvatore's arm, which he's kept around my waist for the entire event. No one has approached us except for Arturo. And he only came by to share some confidential information with Salvatore.

"I like the dress," Salvatore says and places a kiss on my bare shoulder. "Goes well with the bracelet."

"It seemed shameful to let it lie unseen in a shoebox under the bed."

"You're keeping the bracelet in a shoebox? Under our bed?"

"Where the fuck should I put the million-dollar thing?" I whisper. "You won't let me use the safe."

"There is only one place where it deserves to be, Milene." He traces the tip of his finger along my neck and down my arm to my wrist.

The intensity with which he looks into my eyes feels like a living thing, and a slight shiver passes me.

I've watched Salvatore interact with his men. He doesn't talk much. And while he listens attentively as they speak, he also seems to keep the rest of the room in sight. This, the way he's looking at me now, is different. It's both alluring and frightening to be the sole focus of a man like Salvatore Ajello.

"Time for the fireworks!" someone shouts from the other part of the room.

A collective cheer fills the room, and from the corner of my eye, I see guests heading toward the exit. Salvatore doesn't move from his spot but continues tracing my forearm with the tip of his finger. His left hand cups my cheek, thumb caressing the skin below my eye.

"You forgot to put your glove on," I say, not taking my eyes off his, and lift my hand to cover his. At first, he was only removing it after he came home in the evenings, but now, I can't remember the last time I've seen him wear it.

"I don't forget things, Milene."

The first explosion booms outdoors as colorful lights flash against the inside walls, the brightest of these accentuating the hard lines of Salvatore's face.

I tilt my head to the side, leaning further into his touch. "I thought seeing your hand bothered you."

"It does." He bends his head and places a kiss on my neck, below my ear.

The bangs of the fireworks continue, but my heart is beating even louder. Burying my hands in Salvatore's hair, I crush my lips against his. He takes a step forward, and then another, forcing me to move back until I'm pressed against the cold surface of the floor-to-ceiling window overlooking the garden.

"Why has no one approached us this whole evening?" I ask, then shudder when I feel his hand on the inside of my thigh, inching upward.

"Because I made sure they all knew I didn't want anyone coming near you."

His hand reaches my panties and deft fingers pull them to one side, exposing me.

"Why?"

"I wasn't in the mood"—his finger teases my clit and moves to my entrance, while his amber eyes stare at me with the intensity of a bird of prey homing in on its next meal—"for sharing your attention with anyone."

"You're so unbelievably self-centered." I smile, then suck in a breath as his finger enters me.

"Yes, I am." Another finger slips inside.

I quickly glance over Salvatore's shoulder and see Aldo and Stefano standing in the opposite corner of the otherwise empty room. They are both staring at the ceiling, offering us their discretion in the process.

The fireworks are still lighting up the sky, and everyone is in the front yard, some distance beyond the window. It's dark outside, and with the bright lights in the room, anyone who looks in our direction will have a prime view.

"People will see us," I whisper, then let out a low moan when Salvatore's thumb presses on my clit.

"I don't care about people." He bites my lower lip and moves to my chin. The fingers inside me keep moving, stretching my inner walls.

"I am people, too, Tore." I breathe, then gasp when he bites my lip again.

"You are not people."

"Oh?" Tremors rock my body so hard I can barely manage words. "And what am I?"

His mouth stills. Slowly, he lifts his head and stares into my eyes.

"Mine," he says and thrusts his fingers all the way in, hitting that spot only he has ever found. "You are mine, Milene."

I shudder as I come, sagging against his chest for support.

Salvatore removes his hand, then grabs under my thighs and lifts me. I wrap my legs around his waist and attack his sinful lips, feeling his hard cock behind the fabric of his dress pants as it presses into my core.

The sound of screeching tires somewhere outside reaches us. Salvatore's head snaps up, and he looks over my shoulder toward the front yard, visible beyond the window.

"Stefano! Aldo!" he shouts, turns around abruptly and heads across the room, still holding me tightly. "Go through the kitchen. Aldo first."

As Salvatore barks the orders, I stare over his shoulder at the yard through the window. Two black cars have parked at the edge of the lawn, and men with guns are getting out. Shots ring out a second later.

Salvatore lowers me to the ground and takes my chin between his fingers. "You're going with Stefano."

I blink at him, terrified and confused. The next moment, Stefano's hand grips my upper arm, pulling me away.

"What... Tore!" I yank my arm, trying to free myself from Stefano's hold. I'm not going anywhere without my husband.

Salvatore looks at me, then moves his gaze to Stefano and gives him a nod. "With your life, Stefano."

"With my life, Boss," Stefano says next to me, grabs me around the waist, and runs.

Salvatore remains standing in the same spot, watching us for a few seconds as we retreat, then reaches inside his jacket. I stare in horror as he takes out a gun and turns in the direction of the double glass doors on the opposite side of the room. The doors that lead to the front yard where, based on the screams and the sounds of gunfire, all hell just broke loose.

## Salvatore

It's chaos.

Some of the guests are running, trying to find cover or shelter within the house. More than a dozen bodies are scattered around the lawn. I've spotted at least eleven shooters. Two are lying on the grass, probably dead already. Six are using the cars as cover, shooting at Rocco's security detail. The rest are scattered, firing randomly.

Arturo is standing at the edge of the lawn, taking out the shooters with his guns. He's the only man I know who shoots equally well with his left and right hand. Learning to aim and shoot with the non-dominant hand requires immense determination and practice, something I know from personal experience.

One of the gunmen separates from the group behind the cars and heads toward the house, hitting Rocco's man with a well-aimed bullet along the way. I raise my gun and fire off two shots in his direction. The first bullet misses, but the second gets him in the chest. He stumbles. I shoot again, this time hitting his stomach, and he ends up facedown on the grass. A bullet whizzes by my head, and I quickly step back, taking cover behind a thick stone column on my right. Five more of Rocco's people run out from the house and charge toward the shooters on the lawn, picking them off first before focusing on the group behind the cars.

The phone in my pocket vibrates once. Stefano's signal that he has Milene secured in the vehicle. The pressure in my chest loosens.

When I leave the porch and head toward the attackers' cars, most of the shooters are already dead. Rocco might be a little slow where business is concerned, but he knows how to choose his security.

The last two assailants are crouched behind one of the vehicles, hiding from Rocco's men, who are peppering them with bullets from high-powered weapons somewhere on my right. The hostiles don't notice me approaching since they're too focused on keeping their heads low and returning fire. I aim for the head of the shooter closest to me and let a bullet fly. His head snaps to the side, and he crumples instantly. The other shooter looks down at his fallen comrade, then lifts his gun to aim at me. I shoot him twice in the chest before he has time to pull the trigger. The gunfire ceases. Rocco's men scatter around to check for life among fallen people.

"Irish?" I ask as I approach Arturo while he's looking over one of the dead shooters.

"Most likely," he says. "How do you want this handled?"

"With the spilling of blood." I take my phone and call Nino.

"I need twenty armed men," I say the moment he picks up the call. "I'll meet them in an hour at the gas station near Fitzgerald's house."

"They'll be there."

"Good."

"Boss?" he adds. "Are you okay? Stefano called to tell me what happened."

"Yes," I answer. "Rocco lost three men. A dozen or so guests are wounded. A few of them seriously. At least two dead."

"Should I call Ilaria?"

"No. This it too big of a fuckup to be covered up. Somebody's probably already called 911. I'm leaving. Rocco will have to deal with the authorities. Call Greg. They're going to need a lawyer here right away, before the police arrive." I cut the call and turn to Arturo. "Go. I don't want you here when the authorities show up."

"You think Rocco can handle this?"

"I don't give a fuck. He's disposable. You're not," I say and head toward my car. It's time to deal with Patrick Fitzgerald.

I'm turning on the ignition when my phone rings. Stefano's number.

"We're just entering the garage," he says.

I lean back in the seat and close my eyes. She's safe.

The sound of jostling comes from the other end of the line.

"Give me that fucking phone!" I hear Milene shout. "Jesus fuck, Salvatore! Are you okay?"

"Yes."

"Sure?"

"I'm fine, Milene. There's something I have to handle. I'll be home in a couple of hours."

A few moments of silence follow before she speaks again. I notice her voice is shaking.

"You scared the fucking shit out of me. Don't you dare send me away like that again," she whispers. "Next time, you're coming with me."

I grind my teeth. She has no idea how hard it was to trust her safety in Stefano's hands instead of getting her out of harm's way myself.

"Stefano is faster than me, cara."

"I don't fucking care!" she snaps, and the line goes dead.

I lower the phone and stare at it. No one ever dares to hang up on me, and yet, she does it all the time. It's strange.

I park my car in Fitzgerald's driveway and head toward the front door, where Nino is waiting.

"Fitzgerald's not here," he says.

"Deegan?"

"Pasquale has him in the kitchen."

"Let's go and chat with him," I say and walk inside the house, avoiding the fresh array of bodies under the dim porch lights.

We've had people watching Fitzgerald's house for weeks, so getting inside didn't pose a problem. They already knew the guards' routes and Alessandro disarmed the outdated security system in less than five minutes.

When I step inside the house, I pass the house staff, gathered together in a corner and facing the wall, some of them visibly shaking. Two of my men stand guard over them. I follow Nino toward the rear of the house.

Fitzgerald's second-in-command is sitting at the dining table with the barrel of Pasquale's gun pressed against his left temple. The Irishman looks up, then follows me with his eyes as I approach the table and take a seat across from him.

"Where's Patrick?" I ask and lean back in the chair.

"I don't know," he snaps.

I nod at Pasquale. He lowers the gun and shoots Deegan in his thigh. The Irishman screams.

"Where is Patrick, Deegan?" I ask again.

"I don't know!" he chokes out. "When he heard the raid had failed, he got into his car and disappeared. He's probably in one of his safe houses."

"Figures." I will never understand how a coward like Fitzgerald ended up as the head of a major criminal organization. The Irish were probably in disarray when the Bratva killed off most of their leaders four years ago, and he took an open opportunity to rise fast within their ranks. "Do you know the locations of the safe houses?"

"No. Patrick never shared those with me."

"Too bad." I look up at Pasquale. Another gunshot pierces the air. Deegan twitches once, then slumps forward, blood pooling from the fresh hole in the side of his head.

"What should we do with the staff, Boss?" Nino asks.

"I'll leave it to you to decide. If you think any might talk, dispose of them." I stand up. "Tell Alessandro to burn down the house. I don't want any evidence we were here."

It was by accident that I found out about Alessandro Zanetti's skills with fire. I sent him to dispose of some competition a while back, assuming he would shoot them. Instead, he tied them up inside an abandoned shack and set the thing on fire. It burned down so thoroughly and so fast the bodies couldn't be identified.

I'm halfway to my car, with Nino at my side, when the sound of gunfire rips through the air. It's coming from the direction of the garage to our left. Nino takes out his gun and runs toward one of our soldiers, who is already returning fire by the overhead door. It looks like some of Fitzgerald's men decided to hide in the vehicles. Nino slips inside while I take my gun out of the holster and head to the other side of the building's door to cover him.

A man, gun in hand, rushes out of the garage and turns to aim at one of my men changing his magazine next to the door. I send a bullet flying. The Irishman falls, blood oozing from his neck. There's another body sprawled on the ground a few yards back.

Inside the garage bay, Nino is crouching behind a vehicle, trying to neutralize the last two shooters, who are raining bullets in his direction from behind another car. I fire a few bullets in their direction, but they both duck. Nino straightens and runs toward the other car while one of our soldiers and I cover for him. He kills one of the foes immediately, but the last one launches toward the exit, shooting randomly. Bullets tear into him from all directions, and he falls to his knees, then topples over.

I throw my gun on the ground and take off my jacket, pressing it over the bleeding wound on my left side.

Milene

I check the time on my phone. Half past two in the morning. Where is Salvatore? He told me he needed to take care of something. That was hours ago. I open the call log and swipe over his name again. He didn't answer on the last two calls. That never happens. I half expect this one to go unanswered, too, but a sigh of relief escapes my lips when I hear his voice on the other end.

"Tore? Is everything okay?"

"Yes," he says in a clipped tone.

"Where are you? Has something happened?"

"No. I'll be there in ten minutes." He cuts the call.

I grip the phone tighter as my hand shakes for a moment. Taking a deep breath, I open the contact list, find Nino's number, and hit the green call button.

"Mrs. Ajello?"

"Where is he?" I bark into the phone.

"Who?"

"Don't fuck with me, Nino. Where is Salvatore, and what happened?"

A short silence falls across the line before he answers. "We're downstairs."

"In the office?"

"No. The infirmary."

"Why? Did someone get shot?"

"Yes."

"Jesus! Who is it this time? Why didn't anyone call me, damn it?" I spin around and head toward the front door. "I'm coming down."

"I don't think that's a good idea, Mrs. Ajello. Boss said he doesn't want you here."

I still as I'm about to turn the handle. "Why the fuck not?"

"Because it's him who got shot."

"What?"

"The doc is digging out the bullet."

The phone falls from my hand, and I run out of the penthouse. I don't wait for the elevator. Dashing, instead, down the stairwell, I run across the hallway toward Stefano at the entrance to the infirmary. When he sees me coming, he blocks the way and raises his hand as if to stop me.

"Mrs. Ajello, Boss said I can't let anyone in."

"Fucking, move!" I swat his hand to the side, grab for the door, and get inside, only to stop dead at the threshold.

Salvatore is sitting on one of the gurneys. Ilaria is next to him, sewing up a wound in his side. A bunch of bloody gauzes are scattered on the floor around her feet. I suck in a breath, and upon exhaling, something like a whimper leaves my mouth. Salvatore looks up at me and lets out a curse.

"What the fuck is wrong with you?" I yell, brushing the tears from my face and marching toward him. "Can't someone else get shot for a change? Or is that your exclusive right?"

"Milene, calm down," he says as Ilaria ties the last stitch.

"Don't you dare tell me to calm down, you reckless, negligent idiot." I grab at his shoulders and continue shouting, paying no heed to Ilaria and Nino, both of whom are standing to my left and staring at me with shocked expressions on their faces. "I'm done counting the gunshot wounds on your body! Do you understand?"

"Milene—"

"This is the last one!" I bark into his face, then burst out crying. "Promise me!"

"It was probably a ricochet. It barely went in."

"I don't give a fuck if it's a bloody paintball capsule, Salvatore!" I sniff and grit my teeth. "Next time you get shot, I leave."

His left hand grabs me at the back of my neck, and he stares at me with his nostrils flaring. "You will never say that again, do you hear me, Milene?"

"I. Will. Leave." The words tumble out as tears continue to roll down my cheeks. I reach for him, pull his face to mine, and slam my lips to his. "Damn it, Tore."

Someone clears their throat, and I turn my head to find Ilaria standing next to me, one hand on her hip and the other holding a roll of bandages. "If you two are done, I'd like to proceed," she says, then looks at Salvatore. "And I'd like to join the 'last time' club for good measure. I'm done patching you up. Next time, find someone else. Milene, he'll have to take antibiotics for the next ten days, can you check whether we have any in the locker?"

"No." Salvatore grabs me by the waistband of my shorts, keeping me in place. "Nino, go check the locker."

Nino nods and goes to rummage through the drawers while Ilaria bandages Salvatore's wound. I caught a glimpse of it before she started, and it didn't appear too bad. Still, I can't make myself stop shaking. When Nino told me Salvatore had been shot, the worst of all scenarios flashed before my eyes. Even seeing he's okay does little to quell the feeling of dread.

"I'm going to get you a shirt," I say and turn toward the elevator, but Salvatore's hold on my shorts tightens.

"Nino, have someone go upstairs and get me a shirt."

Nino throws Ilaria the box of antibiotics and takes out his phone.

"I could have gotten your shirt," I say.

Salvatore presses his lips together, then bends to whisper in my ear. "You said you were going to leave me. Until I manage to forget that, Milene, I'm not letting you out of my reach."

"No physical activity for at least a month, Salvatore." Ilaria states.

"Don't be ridiculous." He gets down slowly off the gurney. "It will heal in a few days."

"Oh, for all that's holy." She shakes her head and turns to me. "Please try to reason with him."

Stefano rushes inside, carrying a white dress shirt in his hand, and offers it to Salvatore. Reluctantly, my husband finally releases his hold on me. He puts the shirt on, but when he tries to fasten the buttons, I move his hands away and take over.

"There's no reasoning with him, Ilaria. He's as stubborn as a mule," I mumble as I move down through the buttons.

Only when I'm on the last one do I become aware of an eerie silence in the room. Nino and Stefano are frozen in place a few feet away, their eyes glued to my hands and the front of Salvatore's shirt. On my other side, Ilaria's clutching the box of antibiotics, staring at my hands in a similar fashion. I run my finger down the row of buttons on Salvatore's shirt, wondering whether I've accidentally skipped a hole. I haven't. Shaking my head, I finish the last one.

A kiss lands on my forehead. "Let's go upstairs."

"Sure." I nod and turn to Ilaria. "Would you like to come?"

She doesn't reply right away. She seems too preoccupied with my hand clasped in Salvatore's, our fingers entwined. "No . . . I have some things to do." She looks at me, then quickly turns and heads toward a chair to take her coat and purse. Things to do at three in the morning?

"I'll call you tomorrow. Don't tear your stitches," she throws the words over her shoulder, and then she's gone. I'm not exactly sure, but I think I saw tears in her eyes before she hightailed it out of the infirmary and into the elevator, the doors of which promptly closed.

When we get to the penthouse, I head toward the kitchen. "Do you want something to eat?" I ask.

"Yes."

"Okay, I'll check if Ada left anything in the fridge. Do you want something in particular?"

"Yes." Salvatore pulls on my hand and turns me toward him. "You. Get on the counter."

I raise my eyebrows.

He takes a step toward me. "Now, Milene."

When I don't make a move, he takes another step forward, forcing me two steps back. And another. My back makes contact with the cabinet.

"Up."

I grab the edge of the countertop and hoist myself up to sit.

"You'll tear your stitches," I say.

"I won't. Stand up."

Wondering what he has in mind, I do as he says, watching him all the while through narrowed eyes. He takes a step closer, places his hands on the counter, one on either side of my feet, and looks up at me.

"Take off your shorts and panties."

He can't be serious.

As I look on, Salvatore grips my ankles and leans forward.

"Now," he says and bites at the denim covering my pussy.

My hands are shaking slightly as I unbutton my shorts in haste and kick them off, along with my panties. The moment I straighten back up, Salvatore buries his face between my legs. I expected him to start slow. I was wrong. He sucks on my clit with such vigor, I scream and thread my hands in his hair, squeezing at the dark strands as he licks and laps with his tongue. His right hand moves upward along my inner thigh, higher and higher.

"Stitches," I rasp, then whimper when his tongue licks at my folds again.

"They're on my left side," he says as he slides his finger inside me.

My eyes roll back into my head, and my legs shake. Another finger enters me. I gasp and reach to grab the shelf on my right. Salvatore keeps licking at my pussy while his fingers move inside me, stretching my walls, once again, sending me into a state of total bliss.

"Dear God," I moan and throw back my head. When I feel the slightest of bites against my clit, I come so suddenly, I almost fall off the damn countertop.

"Your legs are shaking," Salvatore says and slowly slides out his fingers.

It's not just my legs. My fucking brain is shaking along with the rest of my body. I let go of the shelf I've been clutching and lower myself down to sit on the counter.

"We could have both ended up on the floor," I say when I manage to catch my breath. "You're insane."

He cocks his head to the side and places his palms on my cheeks, watching me with hooded eyes. "I thought I was 'dear,'" he says, "and 'god.'"

I snort in exasperation. "And humble, too." Then, I shake my head and press my mouth to his, tasting myself on him.

"No, not really." His hands squeeze a little. "And I would never let you fall, Milene."

"I know," I whisper.

Milene is standing in front of the medicine locker on the other side of the room, going through the contents, and making notes on a pad of paper. Probably doing inventory. It takes great willpower to remain seated instead of going to her and bringing her back with me, so she's by my side.

"You let her button up your shirt," Ilaria says while changing my bandage.

"I did," I say.

Ilaria stays silent for a few moments, fumbling with the bandage, but I know she won't let the subject slide.

"Was it a one-time thing? You didn't want to distress her even more yesterday?" she asks, her tone a forced kind of casual.

"No. She's been doing it for quite some time."

My mother's hands go still momentarily while dressing the wound. She looks up, an expression of shock written across her face as our gazes connect. With two unusable fingers and nerve damage to the other three, doing things that require finesse has been a problem of mine for years. A weak spot. Letting someone button up a shirt for me is something I would never have allowed. Especially in front of witnesses. And she knows it.

Ilaria's eyes travel down, stopping on my left hand, which is gripping the edge of the gurney. She reaches out and brushes the back of my hand with the tips of her fingers.

"I forgot how bad it was," she says.

I attempt to straighten the fingers but can't. I went through six rounds of surgery on that hand alone. And still, it wasn't enough. My nerves are too damaged. I hate it. Just looking at the scars, and remembering what they represent, makes me want to kill someone. I never tolerate weaknesses in others, but especially in myself.

There is a question in Ilaria's eyes as she waits for me to respond.

"I want to feel her skin when I touch her," I answer. "And I can't do that if I'm wearing a glove."

She watches me for a few moments, then whispers, "Are you in love with her, Salvatore?"

For that question, I don't have an answer. Yet, I can't keep my attention away from the other side of the room where Milene is still studying the medical supplies intently. She's wearing jeans and an awful yellow T-shirt I can't stand. Her hair is gathered into a bun at the top of her head and secured with two pencils.

"I have no idea, Ilaria," I say. "You know I'm not good with emotional shit."

"I do know."

I'm getting up from the gurney, intending to leave, when Ilaria speaks again.

"What would you do if someone hurt her, Salvatore?"

I turn my head rapidly to face her, pinning her with my stare. She takes a step back, but I know it was unconsciously done. Everyone does it. Except Milene. She usually juts her chin up. Or smirks.

"If even a seed of an idea of hurting my wife formed in anyone's head, I would smash said head open with my bare hands like it's a fucking watermelon," I spit out. "Next, I would take out their sick brain and squeeze it so hard the only thing left would be mush."

My mother smiles and heads toward the medicine locker, humming to herself.

# Chapter Twenty Three

Milene

"I'M GOING TO DROP BY TO SEE PIPPA LATER," I THROW OVER MY shoulder and turn on the coffee machine. "I promised I'd go shopping for a dress with her afterward. They're throwing a banquet for the hospital staff on Saturday." There's no returning to the residency program for me—not after the Family changed my life a couple of months back. And since the attack a month ago, Salvatore's reasons for not letting me work as a nurse in a public hospital are more understandable.

"Do you miss it? The work," Salvatore asks from his spot at the dining table.

"You know I do." I shrug.

"Nino is still trying to locate where the Irish are hiding so we can wipe them out. When I'm done with Fitzgerald, we'll figure something out."

The cup I'm holding almost slips from my fingers. I turn around and stare at him. "What do you mean?"

"If it means that much to you, we can try to find a hospital nearby that might allow bodyguards," he says while watching me with a grim-looking face. "Or you can take over the infirmary downstairs."

I squeeze my lips together, then smile. "Thank you."

Salvatore nods. "About that shopping spree. How long?"

"Three hours. Maybe four."

He glares at me for a few moments, lips pressed into a thin line, then nods. I take my cup of coffee to the table, sit myself down on Salvatore's right thigh, and reach for the basket of breakfast pastries. His right arm comes to rest around my waist, and he continues eating.

Sitting on Salvatore's lap during meals was a little strange in the beginning, but I've gotten used to it. It started a month ago, right after the skirmish with the Irish. At first, he would insist I sit on his lap when we were having breakfast. Then it was dinner, as well. Now, it's every meal. When I asked him why, he said that he still hadn't forgotten that I told him I was going to leave if he got shot again, and this was my punishment. It doesn't seem like a punishment. In fact, I quite enjoy being so close to him in this way. His explanation was transparent bullshit, of course. Salvatore has problems recognizing his own feelings, so it's no wonder he has equal difficulty in expressing them.

"You'll call me every hour," he says and squeezes my waist.

"You know I will." I place a kiss at the corner of his tightly pressed lips.

"Don't forget, Milene."

I sigh, take his face between my palms, and tilt his head. "How about we make it thirty minutes? Would that make it easier for you?"

He just watches me in that unusual way of his, as though he wants to absorb me into himself through his eyes.

"Thirty minutes it is, then." I smile and kiss him. "You need to start talking about these things, Tore. I can't always guess when something's bothering you."

"You've been doing well so far."

There is a sound of something crashing to the floor, followed by angry mewling as Riggs runs out of the kitchen and dashes across the living space. A second later, Kurt lunges after Riggs at breakneck speed, but he loses traction on the polished floor and ends up sliding across the hallway on his side, hitting the wall at the end with his butt.

"That cat needs a brain transplant," Salvatore deadpans, and I burst out laughing.

"If that was your attempt at making a joke, you need to work on your delivery."

"You're laughing, aren't you?"

"Yeah,"—I snort—"but only because you're mine, and I don't want to discourage you."

He arches an eyebrow.

"You can't deliver a joke with the same intonation you use for death threats, Salvatore." I place one more kiss on his mouth, grab another pastry from the basket, and stand up. "I'll call you. Promise."

"I really don't see how this is necessary," Pippa grumbles as we reach the perfume store. "It was fun the first few times, but now it feels weird."

I glance over my shoulder. Alessandro's walking a few paces behind us, looking dangerous in a dark suit, his earpiece visible. I wonder where he finds suits in his size. The guy is at least six and a half feet tall and has the muscle mass of a medium-sized mountain. Vincenzo is standing near the cash register at the opposite corner of the store with his hands clasped behind his back. Two more bodyguards are by the entrance, one out front, and the other inside.

"Ignore them." I shrug.

"I need to go to the restroom," Pippa says. "I'll catch up with you."

"Again? Your bladder's the size of a peanut."

"I'm on a detox program. Liquid food for the next seven days. It sucks." She dashes to the exit.

I walk toward the men's section and pass a shelf with the sign "New Arrivals" near the middle of the store. I reach for a bottle of cologne to take a sniff. Nope, too strong. Salvatore wouldn't like it. I'm putting the bottle back when the sound of a gunshot pierces the air.

The bottle slips from my hands, crashing to the floor, as I stare at the bodyguard who was positioned outside the entrance. He's spread-eagled on the ground, blood pooling all around him. A huge male body materializes in front of me at the same moment another shot rings out. Rooted to my spot, I stare at Alessandro's back, which is obstructing my view of the entrance, and try hard to get enough air into my lungs. It doesn't work. All I can manage are quick, sharp breaths. I can't see anything, but based on the proximity of the bangs, I know it's Alessandro's gun firing. Once, twice . . . seven times. The sound mixes with the noise of other shots, and it seems as though gunfire is raging all around us. People are screaming. My heartbeat skyrockets and I frantically look around for Pippa. Where is she?

"Vincenzo," Alessandro says. "The door. Cover us."

Vincenzo leaves his spot behind the shelf to our left, runs toward the entrance, and continues returning fire.

"Take off your shoes," Alessandro's deep voice says as he changes the magazine in his gun and resumes shooting.

The moment I have my heels off, his fingers wrap around my wrist and move my hand to the waistband of his pants at his back.

"Hold on. Walk behind me," he commands in an even voice. "We're leaving."

The sleeve of his jacket has ridden up, revealing a leather bracelet around his wrist. At the knot where the leather string is tied, there's a small silver pendant in the shape of a teddy bear with a pink bow atop its head.

"Milene."

I firmly grab his belt, and his hand vanishes from view.

Alessandro walks toward the exit. One step. I follow, holding on for dear life and staying as close to him as possible. Several more gunshots. I wince with each boom. Another step. One more round of firing. He changes the magazine again. Two more steps. We stop at the door, and my eyes fall to the prone body on the ground to my right. The bodyguard's eyes are open but glazed over. I realize for the first time how young he looks. There's a hole in the side of his neck which is oozing blood, and a few more on his chest. I press my lips together, trying to keep the tears from falling.

"Vincenzo." Alessandro's voice. "Behind Milene. Cover our backs."

We step out of the store, Alessandro first, with me following. Vincenzo comes out after us, his back pressed to mine, holding his gun at the ready.

A shot rings out, shattering the store's window to our left. Another one follows. Alessandro keeps walking down the aisle, firing off bullets ahead of us. His left sleeve is wet. When I lower my gaze, I see blood dripping down his hand and onto the white tiled floor. Bodies lay scattered around us. There must be at least twenty. My eyes flit over each one, afraid I'll find Pippa among them. It's only men, however, and some of them still have their weapons in hand. Police sirens blare from the street outside, but they seem distant and somehow otherworldly.

"That's all of them," Alessandro declares as if he's discussing the weather. "Let's go to the car."

Suddenly, Vincenzo's arm wraps around my waist, and he tugs me toward him. I gasp as my hand slips from Alessandro's belt. He spins around as Vincenzo lifts his gun and sends five bullets into the big man's chest. I scream as Alessandro drops to the floor.

"Move." Vincenzo painfully grips my upper arm and drags me backward to an emergency exit, my eyes glued to Alessandro's unmoving form.

"You piece of shit!" I yell as Vincenzo keeps on dragging me. We're in the underground parking lot and heading for a black van parked at the far side of the dimly lit garage.

"Shut the fuck up, or I'm going to silence you with my fist." He squeezes my arm harder and jerks me along.

The van's side door slides open to reveal two men.

"Where are the others?" the huge bald guy next to the door asks.

"Gone," Vincenzo says, grabs me by the hair, and pushes me inside.

"What do you mean, gone? We had twenty-five people!"

"Zanetti killed them all."

"Why the fuck didn't you kill the bastard?"

"I had to at the end," Vincenzo snaps. "I was paid to get the woman out. Not to help a bunch of idiots who are incapable of taking out one man."

"Fucking coward," the bald guy spits out, raises a gun, and shoots Vincenzo in the face.

The sliding door closes with a firm click as the engine comes to life.

Salvatore

The phone on my desk rings while I'm in a meeting with Cosimo. The moment I see Alessandro's name, a feeling of dread forms in the pit of my stomach. He could be calling me to approve a change of route because Milene decided to go somewhere else after the mall, but I somehow know that's not it.

"What happened?" I bark into the phone.

"The Irish attacked us while we were at the mall," Alessandro says. His breathing is labored, wheezing. "I managed to neutralize them, but before we reached the car, Vincenzo grabbed your wife and pumped half a magazine into me."

I squeeze the cell in my hand. "Where did he take her?"

"I don't know." Alessandro coughs. "I was wearing a bulletproof vest, but I passed out from the impact. They're gone."

"Get out of there and call someone to pick you up." I cut the line and look at Cosimo. "Leave. Send Nino here. Right now."

I open the GPS tracking software on my laptop and stare at the red dot that shows Milene's location. The signal is moving along the highway. They're taking her out of the city.

"They won't touch her, Boss," Nino says. "It's you they want."

"I know," I say and continue staring at the red dot flashing on the screen. I haven't taken my eyes off it since the moment I opened the tracking app, as if it will disappear if I so much as blink. Something dark and hungry for destruction awakened inside my chest when Alessandro called. An abyss of darkness grows with every passing second, yearning for slaughter. A black hole ready to swallow the entire universe. They dared to take my Milene. Oh, how they will pay.

The pulsing dot stops. My heart skips a beat. A minute later, the phone on my desk rings. I grab the phone and take the call.

"Ajello," the voice on the other side says. "I heard you lost something."

"Where is my wife, Patrick?"

He laughs. "Oh, wouldn't you love to know?"

"Where. Is. She?"

"Get into your car and drive south. Someone will call you with further instructions. When you reach the destination, we'll make a trade. You for her," he says. "If you are not alone, I'll tell my men to snap her neck."

The call disconnects.

"Take thirty men," I say to Nino. "They're holding Milene somewhere west of the city, probably in the industrial zone. You can get the exact coordinates off this. Take it with you." I nod toward the laptop.

"I can have them ready to go with you in ten minutes."

"They won't be coming with me. You'll take the men directly to wherever Milene is and find cover close by. I'll call you when I get there. Patrick will probably lead me around in circles for a while to make sure no one's following, so you'll be there before I arrive." I pin him with my stare. "Don't even think about sending anyone after me," I whisper.

"But, Boss . . ."

"Don't you fucking dare!" I snarl and strike the desk in front of me with my palm. "I will kill anyone who follows me, and I will end you too for disobeying orders! Do you understand?"

Nino grinds his teeth. "It's a trap."

"Of course it's a trap." I put the phone in my pocket and take the car keys off the desk. "When I get there, wait twenty minutes, and then you and the men can go in with guns blazing. Not a second sooner, Nino."

"They'll kill you."

"They won't. Not right away, at least. I want them focused on me, not on Milene, while you storm the place." I get up and walk around the desk until I'm right in front Nino. "Whatever you find when you go in, you will get Milene out first. Only when she's safe are you are allowed to come back for me. Nod if you understand."

He stares at me with wide eyes.

"Fucking nod!" I yell into his face.

Nino closes his eyes and nods.

"Good." I turn and leave the office.

# Chapter Twenty four

Milene

THE VAN DOOR SLIDES OPEN TO REVEAL BRIGHT DAYLIGHT. A HAND wraps around my upper arm, dragging me outside. I squint at the sun, my eyes having become accustomed to the gloominess of the van. I try to see the place they've brought me to. A big metal hangar that looks like some kind of a warehouse looms a few feet in front of me. It could be anywhere. I don't manage to see more because one of the men, the bald hulk, ushers me toward the building. Stones and other debris press sharply into the skin of my bare soles.

What will they do to me? If they planned on killing me, they would have done it already. I cast a glance down at my tied hands and the gold band around my left wrist. Salvatore's OCD is going to save my life. He'll send someone to get me out. I just need to stay alive until they get here.

The inside of the warehouse is nearly empty, with only a few random pieces of furniture scattered around. In the far-right corner, there are a few mismatched chairs next to a long Formica coffee table. Eight men are sitting around it, drinking and laughing. I quickly drop my head to keep my eyes fixed on the hard ground between my feet. The guy holding me drags me toward the wall on the left and pushes me to the ground. With my hands tied, I don't manage to soften the fall, and land hard on my shoulder, my nose against the damp and dirty floor.

"Don't fucking move," the bald guy barks and crosses his arms in front of his chest, looking in the direction of the wide sliding doors they've left open.

Looks like we're waiting for someone. Probably the head of the Irish clan. I wiggle into a sitting position and lean my back against the wall, turning so I can see the entrance.

It must have been two or three hours since I've been brought into the warehouse. I can't be sure since I don't have a watch. I've spent most of that time on the cold floor, looking around, searching for a way out. Nothing has come of it. The bald guy keeping guard over me hasn't said a word.

When I wasn't looking for an opportunity to escape, I thought about the three men who died for me today. I didn't know the two bodyguards who remained at the store's door very well. I can't even remember their names, and it's eating me up inside. How can I not remember their names? I think about Alessandro. He might have been a big sullen grouch, but he saved my life today, probably several times, only to end up dead because of it. I wish the bald guy hadn't shot Vincenzo. That fucking traitor deserved a much more painful death.

What do they plan to do with me? Are they going to ask for a ransom? Why haven't they done something already? Other than maybe a few missing strands of hair, some cuts to my feet, and bruises on my arms from being manhandled, I'm pretty well intact, at least on the outside. At one point, I thought I might be gang-raped over a rusty oil can, but aside from the dirty jokes I've heard from the men around the table, I've been largely ignored. Obviously, I'm a pawn in a much larger game. Is that a good thing? Will they get more money from Salvatore if I'm unharmed?

A phone in the bald guy's pocket rings. He takes it out, listening to the person on the other end for a while. Then, he looks over at the men who are gathered around the coffee table, watching some videos on someone's phone and laughing.

"He's here," the bald hulk barks. The men jump off their chairs and rush to pick up their weapons resting against a wall nearby.

A large silver car pulls through the open doors. One of the men runs over and shuts the warehouse door behind the vehicle while the other seven stand in front of the car, their guns pointed toward it. The driver-side door opens and Salvatore steps out. I fumble my way up from my spot on the floor, intending to run to him, but the bald guy wraps his meaty hand around my upper arm, holding me firmly in place.

Salvatore closes the car door and looks around, paying no heed to the men pointing their guns directly at him. It's as though he's entered a 7-Eleven to buy a fucking carton of milk. I hold my breath, waiting for his men to barge in. Nothing happens. What the fuck? Why is there no one with him?

His gaze reaches me and stops. His eyes move down my body. I can only imagine what he must be thinking as he sees my tangled hair and the scratches on my left cheek that I obtained when the bald Irishman pushed me roughly to the ground. His eyes roam over my stained powder blue dress and finally down to my bare feet. The men around yell at Salvatore to raise his hands, but he ignores them. His gaze travels back up my body until it reaches my eyes, where it remains fixed. Three of the Irishmen circle behind him, their guns trained on Salvatore's back. They're still shouting.

Two of the men grab Salvatore's biceps and drag him to the chair at the center of the huge space. And he lets them. What the hell is going on? Where the fuck is his backup? They have the GPS coordinates from my bracelet, so why has Salvatore come alone, damn it? I watch in horror as they push him down onto the chair, and a short stocky man proceeds to tie Salvatore's hands behind his back.

Salvatore doesn't try to resist and says nothing. He just sits in the chair and stares directly at me.

The stocky guy pulls his fist back again and punches Salvatore in the stomach once more. I stifle a whimper and close my eyes for an instant as his fist makes contact.

"I think we should keep him alive for at least a few days," one of the men standing by the wall says and laughs. "Until everyone gets their turn."

When the stocky guy swings his fist again, I pull on my arm in an effort to get away, but the bald Irishman holding me tightens his grip. He'd moved me so I was standing in Salvatore's line of sight. The only thing I can do is watch as another blow hits home.

Since the moment Salvatore entered ten minutes earlier, the Irish have focused all their attention on him, leaving me on the sidelines with the heavy-set bald man. I was bait, used to get Salvatore here.

He hasn't uttered a word since he arrived. Not when they dragged him to the chair in the middle of the room and tied him to it, and not while they've been hitting him. He just sits there in silence and watches me—his piercing eyes never leaving mine.

The stocky guy hits him again, this time on the chin, and Salvatore's head snaps abruptly to the side. I try to blink back tears, but they fall anyway. Some trickle down my cheeks to land on my ruined dress. They're going to kill him, and he knew that the moment he stepped inside the warehouse. Still, he came. Salvatore takes a deep breath, lifts his head and returns his eyes to mine. I sniff and tug at my arm again, trying to lurch forward, but the hand holding me only tightens. I'm powerless against its vice-like grip.

The wide metal doors on the right slide open and a car moves inside, coming to a halt close to the chair where Salvatore is bound. The driver gets out and opens one of the back doors. A man in a navy suit emerges. He throws a look in my direction, then shifts his gaze to Salvatore as a wicked smile spreads across his lips.

"You know," he says as he walks toward Salvatore. "If anyone had told me a woman would be your downfall, I'd have laughed them out of the room. I wonder what's so special about her."

Salvatore's eyes leave mine and focus on the man in the suit. "Patrick," he says in an even voice. "How nice of you to join us. I expected you to hunker down in your hole and let the others do your job for you, as is your usual style."

What the fuck is he doing? Why is he provoking the Irish leader?

"Always so composed." Patrick shakes his head and looks at me over his shoulder. "Will you maintain composure when I start playing with your wife? She is a pretty thing, I'll give you that."

"I had an interesting chat with one of your men," Salvatore continues. "I wasn't aware you had a gambling problem, Patrick. Do your people know you're spending the organization's money like water?"

Patrick's head turns rapidly back to Salvatore, and he backhands him. "Shut the fuck up!"

Salvatore spits blood on the floor, then looks up. "Two million is a lot of money to lose, Patrick."

I gulp, and tears stream from my eyes as I realize what he's doing. Damn you, Salvatore. He is trying to make Patrick focus on him instead of me.

"I planned on toying with you for a while before killing you," Patrick says. "But perhaps I've changed my mind."

As he reaches inside his jacket, the sound of gunfire erupts outside. The sliding doors open, and men with guns rush inside, shooting with accuracy at the Irish. I recognize Carmelo and Aldo among them. The windows on the other side of the warehouse shatter under the gunfire, and the Irish mob suddenly slides into disarray, running this way and that, seemingly unprepared for any such intrusion. My captor vanishes from view, his bald head moving toward the open doors, gun in hand. I turn to Salvatore, who's still tied to the chair, directly in the crossfire, and run toward him.

"What are you doing! Get down!" he shouts as I reach him. I ignore his yelling and go around to the back of the chair. My hands are tied at the front, so I should be able to release him, but when I reach for his wrists, cold panic rises inside me. They didn't use rope the way they did with me. Both of Salvatore's hands are handcuffed to the back of the chair. A metal chair. Bolted to the floor.

"Milene! Get the fuck down!"

From all around us comes the sound of shouting and gunfire, but it appears most of the gunfire is taking place around the doors. I take a deep breath, move around to face Salvatore, and hook my tied hands around his neck. I climb onto his lap, straddling him, my back toward the doors and the shots being fired around us.

"Milene! What the fuck?! Get down!" he snarls, shaking his body, trying to throw me off, but I plaster my chest to him and squeeze my arms around his head, pressing it to my chest.

"Damn it, Milene, I'm going to fucking kill you! Get off me and lie on the floor!" he yells at the top of his lungs. "Right now!"

"You're a damn magnet for bullets, Salvatore." I kiss his hair and tighten my grip. "And I'm pretty sure you've already used up your nine lives, so you're not getting shot again today."

His chest rises and falls. Several bullets whizz somewhere close to my head and hit the table further back in the room, sending it toppling to the concrete floor. Salvatore's body starts to shake in my embrace.

"Vita mia," he whispers. "Please. Get down."

Another bullet ricochets off the floor to our right, and I press myself more tightly to him. His body is shaking as though he has a fever. "I love you, Tore," I say into his ear.

"Milene." His eyes are red. "I'm going to bite you. With all my strength." The gunfire still rages, but I hear now how his voice trembles. "It's going to hurt, Milene. Very much. Get. Off. Me."

I smile. "Be my guest. I'm not moving."

Bullets hit something over our heads and part of the metal construction comes crashing down behind us, sending dust and shards of debris into the air. Salvatore's breathing becomes erratic, his chest rising and falling at a maddening speed. As I watch, a tear rolls down his cheek.

"Please," he whispers.

"No," I say, and squeeze my arms around him, tucking his head into the crook of my neck. He thrashes around again, and I barely manage to keep myself from falling off his lap.

More yelling and gunshots reach my ears, the sounds lasting a couple of seconds more before the action quiets. Soon after, only voices and rapid footfalls can be heard. Nino jumps down to the warehouse floor through a large broken window at the back and runs toward us, with Pasquale and another man following. As I watch them over Salvatore's head, Nino and Pasquale stop abruptly and raise their guns in our direction. My eyes widen because, for an instant, I think they might actually shoot at us. Before they're able to pull the triggers, a gunshot explodes somewhere behind me, and pain erupts in my arm.

I stifle a scream and almost faint on the spot as I stare at the big red hole in my arm oozing blood. It's different to see a wound on my own body, and no amount of experience could have prepared me for it.

"Nino!" Salvatore yells, staring at my arm and the blood pouring from the wound. He's breathing hard, and when he looks up at me, there's a crazed look in his eyes.

Nino comes running, presses a bundle of material that looks like someone's shirt onto my arm, and I scream.

"To a hospital," Salvatore barks. "Now, Nino!"

"What about you, Boss?" Nino asks as he gathers me up in his arms.

"If you don't get my wife to a hospital in under five minutes, Nino, I will fucking end you! Carmelo, go with them and take Pasquale. Fucking now!" he shouts.

Nino nods and carries me out, running toward an SUV parked outside.

## Salvatore

It takes forty minutes for Stefano to find the keys to the handcuffs and release me. Forty fucking minutes of me sitting there while Milene loses blood. Shot. Because of me.

A sound of a phone ringing comes from my left.

"It's Nino," Stefano says and passes me his phone.

My hand is shaking as I take the device and stare at the screen. It's an arm wound. It shouldn't be serious unless the bullet hit an artery. The shaking of my hand intensifies, and I manage to hit the answer button only on the third try. I position the phone next to my ear and close my eyes.

"Nino?"

"She's going to be okay."

I grab the back of the chair and exhale. "How bad?"

"Some muscle damage that should heal fine."

"She's expected to have a full recovery? No consequences?"

"They'll release her tomorrow. Your wife is okay, Boss."

I cut the call, then turn to look at the bodies of the Irish men strewn all around. Most of them are dead, but there are others still alive, whimpering or panting. Turning my head to the side, I fix my gaze on the man Aldo is holding pressed onto the hood of a car. Fucking Patrick Fitzgerald! He was hiding in his car while the gunfire was raging, and then tried to shoot me when everyone lowered their guard. Only, the bullet hit my wife.

"A knife," I say without taking my eyes off the Irish mob leader with only a few hundred heartbeats remaining in his pathetic life.

Someone presses the handle of a knife onto my outstretched hand. I take a step forward, bend, and grab the first groaning Irishman I see by his hair. Fitzgerald is staring at me, eyes wide, and I keep my gaze on him as I press the knife to the side of the man's neck and draw the blade across his throat. Warm blood flows over my hand. The warehouse, which was brimming with shouts and noise, goes silent.

I let the body fall at my feet, step over it, and walk toward the next man. This one is passed out, but he's still breathing. I grab him by the hair, too, and press the blade to his Adam's apple.

A strangled sound leaves Patrick's lips as he tracks my hand with his eyes and watches the blood spray over my arm and shirtfront. When I let the body fall and take another step toward him, Patrick looks up. I take a further step and proceed with creating a path of dead Irishmen, not taking my eyes off his. The terror on his face is delicious. He knows I'm saving the best for last. I smile and take another step. Oh, how I will enjoy filleting the man who hurt the only thing in this world I love.

✕

I enter the small private hospital that treats my men when Ilaria can't care for them in the infirmary, and turn toward the hallway on the left. Two nurses at the main desk stand up abruptly, but when I don't acknowledge them, they sit back down. There's a piercing pain in my left side. Patrick's goon probably broke one of my ribs, but I ignore it and keep walking, with Stefano following a few paces behind.

I don't remember ever being as scared as I was when I saw blood pouring from Milene's arm. It was as if someone had lodged a knife in my stomach and dragged it upward, opening my chest.

People who see me pass step aside, staring at the blood still covering my arms and hands. It's a good thing I wore a black shirt for the occasion. It means they can't see the blood soaked into that, as well.

The doctor who usually treats my men looks up from the chart in his hand and rushes toward me. "Mr. Ajello! What—"

"Back off," I snap, turn around the corner, and rush down the long hallway toward the door at the end, where Carmelo and Nino stand guard.

"Open the door," I say.

"Boss. You may want to wash the blood off first." Nino nods toward my hands. "She may freak out if she sees you like that."

I hadn't thought of that. "Find me a shirt."

It takes me five minutes to scrub my hands and arms. The black T-shirt Nino brought for me hides the stains on my chest, which I didn't bother cleaning. When I throw open the door to Milene's room, I'm in a semi-presentable state. Outwardly, at least.

"Tore!" Milene sits up in bed and swings her legs over the side.

I grab the metal cart standing at the foot of the bed and squeeze the edge with all my strength.

"Don't you dare get down from that bed," I whisper, eyes focused on the bandage around her upper arm and the IV stand next to the bed. She could have died. I close my eyes and take a deep breath, trying to compose myself. It doesn't work.

I grip the frame of the cart harder. There's a shitload of something inexplicable building up inside me, and it feels as though I'm going to explode like a fucking supernova.

"How could you do it?" I ask quietly, then switch to yelling. "How the fuck could you do that! I wanted to die on that chair, knowing you were in the direct line of fire, waiting for a bullet to hit you! Because of me!" I squeeze the cart and launch the thing at the wall behind me. "You. Cannot. Do. That!"

"Tore—"

"No!" I snarl. "Never! Never, Milene! I can't . . . I can't bear even the thought of what could have happened! How the fuck do you expect me to deal with this? You, getting hurt, for me? You will never do that again!" I bury my hands in my hair and pull. "Fuck!"

Milene cocks her head and watches me. Apparently coming to some mysterious conclusion, she slides down off the bed and takes the IV pole in her hand. With it at her side, she comes to stand next to me.

I take a deep breath, then exhale and grab her by the back of her neck. "Never, vita mia," I whisper.

"Did you have a doctor check you out?" she asks.

"No."

Her right eyebrow lifts in one perfect arch. "Why?"

"I was busy."

"Busy with what?"

Killing the Irish and freaking out. Not that I plan on telling her that. "Doesn't matter."

She sighs. "You look awful, baby."

"I know."

She places her palm on my cheek and pulls me down for a kiss. "Let's find someone to have a look at your lip. And your eye. Your face is a mess."

"The fuck with my face."

"Can I have a hug?"

"No."

Milene blinks in confusion. "Why the hell not?"

"I'm afraid I'm going to hurt your arm." My gaze moves down to the bandage, then I quickly avert my eyes and place a kiss on her forehead. "I can't bear to even look at it."

"Tore . . ."

"I was so scared, Milene," I whisper again, tracing the line of her eyebrow with the tip of my finger. "I don't think I've ever experienced anything like that before. It's like I jumped off a cliff and watched the earth rise up to meet me, just waiting for the impact." My finger travels down until it stops on her bottom lip. "I'll get a fucking aneurysm because of you."

Milene leans against me, wraps her hand round my neck and tilts her head up. "A kiss. Then a hug."

I narrow my eyes and grab her face between my palms and press my lips hard against hers. The pressure in my chest builds, my heart beating so fast it feels like it might burst out. I press her harder to my body, careful not to hurt her arm.

"You don't understand, Milene," I say into her mouth.

"Of course I do." She smiles and looks right into my eyes. "I love you, too, Tore."

# Chapter Twenty-five

Milene

*Six weeks later*

A DOOR CLICKS OPEN AND THEN BANGS CLOSED.

"Milene!"

I let go of the curtain I was in the process of hanging and turn to see Salvatore marching across the living room toward me.

"Standing on a coffee table? Really?" He grabs me around the waist and lowers me onto the floor. "You could have broken your neck! That thing is two hundred years old. It could have collapsed underneath you."

I roll my eyes.

"Don't roll your eyes at me. I'm serious. I'm going to go completely gray in a year because of you."

"Oh, don't you dare blame me for your gray hairs." I press my hands to his hair, combing my fingers through it, and savoring the moment. "You came to me like this. Very dashing, I must admit."

"You know very well you're responsible for half the grays." He squeezes me around the waist and nods toward the half-hung curtain. "New ones again?"

I cringe. "Yup. I hoped you wouldn't notice."

"I hate those cats."

"I saw you scratching Kurt behind his ear this morning." I rise up on my toes and kiss him. "Don't worry, I won't tell anyone. If you find a way to convince me to keep my mouth shut, that is."

"All right." He scoops me up and carries me to the bedroom, where he throws me on the bed and sits down to remove his prosthesis.

"You know, I was thinking," I say as I place my chin on his shoulder and wrap my arms around him from behind, unbuttoning his shirt. "How would you feel about getting a dog?"

Salvatore's body goes so utterly still that I pause in my task and arch my neck to find him staring at the wall.

"If you bring another animal in here, I'll kill someone, Milene."

"Please?" I take his chin between my fingers and turn his head toward mine. "It can be some small breed and—Why are you keeping your eyes closed?"

"No reason."

"Salvatore Ajello, open your eyes. Right now."

He sighs. Opens his eyes.

"Pretty please?" I ask and smile widely.

His gaze travels to my mouth, then he reaches with his hand to trace the line of my lips with the tip of his finger.

"I want a psychological evaluation from a licensed animal psychologist, on paper, before it sets its paw in here."

I squeal in delight and kiss the tip of his finger.

"You're doing it on purpose," he says, without taking his eyes off my lips.

"I have no idea what you're talking about."

"You know very well what your smile does to me, and you're using it shamelessly." His finger stills at the middle of my bottom lip. "I wonder if you are aware of what a weapon you are wielding."

"It's just a smile. Not a weapon."

"And a gun is just a piece of metal. It can still take a life in a second, if used properly." He takes my chin between his fingers and leans in, pressing his lips to the corner of my mouth. "You should be very careful with that smile, vita mia. People may end up dead because of it."

"Smiles don't kill, Salvatore."

"Yours does. Try giving one of the smiles that belong to me to someone else and watch the river of blood ensue."

"Such a poet, my husband." I smile against his lips. "Maybe I should stop smiling, then. I don't want to risk killing someone by accident."

The hand holding my chin tightens. "You will never stop smiling, Milene," he says. "If anything, or anyone, ever makes your smile falter, even a fraction, I'll destroy them."

"So vicious." I smirk and drop down onto the bed, pulling him with me. "Would you mind destroying my pussy instead?"

The corners of Salvatore's lips curl upward. It's not exactly a smile, but it's close. His hands travel down my body pulling down my shorts and panties.

"I would like that very much."

The moment our clothes are off, he lies on top of me, and buries himself inside me. I gasp from the sudden intrusion but recover and wind my legs around his waist, opening myself even more. Salvatore doesn't move but watches my face as my pussy pulsates with need. I lift my pelvis slightly, wriggling my hips, trying to coax him to move, but he remains motionless, with his huge cock lodged inside me, stretching me in ecstasy.

His hand slides between our bodies, down my chest, then along my stomach until he reaches my pussy. A shudder passes through me when he moves his finger between my folds and presses it against my touch-hungry clit. I pass my fingers through his thick hair and bite at the side of his chin. The pressure between my legs builds as he keeps teasing me with his finger, and I want to scream from the need to have him move inside me. Still, the devil stays stone-still.

"Salvatore!" I snap, then whimper when he pinches my clit.

"Yes, Milene?" He bites my lip.

"Stop torturing me."

"All right." He removes his hand, and I scream in frustration.

"You are a dead man," I say through my teeth.

"Make up your mind, cara." He bends his head to lick my neck, then slides his cock inside me. "Is this what you want?"

I squeeze my legs around his waist and tighten my hold on the hair at the back of his neck, then tilt my head to the side and bury my teeth into his biceps. "Yes."

I feel him swell inside me. Threading his fingers in my hair, he slides out only to slam back inside with such force he pushes me all the way up the bed, and my head almost hits the headboard. It probably would have, if he hadn't had a protective hand ready in place.

"Always planning in advance," I breathe, then moan when he slams into me again.

"Of course." Another thrust. "Did you think I would ever let you get hurt?"

I open my mouth to say no, but his next forward motion forces his cock so deep inside I choke on my own breath. My walls spasm, and I move my hand to place it at his throat, using a little pressure. Fingers in my hair curl into a fist. Salvatore's hand moves down my thigh, pulls my leg up and to the side, and he thrusts deeper into me. His lips trail kisses along my jaw toward my mouth until they finally reach mine. I take his lower lip between my teeth and bite. The pounding intensifies. I put a bit more pressure into my bite until I taste the metallic tang of blood. Salvatore goes into a frenzy.

The bed screeches under me, headboard banging against the wall in time with his pounding. It's like we're in the middle of a damn earthquake, and I'm being ruthlessly—bang—beautifully—bang—destroyed.

I scream as I come, white stars exploding behind my eyelids as Salvatore keeps on driving into me. His enormous cock assaults my pussy until he finds his own release, and the heat of him pours inside me. He thrusts one last time. The sound of breaking wood fills the room.

I lift my head from Salvatore's chest and trace the line of his eyebrow with my pinkie, then let it travel down and along his chin. "I can't believe you broke the fucking bed."

"It was old," he says and turns his head to the side to plant a kiss against the tips of my fingers.

There's a long horizontal crack along the entire length of the headboard. With the decorative curlicues along its sides, it certainly does appear ancient. "How old, exactly?"

"A hundred years, or something like that."

I gape at him. "You destroyed a fucking antique. Barbarian."

"You curse too much, Milene."

"No shit?" I laugh. "We're getting a new bed from Target."

"We are not buying a bed at Target."

I raise an eyebrow. "Snobbish much?"

"I am," he says and takes my chin between his fingers. "But you love me anyway."

It's a statement. Delivered in his even tone, the one he uses when ordering people around. However, there is a question in those light brown eyes that watch me so intently.

"But I love you anyway, Tore." I smile.

His gaze moves to my lips and stays there. "I love you, too."

My breath catches. His eyes move back to mine as his other hand comes to stroke my ear. "I'm sorry," he says. "I know it's not easy. Being loved by me."

I bite my bottom lip and take a deep breath. "You're wrong." I know he loves me, but it's different when he says it. That he's reached the point where he can utter those three little words means more than the sentiment itself. "Being loved by you, is the best fucking feeling in the world."

His lips press against mine. "Are you sore?" he whispers.

"Oh, you are *not* getting your barbarian cock anywhere near my pussy within the next twenty-four hours, at least, Salvatore."

"What about my mouth?"

I smirk and kiss him again. "That might be a possibility."

He rolls us until he's on top of me again, and my eyes follow him as he moves down my body, trailing light, airy kisses along the way. When he reaches my pussy, he brushes it with the tip of his finger, then replaces that with his lips through a kiss.

Salvatore's phone rings on the nightstand. I grab the bedsheet with my hands and moan as he sucks on my clit and slides a finger inside me. The phone keeps on ringing.

"Tore."

"What?" he mumbles into my pussy, then resumes the pressure of his lips and tongue, his five-o'clock shadow scratching against me and turning me on even more.

"Do you want to take that? It might be important if they're calling at eleven at night."

"Look at the caller," he says and squeezes my clit lightly between his lips, making me shudder.

I reach over and feel around the nightstand for the phone, grab it, and look at the screen.

"It's Arturo."

"Take the call and put him on speakerphone."

I lift my head from the pillow and narrow my eyes at him, then bury my fingers into his hair and tug on it until he returns my stare. "You are not taking business calls with your face buried between my legs, Salvatore."

"Put him on speakerphone, Milene." He slides another finger inside me as he resumes licking my pussy.

"Unbelievable," I mumble and hit the speakerphone button to take the call.

"Boss," Arturo's voice fills the room. "We have a problem."

"Be quick," Salvatore says between the motions of his tongue.

"Rocco killed another one of his men assigned as his wife's bodyguard. He said the guy was flirting with her."

"He said the same for the previous one." Another lick. "And the one before."

"Yeah. I don't know what to do."

Placing his hand on my thigh, Salvatore opens my legs wider and blows a hot breath against my wetness. I stifle a moan as my body shakes.

"Tell Alessandro I want him in my office tomorrow at nine." Salvatore barks, removing his fingers from inside me, and moving his body upward so he can enter me with his cock. I grab his firm ass with both hands as he pushes himself in, enjoying every inch of him, as I always do.

"What about Rocco?" Arturo's voice continues from the phone. "I can try reasoning with him, but maybe it would be for the best if—"

I groan, grab the phone, and launch it toward the other side of the room where it shatters against the wall.

Salvatore stops in midthrust. "I liked that phone."

"No more multitasking," I breathe, then push my tongue into his waiting mouth.

I watch Alessandro as he enters my office and comes to stand on the other side of my desk, his hands clasped behind his back.

"Are you gay?" I ask.

He blinks at me. I think this is the first time I've seen Alessandro Zanetti look confused.

"No."

I lean back in my chair. "You're being transferred to one of my capos. You'll work as a bodyguard to his wife. While you're there, if anyone asks, you *are* gay."

"Why?"

"Because he's pathologically jealous, and he's already killed the previous three men assigned to that position. He thinks you're gay anyway, so I hope it'll make things easier."

"All right." He nods. "Which capo?"

The phone on my desk vibrates.

"Rocco Pisano," I say and read Nino's name on the screen. "You can go. Arturo will give you the details."

"Yes, Boss."

As Alessandro turns to leave, I catch a glimpse of the expression on his face. He's smiling.

"Yes," I say into the phone.

"Boss. Arturo's sister is missing." Nino's grave voice says from the other end.

"Which one?"

"Asya. She and Sienna snuck out and went to a bar last night. Sienna returned home around midnight. Asya never came back."

"Phone?"

"Found in the bushes some distance from the bar, along with her purse," he says, "I'm here with Arturo. There is no sign of his sister, but . . ."

"But?"

"One of the guys found blood in the snow, Boss. Her glasses were next to it."

Shit. "Send me the address. I'm coming."

I grab my car keys off the desk and leave the office. As I am walking toward the elevator, I pass by Alessandro who's talking on his phone with someone. His tone is low, but I still manage to catch one sentence.

"Felix," Alessandro says into the phone, "It's Az. I need you to do something for me."

# Epilogue

Milene

*Two years later*

I CAN'T BELIEVE HE DID IT AGAIN.

The elevator pings open. Paying no heed to Salvatore's secretary who is gaping at me from behind her desk, I march across the office foyer toward the big ornate door on the right.

"Mrs. Ajello?"

I stop and throw a look over my shoulder. "Yes, Ginger?"

"Is everything . . . okay?" the secretary asks, her eyes going from my tangled hair, over Salvatore's gray T-shirt which I'm wearing, to my bare feet.

"Of course it is." I grin widely, grab the knob and enter my husband's office.

With hands on my hips and a scowl on my face, I walk around his desk and come to a stop next to him. Salvatore looks up from the laptop, then leans back in his chair.

"Did you sleep well, vita mia?"

I narrow my eyes at him and point at the small bundle he's holding on his chest. "Stop stealing my baby."

From the moment we came home from the hospital a month ago, Salvatore has been using every opportunity he can to sneak into the nursery, take Mia and carry her around with him everywhere. His explanation—she likes sleeping in his arms better than in the bed. And if it wasn't enough, he's been the one holding her while she's awake too. All. The. Time.

Salvatore cocks his head and does that thing with his eyes, the one when he pins me with his gaze and slowly blinks. Damn, it still makes me weak in the knees.

"You had her to yourself for nine months, Milene," he says in that grave tone that makes even the most bizarre statement sound absolutely solid. "It's my turn now."

"She was inside my belly, Salvatore. It doesn't count."

"In my book, it does."

I sigh and take his face between my palms. "What's going on? And don't tell me 'nothing,' because I know you all too well. So, spill it."

He holds my gaze for a long moment, then closes his eyes. "I'm afraid she won't love me."

"What?" I tighten my hold on his cheeks and shake his head slightly. "Of course she'll love you, baby. You're her dad."

Salvatore's eyes open and even though he doesn't say anything, I see worry deep inside his amber depths.

"She *will* love you," I say again and press my lips to his. "She'll fucking adore you. Like I do."

"You promise?" he whispers into my mouth.

"I promise." I reach out and place my hand on our daughter's head, brushing back the short blond strands. "Just look at her. She already loves you unconditionally."

He looks down at the baby sleeping on his chest. Mia's eyes flutter open and a moment later two amber gazes collide.

And then, my husband smiles.

PERFECTLY IMPERFECT
BOOK SIX

# Fractured souls

PERFECTLY IMPERFECT SERIES

Pavel & Asya

# AUTHOR'S NOTE

Dear reader,

*Fractured Souls* has been my hardest book to write so far. Because of the delicate subject, it's different from the previous books in the series. *Fractured Souls* focuses mainly on the characters, and while there is a Mafia/crime subplot present, it's secondary to the characters' story. Also, if you've read the previous books in the series, you know I love to throw a bit of humor into each story. This book, however, won't have that element. It deals with an extremely heavy subject, and the inclusion of humor would have been distasteful.

Please read the trigger warning on the next page. If you feel like you may find the subject matter disturbing, or it may cause you harm, please skip this story. Don't worry, if you do decide to pass on this one, you won't miss any revelations critical to the rest of the series, and you will be able to return to the Perfectly Imperfect world in the next book. However, if you're still uncertain whether you should read it, please feel free to email me or reach out via TikTok or Instagram message (my contact information is on my website at www.neva-altaj.com/contact) and share your concerns. I'd be happy to give you spoilers so you can decide if you want to read the book or not. Your mental health matters.

I would like to express my gratitude to Ruthie, who did a sensitivity read for Fractured Souls and offered advice for improvement so that Asya's struggles, and her journey, are presented realistically and tactfully.

If you choose to read *Fractured Souls,* I hope with all my heart that you'll like Asya and Pavel's story. It might be a part of a Mafia series, but above all else, it's the story of love, overcoming hurt, the strength of family, and the perseverance of the human spirit.

# Trigger Warning

This book contains topics that may be difficult for some readers, such as an on-page sexual assault (including rape, but not between the main characters), post-traumatic stress disorder (PTSD), mention of attempted suicide, mention of sexual slavery, mention of drug use, explicit scenes of violence and torture, and gore. If you are a survivor of sexual and/or physical abuse, parts of this story may trigger memories that can cause stress or sadness.

Our heroine deals with her situation by relying on the strength and support of our hero. While we believe that love can heal, please keep in mind that this story is a work of fiction. I encourage you to seek out help from a support organization and/or a trusted health professional. You do not need to suffer in silence.

# Character Notes

Asya—pronounced as [ˈaːzja].

Pasha—Russian nickname (short form) for Pavel, used in casual settings.

Pashenka—a variation (affectionate diminutive) of the name Pavel/Pasha, used as a term of endearment by close family members/relations.

Mishka—a Russian term of endearment, meaning little bear or teddy bear.

*In case you need to refresh your memory on the Bratva hierarchy and family ties, check out the "Extras" page on my website.*

# Playlist

There are several classical pieces mentioned throughout the book. Here's the list in case you want to check them out.

"Moonlight Sonata" by Ludwig van Beethoven

"Flight of the Bumblebee" by Nikolai Rimsky-Korsakov

"Gymnopédies" by Erik Satie

"In the Hall of the Mountain King" by Edvard Grieg

"The Rain Must Fall" by Yanni

"Für Elise" by Ludwig van Beethoven

"River Flows in You" by Yiruma

# Prologue

Asya

IT'S SNOWING.

The ground is cold on my back, scraping my shoulder blades, as I stare over the man's shoulder into the dark expanse above me. Everything seems blurry. I can't discern separate snowflakes, but I can feel them falling on my face. Fragile. Delicate. They remind me of the notes in one of the pieces by Erik Satie so I hum the tune while a searing pain keeps tearing at my insides.

Should it hurt this much? I know it was supposed to hurt at first, but I never imagined it would keep hurting.

The man grunts and the weight is suddenly gone. I slide my hand down my stomach and over the fabric of my torn dress to press my palm between my legs. Wetness. Too much. Way too much. I raise my hand in front of my face, staring at my blood-covered fingers while the melody still plays in the back of my mind.

"Well, you've ended up being quite a treat, sweetheart," the male voice says. "I had my eye on your sister initially. You may look the same, but there is just something about her that oozes class. The clients do tend to prefer more polished ones, but you'll do."

Panic, as I've never felt before, explodes in my chest, breaking me out of the stupor I'd fallen into. I roll to the side until I'm lying facedown on the ground. Energy surges through my veins, and I spring to my feet. And then, I run.

The pain between my legs is excruciating. With each step I take, I feel a stabbing jolt. My whole body is shaking, but I'm not sure if it's from the cold, the pain, or the shock. Maybe it's just the horror of what he did and said. I risk a quick look over my shoulder and a low whimper leaves my lips when I see my rapist following and gaining on me.

There are streetlights some distance in front of me, so I change my course to run in that direction. The faint, slow melody playing in my head transforms into a battle march as if urging me to go faster. The ground is uneven, making it hard to run. I keep tripping over the roots of the nearby trees and the small bushes that are hard to see in the dark. My vision is blurry—I lost my glasses—but I focus on the light that I can see through the branches like it's my only lifeline and keep running. The ripping and burning sensations in my lower belly are almost too strong to ignore, but I grit my teeth and try to keep my pace. The air leaves my lungs in short bursts while snowflakes fall on the exposed skin of my arms. Just a few dozen yards to the street. I can hear the vehicles. I just need to reach the street, and someone will stop and help me.

I'm almost there when my bare foot catches on something and I stumble, falling with my face hitting the cold, hard ground. No! I get up, intending to keep running toward the lifesaving light when an arm wraps around my middle from behind.

"Got you!" The son of a bitch laughs.

I scream, but his other hand covers my mouth, stifling the sound.

"It looks like they will have to reeducate you, honey," he says next to my ear. "I might visit you again when you're more docile. Boss lets me fuck my finds for free once a month."

"Please," I whimper into his palm while kicking my legs.

"Perfect." He lets out another wicked laugh. "See, you're already learning."

I try hitting him with my elbow and almost escape his grip when I feel the prick of a needle on the side of my neck.

The man shushes me. "Easy, now. Just a few seconds and it'll all get better."

My vision blurs until there is nothing left but darkness.

The music stops.

# Chapter one

## Pavel

*Two months later*

NEON LIGHTS SHINE DOWN ON PEOPLE CRAMMED TOGETHER, moving to the music which is blasting from the overhead speakers. The smell of alcohol and competing fragrances permeate the air, even up here, in my office. I step toward the floor-to-ceiling glass wall and cross my arms over my chest, watching the crowd on the dance floor below. It's not even midnight, but it's packed with hardly any breathing space.

A commotion at the far corner of the dance floor attracts my attention. Vladimir, one of the club bouncers, is holding a man by the back of his shirt, dragging him toward the stairs that lead to the upper level. If the man was starting a brawl, security would have thrown him out. This must be something more serious if he is being brought to me.

The door behind me opens five minutes later.

"Mr. Morozov." Vladimir pushes the man inside the office. "We caught this one dealing in front of the restrooms."

I walk toward the man sprawled on the floor and put the sole of my right shoe over his hand. "Distributing drugs in my club?"

The man whimpers and tries to remove my foot with his free hand, but I press harder. "Talk."

"It was just some pills a friend gave me," he chokes out and looks up at me. "He said it's some new stuff he swiped from his work."

I cock my head to the side. "His job? What does he do?"

"I don't know. He never talks about it." He tries to free his hand again but fails. "I'm so sorry. It won't happen again."

I motion for Vladimir to hand me the small plastic bag he's holding and look it over. There are a dozen white pills inside. "Have you tried this?"

"No . . . I . . . I'm not into drugs," the man says, then whimpers when I apply more pressure to his hand.

"So you brought them here to sell. Very wise." I throw the plastic bag back to Vladimir. "Take this to Doc. We need to check what's in that crap."

"What should we do with the dealer?" Vladimir nods toward the man on the floor.

Based on the panicked look in the man's eyes and the shaking of his hand, it wouldn't take long to break him. I could take him to the storeroom and question him. But we have rules in the Chicago Bratva, and my scope of work doesn't include information extraction.

"I think he would enjoy a little chat with Mikhail. Get him out of my sight," I say and turn around to walk back to the glass wall overlooking the dance floor.

I can hear yelling and a lot of kerfuffle behind me as Vladimir drags the man out. The racket ceases when the door closes behind them. My eyes scan the people milling around and dancing, stopping at the booth in the far-left corner. Yuri, the man in charge of the Bratva's soldiers, is sitting in the middle with a blonde-haired woman by his side. On his other side, laughing about something, are the brothers Kostya and Ivan, who manage the finances in our organization. Seems like some of the guys got a free night.

The phone in my pocket rings. I take it out and see Yuri's name on the screen.

"Is something wrong?" I ask when I take the call.

"No," he says, looking up at me from the booth. "Come down and have a drink with us."

"I'm working."

"You're always working, Pasha." He shakes his head.

He's right. Unless I'm sleeping or working out, I'm at one of the Bratva's clubs. Spending time in my empty apartment since I moved out of the Petrov mansion when the pakhan's wife had a child has always been hard. But in the last few years, it's gotten even harder. The fact that I've been running two nightclubs for the last seven years, spending most of my time surrounded by people, should be enough to make me want to seek solitude. It's not. It just reminds me that I have no one to go home to.

"Come on, just one drink," Yuri urges again.

Kostya's deep laugh comes through the line. Looks like he's fooling around again. Always a trickster, that one. "Some other time, Yuri," I say.

I end the call but don't move away from the glass wall, watching my comrades having a great time. Maybe I should join them. It would be nice to relax and talk about nonsense sometimes, but I never can. The problem is, on the few occasions I have gone out with them, I ended up feeling even more alone.

The Bratva is the closest thing to a family I've ever had. I know for sure that each one of them would take a bullet for me. As I would for them. And still, even after ten years in the Bratva, I can't let myself get too close to my friends. With my past, I guess, this may be expected. When you're discarded by the people who should have been your safe harbor, it's hard to allow yourself to get close to anyone because, at some point, they will leave, too.

Sooner or later, everyone leaves.

I stand there for a long time, watching the guys laugh, then turn away and go back to work.

## Asya

I walk inside the office and come to a stop in the center of the room. Dolly, the woman in charge of the girls, is sitting behind her desk, her attention focused on the small leather-bound notebook in front of her.

"You'll be entertaining Mr. Miller tonight," she says as she scribes something in her ledger. "He prefers it slow. Start with a massage and go from there."

I nod. "Yes, Dolly."

"Oh, and no blow jobs. Mr. Miller doesn't like those." She closes the notebook and walks around the desk, her heels clicking against the linoleum. I bow my head and focus my gaze on the floor so she won't be able to see my eyes. Her pink shiny heels enter my field of vision as she comes to a stop right in front of me.

"He's a very important client, so make sure you fulfill his every need. If he likes you, he may request you again. He's very mild-mannered. He doesn't hit girls often, which is rare as you already know. And don't forget the condom. You know the rules."

I nod again and raise my hand, palm up. Dolly places a single white pill on my palm.

"What about the rest?" I ask. "I need more. Please."

"Always the same tune with you girls," she barks. "You get the rest when you're finished with the client. You know that already."

"Just one more," I beg.

"I said after you are done!" she yells and slaps me across the cheek. "Get back to your room and be ready in an hour. You've been out of commission for almost a week. We're losing money."

"Yes, Dolly," I say in a small voice and turn toward the door.

"Oh, and don't forget to take off the glasses. Mr. Miller doesn't like those."

"Of course," I say.

After exiting Dolly's office, I turn left and hurry down the hallway, passing the doors to other rooms. I'm one of five girls here at the moment. There used to be six of us, but two days ago, one of the girls disappeared. Since I try to keep to myself, I didn't know her other than seeing her in passing. I remember she had long blonde hair which she wore braided down her back. No one knows what happened, but I heard the other girls gossiping about her meeting with a client who is known to be rough.

I reach the last door at the end of the hallway and walk inside. After a quick look around to make sure my roommate isn't here, I rush toward the small bathroom on the other side of the room. I lock the door and turn toward the toilet.

Opening my right hand, I stare at the white pill in my palm. Such a small thing. Harmless looking. Who would guess that something so tiny can keep a person willfully enslaved, living in a prison without bars? It would be so easy to put it into my mouth and just . . . let go.

It is always the same setup. One pill before the meeting with the client. Three more after I'm done. The first one is meant to keep me high and, therefore, more obedient. It doesn't make it hurt less, but it does make me not care. It's also highly addictive. If I take it, it will ensure I'll come rushing back for the three pills afterward to satisfy the craving brought on by the first. The cycle would repeat. Again, and again. Keeping my brain in a haze, constantly on some level of high, needing more each time, not capable of thinking about anything else.

An addict, that's what I've become. Just like the rest of the girls here.

I squeeze the pill in my hand, then throw it into the bowl and flush it. The pill makes two circles before disappearing down the drain, but I keep standing there, staring into the toilet.

It's been six days since I stopped taking the drugs. It happened by accident. I caught stomach flu last week, and for three days, I vomited nonstop. My body wouldn't keep anything inside, including the pills Dolly continued to shove down my throat. By the time I felt better, my brain was clear of the drug-induced stupor for the first time in two months.

That day was the hardest. Even though I was constantly cold—God, I don't ever remember being so cold in my life—I was sweating. Everything hurt. My head, my legs, my arms. It was like every single bone in my body had been shattered. And then there were the tremors. I tried to control the shaking for fear my teeth would fracture, but couldn't. Dolly thought it was the fever finally breaking, but it wasn't. It was withdrawal. The urge to just swallow the pills she gave me was almost too much to fight, and only pure stubbornness kept me from succumbing.

It got easier after that. I still randomly got the chills, but it was nowhere near what I experienced that first drug-free day, and my limbs and head hurt significantly less. I pretended to swallow the pills and made sure to act the same as I did before, begging for more all the time, while secretly throwing the drugs away. Amazingly, my deception worked. Now it's just a question of how long I'll be able to keep the pretense before someone notices.

I take off my glasses and leave them next to the sink. They aren't even the right prescription, just something Dolly got me so I would stop stumbling and squinting. My own were lost during my last night in New York.

I look away from the reminder, take off my clothes, and step inside the shower stall. Turning the water to scorching hot, I move under the spray and close my eyes. There is a washcloth on the small shelf to my right. I take it and scrub my skin until it's red, but it doesn't help. I still feel filthy.

I don't understand why I haven't fought harder. Yes, the drugs kept my brain in a haze, but I've always been aware of what was happening. Still, I've just . . . capitulated. Let them sell me, night after night, to rich men who are willing to pay an enormous amount of money to fuck a pretty, polished doll. Because that's what we are. They wax us, have our nails and hair done, and make sure we wear expensive clothes. The full face of makeup is mandatory, and it smears quite nicely when a girl cries after the session. So many of the men like to see us break.

I haven't cried once. Maybe something broke inside me that first night. A million particles of my fractured soul mixed with the snow and blood. I just didn't care anymore.

The driver comes to pick me up an hour later, and during the drive, I stare blankly through the window at the people rushing along the unfamiliar sidewalks. When I was taken, at first I thought I was being held somewhere on the outskirts of New York, but I now know that I've ended up in Chicago. As I watch "normal life" passing me by, for the first time in two months, I'm tempted to grab the handle and try to escape. I'm sickened at the realization that it's taken me this long to think about running away. But I consider it now. I want to feel clean again. That may never happen, but I want to try.

I've heard what they do to girls who try to escape. As long as we are obedient, we get the pills, because high-paying clients don't like girls with needle marks on their bodies. But the moment a girl creates problems, they switch to the syringe. And it's over. Was that what happened to the girl who disappeared?

Leaning back in the seat, I close my eyes and exhale. I'll keep pretending I'm still an obedient little slut, ready to endure everything and wait for my opportunity. I will have only one chance, so I better make sure it counts.

They always wear suits.

I regard the man sitting on the edge of the bed in this fancy room where the driver escorted me. Late fifties. Receding hairline. He's wearing an impeccable gray suit and an expensive watch on his wrist. Two phones on the nightstand. Probably a banker. Again.

The room is as expected for a client like him. Heavy luxury curtains in deep red—the color of blood—and a four-poster bed with black silk sheets to hide the bloodstains. A tall lamp in each corner and a wooden mobile bar stocked with different liquors. Only the best labels, of course. I've been in this room once before, but I remember that the bathroom is equally chic, with a large tub and a shower. There's a first aid kit under the sink there. The driver used it because the client I was with that night left me with a nasty cut on my lip.

Mr. Miller motions for me to approach. I close the distance between us and stand between his legs, trying to detach myself from what will follow. It was much easier with the pills.

"Pretty," he says and places his palm on my thigh just below the hem of my short white dress. Seems like it's the favorite color of every client. "How old are you?"

"I'm eighteen, Mr. Miller."

"So young." His hand travels upward, pulling my dress. "Call me Jonny."

"Yes, Jonny," I mutter.

"Dolly said your name is Daisy. Small and sweet. Fitting." A shiver passes over my body upon hearing the name they gave me because they found my own too unusual. I despise it. Just hearing it makes me want to throw up.

Mr. Miller lifts my dress over my head and throws it onto the floor. It falls as a small white bundle at my feet. I don't know why, but clients removing my dress has always hit me harder than them taking off my panties. Each time it happens, it feels like the last layer of my defense is stripped away from me. I shudder.

"Do you find me attractive, little Daisy?" he circles my waist with his hands.

"Of course I do, Jonny," I say automatically. It had been ingrained in my brain with fists during my first day of training.

"Hmm . . ." His hands squeeze my waist, then pull my lacy thong, white as well, down my legs. "I usually like it slow. But you are too sweet. I don't think I can wait."

The moment he has my panties removed, he throws me onto the bed. I lie there, unmoving, and watch him take off his jacket. His tie is next, and my body shakes as he loosens the knot. One of my previous clients wrapped his tie around my neck while he fucked me from behind, pulling on it every time he thrust into me, cutting off my air. I close my eyes in relief when Mr. Miller throws his tie to the floor. He starts on his dress shirt, but only undoes the first two buttons and moves to his pants. My breathing pace picks up. At least he removed the tie. I can handle the shirt.

"Open your legs wide, honeybee," he says as he puts on the condom. The guy who runs the organization is very strict on protection, but it's more about making sure the clients are safe than the girls' safety.

Mr. Miller crawls across the bed until he is looming above me. The vein at the side of his neck pulses. He watches me with wide eyes, then dips his head and licks my naked breast. I grit my teeth together, willing myself not to recoil. It doesn't end well when I recoil. I hope the music will come, making this a little easier to block out. It doesn't. The last time I heard the music was that snowy night. Sometimes, when I lie in bed, trying to sleep, I drum my fingers on the bedside as if it'll help call the melody. But I don't hear it like I used to.

Mr. Miller's meaty hands grip the inside of my thighs, spreading my legs apart. The next moment, his cock thrusts inside me all at once.

It hurts. It always hurts, but without the drugs to scramble my mind, it's a thousand times worse. I tilt my head up and stare at the ceiling as he slams into me again. At times like these, I try to disconnect, to mentally pull away and toward a happy memory, hoping to detach myself from yet another rape.

Thank God, a memory pops into my brain.

*It's the summer before my sophomore year of high school. I'm sitting in the garden, reading, while my twin sister chases her Maltese—Bonbon—across the lawn. Poor animal. She even put a yellow silk bow on his head. When Sienna said she wanted a dog, I was sure Arturo would say no. Our brother is not a fan of keeping animals inside the house. I have no idea how she managed to convince him to let her have one.*

*"Asya!" Sienna yells. "Come!"*

*I wave my hand at her and keep reading. The murder mystery is just being unraveled, and I'm eager to see who the culprit is. I'm sure it's . . .*

*A spray of cold water splashes my chest. I scream and jump up off the chair, glaring at my sister. She's holding a watering hose in her hand, laughing like a madwoman.*

*"You're dead!" I chuckle and dash toward her. She's still doubled over from laughter when I reach her. I grab the hose, pull the collar of her top, and send the water stream down her back.*

*Sienna shrieks and turns, then grabs the hose, trying to direct it at me, but it just ends up spraying her face. I'm still laughing when I lift my free hand to wipe the water from my eyes, but I stop mid-motion. My hand is red. I look at the hose in my grip. It's pouring red liquid onto the ground around my feet. Blood.*

I open my eyes and stare at the white ceiling above me while the smell of sweat infiltrates my nostrils. Yeah . . . the happy memory trick never works that well.

Mr. Miller keeps pounding into me, his labored breaths blowing into my face, and beads of sweat dripping onto me. He groans loudly, the sound reminding me of some huge animal in rage. Abruptly, he stops and pulls out. His weight disappears. I lift my head off the pillow and see him slumped on his knees at the foot of the bed, his hands clawing at his chest. He's breathing hard. His face is red as he stares at me with wide eyes.

"The . . . pills," he chokes out. "In . . . the jacket."

I just gape at him for a few moments before getting up off the bed and running toward his jacket where he had left it on the back of a chair. I find an orange bottle in the left pocket and take it out. Mr. Miller is slumped on all fours, trying to draw breath.

"Give me . . ." he wheezes, raising his arm in my direction.

I look down at the bottle in my hand and back up, taking in his flustered face and rheumy eyes. Slowly, I step further back. Mr. Miller's enormous eyes glare at me. I retreat a few more steps until I feel the wall behind my back.

And then, I watch.

It lasts less than two minutes. Wheezing. Shallow, labored breaths. And finally, a choking sound. Mr. Miller collapses sideways onto the bed, his head tilted up in my direction, eyes bulging. It looks like he is trying to speak, but the words are jumbled. I can't make out what he's saying, but I see it on his face. He is begging. I stay rooted to the spot, clutching the medicine bottle in my hand, and watch a man dying before my eyes. With each breath he takes, I feel the remains of my soul, or whatever is left inside me, die a little more. Until there is nothing, just a black hole.

The door on my left bangs open and my driver barges inside. He runs toward Mr. Miller's body, which is lying still across the bed, and places his fingers on the man's neck.

"Fuck!" the driver spits out and turns to me. "What have you done, bitch?"

I ignore him. For some reason, I can't take my eyes off the body on the bed. The eyes are still open, and even though I can't see them clearly, it seems like they are still looking directly at me. A slap lands on the side of my face.

"Wake the fuck up! We need to leave," the driver barks.

When I don't move, he grabs my arm and starts shaking me. A moment later, I feel the prick of a needle in my arm.

No!

That prick awakens whatever is left of my self-preservation. The pill bottle falls out of my hand. I pull my arm away, turn, and run out into the hallway.

It's well into the night and the inside of this place seems deserted. The two wide yellow stripes running the length of the carpet help me orient myself, and I follow them, running along several hallways in search of an exit. My vision clouds, and I'm becoming lightheaded. Every step I take is harder than the previous one, and it feels as if my legs are weighed down by concrete blocks. I turn the corner and keep running until I see a door at the end. There is a green-lit sign above it. I can't read the letters, but there is only one thing it could be. The exit.

As soon as I reach the door, I grab the knob and dash outside. It's a fire escape. I'm seeing double and my head spins, making me dizzier with each passing second, but I manage to grab the railing on the third try. Clutching the cold iron, I fumble down the steps, miraculously without falling. The moment my bare feet reach the ground, I turn left and run into a dark alley. A car horn blares on my right, and I turn just in time to see blinding lights shining into my face before the darkness swallows me.

"Shit!"

I open the car door and dash out, running to the front of my vehicle. On the road, barely a foot from the front bumper, lies a completely naked woman. I know I didn't hit her. I managed to stop the car before I reached her, but it looks like there is something wrong with her. Her body is shaking as if she has a high fever.

I bend and scoop her up into my arms. The smell of rancid male cologne invades my nostrils as I adjust my grip. The woman's skin is unusually cold and she is trembling so much that, if I wasn't clutching her to my chest, she'd slip from my grasp. Turning on my heel, I carry her to the car. Shifting her meager weight in my arms, I somehow manage to reach the handle and get the back door open. I don't have a blanket, so once I gently lower her onto the seat, I remove my jacket and drape it over the girl's naked body. She immediately curls into a fetal position while tremors continue to shake her slight form. As soon as I'm back behind the wheel, I hit speed dial on my phone, and floor the car.

"Doc!" I bark the moment he takes the call. "I have a girl in my car who seems to be having a seizure, maybe. Should I try to do something or drive straight to a hospital? Or should I bring her to you? I'm five minutes away."

"Symptoms?"

"She's shaking really bad, and her arms and hands are twitching." I throw a look over my shoulder. "Doesn't seem coherent."

"Foam at her mouth? Vomiting?"

I look over at the girl again. "No. Not at the moment."

"Bring her here," he says. "If she vomits, you need to stop the car and make sure she doesn't choke. It could be an epileptic seizure or an overdose."

"Okay." I toss the phone on the passenger seat.

Luckily, the traffic is light, so it takes me under five minutes to reach the building where the doc has a small clinic on the ground floor, just below his apartment. Since he mostly does house visits for the Bratva, he only uses it when someone needs an ultrasound or an x-ray.

I park at the front and lift the girl from the back seat. Her limbs are still twitching uncontrollably, but she's not vomiting. Holding her in my arms, still wrapped in my jacket, I run toward the glass door the doc is holding open.

"Put her on the gurney," he says and rushes toward the medical cabinet. "Why is she naked?"

"No idea. She ran out of a building, disoriented, and collapsed in the middle of the street. I almost hit her with my car."

The doc comes over carrying a syringe, leans over the girl, and pulls open her eyelid. "Overdose. Move away."

I take a couple of steps back and watch as he gives her an injection of something, then proceeds with attaching an IV with saline into her arm.

"I'll take a blood sample so we know what she's taken. But I won't have the results before tomorrow. I assume it was one of the common drugs so I've given her something to counteract it. It will reverse the effects." He grabs a blanket and places it over the girl. "Unless she is a heavy user, she should be okay in a couple of hours. Just drive her to a shelter or something and leave her for them to deal with."

I look down at the girl. Long dark brown strands are falling over her face, hiding it from view. She is still shaking under the blanket, but there is no twitching. Her breathing also sounds slightly better. What the fuck happened to her?

"I'll take her to my place for tonight," I say without taking my eyes off the girl. "When she's better in the morning, I'll take her home."

"Are you serious?"

"Yes." I look up and find Doc staring at me.

"You can't take a drug addict to your place."

"I won't drop her off at the shelter as if she's a bag of junk, Doc." One of the girl's arms is hanging down. I take her small hand and tuck it under the blanket next to her side. "And it will be just for tonight anyway."

The doc sighs and shakes his head. "If she is an addict, which I'm pretty sure she is, she will go through withdrawal. With the medicine I gave her, it'll probably start right away. Depending on what she took and how heavy a user she is, it could take anywhere from a couple of days to two weeks for it to pass."

"Even though she is naked, her hair is clean, and her nails are manicured. It's more likely that someone drugged her while trying to sexually assault her, or she escaped an abusive partner."

The doc watches me, then nods. "All right. I'll see if I have a rape kit. I'll also do a basic exam. Wait outside."

I glance at the girl, who seems to be sleeping, and head toward the exit. It's started snowing. I lean back against the wall and stare at the street in front of me, wondering what the hell happened to that girl.

Fifteen minutes later, the doc comes out and stands next to me.

"So?" I ask.

He doesn't say anything at first, just peers into the night.

"Doc?"

"They didn't 'try' to rape her," he says finally. "They demolished her, Pavel."

My head snaps to the side. "Explain."

"Someone tore into her; there is definitely evidence of forced trauma. Looks likes this may not have been the first time, either. She has older scar tissue. I took samples for STD tests and did a pregnancy test." He sighs and removes his glasses. "I've treated her the best I can, but she will need painkillers. I'll check if I have something nonaddictive she can take that won't react with the meds I gave her to reverse the overdose. She also has bruises, but they seem several days old. There is only one needle mark on her forearm, and it's fresh. They probably injected her with whatever she overdosed with."

"Send me the test results as soon as you get them," I say through gritted teeth.

"You're really taking her to your place?"

"Yes." I head back inside.

"Pavel," the doc calls after me. "I don't know what her mental state will be when she wakes up. Don't ask her what happened, just get her to her family. And tell them she'll need psychological help."

"Okay." I nod.

I sit down in the recliner and watch the sleeping girl curled up in the middle of my bed. At first, I thought about placing her in one of the other two bedrooms but decided against it. Better to be close in case her state worsens.

She seems better. Her breathing sounds normal, and the shaking stopped completely. I tilt my head, watching her small frame under the thick duvet. She's still naked under the covers. I didn't want to risk maneuvering her arms and legs to get her into one of my pajamas. What if she woke up and thought I was trying to hurt her?

I grip the sides of the recliner and draw a deep breath. What kind of sick bastard would abuse a woman in such a way? Especially someone so tiny. I close my eyes and try to subdue the urge to run to my car, drive back to where I found her, and search for the motherfucker who hurt her. I can't risk leaving her alone, though. What if she has another seizure? But I will find the man who dared beat and rape her, or whatever other torture the sick fuck subjected her to. And I will make him pay. My hold on the armrests intensifies, and the faint sound of wood squeaking follows. The sleeping girl stirs, and I release the recliner, not wanting to wake her.

I don't know what came over me and made me decide to bring her to my place. I could have easily left her at a hospital and told them to send me the bill for the services. It doesn't make sense, but I couldn't make myself leave her somewhere. It's been years since I felt any kind of connection with a person, even those closest to me. But seeing this girl, so hurt and unprotected, stirred something deep inside my soul. The need to shield her from anything that may try to hurt her again came viscerally, but with it, I also had the urge to destroy. It's strange to have this hunger for violence rising inside of me again after so many years.

The girl rolls to her other side, and one of her legs slips out from under the duvet. I get up and tuck it back under the covers.

She seems fine for the moment, sound asleep, so I decide to take a quick shower. Inside the walk-in closet on the other side of the room, I use the flashlight on my phone to find a pair of black pajama bottoms and boxer briefs.

I'm already at the bathroom door when a thought surfaces, and I return to the closet to grab a T-shirt, as well. When I'm home, I usually wear just pajama bottoms, but the girl could get scared if she sees all the ink on my torso. She will probably be scared when she wakes up in a strange place, and there is no need to distress her more than necessary.

I turn the water to cold in the shower, hoping it'll help me shake off the persistent urge to kill someone. It doesn't help much. Pressing my palms to the tiled wall, I lift my chin and let the cold spray hit me right in the face. As the freezing water runs down my body, I dig inside my brain, pulling out the memory of one of my last fights. The most violent one, since I need some way to deal with this urge to destroy someone. My opponent snuck a knife inside the ring and managed to slice my side twice before I overpowered him. I made sure he knew what I thought about his actions by breaking his back and burying his own blade to the hilt at the base of his skull. Violence isn't something I enjoy, but when I find myself in a beast's den, I inevitably become the very beast I'm fighting. It's nothing more than survival. Reliving that scene helps feed my thirst for destruction. Somewhat, at least.

I take no more than five minutes in the bathroom, so I expect the girl to still be sleeping soundly. Instead, she is tossing and turning in the bed, her body shaking. I rush over and press my palm to her forehead, finding it hot. She is mumbling something I can't decipher because her teeth are chattering too much. I bend my head trying to catch what she's saying.

"Cold . . ." her small voice whimpers. "So, so cold."

I grab the blanket folded at the foot of the bed, throw it over her, then take my phone from the nightstand.

"Doc," I say the moment he picks up, "the girl has a fever and is shaking like a leaf, saying she's cold."

"Withdrawal," he says. "It's a normal reaction."

"What can I do?"

"Nothing. Her body needs to go through that. She'll be better in a couple of hours. But it may happen again over the next few days. Make sure you tell the family that tomorrow."

"Okay. Anything else?"

"She will probably feel sick tomorrow, but she needs to drink liquids. Try giving her water the moment she wakes up," he says. "Oh, and Pavel, I probably don't have to tell you this, but it would be best if you don't touch her or get into her personal space. If she freaks out in the morning, give me a call and I'll go get Varya. She can stay with the girl until her family comes to pick her up."

"Thanks."

I lower the phone and observe the girl again. She is still shaking, but I don't think I should cover her with anything else. She'll get too hot. There's the mumbling again, but she's turned with her back to me so it's hard to hear. I put my knee on the bed and lean closer, trying to understand. She's crying. The whimpers are very low, broken, and that sound is so fucking heartbreaking.

The doc said I shouldn't try to touch her, but she's delirious now and probably doesn't know what's happening around her. I can't bear the idea of doing nothing any longer. I reach out and place my palm on her back, over the blanket, and brush it lightly. She doesn't pull away, so I sprawl down onto the bed behind her, making sure my body doesn't touch hers, and continue stroking her back. After some time, the crying stops. I pull my hand off, intending to get up when the girl suddenly turns around and buries her face into my chest. I lie there, not moving, not daring to touch her, but also unable to move away. Her hot breath fans my chest as she lies with her hands squeezed into fists and tucked between our bodies. She's still shaking.

A barely audible whisper reaches my ears. "More."

I look down at her, having no idea what she meant by that.

"Please."

The way she says it guts me. It's like a call for help from a drowning person. Slowly, I place my palm where I think the small of her back may be. I can't really tell with her bundled under the covers. I move my hand across her back, up then down. The girl sighs, snuggles closer, and buries her nose in the crook of my neck.

It must be dawn already, but I'm not certain because I pulled the heavy drapes over the windows. I should get some sleep. I have a meeting with the pakhan this afternoon, after which I'll be stuck at the club until at least three in the morning. Instead of doing what I'm sure the doc would advise—going to another room—I stay where I am, with a girl whose name I don't even know, and stroke her back until her breathing evens out and she falls asleep again.

# Chapter Two

Asya

THE DOOR ON THE OPPOSITE WALL IS HUGE AND IS MADE OF THE darkest wood I've ever seen. An hour must have passed since I woke up. I can't be sure, though. There's a clock on the wall, ticking, but it doesn't help because I can't see the details of the face or hands. Based on the sliver of light visible between the drapes, it must be midday.

I desperately need to pee, but I'm afraid to move from my spot in this bed. The last thing I remember is following the yellow hallway lines after I ran out of Mr. Miller's room and finding the door with the exit sign. I don't have a clue where I am. I don't know how I got here. And I have no idea what they are going to do with me. My body is shaking. The pain between my legs is still there but not as strong, and my head hurts as if it's going to explode. Other than that, I feel fine. Physically, at least. Mentally? Mentally, I feel fine, too. In fact, I feel great.

That can't be good.

The door opens and someone walks in, then stops abruptly. It's a man, that much I can discern even from this distance. He's tall and very muscular, wearing a black T-shirt and baggy black pants. His hair is either dark blond or light brown. That summarizes everything I can make out. I had a week left until my scheduled second eye surgery, but then . . . everything happened. The doctor said he expected to correct my nearsightedness almost entirely.

The man just stands there, and I wonder how long he plans on just staring at me.

"Good morning," he says finally, and a pleasant shiver passes down my body. I've never in my life met a man with a voice so deep. "How are you feeling?"

I squint my eyes, trying to see him better, but he's still just a blurred shape.

The man takes a tentative step forward. "Can you tell me your name?"

I can, but I don't feel like talking right now. I don't know why. I just don't. Another step. He's in the middle of the room now.

"Your family is probably worried about you. Can you give me their number to call them? So they can come to take you home?"

Yes, my brother and sister are probably going out of their minds. I've been missing for two months. Arturo must be feeling crazy with no information on me. He's been both a father and a mother to me and my sister since we were five. And Sienna, oh my God, I can't even think about it. I need to call them to let them know I'm okay.

Nausea claws its way into my throat. I don't want to call Arturo, because I'll have to tell him what happened. What I did. I don't want my family to know that their sister is a prostitute and an addict. They'll probably tell me everything will be okay. My body starts shaking. It's not going to be okay.

Nothing will ever be okay again.

"What's wrong?" the man asks and takes another step toward me.

They probably think I'm dead. Good. It's better that way. I'm not worth their worry. I'd never be able to look them in the eyes. The sister they knew doesn't exist anymore. She's gone. And in her place is this disgusting, filthy creature who lets people violate her and sell her body while she does nothing to stop it. Nothing! My teeth chatter and I can't breathe.

"Please, tell me what's wrong."

His voice is so calming. I should be scared shitless, having an unknown man here, considering what I've gone through. I'm not. The thing is, I had so many nasty things done to me that there is nothing he can do to hurt me. I'm more scared of Arturo and Sienna finding out than being violated again. I try breathing deeper but can't. I can only manage small gasps.

A hand enters my field of vision and I flinch, expecting him to hit me. Instead, the man takes the blanket that has fallen off my shoulders and wraps it around me. His palm rests on my back and slowly moves up and down. He did the same thing last night. I remember waking up and being freezing cold when a hand started comforting my back. It made me feel safe, something I thought I would never feel again. I did last night.

My eyes focus on the blanket wrapped around me because I can't look at him right now, but I can finally fill my lungs. I close my eyes, and a faint melody plays somewhere deep inside my mind. The notes are soft, barely recognizable, but still, my heart skips a beat. I thought I had lost my music. As the hand on my back continues its path, up then down and up again, the music gets a little louder. Beethoven's "Moonlight Sonata." Deep. Soothing. Just like his voice.

"I'm going to get you some water," the man says, and his hand vanishes off my back as he moves away.

I scream.

I freeze. Did I accidentally touch her skin or do something to trigger her?

Careful not to touch her, I step away from the bed, but the girl suddenly leaps toward me. Her arms come around my neck, squeezing it in a vice-like grip, while her legs wrap around my waist. I stand next to the bed, stunned, with the girl clinging to me like a baby koala. She tucks her face into the crook of my neck and is humming something. Now what? Should I try putting her back on the bed? Or should I just wait until she decides to get down?

I wait for a couple of moments to see if she'll let me go, but she clings to me relentlessly. It looks like I'm stuck with her like this for now. Carefully, I wrap one arm around her back and lean to take the package of painkillers the doc gave me from the nightstand. I put the medicine in the pocket of my pajama bottoms and place my hand under her thigh. Since she is still completely naked, I pull the blanket off the bed and cover her body, tucking the ends under her chin.

"Let's go get you some water," I say and head out of the bedroom.

I carry the girl into the kitchen. She doesn't let go while I get a bottle of water from the fridge and walk toward the cupboard to take a glass. I do it with one hand since I'm still holding her with the other one, afraid she might slip and fall.

"Want to come down and drink your water?" I ask.

She squeezes her arms tighter around my neck. I look at the glass I placed on the counter, then at the bottle standing next to it. Okay. I have no fucking idea what to do.

"Listen, mishka, the doctor said you need to drink something. Please don't make me force you."

The arms around my neck tighten, then loosen, and I carefully put her down. The girl stands in front of me, clutching the blanket with her hands. Her head is bent down, hair has fallen on either side of her face, hiding it from view.

"Here." I pass her the glass of water and take the medicine out of my pocket.

The second I place the pills on the counter, the girl abruptly steps back.

"They're painkillers. Look." I take two pills from the bottle, throw them into my mouth, and offer one to her.

She stares at the pill on my palm, steps backward again, and bumps into the kitchen island.

"Okay." I put the pill and the bottle on the counter and hold the glass of water out to her. "Just water. All of it, please."

When she drinks the water and hands the glass back to me, I nod and take it. "Good. Do you want to take a shower?"

The girl doesn't reply.

There isn't much light in the kitchen. I usually keep all the blinds down during the day because that's when I sleep. I tilt my head to the side, trying to gauge the look on her face. She seems confused. I know she can speak, so I don't understand why she's not answering any of my questions.

"Do you want to shower?" I try again.

She bites her lower lip and something close to frustration passes across her face, but she doesn't reply. Not even a nod. What am I going to do with her? There is mud on her right shoulder and arm, and some in her hair. Probably from when she fell on the street.

"All right, I'll take you to get a shower. Nod, mishka."

An exhale leaves the girl's lips, and she nods. I turn toward my bedroom, but immediately feel a tug on my T-shirt and throw a look over my shoulder. The girl is right behind me, holding the blanket with one hand and clutching the hem of my T-shirt in the other.

She follows me across the living room and into my bedroom, hanging on to my shirt all the way. When we reach the bathroom, I nod toward the cabinet on the right. "You'll find towels and some basic toiletries there."

The girl remains behind me, still gripping my shirt. I turn to leave, but a low whimper stops me in my tracks. When I look over my shoulder, I find the girl with her lips pressed tightly together and her eyes wide and searching my face.

"Want me to stay?" I ask.

She doesn't reply. Not that I expected her to. But her eyes peeking between the tangled dark strands and boring into mine say enough. Without thinking, I reach out to sweep the hair off her face, but abruptly pull my hand away when I realize what I'm doing.

"All right. I'll wait here." I face the door. "Let me know when you're done."

Nothing happens at first, but a couple of moments later she releases my T-shirt. I hear her pee and flush the toilet. The shower turns on shortly after.

I stare at the door in front of me, thinking. I'm no expert on mental health, but I know that her behavior is way off. It seems the total opposite of what I would expect from a woman who's experienced sexual assault. I assumed she wouldn't want to go within a ten-foot radius of an unknown man. I didn't expect this, and I'm not sure how to behave.

A sound of rapid breathing, like she's hyperventilating, reaches me. "Is everything okay?" I ask over my shoulder without looking toward the shower.

There is a sniff and more heavy breathing. I finally look inside the stall and see the girl sitting on the floor with the blanket still wrapped around her. She is frantically scrubbing the washcloth over the inside of her legs. The skin there is so red, it looks raw.

"Fuck." I dash across the bathroom, get into the shower, and crouch in front of her. "That's enough. You're clean." I take her hand and untangle her fingers from the washcloth. Almost reluctantly she lets it go, loosening her hold on the blanket at the same time. The wet mass falls off her shoulders. "It's okay."

The overhead spray is scorching hot as it rains down on us, but her body is shaking. I scoop her into my arms and step toward the bathroom vanity, carefully setting her down on the counter. The towel I used earlier is hanging on the wall next to me. I grab it and wrap it around her shoulders.

"Mishka, look at me," I say and grasp her chin between my fingers to tilt her head up. "I need to take off my T-shirt or I'll get you wet again."

My clothes are completely soaked, but I don't think it's a good idea to leave her here alone while I go to change.

"Is that okay?" I ask.

Her red-rimmed eyes regard me, and they're darting back and forth as if she wants to say something, but her lips remain sealed. Then, she parts them and sucks in a small breath, followed by the sound of her chattering teeth. The harsh LED light above the sink is shining directly onto her. I look over her small body wrapped in my towel and the dark brown hair hanging down around her face. I haven't had the opportunity to see her that well until now, and it strikes me how young she looks.

"Christ, baby. How old are you?" I whisper.

And, of course, there is no answer.

I grab a handful of the material of my T-shirt at my back and pull it over my head, dropping it to the floor. "Don't be scared. They're just tattoos," I say.

The girl's gaze moves to my torso as she takes in the multitude of grotesque scenes covering my skin. She squints and leans forward, examining the black shapes. Her gaze travels upward until her face is right in front of mine, two brown eyes staring me down.

"Can you please say something?" I ask. "Your name?"

Nothing.

"I'm Pavel. But people usually call me Pasha. It's a Russian nickname."

Her eyes widen at that, but she doesn't utter a word.

"Okay. Let's take you to bed and get you warm."

The moment the words leave my mouth, she clings to me again, wrapping her arms and legs as before. I pick up the towel that fell next to the sink, put it around her shoulders, and carry her to my bed.

"I need to change," I say as I cover the girl with a blanket. "I'll get you something to wear, too. Is a T-shirt okay?"

I don't know why I keep asking her questions when she never replies. After I have her tucked into bed, I cross the room and enter my walk-in closet. I change into dry pajama pants and put on another T-shirt, then I rummage around trying to find a smaller T-shirt. I know I have one that Kostya gave me a couple of years ago which was several sizes too small. He had it custom ordered with "Classy but Anal" printed on the front. Idiot.

There's a shuffling sound, and I look over my shoulder to find the girl standing in the doorway, with the blanket wrapped around her. She takes a step inside and looks at the shelf where I keep my T-shirts. There aren't that many, maybe ten in total. I only wear them when I work out. The rest of my wardrobe consists of underwear, pajama bottoms, dress shirts, and suits. I don't own any jeans, sweatshirts, or other casual clothes. I swore to myself years ago that I would never wear jeans again.

Her gaze falls to the bottom shelf where I keep my shoes, then shifts to the right where a rack runs the length of the space. There are at least thirty suits and twice that number of shirts hanging off it. The moment she sees this, she stiffens, takes two steps back, and dashes away.

I grab the first T-shirt off the shelf and exit the closet, finding the girl curled up on the bed with her back toward me.

"I'll leave this for you here," I say and put the folded shirt at the foot of the bed. She doesn't react.

I should get her something to eat, but it can wait. She needs sleep more. I take a seat on the edge of the bed, watching her small form. The edge of the blanket is pulled up all the way to her forehead. I reach out to place my hand on her back, over the blanket, and stroke it. She releases a small sigh and relaxes slightly under my palm. She's all the way on the other side of the bed, so I climb up and lie down a safe distance from her, and resume soothing her back.

Something warm presses into my side. I open my eyes and find the girl snuggled into me with her arm thrown over my chest and her face pressed to my upper arm. Seems like we both fell asleep. The clock on the wall across the room shows four p.m. Shit.

As carefully as possible, I untangle myself from the sleeping girl and head into the bathroom to get myself ready for work. When I emerge fifteen minutes later, she is still asleep. I consider waking her to let her know I have to leave but decide not to disturb her.

There isn't much in the kitchen or fridge because I usually order food or eat at work. I find some eggs, a loaf of bread and some marmalade, and place it all on the counter for her. With that done, I scribe a quick note saying I've gone to work and she should eat. Then, I leave it on the nightstand next to the bed. The blanket has slid from her body, so I cover her again, but instead of leaving right away, I watch her for several long moments.

Cold. So cold. I wrap the blanket tightly around myself and sit up in bed. There's no one around. Where is he? Maybe he's in another room. I listen for sounds, any sounds, but there is only silence. The floor lamp next to the bed is on, throwing light on a piece of paper lying on the nightstand. I take it and bring it closer to my face. I've been nearsighted all my life; I need to hold the note a foot in front of my eyes to be able to clearly make out the writing.

The note says he won't be back before late tonight. I put the paper back on the nightstand. He left me alone in his apartment. I shudder and wrap the blanket tighter around me. What time is it? How long will I have to wait until he's back? I scoot back in the bed until I'm huddled in the corner, wedged between the headboard and the wall, and close my eyes.

What the fuck is going on with me? When I woke up this morning, I felt completely fine until he mentioned my family. Just the idea of them finding out what happened to me made me lose it. It was as if I was suddenly thrown into a black abyss. The darkness is too familiar. It was the same void where I spent the last two months, completely detached from everything happening around me. Or to me. It felt like it would swallow me whole. Like invisible, poisonous gas, its toxic whisp encircled my mind, wanting me to let it inside. *Dirty*, it whispered. *Filthy. No one will ever want to touch you again.* But then, Pasha stroked my back. He didn't find me repulsive. The voices stopped, and the black hole closed.

I'm left with this strange conviction that it won't come back while he's nearby. But he's not here now.

*When your brother finds out what happened, he'll be disgusted,* the voice whispers in my ear. *He won't love you anymore. No one can love such a miserable creature. Letting strangers fuck you, while you did nothing to fight back. Repulsive.*

I breathe slowly in and out, trying to block it out. It doesn't work.

*It's all your fault. You brought this onto yourself. It was your decision to go with that guy.*

I drag my hands into my hair and squeeze as if pulling at the roots will rip the voice out of my head. But it continues.

*You thought he was nice. He was a sexual predator who raped you and threw you into a prostitution ring, and you found him nice! You're not capable of sound reasoning.*

I reach out to grab the note Pasha left and focus on the first couple of lines.

*"When you wake up, you can explore the apartment. I left some food on the counter in the kitchen. Eat."*

It's an instruction. Not a question. I don't have to make the decision myself. I just need to follow what he said. A sigh of relief leaves my lips. Clutching the note in my hand, I climb down off the bed and, taking the T-shirt he left, head out of the room.

Pasha's place is very upscale. Everything—from the modern dark furniture to the soft, thick carpets and heavy curtains—looks expensive. There is no clutter, no little trinkets on the shelves, or anything like that. I found two other bedrooms, significantly smaller than the one where I slept. They don't seem to be in use.

The living room is the largest space in the apartment, with a TV mounted on the wall and a couch and two recliners in front of it. I stand in the middle of the room and look around. One bookshelf. Several modern paintings on the walls. It's nice, but it all seems staged as if it's a setup for an interior design magazine or a showroom. It feels strange to be in a place like this.

At home, all our shelves and walls are covered with photos of Sienna and me, with a random one of Arturo when we managed to convince him to take a picture with us. Sienna's fashion magazines and my music sheets are strewn around. The throw pillows on the sofa are mismatched. There are dog toys everywhere. Random hair products and body balms usually litter strange places like the kitchen counter or the TV shelf. Something squeezes in my chest when I think about home. It seems foreign, somehow, as if my home belongs to someone else.

I clench the paper in my hand tighter and head into the kitchen. The countertops are shiny and black, with a glass stove that looks like it has never been used. The size of the black fridge seems like it could store enough food to last ten people a week, but when I open it, the only contents are several bottles of water, a carton of milk, three tomatoes, and an unopened pack of cheese.

The countertop runs the entire length of the wall, but the only item on it is a coffee machine. No spice jars, no holder for cups. Nothing. Just a coffee machine. On the island, he left out some breakfast food for me. Should I cook some eggs, or just have some marmalade on the bread? An unpleasant tingling spreads through my insides. It's either eggs or marmalade; I don't think I can eat both. But when I think about picking one, the anxiety in my stomach intensifies.

What the fuck is wrong with me that I can't make such an idiotically small decision? The same thing happened this morning when Pasha asked me if I wanted to take a shower. I was filthy. I needed a shower. But when he asked, I couldn't make the decision. I grab the edge of the island and stare at the stuff left out for me. Eggs or marmalade? It's a simple choice, damn it! Why can't I fucking decide?!

After twenty minutes of staring, I end up frying the eggs while eating a slice of bread with marmalade and feeling like an idiot the whole time.

At least the fever I had has passed.

By the time I'm finished with my meal, it's already dark outside, and I don't know what to do. The note said to explore and eat. Not what to do after that. I could go back to sleep or maybe read something. There is a bunch of books on the bookshelf in the living room. I can't watch TV without my glasses unless I stand right in front of it. Read? Sleep? I need to make a decision again, but I can't!

Grabbing the sides of my head, I pull on my hair and a frustrated whine leaves my lips. I read the last part of the note again.

*"I went to work and won't be back till 3 a.m. If you're thinking of running away, please don't. Wait until I'm back."*

He said to wait for him. Simple. Direct. Unquestionable. The pressure in my chest dissipates. I stand a couple of steps from the front door. And wait. Anyone looking at me now might think they are seeing a trained dog. I don't give a fuck. The only thing I care about at this moment is not feeling this overwhelming anxiety anymore. I'll deal with my fucked-up psyche some other day. I sit on the floor, wrap my arms around my legs, and stare at the front door.

My phone rings as I'm parking my car at the end of the long row of vehicles pulled up in front of the pakhan's house. The last in line is a big red bike. Something major must be up since Roman's called the top brass, including Sergei. I grab the phone from the passenger seat and take the call.

"Doc?"

"I have the girl's results. As far as STDs are concerned, she's clean. Negative on the pregnancy, too. The bloodwork shows she's a bit anemic, but that's it."

"What about the drugs?"

"Well, that's the interesting part. The substance found in her system isn't listed. It looks like it may be something new, something that hasn't hit the mainstream, yet."

"That's strange."

"Wait, there's more. The test came back on the pills Vladimir dropped off the other day. It's the same stuff."

"Are you sure?"

"Yes."

"Did you tell Roman?"

"I did. Just got off from the call with him."

I stiffen. "So . . . you told him about the girl?"

"Of course. Why? Should I not have?"

"Nope, just asking," I say and squeeze the steering wheel until my knuckles go white. The fact that he told Roman about the girl doesn't sit well with me, and that doesn't make sense. I've never felt the need to hide anything from the pakhan.

"How is she?" the doc continues. "Did her family come to get her?"

"She's still at my place."

"What? Why didn't you call her parents or someone?"

"She won't talk. In fact, she hasn't said a word."

"Shit. She must be scared shitless. We should have had Varya stay with her until her family is able to come. You should probably stay away while she's there."

"About that." I rub my neck. "She doesn't seem scared of me. She's actually been glued to my side since the moment she woke up this morning. Won't let me leave her sight. She even insisted I stay in the bathroom while she took a shower."

"Hmm. This isn't my specialty, but I do know that assault victims can react in multiple ways. Does she flinch when you come close?"

"When I tried to leave the room to get her a glass of water, she screamed and jumped into my arms. Naked," I say. "Do you have any advice on what I should do? How to behave until I can reach her family?"

"No idea. I'm not a psychologist. But, I'll make a few calls and let you know what I find out."

"Thanks, Doc."

I put the phone in my jacket and look down at my watch. I shouldn't have left her alone, but all this is new to me. I've never had anyone to worry about. Never had to take care of someone. And no one ever took care of me, so I haven't a clue what I'm doing.

As I assumed, almost everyone from the Bratva's top circle is here.

The head of security, Dimitri, is standing next to Roman's desk, while Mikhail is sitting in the chair near the window. Mikhail oversees the transport operations involving the Bratva's drug products, and he's also in charge of information extraction. In other words—torture, when necessary. Sergei, the pakhan's half brother, is leaning on the wall beside the door, flipping a knife blade in his hands. He handles the negotiations with our suppliers and buyers. And kills them occasionally.

"Fyodor's daughter, Ruslana, has been found dead," Maxim, the second in command, says and places a yellow folder in front of Roman. "The body was found in a dumpster in the suburbs. Some homeless man stumbled upon it."

"Cause of death?" Roman asks.

"Suspected overdose."

"Ruslana was a good kid. Sophomore in college. It doesn't sound like her to get mixed up with drugs." Roman nods toward the folder. "When did she go missing?"

"Last month. Her father said she went to a store and never came back."

"Did he file a missing person's report?"

"Yes. Nothing came of it. It was as if she fell off the earth. But that's not the strangest thing." Maxim takes a piece of paper out of the folder and passes it to Roman. "Here's the medical examiner's report. She was high on heroin, but they also found traces of an unidentified substance. I pulled some strings and had the results cross-checked against the pills taken from the dealer at Ural. Same thing."

After a brief scan of the contents, Roman asks. "You think the heroin is a cover-up?"

"Probably." He nods.

"Drugs are not ice cream. You can't just whip up a new flavor in someone's kitchen." Roman drums his fingers on the desk and looks at Mikhail who is sitting to my right. "Did you get anything from the dealer Pavel caught?"

"He just kept repeating what he told Pasha," Mikhail says. "A friend gave him the pills in exchange for debt forgiveness. He didn't know how his friend got the drugs or what they were. We have nothing, just the name of this friend. But, it seems his buddy has disappeared. Yuri has men keeping their eyes on his place. As soon as he surfaces, they will bring him in."

I watched Mikhail work over a guy once a few years back. He made torture into an art form. If Mikhail couldn't extract anything else from the dealer, it means there wasn't anything left.

Roman sets the folder aside and leans forward, placing his elbows on the desk. "Now, onto the second issue. What the fuck is wrong with you all—collecting random unconscious women and taking them home with you?"

All heads turn toward Sergei who is sitting on my right.

"Oh, don't look at me!" He laughs, "I got mine years ago and I'm done."

"And don't we all remember the monumental fuckup that resulted in?" Roman snaps. "The speculations are still rampant all over Mexico about what happened to the Sandoval compound. Some people don't believe the bullshit that the government is pushing about it being an earthquake, and think it was a meteorite strike instead."

"Well, since Pasha doesn't know shit about explosives, I'd say we're good." Sergei smirks at me. "Wanna share something about the girl Roman told me you have at home?"

Everyone's attention immediately switches to me.

"I have no idea who she is. She won't talk," I say. "But when I found her, she was spiked with the same crap that was being peddled at Ural."

"I need updates on this new drug," Roman says. "I want to know who's making it and for what purpose. And I want them dealt with. Fyodor's daughter was a good kid. Everyone who was in any way involved in her death will pay for it. In blood."

He jerks his head toward the door, which means the meeting is over. Kostya and Mikhail leave the office first, and the rest of us follow.

I'm crossing the foyer toward the front door when I hear high-pitched, female screams. I turn around, spotting Kostya cowering in the corner, protectively holding his hands over his head. Olga and Valentina have him pinned, crying and hitting him with kitchen rags. Looks like they still haven't gotten over the fact that he broke up with both of them. The poor bastard had to move out of the mansion on the same day he told them they were done to avoid bodily harm. I leave Kostya to his misery and head outside.

My phone rings as I'm getting into my car. It's the doc.

"Where are you?"

“Just leaving the pakhan’s house, heading to Ural,” I say. “Why?”

“I just spoke with a friend who’s a psychologist. She often works with assault victims. I explained the situation to her and told her about the girl’s behavior.”

“And?” I switch the phone to hands-free and put the car in reverse. “Did she have any idea what’s going on?”

“She wasn’t surprised and surmised that the girl has developed an attachment to you,” he says. “Apparently, some assault victims tend to stay away from men. Especially strangers, but sometimes even family members. Others, however, form a strong bond to whomever has saved them. They latch onto their protector, even if it’s a male.”

“I don’t understand,” I say.

“The trauma of being sexually assaulted is an experience filled with violence. It transforms a person’s sense of safety, the way they look at the world, and their relationships with other people. Looks like this girl started to associate the feeling of safety with you. She sees the rest of the world as unsafe. As her savior, you’ve become her ‘safe place.’ ”

“I didn’t save her. She saved herself. Ran out of that building.”

“Realistically speaking, yes. But in her eyes, you’re the one who saved her. We don’t know how long she was held captive and sexually assaulted. You taking her to your place could be the first time she’s felt safe in days. Weeks. Maybe months.”

“Jesus fuck.”

“Go home. Talk to her. She needs professional help, and she needs her family,” he says in a grave voice. “And she shouldn’t be left alone.”

As soon as I cut the connection, I call Ivan and send him to Ural. It’s an hour-long drive from Roman’s to my place, and the whole time I mull over what the doc had said. I should have stayed with the girl. What if she woke up and was scared because I was gone? No one in their right mind would have left the girl in that state alone in a strange place. I wasn’t thinking.

I hit the steering wheel with my hand and press the gas pedal harder.

When I open the front door, it’s pitch black inside. Could she still be sleeping? I reach for the switch, turn on the lights, and stop dead in my tracks. The girl is sitting on the floor a few paces from the door with her arms wrapped around her legs. Her body is shaking uncontrollably.

"Shit." I crouch down beside her, intending to scoop her up, but as soon as I reach for her, she leaps into my arms. Wrapping herself around me like a koala bear again, she buries her face in the crook of my neck.

Holding on under her thighs, I carry the girl to my bedroom. My intention to gently lower her onto the bed doesn't go as planned when her arms and legs squeeze me in a tight hold.

"I'm so sorry for leaving you alone," I whisper and sit down on the edge of the bed.

There is a bundled blanket next to me, so I reach for it and wrap it around the girl's shoulders. She doesn't move, just clings onto me, still shaking.

"You're safe." I place my hand on her nape and stroke her back with my other one in what I hope is a soothing motion. "You're safe."

A small sigh leaves her lips, and her body relaxes in my arms. I keep up my comforting strokes for at least half an hour before she lifts her head off my shoulder. I reach for the lamp next to the nightstand, turning the dimmer switch to bring up the lights a bit more. The girl blinks a couple of times, probably adjusting to the sudden brightness, then looks right into my eyes.

"Feeling better?" I ask.

She doesn't reply, just stares at my face for a couple of seconds. Dear God, she is so damn young. She uncoils her arms from around my neck and trails her hands over my shoulders and down my chest, stopping at the lapels of my suit jacket. Her eyes snap down to where her hands are, and her body suddenly goes rigid. I follow her gaze and see that it's focused on my tie. She starts shaking again and a whimper leaves her lips.

"What's wrong?"

The girl's breathing becomes faster and shallower, and her eyes keep staring at my tie in horror.

"Look at me." I cup her face with my palms and tilt her head up until our gazes connect. There's panic in her dark brown eyes. "Good. Now, breathe."

She tries, but her breath hitches. Another try. Her lower lip trembles, and I hear a soft whisper but can't make out what she's saying.

"I didn't hear you, baby. Can you try again?"

She closes her eyes and leans forward. Her words are faint next to my ear, "They always . . . wore suits."

It takes me a few seconds to understand what she's referring to. The moment I do, a cold chill runs down my spine. She said "they." Plural. I thought she may have been in an abusive relationship with some psycho who drugged her.

I let go of her face and quickly remove my jacket, throwing it toward the middle of the room where she won't see it. Then, I start undoing my tie. The girl looks down, her gaze locking onto my hands as I'm pulling at the knot, and the shaking in her body intensifies.

"Look at me." I manage to form the words, speaking evenly so I don't frighten her. It's difficult because the anger raging inside of me is threatening to erupt. "Look at my eyes. Good girl. I'm throwing it away, okay?" I let the tie fall to the floor.

The moment the tie is out of view, her body relaxes a bit, but she's still shaking.

"Shirt as well?" I ask, and without waiting for the answer, I start on the buttons.

The girl bites her lower lip and nods.

"Okay, baby." I undo the last button and yank off the shirt. "Better?"

I stare into her red-rimmed eyes, and God, she seems so lost. She looks down again and slowly places her hand on my naked chest. The tip of her finger moves across my collarbone where my tattoos start, then slowly traces downward. It's a barely there touch, outlining the shapes inked on my skin.

"I'm afraid I can't remove these, mishka," I say.

Her eyes lift back to mine, and as she watches me, the corners of her lips curve upward ever so slightly.

"Is that a smile?"

She shrugs.

It was a tiny smile, but a smile nevertheless. It completely transforms her face, giving me a glimpse of the woman she was before everything that happened to her.

"What's your name, baby?"

The need to know her name, the tiniest of details about her, has been eating me alive.

"It's Asya," she says in a small voice. Unusual name.

"Asya," I try it out. It fits her. "It's a very pretty name. And your last name?"

"DeVille," she whispers.

I raise my eyebrows. "You're Italian?"

She nods.

The last name sounds familiar, but I can't place it. "Are you from Chicago?"

"New York."

The moment she says it, the realization comes. "Are you related to Arturo DeVille?"

"He's my brother." She bites her lip. "You know Arturo?"

The underboss of the New York Cosa Nostra Family. Shit. I haven't met Arturo DeVille, but Roman always makes sure the Bratva has intel on each and every person connected to us in any way.

"I'm a member of the Russian Bratva, mishka. Your don's wife is the sister to the wife of one of our enforcers," I say. "We need to call your brother right away and let him know you're here."

Asya's body goes stone-still. "Please . . . don't."

"Why?" I ask as nausea suddenly comes over me. "Does he have something to do with what happened to you?"

She shakes her head, then wraps her arms around my neck and snuggles into my chest. "He probably thinks I'm dead. I want to keep it that way."

"But, he's your brother. He's probably going nuts with worry." I pass my hand through her dark brown strands. "You need to tell him you're okay."

"I'm not fucking okay!" she snaps, then climbs down off my lap and pins me with her gaze. "Those people have been pumping me full of drugs and selling my body for months. And I let them! I did nothing! What kind of pitiful being just lets that happen without fighting back?"

She's crying while yelling. And I let her. Anger is good. Any kind of reaction is good. So, I don't make a move. Don't try to calm her down. I just sit on the edge of the bed and watch her in silence.

"Do you know that last night, when you found me, was the first time I tried to run away?" she continues. "You want me to tell my brother that? He raised me better than to be a fucking doormat! I would rather never see him again than have him learn what I allowed them to turn me into!"

She takes a deep breath and grabs my shirt off the floor near her feet. Stepping onto the edge of it she uses both hands to pull on the material, throwing her whole weight into her task, until the shirt rips. Then, she starts shredding it. I watch her in amazement. I thought she was meek and delicate, but as I observe her glorious rage, I realize how very wrong I was. There is fire in her and fierce life. The people who hurt her, who broke her spirit—they haven't banished it completely. And I will find every single one of them and make them pay.

"I hate them! I hate them so much!" she roars and looks up at me. "And you? Why the fuck are you just sitting there? How can you simply be watching me have a mental breakdown and do nothing?" She throws a torn piece of material in my face and screams in frustration when I don't make a move. "What the fuck is wrong with you?" She places her hands on my chest and shoves me. "Shouldn't you try to calm me down?"

"No," I say.

"No? You'll just watch me fall apart?" she shoves at me again. Then one more time.

"You're not falling apart, Asya." I reach out and trace the line of her chin with my thumb. "You're pulling yourself together."

"Pulling together?" Her eyes widen, and she bursts into a fit of hysteric laughter. "When I woke up, I couldn't decide if I should eat the eggs or marmalade! I couldn't make the most basic decision. I spent twenty minutes staring at the stuff you left out on the counter and had to eat both because I couldn't choose!"

The last words get lost in a fit of crying. Her shoulders sag and she looks down at her bare feet. Placing my forefinger under her chin, I tilt her head up until our eyes meet.

"What do you want?" I ask.

She blinks at me, and two tears slide down her cheeks.

"Do you want them dead?"

There is a sharp intake of breath, but she doesn't reply. I reformulate my question into a statement.

"You want them dead."

Squeezing her lips tightly together, she nods.

"They will die," I say. "What else do you want?"

No reply.

"You don't want your family to see you like this."

Another nod.

"I'll never be the person I was before," she whispers.

"No. You won't." I lightly pinch her chin. "And that's okay. They'll love you just the same. What happened to you, changed you, Asya. It would change anyone. Irrevocably. You need to accept the person you've become. You're still you. Changed, yes, but that shouldn't keep you from the people who care about you."

She sniffs and climbs back onto my lap. Again her limbs wrap around me, and she buries her face in the crook of my neck. Barely audible murmurs escape her lips, and I tilt my head to the side to hear her better. Once she's done, I stare at the far bedroom wall for a long time, thinking about what she just asked of me.

If Roman finds out, it won't end well. We've been maintaining a good relationship with the Cosa Nostra, but if I let her stay, it may mean war. And if Asya's brother finds out, he will probably kill me.

I inhale and nod. "Okay, mishka. You can stay."

# Chapter Three

Asya

"IS MARMALADE OKAY?" PASHA ASKS AND PLACES THE JAR ON THE counter.

I grip the hem of his T-shirt harder as he turns to face me.

"I don't have anything else here, but I'll run to the store later and buy more food. I rarely eat at home. We'll order some clothes for you, too."

I tilt my head up and find him watching me. "Thank you."

I'm wearing another of his T-shirts with nothing underneath. No panties. No bra, either. It feels strange.

When I woke up this morning, I had a fever again. Pasha wrapped me in a blanket and pulled me against his chest. We lay in his bed for what felt like hours until my body finally stopped shaking. He carried me into the bathroom and stayed there while I did my business and took a shower. After I brushed my teeth, he wrapped me in a fluffy towel and led me back to bed, where I waited with my eyes glued to the bathroom door while he had a shower.

"Do you want coffee?"

I look at the coffee machine, feeling like the most pathetic being on earth. "I don't know."

Pasha's palm gently presses against my back, moving up and down in a soothing motion. I take a deep breath and look up to find him watching me. There is no reluctance in his eyes. No reproach. And no pity.

"Did you drink coffee before?"

"No," I whisper.

"How about tea? I have chamomile, I think." He opens the cupboard, takes out a metal container and places it in front of me.

I just stare at it.

He lifts my chin with his finger. "Did you like drinking tea, Asya?"

"Yes."

"Let's assume you still do." He smiles, and it's so beautiful. "What did you like to eat for breakfast before?"

"Cereal with raisins," I say. "Sometimes, I'd have some with chocolate chunks instead."

"Then I'll buy a few of those. How about other food? What were your favorite dishes? Were you allergic to anything?"

I sniff, trying to stifle the urge to cry. He's asking the questions in a way that makes it easier for me to answer. He's not asking me to pick, which would raise my anxiety, but rather asking me about facts.

"I never liked broccoli or green peas. Everything else was okay with me," I say. "No food allergies."

"Did you prefer ordering takeout or cooking for yourself?"

"I liked cooking."

He nods. "Make me a list of ingredients, and I'll go to the grocery store tomorrow. We'll order something to eat today, but tomorrow, you can prepare one of your dishes."

I bite my lower lip. That would require picking one of many.

"How about lasagna for tomorrow? I don't think I've ever tried one. Did you like making lasagna?"

The weight pressing on my chest dissipates. I nod.

"Good. I'll go get my phone so you can make that list for me, but first, let's have some breakfast. Okay?"

"Okay."

I follow him around the kitchen as he puts the kettle on to boil and takes out the bread. He spreads the marmalade methodically, making sure it's evenly distributed over the whole slice.

There is a multitude of small scars that cover his knuckles. His hands and fully inked arms seem at odds with the posh, almost clinically impeccable surroundings. I take the opportunity to inspect his face a bit better, including his strong jaw and sharp cheekbones, noticing a few scars on his forehead and several more on his chin, too. Finally, I peer at his eyes. I can't make out their color, however, since he towers over me by at least a foot.

Pasha stops what he's doing and looks down at me. Why are his eyes so sad? I let go of his T-shirt and place my palm over his forearm. The muscles under my fingers tense, and I expect him to pull away, but he doesn't.

I tighten my hold on him and lean into his side to get closer to the warmth of his big body. The faint sound of music reaches me. Someone, a neighbor probably, must have turned the TV too loud, and without thinking about it, I hum along to the tune.

## Pavel

Asya is bundled under the covers. I gave her an extra blanket when she wouldn't stop shivering earlier. She is asleep now, while I'm still awake, listening to her breathing.

She was okay this morning, but after lunch she got sick, and we barely managed to get to the bathroom in time. I held her hair while she emptied her stomach into the toilet, then helped her brush her teeth and carried her to the bed. Her fever spiked again, but it wasn't as bad as it was the first time. I don't have a thermometer, so I kept pressing the back of my hand to her forehead every five minutes, but it seemed like her temperature was only slightly elevated. The fever broke an hour ago, and she finally stopped tossing in bed.

I reach for my phone on the nightstand and type a message to Kostya, asking about the situation at the clubs. A minute later, I receive the reply—a bunch of Russian curses and wishes for my slow and painful demise. Apparently, he's not happy about having to fill in for me.

When I called the pakhan earlier today and asked for a few days off, I suggested having Ivan take over. Roman laughed and said he'd give the clubs to Kostya because it was time for him to start doing actual work instead of only chasing women and burning rubber on a regular basis.

Kostya started working alongside his brother, helping with the Bratva finances when he was barely twenty, but he's always been a problem child. Roman has a soft spot for him, though, since Kostya's the youngest in the inner circle. I guess we all do. Kostya is like everyone's little brother, and he shamelessly uses that to his advantage, constantly getting off the hook because of his age. Hopefully, he won't get any crazy ideas while he's filling in for me. If he decides to transform my clubs into strip clubs, I'm going to strangle him.

Asya stirs next to me, and I quickly feel her forehead. No fever, thank fuck. When I pull my fingers away, she grabs my hand and lays it on her chest. It looks like I'll be sleeping in the same bed with her again. I sprawl out next to her and watch her face. I kind of understand her reasoning for not letting me call her brother, but then again, I don't understand it at all. Wouldn't it be easier for her to be back home with her family? I've never experienced family dynamics, but I'm sure her brother and sister would do a much better job than me.

I reach out and turn off the lamp, closing my eyes. But sleep evades me. How did Asya end up in Chicago? Who are the people who took and kept her? Is there a connection to Fyodor's daughter? I have so many questions and zero answers.

Tilting my head to the side, I watch Asya's sleeping form. She's still clutching my hand in her own. I need to buy groceries first thing in the morning. I can't have her eat bread and marmalade three days in a row. I need to get some toiletries for her, as well. And clothes. But I kinda like her in my T-shirts.

A brown strand of hair has fallen over her face, so I reach out and carefully move it. Why did I let her stay?

# Chapter four

Pavel

I STAND IN FRONT OF THE BATHROOM MIRROR. GRAY JEANS AND A BLACK T-shirt are lying folded on the counter next to the sink. They disgust me. I don't recall how long it's been since I've worn jeans, probably more than a decade.

It's not the garments themselves that are the problem, but rather the memories of digging through heaps of discarded clothes, mostly jeans, trying to find something that fit. Everything was always torn and dirty, and I didn't have the money for laundry before putting them on. People avoided me when I took the subway, making my shame nearly palpable.

The moment I started earning serious money through underground fights, I traded in my entire secondhand wardrobe for slacks and dress shirts. Eventually, I switched to suits. As time went on, I switched to more upscale clothes and added expensive watches and other accessories. It was all a means to forgetting what I had been for the first twenty years of my life. Trash. Someone from whom people would quickly turn away, ignoring my presence. The funny thing is, even though it has been nearly fifteen years, I can still smell the stench, whether from the clothes or the half-rotten food I dug out of the dumpsters in alleys behind restaurants, that always surrounded me.

I look at my face in the mirror, regarding the small scars scattered across my temples, the bridge of my nose, and my chin. They are faded now, barely noticeable, but I can still recall the fights that left me with each mark. I'm not even sure how many times my nose has been broken. Seven? Probably more.

I was barely eighteen when I started fighting for money. At first, it was a way to put food in my mouth, but as time passed, it transformed into something else. The people who came to watch, who chanted my name . . . they fed the deep yearning I've always felt in my soul. The need to belong. Somewhere. Anywhere. The excitement of the crowd as it cheered for me, made me feel less alone.

I'm not exactly sure why I said yes when Yuri approached me after one of my fights and offered me a position in the Bratva. Maybe I wanted to feel closer to my heritage. There weren't any Russian kids in the foster homes when I was growing up. By the time I aged out of the system, I had almost forgotten my mother tongue. Years with the Bratva helped me regain it, so I have no trouble with the language anymore. But it's not the same. It no longer feels like my first language, but neither does English.

I trace the more prominent scar on the left side of my jaw with my index finger. No matter how hard I try to hide the past, some reminders, visible or not, will always remain.

Is that why I let Asya stay? Maybe, I recognized a kindred spirit trying to outrun the past and wanted to help. After all, I know how it feels to not have anyone to turn to. But I'm afraid that it's only part of the reason. My true motivation is much, much more selfish. I've been alone all my life and have gotten used to it. It's the way I function. But after Asya stumbled onto my path, I realized how lonely I'd been and how much I enjoy having her here, in my home. I relish the comfort her presence brings me. Crave it, in fact, so much so that I agreed to hide the reality that she's alive from her family.

I reach out and pick up the jeans. It's one of five pairs I ordered online yesterday after I realized the effect suits had on Asya. I can't keep walking around in my pajamas all day, and I definitely can't wear them out to the store.

Taking a deep breath, I put on the jeans.

At least fifteen bags line the counter in a perfect row. Pasha bought way too much stuff.

When he returned from the store an hour ago, he had to go back to the car twice to bring everything up. After he placed the last bag at the end of the long line, he asked me to put away the groceries he brought and to make lunch. Then, he took his laptop and, saying he has some work to do, disappeared into his bedroom.

I unpack the groceries from the first bag, leaving the things I need for lasagna on the kitchen island and storing the rest. I should have been more specific with my grocery list. I assumed he'd get whatever brand of pasta or tomato sauce he comes across first, but instead, he must have purchased every kind available in the store. There are four different brands of lasagna noodles, three tomato sauces, six types of other pasta, and at least ten varieties of cheeses inside the first few bags.

I pull the cereal boxes from the next three bags and count them. There are twelve different kinds: oats, soya, wheat, some with dried fruit or raisins, one is with honey, others include chocolate, and a couple more with almonds.

I glance over my shoulder at the bedroom door. I hoped Pasha would stay in the kitchen or the living room, but he hasn't returned. However, even when he's not in the same room with me, knowing he's here, makes the dreadful voice in my head retreat.

After I'm done putting away the groceries, I look at the last few bags on the counter. They are big boutique bags with wide ribbon handles. Pasha said he would buy something for me to wear. I expected some sweatpants and a few T-shirts, but the bags in front of me are stacked full of clothes. Should I unpack these? He only mentioned the groceries when he asked me to put away the things he bought. I turn around and move to the kitchen island to prepare the lasagna.

Making lunch while only wearing someone else's T-shirt and nothing underneath is weird. Especially in a kitchen belonging to a man I don't really know. Weird, but at the same time liberating. I focus on the task in front of me while a faint melody plays in the back of my mind.

"No, you can't bring the buyers to Ural, Sergei," I say into the phone and sigh.

"Why the hell not? Did you look outside? It's fucking freezing. My balls are going to fall off if I take them to the unheated warehouse and have to listen to their rambling for more than ten minutes."

"The last time you conducted a meeting in my club, the cleaning crew spent two hours trying to wash away the blood and brain matter from the VIP booth."

"That was years ago, Pasha!" he barks. "And you changed the upholstery to dark leather last month. Washing the blood off that is a piece of cake."

"I said no."

"*Mudak*," he mumbles and hangs up.

I shake my head and switch back to the liquor order I've been reviewing on my laptop. Since I won't be heading to the club, I had to take care of the most pressing matters and brief Kostya on the rest. He might be good with numbers, but logistics is not his strong suit. I glance at the time in the corner of the screen and see that it's just after noon. I should check on Asya again.

I've been holed up at the desk in my bedroom for the past three hours, but I've been taking peeks at Asya every fifteen minutes to make sure she's okay. She seemed immersed in cooking lunch, and her relaxed posture said she was enjoying the process. The last time I checked on her, I heard her humming a complicated tune. I expect to find her buzzing around the kitchen this time too, however, she's nowhere in sight.

"Asya?" I call as I hurry across the living room, but there is no answer.

I pass by the dining table, where plates and salad bowls are set for two. A big tray of lasagna, cut into squares, sits between them. I round the kitchen island and come to a halt. Asya is sitting on the floor with her back pressed to the cupboard, arms wrapped tightly around her legs. She's staring at the window on the far wall with panic in her eyes.

"Asya?" I crouch next to her and place my hand on the back of her neck. "What's wrong?"

"It's . . . snowing," she whispers, eyes locked onto the scene before her.

"You don't like snow?" I ask.

"Not anymore," comes her barely audible answer.

"Asya, give me your eyes, baby." I brush my thumb down her cheek. "Please."

She takes a deep breath, then turns her head. There's such a haunted look in her eyes. Seeing it hits me right in the chest.

"I'm going to pull down the blinds," I say. "Okay?"

"Okay."

Quickly closing the blinds in the kitchen, I head to the living room to pull the heavy curtains over the windows there and rush back. Asya hasn't moved, but now she's staring at the floor.

"I'm sorry," she mumbles and looks up at me with watery eyes.

I crouch in front of her and cup her face between my palms. "You have nothing to be sorry for."

"I'm such a spineless person," she says and presses her lips tightly together.

I lean forward until my face is only inches from hers. "You're reacting because of the reminders. Your mind is being triggered by various things, but it doesn't mean you're weak. Do you understand?"

She sighs and closes her eyes. Something breaks inside me to see her so defeated. I grit my teeth. I need to stay calm for Asya's sake now, but eventually, I'm going to annihilate the sons of bitches who did this to her.

"Mishka. Look at me."

Her eyes open.

"You are not weak," I say. "And you will fight and get better. I promise."

She watches me for a few moments, then leans forward so her mouth is right next to my ear, sliding out of my hold in the process.

"I killed a man," she whispers. "That night, I escaped. I killed my client."

I bite down to hold my rage inside. "Good," I say through gritted teeth.

"I don't regret it. I should. But I don't." Her arm comes around my neck as she presses her cheek to mine. "Does that make me a bad person?"

"No. You defended yourself from a sexual predator who violated you in the most terrible way. In fact, you did him a favor."

"A favor?"

"Yes. Because if you hadn't killed him, I would have. And believe me, whatever you did wouldn't even come close to what I would have done to him." I squeeze the back of her neck lightly. "Come show me what you prepared. It's the first time someone has cooked for me."

Asya leans back, her face right in front of mine again, and places her hand against my cheek. "Thank you. For everything."

# CHAPTER *five*

Asya

I PUT ON THE PAJAMAS PASHA BOUGHT FOR ME AND LOOK AT MYSELF in the bathroom mirror. The top is not that bad, maybe a size or two too big. The bottoms are a different story. I had to roll the waist and cuff the legs more than twice to make sure they'd stay on and I wouldn't trip while walking. I checked the label and saw that it's size medium. I usually wear extra small.

The rest of the clothes he got lie folded on the long counter next to the sink. All of them are mediums, too. Either Pasha has never shopped for female clothes, or he can't guess sizes that well. I noticed two empty shelves in the cabinet at the other end of the bathroom, so I put the clothes there. I don't want to intrude on his space any more than I already have. I still can't believe he's let me stay.

When I exit the bathroom, Pasha is stepping out of his closet, wearing dark gray pajama bottoms and a black T-shirt.

"I'll leave the door open," he says. "If you need anything, I'll be in the room across the hall."

My body goes rigid upon hearing his words. Wrapping my arms around my middle, I nod and head toward the bed.

"Asya? Is everything okay?"

"Yeah." I climb in bed and turn to face the wall, pulling the blanket all the way up to my chin.

The room falls silent for a moment, but then I hear the sound of bare feet approaching.

"What's wrong?"

I grip the blanket in my hand. "Can you sleep here again?"

"Here? In this bed?"

"Please."

He doesn't say anything. I squeeze my eyes shut, hating myself for asking him. He probably thinks I'm a weakling. As if usurping his life and his space is not enough, I'm asking him to keep sleeping in the same bed with me. I open my mouth to tell him I've changed my mind when the bed dips behind me.

I slide my hands under the pillow, hoping it will stop me from turning toward him and snuggling into his chest. This inexplicable pull I feel toward him confuses me, but it also makes me feel disgusted with myself. I've been assaulted and used in the most degrading ways, so what I should be feeling toward Pasha and any other man is loathing, fear, and repulsion. Instead, I'm attracted to him. But the entire time I've been here, he hasn't once tried anything, hasn't touched me in any way that could be considered sexual.

*It's because you're filthy,* the voice in my mind whispers. *Spoiled goods no man would ever want to touch. How many dicks have been inside your pussy? Too many to count?*

I turn my face into the pillow. I need it to stop!

*You know what you are? A slut. A dirty, filthy whore.*

Pasha's thick arm wraps around my waist and pulls me into his body until my back is pressed to his chest.

"Talk to me," he says into my hair.

A shudder passes through my body because of his closeness, and it's not a bad shudder.

"Why didn't you call my brother and get rid of me?" I ask.

"Because I understand the need to deal with your shit yourself. And because I know how it feels to have people get rid of you." The arm around my waist tightens. "I would never do that to anyone."

"You're holed up here with me. Don't you need to go to work?"

"I had someone fill in for me. But I'll have to go for a meeting with the pakhan tomorrow. I won't be long."

My body stiffens as panic rises in the pit of my stomach. It's completely unnatural, the way I have become attached to him, but I can't shake off the feeling of dread that forms from the idea of him not being nearby.

"Okay," I whisper.

"Will you reconsider talking to the psychiatrist?"

I squeeze my lips together and shake my head. Pasha has been trying to convince me to talk with the mental health doctor since this morning. He said she has experience with cases like mine. I can't do it. The thought of talking about it with anyone other than Pasha makes me sick.

"All right, mishka. Let's give it a few more days."

"Does it mean something? Mishka?"

"A bear cub."

He calls me a bear cub. What a strange endearment. I turn my head to look at him. "Is it because I like clinging to you?"

"Yeah." He lifts his hand as if he's going to touch my face, but pulls back. "Let's go to sleep."

I nod and turn back to the wall, pretending I'm trying to sleep. I can't get over the fact that he said yes when I asked him if I can stay instead of sending me back to my family. It was so outrageous, I was a 100 percent sure he'd refuse. He didn't. And I still find it hard to believe that he agreed not to tell anyone who I am.

A light touch grazes the back of my head. I'm not sure what it is, but it seems like a kiss.

# Chapter Six

## Pavel

"Is that girl still at your place?" Roman asks as soon as I enter his office.

"Yes." I nod and take a seat next to Maxim.

"Good. You need to ask her how she got the drugs. Yuri still can't locate the guy who supplied the pills, so your girl is our only lead."

I meet my pakhan's gaze and shake my head. "No."

"No?" He widens his eyes at me.

"If she tells me something herself, I'll let you know. But I'm not making her talk unless she wants to."

"Why wouldn't she?"

"Doc hasn't told you?" I ask.

"Told me what? He said you found the girl, she overdosed, and you took her home."

"She was sexually abused, Roman. I think the people who had her were running a prostitution ring."

Roman stares at me, a muscle ticking in his jaw. The pen in his hands snaps in two. The topic of abused women has always been a sensitive subject where he's concerned.

"Is the girl okay?" he asks through clenched teeth.

"She's better."

"Good. Don't ask her anything." He nods and turns his attention to Maxim. "What's the issue with the Albanians you wanted to discuss?"

Maxim takes off his glasses and crosses his arms over his chest. "It seems like they have suddenly obtained a huge amount of money. One of Anton's guys reported that he saw Dushku's son-in-law spending an insane sum at one of the Cosa Nostra casinos."

"How much?"

"Tens of thousands per night. Several nights in a row."

"Julian is an idiot who never earned a cent himself. He's been milking money off Dushku for years."

"Well, it looks like he suddenly has more than he can spend," Maxim says. "Could he be involved in this new drug thing?"

"He better not be. Because if anyone from the Albanian crime organization dared to bring their drugs into my territory, they won't be liking the consequences of their decision. I made things very clear to Dushku when we had our little chat a few months ago after the fuckup with the Irish."

"What happened with the Irish?" I ask. Since I'm mostly focused on running the clubs, I'm not always up-to-date on other business issues. The latest thing concerning the Irish I remember is that they tried to wipe out the Bratva a few years back and almost killed Kostya. Sergei eliminated their leader and several other top-tier men, and Roman threw the rest out of Chicago.

"They've set up base in New York," Roman says. "Don Ajello sent me a message a few months ago, saying that Dushku started collaborating with the Irish and delivered a large shipment of guns to them. Dushku did this despite knowing very well my stance on the Irish."

"Was it only one shipment?" I ask. "Or does Dushku still work with them?"

"Just one. Shortly after that, Ajello took care of the Irish because the idiot Fitzgerald kidnapped his wife. Ajello went ballistic."

"He killed Fitzgerald?"

"Filleted him with a knife himself." Roman grins. "I don't know the man, but I like him already."

"What do you plan on doing with the Albanians, Roman?" Maxim throws in.

"Do we have anyone inside who can keep an eye on what they are doing? We need to know where that money came from."

"One of the Baykal waitresses visits Dushku regularly," I say. "Maybe she can persuade him to talk about his business."

"Let's try that for now." He nods. "If it does end up that Dushku is behind this, I'm going to personally gut him."

As I exit my car, heading to the front of my apartment building, I notice a familiar vehicle parked outside the entrance. Yuri is sitting behind the wheel of his white SUV, waving me over.

"What's going on?" I ask as I slide onto the passenger seat.

He leans his elbows on the steering wheel and pins me with his gaze. "I don't know. You tell me."

"Nothing. Why?"

He shakes his head and looks toward the street beyond the windshield. "I've known you for ten years, Pasha, so don't give me this shit. Are you planning to leave the Bratva?"

"No. Why would you think that?"

"You let Kostya take over your clubs. You've practically lived at Ural and wouldn't let anyone cover for you, ever. When I tried convincing you to take a break a few months back, you said you can't function unless you're working."

"Well, I've decided to take that break now."

"So, you're coming back?"

I slouch back in the seat and look up at my building. It's been about three hours since I left for the meeting with Roman, and I've spent every single second of that time thinking about Asya. Is she okay? Has she eaten? What if she's hungry and can't decide what to make? Is she scared having been left alone? What if I come home and she won't be there?

"I'll come back, Yuri. Don't worry."

"When?"

"When she leaves," I say, looking up toward the windows on the third floor. I can't see the lights inside because the blinds are closed. What if she got scared again? I hate leaving her alone.

"She? The girl you have at your place?"

"Yes."

"Are you two . . . in a relationship?"

"No."

"I don't understand."

I glance at my friend. His jaw is clenched tight and there is a concern in his eyes. At sixty-five, Yuri is the oldest in the Bratva's inner circle. He has become a father figure to the soldiers who work under him, but he's also fiercely protective of the rest of the Bratva's men, regardless of their position. I've always found it strange, how he can care so greatly about the guys who aren't his family, while there are people in the world who don't give a fuck about their own flesh and blood.

"Have you ever met someone who feels like they are a missing piece of you?" I ask. "A piece you didn't even know you were missing until they stumbled into your life?"

"No, not really. You think that girl is yours?"

"I've known her for a week."

"That's not what I asked."

"I know. But it doesn't really matter. She'll be leaving soon, anyway." I grab the door handle. "I'm coming back to work as soon as she does."

"Maybe she won't want to leave."

"Yeah, sure," I say and exit the car.

I AM STANDING IN THE MIDDLE OF THE SHOWER STALL, STARING AT THE two bottles on the corner shelf. The black one is the bodywash for men I've been using since I got here. It has a woodsy scent with a hint of citrus and sage. It was there from the start, and it was the only one. Now, there is a different shower gel next to it. A pink bottle with flowers on it. Pasha must have brought and left it here for me. I take a deep breath and reach for it, but the instant my fingers come close to the bottle, anxiety rises within my chest. I look back at the black bottle and move my hand to it. The anxiety intensifies. I let my hand fall. I spend more than fifteen minutes watching the stupid soap bottles and gritting my teeth to the point of my jaw hurting. I finally grab both and send them flying across the bathroom, where they hit the wall and fall to the floor.

A bang sounds on the door. "Asya!"

I lean my back against the tiled wall as my breath comes in shallow bursts. This is the first time I've tried to take a shower without Pasha being in the bathroom with me. I felt so proud of myself earlier when I told him he didn't have to come in with me. He smiled a little and said he would stay on the other side of the door just in case.

"Asya?" Another bang. "I'm coming in!"

The door bursts open and Pasha rushes in, looking around himself. His eyes fall to the bottles on the floor, and then his gaze snaps to me. His metallic gray depths, not light blue as I originally thought, scan me from head to toe—questioning, assessing . . . worried. Their intensity draws me in, grounding me in a way that eases my anxiety.

"I couldn't choose which fucking bodywash to use," I say and close my eyes, feeling completely defeated.

"Shit," Pasha mumbles. A few seconds later, his rough palm caresses my cheek. "I'm sorry. I wasn't thinking."

"It's not your fault I'm a basket case." I sigh.

"You're not a basket case, mishka."

"Yeah, sure." I snort. "You should take me to the nearest mental hospital and leave me there."

"Asya, look at me."

I open my eyes to find him standing in front of me, his hand still on my cheek, and the other on the wall next to my head.

"It will get better," he says. "I promise."

"You don't know that."

"I do. You're a fighter. It'll take time, but you will get better. Come on, let's get you washed up. Okay?"

I nod reluctantly.

"Good. I'll go get that shower gel."

I watch him walk toward the other end of the bathroom and pick the bottles off the floor. Then, he returns inside the shower stall.

"This one is mine," he says as he places the black one back onto the shelf, "and the pink one is yours. You'll use that one."

How can he be so calm? It's as if my throwing a fit doesn't bother him in the least.

"Now, what else is the problem?" He looks down at me.

I bite my lower lip. "The towels."

"The towels?"

"Bath towels. You have blue and white ones." I keep using the hand towels after my shower because those are all white.

"I'll use blue. You have the white. Does that work?"

I nod, feeling like a complete idiot. Pasha's fingers lightly grip my chin, tilting my head up. "Any other problems with the bathroom?"

"No," I whisper.

"Okay. Should I wait here?"

I don't want him to leave, but I shake my head anyway. It's not easy, but after his instructions, I can handle the shower alone because I know he will still be close by.

He smiles. "Shower. Dress. I'll be waiting outside, and we'll have breakfast when you're done."

Pasha's thumb brushes lightly along my jaw before his hand falls away from my face. He turns and leaves the bathroom. Slowly, I raise my hand and retrace the path of his touch.

## Pavel

I place a cereal box on the counter in front of Asya and head toward the fridge to get the milk. When I put the carton next to the cereal, she reaches for it, but I take her hand in mine.

"Not yet," I say.

With my free hand, I open the cupboard and take out a jar of marmalade. I place it next to the cereal box, grab the peanut butter and bread, and line everything up on the counter. Asya tilts her head to the side, watching me.

I move to stand behind her and nod toward the things on the counter. "What would you like to have for breakfast?"

Asya looks over the assortment of food and flattens her lips.

She's been here for two weeks. Every morning I've given her milk and selected a cereal, making sure it was a different flavor each time. Asya always made us both a bowl, and we had breakfast in the dining room. It distresses her when she needs to make even the most trivial decision, so I've tried my best to make it easier on her. But it's time she pushes beyond her comfort zone, even a tiny bit.

"Why are you doing this?" she asks through her teeth.

"What?"

"Asking me to choose."

"If you can't, I'll help you." I reach to place my hand on her waist, but I catch myself and press my palm onto the cold counter instead. "But maybe you can try. It's just food. You can't make a wrong choice, so don't worry."

She grabs the edge of the counter in front of her and stares at the items. A minute passes. Then five more.

"It's okay," I say. "Take your time."

The need to stroke her back or place a kiss in her hair is eating me alive. I forgot myself once and kissed her on the back of the head. Hopefully, she was already asleep and didn't notice it. She would probably feel revolted if she finds out I'm attracted to her. It's wrong on so many levels. When she mentioned the other day that she's only eighteen, it only made the situation worse. She is fifteen years younger than me. I need to keep my distance as much as possible.

"I can't." Asya's nails scrape the top of the counter as she tightens her grip, her gaze fixed on the cereal box.

"Of course you can," I say as I battle the need to touch her.

It guts me each time I see her struggling to make even the most basic choice. She still doesn't want to talk with the psychologist, so I've been calling every two days to ask for guidance. The psychologist recommended I create a situation where Asya would need to make a small decision, but I'm not supposed to insist if it makes her too uncomfortable. The doctor tells me every time that for Asya to get better, she needs professional help. However, it can only happen if Asya is ready to accept it.

A few seconds later, I see Asya's right hand creeping forward, toward the cereal, then it stops. I move the box closer but make sure it's still far enough that she needs to reach for it.

"You said you liked to eat cereal at home," I say. "Do you think your preferences have changed?"

"No."

"Then it's safe to say that you'd pick cereal. Come on, just a few more inches."

Asya purses her lips together and, the next moment, her hand closes the distance to the box. She grabs it and presses it into her chest as if it's something utterly precious.

"I did it," she mumbles.

"See? It'll get better."

She spins and wraps her free hand around my wrist while her gaze bores into mine. Her palm moves upward, along my forearm.

"Thank you," she says and leans into me slightly.

"Any time, mishka." I reluctantly take a step back. "Let's eat. I'm starving."

A strange expression crosses Asya's face as her hand falls from my arm. She turns away and busies herself with pouring the milk and cereal into matching black bowls. I don't think I ever used these before she came. In fact, more than half of the kitchen wares were unused, tidily stored away in drawers and cupboards. Of all the stuff I own, I've only used two plates, some glasses, and a few coffee cups. I'm not certain, but I may have used the stove only a time or two.

When Asya is done pouring the cereal, I carry the bowls to the dining room. She follows a step behind me, clutching the hem of my shirt in her hand, something she still does most of the time. Only after I reach the table does she let go of my tee and take the chair on my right.

She is so quiet all the time. When she eats. When she walks around my place. Even when she cooks. There is no clanging of pots or silverware, no noise whatsoever unless she's humming to herself. I can't decipher the song, but the melody sounds familiar.

I wonder if she was so quiet before, or if it's a consequence of everything that's happened to her. But there's still fire left in her. It might be suppressed deep inside, but it's there. Whoever hurt her, didn't extinguish it completely.

# Chapter eight

Pavel

"Ready?" I ask.

Asya is standing in the middle of the bedroom with her arms wrapped around her midsection. "No."

"We need to get you some clothes. Nothing I bought fits." I nod toward the shirt she's wearing which is at least two sizes too big. The legs of the blue jeans she's got on are rolled up, as well. How did I fuck this up so much? When I was buying the clothes, they seemed small to me. Asya might only stay with me for a short time, but I won't let her go around pulling the sleeves of her shirts nonstop. I want her to feel comfortable. "The store is close by and we'll be the only ones there."

Asya looks down at the floor, biting her lower lip.

"Asya. Look at me, baby," I say, and she reluctantly lifts her head. "I won't let go of your hand, no matter what. You will be safe."

"You said 'safe,'" she mumbles. "You didn't say 'it's going to be okay.' Why?"

"Because it probably won't be okay. You may get scared because it's the first time you're going out in public after almost three weeks. You may even freak out." I squeeze her hand. "But you will be safe the whole time. Do you understand what I'm saying, mishka?"

Asya's eyes find mine and, for a moment, I'm taken aback by the trust I see in their depths. Roman trusted me with his clubs when he assigned me to manage them. But no one has trusted their life to me before. Feeling safe is one of the most basic human needs, and she just placed her faith in me.

"Do you want to take the car or walk there?" I ask. "It's just two blocks away."

She just watches me, her lips pressed tight. Looks like she's still having trouble making decisions herself, but she is getting better. This morning she opened the fridge and took out the milk to make cereal for breakfast, she probably did it without thinking about it. Before today, she would just open the fridge and stare inside until I came and picked up the milk for her. I would never admit it, because it's absolutely selfish, but I secretly enjoy it.

I have never needed anyone, or better said, I've never let myself need anyone. And no one has ever needed me. That concept was completely foreign to me until now. The idea of Asya needing me feeds a yearning that I couldn't name before.

We're still sharing my bed. For the first couple of nights, I thought about using one of the other bedrooms, but I'd see the fear in her eyes when I tried to leave and go back to lie next to her instead. At some point, I stopped trying. I love how she snuggles into me when she awakes from a nightmare, as if being close to me is enough to chase away the monsters.

"We'll head out on foot, then," I say and leave the room with her following, her hand tightly clasped in mine.

We are the only customers in the small boutique I picked. I called the owner earlier and instructed him to make sure no one else is let inside until we're done. I also requested to have the store cleared of all personnel except the one attendant at the cash register, who was also told not to leave her spot.

Asya comes to a stop in the middle of the store and looks around, her eyes skimming along the long racks of clothes and the shelves of shoes. She takes everything in, inhaling a deep breath, and squeezes my hand.

"Let's start with underwear," I say and lead her to the far corner of the store.

Asya peruses the things on display but doesn't make a move to pick anything up. Her eyes wander over the underwear, lingering on some items for a few seconds longer than others. It's usually the bright colors that draw her attention. She passes over the white pieces as if they're not even there.

I pay attention to her gaze as she looks at the displayed undergarments, noting every article her eyes land on for a split-second longer than the rest. After she's done with the displays, I pick up the smallest size of every item that caught her attention.

"All good?" I look down at her and find her watching me. Her eyes are brimming with unshed tears. I brush her cheek with the back of my hand, then nod toward the rack on my left. "Let's do shirts next."

We repeat the ordeal in every section of the store, and since my hands end up filled with clothes, Asya switches to holding the sleeve of my jacket. When we reach the changing room, I enter the stall and place the heap of clothes, along with the yellow coat she ogled for almost a minute and two pairs of shoes, onto the bench by the mirror.

"You can let go of my jacket and try on everything," I say.

She nods but doesn't let it go.

I reach for the first shirt on the pile and offer it to her. "You're safe, mishka. No one can hurt you while I'm here."

The corners of Asya's lips lift a little, and she slowly releases her hold.

It takes her more than half an hour to try on everything, and only a few items end up being too big. I collect the clothes that fit under one arm and, taking her hand in mine, we leave the changing room. As I'm paying at the cash register, the chime of the bells over the door rings out behind us. I turn around just in time to see an older man in a gray suit coming inside the store.

"Mr. Morozov!" he smiles, walking toward us. "I hope your shopping experience went as requested?"

Asya stiffens, her hand squeezing mine in a mad grip. I look down at her to find her staring at the boutique manager with horror in her eyes.

"Come, baby," I say, sliding my arm around her middle. She jumps up and tightly wraps her arms and legs in a familiar pose.

"Was everything to your liking?" the idiot keeps rambling as he approaches us. "I specifically—"

I grab the store manager by the collar of his dress shirt with my free hand while supporting Asya with the other. I jerk him around and slam him against the concrete pillar next to the cash register.

"What the fuck did I tell you?" I bark into his face.

"I . . . I . . . please!"

"I said only one person, a female, is allowed in here until we leave." I shove him into the pillar again, then one more time for good measure. "Are you a fucking female?"

"No . . . please . . ."

"No. You are not!" I snap.

Fingers are in my hair, passing through the strands. Once. Twice. I turn my head to the side slightly and my cheek presses to Asya's.

"He meant no harm," she whispers next to my ear.

"The road to hell is paved with good intentions," I say. "Do you know that quote?"

"Yes." Another stroke through my hair. "It's both true and idiotic. Let the man go."

"No one scares you and gets away without punishment." I release my hold on the store manager's shirt and backhand him before turning to the counter to collect our bags.

I leave the store with Asya in my arms and carry her the two blocks to my building. A few people we pass throw dumbfounded looks in our direction, but they quickly look away when they see the angry scowl on my face. Most of Asya's tension eased shortly after we left the boutique, but she keeps her face snuggled in the crook of my neck, her arms and legs clutching to me with all her strength. Stupid motherfucker, I should have just snapped his neck for scaring her. I'm still so fucking livid, I have to resist the urge to turn around and do that exact thing.

When we reach my building, I don't even nod to the security guy in the lobby, just head right into the elevator and hit the button for the third floor with my elbow. As soon as we're inside my place, I let the bags fall to the floor and walk to the living room. Asya is still plastered to my body as I sit down on the sofa.

"You can let go, mishka," I say and stroke my palm down her hair.

She just shakes her head and presses her face more into my neck. A soft sigh escapes her, and then I feel something wet on my skin.

"Please don't be sad, baby."

Asya takes a deep breath and leans away, looking at me. Tears are falling down her cheeks, and her eyes are red and puffy. But she doesn't look sad. She looks mad as hell.

"I'm so sick of this," she says through her teeth and grabs at the front of my jacket. "So. Fucking. Sick."

"I know."

Her hands let go of my jacket and she takes my face between her palms, staring into my eyes. "I want to go to the mall."

Our gazes are locked. It feels like I could drown in the dark depths of her eyes, it makes it hard to think straight. "I don't think that's a good idea, Asya."

"I can't live like this. Panicking because of the most basic things. Hiding here, in your place." Her hands move to the back of my head, threading the strands between her fingers. "I want my life back. I want myself back."

Her last sentence is barely audible. I lift my hand and brush the tears from her cheeks with my thumb. "Okay."

Asya nods and her eyes fall to my lips. Her hands are still raking my hair. As I watch, she takes a deep breath and leans forward. She's going to kiss me. God, I've been thinking about kissing her for days, hating myself for having the idea festering in my mind. She is too young, and she's been terribly hurt. Letting her kiss me would be no better than making a move on a traumatized girl.

"Asya," I whisper. "Please don't, baby."

## Asya

My body goes rigid upon hearing Pasha's words. I look up to find his eyes regarding me with concern. Just a couple of inches are separating my mouth from his. If I'm quick, I might be able to steal one quick kiss, even if he doesn't want it.

But as fast as that thought enters my mind, another follows. No, I know what's it like to have something taken from you against your will. I can't do it to him.

"Why not?" I ask. "You don't want spoiled goods, is that the issue?"

Pasha's eyes widen and the next instant his hand shoots up, grabbing my chin. "Don't you ever say that again," he says through his teeth. "Ever."

"Then why, Pasha? Is it bad that I want to kiss you?" I lean into his hand, intending to close the distance between us, but he doesn't allow me to.

He doesn't say anything, just stares at me, his nostrils flaring. I wonder if he's aware that while he's holding me away from him with his left hand, his right is still stroking my cheek. I sigh and straighten, letting go of his hair.

The phone in his pocket rings. He reaches for it and presses it to his ear, listening to what the person on the other side is saying. I can hear the faint voice from the other end. It's male and sounds agitated, but I can't understand what is being said because he's speaking Russian.

"I'll come over," Pasha replies in English, then lowers the phone.

"You need to go to work?"

"Yes. I'm in charge of the Bratva's club business. I'll be back in a couple of hours," he says. "Will you be okay?"

I don't want him to go, but I nod anyway.

"I've ordered some groceries; they will leave them at the front door. If you're tired of cooking, I'll order something for you from the restaurant across the street." He brushes the side of my chin with the tip of his finger. "But if you want to make something for dinner and can't decide what, there is a laptop on the nightstand in the bedroom. Google quick dishes and pick the first one you know how to make. Okay?"

I nod again. He doesn't release my chin. Instead, his fingers move along my jaw to the back of my neck where he buries them in my hair.

"I emptied the dresser in the bedroom, you can put your new clothes there."

So, he noticed that I freaked out when I saw the suits in his closet. "Do you really need to leave?"

"I won't be long." He looks over at the clock on the wall. "I need to go over some paperwork with Kostya before the club opens at ten. I'll be back by ten thirty."

"Can you take the clock down?"

Pasha looks down at me, and I can see the question in his eyes.

"I'm nearsighted," I say.

His hand on my nape moves back to my chin and tilts my head up. "Why haven't you told me?"

I shrug.

"Do you wear glasses or contacts?"

"Glasses. Contacts irritate my eyes."

His other hand cups my face and he glides his palm up, brushing his thumbs along my eyebrows and then over the sensitive skin under my eyes. "We'll get you glasses tomorrow when we go to the mall."

He lets go of my face and removes his wristwatch. "Would this work?" he asks.

I stare at the expensive gold watch he placed in my hand. It's still warm from touching his skin. "Yeah," I choke out.

"Okay." He nods. "Take a shower. You have three pairs of pajamas—they're all the same so you don't have to choose. Put away your new clothes. Eat. Wait for me. In bed, not on the floor in front of the door."

I get down off his lap and watch him leave, then head into the bathroom to have a shower.

I grip the wristwatch in my hand. Half past eleven. I've been sitting in bed for two and a half hours, staring at this thing, and with each passing minute, the panic in the pit of my stomach intensifies.

I did everything Pasha told me to do within the hour, including preparing risotto with chicken. It was the first dish that showed up in my Google search. Making food was usually my task at home. I quite enjoy cooking, so I can prepare almost anything except seafood. The slippery feel of it in my hands always made me cringe, so Arturo was in charge of that. My brother is an amazing cook, and he's the one who taught me everything. He tried to coax Sienna into learning, too, but my sister burned everything. My guess is she couldn't cook and simultaneously post dozens of photos on social media.

I look down at the watch again. Twenty to midnight. Where is he?

# CHAPTER nine

Pavel

*Three hours earlier*

EVERYBODY IS STARING. THE TWO SECURITY GUARDS AT THE BACK entrance of the club. The cleaning lady mopping around the tables. The barman. I ignore them and climb the narrow stairs leading to the gallery housing our administrative spaces that overlook the dance floor.

I pass the room where two security guys are hunched in front of the screens, watching the camera feeds, and enter my office. Kostya is sitting behind my desk, looking at the monitor and clicking angrily on the mouse. The whole tabletop is covered with papers. Off to the side, there are two empty coffee cups and a half-eaten sandwich with crumbs scattered everywhere.

"Such a pig." I shake my head.

"You picked the worst fucking time to take a vacation," he mumbles and keeps hitting the mouse. "The contracts with liquor suppliers need to be renewed. Two waitresses are sick and another is going on maternity leave. The surveillance system crashed twice yesterday. I forgot to order . . ." He looks up and scans me from head to toe. "Who the fuck are you and what have you done with Pavel?"

I nod toward the mess on the desk. "Clean this shit up so I can sit down and see what else you've fucked up."

"Jeans? Really? And a fucking hoodie?" he raises his eyebrows, then bursts out laughing. "Pasha, sweetheart, are you all right?"

"Hilarious. Get up."

"Yuri called," he says and collects the cups. "They found the guy who supplied those pills. He's bringing him here."

"Good." I sit down and sort through the contracts strewn across the desk. Some have round brown stains on them. "Wait for them downstairs and take the guy to the back room when they arrive."

"Okay. Are you sure you don't want me to call the doc to check your head?"

"Fuck off, Kostya."

I'm almost done with the mess Kostya made when gunfire explodes downstairs. Grabbing my weapon from the drawer, I rush into the surveillance room.

"What's happening?" I yell.

"Yuri and two soldiers came in two minutes ago, dragging some guy with them. Those vehicles arrived after them," the security guy says and points to the screen showing the back alley. Two cars with tinted windows are parked just around the corner. "Eight people came out, killed the guards, and came inside the club."

"Call Dimitri. Tell him we need backup and Doc. Then, get downstairs. Now!" I rush toward the door while gunshots keep ringing out below.

The dance floor is covered in blood. Three hostiles are down in the center, and two feet away, the body of a waiter is sprawled with his face to the ground. Across the room, there are two more bodies, probably the soldiers who arrived with Yuri. Kostya is crouched behind the bar, shooting at two men near the entrance. I aim at the first one and shoot him in the head. The other one turns in my direction but falls when Kostya's bullet strikes his neck.

"The rest?" I shout as I'm running down the stairs.

"They went in the back." Kostya jumps over the bar and rushes toward the hallway leading to the storage area. "Yuri is alone in there!"

I don't hear any gunfire as I run after Kostya. That's not good. He turns left and I follow just a few paces behind. We barge into the back room at the same time, our weapons raised.

One hostile is facedown on the floor near the metal cabinet that stores the cleaning supplies. On the right, there are two more men. One is obviously dead, a hole in his forehead. There is a big red splatter on the wall above him. The one next to him is still alive, but he's been shot in the thigh and shoulder. I walk toward him and collect his gun and his comrade's. Another man in cargo pants and a checkered shirt is sprawled on the middle of the floor, several gunshot wounds are in his back. His hands are tied. It's probably the guy who supplied the drugs.

"Yuri!" Kostya yells somewhere behind me. I turn and a chill flushes over me.

Yuri is sitting on the floor with his back on the wall. His whole torso is covered in blood. I rush to kneel next to Kostya, who rips off his shirt and presses it over the wound in Yuri's stomach. I take off my hoodie, too, bundle it up and shove it against the other wound in the middle of Yuri's chest. Kostya's white shirt over Yuri's stomach is already saturated, and blood is seeping through his fingers.

"Where the fuck is the doc!" I bark and grab Yuri by the back of his neck. "Yuri! Open your eyes!"

His eyes slowly flutter open, but the look in them is unfocused.

"Stay with us! Yuri! The doc is coming," I shout.

He tries to tell me something, but it's too faint.

"Don't." I squeeze his neck. "We'll speak when the doc patches you up."

Next to me, Kostya takes out his phone and dials. Dear God, there is so much blood. I carefully run my hands over Yuri's chest and sides and find another wound above his hip.

"Fuck." I frantically take off my T-shirt, pressing it over the injury. "Yuri, no. Don't close your eyes. Stay with us."

He takes a shallow breath and lifts his hand to grab my upper arm, pulling me toward him.

"Albanians," he says next to my ear, then coughs. "I heard them . . . speaking to each other."

The hold on my arm loosens, and Yuri's hand falls to the floor. His dark blue eyes are still on me, but they look glassy. Two rivulets of blood are trailing down from the corners of his mouth.

"Yuri!" I yell into his face. "Don't you dare die on me! Yuri!"

"Pasha," Kostya says. "He's gone."

No! Yuri is responsible for giving me the only family I've ever known—the Bratva. He can't be gone.

"Yuri!" I shake him.

"Pavel, stop," A rough voice says behind me, and I look up to find the doc standing there.

"You're late!" I yell.

"There is nothing anyone could have done," Doc says, nodding to the floor. "He lost too much blood."

I slowly lay Yuri down, stand up, and head toward the opposite end of the room. Grabbing the only living Albanian by his neck, I punch him in the face with all my strength.

"Why?" I ask, then punch him again. "Why were you here?"

"To dispose . . . of Davis," he mumbles.

I punch his head again. And again.

"Pasha! That's enough!"

I ignore Kostya's yelling and continue hitting the motherfucker while the smell of blood invades my nostrils. Someone tries to shove me away, but I shake them off and keep plowing my fists into the Albanian's face until all that is left of it is a mass of blood and red flesh.

When I'm done, I let the body fall to the floor and head toward one of the cabinets. I take out two white linen tablecloths and carry them to where the doc is kneeling next to Yuri's body. I use one to wipe the blood off my friend's face, then close his eyes and carefully cover him with the clean linen.

*"Prashchay, bratan,"* I say, then turn and head toward the door, passing Kostya along the way.

"Jesus fuck," Kostya mumbles, staring at the body of the man I killed with my bare hands. "I'm gonna puke."

When I get back into my office, I grab a vodka from the minibar and take a hefty drag directly from the bottle. It tastes even more awful than I remember. Sitting down in the recliner by the minibar, I take another pull. I don't recall the last time I got drunk.

Someone yells downstairs. Looks like Roman's arrived. I lift the bottle and drink again. Five minutes later, more noise—something's breaking. It sounds like someone is throwing around pieces of furniture. More shouting.

"Dimitri!" Roman roars "Get Angelina on the phone. Fucking now!"

Sounds like Sergei is here, as well. I stand up, bottle in hand, and walk toward the glass wall to look at the scene below. Sergei is standing in the middle of the dance floor, gripping a broken bar stool in his hand. Roman is facing him, his palm is extended toward his brother, and he's saying something to Sergei, who looks like he's going to smash the stool over Roman's head at any second. Dimitri approaches them from the side, holding a phone in his outstretched hand. Sergei's head snaps toward the phone, his gaze zeroing in on the device. The stool crashes to the floor. Sergei grabs the phone out of Dimitri's hand, presses it to his ear, and listens for a few moments. He then throws the phone back to Dimitri and leaves.

I should probably stay and see if they need my help, but I can't stomach the idea. Yuri is gone. The look in his eyes as he stared at me during those last few seconds of his life is going to haunt me for the rest of mine. I shake my head and set off toward the fire escape.

I find Kostya leaning on the wall near the back exit. He looks over at me, then at the bottle in my hand.

"Since when do you drink alcohol?" he asks.

"Since today." I tip my head toward his car. "I need a ride."

We don't speak during the half-hour drive to my place, both of our gazes fixed on the street in front of us. It's started snowing again, and I find myself fixated on the white flakes falling from the sky. I guess I don't like snow anymore, either.

I close my eyes, lean back in the seat, and take another heavy gulp from the bottle.

The front door bangs open, and I exhale with relief. He's back. A moment later something crashes to the floor.

"Pasha?" I shout.

There are a couple of seconds of silence before I hear his voice.

"It's me, mishka." His voice is strange. Strangled.

I expect him to come into the bedroom, but he doesn't. I stare at the open door. Then, there's a sound of glass breaking and a thud.

"Pasha?"

Nothing. I tense. Something's happened. I throw the blanket off, intending to go look for him, but I can't make myself move. He said to wait for him in bed. Should I stay here? Or go and see what happened? I can't decide.

"Pasha?" I call again. No reply.

My hands start shaking. Something bad has happened. I know it because this is so unlike him. I move toward the edge of the bed, and the tremors in my hands intensify while nausea claws its way up my throat. The thought of leaving the bed makes me want to weep. Grabbing a handful of the bedsheets in my fingers, I squeeze and try to swallow down the bile. Finally, I dash across the bedroom at breakneck speed, hitting my elbow on the doorway. I misjudged the distance. Ignoring the pain, I burst into the living room.

"Pasha?"

The lamp in the corner is on, illuminating the room in a dim, dusk-like glow. The front door is hanging wide open. The narrow table near the door where Pasha leaves his keys lies overturned on the floor. He's nowhere in sight.

I head toward the overturned console and feel something wet and sticky on the floor under my bare feet. I know the light switch is close, so I start feeling the wall with my palm. My sight is worse when there's not enough light. Both the switch and the wall are white, making it hard to spot. When I find it, I turn on the lights and look around.

Pasha is sitting on the floor in the kitchen, leaning with his back against the oven door. His eyes are closed. There are pieces of glass everywhere, and the smell of alcohol is in the air.

"Pasha?"

He opens his eyes and cocks his head to the side, regarding me. "I'm sorry I'm late."

Careful not to step on the glass, I cross the kitchen and crouch between his legs. He doesn't look like himself. His hair is a mess, and he's wearing only jeans. His bare chest is splattered with what looks like dried blood. And I'm pretty sure he's drunk. I reach out and cup his face in my palms.

"What happened?" I ask.

He closes his eyes and leans forward until his forehead touches mine.

"Someone died, mishka," he whispers.

I move my hands through his dark blond hair. One of the strands keeps falling forward, across his eye.

"Who?" I try moving that tress of hair off, but it ends up over his face again.

"Yuri. One of the Bratva's enforcers. A friend."

"What happened?"

"Three weeks ago, we caught a guy dealing drugs—pills—at our club. It was the same substance that was used on you. Yuri found the man who supplied the pills and brought him to the club to be questioned."

"Did you get some answers?"

"No. A group of men followed them and charged inside, shooting. They killed five of our men, then went to the back where Yuri was with the prisoner." He shakes his head. "Killed them both."

"I'm so sorry," I whisper and lean forward, placing a kiss at the center of his forehead. "So very sorry."

He looks at me then, our eyes so close, and as I stare into his, my heart flutters. It feels like a butterfly is trapped within my chest. I want to kiss him or comfort him in any way I can. The way he did for me. But I don't know if he'll welcome it. So instead, I just brush the back of my fingers down his cheek.

"Let's go to bed, Pasha."

He takes a deep breath and slowly rises, pulling me up with him. When we're both standing, he looks at the kitchen floor covered in glass shards.

"Shit. Please tell me you didn't cut yourself."

"I'm fine. Let's go."

Pasha's gaze falls to my bare feet. "Step on top of my toes."

"Why?"

"I don't think it's wise to carry you while I'm in this state, mishka."

I'm about to say I can get back by myself but change my mind. Wrapping my arms around Pasha's waist, I place my right foot over his shoe, then the left. His left hand slides to my back, pressing me closer to his body.

"We'll go slow," he says. "Hold tight."

"Okay," I murmur and press my cheek to his chest. I'll probably end up with blood on my face, but I don't care.

Pasha grabs the side of the counter with his free hand and takes a step forward. Then one more. I keep myself pressed to his body as he walks through the kitchen. The glass shards break under the soles of his shoes with each step. When we reach the living room, he braces his palm on the wall and looks down at me. There is no glass this far from the kitchen, but I don't remove my feet from the top of his. Instead, I squeeze his waist tighter. Something passes between us, like an exchange without words being spoken. He's silently telling me I'm safe to let him go, but I answer that I won't, even if there is no need to hold him anymore. As if acknowledging my unspoken reply, Pasha nods and resumes walking us all the way to the bedroom.

When we reach the bed, I release his waist and climb under the covers. Holding up the corner of the duvet, I pat the pillow next to my head. Pasha watches me for a few moments, then removes his shoes and slips under the covers next to me.

"Tell me about your friend," I say and snuggle into his side. "What was he like?"

"I met Yuri ten years ago. He came to one of my fights. After the match was over, he approached me and asked if I'd like to focus my energy and skills somewhere else."

"Fights?" I ask.

The silent pause lasts almost a minute. "Before I joined the Bratva, I earned money by fighting in underground matches," he finally says. I can't see his face, but his voice is clipped. Is he worried that I might think less of him because of how he earned his living?

I press my hand on the center of his chest and bury my face into his neck. "Yuri recruited you for the Bratva?"

"Yes. He was in charge of foot soldiers. Three years later, when the guy who ran the clubs was killed, the pakhan promoted me to the position, saying that my three-piece suits made the other soldiers fidgety. But Yuri was always around, pestering me to go out with the guys. He said I needed to loosen up."

"And did you? Follow his advice?"

"Nope. I'm not really a people person, mishka."

Yeah. I got that impression, too. I move my hand up and thread my fingers through the hair at the back of his head. A melody comes to mind. "The Rain Must Fall" by Yanni. Slow and sad. Peaceful. I hum the tune as I pass my fingers through Pasha's hair.

"Why did you let me stay here?" I ask.

Pasha sighs and places his chin on the top of my head. "I don't know. Why did you want to stay?"

I've been asking myself that question for weeks. "I don't know, either."

# Chapter Ten

Asya

THE ELEVATOR DOOR LOOMS IN FRONT OF ME, AND I DESPERATELY try to control the panic building within. I'm failing miserably.

"Don't let go of my hand," I whisper as bile creeps up my throat.

"I won't," Pasha says next to me.

There is a ding, signaling that we've reached the mall's ground floor. The doors open. The moment I glimpse people milling around, I take a quick step back. Pasha's hand shoots out to the side, hitting the button to close the door.

"You can do this, mishka," he says. "But if you're not ready, we'll try again next week."

No, I'm not ready. I don't think I'll ever be ready. But I'm doing it anyway. And I'm doing it today.

"Open the door, please," I choke out and squeeze Pasha's hand.

The first minute is the worst. It's early, so the mall is not crowded at all, but still, it feels like I'm going to suffocate just by being here. The sight of people in such an enclosed space, the sounds they make, their looks—everything seems too much. Pasha squeezes my hand back and takes a step forward.

Someone is laughing. They are farther away, down the hallway, but it seems like they are right next to me. The sound of feet thumping on the floor and random chatter echo in my ears. I shut my eyes and hold my breath. There is a light touch on my face, the tip of Pasha's finger trailing the line of my jaw. I take another breath and open my eyes. He's standing in front of me, blocking the view of the crowd with his wide frame.

"It's okay, baby," he says. "No one can hurt you when I'm here. Just look into my eyes."

He moves his hand to the back of my neck and takes a step backward, pulling me with him. Without letting go of his gaze, I step forward. His lips curve upward. He takes another step, and then one more. I follow. I can still hear the people, but the sounds don't bother me that much anymore because all my focus is centered on the man in front of me.

I don't think anyone would call Pasha beautiful. The lines on his face are too harsh. His right eyebrow is split in two by a thin scar. His nose is too big and slightly crooked. He doesn't look like a man you'd want to ask on a date, but rather someone you'd want to have by your side when walking in a dark alley. Though, if someone asked me how a perfect man should look, I would point to the one standing before me.

Two more steps. I match his pace. Out of the corner of my eye, I see people looking in our direction with wonder on their faces. Several more steps, and Pasha stops.

"We're here." Pasha nods toward the store on his right.

I throw a quick look to the side. It's the optical retailer.

"Do you want to go inside now, or would you prefer we come back later?" he asks.

"Now." I nod and take another step toward him, molding my front to his.

His hand slides from my neck to my hair, and I can feel the heat of his body seeping into mine. I want more, need more of it. I lift my palm and place it on the center of his chest. People are passing us by, some grumbling that we're in the way, but neither of us moves. Pasha's head dips slightly, and I hold my breath, wondering if he's going to kiss me. He doesn't. Instead, he releases my hair and takes a step away.

"Let's go find some glasses for you," he says and heads inside the shop.

I'm standing next to Pasha as he gives the store attendant his address so they can deliver my new glasses once they're ready when a man enters the store and heads toward the rack of sunglasses. He's holding a phone to his ear, talking to someone. My eyes skim his dress pants and white shirt and stop on his bright red tie. I should look away. Turn and focus on something else. I can't. It feels like my eyes are glued to the red material around his neck. The tie that was used on me by the client was red. I bite my lower lip until it hurts and squeeze Pasha's hand.

"Mishka? Are you all right?"

I close my eyes, trying to suppress the memory of my body being pressed into the bed while I desperately claw at the tie around my neck. My breathing becomes faster. Shallower. I can't get enough air. It feels like I'm suffocating.

"Asya?" Pasha wraps his arm around my waist and turns around, following my gaze. The guy with the tie is still standing next to the sunglasses rack, browsing through the display.

"Wait here, baby," Pasha says next to my ear and, releasing his hold on me, walks toward the man.

I thought he would ask the guy to leave. Instead, Pasha grabs the back of the man's shirt and pushes him toward the door. The man flails, yelling. Pasha pays him no heed, twisting the guy's arm behind his back while continuing to push him toward the exit. The store employee behind me lets out a shriek and grabs the phone, probably to call security. I fist my hands, hating myself for being so weak, then take a deep breath and march out of the store to where Pasha is still clutching the man by his shirt.

"Pasha," I whisper and wrap my hand around his forearm. "Please."

He looks down at me, releases the guy and pushes him away. The man stumbles, then turns around, biting out obscenities in our direction. Pasha takes a step toward him, but I tighten my hold on his arm.

"Please, don't," I say. "Let's go back."

He glares at the tie-clad man for a few more seconds before he takes my hand in his and leads us down the hallway toward the elevators.

As we're passing a restaurant, my eyes fall on the small object sitting atop the raised platform beyond the entrance to the establishment. I stop in my tracks, my feet seemingly rooted to the ground, and stare at the instrument.

I glance at what has caught Asya's attention, and my eyes fall on the piano next to the wall. It's one of those tiny versions—a baby grand piano made of white wood. Its lid is open and some music sheets lie on the small stand above the keys. The bench seat before it is unoccupied.

Asya takes a tentative step toward the platform and stops for a second. The next moment she's rushing forward, pulling me with her. When she reaches the piano, she releases my hand and climbs up to sit on the bench in front of the instrument. She sits there for at least five minutes with her eyes glued to the keys. I stand close by, turned in a way that allows me to keep an eye on her while I can still see our surroundings just in case someone gets a stupid idea of approaching and asking her to leave. One of the waiters looks up and takes a step in our direction. I cross my arms and turn toward him, daring him with my glare to say something. The man sizes me up but quickly goes back to what he was doing. Good for him.

A single low note plays behind my back. Followed by another. A few seconds of silence and then a melody begins. My body goes stone-still as a combination of low tones unfolds behind me in a slow tempo. The tune sounds familiar. It's a popular classical piece, but I can't remember which one. I want to turn around and watch her play, but I'm afraid it'll distract her. Instead, I stand guard, watching the people at the tables around us. All of them have stopped what they were doing, their meals abandoned as they all look in Asya's direction. The melody ends, but she continues with another. I know this one. It's "The Flight of the Bumblebee." Unbelievably fast. Even to a layman's ear, it's clear that she's not an amateur.

I can't fight the urge any longer. The need to see her play is too strong, so I turn around and stare. She might just be wearing plain blue jeans and a navy blouse, but it feels like I'm in a damn concert hall, watching the star pianist putting on a show. The way she holds her body, the movements of her hands flying elegantly over the keys, and the confidence in her posture are all stunning. But what takes me aback the most is the expression on her face. Joy. Elation. Happiness. She is smiling so widely that it feels like her whole being is glowing. I can't move. I can hardly breathe. Seeing her like this is as if I'm meeting her for the first time. There's nothing in common between this maestro and the frightened girl I let stay in my place, the one who still follows me around the apartment, gripping the hem of my shirt in her hand.

Rage boils up through my insides at the thought of this side of her being smothered. I'm going to make the people who broke her spirit pay. In blood.

Asya finishes the melody and looks up, her eyes finding mine. Applause breaks out around us. People are shouting, asking for more. She ignores the noise, slowly rises, and walks toward me without breaking eye contact.

"You didn't tell me you can play the piano." I reach out and move a few stray strands away from her face. She is still standing on the platform, which makes us almost the same height.

Asya just shrugs and takes another step forward, plastering her front to mine. Our faces are barely inches apart.

"Which piece was it?" I ask. "The one you played first."

"Beethoven." She lifts her hand and traces the line of my jaw with the tip of her finger. "It's called 'Moonlight Sonata.' It reminds me of you."

The light falling through the window to the right of us makes her hair glow. A small smile still lingers on her lips. I fight the urge to bury my hands in her dark hair and crush my mouth to hers.

"We should get going," I say but I don't make a move to turn away. "It's almost noon. It's going to get crowded."

Asya's hand slides down from my face, grazing the sleeve of my jacket until her fingers wrap around mine. Her skin feels so soft compared to the roughness of my palm.

"Can we come again tomorrow?" she asks peering deep into my eyes. "I've missed playing."

As if I could say no to her when she's looking at me like this. "Sure, mishka."

A huge grin spreads over her face, making me feel like I'm bathed in its warmth. I want more of it. More of her. I reach out and place my hands on her hips. "Want to hop up?"

She tilts her head to the side, regarding me.

"Looks like a business group just arrived," I lie, then nod toward the left side of the hallway. "They just went into one of the stores."

Asya's hand squeezes mine, and she jumps into my arms the moment after. Her legs wrap around my waist, and she tucks her nose into the crook of my neck. Ignoring the stares of the people around us, I turn and walk toward the elevators, supporting Asya with one hand under her thighs, my other arm wrapped around her middle, holding her tightly against my body.

I should feel bad for lying to her, but I don't. The satisfaction I feel from having her body pressed to mine overwhelms any remorse I might have. I know it's selfish, but I don't fucking care.

# Chapter eleven

Asya

THERE ARE TWO CARTONS OF MILK INSIDE THE FRIDGE. THE REGULAR one and one that's fat-free. Pasha usually buys only the regular full-fat milk. I squeeze the fridge handle and glare at the cartons sitting there so innocently on the shelf. They mock me.

It's fucking milk!

A palm caresses the small of my back. "Problem with the milk?"

"Yes," I say, staring the damn things down. "Was there a two-for-one special on milk at the store?"

"Nope. I bought skim this time too in case you like it more than the other one." Pasha stands behind me and touches my elbow, then trails his hand down my forearm until his palm presses over the back of my hand. Slowly, he lifts my hand to the shelf where the milk cartons are. "Which one do you want?"

"I don't know."

"Of course you do." He moves my hand a little further until my fingers touch the top of the first carton. "I've never liked skim milk. It tastes almost like water. You?"

"I don't like the skim one, either." I blurt out without actually thinking about it.

"There. It wasn't that hard." He moves my hand to the other milk option. "We'll go with this one. You can make some oats cereal for me, too."

His hand falls away, leaving mine hovering just over the cartoon. I grab it and take it off the shelf. "Last time we had it, you said it tasted like cardboard."

"I'm ready to give it another try."

I turn around and look up at him, enjoying seeing him clearly through my new glasses without having to squint to gain focus. The ability to take in every line of Pasha's face surpasses the satisfaction of being able to see everything else around me in striking detail.

A few strands of his wet hair have fallen across his forehead. I try to sweep them away, but they keep sliding over his eyes.

"You need a haircut," I say as I try one more time.

Pasha cocks his head to the side, regarding me, then pulls out a drawer on his left. His eyes remain locked on mine while he rummages around in the drawer and pulls out a pair of scissors, placing them on the counter. They're huge, with white plastic handles. I use them to open pasta packages and other stuff.

"Those are paper scissors," I say, staring at them.

"I know."

He wants me to cut his hair. I move my gaze back to his striking gray eyes. "I've never cut anyone's hair, Pasha. What if I mess it up? Don't you have a hairdresser or a barber who could do your hair?"

"I do. But I'd like you to do it," he says and brushes my cheek with the back of his hand, "Will you?"

My heart skips a beat. I put the milk down on the counter and pick up the scissors. Pasha turns and leaves the kitchen. Two minutes later he comes back carrying a chair in one hand and my pink comb in the other. He places the chair in the middle of the kitchen and sits down with his back to me.

I walk toward him on shaky legs while my heart accelerates to double time. When I'm behind him, he lifts his hand, holding up the comb. I bite my bottom lip, accept the comb, and start passing it through the dark blond strands. His hair is not very long, I would just need to shorten the part on the top of his head that's grown out a little. Instead of starting the cut, however, I keep brushing his hair. Pasha doesn't move a muscle, but I hear his loud inhale when I use my other hand and push my fingers through the strands. I pull up some of the longer hairs, cut off half an inch, and continue running my fingers through.

"I need to go out for a few hours," he says in a clipped voice and leans his head slightly back, closer to my touch. "Yuri's funeral."

"Okay." I nod and make another cut.

"I'll need to wear a suit. I'll change in the other room. You can stay in the bedroom until I've left."

I bend my head slightly and inhale his scent before I shift my hand to the next patch of hair. "Were you close? You and your friend?"

He doesn't reply right away. When I look at his face, I see that his eyes are closed and his lips are pressed into a thin line. "In a way," he says finally.

I finish the last cut and set the scissors and the comb on the counter. Pasha is still sitting with his eyes closed. Leaning forward, I rest my chin on his shoulder and brush his cheek with my own. "I'm so sorry you lost your friend."

His hand comes up and cups my cheek. "Everybody leaves, mishka. One way or another," he says, stroking the side of my face with his thumb. "It's only a matter of time."

I watch him as he stands up and leaves the kitchen, carrying the chair with him. There was a very strange tone in his voice when he said that last sentence. As if he was referring not only to his friend who died.

I HATE FUNERALS.

I guess everybody does, but they disturb me on a fundamental level. The expressions on people's faces. The sorrow. The crying.

When they start lowering Yuri's casket and his sister breaks down, falling to her knees onto the muddy ground, I can't take it anymore. I turn around and head toward the parking lot while cries and pained screams ring out behind me. Even when I'm in my car, driving back home, I can still hear them in the recesses of my mind. The fact that we still have no clear proof of who's behind the attack makes it even harder to process.

As I reach for the bell in my eagerness to hear Asya skirring to open the apartment door, I realize I'm still wearing the suit. I have a black coat over it, but it may still disturb Asya. I planned on taking a change of clothes with me but forgot. If someone told me a few months ago that I'd be concerned about not having some jeans and a T-shirt on hand, I would have laughed in their face. My loathing toward denim somehow got pushed away and dissolved since Asya's arrival. I know it's because wearing casual clothes instead of suits helps her, so I'm no longer bothered by the idea of tattered Levi's.

Pulling my hand back, I remove the coat and unbutton my suit jacket. Only when the jacket, vest, and shirt are all off do I reach for the bell again. A split-second later a thought slams into me that I should have just used my key. Too late.

Asya unlocks the door, opening it all the way. Her eyes go wide as her gaze moves down my naked chest and stops on my hand holding the bunched-up clothes. Slowly, she reaches out to take my other hand and ushers me inside.

"You'll freeze to death." She mumbles as she walks toward the living room with me following.

When we reach the couch, she lightly pushes me down to sit and disappears from view. I toss the bundle of clothes onto the other end of the couch and stare aimlessly at the blank TV screen. I still can't get the image of Yuri's sister sinking to her knees in the mud out of my head.

A light touch on my shoulder pulls me out of my daze as Asya comes to stand in front of me. She's holding a T-shirt and a gray hoodie in her hand. I don't leave my clothes lying around. She would have needed to go into the walk-in closet to get those for me. Where my suits are. I take the T-shirt from her and put it on. Once I have the hoodie on, Asya climbs onto my lap and wraps her arms around my neck.

"Was it bad?" she asks next to my ear.

I place my hand at the back of her head, threading my fingers into her hair, and inhale. "Yeah."

"Did you find out anything more about who the attackers were?"

"No. Just before he died, Yuri said they were Albanians, but we don't have any other info. The guy who supplied the drugs is dead. Without other leads, we can't make any connections."

Her hold on me tightens. I feel her chest rise as she takes a deep breath, then she starts whispering.

"The guy who took me wasn't Albanian. At least, I don't think he was." I say. My voice is trembling.

"Mishka, don't." Pasha places his palm on my cheek. "You don't need to talk about it if you don't want to."

"I was at a bar with my sister," I continue. "We used fake IDs to get in. All we wanted to do was go dancing. A guy approached us. He was handsome. Charismatic. Made us both laugh. He didn't have an accent; I would have remembered if he did. Sienna decided to go home early, she had Pilates the next morning. I stayed."

"Didn't you have bodyguards with you?"

"No. We snuck out of the house and took a taxi to the bar. Arturo always got furious when we did that."

His finger moves down to trace my chin.

"I thought he was funny. That guy," I say. "He said his name was Robert. We talked for an hour, and when I said I needed to go home, he offered to walk me outside to catch a cab. I found it very chivalrous."

It almost makes me laugh, how stupid I'd been.

"He pressed something over my face. A wet rag that smelled harsh. I tried getting away, fighting him. He was bigger than me. Stronger. I lost consciousness soon after."

My voice is shaking. I close my eyes, willing myself to keep going.

"I came to in the dark. I was sprawled out on the cold ground and he was kneeling over me, tearing up my dress. I screamed and tried to fight him, but my mind was still hazy. Then I felt . . . him . . . between my legs." I tighten my arms around Pasha's neck and bury my face into him. His body is so utterly still, except for his chest that's moving due to fast, shallow breathing. "It hurt. So much. It was my first time."

I feel his arms coming around my back and press me into his body. It makes me sick, talking about this, but now that I've started, I can't stop. As if it yearns to get out of me. "I froze. I couldn't move my arms or legs; it was as if I was suddenly paralyzed."

The feeling of utter helplessness, the horror I felt in that moment . . . I don't think I will ever be able to forget.

"After . . . I managed to get away from him and ran toward the street. I ran as fast as I could. He caught me anyway. And then he drugged me," I say. "I woke up alone in a strange room. I was so so scared."

The arms around my body tighten, and I feel his palm stroking my back, just like that first night.

"There was a woman. Dolly. She was the one who gave me and the other girls the pills. And kept bringing them twice a day. She was also the one who instructed the girls and set up the appointments with . . . clients." I tilt my head up until my lips come right next to his ear and whisper, "I didn't fight it. I let them drug me and do whatever they wanted with me. What kind of miserable, disgusting person do you need to be to allow that?"

Pasha's hand comes up to the back of my head, and he tilts my head until our eyes meet. "A young, innocent woman who was so violently abused that her mind shut down in an attempt to shield her. But you fought. Escaped. Survived. It wasn't someone else who saved you. You did it yourself."

"It doesn't make me feel any less disgusting."

"Don't say that, baby." He leans forward and places a kiss on my forehead. "I will find the people who hurt you. And they will scream for mercy as I break them like they tried to break you. Their deaths will not be quick."

My insights twist as I absorb his words. Do I want them dead? I imagine Robert as he pleads for his life. Bile rises in my stomach. But did I not plead also? And what about other girls? Now, as I picture Robert's screams for mercy, a small smile breaks across my lips.

"Can I watch?" I ask hesitantly, simultaneously dreading and craving the idea.

"Every second of it, mishka."

I lower my head onto Pasha's chest and wrap my arms around him. Uncertainty and wariness consume me. "I'm scared," I whisper. "I'm afraid it'll happen again. I don't know if I'll ever be able to go outside and walk down the street by myself without flinching every time someone passes close to me."

"You will." He resumes stroking my hair. "I promise you that."

# Chapter Thirteen

## Asya

"I hope they'll let me play again," I say as I'm walking next to Pasha toward the car.

My anxiety spiked every time I thought about returning to the mall and being among all those people, the noise, and surrounded by all those smells. The memories caused me to shudder. But I also remembered the feeling of utter freedom that engulfed me when I placed my fingers on the keys after so long without music. All the excitement, joy, and happiness I didn't think I would ever feel again came rushing back. I've managed to stifle the need to play again for the past five days, but now I crave it.

I finally caved this morning and asked Pasha to take me over there.

"When did you start playing?" he asks as he fires up the engine.

"I was five. Arturo was trying to find a way to distract me and my sister from what happened to our parents, so he asked a neighbor, who had a piano, to give us lessons." It's hard to think about my brother and sister, knowing how much they must be worried, but the idea of facing them still leaves me with bone-chilling panic.

"What happened with your parents?" he asks.

"There was a raid on one of the casinos where they worked. Someone took out a gun and shot at the police. Then, everything went to hell. A lot of people were killed that night."

"They both died?"

"Yeah." I close my eyes and relax in the seat. "I can't even remember them that well. There are photos, of course, so I know what they looked like. But I can't remember details about them, and if I do, they're fuzzy. I remember my mom singing to us every night before bed, but I can't recall the song."

Pasha brushes the back of his hand down my cheek, and I lean into it. His light touch is there one moment and gone the next. When I open my eyes, he's putting the car into drive.

"I know what you mean," he says as he backs out of the parking spot. "I don't remember my parents, either."

"They died, too?"

"Maybe. Maybe not."

I watch his hard profile, wondering if he'll elaborate. He doesn't, just keeps driving in silence. I look down at his hand holding the stick shift and notice he's gripping it hard. I stroke his white knuckles with the tips of my fingers until I feel his hold loosen.

"Did you play professionally?" he asks after some time.

"No, not really. I played at school a couple of times, usually when we had a celebration. Music has always been something personal for me. I decided to take a year off after high school to figure out what I wanted to do next. I thought about applying to a music conservatory, but that was . . . before."

"Do you still want to?"

I look at the road beyond the windshield. "I don't know."

The elevator dings. I squeeze Pasha's hand and try to bring my breathing under control. The urge to ask him to go back clashes with the need to feel the keys beneath my fingers once again. The doors open. Pasha steps out, turns to face me, and takes both of my hands in one of his.

"Breathe. We'll go slow," he says and takes a small backward step. "I'm here. No one will dare touch you, mishka."

I nod and step out of the elevator.

There are more people around than there were the previous time. A multitude of sights and sounds overwhelm my senses—lights, laughter, footsteps, children running by while their parents are frantically trying to corral them. I close my eyes.

Pasha's rough palm cups my cheek and his thick arm wraps around my waist. "It's okay, baby."

My eyes flutter open and I take a deep breath. Hooking my fingers through the loops of his jeans I look up at him. His head is bent, barely inches from mine.

"You like music," he says. "Let's make this a dance. Almost like a waltz, yes?"

I can't help but smile a little. "People will laugh at us, Pasha."

"I don't give a fuck."

He takes a step back and I follow. Then another one. And another one. It does feel like some strange dance—him holding me close and walking backward—and suddenly, I feel the urge to laugh. So, I do. People around us must think we're nuts, but I don't care. I keep my gaze glued to Pasha's as I follow him, laughing. It's so good to feel joy again. He watches me with a small smile on his face and moves his thumb to my lips, stroking them.

"I wish you'd laugh more often," he says.

"I'll try."

When we reach the restaurant with the piano, he slowly lifts his hand off my face. I turn toward the corner where the piano should be, and my smile falls away. It's not there. Instead, two large flowerpots are in its place. I look around, wondering if they moved it somewhere else, but there's no sign of it.

"Can we get out of here?" I ask, staring at the flowerpots, trying my best to keep the tears at bay.

Pasha turns the key in the lock and opens the door to his apartment, holding it for me. I step inside, heading straight for the bathroom to splash some water on my face. As I cross the living room I come to a stop in the middle of the room. There, by the wall next to the window, is a small white piano. It's the one from the mall. I cover my mouth to stifle a sob.

"How?" I choke out, staring at the piano.

"I bought it last week and had it in a storage nearby, ready to be brought here when we headed out," Pasha says behind me, and I feel his hand on the small of my back. "I wanted to surprise you. You didn't even notice that we took the longer route back—to give the delivery guys more time."

"But, why?"

"Because you didn't feel comfortable at the mall. We will go again, only because you need to adjust to being in a crowd. But you should be able to play where you can enjoy it."

"Thank you," I whisper, pressing my lips together tightly. I want to turn around and kiss him, but I don't think he would let me.

"Will you play something for me?" he asks.

"Yes."

I take his hand and lead him across the room. He even bought the bench that was there with the piano. I take a seat on one end and pull him down to sit next to me.

Leaning forward, I pass the tips of my fingers over the keys, position my hands, and play. I pick one of my favorite modern pieces, Yiruma's "River Flows in You." It's soothing but strong, seductive, and full of emotion. It reminds me of Pasha.

He doesn't speak. Doesn't ask what I'm playing. He just sits there—big and silent—watching my hands as I move from one piece to the next. At some point, his gaze moves from my hands to my face and stays there.

## Pavel

For more than an hour, I sit on the bench next to Asya, listening to her play. Or better said, I stare at her while she plays. I find it impossible to take my eyes off her face, seeing every emotion as it crosses her features. When she's playing a fast and uplifting piece, there is a wide smile on her face. When she switches to something slow and sad, her smile fades. She's not merely playing the notes; she feels and experiences every emotion as the melody gives and flows through her, lighting her up from the inside out.

When I'm finally able to unglue my eyes from her face and throw a look at my watch, I see that it's almost two. We've only had breakfast this morning, and while I don't have a problem with skipping meals, I don't want Asya to be hungry.

I rise off the bench and head to the kitchen in search of the takeout menu from the fast-food joint one block over, but I change my mind and open the fridge. I'm used to having it always nearly empty, so it's strange to see all the shelves packed full. Asya usually orders whatever she needs online with my phone, so I don't even know half of the items in there. I move a bunch of vegetables to the side and take out a package of chicken. Well, at least I think it's chicken. Asya's been preparing food for us every day, so I guess I could handle that task today. I find the frying pan in the cupboard and turn toward the island where she keeps her spices in a wide black basket. There are at least twenty small jars. I take one out and smell the contents. It's labeled as sage. Isn't that tea of some type? I put the jar back and pick up another. This one looks like salt, but it has some green things in it.

"Need help?" Asya's voice chimes behind me.

"You were playing. I wanted to make something for us to eat. I'm looking for salt. The normal kind." I turn around and find her smirking at me.

"So, you know how to cook?"

"I know how to heat the leftovers from takeout. Does that count?"

"That doesn't count." Asya laughs and I absorb the sound. I love when she laughs. "Come on, I'll show you how to prepare something simple."

She takes the jar out of my hand and opens it. Keeping her eyes on mine, she licks the tip of her finger and dips it inside.

"Here. Try it. It's just salt with herbs." She lifts her finger, holding it in front of me.

I stare at her. She's still smiling. Slowly, I take her hand and bring it closer to my mouth. Without removing my gaze, I lick at the tip of her finger, but I can't focus on the taste. All my attention is glued to Asya's face. She's biting her lower lip, looking at me with wide eyes. I take a step forward until our bodies touch. I can feel her chest rising and falling as her breathing quickens. Her free hand comes to land at the small of my back, then slides under the hem of my T-shirt. I can feel the heat of her touch. The urge to grab her, put her over my shoulder, and take her to the nearest bedroom is raging inside of me. Asya's palm moves up along my spine, and my mind is assaulted with images of her naked under me as I kiss every inch of her body. Just as I've been imagining for days. Wrong. So wrong.

I let go of her hand and quickly step back, turning toward the kitchen island. "What else do we need for this lunch?"

I don't miss the soft sigh as I hear her opening the cupboard behind me. "A bigger pan."

Asya walks around the kitchen, collecting everything she needs and cutting up the vegetables while my eyes follow her the whole time. I like having her here, in my space, way more than I should. Turning around, she opens the drawer next to me and reaches inside, but her hand falters. I look down and see that there are two different brands of flour.

"It's the same thing. Just a different manufacturer," I say.

"I know." She nods but doesn't make a move to take one.

For a few moments, I wait to see if she'll choose, but when I notice a look of frustration on her face, I take her wrist and move her hand toward the package on the left. "How about that one?"

"Thank you," Asya mumbles, takes out the flour, and walks toward the stove.

She's mad at me, but it's better this way. Even if there wasn't this age gap, we are from two completely different backgrounds. Giving in to temptation and letting something happen between us is out of the question. I'm already treading a thin line, and every day it's becoming harder to control myself. Sometimes, I wish she'd just call her brother to come and get her, because having her so close all the time, makes me feel like I'm going to combust. Just as often, though, I'm flooded with an urge to find her brother myself... and dispose of him before he has an opportunity to take her away from me.

# Chapter fourteen

Asya

Clutching the coat around me, I stare at the front door. I've been looking at it for at least an hour. First, for ten straight minutes from the middle of the living room, then I managed two steps toward it and continued staring. It took me an hour of this stare-take-a-step-stare cycle to finally reach it. As I'm grabbing the handle, my hand is shaking. Biting at my lower lip, I open the door and exit the apartment.

Pasha's place is on the third floor, but since most of the residents use the elevator, the stairwell is vacant. Tiny shuffle at a time, I make my way down the stairs. It's quite a feat, considering how much my legs are shaking.

Pasha went to a meeting with his pakhan two hours ago, so he should be back soon. I could have waited for him, but I can't bear this feeling of helplessness anymore. I've been hiding in his apartment as if I'm a criminal for more than a month now, and I've finally decided I won't do it a second longer. I'm going to leave the building and take a walk around the block. Alone. It's three in the afternoon; what could possibly happen? Just a small walk, a completely normal thing, and I'll go back. I've been outside several times with Pasha. I will be okay.

When I make it to the foyer, I wave to the security guy sitting behind his desk and head toward the exit. A big glass sliding door allows me to see people as they pass by on the sidewalk. As I approach the door, a wave of nausea comes over me and gradually becomes worse as I get closer. The door swooshes to the side. I swallow the bile and take the last few steps.

My feet reach the sidewalk. I stop and look up at the sky, feeling the sunrays on my face. It wasn't that hard.

Someone moves by me, catching my shoulder with their arm. I flinch and look to the side to see an older woman walking away. She rounds the corner and disappears from view. I'm feeling sick to my stomach and my hands and legs are still trembling slightly, but it's getting better now that I've finally crossed the threshold.

Laughter rings out across the street as a group of kids runs inside a building. To the left, there is a grocery store with a lot of people going in and out, so I decide to turn right. I'm almost to the corner when a taxi pulls over just ahead and a man steps out. I stop and watch as he gets a laptop bag from the back seat. He's wearing a black suit with a white shirt and a dark gray tie under his unbuttoned coat. My heart thumps at double its normal speed. My breath hitches. The taxi leaves and the man slings the bag's strap over his shoulder and heads in my direction. I take a step back. Then another one. The man keeps walking, and with each of his steps, my breathing becomes more erratic. I turn around and run.

People. Too many people. They are all looking at me. I crash into someone's chest. Two hands grab my upper arms, probably just to steady me, but it feels like claws burying into my flesh. I scream and, the moment the hands release me, resume running.

"Did that waitress who's sleeping with Dushku find anything out?" Roman asks.

"No," I say. "Apparently, he talked about some confiscated shipment and complained about his wife spending too much money on shoes. But that's it."

"I've known Dushku for fifteen years. He's a master schemer and he's ruthless when it comes to business. But he would never get involved in human trafficking. If there's a connection here, we're not seeing it." He turns to Dimitri. "What about the men you have following Dushku's son-in-law?"

"Nothing."

Roman hits the surface of his desk with his palm. "What's the name of that guy Julian sends to do his errands? Besim?"

"Bekim," Dimitri says.

"That one. I want Mikhail to have a chat with him. Someone dared to send mercenaries into the Bratva club and kill our men just to silence a seemingly nobody. It means there is a lot at stake. We'll find out who's responsible for Yuri's death, and I will personally slaughter him."

"What if it was Dushku who orchestrated everything after all?" I ask.

"Then he will die. And it will be neither fast nor pretty. Has the girl staying with you said anything?"

"She said the man who grabbed her didn't have an accent. The name he gave her was Robert, but that could be a fake."

"I'll have Maxim get photos of Dushku's men. Would she be able to recognize him?"

"Probably."

"Good. When are you planning on taking her to her family? She's been at your place for a month."

My body stiffens. I've always been honest with Roman. Until today. "She won't tell me her last name or give me their number," I lie. "I have no way of finding them until she does."

"Perfect," he barks. "And how long do you expect to remain on this unplanned vacation? The clubs won't run themselves."

"I've taken everything I need from the office, and I've been working from home. Kostya has been personally handling whatever I can't do remotely."

"All right. But next Saturday I need you at Baykal. I have a meeting with the Ukrainians. They want an in with us."

"They got over the Shevchenko fuckup?"

"Everybody knows Shevchenko was an idiot. Sergei did them a favor by killing him." Roman shrugs. "They're sending a new guy to handle the talks. He's coming with two other men."

"Okay. I'll double the security."

He leans back in his chair and motions with his hand toward my outfit of jeans and a T-shirt. "What's with the new fashion style?"

"I needed a change," I say and see him lift an eyebrow. "Anything else?"

"No. You're free to go. Dimitri and I will go over the rest."

I nod and leave the pakhan's office.

As I'm heading down the hallway, the kitchen door on the other end bursts open, and a petite brunette in a paint-stained dress runs out. Her hands are laden with *piroshki,* and she is struggling to make sure none fall in her haste. At the top of the stairs, a little dark-haired girl starts jumping up and down and clapping her hands. Her sweet giggles echo off the hallway's high walls. Roman's wife and daughter. Nina Petrova sprints up the stairwell, nearly reaching the top when the kitchen door swings open again and Igor—the cook—wobbles out, shouting obscenities in Russian. If Roman catches him cursing in front of his little girl, the old cook will be as good as dead. I shake my head and stride toward the front door as the chorus of Igor's yelling and female laughter rings behind me.

"Mr. Morozov," the security guy in the hall of my building nods as I enter. "How was your day?"

"It was good, Bobby. Thank you."

"Oh, your girlfriend isn't back, yet."

I freeze in midstep. "What?"

"She left half an hour ago. I thought you'd like to know."

"Left?" I ask as panic floods my system. "Where?"

"I'm not sure. She just walked outside. I didn't see where she went."

I rush toward the security desk and come around to the other side. "Show me the camera feed from that time."

He skips the video to the moment when Asya walked out. She stands on the sidewalk, in full view of the camera for a couple of moments, then goes to the right. A few minutes later, she runs past the entrance at breakneck speed. I can't see her face, but based on how fast she's moving, she was scared shitless.

"Call me if she comes back!" I bark and run toward the exit.

I rush along the sidewalk, frantically looking in all directions, but I don't see Asya anywhere. There is a grocery store nearby. I walk inside and ask the cashier if he saw a girl meeting Asya's description, but he only shakes his head. I leave the store and continue down the street, asking people if they saw her, going inside other businesses, but no one has seen a runaway girl. When I reach the intersection at the end of the street, I turn around and head back. It's too crowded here. I doubt she'd go into a big mass of people.

Dread and anxiety keep building within me with every passing minute. She couldn't have gotten far, so why can't I find her? I should have bought her a phone, so she could have called if she needed me. It didn't even cross my mind until now since we were almost always together. Idiot!

I spot a group of kids hanging around the steps in front of a building across the street, laughing, so I sprint toward them.

"Did you see a girl run by about five minutes ago?" I ask.

"Yellow coat. Long brown hair?" a kid of about nine asks.

"Yes." I nod.

"I think I saw her running there." He points toward the alley behind the grocery store. "She seemed scared."

I swivel around and run across the street, nearly getting clipped by a taxi, and dart into the narrow alley. It looks deserted at first glance, but I keep going deeper, passing the dumpster by the grocer's back door. The smell of rotten fruit emanating off the trash cans accosts me, reminding me of a time when the stink of spoiled food was all I could smell. I fist my hands and round the corner, moving between the buildings.

It's my fault. I should have taken Asya outside more often, a bit more every day so she could have gotten used to being around other people again. I should have insisted on her going to the shrink or tried harder to convince her to call her brother. She needs to get back to her life, to her family. I didn't do any of that. Instead, I let her hide in my place. With me.

I like waking up with her curled into my side—her small body pressed to mine as if even in sleep, she subconsciously sought my presence. Or how she climbs onto my lap when we sit down to watch TV in the evenings and rests her head on my shoulder. She usually falls asleep after ten minutes, but I stay on the couch for hours, and only when it's well into the night do I carry her to bed. It feeds whatever longing that's awoken inside me, the inner need to keep her engulfed in my arms all the time, to know she's safe where no one can ever hurt her again. She's been staying with me for more than four weeks now, but she still keeps following me around the apartment, holding either my hand or the hem of my shirt. It feels good to be needed. So, I stopped trying to convince her to call her family. The selfish son of a bitch I've transformed into wants to keep her.

The alley curves to the right and ends in a big concrete wall. A pickup truck is parked beside it. There's no one around. I almost turn to head back when I spot something yellow under the truck. I rush over and stop in my tracks. There, between the truck and the wall, Asya is laying on her side, her face toward the wall and her arms wrapped tightly around her middle.

"Jesus." I kneel and gather her into my arms. She's shaking. The moment I have her in my embrace, her arms envelop my neck, and her legs wrap around my waist. I place my palm on the back of her head, tucking her face into the crook of my neck.

"It's okay, mishka," I whisper. "I have you."

Pathetic.

Weak.

That's how I feel as Pasha carries me back to his apartment. I can't gather the courage to even lift my head and look up because I'm afraid I'll freak out again. Instead, I keep my face buried in his neck.

I don't understand why he keeps troubling himself with me. All I did was barge into his life and make a mess out of it. I've been dreading the moment when he'll sit me down and tell me it's time for me to leave. It's bound to happen, and probably soon. I'm nothing to him. I can't keep disrupting his life. But just the idea of leaving his side makes me shudder from the terror it unleashes inside of me.

"Let's get you showered," Pasha says as he carries me inside the apartment.

In the bathroom, he stops next to the shower stall, waiting for me to let him go. Instead, I cling to him harder.

"Asya, baby. Look at me."

Reluctantly, I lift my head from his neck and look into his eyes. I don't think I ever met someone with eyes like Pasha's—the color is a striking metallic gray.

"You need to wash your hair," he says in his deep voice, and it seems I can feel it all the way to my bones. "You have engine oil everywhere."

"Can you do it?" I blurt out and regret it the moment the words leave my mouth. As if he's not burdened enough with me already.

Pasha watches me for a few moments, raises his hand as if intending to place it on my face but changes his mind and just takes my glasses off.

"Okay." He sets the glasses next to the sink and slowly lowers me down.

I take off my coat and sweater, then remove my shoes and jeans. Pasha waits patiently in front of me, his eyes fixed on mine. Even when I shed my bra and panties, his gaze never wanders lower.

It should bother me, being naked in front of him. It doesn't. Just the thought of a man looking at my nude body usually makes the bile bubble up my throat. Any man except him. I wish he would look lower. Touch me. Kiss me.

I step into the stall and turn on the shower. Water hits me from above, the stream falling straight down onto my head, making the rivulets run down my body. I stand unmoving under the spray and watch as Pasha takes off his jacket, removes his shoes and socks, and steps into the shower fully clothed. He takes the shampoo bottle off the shelf, pours an amount three times larger than necessary into his palm, and looks down at me.

"Turn around," he says, his voice huskier than usual.

I face away from him and reach out to shut off the shower. Once the sound of water ceases, the only thing I can hear is Pasha's deep breathing. His touch starts at the top of my head as his hands massage my scalp. The beating of my heart picks up pace. He took his shampoo, not mine, by mistake. But I didn't stop him. I close my eyes and inhale, letting the scent of sage and citrus fill my nostrils. I don't think I'll ever be able to connect those two scents with anything other than falling asleep next to Pasha.

His hands disappear from my hair. I turn on the shower again and slowly turn around.

The water is cascading down my face, blurring my vision, but not enough to obscure the sight of his wide chest in front of me. His white T-shirt is completely wet and plastered to his body, revealing the images inked on his skin. He rarely removes his shirt in front of me. I think he believes his tattoos scare me. They don't. Nothing about Pasha scares me, just the opposite. The only time I feel absolutely safe is when he is with me.

I tilt my head up and find those gray eyes of his staring at me. God, I want to kiss him so much. I've been thinking about it for weeks, but can't decide if I should or not. Now, however, looking at him—all wet from head to toe because I asked him to wash my hair for me—I don't have to decide. There's no question if I want or not, only the need to feel his lips on mine. I raise my hands to cup his face with my palms and pull his head down.

"Asya." He bends slowly, looking into my eyes.

"I love how you say my name." I smile. He pronounces it with a Russian lilt. Lifting onto my toes, I tilt my head up and lightly touch my mouth to his. "Say my name again. I want to know how it tastes on your lips."

Pasha's hand comes to rest at the back of my neck, stroking the sensitive skin there, while his eyes bore into mine.

"Please," I whisper over his lips.

He touches his forehead to mine and closes his eyes. "You've been hurt."

"I know." I move my hand along his jaw and bury my fingers in his wet strands.

"You're eighteen," he says. "I'm too old for you, mishka."

I bite his lower lip lightly. "Bullshit."

His hand at the back of my neck grips my hair. His breath fans my face as he exhales, and he opens his eyes to look at me. "Asya," he says into my lips, then seizes them with his own.

I grab at the material of his wet shirt to keep myself steady as I let him devour me with his mouth.

"Asya," he says again between kisses, moving his lips to my chin and along my neck. "My little Asya."

I grab the hem of his shirt and pull it up and over his head. Pasha's hands glide down my body, stopping under my thighs as he lifts me. I wrap my arms and legs around him at the same moment, just as I have so many times before. The movement is so natural, it feels like I've been doing it all my life. He carries me out of the bathroom and toward the bed, kissing me the whole way.

"We won't do anything, mishka," he says and lowers me to stand next to the bed. "I will just be kissing you. Okay?"

I nod and brush my palm down his cheek. "Okay."

"I need to grab a change of clothes. Wait here."

Oh, so not happening. I jump back into his arms.

"Asya." He looks down at me. "I need to go into the closet, baby."

I know what he means. His suits are there. "I won't look," I say.

Pasha squeezes his arm around my back. "Okay. I'll be quick."

He runs. I don't even notice the suits because he just rushes inside, grabs a pair of boxer briefs, pajama bottoms, and a T-shirt, and he's out in under five seconds.

When he places me on the bed again, I drift to my spot next to the wall and pull the blanket over my naked body. My hair is still wet and will soak the pillow, but I don't care. Pasha turns his back to me and, in a few quick moves, changes out of his wet jeans and underwear into dry boxer briefs and pajama bottoms.

"Don't," I say when he reaches for the T-shirt.

He looks over his shoulder, then at the tee in his hand. "Mishka?"

"Please," I whisper.

Pasha nods and throws the T-shirt onto the recliner. The mattress dips as he climbs into bed. As soon as he's next to me, I lean forward and place a kiss on his naked chest. His hand comes under my chin, and he tilts my head up.

"Nothing will happen tonight. Just kisses and cuddling. But if you want us to stop, you need to tell me. Right away, Asya."

An urge to cry comes over me at hearing the words, but I bottle it up. Wrapping my arms around his neck, I crush my lips to his. His hand caresses my back, stroking me over the blanket. I shove the blanket off me and continue kissing him. Pasha's palm presses against the small of my back and, for a fleeting second, I freeze. He quickly removes his hand and lies there utterly still.

"It's okay," I say into his lips. "I know it's you."

He slowly puts his hand back, but it's barely touching me. I sigh, throw my leg over his waist, and climb on top of him. "Please, stop treating me as if I'm going to break when a wind blows in my direction."

Pasha's hand cups my cheek, brushing the skin under my eye with his thumb. "I'm afraid you're going to."

"You can't break something that's already been broken beyond repair, Pasha." I press my cheek into his palm. His jaw goes rigid and the vein at his temple pulses.

"We'll fix you up, mishka," he says through gritted teeth and pulls my face closer. "We will piece together every broken shard, I promise you. And then, we'll fucking annihilate the bastards who hurt you."

I crush my mouth to his. I don't think I'll ever go back to who I was before, but I don't tell him that. Only kiss him.

Pasha's arm circles my waist, and he rolls us until I'm on my back with his body looming over mine.

"Okay?" he asks, and I nod.

"Just kissing, and nothing else, Asya. Remember?"

When I nod again, Pasha slides down, his mouth landing on my collarbone and trailing a line down the center of my chest to my stomach. His hands roam over my arms, my sides—his touch slow and featherlight.

"No one will hurt you ever again, mishka," he whispers as he moves down my body, his lips covering every inch of my skin—down my right leg, then my left, all the way to my feet. As he shifts back up, leaving a trail of kisses along my inner thighs, that dreadful voice whispers inside my head.

*You are disgusting. I don't know how he can stomach putting his mouth on something as filthy as you. The only thing you're good for is being fucked without mercy. You don't deserve any better.*

I squeeze my eyes shut and move my hands down my body, pressing my palms over my pussy. Pasha's mouth stills on my hipbone.

"Baby? Do you want me to stop?"

I shake my head. "Please don't," I whisper. "Just not there."

"Okay. I won't do anything that will make you feel uncomfortable."

"It's not that," I say.

Pasha moves up my body and takes my face into his palms. "Give me your eyes, Asya."

I open my eyes to find him looking at me with concern. I don't deserve this. I don't deserve him.

"What did I do wrong?" he asks, and I feel the tears gathering in the corners of my eyes.

"You did nothing wrong," I choke out. "I just don't want your lips there."

"Why, baby?"

"Because . . ." I shut my eyes again and squeeze my legs together. "Because I'm dirty."

I feel the kiss land on my lips. "There is nothing dirty about you," he says. "You are the most beautiful, pure thing I've ever encountered, Asya"—another kiss—"and I will erase every bad memory you have, if you'll let me."

The tip of his finger traces along my eyebrow. "Please?"

"Okay." I nod.

Pasha takes my hand and places it on the back of his head. "Grab and tug it."

I bury my fingers in his hair and grip the silky strands.

"Harder, mishka," he says and nods when I do. "Good. I want you to do that the moment you want me to stop. Deal?"

"Yes"

He kisses my lips again before moving his mouth lower, to my chin, my neck, across my collarbone and over my breasts to my stomach, then he pauses. When I don't do anything, he slides even lower until his lips reach my pelvis, and he waits again, looking up at me. He's pausing to give me a chance to stop him, but I don't. I take a deep breath and nod.

A kiss lands at the center of my folds. Then another one. A pause. Two more kisses, and I shudder.

"Asya?"

"I'm okay," I mutter.

Another kiss. A tentative lick. Pasha's hands push on the inside of my thighs, opening my legs wider. In the next moment, his tongue presses to my clit. I inhale and shudder again as a tingling feeling unfurls in my core.

Several more licks, and another kiss. His lips mold to my pussy and suck. A moan leaves me, and I squeeze at his hair without thinking.

Pasha's head snaps up. "Baby?"

"Sorry." I let go of his hair and push his head down between my legs again. "More."

He resumes licking me—slow at first, then faster. The pressure between my legs builds, but I need more. Pasha's mouth slips lower, his tongue entering me, and I gasp at the sensation. My body starts shaking.

"I need . . ." I mutter, arching my back. "More."

"Just my mouth today, mishka," Pasha says and moves to suck on my clit again. My body is trembling, yearning.

"More!" I scream and grip his hair with all my strength.

He keeps teasing my clit, switching between licking and sucking while his hand moves along my inner thigh closer to my core. My breathing picks up the moment I feel his finger at my entrance, I'm already close to combusting. Slowly, his finger slides inside, so impossibly carefully, it makes me want to weep. He's acting as if it's my first time. As if there weren't dozens of other men who already plunged their way inside me by force. I throw my head back and moan, riding the unfamiliar feeling of floating that comes over me while wetness pools between my legs. When he has his finger fully in, he presses his lips over my clit and sucks, hard, and it feels like I burst into a million tiny butterflies. I never imagined that it would feel so whimsical to have an orgasm.

My body is still trembling when Pasha lies down beside me. He wraps his arm around my front, placing his hand on the back of my head, and tucks my face into the crook of his neck.

"I wish my first time was with you," I whisper.

"It will be."

"Pasha, you know very well—"

His hand covers my lips. "Your first time is going to be with me," he says next to my ear. "All that from before, it doesn't count. Do you understand?"

I press my lips together, trying not to cry while something warm swells inside my chest, gluing together a couple of the broken pieces of my soul.

# Chapter fifteen

## Pavel

"Pasha, *ma che fai*?"

I look up from the spaghetti I was just going to place into the pot. Asya is standing on the other side of the kitchen island, staring at my hands in horror.

"You do not break spaghetti!" She walks around the island, shaking her head.

"They're too long. Can't fit into the pot," I say.

"No, no, no, you can never do that." She takes the spaghetti noodles out of my hands and throws them into the trash can in the corner. Then, heads to the cupboard, probably to get another package. She stiffens the moment she pulls the cabinet door open, her hand squeezing the handle as she stares at the bags of different pasta lined up on the top shelf. They are all different brands. I walk up and lift her free hand until it's hovering right before the bags.

"Take your time," I say next to her ear and let go of her hand.

Asya stares at the shelf. With her hand still hovering in midair, she bites her lower lip, then grabs the middle bag.

"I did it," she says, squeezing the bag.

"You did." I smile and place a kiss on the side of her neck.

She tilts her head, giving me more access.

"I'm so proud of you, baby."

"I never would have managed it without you." She turns to face me. "You know that, don't you?"

"You would have."

"No. I probably wouldn't." She places her hand on the back of my neck, pulling me down for a quick kiss. "Thank you."

She rushes around the kitchen, getting the pasta into the pot and the cheese out of the fridge. There's a small smile on her lips, and I feel the warmth in my chest upon seeing it. I'm so fucking proud of her. It took weeks of practice to get to this point, and she's doing considerably better. It may take us a little more time for us to be where she won't need me to steer her toward the decision, but we'll make it there eventually. Suddenly, panic replaces the warmth in my chest. Will she leave when she gets better? She probably will.

## Asya

"I should be back shortly," Pasha says as he walks inside the closet. "I need to sign some contracts and check if Kostya made another mess with the orders. If it happens to take more than two hours, I'll call you."

I look down at the phone in my hand. He went out yesterday, saying he had an errand to run, and came back half an hour later with a white paper bag. Inside was a brand-new phone and a pair of headphones. He said those are in case I wanted to listen to music.

I leave the phone on the nightstand and walk across the bedroom, stopping at the closet threshold. Pasha is standing in front of the shelf on the left, rummaging through a stack of T-shirts. I let my gaze dart to the rack on the right side where dozens of his suits and dress shirts are hung in perfect color order, from black to light gray. Biting down on my lower lip, I enter and approach it. Slowly, I reach for the hanger with a charcoal gray suit. My hand shakes as I touch the elegant fabric, taking the garment off the loop.

"I think you should wear this today," I say and turn around to face him.

Pasha's eyes fix on the suit I'm holding to my chest and then move up until our gazes connect. "Baby . . . I don't . . ."

"Please." I extend my hand, offering the outfit to him. "It's you. I would never be scared of you, Pasha."

He regards me with concern in his eyes, but reaches out and takes the suit from me. I offer him a small smile and walk toward the far end of the rack where his shirts are hanging. I slide my fingers across the hangers until I reach one of the white shirts, then take it off and return to Pasha. He lays the suit on the shelf and takes the shirt from my hand.

He slowly puts the shirt on, his eyes glued to my face the whole time as if he's waiting for me to freak out. I'm certain that if he spots even the slightest trace of fear on my face, he'll have the shirt off in a second. But he won't see it. He will always be my Pasha, no matter what he wears.

Once he has the shirt buttoned, he waits a few moments before reaching for the pants and putting them on. Finally, he grabs the jacket.

"Okay?" he asks.

I nod and smile. When he gets the jacket on, I reach out and straighten his lapels.

"One more thing," I say and turn to open the drawer behind me.

A variety of silk neckties in multiple colors are rolled and stuffed in small compartments within the drawer. My eyes skim over them until I find one that's the same shade as his suit. As I extend my hand to take it out, an image of me restrained on the bed flashes through my mind. My hand falters just above the tie. I push the memory away, replacing it with thoughts of Pasha. Pasha embracing me in bed, stroking my back. Pasha moving the cereal box closer to my hand, encouraging me to make a choice. Pasha carrying me safely home even though I was dirty and smeared in oil. Pasha washing my hair. Pasha kissing me. I wrap my fingers around the silky material, take the tie out, and turn around.

"Can I . . . can I put it on you?" I choke out.

He doesn't say anything, just bends and cups my face in his palms. There's a strange look in his eyes as they bore into mine—a mix of concern and wariness but there's awe, too. And pride.

I drape the tie around his neck and begin making the knot, looping the wide part over the thin one. My fingers are trembling, and the fabric slips from my grasp. I take a deep breath, pick up the loose end, and resume my work. When I'm finally done, I let go of the tie and look up. That's when I become aware that Pasha is still holding my face.

"You are the strongest person I know," he says and presses his mouth to mine.

The kiss is gentle as if he's afraid I'll get scared. I might be broken, but what's left of me is desperately in love with him. I don't want him to hold back on me. I don't want gentle. I want all of him. I fling my arms around his neck and jump, clinging to him as if he were a tree. His hold on me is instantaneous, supporting me while I pull down his face and bite his lip. Hard.

"I want you to make love to me," I say into his mouth. "And I don't want you to hold back."

"Okay, mishka," he says between kisses. They're still delicate.

"Pasha." I squeeze the hair at the back of his head. "No holding back. I need you not to hold back. Promise me."

"Asya, baby, I don't want to—"

I press my finger over his lips. "I don't want to feel broken when I'm with you. So, I need you to treat me as if I'm not. Give me everything you have. Please. Promise me."

Pasha's arms tighten around my waist. "I promise," he says and crushes his mouth to mine.

It's a whirlwind of hard, fast kisses and bites. Clashing teeth and dueling tongues. We are a tangled mess of lips and limbs. He's holding me so tightly pressed against his body that I'm certain no tidal force in the universe could tear us apart. And I'm marveling at every second of it.

A melody pops into my mind and plays in the background as we attack each other's lips in a frenzy. "In the Hall of the Mountain King" by Grieg. My arms around his neck tighten. We don't stop kissing as he carries me to the bedroom until we reach the bed.

"I need to take off my clothes," he says into my mouth and lowers me to the bed.

I nod, reluctantly releasing my hold of him. He removes his jacket first and lets it fall to the floor. The tie is next. I see the concern in his eyes as he reaches for it. Leaning forward, I brush the back of my fingers down his cheek. "You promised."

The tie falls down, too. His shirt and pants follow and, soon, he's standing in front of me completely naked. My mountain king.

Getting closer I press my lips to his. "Now, please help me take off mine."

I take a deep breath and circle my hands around Asya's waist. It doesn't matter what I promised. I can't make myself do anything that may lead to triggering her trauma, even if it means going back on my word. Focusing on her face, I hook my fingers in the waistband of her sweatpants and start pulling them down, inch by agonizingly slow inch. If I notice even a speck of distress, we're stopping. Then, I slide my palms up her legs, over her panties, and pull up on the hem of her top. She smiles and lifts her arms, shaking out her dark hair as the shirt comes free of her body. Unclasping the bra, Asya tosses it to the floor and stands in front of me, clad only in her panties. She tries to make herself look unfazed, but I see the restrained terror in her eyes. And also, the fierce determination to show me that she won't cave, no matter what I say. I caress her face and lean forward until we're nose to nose.

"You are the purest thing I've ever touched in my life," I say holding her gaze, "and I will never, ever hurt you."

"I know," she utters, then places her palms over mine and lowers herself onto the bed, pulling me down with her.

"Grab my hair, mishka."

Her right hand moves to the back of my head, fingers threading through the strands.

"Good. Now I need you to promise something," I say.

"What?"

"Even the smallest discomfort, you pull, and I'll stop."

"I promise."

I kiss her lips, along her chin, and down her neck. My cock is so hard it hurts, but I ignore it and continue peppering her body with kisses. Her small hand, arm, shoulder, across her collarbones to the other arm. I am going to erase every single evil touch she's had on her skin with my lips. When I reach her panties, I halt for a moment, waiting to see if she'll stop me. She doesn't. I trail a line of kisses from her midriff down, over her still-covered pussy, and back up to her stomach. Asya's free hand slides to the lacy material and pushes it down. I drop a kiss on the back of her hand, then take the sides of her panties and slowly pull them off.

"I will never hurt you." I lean forward and capture her slightly trembling lips with my own. "Hair, baby."

She takes a deep breath and takes a hold of my hair again.

"Never," I repeat, leaving a path of kisses from her neck all the way to her sex.

When I slide my tongue over her pussy, Asya's breathing picks up. I keep licking, then add my thumb and start massaging her clit. A small sound of pleasure leaves her lips, and I feel her wetness on my face. I quicken my licks and keep teasing her with my finger until I'm sure she's close, and then I suck on her clit. Asya arches her back and moans while the tremors pass through her body. Carefully, I lower myself over her, but keep most of my weight on my elbows. Her eyes flutter open, and our gazes connect.

"Yes," she answers my unspoken question and widens her legs a bit more.

I position my cock at her entrance, then slowly begin sliding inside. It's hard to hold back because the need to lose myself within her is overwhelming, but I keep my pace steady, half an inch at a time. And I don't break our eye contact the entire time.

Her breaths are coming fast, and her eyes are wide, but her grip on my hair doesn't waver. Once I'm fully inside, she gasps, her lips spreading into a smile. And then, the hold on my hair loosens and vanishes completely.

"Now, I need you to keep your promise," she says and kisses the side of my jaw. "I need you to treat me as if I'm not broken."

"You are you, mishka." I pull out, pause, and slowly slide back in. "Absolutely perfect . . ." I retreat, then slide inside again, but a little faster. "Just the way you are."

It's almost impossible to restrain my impulses, but I rein myself in and adjust the tempo so it builds slowly, making every thrust just a little bit faster and harder than the previous one. Asya's legs wrap around me, and she tilts her chin up, staring into my eyes.

"Prove it to me," she digs her nails into the skin of my arms. "Give me everything."

My control snaps in an instant. I bury myself in her to the hilt. Her body starts trembling under me.

"More," she chokes out.

I pull out and immediately thrust back inside, bottoming out in her heat.

"Faster!"

Grabbing the back of her neck, I pound into her—fast and hard—the sight of her flushed face etched forever on my mind. The bedframe creaks beneath us. I hook my fingers behind her knee, raising her leg and opening her more so I can slide in deeper. Asya's hands squeeze my arms, then move up to wrap behind my neck, pulling my head down for a kiss. I consume her lips like a starved man, taking more and more while rocking into her.

A moan escapes from Asya's delicate throat. I pull out completely and just watch her for a moment before slamming back inside. Her pussy spasms around my cock while her hot breath fans my face. She cries out as she comes. Hearing the sounds of her pleasure and seeing her come apart under me sends a jolt to my system, and I explode with a groan the very next moment.

*I'm in the room with the red drapes again. The heavy scent of male cologne clings to the air. My hands are tied to the headboard, and a huge male body looms above. Droplets of stinky sweat fall from his forehead onto my breasts. Pain spreads through my whole being as he thrusts into me again and again. I scream.*

"Shh. It's just a dream," Pasha's deep voice says into my ear. "You're safe."

The panic recedes and extinguishes completely when he pulls me closer toward him, wrapping his arm tightly around my waist. I don't have nightmares that often anymore, but when I do, they are bad.

"Are you okay?" Pasha asks and places a kiss on my shoulder.

I flip around so I'm facing his naked inked chest. The lamp by the nightstand is on but dimmed, throwing a soft yellow light onto the black and red shapes. I reach out to stroke the line of a skull bathed in blood. It's one of many. There must be at least ten different skulls on his chest alone. The rest of the tattoos are of similarly disturbing scenes.

Most men in the Cosa Nostra have some ink. Even my brother has a full sleeve tattoo. But I don't think I know anyone who has their entire upper body tattooed like Pasha.

"Why so many?" I ask.

"Everyone has a different way of coping with the shit life throws at them. This was mine."

"What kind of shit?"

Pasha looks down at me and places the tip of his finger on the corner of my lips. "Abandonment. Low self-esteem. Loneliness," he answers, then looks away. "Humiliation. Hunger."

I blink at him in confusion. It's obvious he has money. His watch costs at least twenty grand.

"It wasn't always like this for me," he says, guessing my thoughts. He looks down at me again and traces his finger over my eyebrow. "I was left on the doorsteps of a church when I was three. The earliest memory I have is of a woman leading me up the steps to a big brown door and telling me to stay there. Then she left. It was probably my mother, but I can't be sure. I don't remember what she looked like. I don't remember anything prior to those five stone steps and the brown door."

I slide my palm across his chest and examine the design on his left pec. It shows a dark double door. Thick black vines wrap around it several times as if to keep it shut. The details are amazing; the images are almost photo quality.

"You did that?" I point to the design.

"Yes. As well as most of the rest. Except for the ones on my back and other places I couldn't reach."

"Can I see those?"

He turns so his back is to me. Skulls again. Snakes. Lots of red. Spiders. Some strange, winged creatures. The style is similar to those on his front and arms, but they don't look as good as those he did himself.

"A jail buddy did those for me," he adds and turns back to face me.

My head snaps up and I stare at him. "You were in jail?"

"A couple of times."

"What for?"

"Police often raided the clubs where the underground fights were held. The charges varied from disturbing the peace to assault. I did four months for that last one."

"But you're so levelheaded. You even organize your T-shirts by color."

He smiles at me. "I organize everything by color, mishka."

I reach out and brush the side of his face with the tip of my finger. Such a hard-looking man. Yes, looks can be so deceiving, because his rough exterior hides an amazingly beautiful soul. How can someone who experienced the things he did have a heart as big as his? Is it big enough to include me, too? I lean forward and kiss him. The moment our lips touch, my soul begins to sing.

For as long as I can remember, I have associated music with the feeling of joy. Whenever I was feeling down or scared, I'd play the piano Arturo bought me. Sometimes, I played for hours until sadness or fear was replaced with joy. Right now, it seems that my relationship with music has transformed. I don't need to play anymore to feel better. I just need to be close to him, to my Pasha, and the melody fills me.

"How old were you when you started fighting?" I ask.

"Eighteen."

"Were you good?"

Pasha laughs into my lips. "Not in the beginning. The first few months, I got the shit kicked out of me."

"But you kept doing it?"

"The money was good. And as I got better, I earned larger sums. So I practiced every day and made sure I was the best I could be."

"So it was all about the money?"

"At first, yes," he says as he traces my chin with his finger, "but there was something . . . primal that rose within me when I heard people cheering and yelling my name. I got addicted to it, in a way. It was very fulfilling. Well, for a period of time, at least. I was twenty-three when I joined the Bratva. I can't believe it's been over ten years."

"So you went from a fighting ring to an upscale club. It's a big change."

"I started as a soldier. Sometimes running errands, but most of the time, I was sent to collect debts. I'd never even held a gun back then, so Yuri had to teach me how to shoot before I could be given more serious assignments."

"Do you like it? Running a nightclub?

"Two clubs, actually. I'm at Ural most of the time. It's a bigger one. The second club, Baykal, is mostly used to launder money. But yes, I like it."

I lean my head on his chest and stroke the inked skin of his stomach. "I've never been to a club. The New York Family isn't involved in the entertainment business, so Arturo only let me and Sienna go to bars owned by someone within the Cosa Nostra. And even that was rare."

"Why?"

"He was scared that something would happen to us. Sienna always wailed about how paranoid he was. I guess he was right to be."

Pasha's hold on me tightens, and he strokes my back.

"How does it feel?" His voice is soft, almost reverent.

"What?"

"To have a family. Someone who'll stay with you, no matter what. Even if you make a mistake. Even when you're angry. Someone who'll be in your corner even when they know you're wrong. To have someone who is . . . yours?"

The look in his eyes . . . I can't describe it. Longing. Hunger. And so much sadness.

"It's like warmth," I whisper.

"Warmth?"

"Yes. When you find yourself in a frigid, raging storm, they are the people who will do anything to make sure you don't get cold. They will wrap their arms around you, shield you, surround you in their own warmth while the icy wind beats on their backs."

"Is your family like that?"

"Sometimes, Sienna and Arturo are hard to deal with. The three of us have very different personalities. But yes. They are both like that."

"Will you tell me about them?"

"Sienna is . . . a force of nature. She's loud. Outspoken. One moment, she would be laughing like crazy, and the next, she'd be crying her eyes out." A nostalgic smile spreads across my lips. "Sienna loves to pretend that she's shallow. She posts a gazillion photos on social media, wearing ridiculous clothes that usually make people think she's a bit whacky. Sometimes, she gives them the impression that she's not very bright."

"Why?"

"I have no idea." I reach out and trace the line of his brow with my finger. "My sister is the most intelligent person I know, but instead of doing something with her amazing mind, she'll just . . . fool around. The only thing that truly interests her is her writing."

"What does she write?"

"She's never shown me." I smile. "But I snuck a peek at some of her notebooks when we were younger. They were hidden in a box under her bed. She writes romance novels."

"Romance novels?" Pasha raises his eyebrow. "Is she good?"

"Yeah. Very good. Sienna has a thing with words. Other than English and Italian, she can speak four other languages. And she learned them on a whim."

"I don't think I've ever heard of anyone learning a language on a whim."

"My sister learned basic Japanese in a month, all on her own, just because a boy from school called her stupid." I laugh. "She was fourteen at the time."

Pasha smiles, but his eyes stay sad. "That's quite the talent. Most people would be hard-pressed to learn and speak one foreign language, never mind five. I don't like speaking Russian. I understand it completely, but I almost never converse in it."

"I've noticed." I lean forward and press my lips to his. "Why?"

"Because I have an English accent if I do. None of the kids at the foster homes or schools spoke Russian, so during that time I kind of . . . just forgot it, I guess." He nips at my lip. "What about your brother?"

"Arturo is like all older brothers. Just a hundred times worse."

"Protective?"

"To a point of driving me insane. He was twenty when our parents died, so he took on their role."

"You didn't have any other family members?"

"We had an aunt. Dad's half sister. She offered to take me and Sienna in, to live with her. Arturo said no." I shake my head. "I'm worried about him.

I think, something flipped in his mind when our mom and dad were killed, and he focused all his attention, outside of his work, on the two of us. He's thirty-three, but he's never brought a woman to our house. I know he had several relationships; we even met some of his girlfriends. But none of them have set a foot in our home. I think he was so focused on raising us that he actually forgot he's not really our parent."

"Why don't you want to call him? It's obvious he loves you."

"Because I love him, too," I whisper. "At first, I thought he wouldn't be able to get over what happened to me. So, I didn't want to call him."

"And now?"

"Now, I don't want to call because I know how much he'll hurt if he learns the truth. Arturo will put two and two together, even if I don't tell him everything. He'll blame himself. I can't allow that. He has enough on his shoulders, and he's shielded me from enough storms in my life." As I say this, something else crosses my mind. "There was a girl. At Dolly's place. I think she may have been Russian. She was brought in about a month after they took me, but she disappeared a few days before I got away."

His palm stills on my back. "Do you remember her name?"

"Rada, or something like that. I'm not sure. Why?"

"Could it have been Ruslana?"

My head snaps up. "Yes. It was Ruslana. Do you know her?"

"She was the daughter of one of the Bratva's soldiers."

"Was?"

"Her body was found around the time you escaped. A day or two earlier, I think."

I shudder and bury my face in the crook of his neck. She couldn't have been more than a year or two older than me.

"Will you be in trouble because you didn't go to the club tonight?" I ask, trying not to think about the girl with a long blonde braid and how it easily could have been me.

"I'll go tomorrow."

"Can I come with you?" I ask.

A kiss lands on the crown of my head. "Of course."

# Chapter sixteen

Pavel

Soft tones of a delicate melody reach my ears as I exit the elevator. I walk up to the door of my apartment and pull the keys out of my pocket. Lately, I've been pretending that I've forgotten my keys so I can ring the bell and hear Asya's hurried steps as she runs toward the door to let me in. When she opens it, it's as if she has missed me, even though I've only been gone for a short time. It feels good to come home and know that she is waiting for me. So, I keep pretending to forget my keys and ring the bell each time.

But I don't want to distract her from her playing today. Opening the lock, I walk inside. Asya is sitting in front of the piano, her phone is on the small stand above the keys. She probably found new sheet music online and downloaded it. I should buy her actual sheet music books. It can't be easy to follow along on that small screen. Trying my best not to make any noise, I leave the grocery bags by the door and walk into the living room. I lean my shoulder on the bookshelf on my right and watch her.

Her hair is loose, and it sways left to right when she bobs her head along with the melody. I can't see her face from my spot, but I'm pretty sure she's smiling.

Something squeezes in my chest. Will she take the piano with her when she leaves? Because she will leave, eventually. I won't delude myself into believing she'd want to stay with me when she has a home, a family, probably a bunch of friends, and plans to attend a music conservatory. Her life might have been placed on hold with what happened to her, but she'll bounce back. I've seen her strength and determination. Her courage. All those things that make her *her*—the same traits that made me fall so desperately in love with her, they will also take her away from me.

We need to get to the club soon if we want to arrive before the opening and avoid the crowd, but I can't make myself ask her to stop. The melody changes as she switches to my favorite one, "Moonlight Sonata." I'm not sure why I love hearing her play that one the most. Maybe because of the first time I heard her play. I've even set it as her ringtone on my phone. I grip the back of my neck in frustration. I hope she takes the piano when she leaves. Because if she doesn't, I'm going to smash it until there is nothing left of it.

"If you get uncomfortable, even a little bit, let me know and we'll leave. Okay?"

I nod and squeeze Pasha's hand.

As we walk toward the entrance of the club, I look up at the dark sky, searching for the small white flakes. The temperature has dropped significantly, and there is a crisp feel to the air. It's been clinging to my senses since the moment we left Pasha's building, along with the panic that's been rising in my chest. I almost asked Pasha if I could return to his place, fearing that it would start snowing. I thought I was getting better. In some ways, I was. But the idea of seeing the frost-covered ground makes my heart pound at double its normal rhythm.

A man standing at the entrance opens the door for us when we approach. He's wearing an unbuttoned black coat, revealing a black suit underneath. I tighten my hold on Pasha's hand and will myself to offer the bouncer a small smile as we pass.

Pasha leads me across the spacious area decorated in shades of black and gray. Tall tables surround the edges of a currently empty dance floor. Along the wall, a raised platform holds several large booths containing luxury leather seating. The space is completely empty, save for a girl who is cleaning at one of the booths, making the sound of our footsteps echo off the walls.

Finally reaching the opposite side of the floor, we climb the stairwell to the upper level. This space has been made to look like a gallery of sorts. The floor-to-ceiling glass wall leans out over the dance floor, exposing the entirety of the club's interior to anyone standing up here. We enter a room where a man in his early forties sits in front of a block of monitors showing various camera angles of different areas in the club. Pasha nods at the man and heads toward another door on the right.

As we enter, I spot a blond man in his twenties sitting behind a desk covered with papers. He's mumbling something to himself while glaring at the computer screen in front of him. His longer-cut hair is tousled but it doesn't hide the fact he's very handsome. A few months ago, my face would have flushed red if I saw him. But that was before I met Pasha. This guy may be attractive, but his looks have no impact on me.

"I see you finally decided to drag your ass here," the man grumbles then looks up from the screen, his eyes zeroing in on me and going impossibly wide.

"Kostya, this is Asya," Pasha says and leads me around the desk until we're standing in front of his friend. "Where are the contracts that need my signature?"

Kostya's gaze drops to my hand clasped in Pasha's before it flips back up to my face. His eyebrows shoot all the way up to his hairline.

"Eyes on me, Konstantin!" Pasha barks.

"Jesus fuck, man!" Kostya cringes. "Don't do that. Only my *babushka* calls me by my full name, usually when I've fucked something up."

"Contracts. Now."

"What the fuck has gotten into you? Did you change your fucking personality along with your wardrobe? Christ." He grabs a stack of papers out of the drawer and tosses them on the desk in front of Pasha. "Here."

Pasha starts signing the contracts, but his left hand retains its hold on mine the entire time. He's wearing jeans and a black sweater today. I tried to convince him to put on a suit, but he said no.

Kostya pretends to be busy with something on the computer screen, but I notice him throwing a quick look at me every few seconds.

Once Pasha is done signing, he pushes the papers to the center of the desk and straightens. "Is that all?"

"Yup."

Pasha nods and heads toward the exit. I wave at his friend and follow. We're at the threshold when Kostya calls out, "Oh, Pasha! You may want to drop by the old warehouse later."

"What for?"

"We've caught one of Julian's men. Bekim. Mikhail will be questioning him."

Pasha's body stiffens. He turns slowly and looks at his friend. "Call Mikhail. Tell him he can stay home with his family tonight."

"What? So, who's going to have that chat with the guy?"

Pasha looks down at me. "I will."

## Pavel

When I enter the warehouse, Kostya is already there, leaning against the wall and fumbling with his phone. In the opposite corner, with his face to the floor, lies a man in his early thirties. His legs are bound with silver duct tape around his ankles and knees. His hands are tied behind his back. A dirty rag protrudes from his mouth.

Even after all these years, a faint scent of burned wood still lingers in the air. This is one of the warehouses that the Italians tried to burn down before we signed the truce. The basement in the pakhan's mansion has been out of commission since then—his wife doesn't appreciate the smell of blood in her house—so we decided to leave this warehouse as is and conduct our interrogations here.

I glance at the soldier standing a few paces from "our guest" and tip my head toward the exit. "Leave. I'll call you when I'm done."

The man nods and heads outside.

I don't waste any time and grab Julian's man by the back of his jacket, dragging him away from the wall to give me more room. He whines and starts thrashing, then moans when I let his body fall back to the floor. I place my foot on his back and wrap my hand around his thumb. The sound of bones breaking is followed by a muffled, pained whimper. I press my foot harder and take the next finger.

"You need to ask Mikhail to give you a quick course in torture," Kostya says from his spot by the wall. "The rule is: ask questions first. Then start breaking shit."

Another snap.

"Our methods differ," I say as I continue.

Once I've broken all ten fingers, I leave the man to weep on the ground and pick up a knife off the nearby table. I step on his back again and cut the tape binding his wrists. The man thrashes, trying to wriggle free. I grab his right forearm with one hand, his palm in the other, and twist them in different directions. The man screams around the rag as his wrist snaps. I repeat the action with his other arm.

I consider breaking his ankles next but decide I don't want to risk him passing out on me. Moving my foot to his side, I push at his body until he's facing up and yank the rag out of his mouth.

"Is Dushku distributing the new drug?" I ask.

"No," the man chokes out. "It's Julian. His son-in-law."

"Is Julian involved in the high-end prostitution ring, as well?"

"Yes. He's running it."

"Does Dushku know?"

He shakes his head and whimpers. I place the sole of my shoe on the broken fingers of his right hand and put pressure into my step.

"He doesn't know! It's all Julian and some of his college friends!"

"What do you know about the Russian girl who was found dead a few months back? She had your drug in her system."

"It was an accident," he wails. "A client got too rough, and she died. We had to get rid of her, and make sure she wasn't linked to us through the drugs we use. So we pumped her full of heroin."

I press my heel on his throat, enjoying the choking sound that leaves his mouth. "You will give my friend here the names and addresses of everyone who's involved in this scheme. Including the clients. Even the fucking janitor. Make sure you give the details about the woman—Dolly—in charge of the girls, too. And the address of where you're keeping them."

He nods.

"I also need the names of the men abducting the girls."

"Robert is in charge of that," he squawks when I ease my foot off a little.

Robert. The motherfucker uses his real name when luring the girls.

"American?" I ask.

"Yes. He's been working for us for the last three years. Julian brought him in."

"Last name and address."

He rattles off the information, and I commit it to memory.

"Kostya," I call. "Our guest is ready to talk. Come here to take notes and relay everything he tells you to Maxim."

I throw one last look at the man on the floor. "If you happen to forget a name, I will come back and finish what I started. And I'll make sure you stay alive and coherent until I'm completely done."

Leaving the warehouse, I call Asya to let her know I won't be back for another couple of hours. Inside the car, I enter the address Bekim gave me into the navigation system.

Seems like I'll be having another chat tonight.

I WAKE UP TO THE FEELING OF FINGERS COMBING THROUGH MY HAIR. Pasha is lying on the bed next to me, still wearing the same clothes he had on the previous evening.

"When did you get back?" I ask.

"Five minutes ago," he says and continues stroking my hair. "I need to show you a photo of someone."

"Okay." I nod. He'd already shown me photos of more than a dozen men the other day, asking if I recognize anyone, but none of them seemed familiar.

Pasha releases my hair and reaches behind him to take his phone off the nightstand. I take the phone when he holds it out to me and look down at the screen. The image is of a man suspended upside-down from a ceiling. I can't make out his face too much, so I zoom in. The phone nearly slips from my hand.

"Is this him? The one who took you?" Pasha asks. His voice is strained as if he's speaking through gritted teeth.

I swallow the bile that has suddenly risen up my throat. "Yes."

Pasha nods and takes the phone from my hand. He grasps my chin between his fingers, tilting my head up until our gazes meet. "We've got all the names. Everyone who was involved. The Bratva will deal with the rest of their organization, but I told Pakhan that this one is mine." He leans forward and presses his forehead to my own. "You said you wanted to watch."

"What?"

"Him, dying. Slowly. As I cut him piece by little piece."

I look into his gray eyes as they stare back at me and take his face between my palms. "Yes."

Pasha nods. "I'm going to shower and change. And then we'll leave."

It's a two-hour drive west of the city to a rundown house that's not much more than a shed. Pasha parks the car and turns toward me, taking my hand in his.

"If you've changed your mind, I'll drive you back," he says. "It's okay if you can't handle seeing that motherfucker again. I'll come back tonight and take care of him."

I look through the windshield at the house. The man who destroyed my life and messed up my mind is beyond that wooden door. Panic started brewing the moment I saw his image on Pasha's phone and multiplied tenfold during the drive here. The idea of seeing him again makes me sick, but I need this. I need vengeance. Maybe seeing him die will help me get myself back.

"I'm ready," I say.

The first thing I notice when Pasha opens the door of the house is the stench, a mix of vomit and piss. It's so foul, I barely manage not to immediately empty the contents of my stomach. It's dark inside. The windows are covered with shaggy drapes or nailed-on boards, and the only illumination is from the sunlight coming through the open door. I follow Pasha as he takes two steps to the left, squeezing his hand with all my might. There is a click when he flicks on the light. It's a small sound, barely audible, but in my head, it reverberates like an explosion. I want to turn around and look the asshole in the face, but I can't make myself move.

"It's okay, mishka." Pasha wraps his arms around me and presses my face into his chest. "He can't hurt you anymore. And I'll make sure he doesn't hurt anyone else, ever again."

I inhale deeply, savoring Pasha's scent. It's the scent of safety. And love. It would be so easy to ask him to kill the son of a bitch for me. But deep inside, I know I need to play this tune myself.

"Do you have a gun?" I mumble into Pasha's chest and feel him go still.

"Yes."

"Can I have it? Please."

His hold on me loosens, and his hands travel up my arms until they reach my face.

"You don't have to do this. I'll make sure he suffers."

I lift my hand and cup his cheek. My Pasha. Always ready to fight my battles for me. "Please."

He closes his eyes for a second, reaches into his jacket, and takes out a gun. "Do you know how to shoot?"

"No."

"Okay. Hold it like this." He places the weapon in my hand and moves my fingers to the correct position. "The safety is on. When you're ready, you switch it off. Here. You need to hold the gun tightly. This one has a bit of a recoil."

I stare at the handgun. It's heavy. Much heavier than I expected. I swallow and turn to face the man who ruined my life.

He's still in the same position as I saw in the photo. His feet are tied to the beam above, his arms are dangling. Something is wrong with them, however. They hang at an unnatural angle. It's hard to believe this is the same man I met at the bar. His dirty clothes are torn in several places. Dried blood is smeared over the exposed parts of his body, staining his shirt, and the floor below. His eyes are closed and one side of his face is swollen. He's not moving. I'd think he's dead already, but I can see his chest rising and falling.

I've imagined this moment so many times. Dreamed about making him pay for every fucking second of my pain. I thought that if I ever got the opportunity to avenge myself, I would want him to suffer as I did. But now, seeing him like this, I just want it to be over.

I cover the distance between us in quick steps until I'm standing right in front of him. His head is level with my chest, and the foul smell is even worse up close.

"I hope you burn in hell," I choke out and spit into his face. Robert's eyes flutter open, meeting mine. I flip the safety switch and press the barrel to the bridge of his nose.

And pull the trigger.

A loud bang erupts through the room.

I wrap my left arm around Asya's middle, pulling her out of the way so the dead man's body won't hit her when it swings back. I don't think she even noticed me standing right behind her. I take the gun out of her hand, sliding the safety on, and carry her out of the house.

When we reach the car, I throw the gun onto the back seat and lower Asya to the ground, turning her to face me. Her hand and the sleeve of her yellow coat are covered in blood spatter. I unbutton and take the coat off her, throwing it onto the back seat, as well. Then, I pull off my own jacket and manage to get Asya's arms into the sleeves, zipping her into its warmth. She doesn't say anything while I get her dressed. Her eyes seem vacant as she stares in front of her. I don't think she's even aware of me.

I shouldn't have let her do this. When she took the gun and turned toward the son of a bitch, I was certain she'd change her mind. I don't think the sound of a gunshot has ever shaken me this much.

"Mishka," I prompt her as I wipe the blood off her hand on the front of my hoodie. "Please say something."

Asya just blinks. Her eyes remain unfocused.

A small white flake lands on her cheek. Another one follows. I look up at the sky. It's snowing. I quickly grab the hood of the jacket and pull it over her head. "Let's go home, baby."

By the time I park the car in front of my building, the light snow has turned into a full-blown blizzard. Asya spent the entire two-hour drive curled up on the passenger seat with her face pressed to my shoulder.

"We're here," I say.

She nods and straightens up, but keeps her eyes closed. I exit the car and walk around the front. However, when I open the passenger door, Asya makes no attempt to move.

"Let's get you inside." I bend and scoop her into my arms.

The wind blows in my face, sending snow into my eyes as I carry her toward the building's entrance. The parking lot is barely forty feet away, but by the time we reach the doors, we're both covered in flurries.

As soon as we get inside the apartment, I set Asya down and remove her jacket. I take off my hoodie next. It's black, like the jacket, and the snow hasn't had a chance to melt off it, yet. I throw the hoodie behind me and crouch to unlace her boots. I need to call the doc's psychologist friend again and ask what to do. I can't tell her that I let Asya kill a man, but I need some kind of advice. What if she regresses? Her silence is freaking me out.

As I'm untying Asya's other boot, I feel her hands in my hair. Slowly, I look up and find her watching me with a strange look in her eyes.

"I never should have given you that gun," I whisper. "I'm so sorry, baby."

Asya cocks her head to the side and glides her hands down my neck and further, to the center of my back. Grabbing handfuls of material with her fingers, she pulls the T-shirt over my head and then starts unbuttoning her shirt. I regard her as she removes it and her bra and starts on her jeans. I'm still crouching in front of her as she pushes the discarded clothes to the side and stands bare before me.

Taking my hand in hers, she pulls me up and unbuttons my jeans. I can't take my eyes off her while she removes my shoes and the rest of my clothes, leaving us both naked in front of each other.

"Asya, baby?" As I reach out to caress her face, she jumps on me. I barely catch her in time, managing to grab a hold under her thighs. Her arms lock around my neck, legs wrap my waist as she dips her head until her lips touch the shell of my ear.

"Yes, Pashenka?" she whispers.

I suck in a breath. No one has ever called me that. The pakhan and a few others use my full name, but the rest call me Pasha—the Russian short variant for Pavel. But no one has ever used a diminutive name. In Russia, those are usually reserved for someone's closest family members and spouses.

"How do you know about that endearment?" I ask.

"I found a website about Russian names," she says and places a kiss on the side of my neck. "It mentioned that it's a very personal and affectionate name, and it's best to ask for permission before using it." She trails her mouth to the side of my jaw. "Do I have your permission to use it?"

"Yes," I whisper.

Her lips reach mine and hover just a breath away. "I want you to fuck me, Pashenka."

My cock swells upon hearing her say it. Squeezing her thighs, I turn around, pinning her to the front door. I can feel her dripping pussy against my abs, and it takes all my restraint not to bury my dick inside her. Asya bites my bottom lip, and my control snaps. Positioning her above my rock-hard cock, I start lowering her, inhaling her trembling breath as I fill her up. She moans into my lips, then squeezes my hair when I pull out.

"Harder." Her soft whimper transforms into a scream when I slam back inside.

As I drive into her pussy, I can feel her warmth, and it feels like coming home. I don't think I really knew what that phrase meant before meeting Asya. But this—her body pressed to mine, her hands in my hair, and her lips crushed against my mouth—it finally feels like home. She is my home. Squeezing her thighs, I thrust hard, wanting to imprint myself on her. To mark her as mine in some way.

"Harder." She moans and sinks her teeth into my shoulder.

I've long since lost the ability for rational thought. Purely on instinct, I turn around and carry her across the room to the dining table. Ignoring the neat stacks of financial documents I labored over yesterday which are now lining the tabletop, I lower Asya directly on one of the contracts. She's so wet that the paper under her ass gets instantly saturated.

"Lie down, baby." I grab her behind her knees and pull her closer, placing her feet at the edge of the table. She watches me through her spread legs, a tiny smirk lighting up her face.

"I'm waiting," she says.

I smile and take a step closer, letting just the tip of my cock find its home, and press my thumb over her clit. She sucks in a breath. I rub small circles on her nub, teasing her, then slowly push further in as I increase the pressure with my thumb. Before I'm even fully inside, her body starts trembling. My cock hurts because of how hard it is, but I keep up my slow movements, watching her body arch off the table and reveling in each sound of pleasure she makes. With one last circle on her clit, I take her ankles and slowly straighten her legs to a perfect V. I pound into her, narrowing and widening her legs with every thrust and retreat.

"Harder!" she yells.

I rest her calves on my shoulders, press her knees together, and slam back inside. She orgasms, screaming out her pleasure while tremors shake her body. I can feel her pussy spasm around my cock, and it sends a jolt up my spine. I roar and explode into her.

I stroke the length of Asya's hair, then leisurely run my palm up and down her back. She's been sleeping on top of me for two hours now. I should try getting some sleep, too. I spent the previous night chasing and, once I caught him, beating the shit out of the motherfucker who hurt my girl. But I can't sleep. I keep thinking about Asya as she pulled that trigger.

It feels as if a countdown has begun with that bullet. The man who tore apart her life is gone. Roman assured me that the rest of the organization will be dealt with, so I'm sure they will all be dead by this time tomorrow.

I look down at Asya's face resting on the center of my chest. She usually tosses and turns in her sleep, but she hasn't moved a muscle since falling asleep earlier. I tug on the blanket at her hips and cover her fully.

How much time do we have left? She's been doing much better these past few weeks, and I very rarely need to help her with decisions anymore. Men in suits still make her uncomfortable, but she's come a long way toward overcoming that, too. The nightmares have stopped, and the only thing that still distresses her is snow. I'm so fucking proud of her.

As good as her progress is, it fuels the utter panic rising within me. Will today be the day she'll tell me it's time for her to leave? Or will it be tomorrow? It's been weeks since I stopped urging her to contact her brother. I convinced myself that I did it to give her time and space to heal, but I've been lying to myself. I did it because I want her to stay. Forever.

As I watch her sleeping form, her presence lessens the gaping hole inside my chest, but the sound of a ticking clock echoes through my mind. Counting down the days, or maybe mere hours, I have left with her.

*Tick. Tock.*

*Tick. Tock.*

Pavel

"Are you sure, Asya?" I ask as I hold the car door open for her.

"Nope." She takes my hand and exits the car "But I need to do it anyway."

"Okay, baby."

With Asya's hand clasped in mine, I head toward the back entrance of Ural. I still don't think it's a good idea to come to the club during the hours it's open to the public. It's not the same as going to the mall. Here, there will be more people in a smaller space, all crammed together. And since Ural is a more upscale place, most of the clubgoers will be wearing classy clothes, including suits on men. I know she needs to face her fears, but I don't like the idea of her getting stressed for any reason. I want to shield her from harm. But Asya has been insisting for two weeks, so I finally caved.

We leave our jackets at the coat check and enter the main space. There are already more than a hundred people inside. Asya wraps her arm around my forearm and leans into my side, but she doesn't falter as we head around the dance floor toward the opposite corner, bringing us near the stairs that lead to the upper level. I told the staff to remove the tables from that spot. We're halfway to our destination when a man waves at me from one of the VIP booths and then heads in our direction. Damian Rossi. The Chicago don's brother. He navigates through the crowd and meets us near the stairway.

"Pavel, I've been looking for you. How does renting this place for a night work?" He grins and looks over at Asya, offering her his hand. "I'm Damian."

"Hi," she says quietly but doesn't make a move to shake his hand.

I'm barely containing my urge to tell the Italian to go to hell, but Asya seems fine. I don't want her to think I doubt her ability to deal with the situation. She said she can handle it and, unless I notice distress, I won't interfere.

"Rentals are limited to the Bratva members only," I say. "What's the occasion?"

"Oh, nothing special. Some friends and I would like to throw a party, and we're looking for a venue." He shrugs, then turns back at Asya and his smile widens. "Would you like to come, *bellissima*? I didn't get your name."

Asya's hold on my forearm tightens.

"Leave, Damian," I say in a curt tone.

"What? I was just—"

I grab the front of his shirt and shove my face in his. "Turn around and leave. Right fucking now." I snarl through my teeth.

He blinks at me in confusion and raises his hands. "Okay, man. No need for a spat, especially in front of a lady."

I let go of his shirt and watch as he walks back to his booth.

"Do you want to leave?" I look down at Asya.

"I'm okay." She offers me a small smile. "Let's stay for a bit."

When we reach my intended spot, I lean against the wall and pull Asya to stand between my legs with her back pressed to my chest. She's wearing jeans and a simple sleeveless top with a high neckline. The fabric is soft lightweight wool and it's in the same shade of brown as her hair.

"All good?" I ask as I wrap my arms around her waist.

"Yeah."

We stand in silence and people watch for about ten minutes. She seems relaxed at first, but then leans more against me. Her hands come up to cover mine, squeezing my fingers.

I dip my head until my chin lands on her shoulder. "Talk to me."

"I'm okay. Just a little uneasy. There are a lot of people."

"Want to leave?"

She seems to be undecided for a few moments but then shakes her head. "Not yet. It's a bit unnerving, but I can handle it. I want to experience this a bit longer."

I grit my teeth. I don't want her around anything that makes her uncomfortable. And I certainly don't like the fact that she's feeling unsettled. If she wants to stay, okay. But it'll be under my new conditions. I spin her around, grab her under her thighs, and lift her.

She yelps in surprise and locks her feet behind my back. "Pasha?"

I face the wall, bracing her on it and letting her see the dance floor.

"Now you can keep checking things out," I bite out.

Asya arches her eyebrows at me and smiles. "I like the new view even better." She leans forward and presses her lips to mine. "So much better."

I nip her lower lip. Asya sucks in a breath and tightens her legs around me. My cock swells. I can feel the heat of her pussy next to my hard length, and my dick hardens even more when she grabs at the back of my neck and sinks her teeth into my chin.

"Maybe we could head home after all," she says into my mouth. "What do you say, Pashenka?"

I don't reply, just turn around and carry her toward the exit.

I almost trip trying to get out of my pants without letting go of Pasha's neck. My shoes and top are somewhere in the living room, along with his jeans and T-shirt. I'm not sure, but I think our jackets may be in the hallway in front of the elevator. Finally free of my jeans, I walk backward to the bed, trying to unclasp my bra with one hand. Pasha slips off his boxer briefs, grabs me around the waist, and throws us onto the bed. I end up sprawled on top of his chest.

"I want us to try something," I say and nip at his chin. "I saw it online."

"What?"

"Umm . . . it's a position." I smile sheepishly and scrape my teeth over my lower lip.

Pasha lifts an eyebrow. "Oh? Something specific?"

His hands slide down my back and squeeze my ass. In his hands, every inch of my skin feels as if it's been zapped by a live wire. I still find it hard to believe how much I enjoy him touching me. Kissing me. Making love to me. I was afraid, at first, that I might freak out at some point, forgetting who he is, and flinch at his touch. The idea that it may happen was constantly present in my mind for a while. I loathed the possibility of unintentionally hurting him if I involuntarily recoiled, making him think he did something wrong. I'm not afraid of that anymore. Both my body and my mind recognize him, no matter what's going on. Even when he's rough. Even when he pushes me against the wall and takes me from behind. There's not a speck of fear. Just mind-blowing pleasure.

"Yes." I smirk and feel the heat in my cheeks.

Pasha moves his hands up my back, then takes my face between his palms, pulling me in for a kiss. "Turn around."

"You know what I have in mind?"

"Based on how red your face is, I'm pretty sure I do." He bites at my lip. "Come on, give me your pretty pussy."

I flip and face his cock, leaving my pussy exposed to his mouth. Pasha grabs at my butt cheeks, pulling me closer, and buries his face between my legs. His tongue circles my entrance, then slides inside, making me gasp. As I reach for his cock, my hands are trembling from the overwhelming sensations. I squeeze his hard length and take the tip into my mouth. Pasha changes his tempo—slow licks and kisses turn frenzied—eating my pussy as if it's dessert. The combined feeling of his tongue on my pussy and his cock in my mouth isn't comparable to anything I've ever experienced before. He adds his fingers and then pinches my clit, and I come all over his face.

It takes me a few moments to recover from the high, and then I take him deeper into my throat as he keeps lapping up my juices. His breathing is labored. I can tell he's close. I leisurely ease my mouth off his hard length and turn around to face him. Locking my eyes with Pasha's, I position myself over his straining cock and slowly lower myself, marveling at the feel of him filling me up. Pasha's hand shoots up, grabbing me behind my neck, and stays there as I rock my hips while he stares into my eyes, unblinking. Strained breaths leave his lips, and the muscles on his chest are taut under my palms, but it's the look on his face that holds my attention. His jaw is clenched, his lips flattened. It seems like he wants to say something, but he's holding back.

"What's wrong, Pashenka?" I ask as I lift my ass, then drop back down, gasping as his cock drives deep into me.

His hold on my neck tightens, but he doesn't utter a word. Just slams into me from below so hard that my mind goes blank. The next moment, I find myself on my back with Pasha's body over mine. He continues to grip my neck while thrusting so fast that my body shakes and I can barely get enough air into my lungs. I love when he lets go of his steely self-control and fucks me with all his power. There's nothing better than having him screw me until we come at the same time. It makes me feel strong, fearless, and happier than I've ever been. I grab his arms and shout out his name as another orgasm erupts.

# Chapter nineteen

Pavel

Slow, emotional notes drift in from the living room. I open my eyes and stare at the ceiling. A little while ago she played "Für Elise." I don't know the name of this particular melody, though, and I rarely ask because I prefer when Asya tells me on her own. Her music is very personal to her, so the fact she shares something she feels this intimate about, without me asking for it, strikes a deep chord in my soul. Early on, I got used to not asking for things in my life, and it became a habit. Why ask for things when the answer will almost always be no? Yes, there's a possibility for a different outcome, but I guess I prefer not asking over dealing with disappointment.

My first few years in foster care, I kept asking the same three questions. *Did my mother call? Did anyone call looking for me? Will my mother come back?* The answer was always no. Then, the questions changed. *Do I have any other family? Will another family pick me like some of the other kids?* Like that troublemaker, the boy who kept fighting with the other boys at one of the homes I lived at. I don't remember his name. Was it Kane? Or maybe Kai? Two of the other foster kids ended up in the emergency room when they teased him about his long hair. The crazy fucker bit off a chunk of one's ear and stabbed a fork into the other's neck. That boy disappeared after that, and we all thought he ended up in juvie or a mental institution. But a few months later I overheard the social workers saying he was adopted. So, I resumed pestering the foster parents and the social workers day after day, asking if someone would adopt me, too. I asked and asked until my foster dad got fed up with it and yelled into my face to stop asking idiotic questions. I followed his advice.

Is it my fear of rejection that makes it so hard for me to ask Asya to stay with me? Last night, I almost did. I wanted to ask her so much that I barely managed to stop the words from exploding out of my mouth. She might have said yes. I know she likes spending time with me. I think she even likes me, but remaining with me would mean not returning to her family. Does she like me enough to choose me over them?

The melody in the living room changes. I know this one. It's the piano version of the *Game of Thrones* intro. Asya loves that one. I roll out of bed, intending on dragging her back to bed, just as my phone rings on the nightstand. Roman's name lights up the screen.

"Pakhan?" I ask when I answer the call.

"I need to talk with you, Pavel."

"All right." I nod and sit on the bed.

"In person," he adds in an ominous voice. "I'll expect you at the mansion in an hour."

The line disconnects.

I step inside the pakhan's office and find him seated behind his desk. Mikhail and Sergei are there, too, lounging in the recliners by the bookshelf.

"Pakhan." I close the door behind me and head toward his desk. "Is something wrong at the clubs?"

"Not exactly," he says. "Tell me, Pavel, is there anything I need to know? Something you forgot to mention, maybe?"

"About what?"

He tilts his head to the side, regarding me. "Does the name DeVille sound familiar to you?"

A chill runs down my spine.

Roman smiles. It's not a nice smile. "I see it does." He leans forward and hits the desk with his palm. "What the fuck were you thinking, hiding Arturo DeVille's sister at your place?"

It takes me a few moments to recover. How the fuck did he find out?

"She doesn't want anyone to know. Her brother included," I say through my teeth. "When she's ready, she'll call him."

"I don't give a fuck what she wants!" Roman snarls. "Her brother has been searching for her for months, thinking she's dead! Can you at least imagine what it's been like for him? His baby sister, gone, not knowing if she's dead or alive?"

I fist my hands and grind my teeth. "Asya doesn't want to call him, Roman."

"Do you know she has a sister, Pavel?" Roman continues. "A sister who spent two weeks in the hospital after she swallowed a bottle of sleeping pills because she believed it was her fault that Asya went missing?"

"Shit." I close my eyes. "Is she okay? Her sister?"

"She's okay."

"How do you know all this?" I ask and look at him.

"When Asya went missing, Ajello sent a message to all Cosa Nostra Families, demanding they report it if anyone sees her. He sent her photo." The pakhan sighs. "Damian Rossi saw you two at Ural last night. Arturo was at my door at six this morning."

I grab the back of the chair in front of me, gripping it hard enough to make my knuckles turn white. "Did you tell him where she is?"

Roman throws a look toward where Mikhail and Sergei are sitting. "He's currently on his way to your place, Pavel."

I stare at him while fear worse than any I've ever experienced spreads from the pit of my stomach. He is going to take her away. I turn on my heel, ready to rush out of the office and head home, only to find Sergei blocking my exit.

"Move!" I snarl and lunge at him, but two arms grab me from behind.

"Pasha. Calm down," Mikhail says, restraining me.

I thrust my head back, headbutting his forehead. Mikhail's hold falters and I use the opportunity and lunge at Sergei. He gets my head with his fist, but I throw my elbow into his stomach. I dodge, avoiding his next punch, and take a swing at his face just as Mikhail rushes me from behind, pinning me against the wall beside the door.

"You can't fucking keep a person from their family!" he roars next to my ear and bangs my head against the wall.

"He'll take her away!"

"He can't take her away if she doesn't want to go," Mikhail says. "But if she wants to, you don't have the right to make her stay."

"I know." I close my eyes and slump against the wall, defeated.

"Let him go, Mikhail. You can leave," Roman says from somewhere behind me. "You, too, Sergei."

I hear the door opening and retreating steps, but I don't move. My forehead rests on the cool surface. I'm slowly going numb.

"Pavel, look at me."

I open my eyes and tilt my head to the side. Roman is standing next to me, leaning on his cane.

"You need to let her go. If you don't, neither you nor her will know if she's with you because she loves you. Or if it's because she's afraid to leave."

"You don't understand," I say. "I've never had anyone, Roman. Until her. I can't imagine my life without her anymore."

"She needs to go see her sister. She needs her family. And her family needs her. But she will return."

I look at the wall again. "She won't. If she leaves, she won't be back."

"Why are you so certain?"

"Because she doesn't need me now, Roman. She needed me before. Not anymore."

"Do you want her to stay with you just because she needs you? You deserve better than that. Both of you do."

"I know." I bang my forehead on that goddamned wall as if it'll help stifle the terror raging inside me.

"Go home. Talk to her. Talk to Arturo, he deserves an explanation." Roman places his hand on my shoulder and squeezes. "Take a few days off if you need to. And please stop banging your thick head against my wall. You'll break the fucking thing."

"My head?" I ask.

"The wall, Pavel. If your skull didn't crack during all those years of fighting, it certainly won't now."

I snort and shake my head.

## Asya

There is a knock on the door.

My fingers still on the piano keys. Pasha never knocks. He always rings the bell. It must be a neighbor wanting to ask me not to play so loud. I cross the living room and open the door. When my eyes land on the man standing on the other side, I quickly take a step back.

"Dear God," my brother chokes out and pulls me into a bear hug, squeezing me so hard that it's impossible to move a muscle.

I try to gulp a deep breath, but no air seems to enter my lungs. Another try. Arturo eases his hold and looks down at me with a slightly crazed look in his eyes. And then, he's squishing me to his body again. My arms are shaking as I embrace him and press my cheek to his chest.

"I thought you were dead," he says into my hair. "I thought someone took you, and I've been waiting for someone to call and ask for a ransom. The call never came."

"I'm sorry," I mumble, tears gathering in the corners of my eyes. It's hard to believe he's here after all this time. And it feels good. "I'm so sorry, Arturo."

"Why, Asya? Why not let us know that you're okay?" He cups my face between his palms and tilts my head up. "Where have you been all this time?"

I watch my brother while worry ignites a foreboding feeling in the pit of my stomach, spreading the heated pulses of dread up my chest.

"We found your purse and glasses behind that bar. And blood. What happened?"

I open my mouth, but no words leave my lips.

"Jesus fuck, Asya, say something, damn it!"

"I was raped!" I yell into his face.

All color leaves Arturo's face. He blinks. His hands on my cheeks start shaking. I wrap my arms around his back and bury my face into his chest.

And then I talk, but I don't tell him everything.

When I'm done, Arturo lowers himself to his knees in front of me, still holding me in his embrace. I thread my fingers in his hair and lean my cheek on top of his head, listening to him as he mumbles how he's going to crucify the son of a bitch who hurt me, then how much he loves me.

"I love you, too, Arturo," I whisper.

And that's why I haven't told him the whole story. I skipped the worst part. It's better like this.

"We need to call Sienna," Arturo murmurs. "I didn't want to tell her anything until I was sure. In case . . . in case it wasn't you, I couldn't risk her doing something stupid again."

"What do you mean?"

He shakes his head and holds me harder.

"What did she do, Arturo?"

## Pavel

The first thing I notice when I step inside the apartment is a dark-haired man sitting on the sofa in my living room. He's looking at the floor between his feet, elbows leaning on his knees as his hands grip his hair.

"Where's Asya?" I ask.

"Taking a shower. Preparing to leave," he says, still looking at the floor.

"She told you everything?"

"Yes. I also know she's been here this whole time."

I cross the living room and take a seat on the recliner to his left. "I need to give you some pointers on Asya."

His head snaps up, and two dark brown eyes, the same shade as Asya's, pin me with a stare full of hatred. "I don't need you to give me fucking pointers on my sister. I raised her since she was five."

I ignore his hostility. "She still has problems making some decisions. We worked out almost everything, but she may need help from time to time. Try not to give her specific direction, but rather steer her toward it."

He stares at me in silence.

"No daisies. Not flowers, and nothing else, either, like curtains or whatnot with pictures of them," I continue. "She's not triggered by suits anymore, but men's ties can still distress her. If you're in public, and the place is crowded with unfamiliar men wearing suits, you need to hold her hand."

He looks down at himself, focusing on his silk gray tie, then lifts his head and passes his eyes over my T-shirt and jeans. When he moves his gaze up and our eyes meet, I see the loathing there.

"Jesus fuck!" he barks. "You're in love with her."

I don't look away as I reply, "Yes."

"She's eighteen, for God's sake! You are too old for her. Asya needs someone her age. And definitely not an ex-convict."

"You checked me out?"

"Of course I checked you out. I wanted to know the man who was keeping my sister from me. I even dug up videos of some of your fights."

"Well, I hope they were entertaining."

Arturo leans forward and pins me with his gaze. "You tried to steal my baby sister! An abused, hurt girl. You kept her from her family, even though you knew she needed us," he spits out. "I don't know what kind of sick fantasy you created, playing house with a teenager, and I don't care. I won't let you get near her again! Ever! My sister deserves better."

"I know." I rise and head to the stand by the front door where I keep some pens and paper. "I'll give you my number. Call me if you need any help."

I walk back and drop the paper on the coffee table in front of Arturo, then head toward the front door. "I'll come back in two hours. Will you be gone by then?"

"No goodbye?" he raises his eyebrows.

"No," I say.

"Good."

I nod and leave the apartment.

I'm sitting in my car two streets down from my building when my phone rings. "Moonlight Sonata" surrounds me. I lean my head back and watch the cars passing down the street. The ringing stops but immediately starts again. I let it run its course, the sound reverberating through the small space. I could have silenced it. Every fucking tone feels like a knife to my chest, but I didn't. The phone rings four more times, and I let it ring through every fucking time.

A message arrives. I take the phone off the dash and look at the screen. It's a voice mail. I hit play.

"Pasha? What's going on? Arturo said that you came home and left? Did something happen?" Rustling in the background. "We're heading to the airport. I need to go see Sienna. She . . ." Sniffing. "My sister tried to kill herself. She thought what happened to me was her fault. I'll stay with her for a few days and then I'm coming back. I'll call you when I get there" Her voice sounded shaky. Was she crying?

The message ends. I hit play again. And again.

It's almost midnight. I'm lying on the couch, gripping the phone as it continues to ring in my hand. I want to swipe that green button and take the call so much; it's making me crazy. I don't. My mind keeps replaying that one sentence Asya's brother said.

*You kept her from her family, even though you knew she needed us.*

He was right. I should have contacted him to let him know she was safe. If I explained the situation, he might have agreed to wait until Asya was ready to face him. But I was too selfish and too fucking terrified that he would take her away from me. I could no longer imagine my life without her. The possibility of her leaving scared the fuck out of me and I was ready to do whatever was needed to make sure she stayed. So, I kept my promise to her and remained silent, a self-preserving son of a bitch. I became her fucking demon. No one deserves to be with such a person, especially not Asya.

I've always believed I would be able to measure love by how much I would want to be with a person. Deciding to be with someone for the rest of my life seemed like the pinnacle of love. Wrong. I understand things much better now. Knowing that Asya, the woman I love, will be better off without me, I had to let her go. Even though it hurts. Even when it's shredding me on the inside. Maybe, if I loved Asya a little less, I would have found a way to keep her with me. I love her too much to do that to her, though, so I've let her go.

I should have answered the call. Said goodbye, at least. But I couldn't. Hearing her say she'll come back, but knowing that she won't, I couldn't risk speaking to her. I would have done something stupid, like make her promise she'll return to me.

My eyes land on the piano near the living room window. Why didn't she take the damn thing with her? I get up off the sofa and head into the kitchen to grab the toolbox from where I keep it under the sink. When I come back to the living room, I'm holding a hammer in my hand. Walking to the instrument, I intend to smash the thing until there is nothing left of it, but instead, I end up staring at the keys for an hour. Asya loves this piano. The hammer falls from my hand, hitting the polished floor with a loud thud. I can't make myself destroy something that brought her joy.

My phone rings. I grab it and throw the fucking thing across the room.

It's better like this for her. She won't feel obliged to call me out of some misplaced sense of gratitude or whatever. It might be hard for her to adjust for the first few days at home, but she has her family now. Friends, too. Soon enough, she'll forget all about me and continue with her life. Maybe I'll do the same.

The phone rings again. It rings two more times that night.

It keeps ringing at least ten times every day for the following five days.

On the sixth day, it rings only once, and then the calls stop.

# Chapter Twenty

Pavel

*Three weeks later*

I park my car a block away from Asya's home and head up the street.

Flying in would have been much easier. Instead, I drove thirteen hours, hoping I'd change my mind along the way and turn around. I stopped three times and almost convinced myself to do exactly that, but when I got back on the road, I just continued heading east. The need to see her again is an obsession, the only thing I've thought about for days. Just one quick glimpse, and I'll be gone.

Something wet lands on my cheek, so I peer at the night sky. It's snowing. My chest tightens at the sight of the white flakes as they fall on my face. My mishka doesn't like snow. It's the one thing we weren't able to overcome.

I promised myself that I won't keep hoping for her return. I knew she wouldn't, not after all the calls I didn't take and the messages I left unanswered. Yet, I still hoped.

Last week, feeling more miserable than ever, I dug out the box with my tattoo kit from the back of the closet. Why I've kept that thing, I don't have a clue. I stopped adding tats more than a decade ago. That night, though, I sat down at my dining table, in my empty apartment, and got working on new ink. Since there weren't any free spots on my torso or my arms, I did it on the back of my hand. When Kostya saw me the following day, he asked if it was one of those temporary things because I'd never tattooed a part of my body that was visible before. I told him what I thought of his opinion with my freshly inked knuckles.

I can see only the upper part of the house at the top of the street. Most of it is hidden behind the high gated fence and greenery, but it matches the description Dimitri was able to find. Asya's home.

I'm still observing the house, trying to spot the light in one of the windows, when a flashy car rounds the corner and parks right in front of the gate. There's a streetlight close by, so I step back into the shadow of a tree. The man who gets out of the driver's side is young, probably in his early twenties. He's smiling, obviously in a great mood. He opens the passenger door, and a woman takes his hand and steps out. She's wearing a white coat, unbuttoned, revealing a blood-red dress underneath. It's snowing harder now, and snowflakes stick to the dress's feathered skirt. The man grabs her around the waist, crashing her into his body. The woman laughs.

I know that laugh. I want to turn away and leave, but I can't take my eyes off the woman as she tilts her head and kisses the man. It's not a friendly kiss, but a passionate one. The man's hand glides up her back.

The gate slides to the side, and the woman untangles herself from the embrace. A moment before she disappears through the gate, I catch a glimpse of her face. She's cut her hair. It's shoulder-length now, but there is no doubt.

It's my Asya.

Something breaks inside my chest. I'm pretty sure it's my heart.

The gate closes and the car leaves, but I keep standing in the shadows, staring at the house beyond the fence.

She's okay. I'm not sure if the man I saw is just a date or a boyfriend, but it doesn't really matter. She's moved on. I expected her to, but seeing it hurts so fucking much. She deserves to be happy, though. And I'm glad she is.

I turn around and head back to my car, snow crunching under the soles of my shoes. I couldn't sleep in my own bed after she left, so I spent the first few nights on the couch, then moved into one of the empty bedrooms.

But I can't do it anymore. I can't be in that place or pretend to live my old life.

When I'm inside my car, I call Roman.

"Pavel?" comes his voice from the other side.

I look at the house up the street one last time.

"I quit," I say and cut the connection.

## Asya

I put down the phone and watch my sister take off her heels and head into the closet.

"That thing is awful," I say.

"What?" Sienna turns around and juts her hip. "This is from the newest collection."

It always amazes me how two people can look identical on the outside but have widely different personalities and tastes.

"It has fucking feathers, Sienna. How do you even wash it?"

"Dry cleaning," she says and unzips the red monstrosity. "When are you planning on getting out of the house? We can go hiking in the Catskills."

"Hiking?" I arch my eyebrows. The highest my sister has ever climbed was onto a stool to get the old hairdryer off the shelf when her regular one died.

"What? It could be fun."

I shake my head and look back down at my phone. "I'm not in the mood."

Sienna stops fumbling with her dress and plops onto the bed beside me. "You need to forget that guy, Asya. He doesn't want anything to do with you. You should have clued in already."

"You don't know that."

"You've phoned him over fifty times! I checked your call history," she says and grabs my phone. "Please don't tell me you called him again."

"Give that back!" I jump at her, trying to get my cell. "Sienna!"

"You did! I can't believe you."

"I haven't called him." I take my phone from her. "I was looking at some photos."

"What photos?"

I shrug.

"You never told me you had a photo of him!" Sienna widens her eyes at me. "Let me see! Please? Please? Please?"

I unlock my phone and reluctantly pass it to her. She grabs it with a squeal and starts going through the folders.

"Oh, I can't wait to . . . holy fuck, Asya! Is this him?"

I glance at the screen, at the photo of Pasha I secretly took one morning while he was still sleeping. He's on his back with his arm thrown over his face. The blanket is bunched up around his waist, leaving his tattooed broad chest fully on display.

"Yeah." I nod.

Sienna flips to the next image. That one's a little blurry, taken the day he gave me the phone. I was trying out the camera with a selfie but moved my hand too fast. In the photo, I'm leaning against Pasha's chest and gazing at the camera. He has his arm wrapped around my waist and is looking down at me.

"I still don't understand what happened," I say, looking at the screen. "Why did he shut me out? Did I do something? Did he decide he can't deal with my issues anymore?"

"Asya, stop." Sienna takes my hand. "You didn't do anything wrong. You hear me? He doesn't deserve you, not after how he acted."

"I miss him so much," I whisper and look back down at the phone. I wish I took more photos of him.

"It'll get easier. You'll meet a guy, fall in love, and forget all about the Russian." She wraps her arm around me and pulls me into a hug. "When you're ready, we'll go out together and find the most handsome, sweet guy for you. Okay?"

A heavy feeling settles over me, and I close my eyes. I don't want a sweet, handsome guy. I want Pasha. Just the thought of any other man touching me makes me sick to my stomach. Acid rises up my throat, so I fan my face, hoping the nausea will pass. It doesn't. It only gets worse. I jump off the bed and dash to the bathroom, barely managing to reach the toilet in time. Sienna runs in after me and lifts my hair away from my face as I empty the contents of my stomach. When I'm done, I slump to the floor next to the toilet and stare at the ceiling.

"I can't even think about other men without vomiting, Sienna," I whisper.

# Chapter Twenty-one

Asya

*One month later*

My phone rings as I'm rearranging my closet for the third time this week. I found that folding stuff helps me keep my mind thought-free. Funny thing, I've also started sorting my clothes by color.

I reach for the cell and see that it's an unknown caller. Only a couple of people have this number because I'm still using the phone Pasha gave me. Somewhere deep inside, I'm still hopeful he'll call, but it's been nearly two months.

"Yes?"

"Asya?" a vaguely familiar male voice asks. "Can you please put that piece of shit on the line? He's been ignoring my calls for weeks, and I have a clusterfuck on my hands at Ural."

I raise my eyebrows. "Kostya?"

"Of course, it's me, sweetheart. Who else has such a sexy voice? Oh fuck, please don't tell him I called you sweetheart."

"Tell who?"

"Pasha, of course. Can you please put him on? It's taken me two days to crack the password on his email account to find your number. Things here are getting disastrous."

Why would Kostya think Pasha's with me? I swallow the lump that's suddenly formed in my throat and close my eyes. "He's not here."

"Please tell him to call me when he—"

"He is not here, Kostya. I haven't seen him since I left Chicago," I choke out.

"What? He's not with you? Did he call you recently?"

"No. I've called him, but he never answered," I say. "What's going on?"

For a moment, there's nothing but silence before Kostya replies. "Pasha quit a month ago."

"Quit? You can't just quit the Bratva. Petrov is going to hunt him down and kill him!"

"Roman won't kill him, but I don't think Pasha cares." A Russian curse comes from the other side, then a sound of something breaking. "No one knows where he is. He took my calls the first week, but then nothing. He hasn't been at his apartment, so I hoped he was with you."

Dread pools in my stomach. "Has he disappeared before?"

"Pavel?" he laughs, but it sounds forced. "He hasn't taken a single day off since he joined the Bratva. Well, before you, I mean."

"Where is he, then?" I mean to ask the question calmly, but I end up sounding like I'm yelling because my voice is higher than normal and trembling.

"I have no idea, Asya."

I pace the room, trying to calm down, but my chest is tight and my heart is racing. I have a bad feeling that something truly awful is about to happen. "I need you to call me the moment you hear from him. Please."

"Sure, sweetheart. I'll make a few calls to see if anyone's seen or heard from him and then I'll let you know."

When we end the call, I walk to the window overlooking the garden and stare at nothing in particular. I promised myself I wouldn't call him ever again. If he wants to talk, he can call me.

I look down at my phone and press the speed dial number. It rings. And rings. Closing my eyes, I lean my forehead against the window and keep listening to the ringing sound until it disconnects without rolling over to voice mail. I call again. And again. After the fourth try, a message arrives. I'm afraid of what it may say, so I stare at his name for at least ten minutes before I gather the courage and open it.

**23:15 Pasha:** Stop calling, mishka. Please.

"Fuck you!" I yell at the screen and throw the phone on the bed. And then I cry.

The familiar sounds of cheering and yelling surround me. Just as the stench of sweat mixed with the faint smell of mold does, too. Laughter rings out and then more hollers. I lean my back on the concrete wall and stare at the phone in my hand and the text I just sent.

She called. Staring at her name on the screen, not answering those calls, was the hardest fucking thing I've ever done. If she continued calling, I would have probably caved.

I check the call log. There're hundreds of missed calls over the last few weeks. At least fifty are from Kostya, but there are dozens from Roman, and Mikhail, too. The rest of the guys have been calling, as well. Even Sergei. I never answered. I didn't feel like talking. What was there to say, anyway?

I press my thumb over Asya's name at the top of the list, swipe to the side and delete the entry. Then, I flip back to the sent message and delete that, as well. Seeing her name hurts too much. I should clear her number, but it wouldn't do any good. I memorized it the moment I bought the phone for her.

A metal door on the other side of the room screeches as it opens, and a man enters. In his black suit and tie, he looks like a businessman. Well, considering the people who come to watch these fights and the amount of money that changes hands every night, they do need to keep it sleek.

"You're next," he says a moment before the bell chimes, followed by excited shouts. "Try not to incapacitate your opponent in the first round this time. The crowd likes to watch them struggle a bit."

I finish wrapping my hands, get up, and head toward the door while more cheers erupt from the direction of the fighting cage.

# Chapter Twenty Two

## Asya

The phone vibrates next to my pillow. I spring up in bed and hit the button to take the call, then press the phone on my ear.

"Did you find him?" I whisper.

"Yes," Kostya says from the other end.

I close my eyes and breathe. Four fucking days have passed. "So, he's okay?"

"He is. In a way."

My eyes snap open. "What do you mean 'in a way?'"

Kostya sighs. "He's fighting again."

"What?"

"Yeah. I tried talking to him. It didn't go well. Roman called him, as well. He even went to his last match. Pasha doesn't want to come back."

"But . . . why? He told me he quit fighting ten years ago!"

"Pasha is a very closed-off guy, sweetheart. Who knows what's going on in that head of his?"

I bury my hand in my hair, squeezing it. "Are those matches dangerous?"

He doesn't reply.

"Are they, Kostya?" I scream into the phone.

"It's underground fighting, Asya. What do you expect?"

"I don't know! I've never been to a boxing match!"

"It's not a boxing match, sweetheart. Boxing has rules. These fights don't," he says in a grim tone as my phone pings with an incoming message. "I sent you the link to the club website and a password to access it. Search for 'Pavel Morozov fights' and see for yourself. But skip the last match."

"Why?" I choke out.

He takes a deep breath. "I know you like him, sweetie. Please, don't watch the newest video."

When Kostya ends the call, I open the message with the link and click on it. At first glance, the website looks like an ordinary gym promo site with images of exercise equipment and people stretching or lifting weights. In the upper right corner, I find a login button. I click on it and enter the ten-digit password Kostya sent with the link. A new window pops up and I immediately notice the chart. The first column shows names, and I spot Pasha's listed second from the top, just under another guy's name. Next to the names are rankings and number of wins. Pasha is currently ranked second. Below the standings chart is this month's schedule. I scroll to the bottom and note there is only one match left this month, set for tomorrow night. It's between Pasha and the guy ranked first. I scroll back up to see the number of wins. Next to Pasha's name is twelve. I glance at the number for the other competitor and my blood goes cold. It's fifty-four.

"Jesus fuck." I sink to the floor and lean my back to the wall, then type "Pavel Morozov" into the search. A collection of videos pops up. The oldest one is dated a month ago. I hit play.

I'm not sure what I expected. Probably a fighting ring and some people standing around it. At least, that's how I imagined boxing matches to be like. What I'm seeing looks nothing like that. The video starts with the view from above, showing the inside of some abandoned factory or a warehouse. In the center, set on a raised platform, is an octagonal cage. Around the cage, men and a few women are seated on cushy chairs. All of them are impeccably dressed as if they came for a business meeting and not to watch a fighting match. Some even have bodyguards standing nearby.

A metal door across from the cage opens and two men enter. The camera zooms in on the fighters, and I almost don't recognize him. Pasha shaved his hair—all of it. But somehow, that's not the biggest change. His posture, the way he walks, and the grim expression on his face make him look as if he's someone else. He climbs into the cage and takes the spot on one side while his opponent heads for the opposite end. The referee signals for the start.

Pasha and his rival circle each other. He swipes at Pasha's side, but Pasha dodges and grabs the man's head, kneeing him in the face. Blood bursts from the guy's nose, and I look away from the screen. When I gather enough courage to look again, Pasha is standing over his opponent, pressing the fallen man's face to the floor. I've never watched a boxing match, but I had the impression those lasted for at least half an hour. This one is done in less than two minutes. The referee signals Pasha's victory and the video ends. I steel myself and click on the next recording.

It takes me almost an hour to watch the first ten videos. I have to pause and collect myself several times before continuing. So much violence. Blood. Broken bones. Each video is more violent than the previous one. It's killing me to watch my Pasha become so vicious. Bloodthirsty. I don't recognize this person as the man I spent three months with. What happened to him? Why is he doing this? There're two videos left, but I can't make myself watch them. It hurts too much.

Sometimes, I wish Arturo hadn't found me. I know it would have destroyed him and my sister. Sienna still blames herself, even though I've explained at least a hundred times that it was me who made the decision to remain at the bar that night. Still, sometimes when I can't sleep, which is often lately, I imagine what my life would be like if my brother hadn't come and I stayed in Chicago.

I still don't understand why Pasha pushed me away. I tried to think of a reason for his behavior, but I can't.

It's almost seven in the morning, but I can't sleep. Not after what I've just watched. I'll wait for Arturo and Sienna to wake up, then try playing the piano again. I haven't been able to complete a full melody since returning home. At least twice a day, I've gone to the ground floor and sat in front of the big black piano, staring at the keys. Most of the time, no music came, and I left it as quiet as it was when I arrived. Other times, when I actually tried to play, every note came out wrong.

I take my cardigan off the chair and leave my room, heading downstairs to grab some breakfast. As I'm passing Arturo's room, I overhear my name being mentioned, so I stop. He's talking with someone on the phone. I lean forward and press my ear to the door.

"She's not the same, Nino," my brother says. "I don't know what to do. She barely leaves her room."

There are a few moments of silence while he probably listens to what Nino is saying.

"No!" Arturo barks. "I'm not calling that son of a bitch. I told him what I thought about him and his attempt to keep Asya from us. Hiding my sister and not allowing her to contact us? What kind of sick bastard does that?"

What?! I grab the knob and throw open the door, heart pounding a rapid tattoo against my ribs. My brother stands by the bed with the phone pressed to his ear.

"What exactly did you tell Pasha, Arturo?" I shout.

"I'll call you later," he mumbles and throws the phone on the bed.

"What?" I yell.

"The truth," he says. "I told him the truth—that he kept you hidden to serve his own selfish needs. That he used a young, wounded girl and made her stay with him instead of returning her to her family. To her life. That he's a sick bastard. That's what I told him."

I stare at my brother, stunned at what I'm hearing, then take two steps until I'm right in front of him. "He saved my life, Arturo."

"Any normal person would have helped a woman in need. But they wouldn't have tried to hide her."

I close my eyes. When Arturo came to get me, I only told him about what Robert did. He thinks I spent the entire time with Pasha. I hoped it wouldn't come to this, that I wouldn't need to tell him what happened during those first two months or what those people did to me. What they made me do. I should have, but I didn't want to hurt him.

"Sit down, Arturo," I say, and when he does, I start talking.

I tell him everything this time.

When I'm done, he's looking at me with red-rimmed eyes, hands gripping his hair while he's barely keeping himself on the edge of the bed. I don't think I've ever seen my brother cry, not even when we were told our parents had been killed.

"Why didn't you tell me?" he chokes out, then grabs me and engulfs me in a hug, crushing me against him. "Why, Asya? Why?" he whispers.

"I was in a very bad place when Pasha found me," I say into his neck. "Something had broken inside me, Arturo, and it felt as if I was trapped in a black hole with no way out. He saved me. And not only my life. He saved my soul, too. He helped me collect all my broken pieces and glued them back together."

"It should have been us," he says into my hair. "Sienna and I should have been the ones who helped you go through that."

"I couldn't make myself tell you. I didn't want to see you or Sienna. I would have rather died than told you."

"Why?"

"Because I wasn't ready. And because I love you and couldn't bear the thought of what it would do to you." I lift my head and take my brother's face in my palms. "I begged Pasha not to call you. I asked him to promise he wouldn't call you until I was ready. It wasn't him who kept me from you. I did that. It was my decision."

"I should have kept you safe," Arturo persists. "I will never forgive myself."

"Please don't do that. It's not your fault."

"I'm going to kill them all, Asya. Every single person who was in any way involved."

"Pasha and the Bratva already took care of them," I say, then tilt my chin up to whisper into his ear, "and I killed the guy who took me."

Arturo's body goes still. "You, personally?"

"Yes. After Pasha was done with him, I put a gun between the bastard's eyes and pulled the trigger." I smile. "It was the best fucking feeling ever."

"Good." He squeezes the back of my neck.

"I need to know what else you said to Pasha. He's been ignoring me, not taking my calls since I left."

Arturo grinds his teeth and looks away. "I told him that you deserve better, and he agreed."

I take a deep breath and close my eyes while pressure forms at the bridge of my nose. "You had no right," I say. "You had no right, Arturo. It's my life."

"You're eighteen, Asya. He's fifteen years older than you!"

"Yes. And I've gone through tough times most people don't ever experience," I bite out. "I think I've earned the right to make decisions for myself."

Yes, I still have problems picking what to wear or eat sometimes, but I don't have any doubts as far as Pasha is concerned.

"So, what happens now?" he asks. "Are you going back to him?"

"You will always be my big brother, Arturo. You know I love you unconditionally." I look into his eyes. "But I'm in love with Pasha. And I want to be with him."

"Are you sure you're in love with him? Maybe it's just a crush? Maybe—"

I raise my hand and put a finger over his lips to silence him.

"When Pasha found me, I was a wreck, Arturo. Both my soul and my mind . . . fractured. Pasha pieced me back together. And my heart yearns for him because he is the glue that keeps all my broken parts whole. Please, try to understand."

Arturo stares at me while grinding his jaw. "I'm going to drop by your place at least once a month. Unannounced. If I notice anything, even the smallest thing that will lead me to believe you're not happy, I'm going to kill that Russian and drag you back home."

"You won't have to." I smile., "I love him. I'll be okay, Arturo."

My brother closes his eyes and reluctantly nods.

# Chapter Twenty-Three

## Asya

I collect my bag from the baggage claim carousel and head toward the arrivals area where family and friends are waiting for the passengers. It takes me less than five seconds to locate Kostya. He's leaning on the pillar further back while several women stand around, gaping at him. When he sees me coming, he walks over to me and takes the bag out of my hand.

"Are we going directly to the fight?" I ask, focusing on his face instead of people milling about.

Most of the men I've noticed at the airport are wearing casual clothes, but there are a few in business attire. I don't freak out when I see men in suits anymore, but I still don't feel comfortable around them. Thank God, Kostya is wearing a hoodie and jeans.

"Yes." He nods and heads toward the exit as I follow. "But I'm still waiting to get the info on the location."

"You don't know where it's held?"

"They switch the places often to avoid police raids. And since this is the last fight of the season, the exact location will be sent just two hours before the start. I only know it'll be somewhere south of the city."

"Why? Is there something special about it?"

Kostya presses his lips into a thin line and nods toward the parking lot. "I'm parked over here," he says, avoiding eye contact. "We should hurry."

"Kostya? Are you hiding something from me?"

"Of course not, sweetheart." He approaches a black sedan and opens the passenger door for me.

I wait for him to get inside and start the car, then turn to face him. "What's so special about tonight's fight?"

"You haven't watched the last match on the website?"

"You told me not to," I say. "I watched the first ten, but I felt too sick to continue. I assumed the last one was the most violent."

"It was." He nods. "But that's not why I told you to skip it."

"Why then?"

Kostya is silent for a few moments, then takes a deep breath and shakes his head. "I think you should watch it before we arrive, Asya. So you can be prepared."

"Prepared for what?"

When he doesn't reply, I dig out my phone from my backpack and pull up the fight club's website. After I log into the private area, I type in Pasha's name and scroll down to the bottom of the page. Picking the video I skipped before, I click play. It starts like all other recordings, with the aerial view, then zooms in on the fighters. There's an ache in my chest when Pasha's face fills the screen. His left eye is a little swollen, and there's a big bruise on his chin. When the camera zooms out again, I notice that he has a splint from his palm to the middle of his right forearm.

I press my hand over my mouth to stifle a cry. "How was he allowed to fight if he was injured?"

"There are no rules in underground fighting," Kostya says. "As long as he can stand, he can fight."

"What happened?" I choke out.

"He sprained his wrist in the fight before this one."

"Pasha is right-handed. How can he fight with a sprained wrist?"

"He improvises."

I watch as Pasha and his opponent take their spots at the opposite corners. They are more or less matched in size, but the other guy doesn't seem to have any significant injuries. The bell rings and Pasha and the other fighter approach the center of the cage. For a few moments, they stay on the fringe, circling, sizing each other up. Then, Pasha suddenly swings his left hand at his opponent's side. The guy dodges the hit and lunges at Pasha with his fist, aiming for the head. Pasha drops down and swipes his leg just above the floor, catching the guy behind the ankles with his foot. While his opponent is on the floor, he delivers a gut punch with an elbow. Almost as soon as the guy folds, Pasha punches him in the head with his left fist, then kicks him. And again. Blood sprays all over the floor, a few teeth dotting the red stains.

Yelling and cheering erupt from the audience. Pasha rises, grabs the guy by his ankle, and launches him toward the other side of the cage. The fighter lands on his side and stays there. The crowd goes crazy. The camera focuses on Pasha, but I can still see men in nice suits beyond the cage, jumping up, and clapping their hands. The view switches from the fighters to the big screen mounted above the cage. It's an announcement for the next match. The one we're heading to now. Under the words "Big Finale" is a graphic of a red skull and the words "Death Match" are also written in red. The video ends.

I lower the phone to my lap and stare at the road beyond the windshield.

"Are you okay, sweetheart?" Kostya asks.

"No," I say, turning my head to look at him. "What does 'death match' mean?"

He keeps his gaze focused on the strip of dark ribbon ahead and squeezes the steering wheel. "It means the fight only ends when one of the fighters is dead."

I thought I overcame my issue with men in suits.

I was wrong.

The moment we step inside the abandoned factory where the match will take place, I stop dead in my tracks and wrap my hands around my middle. The fighting stage with the chain-link cage is in the center and takes up less than a tenth of the space. Everywhere else, filling the room to near capacity, people are standing in groups, chatting. There are no chairs this time. There must be at least a hundred people, most of whom are men. Some are wearing jeans, like Kostya and me, but most are dressed in swanky clothes. A shiver creeps up my spine, the urge to turn away and run is so strong, I need to gather all my willpower to keep my feet in place.

"Asya?" Kostya asks next to me. "Are you okay?"

I close my eyes for a second. "Yes."

"You don't look okay, sweetheart. Do you want . . .?" He reaches out his hand and is about to put it on my shoulder, but I quickly step back.

"Please, don't touch me," I mutter. "I . . . I can't handle it at the moment. I'm sorry."

"Do you want to leave?"

I look up to find him watching me with concern. "I'm staying."

"Okay. We'll stay here, in the back. If you want to leave, just say so. Sound good?"

I nod and move my gaze to the fighting cage. It's on the raised platform like in the videos. A man wearing black dress pants and a button-down shirt climbs inside and announces the start of the match, but I can't pay attention to what he's saying because I'm staring in horror at the mountain of a man entering the cage. I press my hands over my mouth to smother a cry.

"Jesus fuck," Kostya curses.

We both gape at Pasha's opponent as he paces inside the cage, flexing his monstrous muscles for the audience. He's taller than any man I have ever seen.

"Don't the fighters need to be evenly matched?" I whisper. The guy is more than a hundred pounds heavier than Pasha.

"Not here."

"What are Pasha's chances?"

"Before the injury? Fifty-fifty."

"And now?" I choke out.

"Not good, Asya," he says and looks down at me. "Let's go wait outside."

I want to say yes so fucking bad. That monster is probably going to kill Pasha. I heard it in the tone of Kostya's voice, and I don't think I can watch it.

"I'm staying," I whisper at the same moment Pasha steps inside the cage.

The instant my eyes land on him, the tears I've been holding at bay burst out, blurring my vision. I bite the back of my hand, burying my teeth in the skin with all my strength as if physical pain can somehow dispel the feeling of dread. Pasha walks toward the center of the cage and stops, assessing his opponent. I can't help but compare them. My Pasha is a tall guy and heavily muscled, but compared to the beast standing in front of him? Dear God, there is no way Pasha can beat him.

The referee turns away and exits the cage. There is a ring of a bell. Pasha's opponent swings his fist, aiming at the head. Pasha ducks and kicks the guy in the stomach with his left foot. The brute doesn't even move. He swings again, aiming for Pasha's chest this time. Pasha jumps to the right, but not fast enough, and takes the hit to his side. I can't breathe as I watch the opponent close in on him. But before the monster is able to strike, Pasha does a three-sixty spin, and the heel of his foot catches the guy on the neck. Pasha's attack is cut short, however, when a large fist clocks him on the chin.

A scream escapes me as I witness Pasha drop to his knees. He spits out blood and makes a move to stand, but the beast kicks him in the back. The blow is so strong Pasha ends up sprawled facedown on the mat.

"Get up," I whisper into my hand.

My heart is beating out of my chest as I watch Pasha push up, propping himself onto his elbows. He can do it. I know he can do it. He is almost up when his opponent approaches again and kicks him in his kidney. Pasha falls back down, rolling to his side. His face is turned toward the chain-link cage, directly in front of us. The crowd goes crazy. The applause, chants, and hollers are deafening. That damn beast walks around the cage, shouting something at the audience, laughing.

"Finish him!" someone from the crowd yells.

I stare at Pasha, waiting for him to get up, but he just keeps lying there, unmoving. He needs to get up, or the guy is going to kill him. I take off toward the cage.

Several more voices join in the cheering. "Finish him! Finish him!"

People are standing too close together, so I have to squeeze myself between them to get to the front. Bodies are touching me from all sides, making me want to throw up, but I keep pushing myself forward.

"Finish him! Finish him!" the chorus rings all around me.

I finally reach the cage and my eyes find Pasha again. He is still lying on the floor, his face is turned toward me, but I don't think he sees me.

"Pasha!" I yell at the top of my lungs and vault at the cage.

"Pasha!" a female scream reaches me.

I blink and focus on the person clinging to the outside of the chain-link cage.

"Get up!" she yells, grabbing the mesh structure with her fingers. "Please!"

I close my eyes. As if it's not enough that I dream about her every single night, now I'm hallucinating that she's actually here.

"Pasha! Look at me!"

When I open my eyes, she's still there, just a few feet in front of me. If I reach out with my hand, I could touch her fingers where they're gripping at the wire, shaking it.

"Please, baby! Get up!"

My breath catches. "Mishka?"

As I watch, one of the security guys approaches Asya from behind and, wrapping his arm around her middle, pulls her away from the cage. She just grips the metal mesh harder.

"He's coming!" Asya whimpers, looking somewhere behind me. "Get up!"

The guy keeps tugging at her, yelling something. Asya's fingers slip off the links. As the guard carries her away, rage explodes in my chest. He dared to touch her! He put his dirty hands on my girl, and he's wearing a fucking suit!

I roll onto my stomach and rise to face my opponent. He's standing in the middle of the mat, looking at me, blocking my exit. I launch toward him. When my elbow slams into his diaphragm, the air leaves his lungs and he stoops forward. Grabbing his head, I knee him in the face. He stumbles. My leap on his back is swift. Once my arms are coiled around his neck, I squeeze—applying pressure to the back of his head while simultaneously forcing my forearm against his windpipe. The guy starts thrashing around, trying to throw me off. Keeping my choke hold on him, I wrap my legs around his midsection and dig my heels under his ribcage, tightening my grip. He thrashes a few more seconds before he drops to his knees and falls sideways with me still hanging on his back. I keep squeezing, listening to the wheezing sounds coming from his throat. Somehow, I hear them despite the thundering roar of the mob around us. His body goes limp. And I snap his neck. The crowd goes wild. I get up and run toward the cage's exit.

The security guy still has Asya, carrying her toward the back where three other goons are holding Kostya down. A murderous growl leaves my mouth as I sprint toward them. The sea of people splits, letting me pass. The moment I reach the asshole manhandling Asya, I wrap my fingers around his throat and squeeze. His hold on Asya loosens. As soon as she's free, I let go of the man's neck, grab him by the back of his jacket, and heave him to the side.

"Pasha," Asya whispers behind me.

I turn to face her and just stare. I thought I'd never see her again, and having her here, standing before me, is tearing me apart inside.

"What are you doing here?" I bark. It's killing me to be this close to her again.

Her lower lip is trembling as she watches me. The hand she's pressing to her slender neck is shaking. She's trying to keep her gaze on mine, but her eyes wander to the side every other second. I throw a look to the left where she keeps glancing and notice that some of the people from the audience have moved closer and are standing just a few feet away. Most of them are sharply dressed men. Suits and fucking ties!

"Shit, baby," I mumble and take a step forward, wrapping her in my arms and blocking her view of the crowd. "Let's go outside. Okay?"

She tilts her head up and, after a second of hesitation, places her palms on my chest. I close my eyes and inhale deeply. It's hard to have her touching me, to be so close, to know I'll have to watch her walk away again, going back into the arms of that fancy son of a bitch I saw kissing her. But I've already concluded that I'm one selfish bastard, and I'm going to take this opportunity to feel her in my embrace again, even if only for a short while.

I open my eyes and look down at her. "Want to hop on?"

The smile that spreads over her face as she strokes her hands up my chest feels like a knife burrowing itself into my heart. I bend and scoop her up. Asya's arms wrap around my neck like so many times before.

"Release him," I throw over my shoulder at the guys who are still holding Kostya and carry Asya outside.

I can't get enough of his scent. Yes, there's sweat and blood, too, but underneath all that, there's the smell I associate with happiness. Safety. Love. Home. Pasha. Squeezing my legs and arms around him even tighter, I bury my face in the crook of his neck and inhale. I missed him so damn much.

A car door closes behind me, and Pasha gets in the back seat of Kostya's sedan. Even when he's seated, I refuse to let go of him, and plaster myself tighter to his chest. I move my hand up his nape, but instead his dark blond strands of hair, short bristles tickle the skin of my palm.

"Why did you shave your hair?" I ask next to his ear and brush a kiss on the side of his neck.

"Because someone could have used it to gain leverage during a fight," comes his cold answer.

I unwrap my hands from around Pasha's neck and lean back to look at him. His left hand is at my back, caressing me over the fabric on my T-shirt.

"Why are you here, Asya? Did Kostya make you come?"

"No," I say and cup his face with my palms. "I made Kostya bring me here."

"Why?"

I look at his sad gray eyes and lean forward, pressing my lips to his. His mouth is set in a tight line, and he doesn't respond. "Because I love you," I say against his hard lips.

Pasha's body stiffens under mine. "And what happened to your boyfriend?"

"What boyfriend, baby?"

"There's no need to lie. I know."

I straighten on his lap and stare at him in confusion. "What are you talking about?"

He grinds his teeth. "I came to see you last month. I saw you two kiss in front of your house, mishka."

What the fuck? That's nonsense. Today is the first time I've left the house since I returned to New York. I had no desire to see anyone or go anywhere. Unless . . .

I shake my head and reach for my backpack, taking out my phone. "Is this the 'me' you saw kissing a guy?" I ask and turn the screen toward him.

Pasha looks down at the phone, then takes it from my hand and looks closer at the picture on the screen. "Your hair is shorter here." He looks up at me and takes a lock of my hair between his fingers. "And it was shorter when I saw you."

"The woman you saw was Sienna. My sister." I smile. "We're identical twins. I thought I mentioned it."

Pasha lets go of my hair and grabs me behind my neck. "It wasn't you?"

"Of course it wasn't me. I can't even stomach the idea of touching any man other than you."

His jaw clenches and he brings his forehead to rest against mine.

"You're staying," he bites out. "I know I'm selfish. And I know you deserve better. But I don't really give a fuck, Asya. You are staying. And if anyone tries to take you away from me, I'm going to fucking kill them on the spot."

"If you ever ignore one of my calls again, you won't know what hit you."

Pasha crushes his mouth to mine. His hand comes to the side of my face, brushing my cheek with his calloused fingers. His arm around my back squeezes my waist, almost squishing me. I take his bottom lip between my teeth and bite, then kiss my way along his chin to the side of his neck and inhale his scent again. When I get my fill, I move back to his mouth and let his lips devour mine. It's unlike any other kiss we ever shared. Love. Anger. Hurt. Regret. Longing. Healing. There's a lot, and at the same time, there isn't enough.

"Where to, lovebirds?" Kostya asks from the driver seat.

"Home," Pasha says against my lips.

"Home." I nod.

"I can walk," I say as Pasha carries me into his building. He didn't let me move off his lap during the entire drive.

"I know. But I'm not letting you down," he says as he approaches the security guy in the lobby to get a spare key. The poor man looks shocked at seeing Pasha in only his fighting shorts, all bloody, feet bare, and with me clinging to him.

I tighten my hold on Pasha and bury my face in his neck, where I stay until we reach his apartment. He carries me directly to the bathroom in his room and lowers me next to the sink.

"I need to take a shower," he says.

"Okay." I nod, slip off my glasses, and proceed to take off my clothes. Pasha removes his shorts and boxer briefs, then starts unwrapping the bandages on his left hand. I step closer and take over, revealing the bloody knuckles underneath.

"Will you keep fighting?" I whisper, brushing the wounded skin. "I don't think I can bear watching you go into that cage again, Pasha."

His hand cups my cheek and tilts my head up. "Then I won't."

I nod and look down at the splint on his right hand. "Can you get that wet?"

"No," he says and unstraps it.

When he removes the splint I notice something new inked on the back of his hand, but I don't have time to look at it in detail because he grabs me around the waist and carries me inside the shower stall.

"Let me see your face." I motion with my hand for him to bend down. Pasha turns on the overhead shower, but instead of bending, he crouches in front of me. Water is raining down on him, small rivulets rolling down his bruised face. He looks terrible.

"Why did you do it?" I ask, brushing the tips of my fingers over the cuts and bruises scattered all over his face. "Why go back to fighting after so many years?"

"I hoped that if I got my head smashed enough times, I would forget about you. It didn't work, mishka."

"Good." I pick up the soap from the shelf and lather my hands.

Pasha doesn't move from his crouching position, just watches me with his head tilted up as I clean the blood and dirt off his face. I try to be as gentle as possible, especially around the bruises on his chin and under his eye. When I'm done with his face, I move on to his short hair.

"Now for the rest," I say.

He stands up and lets me wash his chest and back. There are more bruises there—on his side, stomach, and some on his back—visible even under the ink.

"Jesus, baby." I brush my palm down a wicked-looking purple mark on his stomach.

His arms are in slightly better shape. I wash the left one and move to the right, starting at his biceps, and continuing down to his wrist which is slightly swollen. I carefully lather the skin, then move his hand under the spray and watch as the water washes away the suds, revealing the new tattoo. The image is of a thorn-covered branch, done in black ink, its sharp spines pointing in all directions. Above it is a red bird in flight, its fluffy wings spread wide. It's beautiful and sad at the same time. I place the tip of my finger on the design and trace the shape of the bird.

"It's you," Pasha says and brushes my cheek with the back of his other hand.

"The bird?"

"Yes."

I look up from the tattoo and find his eyes watching me. "There's only one bird," I say. "Where are you?"

"I'm not there. Just you."

"Why?"

He dips his head to whisper in my ear. "Because there was nothing left of me after you flew away, mishka."

I squeeze my eyes shut, but the tears still escape. The water from the shower cascades down on us, reminding me of the day when he rushed into the stall fully clothed. I wrap my arms around his neck and press my cheek to his. "You shouldn't have pushed me away."

"I know." His arm tightens around me, crushing me against him. "I wanted something better for you."

I move my hand between our bodies and wrap my fingers around his hard length. The moment I start stroking him, he swells even more. "Come with me," I say, taking his hand. I pull him out of the shower and he follows me to the bedroom. When we reach the bed, I push on his chest lightly until he's lying down.

"It doesn't get better than you, Pasha," I say as I climb onto the bed and straddle his legs. "You're the only man I want."

I take his cock in my hand and tilt it to lick the tip. Pasha's hand shoots up and grabs a handful of my hair.

As I suck—slowly at first, then faster—his grip on my locks remains firm. His breathing gets labored, so I switch to licking. I love it, this feeling of elation that spreads through my chest as I see him coming undone. I never would have thought I would enjoy going down on a man, or how much it would turn me on. But this is my Pasha. And I want to do everything with him. I take him into my mouth again—as far as he can go—and he groans as his warm cum explodes down my throat. I swallow it all.

His chest is rising and falling rapidly when I climb on top of him. His hand is still tangled in my hair, clutching at it as if it's a lifeline.

"I love you," I whisper, "so very much."

He stares at me for a few moments, then presses his lips tightly together. "Are you sure, Asya?"

"I'm sure." I lean and press my lips on his forehead. "Can't you see that for yourself?"

He lets go of my hair, sliding his palm around my neck to cup my face and tilt my head up. I expect to see him smiling, but the expression on his face is serious.

"You're very young, baby," he says as he strokes my cheek with his thumb. "What if you meet someone along the way and decide that this . . . us . . . is not *it* for you? I don't think I could survive watching you walk away again, mishka."

I peer at him for a minute, studying his flattened lips, his crooked nose, and his metallic gray eyes that sometimes say more than his words.

"What is love for you, Pasha?" I ask and brush the back of my fingers down his face.

"The feeling of never being close enough." His other hand comes to the back of my neck, squeezing lightly. "I have the need to somehow absorb you into my chest, so you'll always be with me. Safe from harm. Only mine. Forever."

I open my mouth to say something, but he silences me by slamming his lips to mine.

"I love you to the point of madness, Asya," he whispers against my mouth, "and I really need you to be sure. Please."

I bite his lower lip, then trail kisses down his neck and lower until I reach his heart. I can feel it beating wildly. With one last kiss just over his heart, I climb off his body and head into the walk-in closet. I open the drawer and slide my fingers over the ties folded neatly inside until I reach the deep burgundy one. It's not exactly red, but it's close enough. I take it out and head back into the bedroom. Pasha's eyes follow me as I walk toward the bed, his gaze focused on the tie I'm holding.

"Mishka?" he straightens until he's sitting on the edge of the bed. "What are you doing?"

"I want to show you what love is for me."

I come to stand between his legs and take his hand, placing it on my chest, just over my heart. "You never asked me why I freaked out because of the ties. One of the first clients used his tie to choke me while fucking me. I thought I was going to die that night," I say and raise the hand holding the tie, then drape the silky fabric around my neck.

"Asya, no." Pasha reaches for the tie, but I take his fingers in mine and lay his palm back on my chest.

"Can you feel my heart beating faster than normal?" I move his hand a little up and to the left. "No. Is my breathing getting erratic? It's not."

With my free hand, I take one side of the tie that's hanging loose over my front, wrap it around my neck twice and tuck the end into Pasha's palm resting on my collarbone.

"Last week, I tried helping Arturo with his tie. I adore my brother, and I know he wouldn't ever do anything to hurt me. My hands were shaking so much that I asked him to do it himself instead." I lift my eyes to meet Pasha's. "Do you see my hands shaking now?"

"No, baby," he says in a strangled voice.

"Every single part of me is in love with you, Pasha. My body. My mind." I wrap his fingers around the end of the tie and, keeping my hand over his, I pull on it. The silky material tightens around my neck. "Even my subconscious knows how great and unconditional that love is. So, yes. I'm sure."

I release his hand and hold his gaze as he unwraps the tie from my neck. He does it slowly, careful not to pull on the fabric, and throws it to the floor.

"I'm getting rid of all of those anyway." He reaches and scoops me into his arms, then throws me onto the bed.

I bounce twice, laughing. Pasha climbs on the bed, but instead of hovering over me, he takes my ankle and raises my leg to his mouth, placing a kiss on my toes. I giggle and try pulling my leg free, but he keeps his hold.

"Stop!" I wail.

"Not gonna happen," he mumbles and moves his lips to the arch of my foot.

When his lips find the supersensitive spot on the inside of my ankle, I put my other foot on his chest and try pushing him away without success. "I'm ticklish. Pasha! No, not there!"

"Everywhere, mishka. I plan on covering your whole body with kisses. Every day."

He trails the line of kisses up my leg to my pussy. I feel his warm breath as he gently kisses it before he buries his face between my legs, sucking at my clit. His hands glide up my legs and under my butt cheeks, lifting my ass. I choke on my breath and grab the headboard above my head, holding on for dear life as he slides his tongue inside me. My thighs and arms are shaking as if I'm burning with a fever, and my mind goes blank, focused solely on the sensation of his tongue on me. Suddenly, his mouth vanishes but, a moment later, I feel his cock entering me. He isn't even fully inside and I'm already close to coming.

Pasha's hand grabs the back of my neck. I open my eyes and find him looming above me, so big and ferocious looking with all that ink. My mountain king. The most beautiful man, inside and out.

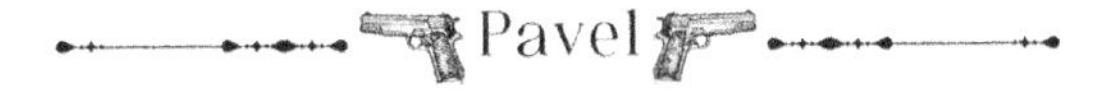

## Pavel

I can't take my eyes off Asya's. It's as if they are holding me enslaved. I still find it hard to believe she's mine. Slowly, I pull out only to thrust back into her again, as deep as possible. A small moan leaves her lips while her delicate arms go taut with strain as she grips the headboard above her. The sounds she makes are addictive. I pull out of her again, wrap my arm around her, and turn her around.

"I wish I had the words to explain," I say next to her ear and kiss her earlobe, "how much I love you."

I let my palms glide down her back while I trail slow kisses along her spine, all the way to her ass. Her skin is so soft it feels unreal, and I experience a slight pang of regret as I bury my teeth into her firm butt cheek. Then, I kiss that spot and position myself between her legs, thrusting into her pussy, absorbing her every gasp and moan. I move my left hand lower, between her legs, and tease her clit. Her body is trembling under my touch as my right palm travels up along her spine. I wish I could touch her everywhere at once. I rock into her with a steady pace for a few strokes, then increase my tempo. Asya lowers her head to the pillow and lifts her ass higher.

"Harder!" she cries out and takes a hold of the headboard again.

I grab her hips and thrust myself deeper. Her walls spasm around my cock, and as I hear her moaning my name when she comes, my restraint snaps. The headboard bangs against the wall while I pound into her like a man possessed.

"Are you mine, mishka?" I bite out between the thrusts. The need to hear her say it is making me insane.

"Always," Asya breathes out.

There are so many things I wished I had in my life, but nothing compares to having her be mine. As long as I have her, I don't need anything else.

"Mine!" I come with a roar, pouring my seed into her.

I tuck Asya closer into my body and pull the blanket over her. It's warm in the room, but I'm always worried she'll get cold. "Does your family know you're here?"

"Yes," she mumbles into my neck.

"And do they know you're not coming back home?" I ask.

I've been dreading this moment. I don't want to fight with her brother, but I will not let him take her away ever again. And if I need to beat the living shit out of him to make him understand, so be it. But what if she can't handle being separated from them?

"I have only one home." She lifts her face to look right into my eyes and smiles. "You. You are my home now."

Something happens inside my chest at that moment. My heart skips a beat, and then I feel something slide into place. The jagged edges finally fitting together.

# Chapter Twenty-four

Asya

I'M TAKING THE BOWLS OUT OF THE CUPBOARD WHEN A KISS LANDS ON the back of my neck.

"I have something for you," Pasha says.

I turn around and stare in confusion at the boxes he's holding in his arms. "New cereal flavors?"

"Yeah." He smiles, but it seems guarded, and places the boxes on the counter. There are five in total.

"Um . . . okay." I snort. "Do you want to pick?"

"No. I want you to choose." He makes sure the boxes are in a perfect line and looks down at me. "Which one?"

I laugh and look at the cereal packages. I rarely have problems with making decisions now, but he still makes sure we practice from time to time. The way Pasha continues to help me is amazing. He even convinced me to meet with the psychiatrist Doc had recommended, and she, too, has been really great. Our sessions are difficult, but I appreciate her care and support.

Reaching out, I grab the box with dried strawberries.

"Does this work for you?" I raise an eyebrow.

"Yes." He leans over and brushes a kiss across my lips. "Now, open it."

Shaking my head, I start opening the box, wondering why he's making such a fuss out of the cereal. I tear the top and stick my hand in to pull out the bag when my fingers touch something hard and velvety. My heart is beating triple-time as I take out a small red box.

"Pasha?" I choke out, staring at the jewelry box. "What is this?"

"I don't know. Let's see" He takes the box from my hand and opens it.

I gape at him as he takes out a gold ring. A radiant-cut yellow diamond shines under the overhead lights. My hand shakes slightly as he lifts it to place a kiss at the tips of my fingers.

"Will you marry me, mishka?"

"Yes," I whisper.

Pasha smiles and slides the ring onto my finger. I sniff and jump into his arms, burying my face in the crook of his neck.

"What would you have done if I picked the wrong box?" I ask.

"You could never pick wrong, baby."

"I could have taken the crunchy cereal."

His palm strokes my back as he laughs. "You hate crunchy cereal."

"Yes, but what if I decided to give it another try?"

He just shrugs.

I lean away and stare at him as realization forms in my brain. "You didn't."

"What?"

I narrow my eyes at him. "Put me down."

"Why?"

"I need to check something."

As my feet touch the ground, I turn toward the counter where the other four cereal boxes are lined up. I take the first one, the one with honey, and open it. A red velvet box sits on top of the cereal bag. When I open it, I find a ring identical to the one on my finger nested on the white silk cushion. I leave the jewelry box on the island and grab the next cereal box. And the next.

The box of crunchy cereal I leave for last. I never would have picked the crunchy one, Pasha knows that very well, but when I open it, the jewelry box is in that one, as well. I put it on the counter next to the other four. He had hidden a ring in each one.

I feel arms wrapping around my waist as Pasha leans on me from behind, but I don't turn. I can't take my eyes off the four extra jewelry boxes holding identical rings.

"Why?" I whisper.

His hold around my middle tightens. "Because I needed you to understand."

"What, Pasha?"

"That as far as I'm concerned, you can't make a wrong decision, baby." A kiss lands at the top of my head. "Even if it's just picking the cereal flavor."

*One month later*

"What if I freak out?" I ask, my voice sounding strangled.

Sienna looks up from the shoe she's helping me tie up. "You won't freak out, Asya."

"Yes, I know . . ." I lift my hand and bite my nail. "But what if I do? There are like . . . two hundred people out there."

Sienna straightens, pulls my hand away from my mouth, and grabs my shoulders. "You won't freak out. You'll go out there, stand beside the man you love and who's crazy about you, and you'll have the best day of your life."

"I know, but . . ."

"You know, I've been thinking," she says. "When you and Pasha decide to have kids, how about you let me pick out their names? Auntie will make sure they are super special."

I stare at my sister in horror. There's no way I would ever let her pick the names for my children. I'd be risking them being named after chocolate bars or some other candy if I do. Or worse.

Sienna looks up at me and grins. "Relax." She giggles. "I'm just kidding. But admit it, going out there in front of all of those people sounds less terrifying now."

I snort. "It certainly does."

"Everything is going to be fine. Don't worry."

I straighten my dress for the umpteenth time, "Maybe I should have picked a white dress. What if people—"

"It's your wedding day. You can wear whatever the fuck you want, Asya." She looks down at my bright yellow lacy dress and grins. "I love it! You look like you walked out of a fairytale."

"You think Pasha will like it?"

Sienna grabs my face between her palms and leans in closer. "That man is so ridiculously in love with you, you could walk in there wearing a kitchen rag and he would eat you up with his eyes."

I laugh. "I can't believe I'm getting married."

"Me either, sweetie." She sniffs. "Come on. Arturo is waiting. And I'm ruining my makeup."

Sienna squeezes my hand tightly as we leave the room and hurry down the hotel hallway toward the big wooden door at the end, where Arturo is waiting. Leaving me with our brother, Sienna slips inside the wedding hall, pulling the door shut after her. A few moments later, the first tones of a melody reach my ears.

It's not the wedding march.

"Ready?" Arturo asks.

I nod, trying to keep my breathing under control.

The music gets louder as the door before us slowly open. It's "Moonlight Sonata." We step into the hall.

Pasha is standing at the end of the aisle, his eyes glued to mine, following our every step. As Arturo leads me forward, a thought crosses my mind that something is out of order. Considering I'm a bundle of nerves, it's not surprising that the realization hits only when we almost reach our destination.

I blink in confusion. Pasha is dressed in black jeans and a black T-shirt. He knows it doesn't bother me when he wears a suit, so why did he come in jeans? I turn my head to my brother, roving my eyes over his jeans and a Henley shirt until I reach his face.

"Your Russian arranged the dress code for the wedding," he says as he keeps walking.

I take a deep breath and glance at the guests sitting on our left. My heart flutters in my chest. I look over to the right side, as well. It's the same. Every single man is wearing jeans and either a long-sleeved or short-sleeved T-shirt. Even our don, who's sitting in the front row with his wife. I've never in my life seen Salvatore Ajello in a T-shirt. In fact, I don't think anyone has. Except maybe his wife.

I shift my eyes back to Pasha and see him smiling, and I can't keep the tears at bay anymore. So, I let them roll down my cheeks and smile widely as my brother hands me off to my future husband.

Pasha lifts my hand to his mouth and places a kiss on my fingers. "Everything okay, mishka?"

"Yes," I say, "everything is perfect, Pashenka."

We're going through the buffet line when Arturo's phone rings. I turn to the side and pass the serving spoon to the older man standing next to me when I note the tension in Arturo's voice.

"How come they didn't find anything? It's been months."

He listens to the person on the other end of the line for a few moments, then squeezes his temples. "All right."

"What happened?" I ask.

"They still don't have a clue why Rocco's house burned down the way it did, but the report will show a suspected gas leak. No remains were found because everything was scorched to ashes, and the building crumbled in on itself. Based on the security footage before the signal cut out, Rocco, Ravenna, and Alessandro were inside. Without any more evidence, they're closing the investigation and pronouncing the three of them dead." He puts the phone in his pocket and looks over his shoulder. "I need to tell the boss."

I'm staring at Arturo's retreating form when I hear subdued snickering at my side. I look over at the gray-haired guy next to me. He's piling meat on his plate while a wide smile spreads across his face. What the hell is wrong with him? Three people died, and he finds it funny?

"Jesus fuck, Albert! Are you done?" The big, blond guy standing on the other side nudges him with his elbow. I think his name is Sergei. "Move already, there are other people here who want to eat. And why are you snickering like a damn hyena?"

"No reason." The old guy shakes his head and leaves, quietly singing something. It sounds like . . . "Poker Face" by Lady Gaga.

# Epilogue

*Five years later*

One. Two. Three. I count in my head as I stare at the plastic stick in my hand. One red line appears in the small display window. Four. Five. Six. Only one line.

I sit down on the toilet lid and look up at the ceiling. After I graduated from the music conservatory, I decided to offer free piano lessons to women who experienced sexual abuse. I hoped music would be helpful in their healing. Yesterday, while going through my booked appointments for the next week, I realized my period is almost a month late. Since I was done with the school, Pasha and I agreed that I should stop taking the birth control pills so we could start trying for a family. I knew that my cycle would get irregular after that, so missing a period didn't necessarily mean I was pregnant. It could simply be the side effect.

"Asya?" Pasha's voice comes from the other side of the bathroom door.

"It's negative," I say, trying to make myself sound nonchalant. To hide the disappointment. I was secretly hoping it would be positive. Just the idea of having Pasha's baby made me want to squeal with joy. I was lying snuggled into Pasha's side when I told him I needed to take the pregnancy test. His body went stone-still for a moment, and then he squeezed me against his body so tightly I could barely breathe.

The door opens and Pasha walks inside the bathroom. "It's okay." He brushes my cheek and takes the test from my hand. The expression on his face seems relaxed, but I see it in his eyes—he hoped, as well.

"You're still young. When . . ." He looks down at the plastic stick in his hand and tenses. "Mishka. How many lines should there be?"

"One. It means negative."

"But there are two."

I jump off the toilet and snatch the test out of his grasp. "But there was only one. Give me the box!"

Pasha passes me the box and I quickly read through the instructions until I reach the part where it says you need to wait for at least five minutes. When I read it the first time, I thought it said five seconds.

"It's positive," I choke out and look up at Pasha. He's staring at me intently. "We're going to have a baby."

Slowly, his gaze glides over my chest to my stomach. He takes a deep breath and lowers himself to his knees in front of me. His big hands are shaking as he takes the hem of my top, pushes it up, and kisses just above my navel. Then, he presses his cheek to my midriff and, wrapping his arms around me, starts humming a lullaby.

Pavel

"I already told you, I don't do OB-GYN exams," the doc snaps.

"We have an appointment with a gynecologist tomorrow," I bark and shove him away from the door so Asya and I can get inside his office. "But I need to know that everything is okay. Now."

"You're overreacting."

"I don't give a fuck." With my hands gently gripping Asya under her arms, I lift her onto the gurney. "You can start."

The doc shakes his head and takes a seat, pulling up the ultrasound machine toward him.

My eyes fixate on the scene before me as I watch while he smears some goo on Asya's stomach and moves the device above the waistband of her leggings. He glides the thing from left to right, then rotates it a bit, while keeping an eye on the monitor and hitting some buttons on the tower unit.

"I'd say you're in week six. They both seem perfectly fine," he says, then looks at Asya. "And you seem fine, too."

I blink in confusion. "Both? Both Asya and the baby?"

"No. Both babies."

My head snaps to the side, staring at Asya who's looking at the monitor with a wide smile on her face. "Are you sure?" she whispers.

"Yes," the doc says at the same time as I say, "No!"

They both turn to look at me.

"Do that again." I point my finger at the ultrasound machine while terror seizes me on the inside.

"I'm pretty sure I know how to count!" the doc exclaims and slams the ultrasound printout against my chest, pointing his other finger at it. "One. Two."

I grab the front of his shirt and get in his face. "Again!"

"Pasha?" Asya grips my forearm. "What's going on?"

I release Doc and cup her face between my palms. "It's dangerous, mishka. And you're so tiny. What if something happens?"

Asya presses her finger over my lips. "I'm going to be fine. There are twins in almost every generation of my family, and no one ever had any problems. Don't panic."

"I'm not panicking. I'm not." I throw a look over my shoulder at the doc. "Should she be admitted to a hospital? I'll drive straight there."

"Pasha." Asya pulls at my shirt.

"Can she walk?" I continue. "No, I better carry her there."

"I'm not going to a fucking hospital!" Asya roars into my ear, grabs my chin, and turns my head to face her. "Let's thank the doctor and head home."

"Mishka . . ."

"I wouldn't advise enraging a woman pregnant with twins, Pasha," the doc throws in.

"He won't." Asya leans forward and presses her lips to mine. "Relax. Everything is going to be okay."

PERFECTLY IMPERFECT
BONUS SCENE

# KURT

A BONUS SCENE FROM
KURT'S POV

*For my readers who insisted on reading the cat's POV :D*

## Kurt

"Down!"

I meet the gaze of the Mean One. The Usurper. First, he confiscated my human, proclaiming her his. Then, he took my spot in her bed. And now, he intends to dictate to me where I should or shouldn't climb. I stride toward the opposite end of the dining table and plant my butt on the papers he's reading.

"Milene," he says without breaking eye contact. "Your animal is sitting on my contracts. I need you to remove it."

"You're running a criminal empire, Salvatore. I'm sure you're capable of putting Kurt down yourself."

The Mean One lowers his head, coming close to my face. "Move."

I lean back slightly and try to keep his gaze. I manage for a full five seconds before I relent. Getting off his precious contracts, I jump down onto the floor but make sure that my tail swats him on his scowling face in the process. He might have won this battle, but not the war. I already checked out the new couch he bought yesterday. He ordered the maid to spray it with lemongrass essence. Someone has been googling cat repellents. Ha! As if it'll do any good. That shit evaporates in about a day, max. The upholstery on the new couch is top-notch. Perfect for sharpening nails.

As I trot across the living room, my eyes zero in on the orange bundle of fur visible in the kitchen. Oh, Riggs the Replacement. How exciting. I change my course and, lowering my body to the ground, start sneaking up on him.

When Milene brought that thing in a couple of months ago, that made me feel so betrayed. He ate my food, tried to take over my sleeping spot on the recliner, and even used my litter box! It looked like Milene wanted to replace me. Me! No one can replace me! But then, I realized that Milene probably took Riggs in because she felt sorry for the idiot. He doesn't know how to play, he's incapable of getting any food for himself, and he sleeps most of the time. The poor bastard wouldn't last a day on the streets. So, I allowed him to stay. But there are limits. I'm not going to relieve myself in the same litter box where someone else takes a piss, and I made sure Milene understands that. I pooped on the floor next to it until she got the memo and bought the second litter box. It was new, shiny, and big. I claimed it for myself, of course.

When I'm just a few steps behind Riggs the Replacement, I charge. He doesn't even notice me coming. I pounce on top of him, grabbing onto his mangy body with all four of my paws, and bury my teeth into the fur at his neck. He yowls and starts trashing around, but I don't release my hold. I don't understand why he's so uncooperative, I'm just trying to play.

"Kurt!" Milene yells behind me.

Reluctantly, I release Riggs the Replacement. Doesn't matter. That cat is a lost cause anyway. He is still puking hair once a week because he won't eat that sticky paste thing Milene keeps trying to give him. I mean, doesn't he have any self-respect?

I jump up on the counter and stroll across its length, along the way brushing my side on the coffee machine. It tickles. I do it a few more times. When I reach the fridge, I jump atop and survey my territory. The Mean One is still sitting at the dining table, leafing through his papers. The Replacement is hiding beneath the couch. In the furthest corner of the living room, Ada the housekeeper is hanging the new curtains. They got short ones this time, reaching just below the windows, so it will be harder to climb them. It must have been the Mean One's idea. Always trying to sabotage me, that one.

As I'm settling in on my perch and contemplating having a nap, the smell of charred meat invades my nostrils. I look toward the stove. Milene put a pan on the burner, but she looks busy cleaning off the hair I left on the coffee machine. Dog's balls! I thought the Mean One forbade her to approach the stove. That woman is incapable of preparing food. She made cookies last weekend. I stole one and played with it around the kitchen. The thing was so hard, it didn't break even when I launched it at the wall. I thought she'd throw the whole batch into the trash, but no. She took the plate to the Mean One and made him eat two of the so-called treats. I almost felt sorry for him. Almost.

The burning food smell is becoming too much to handle. My nose is too sensitive for that crap, so I leave the spot on my watchtower and head into the living room, brushing my flank on the Mean One's leg as I pass him. He gifts me with a murderous glare but doesn't comment. I sprawl down on the middle of a thick Persian rug and eye the Christmas tree in the corner. I tried climbing it twice this morning, but Milene saw what I was doing and chased me away with a kitchen rag. She yelled a lot, but I know it was just for the Mean One's sake. She finds my shenanigans adorable.

With another look at the Christmas tree, I flip to my back and close my eyes. Doesn't matter. As with everything else, I excel at being patient.

Heavy breathing. A moan. Someone screams. I crack my eye open and take in my surroundings. Darkness has fallen, but the light from the kitchen throws a yellowish glow onto the scene happening in the dining room. Milene is sprawled out on the table. Naked. The Mean One is sitting on a chair in front of her, his face is buried between her legs. Oh, for crying out loud, you're not alone here! Exhibitionists. I'll have to scrub my eyes out after seeing this.

Yesterday, I caught them doing it on the couch, and before that, on the kitchen counter. That's not sanitary, you idiots! And don't get me started on what happens during the night. Growling. Wood creaking. Mewling. Headboard banging against the wall. Bang. Bang. Bang. I started sleeping in the damn kitchen sink. What the fuck is wrong with you people? Are you trying to kill each other or is this your idea of mating? Jesus.

I rise, bowing my back and then stretching my body before I head away from this heat-fest when my eyes again fixate on the Christmas tree in the corner. It reaches almost all the way to the ceiling, full of big round objects and dozens of twinkling little things all over it. A look toward the dining room confirms that the two humans are still occupied. Perfect. I zero in on the tree, focusing on the big shiny ball hanging at the top, then run. I jump onto the coffee table, then leap toward the branch just below the beautiful ball. Yes!

The tree starts tilting to the side. Oops! I hold onto the branches for dear life as the whole thing keeps falling. No. No. No!

*Crash*!

Utter silence descends for a few brief seconds. I crouch in the tangle of tree branches and broken decorations. Maybe they haven't noticed.

"I'm going to strangle that cat, Milene."

Shit.

Dear reader,

Thanks so much for reading! I hope you'll consider leaving a review. Reviews help authors find new readers, and help other readers find new books to love!

If you want to be caught up on all the Perfectly Imperfect news, bonus scenes and sales, subscribe to my newsletter or join my FB Reader Group. You can find all the links by scanning the code below with your phone.

I love hearing from my readers, so feel free to reach out.

Made in the USA
Monee, IL
17 September 2023

42881735R00326